ENCOUNTER
—WITH—
TIBER

BUZZ ALDRIN & JOHN BARNES

ENCOUNTER WITH TIBER

FOREWORD BY ARTHUR C. CLARKE

ASPECT®

WARNER BOOKS

A Time Warner Company

Aspect® name and logo are registered trademarks of Warner Books, Inc.

Warner Books, Inc., 1271 Avenue of the Americas, New York, NY 10020

Ⓦ A Time Warner Company

Printed in the United States of America
First Printing: July 1996
10 9 8 7 6 5 4 3 2 1

Library of Congress Cataloging-in-Publication Data
Aldrin, Buzz.
  Encounter with Tiber / Buzz Aldrin and John Barnes.
    p.   cm.
  ISBN: 0-446-51854-9
  I. Barnes, John.   II. Title.
PS3551.L3454E5   1996
813'.54—dc20   95-52190
                                                      CIP

Interior illustrations by Andy Andres (pp. 3, 25, 29, 74, 101, 110, 153, 174, 175, 197, 223, 372, 465, 560) and John Solie (pp. 174, 175)
Book design by H. Roberts

ACKNOWLEDGMENTS

This book would have been impossible without a vast amount of technical assistance and information from a very large number of experts. We would especially like to thank:

Neil Armstrong and Mike Collins for the experence of a lifetime

Arthur C. Clarke for strong words of encouragement during times when we really needed them

Andy Andres for preparation of final art

Dana Andrews for profound insights into the next generation of spacecraft—and several generations after that

Dr. Gregory Benford for consultations, speculations, and arguments without number

John Blaha for expertise and extensive consultation on space shuttle evacuations

Professor Winberg Chai for advice on Chinese politics

Major John G. Cotter of the California Air National Guard for information about the 144th Fighter Wing

Dr. John Connolly for a most helpful review of misssion planning concepts for the Moon and Mars

Hubert Davis for engineering wisdom and the loan of his name

Dr. Mike Duke for notes on space physics and planetary science

Dr. Robert Forward for inspiration and many very advanced concepts in physics

Dr. Steve Gillett for agreeing that our worldbuilding wasn't completely implausible

Dr. William K. Hartmann   for notes on solar system astronomy

Dr. Robert Jastrow   for extensive discussion of astronomy

Dr. Gene Mallove   for information about the ongoing research into cold fusion and potential starship drives

Dr. Gregory Matloff   for his extensive discussion and advice on starship propulsion, and for telling us about the Casimir effect in the first place

Dr. Tom McDonough   for superb guidance on SETI and radio astronomy issues

Chris McKay   for information about Martian surface conditions

Steve Merihew   for orbital mechanics above and beyond the call of duty

Story Musgrave   for an example of astronaut dedication

Paul Penzo of JPL   for Mars trajectory calculating

Dr. Carl Sagan   for *Contact*, and for his many years of devoted effort for a cause we share

John Solie   for sketches and discussions on alien biology

John Spencer   for tremendous help on art

Robert Staehle   for advice about lunar oxygen

Chauncy Uphoff   for cycles orbit mechanics and insight into Chinese politics

Robert M. Zubrin   for a fine eye for detail and a great deal of information about Mars

Dramatis Personae

Aboard the starship *Tenacity*, A.D. 2069–2081
Clio Trigorin, historian
Sanetomo Kawamura, astronomer
Captain Olshavsky

Human beings, A.D. 1990–2010
Crew of the shuttle *Endeavour*:
Lori Kirsten, commander
Henry Janesh, pilot
Chris Terence, mission specialist #1
Dirk Rodriguez, mission specialist
Sharon Goldman, mission specialist
Harold Spearman, mission specialist
J. T. Murphy, mission specialist

On Earth:
Amber Romany Terence, married to Chris
Jason Terence, son of Amber and Chris
Sig Jarlsbourg, businessman and proprietor of ShareSpace Global, later
married to Amber
Allison, Chris's girlfriend after his divorce
Vincente Auricchio, an astronomer

At the International Space Station:
Peter Mikhailovich Denisov, a cosmonaut and engineer
Tatiana Haldin, a cosmonaut and the station commander
François Raymond, a mission specialist
Jiro Kawaguchi, a mission specialist

ON THE SECOND MISSION TO THE LUNAR SOUTH POLE AND TIBER BASE:
Xiao Be, a Chinese astronaut and pilot
Jiang Wu, a Chinese astronaut and secret policeman

On Tiber, 7200 B.C. and before:
Tutretz, meteorologist for the expedition to Kahrekeif
Teacher Verkisus, a scientist
Steraz and Baibarenes, test pilots
General Gurix Zowakou, conqueror of Shulath
Empress Rumaz, Gurix's liege
Captain Wahkopem Zomos, discoverer of Palath
Fereg Yorock, a politician

Crew of the Tiberian starship *Wahkopem Zomos*, 73rd century B.C.
THE ADULT GENERATION:
Captain Osepok Tarov, a Palathian female
Imperial Guard Kekox Hieretz, a Palathian male
Teacher Poiparesis, a Shulathian male
Teacher Soikenn, a Shulathian female
THE SECOND GENERATION:
Mejox Roupox, a Palathian male
Otuz Kimnabex, a Palathian female
Priekahm, a Shulathian female
Zahmekoses, a Shulathian male

Humans of the Real People, 73rd and 72nd centuries B.C.
Rar, first a warrior, later Nim of the Real People
Inok, Rar's heir
Messlah, Rar's grandson
Set, Rar's heir after Inok's death
Esser, Rar's granddaughter

Tiberian slaves of the Real People
Diehrenn, daughter of Otuz and Zahmekoses, a Hybrid
Prirox, son of Kekox and Osepok, a Palathian
Weruz, daughter of Mejox and Priekahm, a Hybrid
Menomoum, a Hybrid male, Weruz's son

Crew of the Tiberian starship *Egalitarian Republic*, 72nd century B.C.
Astrogator Depari, a Hybrid female
Astrogator's Assistant Bepemm, a Hybrid female
Captain Baegess, a Hybrid male
Captain's Assistant Thetakisus, a Hybrid male
Chief Engineer Azir, a Shulathian male
Engineer's Assistant Krurix, a Palathian male
Engineer's Mate Proyerin, a Shulathian male
First Officer Beremahm, a Hybrid female
Ordinary Spacer Tisix, a Palathian male
Political Officer Streeyeptin, a Hybrid male
Ship's Doctor Lerimarsix, a Shulathian female

Humans, 2020–2040
ON EARTH:
Bill Amundsen, commander of NASA's First Aerospace Squadron
Dean, the voice of Mission Control
Mark Bene, astronaut and pilot

ON THE 2033 MARS FIVE EXPEDITION TO CRATER KOROLEV:
Walter Gander, commander
Jason Terence, pilot and second officer
Olga Trigorin, engineer and first officer
Narihara Nigawa, mission specialist
Ilsa Bierlein, mission specialist
Vassily Chebutykin, mission specialist
Dong Te-Hua, mission specialist
Paul Fleurant, mission specialist
Kireiko Masachi, mission specialist
Tsen Chou-zung, mission specialist

SCIENTISTS AT KOROLEV BASE:
Das Chalashajerian (commonly called Doc C)
Yvana Borges
Robert Prang
Akira Yamada
Jim Flynn

ON THE MARS CYCLERS ALDRIN AND COLLINS:
Scotty Johnston, pilot

FOREWORD

BY ARTHUR C. CLARKE

IT DOESN'T SEEM FAIR. THERE WAS A TIME WHEN WE SCIENCE-FICTION WRITERS had Space all to ourselves and could do just what we liked with it. Not anymore . . . people like Buzz have been there, and can tell us exactly where we went wrong.

And now, to add insult to injury, they're *writing* science fiction themselves. Even worse—it's damned good science fiction. Painful though it is to make such an admission, I would have been proud to have written *Encounter with Tiber* myself.

It's true that Buzz collaborated with a master of the genre, John Barnes, but his own contribution is obvious throughout. Anyone reading this novel will learn a great deal about future possibilities in space exploration, some of them very imaginative indeed. I was particularly interested in the use of Zero Point Energy—the imperceptible yet titanic legacy of the Big Bang. The late Nobelist Richard Feynman once remarked that there is enough energy in a cubic meter of space—any space, anywhere—to *boil all the oceans of the world*. If this can be tapped—and there is evidence that this is already happening in some laboratories—travel to the planets, and even the stars, will become cheap and easy.

However, the emphasis in *Tiber* is not on technicalities, but on human relations and interstellar politics. The description of alien societies, their triumphs and disasters, is not only convincing but often very moving. I don't think that Ursula Le Guin has done it any better.

Finally, to prove that I'm not the only one who's enjoyed this book, let me quote from a letter I've just received: "I am midway through *Encounter with Tiber* and find it very engaging. Buzz has put many of his space strategies into the yarn."

It's signed by someone named Neil.

Clio Trigorin:
July 20, 2069

WITH HER IMMENSE BOOSTERS, THE STARSHIP *TENACITY* WAS THE BIGGEST structure ever assembled in space; even when the boosters were gone, in about ten hours, she would still be huge. *And all this for just thirty people,* Clio Trigorin thought. *We first reached the Moon with three, Phobos with seven, Mars five, Titan eleven . . .* She wondered for a moment if it would be worth projecting a power series, and then snorted; carry that one far enough and it would take you to the point where one day the whole human race went to the edge of the universe.

The taxi ship slipped into dock under robotic control, and Clio and the six other people on board got out, vaulting into the huge belly of *Tenacity.* On her way out, Clio caught one last glimpse of the distant Earth, through one of the taxi's windows, just showing bits of Africa, Antarctica, and South America. It might well be the last direct view she would have before departing, but it wasn't quite the sentimental matter for her it had been for other people. She had first seen Earth at sixteen, when she went there for college, and though she had gotten to like her adopted world, her sentimental focus was still on the red plains, sharp crater walls, and immense peaks of Mars, where she had grown up.

Still, she made sure she took a good last look. They were just coming around the Earth and heading back up to apogee, the highest point in their orbit, and below them the southern part of the Indian Ocean receded rapidly, much of it covered by clouds today. One more trip around, in this orbit that swung in close to the North Pole and far out into space over the South Pole; once more they would see Siberia, the Arctic Ocean, and Greenland as huge things filling the whole frame of the video screen; once more they would see the Earth fall away as they swung south—and at last the big antimatter engines on the boosters would push them on so that instead of starting to fall back, high over the South Pole, they would continue on in a straight line, headed for the third brightest star in the sky, the blazing light in the far-southern constellation Centaurus, which now seemed to hang above her head, opposite the brilliant blue-and-white receding Earth.

Clio looked around and saw that everyone else had stopped for a moment to look out as well; then the slow turning of the ship carried Earth out of their view, leaving them only a view of a distant half-moon against a field of stars. The group turned silently away.

They all floated down the corridor, hand-hold to hand-hold, until they came to their quarters. Clio moved her little bag of personal gear into its locker, and then checked her schedule on the screen. Not surprisingly, as the expedition historian she was invited to be in the guest seat in the cockpit for boost, and later for extrasolar injection, but for the hour and a half until then, she was at large.

There was a faint chime for the phone; she turned on the screen and found herself facing Aunt Olga and Uncle Jason. She grinned broadly—they were her favorite relatives, and they had made the long trip back from Mars to the Earth just to see her ship leave (even if Jason stoutly maintained it was mainly to be home for his mother's one hundredth birthday next year). "I'm so glad to see you one more time," Clio said.

Tenacity was still so close to Earth that there wasn't even a discernible radio lag; only near apogee could you readily tell that the radio signal was taking some time to travel back and forth. That would change, Clio thought; eventually they would be four and a third light-years from Earth, and since radio travels at the speed of light, that would mean eight years and eight months, at least, between sending a message and receiving an answer. Even at their farthest separation before, when Mars and Earth had been positioned in their orbits so that the sun was between them and radio had to go through a distant relay, the lag had never been more than forty-five minutes between signal and reply. With a twinge of sadness, she realized that her aunt and uncle were both past seventy now, and that this might well be the last time they had a conversation as opposed to trading video letters.

She would miss them both, but especially Uncle Jason, because Jason's memories were going to be one of the major sources for *From the Moon to the Stars*—the book she tended to think of as her major work.

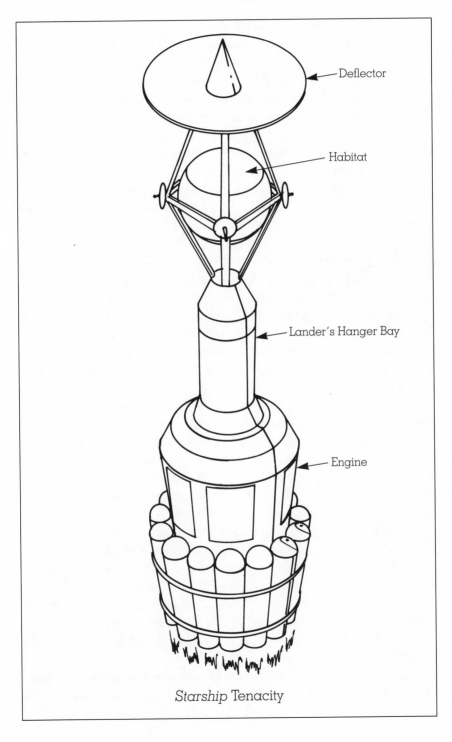

Deflector

Habitat

Lander's Hanger Bay

Engine

Starship Tenacity

"Are you all right, Clio?" Olga asked.

"I'm fine. I was just thinking about how far away I'm going and how long it will be before I see you both again."

"But you will," Jason said. "Most likely you'll be gone less than thirty years—and to judge by the way Mom keeps going, the average life expectancy in my family is about two hundred."

"Give Aunt Amber a hug and apologize for my not being there," Clio said. "I'm sorry to miss her hundredth, but the mission planners planned something else."

"Mom'll understand. She was married to an astronaut once, you know," Jason said. A part of Clio winced at that, for Jason's father, her great-uncle Chris Terence, had died on a mission, decades before Clio was born. No doubt if Clio died out there between the stars, the rest of the family *would* understand.

"Anyway, we just wanted to wish you luck and point out how hard it is to avoid the family occupation," Jason said.

Olga grinned at her and said, "And don't let him harass you. We're very proud. Come and see us when you get back—we'll only be a hundred, and Mars seems to be kind to old people."

"Mars?" Clio said. "You're going *back*?"

"Well, of course," Olga said. "It's *home*."

Jason nodded. "Revisiting Earth has been a great way to remind myself why we took permanent stationing at Crater Korolev. Surely you can remember, Clio? Oh, Earth's got the museums, the libraries, and the night life . . . but when was the last time you climbed a mountain and looked out over a plain and knew for a fact that you could see two hundred sixty miles in all directions and there wasn't a human being anywhere in all that land?"

Trying to be discreet, Clio clicked at the keys on her desktop terminal/communicator, but before she could come up with an answer Jason realized what she was doing, laughed, and said, "Four hundred twenty kilometers. Sorry. I've been using meters all my life, but feet still mean more to me. Anyway, I hope you didn't mind my teasing you before, Clio, but it does seem kind of funny that after you decided that you were going to spend the rest of your life in museums and libraries, and not fly in space like the rest of the family—"

Clio shrugged. "In data storage for the ship, we're taking along practically the whole accumulated knowledge of the human race. And

besides, I'm going out where no one can phone me, there are no com-
mittees to serve on, and there's plenty of time and quiet to read and
think. Historian heaven."

They chatted for a couple of minutes more, but since the only things
they really had to say to each other were that they would miss hearing
from each other as the starship drew further from Earth and radio began
to take months and years to reach between ship and home, and that they
all hoped the person on the other side of the communication link would
be happy and healthy, it wound down fast.

After they rang off, Clio found herself with almost an hour with
nothing to do. She had been on the ship for a total of four months of
shakedown cruises; there was nowhere to explore that she hadn't already
been many times. It was a good thing for this first expedition to another
star system that they had known how important it would be that everyone have enough different projects so that boredom was unlikely, or at
least fairly easy to relieve.

The call from Uncle Jason and Aunt Olga had set her mind drifting
to the "family business" again. When she had left Mars twelve years ago,
as a quiet, studious girl of sixteen, she had mainly been thinking of finally seeing the glories of Earth for herself. Her first couple of years, spending some of the funds her parents had been accumulating for decades in
Earthside accounts, had been wonderful—cities filled with people,
oceans, weather, being outdoors without a pressure suit, museums, con-
certs, theater. Harvard had been a wonderful chance to study all the
things she was seeing in the summers, to learn what all the riot of experience, sound, smell, and color meant, and so she had drifted very naturally into graduate school in history.

There is hardly anything more useful to a historian's career than
access to a unique body of material. And that "family business" Jason
had referred to went far back in Clio's family; many of her relatives had
had a great deal to do with getting humanity to this moment. Jason's
father had died on the Moon, way back when South Pole City had four
people and was known as Tiber Base; Jason and Olga's child, Christopher Terence II, had been the first baby born on Mars. Aunt Olga's
brother Yevan had become the father of Clio just sixteen days after
Chris's birth, so that Clio herself was the second baby born on Mars, a
phrase that she had gotten a little tired of—when she had been in college she had thought that no one remembered Clio Trigorin, except in

occasional jokes (most of them having to do with the difficulty in finding a prom date when the only boy your age on the planet was your first
cousin).

Thus when she entered her grad program in history, because Clio
had a famous aunt and uncle—and through them connections into the
Terence, Jarlsbourg, Trigorin, and Romany families as well—whenever
the subject of her dissertation came up, every professor would lean across
the desk and say, "You have access to information about the most important events of the last century; why don't you do that? It all but guarantees publication."

She hadn't resisted much; at the least it was an excuse to communicate a lot with her family. And it turned out that Uncle Jason was a little
bit of a pack rat. He had diaries and letters from a lot of his family, all
sitting patiently in storage on Earth, since his stepfather, Sig Jarlsbourg,
had kept so much of it for him, always figuring that any year now Jason
would get around to returning. When Clio had begun serious research,
Jason had immediately given permission, and Sig had opened the files
and stored objects to her. She often wondered if Jason realized just how
revealing much of that stuff was. Well, when *From the Moon to the Stars*
was published, he would figure it out.

Besides, he already knew what it meant to be a source for her. Clio's
first book, *A Short History of the Human Emigration Into Space*, had been
not only a critical success but something of a popular one. It had certainly put Clio into a position to write the next, larger and more substantial
book, *From the Moon to the Stars*.

And then her advisor had come to her and mentioned a couple of
connections, and a possibility of being chosen for *Tenacity's* mission,
the first crewed voyage to Alpha Centauri. And though she hadn't been
in space or off Earth for almost ten years, something in the family heritage had sat up and said, "Yes, I need to do this." She had tested, prepared—and, because the primary requirement was to be a historian with
a solid track record of publication, in excellent health, under the age of
thirty (so that there was at least a chance for some years of service after
she got back) she had surprised everyone (except perhaps her family) by
qualifying.

And here I am, she thought. *A little late to have any doubts, and I don't
think I have any anyway.*

She clicked idly through her computer files. Every document she
had found in Sig Jarlsbourg's collections at the ShareSpace Global Cor-

porate Museum, and every interview she had ever done on this project—more than four hundred, with a hundred six different subjects—was there in an ultrahigh-resolution copy. *One more benefit of our study of Tiberian technology,* she thought: *we'll preserve a better record of our journey to go find them, or at least find the place where they were. And still we haven't caught up with them; they made materials we can't begin to duplicate. This very ship's design is built around having to use their awesome power source with our weak and inferior materials.*

She clicked faster, looking at the images of strange objects on the Moon and the Tiberian pictures of their own departure for the stars, millennia ago. *How strange that on our first voyage to the stars, we humans already know, to a great extent, what we will find circling the nearest star. In that, our experience will certainly differ from theirs. And how strange, too—*

Idle clicking through the files landed her on the picture of Chris Terence the day he arrived for astronaut training. Jason's father, the man her cousin had been named after. Unbidden, phrases leapt into her mind—something that might make at least a decent beginning, in rough draft, of *From the Moon to the Stars.*

"Between July 20, 1969, and July 20, 2069, humanity went from a collection of squabbling nations to a more or less unified global civilization, and from barely achieving that voyage to the Moon, one and one half light-*seconds* from the Earth, to attempting one of four and a third light-*years*. I write these words as one who was born on Mars, who will be among this first human crew to leave the solar system, who can almost no longer remember how many times she has been to the Moon, and no matter how many times I compare the numbers to see how far we have come, still there is something lost that is central to the sense of it all.

"At our eventual top speed, we will take 3.75 seconds to go the distance that took Armstrong, Aldrin, and Collins three days in 1969. Or think of it in the way astronomers measure things here within our solar system: the distance between the Earth and the Sun is called one astronomical unit, or one AU. In 1962, Mariner 2—the fastest manmade object up to that time—took more than *three months* to travel about half an AU in a curving orbit on its way to Venus; at peak speed, riding on the beam of a Casimir-effect laser, we will cover the same distance in ten minutes. The Moon is one quarter of one percent of an AU away, and it took Apollo three days to get there; every year on its way around the Sun the Earth travels about six and a third AU and takes a year to do it;

in twelve years, we are going to go 275,000 AU. The difference in speed, and in distance covered, between our *Tenacity* and Yuri Gagarin's *Vostok* is far bigger than the difference between Columbus's *Santa Maria* and *Vostok*.

"And yet, as amazing as the numbers may be, our species itself excels them. Perhaps the most amazing thing is that during the single century in which we went from barely reaching the Moon to voyaging to the stars, we very nearly stood still for the first thirty years—"

PART I
CONTACT LIGHT*—
ANOTHER SMALL STEP

2002–2013

*First words spoken by a human being on the Moon, July 20, 1969; what Buzz Aldrin said when the light that indicated there was something under *Eagle*'s feet came on.

1

A LOT OF TIMES I THINK I REMEMBER, BUT THE MIND PLAYS TRICKS. ONE giveaway, I guess, is that I remember myself from outside, not as if I were seeing things happening, but as if I were watching myself. There's a shrink I know, a guy who only came up to Mars a couple of oppositions ago, who says that's not infallible, but a pretty good indicator that I don't really remember it myself. Probably I heard it told to me so often that now I have a story about it in my head, one in which I picture my four-year-old self sitting there on the living room rug at Grandma Terence's house, watching the TV, listening to my mother explain how my father might be about to be killed.

Talk to the old guys at NASA, the ones who were retiring when I was a rookie, and they call the period that started after the last Moon landing in 1972 the Bad Decades. The exact dates are kind of hard to pinpoint; a lot of people say NASA was still doing okay with Skylab and Viking and the Soyuz rendezvous, fell apart more in the late Carter and early Reagan years, and that they had really pulled themselves out of their slump when they made their commitment to Starboosters for some missions in 2000—which was the year Dad joined the astronaut corps, so I guess you could count him as part of the turnaround. But most of the old guys count the wreck of the *Endeavour* as the last gasp of the Bad Decades, and so you could say that's the period my dad really came out of.

Dad was Chris Terence, astronaut and astronomer, born the year of the first Moon landing. He was what they called a "do-looper" at Cal Tech, because in one of the old computer languages, a do-loop was a group of code that the computer would keep doing over and over, and at Cal Tech, a do-looper was a guy who got his bachelor's, came back for his master's, and then came back again for his doctorate. So Dad was class of '90, class of '93, and class of '97, with as much time spent as possible in the 144th Fighter Wing of the California Air National Guard, getting his jet hours for his astronaut application.

He'd hit on the tactic of going to Cal Tech and joining a Guard squadron that flew fighter jets long before he actually did it. I remember that years later, among his things, we found a list from a student college guide of the top fifty scientific and technical universities, with his penciled-in notes on the nearest Guard airbases; from the date, it had been October of his sophomore year of high school. There at the top of the list was Cal Tech and Fresno ANG Base. Grandma said it didn't surprise her at all to realize he'd started planning that when he was sixteen; she used to say that his next word after "Mama" had been "astronaut"—"There was never anyone who wanted a particular job more than that boy wanted to be an astronaut."

So he'd poured himself into a BS in aeronautical engineering while working as a crew chief in the Guard, a good student job that not only helped him pay for college but got him the leg up for his next steps—a master's in applied physics plus flight school, and finally his doctorate in astronomy with as many hours of flight time as he could squeeze in.

After he picked up the doctorate, he discovered for himself what any number of scientists had been finding out in the USA in the nineties—that unless you were working on something that Xerox or IBM wanted to build this week, or doing medical work under the protection of some congressman with plenty of clout, nobody in the States wanted you. We were training the world's scientists, and they were going home and opening up a thousand frontiers, but we were sending *our* young scientists—the ones who were quite often in their potentially most productive years—off to teach community college, write gaming software, or do routine hospital lab tests. Those were the years, after all, when the woman who won the Nobel Prize in Medicine for her doctoral dissertation pointing the way to making specific viruses against specific cancers got the call from Stockholm at the clinic in Beverly Hills, where she had gone after taking her specialty in dermatology. Whether it was conscious policy or not, America wanted its affluent teenagers to look good a lot more than it wanted to maintain its dominance in science and technology. Boldly going where no one had gone before was all right on television, but in real life people who wanted to do that had to pursue it as an expensive hobby.

So Chris, who was stubborn, shrugged and decided that if he wanted a steady income, he'd have to get the astronaut job sooner than he'd planned on. Between the Guard, adjunct jobs teaching the same beginning astronomy course at each of three different LA-area colleges, and sometimes filling in as a ferry pilot for FedEx, he was eking out a living, able to afford a little apartment all to himself in Saugus.

It just happened that as one of his ongoing projects, he was obtaining deep-sky images (telescope pictures of the sky in areas that didn't have relatively nearby objects like the planets) over the Internet from various observatories. He had set up a program to record the date and time the pictures were taken and see if any similar bit of sky had been photographed at some other time, then compare the two; if any of the stars in the picture seemed to move, his computer would flag the case, because apparent motion indicated that the object might be an asteroid or comet. By having his computer program search the pictures mainly in the plane of Earth's orbit, he could look for ECOs, "earth-crossing-objects"—asteroids or comets that might someday hit the Earth. There were several small journals that were willing to publish any paper that identified a new ECO, and right now one of the things he needed, while looking for a better job and hoping to get into the astronaut corps, was more papers in his *curriculum vitae*, the resumé of publication that a research scientist has to submit with every job or grant application.

It was his fourth find, nothing that could ever either be a threat to the Earth or a reasonable destination for space explorers. It was only a lump of tarry rock, about the size of a smallish mountain on Earth, but at least under the International Astronomical Union rules it was named Terence 1995 BR, which simply meant "the asteroid discovered by Terence in 1995, with the randomly generated code 'BR' attached in case he gets lucky again this year."

And again, more or less by chance, one community college where he taught had an aggressive PR director, who faxed an account of the find to the local television stations. This was during the second week of August, traditionally a slow news time when many programs run large numbers of human interest stories. Consequently, Channel 9, needing a little bit of footage for its 10 P.M. news, dispatched a brand new reporter, Amber Romany, with a cameraman, to get a comment.

Chris was just emerging from his classroom, surrounded by the usual array of bewildered students who were trying to get out of a requirement, or into a class, when he was approached by a young woman with flame-red hair, not much older than his students, who pointed a microphone at him. Behind her a bearded and ponytailed young cameraman with a nose ring, wearing a paint-spattered T-shirt, crouched down and brought the camera up to his shoulder, zooming in on Chris. Startled, he took a step back.

Amber turned to face the cameraman, pushed her red hair up slightly, got the nod from him, and said, "We're here with Dr. Christopher Terence, discoverer of a new asteroid which has been named in his honor. Dr. Terence, any comment?"

"Who the hell are you?" he demanded. Dad was never to be noted for his tact.

"Amber Romany. Channel Nine. Doing my job, at the moment; the station said to interview you and the college said you'd be here. So what's it like to discover a new asteroid?"

"I got home and when I checked my computer screen, the program told me I had done it," he said. "So I rechecked the results from the program and it looked like it was right; then I checked to make sure it wasn't a previously known one; then I notified the IAU, they agreed with me, and that was it. About as exciting as accounting but it doesn't pay as well." He turned to storm off, intending to find out who had gotten TV people involved in this.

Then Amber asked, "Any intention to go there yourself?"

"What?"

"Your vice president said you fly F-15s for the Air National Guard. The 144th's office in Fresno says you fly a lot. You've published a ton of papers since you got your Ph.D. That's just the basic research I could do with some phone calls and an on-line search of scientific abstracts, but I think I see a pattern in it. All that time in jets plus all that scientific work is a guy who wants to qualify for the astronaut corps."

Chris looked around. Some of his students were still hanging around, either watching him or trying to sneak in behind him and Amber to wave at the camera. They were looking at him a little strangely; he shrugged and raised his hands. "All right, caught and convicted. I can't imagine a less interesting rock in space, but I'd be happy to go there or anywhere else."

She smiled at him. "Now will you tell me how you felt about finding the asteroid?"

"Well," he said, "it's always kind of astonishing; there's a lot of space and all the asteroids ever found, together, wouldn't make up one percent of the Moon's mass . . ."

Her interview with him took almost an hour in the hallway; afterwards, as he was grading papers and even as he drifted off to sleep, he kept telling himself that what had happened was that Amber was so pretty that he'd foolishly kept talking, and also kept reminding himself that the interview would probably come out so distorted that no one with any scientific knowledge would even be able to figure out what she had been talking about.

To his surprise, he stayed up later than usual to catch the news, and he had to admit that the interview seemed to be intelligent and seemed to focus on the important issues. Also, looking at Amber on the screen, he realized she was every bit as beautiful as he remembered.

The next day, summoning his courage because he remembered how he had snapped at her when she first appeared outside his classroom, he wrote her a note, in which he grudgingly admitted that she had done a pretty good job on the interview, adding that it was one of the few times he had seen a science story done well. He even apologized for his gruffness when she first approached him—and apologizing didn't come easily to Chris Terence.

Three days later, after he had decided that he'd really made a fool of himself and he needed to stop thinking about her, she phoned him. They met for coffee, and she turned out to be at work on a documentary about JPL, where he knew a lot of people. More or less, that's not only how my parents met, that was to be the whole pattern of their relationship: two smart, talented people yelling at each other, then getting interested in a conversation, and later (sometimes) apologizing.

They were married within a few months, startling all their friends. Following the wedding they had a couple of lean years, during which her salary was three times his and they never bought a car in working order, only junkers he could get to run for a few weeks or months. Afterwards, when they would tell stories about what they had done to keep food on the table and a roof over their heads, I wondered more than once whether maybe those hadn't been the years in which they were happiest.

Anyway, I was born in August 1998, and I guess that made getting a little more cash more urgent, so they borrowed money and put together "Spacetour," a ten-half-hour documentary about the solar system, with Mom narrating and Dad giving some little on-screen lectures, using a lot of footage from public archives. It was a hit with kids and got widely syndicated; I remember it was still showing up on various TV stations when I was about ten because Dad tended to describe the decades-long orbits of the outer planets with phrases like "when my son Jason is thirty . . ." and my friends would hear that and tease me.

It was their last really lean year. By the time I was learning to walk, their careers were taking off abruptly. Dad was accepted into the astronaut corps within a week of Mom getting picked up by the network for their morning show. They moved to Houston, which shortened Mom's commute to Washington and put them near Dad's mother—a very important resource, because they were both away a lot, and sometimes at the same time. I'm told that when Dad flew his rookie mission in late 2000, he was in orbit on my second birthday, and Mom was in Africa somewhere covering a famine. Grandma made them a video of me with the cake; considering the mess that was happening between me and the cake, I wouldn't have wanted to be there either.

Now that I was four, in 2002, I at least could recognize my parents on television when they appeared, which for my mother was every night. Ever since last year, when Mom had switched networks and gotten the evening news anchor job on one of the dozens of little startup networks that had proliferated at the turn of the century, the one firm rule from Grandma was that we never missed the evening news. Dad sometimes teased his mother that what she liked about it was that this way she had a relative on television. Astronauts were never on TV anymore.

So Grandma and I had just tuned in to Mom's show, and neither of us was expecting to hear anything about Dad's shuttle flight on *Endeavour*. The pace of the American space program had picked up a little bit since 1999, when the Chinese had startled everyone by announcing that they would launch a man into orbit on the fiftieth anniversary of their revolution, at the very moment when the Cold Peace was getting underway between the U.S. and China. Even though their first two launches had fizzled, it had still accelerated NASA's program. But though there were more launches, and to everyone's surprise the International Space Station looked like it would get done only about six months late, American manned spaceflight was just not making it onto the news much; it was too routine, and it contained practically no sex or violence.

The broadcast started out with no mention of *Endeavour*, but it was possible that if this were a slow news day, maybe they'd cut to the liftoff, or so Grandma said. I think I remember her saying that as we watched, anyway.

I have a copy of that particular news show, and I've watched it a few times; it's hard to capture, anymore, even in memory, any sense of how much everyone was worried about China. Mom's lead story was about China making new threats against the Republic of Taiwan, and the 82nd Airborne rushing there to back up the Taiwanese Army. It looked like a bad June; the American, Philippine, and Vietnamese navies were already holding joint exercises off the Spratley Islands, intended to put pressure on Beijing not to carry out their announced plans for constructing a missile tracking station there.

In the middle of the story, I saw Mom stop and squint for an instant, looking right at the TelePrompTer, and then she said, "This just in. We're going live to Houston, where there's apparently big trouble on the Space Shuttle *Endeavour*."

The picture jumped and bounced for a second, and then we were looking at Mission Control; instead of the usual laid-back atmosphere, everyone was leaning into his screen, and there was a lot of shouting. One thing I do remember vividly is that Grandma's hand was suddenly on my shoulder, clenching hard enough to hurt, and yet I didn't complain; I needed her touch just then.

To the extent that the television news organizations were bothering to cover a story that had grown stale and routine to them, they were billing this flight as the one that would "finish" the International Space Station (ISS), even though there were several flights to go after it before the station would be fully operational. The reason why they thought this was sitting in the cargo bay: the U.S. Hab Module, the American living quarters for the station. For almost four years, the station had been tenanted by a Soyuz crew of three in rotation (with an additional American, Japanese, or European in the mix). With the U.S. Hab, the constant occupancy could go up to six, and Chris Terence was going to be one of the first "real" scientists to serve a hitch there.

The mission was to take *Endeavour* up and rendezvous with the ISS, then dock the shuttle to the forward node, the cylindrical pressurized vessel that joined the U.S. Lab Module, the European Space Agency's *Columbus* Lab Module, and the Japanese Experiment Module. The node sat in the middle of the enormous truss, its ends festooned with solar panels and its center hung with pressure vessels and solar panels, that was the International Space Station. With the Russian crew, the American team would take the U.S. Hab out of the shuttle cargo bay, attach it to the central node by its hatch, lock it into place, pressurize it, and finally open the door from the node so that the U.S. Hab would become a permanent part of the crew space at the International Space Station.

Liftoff was absolutely normal; NASA engineers could discover nothing wrong afterwards, no matter how many times they played the tapes. The images that had been well-known to Americans for twenty years, by that time, looked the same as ever. In the familiar clear, deep blue light of early evening at Canaveral, *Endeavour* sat on her tail, pressed against the immense external tank that dwarfed her and the two solid rocket boosters beside her. Wisps of fog, caused by the terrible cold of the liquid hydrogen fuel in the external tank, swirled around. The countdown reached zero.

With a shuddering thunder, a white-hot ball of flame, welding-arc bright, appeared beneath the shuttle and grew swiftly into a great column of fire, carrying the shuttle aloft. The exhaust of the solid rockets forming glowing buttresses on that cathedral of light, *Endeavour* roared up into the evening sky, on her way to orbit. The hundred or so people sitting in the guest bleachers—mostly foreign tourists—applauded wildly, but even three miles from the launch site, the thunder of that liftoff drowned out their clapping and shouting. Few noticed at the time, in the reading off of routine information to the crew, that seas were rough in the Eastern Atlantic along its flight path; if all went reasonably well, there would be no need for the information, and all had been going reasonably well for many flights now.

Endeavour rolled over onto her back and continued downrange, shedding the solid rocket boosters, and throttling up engines to 106 percent. Normally the shuttle took off running its main engines at 104 percent of their rated power. With the heavy load of the hab module in its cargo bay, the shuttle was taking off at 106 percent. This had been done several times before; theoretically they could operate at 109 percent without risk.

The mission commander was Lori Kirsten, my father's closest friend from astronaut training, on her own second mission. She'd made her reputation by being the youngest woman ever assigned to a combat squadron, amplified it by transferring in short order to being a test pilot, moved to NASA well before her thirtieth birthday, and flown as the youngest shuttle pilot ever on her first mission. Hotshots are expected to be abrasive, for some reason, which I think is the only thing that saved her politically, because she had a knack for yanking people's chains (which was the surest way to earn Dad's respect). She sat in the left-side seat at the front of the highest of *Endeavour*'s three decks, the flight deck.

Chris sat in his seat behind her, to the right, tensely watching over Henry Janesh's shoulder. Janesh was on his first mission as pilot, but his reputation was good and no one was expecting any trouble.

NASA has had two kinds of astronauts since the early days: pilots and mission specialists. Every astronaut can fly, but not every astronaut is a pilot—a person whose job is to get the spacecraft to where it's going, and back. Most are mission specialists—they could fly the craft if they had to, if a pilot were disabled, but their main function is actually to carry out scientific research or do engineering construction in space. Chris, as the number one mission specialist, was in a different structure of authority than Henry, the pilot; both of them were answerable directly to Lori but not to each other. So Chris was watching over Henry's shoulder not because it was any of his business but just to have something to do—his job didn't really begin until they reached orbit. He listened as routine information came in over the headsets; at four minutes and five seconds into the flight, Mission Control told Henry that they were now "Negative Return," a routine warning. Henry acknowledged that they were now past RTLS, Return to Landing Site, the last possible point at which *Endeavour* could turn around and fly back to the Cape.

Any abort now would have to be a TAL—TransAtlantic Landing. Right now they were at a speed and altitude where as long as only one engine failed at any time in the future, they could make it to the emergency landing field near Zaragosa, Spain. As they gained more speed and height, in twenty-five seconds they would reach the point where up to two engines could fail and still leave them with enough momentum to get all the way across the Atlantic. If the first engine failed during these twenty-five seconds, they would then *have* to have the remaining two engines for the rest of the flight, and a second engine failure might prevent their reaching Zaragosa. If the first engine failed *after* those twenty-five seconds, then even a second engine failure would not keep them from a successful TAL. Thus during those brief seconds they would be passing through an area where if trouble started, they couldn't quite make it back to Canaveral, and everything would have to go right for them to reach Zaragosa. It wasn't so much a time of maximum danger as of minimum slack, but that was just enough to make Chris pay a little more attention over Henry Janesh's shoulder.

Chris did have one good professional reason for wanting to know instantly about any trouble during launch: he was the jumpmaster for this mission. Not every shuttle mission had one—emergency evacuation procedures were to some extent up to individual crews, who based what they did on a standard Egress Cue Card, a list of the tasks that would be necessary to get astronauts out of a shuttle that was headed for a crash. How they implemented the card was up to the mission commander, and as it happened Lori was a strong advocate of having a jumpmaster.

When she had been rotated through her turn at desk duty, she had been assigned to "contingency abort development"—figuring out what to do when the shuttle was in serious trouble—and like everything else she did, she had thrown herself into it eagerly, becoming convinced that evacuation would work best if there were a jumpmaster, someone whose job would involve getting the whole crew out safely. Several other crews had had them, so the idea itself was nothing new; whether a jumpmaster would be useful in a bailout was of course an unsettled question, because no bailout had happened yet. Still, it seemed to Lori that if anything unpredictable went wrong with the bailout procedure, it would be a good thing to have someone right there whose job was to fix it, because shuttles come down very fast, and there might not be much time if anything should hang up. After long study of the positions people sat in and what they would have to do, she had decided that the jumpmaster ought to be Mission Specialist Number One, who had the optimum combination of a clear pathway to the door and a clear view of every other crew member.

Chris might have gone along with it anyway, just because it was Lori asking him to do it, but after the volume of drill she'd made him work through on the subject, he had caught something of her sense of urgency about it.

Still, Chris relaxed a little when they passed "Negative Return," because the maneuver involved in getting the shuttle turned around and headed back was difficult and dangerous. They really needed to keep all three engines for the next twenty-five seconds to preserve some margins for dealing with trouble, but after that they would be in a position for a safe TAL even with multiple engine failures, and thus they would face no more than the usual dangers. Things were looking good.

The solid fuel boosters for the shuttle had never quite lived up to their potential; to compensate for thrust that was not quite up to the job, NASA had chosen to run the Space Shuttle Main Engines (SSMEs), the big engines that burned the liquid hydrogen from the external tank, at 106 percent for a heavy load like the U.S. Hab today. It wasn't *much* outside of what the SSMEs were supposed to be able to do without danger or damage; furthermore government high-tech hardware, especially aerospace equipment, is often drastically overbuilt. Thus they were running a risk, but a slight one, and one that many others had run before. In the event of an engine out, you'd have to go to 109 percent on the remaining two SSMEs; and tests at 109 percent had worked well enough in the past.

It wasn't much different from a family that is spending everything it earns, deciding that it is entitled to a little luxury, and spending a bit more, with the help of a credit card, and then a bit more than that, with the same card, because after all it's Christmas, and it's only a little more. It works for a while, and when it stops working, it seems very sudden and unfair.

Probably none of that was passing through either Henry or Lori's mind when Number One Main Engine flared and died. Per standard procedures, Henry powered up Number Two and Number Three, taking them to 109 percent, to inhibit SSMEs Two and Three from complete shutdown, since it was now vital that they keep running for the rest of the flight.

"Houston," Lori said, her voice level and calm, "we've got Performance Yellow; powering up Two and Three to one oh nine."

"Roger, *Endeavour*, you are go for TAL."

It was disappointing not to make it to orbit, Chris thought to himself, but after all, there would be other missions. So far there was cause for concern but not for alarm. The two still-running engines would just have to run a bit longer, against somewhat greater resistance, at 109 percent instead of 106 percent of design load.

"Roger, Houston, we are pressing on to Zaragosa with two engines."

Everyone was tense; you didn't need to have spent as much time as Chris and Lori thinking about ways things could go wrong to be aware that they were now at great risk. The seconds crept by as they climbed higher and higher on the two engines, gaining the forward momentum they would need to reach Zaragosa, in the northeast corner of Spain, most of the way across Iberia. Chris stole a glance to the side to nod at

Dirk Rodriguez, the Second Mission Specialist, who smiled back. Probably they were each trying to reassure the other. He hoped Sharon Goldman, Harold Spearman, and J. T. Murphy, the mission specialists sitting down on the mid deck, were all right as well and ready to move if necessary, but there was no way to check with all of them tied into their chairs, and comm lines needing to be kept clear for more urgent purposes.

There was an abrupt change in the feel of the ship; the power output from Engine Three fell to zero. At 350,000 feet, moving at Mach 17, *Endeavour* had two engines out.

"Shit," Henry muttered, but his hands were already triggering the software that would control the ship for this emergency abort. "Houston," Lori said, "this is *Endeavour*. We are at Performance Red. Do you confirm negative TAL—we'll have to bail out?"

The emergency abort software kicked in, whipping *Endeavour* around to stand on its tail. The one still-working main engine continued firing straight down at the Earth; the computer had already estimated that they would need all the altitude they could get to carry them as close as possible to the coast of northern Portugal, to make things easier for the rescue crews.

As the *Endeavour* stood up, she rotated slowly to "get the wind on her belly," putting the huge external tank under her, and to tilt slowly forward into a steep fifty-degree angle of attack—leaning high against the wind.

Even with the engine firing, the ship sank terribly fast; in a matter of seconds they reached the 280,000-foot altitude. Deceleration was now 2.9 g's, making everyone and everything feel almost three times as heavy as normal. Henry activated the "pitch forward" to get rid of the tank; slowly *Endeavour* began to level off, dropping her nose at four degrees per second, two-thirds the speed at which the second hand of a clock moves. When *Endeavour* was far enough forward, the remaining engine continued firing until the last moment, getting every last bit of fuel out of the tank and every last bit of velocity and altitude available. When they reached the point where *Endeavour* had to jettison the tank to reduce wind resistance for the rest of the flight, the shuttle itself flew a little forward and up, the wind drag pressed the tank downward, and with a thud the tank separated and fell away from them, hurtling down to the Atlantic far below.

The more nearly level flight slowed their rate of descent; deceleration was still increasing but not as terribly as before. At 250,000 feet, as they were crushed into their chairs at the moment of peak deceleration, Lori turned slightly and flashed them all a ghastly grin. "Well," she said, "now we're in good shape. From here on out it's just a regular reentry."

"Except we're going to miss the abort field by a few hundred miles," Henry added. "I guess here's where we find out if your abort procedure works."

"Oh, it'll work," Lori said. "I've *trained* that jumpmaster." She half-turned and poked Chris's leg through his pressure suit; he barely felt it through the heavy fabric. "It'll be almost twenty minutes till we're at jump height; everyone start checking your sea survival gear. In ten minutes I'll give a warning, and then five after that we put visors down and get ready to go."

The time seemed to race by as Chris and Lori confirmed, over and over, that everyone knew what to do, and everyone had a full, working kit. It seemed to Chris that the warning came almost right away; there was almost no time before Lori called for visors down, and they began the process.

By now they had slowed down enough to be moving at subsonic speeds as they came down through 45,000 feet. The sky was blue again and the sun shone on the ocean below them—but not for much longer. "Looks like we're going in past the terminator line," Lori said, her voice crackling in everyone's headphones. "Doesn't make much difference. Water is water whether there's light on it or not, and by the time the C-130 gets out there to pick us up, it will be dark and they'll have to use the radar beacons anyway."

Still, as they flew on away from the Sun, the dark rushed toward them over the sea terribly fast.

"Houston, we are beginning bailout procedures," Lori said, over the radio.

"Roger, *Endeavour*, we're tracking you and the C-130 is on its way out of Zaragosa right now. Weather on the North Atlantic is looking a little rough, but it's within design limits for your dinghies. Good luck!"

Lori turned back to Henry Janesh and said, "All right, start venting at forty, door jettison at thirty. Chris, plug in your long line, and as soon as the door goes, move to assist. By my procedure on this one, Henry, you go before Chris, I go last."

"Roger," Chris and Henry said, simultaneously.

While he waited for them to reach the 40,000-foot level, Chris made sure his long line would work; it was the comm line that would allow him to speak to all the others on board while also moving around down on the mid deck. Story Musgrave, the astronaut who had refined and developed the role of the jumpmaster, had come up with that device as a way to let the jumpmaster both communicate and assist at the same time. Chris thought a silent thanks to Story, who had also been one of his instructors in training.

Chris had just made sure for the third time when Lori said, "Forty thousand feet," and Henry said, "Venting," at the same time. Henry began to release the air pressure from the cabin; with their visors down, none of them could hear anything, but the fit of their suits changed subtly as the air pressure in the cabin equalized with that outside.

"Thirty thousand," Lori said, as Henry said, "Door jettison." Chris felt a sharp lurch as Henry triggered the charges that blew the door; the door whirled off into the darkening evening sky, out of sight in an instant. "Deploying the pole now," Henry said, dispassionately. Chris had just a moment to see the fourteen-foot pole move into place at the top of the yawning doorway, sticking out into the dark night, but he was busy releasing himself and getting down onto the mid deck.

He undid his lap belt and then threw his harness back over his head. He disconnected the tube that supplied him with breathing oxygen from the place where it entered his suit on his left thigh. He made sure the extra-long comm line was still in place and had not snarled in his harness. Then he unhooked the hose that supplied cooling water to the suit from the thermal electric cooling unit under the seat. He should be free now; he tried to stand up. "Comm check," he said.

"You're fine," Lori said. "Get 'em out, Chris."

He climbed down onto the mid deck below, trying to sound both confident and casual as he said, "All right, in order and by the book, people. Sharon, you're first."

At once she undid her lap belt, threw her harness back, and unhooked oxygen, comm, and cooling water lines. She stepped forward to meet Chris at the base of the pole, by the dark open doorway.

The curved metal pole protruded fourteen feet from the side of the ship into the howling wind outside. The purpose of the pole was to carry the crew out beyond the slipstream before releasing them. *Endeavour* was still moving at nearly two hundred miles per hour; if they just stepped out the door, they would be caught in the slipstream and hurled against the fuselage, wing, or rudder.

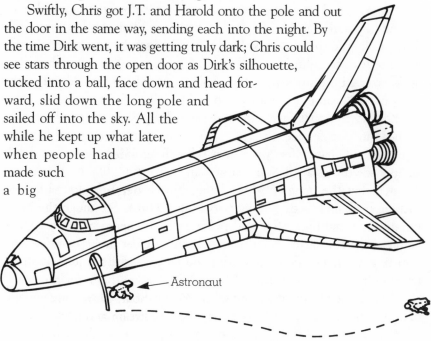

With a tug, Chris undid the Velcro on the upper right strap over the shoulder of Sharon's suit, exposing the ring there. He guided her to the row of hooks that waited, hanging from the base of the pole by short straps, and fastened the ring on Sharon's suit to the hook. "Grab it," he said, over the suit radio, and Sharon took the strap in both hands, reaching up to do so—she was a small woman, just a couple of pounds over the minimum weight and exactly the minimum height. "Tuck hard, and stay tucked!" Chris added. "I'll give you the pushoff."

Sharon picked her feet up off the floor so that she hung from the pole by her right shoulder. Chris shoved her forward and the hook slid through the securing mechanism; another push, and she slid outward away from *Endeavour*. The 200 mph wind yanked her around so that her head pointed toward the ship's nose and she hung face down over the cold black sea more than five miles below. The pole was curved so that the wind would move her gently along it; she accelerated down the pole to its end and sailed off the end into the ever-darkening sky. The release of tension from the hook would arm Sharon's chute, and an automatic altimeter would deploy it when she reached a safe altitude; all she had to do now was carry out the basic procedures for waiting to be rescued.

Swiftly, Chris got J.T. and Harold onto the pole and out the door in the same way, sending each into the night. By the time Dirk went, it was getting truly dark; Chris could see stars through the open door as Dirk's silhouette, tucked into a ball, face down and head forward, slid down the long pole and sailed off into the sky. All the while he kept up what later, when people had made such a big

Astronaut

Space Shuttle Bailout Procedure

deal out of it that he didn't want to hear about it again, he called a "running line of patter," reassuring each crew member, checking through every small detail, trying for a perfect by-the-book bailout and plenty of assurance to his crew.

Henry came next, as Lori had told him to. The ship was now on autopilot; since all it had to do was descend straight ahead for another two hundred seconds at most, and the shuttle autopilot was so sophisticated that theoretically it could land the ship even if the whole crew were incapacitated, Chris didn't spare much thought to worry about there not officially being a pilot anymore. He yanked the Velcro and pulled the ring as he told Henry, "Okay, just like the others, so far I've had perfect tucks from everyone. A bit to the left—there." He slid the ring from Henry's suit onto the hook on the pole. "Tuck up and let's go, see you in Spain—okay, good."

Henry had pulled his feet up into a tight tuck. Chris shoved the large man hard, using his shoulder, and Henry's hook slid out of its restraining mechanism and down the pole, Henry swinging under it, suddenly lining up with the wind, hurtling down the pole, and disappearing out into the stars.

Chris turned to assist Lori and she wasn't there. He looked back behind him and there she was; as she had been climbing down from the flight deck onto the mid deck, her harness had snagged on her chair, and now she was struggling to free herself. Chris jumped up onto the upper deck, grabbed the stuck part, and yanked as hard as he could, but without success. "Lean in toward your chair," he said. "It's almost free."

She did, and that gave him some slack. He pushed the stiff hose a bit farther into the crevice, the thick gloves making him do it all by sight since he could barely feel what he was handling. His pressure suit didn't let him see things at his waist either, and something like Murphy's Law dictated that the hang-up would be at waist level, so he found he was rocking back and forth to take a look and then try to move the hose. Finally by pinching it flat and pulling gently, he gained some slack before it caught again. Another pinch and a twist broke her free, and Lori finally climbed down onto the mid deck. "Not bad, jumpmaster. I knew I hired you for something," Lori said.

They leaped to the door and Chris hastily deployed her ring and got her onto the second hook on the pole. "Remember to tuck!" he said.

"Thank you," she replied. "Now get in place yourself. Captain gets off last."

He stood in front of her and felt her pop the Velcro to free the ring on his right shoulder, something pulling upward, and then a firm tug as she made sure the hook was really on his ring. "And don't you forget to tuck, either," she added. "Just like all the drills, Chris; see you in the bar later tonight."

He kicked forward hard, felt the mechanism release him down the pole, and, hands still clutching the strap, slid out and down the pole, pulling his legs up tight to his chest and tensing his arms.

When the wind grabbed him it was as if a giant hand had seized his whole body and tried to pull it off the pole behind *Endeavour*. He was abruptly flying forward, headfirst, perpendicular to the pole face pointed down at the sea below, and then he swooped down the pole in a motion that felt like some exotic amusement ride, the hook running over the pole making a terrible thunder through his helmet.

The rumble of the hook and its pull on his shoulder ceased, and he was weightless, falling through the starlight toward the little glimmers that danced on the dark sea three miles below him. In the corner of his eye he saw *Endeavour* shoot away forward in front of him, as his much greater wind resistance caused him to slow down abruptly while the ship flew on ahead.

A long few breaths went slowly by and then Chris's altimeter decided he was at a low enough altitude; the chute deployed and he found himself yanked savagely upward for a moment, then drifting down. He could feel a great deal of motion and realized, with a grunt of irritation, that there was a fairly high wind tonight; not only had the seven crew members, released across a period of four minutes or so, been scattered along twelve miles of *Endeavour*'s trajectory, but now the wind would scatter them further. He could see stars off to the sides in several directions as he floated down on the chute, so apparently, even if the waves were bigger and the wind stronger than he'd have liked, at least there would be clear light to see them by. As he descended, the Moon, not far from full, rose majestically out of the sea to the east. Twisting to look that way, he picked out Lori's parachute, so at least everyone had gotten out the door all right.

The Moon had nearly cleared the surface of the water, a huge glowing orb like a monstrous eye against the horizon, when Chris triggered his life preserver so that it was fully inflated by the time that he plunged into the water.

One of many strange things was that there was no sensation of wetness; the pressure suit was still sealed and though there were only about ten minutes or so of air in it, that was more than enough for the purpose. Chris felt a strange shove on his back and looked around to see his dinghy automatically deploying. It swelled up behind him, forming a little platform on the sea, and he gripped the side, pushing down and hauling himself up. One hard heave put him into the dinghy, and now he was able to open his visor and let himself cool off and breathe comfortably. He activated the survival radio to help them find him; his personal locator had been on since he left the ship, so he was sure they knew where he was.

He looked over toward the Moon; a full Moon means a high tide when it passes directly overhead, but here in the middle of the ocean he couldn't think of what difference it would make to him. As he watched, he caught another glimpse of Lori as she splashed down all but due east of him, shadowed against the Moon. If the rescue crew got here soon enough, he could possibly point her out to them; he could just see her dinghy from where he bobbed on the waves.

Far off in the distance he heard the rumble of a jet, but it didn't seem to be coming this way; a couple of hours later, as he lay in the dinghy, a helicopter approached and dropped a specialized, larger dinghy—one in which they could haul him back up—plus a pararescue jumper to help get him into it. Assisted by the pararescue diver in his wet suit, Chris climbed over to the lift dinghy, and the rescuer joined him. Then suddenly the cables overhead tightened and hauled them up toward the belly of the chopper. It was less than three hours since they had lifted off.

The two things that were to make it a bigger event had already happened, but no one knew yet. A CNN camera crew, en route in a Learjet from London to cover a civil war in Africa, had heard the news and managed, using their radio scanners, to listen in on NASA communications and figure out the position that *Endeavour* was headed for. As they diverted to the site, they found that one of their scanners could pick up the shuttle's radio beacon, and thus, between further announcements of the position and following the path along which the signal grew stronger, they rapidly closed in on *Endeavour*.

As they raced after it, phone calls were fanning out of Atlanta to everywhere, offering rights and collecting money; by the time *Endeavour* finally hit the Atlantic, four networks were carrying it besides CNN, right at the beginning of prime time, and so an estimated 128 million viewers saw it happen.

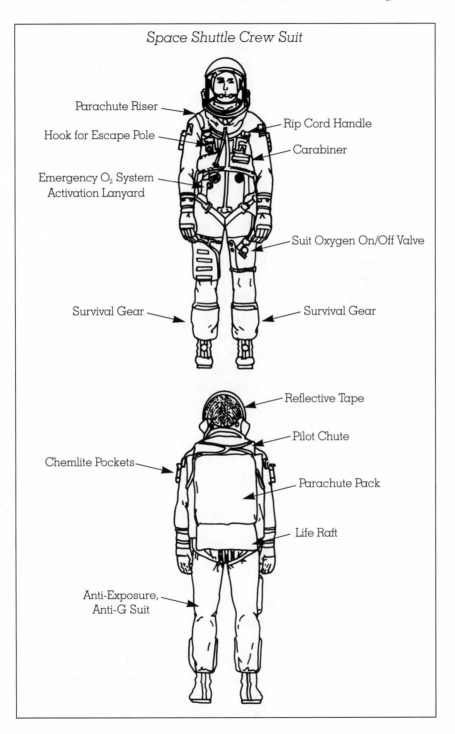

Space Shuttle Crew Suit

The shuttle had never been designed to ditch in water; it had pushed the edge of the technology of the early 1970s, when it had been designed, and many desirable features had had to be sacrificed.

It also had "the glide ratio of a brick," as the first pilots to fly it tended to say, meaning that compared to other aircraft, the ratio between how far it moved forward and how far it fell in a given time, when gliding, was extremely unfavorable.

This wasn't obvious at first when *Endeavour* was still fairly high above the water. It seemed to be flying along more or less as usual, except that its door was open and a pole protruded from it. Still guided by its autopilot, it stayed straight and level.

But as it dropped closer to the water, you could see from its relative motion that it was coming in very fast. Now millions watched as it fell fast and hard, flat bottom to the water.

The impact was partly masked by a great plume of white water as *Endeavour* made contact. The force broke her in half; the crew cabin, in the forward part, went under and sank like a stone, but the largest part, with the wings, cargo bay, and engines, tore free of the cabin and flipped over on its back, rudder-first into the water. With a great eruption of air bubbles, *Endeavour* slipped down into the dark green water and was gone, on its way to the mud a mile below, taking the U.S. Hab with it. In the bright moonlight, the CNN crew captured the whole eerie spectacle, the crewless *Endeavour* flying mindlessly down onto the sea surface, breaking apart in an immense spray of white foam, and sliding into the dark, choppy sea. Within a day, one out of every six people on Earth—a billion people—would see that spectacular crash on the moonlit sea and would hear some announcer intone that the United States had lost not just a shuttle but also the living quarters for the International Space Station.

The other thing that was memorable was still worse; no one knew how it had happened, but Sharon Goldman's arm was broken when they found her. Broken arms are common enough even in sport parachutists and military ejections—the force of the wind when you jump out of an airplane is strong enough to break an elbow or pull an arm out of its shoulder socket, if it catches you the wrong way. And she had been bailing out at far greater speeds. In any case, with a broken arm, she had been unable to climb into the dinghy. When they found her, she was hanging by the wrist she had knotted into one of the grab lines, from the side of the upside-down dinghy, only her hand above the water, drowned.

The inquiry couldn't reconstruct exactly what had happened; clearly she'd had to open her visor to breathe, but so had everyone else. There was nothing wrong with her life preserver as far as they could tell, except that at some time or other it had deflated after being inflated. Theories abounded—that she had panicked, that she had been unable to bear the pain in her broken arm from being yanked through the water and had deflated it herself trying to get a more stable position, that she had been overcome by hypothermia and become irrational, that something had gone wrong because this was her first time in the new improved suits, or that her life preserver had simply failed in a way no one could duplicate afterwards.

I was sort of sad, but at the age of four the concept of death isn't there yet, really; I knew death was something that could happen on a space voyage, and I knew that it was bad, but beyond that I had no real appreciation at all for what had happened. I was just glad that Dad was safe and would be home much sooner. If he had gone up to ISS as planned, he'd have been there for six months, and now I would probably see him in a day or so. Grandma, who had a pretty good idea of what space politics was like, and what kind of trouble was ahead with the loss of so much of the space program's physical capital in one accident, simply told me, "Now, don't be surprised if your father is very sad and upset when he gets back. He might not have a lot of time for you, or want to do anything together. He's just had a really, really bad day."

2

IT SELDOM TAKES THE NEWS MEDIA MORE THAN AN HOUR OR TWO TO DECIDE what the essence of a story is, what kind of tale to tell to the public. Four images stayed in the public mind from the initial coverage, and television reporters quickly found a simple way to link them.

The first of these was the *Endeavour* crash itself. The sheer violence and power with which a symbol of American prowess had been torn apart guaranteed that the media would run it over and over; if the media lives for nothing else, it's image and impact, and here was an image with a powerful impact. The second was of the dinghy floating on the sea, Sharon Goldman's lifeless hand reaching for the help that had come far too late.

Set against those overwhelming images of loss and destruction, which played over and over on television for days afterwards, there were two countervailing ones. One was of a grinning, laughing Lori Kirsten being pulled from the water. (For years afterwards, Aunt Lori used to get annoyed by that photo—enough so that Dad and later Sig knew they could always get a rise out of her by asking what joke the rescue crews had been telling her. She said nobody should be held responsible for the way they looked when they had just missed being killed, and that she was laughing not because she was having fun but because she was relieved.)

And the other was the voice of Chris Terence, carefully and calmly helping each astronaut onto the pole and out the door, and finally freeing Lori from the tangle that one of her suit hoses had made in her seat.

That one used to make Dad angry, too. "What I was doing was just following the manual, damn it. Same thing Lori was doing. We were following standard procedure for that situation. If that's what makes a hero, then every postal clerk who sells you a stamp for the right price is a hero. And I don't see why—"

That was about the point where he would normally get cut off, because he would be having the argument with Grandma, Mom, or the NASA PR people. Grandma would point out that his career was advancing and that it was about time. Mom would sit down and patiently explain, once again, that nobody in the business, with the possible exception of Mom herself, was interested in any of that, that TV news exists to sell shampoo, not to inform the public, and that holding up someone as a hero is much more important, from a standpoint of shampoo sales, than examining whether there is anything heroic about that person.

And some NASA Public Affairs Officer or other—the kind my father called a "PR clown"—was usually on the other end of a phone line, so at the time I didn't hear what they were saying. I asked Dad what PR stood for, and he said "Privacy Rapists," a term which Grandma and

Mom refused to explain, except to tell me that Dad was kind of upset and I shouldn't take anything he said too seriously.

Years later, when I had a little more experience with such things myself, I understood a lot more of what had been going on. NASA was in deep trouble. The budget cuts of the last few years had always been imposed with the insistence that the space station would go forward, if for no other reason than the sheer embarrassment that would ensue if, having lured the Russian space program, Japan's NASDA, and Europe's ESA into this thing, we then backed out of the deal. So the agency had little discretion in how it spent its funds; ISS had to be their top priority. Other missions had been restricted to what could fly on the old, heavy *Columbia*, mostly smaller-scale science missions. *Atlantis*, *Discovery*, and *Endeavour* had been almost dedicated to ISS.

Nor was there any apparent easy way to replace *Endeavour*. The Balanced Budget Act of 1996 had made deficit spending impossible in 2002, so any extra funds would have to come from somewhere else. There was little prospect of building a new shuttle, as had been done after the *Challenger* disaster fifteen years before; the replacement had been *Endeavour* itself, and besides the design was almost thirty years old now.

But there was no way that the remaining three orbiters, *Discovery*, *Atlantis*, and *Columbia*, could carry the necessary traffic for the station, most especially because only *Discovery* and *Atlantis* were equipped to dock there. *Columbia*, too old and heavy to be equipped for docking, was picking up many of the other NASA missions that called for a shuttle.

There had been a serious effort to find a new launch vehicle to take the shuttle's place, but that too had run afoul of simple bad luck. In the early 1990s, experiments had begun in the Strategic Defense Initiative Office to try for a single-stage-to-orbit (SSTO) vehicle—a craft that would have "airliner like" operations, with no staging necessary to reach space, deliver astronauts and cargo, and return, with a quick turnaround at every point—what most ordinary people pictured when they thought of a "spaceship" or "rocket ship." The initial test vehicle, the DC-X, had demonstrated that the necessary maneuvering capabilities were indeed available; it could take off, hover, go from flying nose-down to flying tail-down, and land on its exhaust quite successfully.

Unfortunately, the next step, the X-33, had revealed where the problem would be. With the materials and fuels of the 1990s it looked like perhaps, just barely, it could be done. The DC-X experiments in 1993–95 were indeed encouraging—except that relative to fuel weight, the dead weight (percentage that wasn't fuel) of the DC-X was 80 percent too heavy, and still it was too fragile to hold up under the forces generated in test maneuvers—and those forces were a small fraction of what could be expected in an actual trip to and from orbit.

The specific weak link became clearer with the tests in 2001. A single stage to orbit vehicle, in order to get to orbit, needed to be about 90 percent fuel by weight, and the fuel-engine combination had to be something with a very high specific impulse. The specific impulse is the number of seconds that one pound-mass of fuel can put out one pound of thrust.

One of the many confusing things you have to deal with once your imagination gets off the ground and into the sky is that weight and mass are different things. The mass of an object is the same no matter where it is; you could think of it as the amount of matter in the object, or as the thing that causes the object to have inertia. The weight depends on where you are; it's the downward force of gravity and it can vary from enough to crush atoms (in a neutron star) down to almost zero (in orbit). Imagine a fifty-pound ball on a frictionless table: on Earth, you would need quite an effort to lift it; on the Moon you could lift it easily; on Jupiter you probably couldn't lift it at all. But if you gave it a push to start it rolling, regardless of where it was, the same push would always start it rolling at the same speed; and the same amount of force would be required to stop it.

A pound-mass, then, is simply the mass that, on the Earth's surface, would be pulled downward by gravity with a force of one pound. Thus on Earth, specific impulse is the number of seconds that a pound of fuel would burn with enough power to keep one pound of weight in the air. It is a measure of how much energy is left over after the rocket fuel has lifted its own weight and so of how much energy is left over to do anything useful.

The highest specific-impulses achieved with any common fuel could be gotten with liquid hydrogen—which was both very bulky (so the tanks would have to be large) and had a very small molecular radius (which meant it leaked out easily, through any kind of pores in the material enclosing it). So a tank to hold liquid hydrogen for an SSTO would have to be very large, extremely strong, highly resistant to cold (at normal air pressure, liquid hydrogen must be kept colder than minus 425 degrees Fahrenheit), very small in its pores, and extraordinarily light in weight. There simply was no such material, nor any prospect of it anytime soon.

The X-33 tanks, made with the very best available materials, were much too heavy and leaked frequently, and some cryonic vibration tests suggested the risk of cracking over time. There would be an SSTO, someday, just like in Buck Rogers—but the time was not yet. And meanwhile, the most promising effort to find something to replace the shuttle had run into a dead end that would probably stay dead for at least another decade.

All this trouble was made far worse by the loss of the U.S. Hab. First of all it had been a large fraction of the total American investment in ISS, and as such it was a great deal of money down the drain, with little prospect of finding more. To replace that module, Congress would have to cut something—a couple of bombers, a major dam, an urban interstate spur, a dozen rural hospitals—that had already been promised to constituents somewhere and would have to be taken away from them. The prospects of this were zero; some money might be scared up somewhere, but nothing like what was going to be needed to replace the hab module.

For some of those in Congress, there was an obvious solution: shut down the space program, hand over the surviving three shuttles to some private commercial operator, and offer to let the Europeans, Japanese, and Russians buy out our interest in the ISS—something which they didn't have the money to do, and which was even dumber when you considered that we were getting embroiled in the Cold Peace and badly needed Japan and Russia, at the least, as allies.

The president knew all this, of course—he could hardly have avoided knowing it—and he also knew that a large part of Congress had perfected the art of running against government programs. Where fifty years before, a congressman's standard move to get reelected was to talk about the programs he had voted for, nowadays it was to talk about what he had blocked, stopped, frustrated, investigated, or marginalized. Now that the space program rested on international cooperation, it made an even better target—no one had ever lost a seat if he could run against the Russians or the Japanese, demanding that they "carry their fair share" (though they were spending a higher proportion of budget than the United States) and that they "stop their free ride on the U.S.A." (even though for the last three years other nations had been lifting a lot of American payloads while we tied up the shuttles in the ISS, which had always been an American sponsored and operated project).

Against all this, there were two factors that were favorable: the president had a vision of where the space program fit into the national purpose, and like it or not the United States was going to *have* to do something, for a variety of reasons. First of all, there was the emerging Cold Peace with China. During the nineties, relations had veered all over the place between China and the other major powers, but for the last few years, several concerns had defeated every attempt to improve relations, and whether the United States liked it or not, we had drifted into the Cold Peace. First of all, under the gun to improve economic conditions in the countryside, especially in light of an abysmal human rights record that had alienated most of the young educated class and a ferocious population-control policy that had infuriated the peasant majority, the government in Beijing had responded by a program of "rural industrialization," chiefly meaning that they were going to get electricity and hot and cold running water to everyone, ASAP, regardless of cost, to be followed as quickly as possible with refrigerators and motorbikes. That required energy, and as strapped as the PRC was for foreign capital, energy meant burning their vast reserves of coal at an unprecedented rate.

By 2000, the Japanese and Koreans, who had cleaned up their own environmental problems a decade before, were infuriated by the sheer quantity of foul-smelling gases drifting downwind onto them; Chinese diplomats in Seoul and Tokyo had to be escorted to and from their embassies by police and were often pelted with rocks and bottles by gas-masked protesters. Acid rain in the South China Sea and northern Pacific was killing the surface-level microorganisms upon which the ocean food chain depended, wreaking havoc on already-depleted fishing grounds and threatening the Asian part of the Pacific Rim with protein starvation. There were unmistakable signs of forest die-offs from southern Alaska down through British Columbia to as far south as Eureka, and measurable damage extended as far inland as Banff, Helena, and Pocatello; the scientific basis had been well established decades before when power plants in the American Midwest had been killing forests in Scotland and Norway, and better satellites and remote sensing equipment meant that this time the world didn't have to wait for trees to die by the square mile before both the damage and the culprit could be identified.

All this earned China intense anger from its neighbors, but matters grew worse with a long string of "incidents" (the polite code word for "petty human rights outrages") associated with the British return of Hong Kong to China in June 1997. Objectively speaking, China's occupation and "firm hand" policy in Hong Kong probably had been gentler than the old Soviet Union's occupation of Prague thirty years before. But Hong Kong was a modern and well-equipped city, intimately tied into the global information net, and China had wanted it for its modernity; they couldn't shut down the modems, phones, and fax machines without destroying everything they had gained. So accounts of arbitrary arrests, police brutality, and sporadic rioting came not just from journalists interviewing refugees weeks or months later, as with earlier resistance to Communist occupations, but live as it happened, pouring over the broadcast systems and computer nets.

The embarrassment was compounded by China's failures in space. The first Chinese astronauts had been scheduled for 1999, in a licensed version of the old Soyuz capsule mounted on a purchased Russian Soyuz launcher, but had not flown till 2001. Now the launch facility on the island of Hainan was expanding rapidly, and the Chinese began to demand agreements from Vietnam and the Philippines to place downrange tracking stations in the Spratleys, access to the Philippines for an abort field, and a dozen other requirements for operating a large seacoast launch facility, all of which alarmed China's neighbors. Persuaded by the U.S. and Russia, an embargo against oil and uranium for China was imposed; the Chinese burned still more coal and began trying to jam satellite broadcasts into China; and as Chinese missile "tests" splashed down off California, the design teams who had been working on space-based missile defenses, quietly and on shoestring budgets, for decades, suddenly found that they had more money and attention.

Matters had only gotten worse with the Chinese attempt to upstage the 2000 Olympics (which they had wanted for Beijing and which had gone to Sydney instead on human rights grounds). Their second attempt to launch a manned Soyuz had ended ignominiously with the rescue of Chinese astronauts from the South China Sea in front of foreign journalists.

The eventual success of their first crewed launch the following year did not seem to remove the sting. Following that success, they announced the intention to construct a permanent base on the Moon, with their first landing to occur in 2011, to coincide with the hundredth anniversary of the outbreak of the Chinese Revolution. Since that time they had been launching with, at the least, an aggressive frequency, apparently driving to build up a base of experience as quickly as possible. Though they had not suffered any more serious mishaps, there always seemed to be a chip on the shoulder of their press spokespeople, and it probably didn't help that most of the global newscasters seemed to regard every Chinese launch as an occasion for crossing their fingers and holding their breath.

Thus China had become intensely determined to succeed in space, defiant on environmental and human rights issues and, because of the coal-burning problem and the festering embarrassment of Hong Kong, more and more antagonistic.

The foreign policy experts of both parties thought this was the wrong time to cut back on space; the Chinese had clearly signaled their intention to compete there, and leaders of both political parties agreed that this was a challenge we had to take up. Further, the *Endeavour*/U.S. Hab disaster, by producing a new set of heroes, had given the administration a set of ideal tools for selling the American public—and with them, the Congress—on a renewed and expanded effort in space.

The way to sell it, and the makings of such a program, were there. After every major disaster in American policy, there is almost always a presidential commission intended, at the least, to persuade people that things are being looked into and that the government is thinking about the problem. Historically, every so often such a commission exceeds its mandate drastically—just such maneuvers brought the Federal Reserve Board into existence after the Depression of 1907, and produced the basic American policy on nuclear nonproliferation in the late 1940s.

"Aunt Lori" always told me afterwards that when she got the phone call from the president and was told that she would be on the commission to review the *Endeavour* disaster, the next thing the president said was, "Now partly I want you on that commission because after that accident you and Chris Terence are the most publicly credible astronauts since Story Musgrave; people know you know your stuff. And Terence is not a real political guy, but I have a feeling you could be if you put your mind to it. Now, about the job itself, what your mission is for the inquiry. You're supposed to just figure out what happened and tell us how not to have it happen again. But if you maybe see some other improvements that could be made . . . or if you think more than just the shuttle needs overhauling . . . well, I can't say I would object to reading the report. I read too many reports that only talk about one little problem, right now."

Whenever she told that story, her eyes would twinkle and she'd say, "Jason, if you want to get ahead in the astronaut racket, you have to learn to recognize an order when you hear one. Especially when it's an order to exceed your orders."

Eight months after the accident, the commission made its report. Less than twenty pages of that report dealt with the accident and its causes; they said only that the SSMEs were getting old and had to be run at very high power, and it wasn't altogether surprising that the technology that had stretched the envelope in 1975 wasn't completely up to the challenge twenty-seven years later. A new program was needed—first a way to use off-the-shelf equipment to keep operating in space, because we could no longer afford the kind of shutdown that had happened after *Challenger*; then a conservatively designed, proven-technology replacement for the shuttles; then systematic movement toward better long-range solutions.

Luckily for the commission, the president, and NASA, all of the pieces for such a program were there already, not so much by design as by good luck. The worldwide space doldrums of the 1990s had allowed large quantities of unrealized designs and ideas, and underused hardware, to accumulate, and the Russian need for hard cash plus their decade of experience working with American companies had brought some of that hardware to a high degree of reliability. Thus the new plan could be presented as making maximum use of off-the-shelf technology and offering relatively few new risks.

Foremost of these opportunities was the remarkable Zenit, a workhorse rocket that Boeing was making under license from the Russian and Ukrainian firms that had privatized it. The Zenit had been originally intended as a strap-on booster for Energiya, the giant Russian booster rocket. Boeing had found another use for the Zenit in sea launches from a floating oil-drilling platform, where it had also performed well.

The Zenit was rugged and simple in design, and in particular its engines, once they were being made by Pratt and Whitney with better-quality Western materials, were simple, efficient, powerful, and cheap. Boeing had enhanced the Zenit further by creating the "Starbooster"—a standard Zenit first stage, surrounded by a shell equipped with fixed wings, a V-tail, landing gear pods, and two off-the-shelf, high-reliability fan-jet engines (the same model that had flown in the 737 for decades) in the nose. The Starbooster was the first really reusable rocket booster: when the fuel in the first stage burned out, the heat shield built into the shell allowed a Starbooster to return to the lower atmosphere without burning up, and the engine and wings allowed robot systems to fly it back to its base. Whereas the shuttle boosters had to be parachuted into the sea, fished out, and reconditioned after a dunking in saltwater, the

Starbooster flew back to a runway and could be rolled straight to the mechanics. Turnaround on reconditioning and reflying the solid fuel booster was measured in months; for the Starbooster, in days.

The commission had first considered the possibility of upgrading the shuttle by replacing each of the solid rockets with a "Twin Starbooster"—two Zenits in the same shell, with a "scissor wing" that folded against the body like closing scissors for launch and reentry, then unfolded for flyback. This gave better streamlining and performance on liftoff, made for an easier reentry from the higher flights that the twin engines allowed it to achieve, and most importantly, created a configuration big enough to do the job formerly done by America's aging fleet of disposable Titans and Atlases—early 1960s technology that was still in use forty years later—and be much cheaper than the Air Force's proposed EELV (Evolved Expendable Launch Vehicle), then being proposed for the same purpose.

Boeing had also pointed out that if you used Twin Starboosters on the shuttle, it would *more* than replace the dangerous solid fuel boosters—so much so that you could run shuttle main engines at well below 100 percent, gaining greater performance while avoiding both "*Challenger*-class" and "*Endeavour*-class" disasters.

But the commission noted with some regret that the time to do that had been some years ago; the shuttles were now getting old, nearing the end of their usable lives, and a better shuttle booster could only help the system limp a little faster. Ten years before, with four shuttles flying and the prospect of keeping them operating for a long time, two Twin Starboosters on each shuttle would have greatly enhanced capability and reduced cost; now it was an idea whose time had come and gone. The Starbooster had many uses, and it was a good idea to make use of it; the Twin Starbooster would simply go to the museum with all the other valid ideas that get bypassed on the road to the future.

Rather, they suggested, the thing to do was to concentrate on three problems:

- How can we get people and supplies to orbit at acceptable cost and safety, ASAP?
- How can we use the best of three decades of well-proven technology to create a certain-to-work low cost shuttle replacement?
- How can we eventually achieve the best possible space program combining what we can afford to pay and what we need to do?

Boeing had lost out on the bid for the EELV, but Boeing management had felt very strongly that there should be a market for their simple, proven-technology booster—putting one or two Space Shuttle Main Engines, with their more-than-twenty-year track record, directly under a large hydrogen/oxygen tank (derived from the shuttle's external tank with minimal modifications), and equipping it with the bare bones of guidance systems and a payload rack on top. The idea was that such a lightweight gadget—it was practically all engine and fuel—equipped with a good booster, would easily put itself into orbit. The reusable engines could be loaded into a shuttle cargo bay or otherwise wrapped up in a heat shield to bring back to Earth; the tank could stay up there to be used for construction. They had dubbed this simple, effective rocket the Centurion.

The prospect of sending large, empty pressure vessels into space for use there, as a side benefit to their use as boosters, led the commission to endorse the idea that NASA and the aerospace companies called the "HT Option" and everyone else called "the Big Can." HT stood for "hydrogen tank."

The idea was to make an advantage out of something that had always been a little bit of a problem. Liquid hydrogen burned with liquid oxygen has the highest specific impulse of any ordinary chemical rocket fuel. The higher the specific impulse, the more push you get per pound you have to lift (and the faster the rocket is at burnout velocity, the speed it is moving when the last of its fuel is gone). So liquid hydrogen was obviously the fuel of choice for space launches.

Unfortunately, it is also one of the least dense liquids known; it takes up a great deal of volume for a small weight. Liquid oxygen is denser than water; a pint of it weighs a bit over eighteen ounces. But a pint of liquid hydrogen—taking up just as much space—weighs barely more than one ounce. Thus most of the space taken up by fuel tanks was taken up by liquid hydrogen; the gigantic tank on the side of the space shuttle, for example, was mostly liquid hydrogen.

The sheer bulkiness of hydrogen had always been an annoyance to designers—until now, when it was realized that an empty hydrogen tank was a perfectly good pressure vessel, and that once its contents had been drained, you could simply put racks inside it, attach life support and other equipment to those racks, repressurize it with air, and have a workable habitat for human crews. It wasn't even a hassle to get the last of the hydrogen out—all you needed to do was open it to space while the tank was in sunlight, and the liquid hydrogen would boil away, leaving the tank completely clean (liquid hydrogen isn't sticky and it boils at very low temperatures). And for many missions the tank went to orbit anyway; being able to use it as a habitat would be just a matter of giving it an extra boost and putting it into a specific orbit. Best of all, once you selected the technique for converting tanks into habitats, you could have about as many habitats in orbit as you wanted to launch; the unit cost of carrying the tank up to orbit, plus outfitting it with racks and supplies, would be far below that for custom-built space stations. And besides, the idea of reusing something that was already going to orbit anyway wasn't new—America's first space station, the *Skylab* of the late 1970s, had been the upper stage of a Saturn 1-B.

In fact, the commission pointed out, to get a quick replacement for the U.S. Hab, as long as you were going to be making Centurion tanks, you might as well just take one of the tanks, modify it to attach to the ISS's node, put the racks and equipment into it on the Earth where working conditions were so much easier, and then let a Centurion, assisted by a strapped-on Starbooster, heave it up to a rendezvous with the ISS.

Congressional critics of NASA, and those who wished to discontinue the space program, generally conceded that Starboosters, Centurions, and Big Cans were reasonable enough ideas, and that if the space program had to be conducted at all, it might as well be conducted with those, which was to say cheaply. Thus, those parts of the commission's report were not really controversial; neither was the next part, which dealt with the problem of coming up with a suitable crew compartment to fly on top of a Centurion/Starbooster combination. As the commission pointed out, their solution involved spending no American money for development of new technologies, but only to purchase a well-established and tested product—and one that many Americans would be happy to see used again.

Using an enlarged Apollo II capsule, with its strong reminder of NASA's glory days, was about as close to a public relations winner as NASA could manage at the time. And speaking now, from the other end of my life, the decision to buy them then was to have a profound effect on me, for the Apollo II—later to be nicknamed the Pigeon by pilots who had grown to love it—was one of the great workhorses of space, a ship so useful that nowadays it's hard to imagine how anyone could have thought of going into space without it.

Though the Apollo II came by its legitimate name honestly enough, its lineage was still confusing and strange. Back before it had become clear that the Nixon Administration was going to shut down the Moon landing program permanently, just as soon as they possibly could, Rockwell, the primary contractor for the Apollo capsule, had designed a bigger, more capable six-person version. The plan languished, but never quite died, after NASA committed to the Space Shuttle.

It survived because for so many years there were a variety of plans for the American space station, and one overriding political necessity: if anything went wrong aboard the space station, there had to be a credible way to return the crew to the Earth's surface. Hence there was a need for an "ACRV"—an "Assured Crew Return Vehicle"—which could be moored permanently at the space station, so that, if necessity should arise, the crew could climb into it and make a safe return to Earth. Apollo II was a workable idea for an ACRV; it was a simple, rugged, proven technology that could get people from orbit to Earth.

Apollo II very nearly did die when ESA, the European Space Agency, proposed to be the primary builder of the ACRV. Their version, hastily redubbed the Crew Transfer Vehicle (CTV), to downplay its emergency function and emphasize its role as "Europe's spaceship," would have been an upgraded Soyuz, and for almost two years it looked as if Apollo II would pass into the technological neverland of the thousands of workable ideas that are proposed and developed but never built.

Then in August 1995, budgetary reality stepped in and started the chain reaction that led to Apollo II. ESA was on an even tighter budget than NASA; they had proposed, originally, for the ISS, that they would build both the CTV and the *Columbus* lab Module. It was becoming abundantly clear that they could not afford both without increasing what they were willing to spend, and of the European nations that made up ESA, only France was willing to spend more (perhaps because so much of the hardware would be built in France—or perhaps because, alone among the European powers, the French still had dreams that a nation might be known for something more than material comfort and a gradually rising trade surplus). ESA committed to *Columbus*, and thus by default declared that the CTV for the International Space Station would be the "plain vanilla" Russian-built Soyuz.

But dumb and timid decisions have a way of undoing themselves. The French had wanted to build the CTV, and they had been defeated a little too often within ESA by the cautious, stingy voices. Further, since

Soyuz could carry a maximum crew of three, if Soyuz were the CTV, there would need to be two of them parked at the ISS all the time, and for evacuations each of them would have to have a Russian commander . . . which meant that two ranking officers on the ISS would always be Russian. The French, proud and sensitive as always, had begun to realize that as long as they were tied into ESA, and ESA was dominated by penny-pinching Germans and timid Britons, they would be locked into a permanent last place in space—and that position, in any field of endeavor, has been intolerable to the French since the days of Joan of Arc.

In December 1998, Jacques Chirac, having concluded a secret deal with Rockwell, abruptly announced that France was suspending its active participation in ESA, and that from now on it would sell Ariane launches, staff services, and satellites to the European agency, but its first priority would be the French national space program. President Chirac made a direct comparison between this surprise move and De Gaulle's withdrawal from NATO; it was a matter of sovereignty, and a simple statement that only the French could really be trusted to look after French interests.

And almost as an afterthought, he announced that the newly re-created French space agency, and the government-owned company Aerospatiale, recently merged with Dassault, would be working with Rockwell to re-create Apollo II, which he believed would become the CTV of choice for the ISS, and might well be of use to all spacefaring nations, just as the Ariane had proved to be. As always, France was roundly denounced in the European Parliament and in the national legislatures—and did what it wanted to.

By 2003, when the great debate surrounding the commission's report was boiling in the American Congress, more than a dozen French crews, the last several of them crews of six, had flown in the Apollo II, launched on Ariane, and Rockwell's French section of its spacecraft division was the pride of the company. Thus part three of the commission's report, to buy Apollo IIs as a temporary vehicle for supplementary missions, could be sold—and was sold—as "bringing Apollo back home."

I remember Dad having a long argument with the NASA Public Affairs Officer about that; she had actually come out to the house to brief him on what to say, and she stressed to him, over and over, that "the most important thing to remember is to emphasize just how much you'd like to be flying an Apollo, a proven American technology."

"But I never have. I've never even really looked at the controls on one. And anyway I'm not a pilot." He sounded the way he did when he wanted you to understand something that he thought was obvious.

"You want a space program? If we have one at all, it's going to have to be built around Apollo II for the next two or three years, and that means you're going to say you'd like to be in it. It's not like you're lying, Dr. Terence. You're just stressing the parts of the truth that will do the most good. Now what are you going to say?"

"That Apollo II hasn't killed a Frenchman yet. I wouldn't mind fly-ing one, and besides it's really an American ship if you look at the fact that it's an American company making it—they're just using French labor to build a French design."

She sighed and pushed her glasses up onto her forehead. "You aren't making this easy for us. Don't you *want* to go into space in one of these?"

"I want to go to space in anything and everything, including a bath-tub. All I'm saying is, if you want me to endorse this thing, you've got to let me look at one."

Dad won that one; they let him go to Paris for three weeks to play around on the simulators and talk to French astro-Fs (*astropilots de France*—since the Russians insisted on "cosmonaut" and the Americans on "astronaut," patriotic Frenchmen were not about to have their space explorers called by anything other than a French name). Mom and I vis-ited him there and he dragged us around to a thousand little cafés and historic sites, mostly in the company of several astro-Fs with whom he had become friends. When NASA finally got him back to the U.S. Dad was the Apollo II's most enthusiastic salesman. The whole thing must have taught NASA a lesson about how to cope with Chris Terence, because from then on whenever they had a message to get out to the public, Dad got to take a trip and spend a lot of time with interesting people before they officially asked him.

But in return, Dad would get out there and appear on the talk shows and talk to the reporters, with indefatigable energy and utter passion, for days or weeks until the public was sold on the idea. He got great trips which he paid for by giving great tours; NASA understood the deal and liked it, and although Dad complained endlessly about it all, griping that he was really a scientist and not some stupid celebrity, he did it over and over. Maybe he liked visiting other space programs and special projects so much that it compensated him, or maybe he secretly reveled in the publicity. I'm really not sure whether even he knew which it was.

3

IF THE COMMISSION'S REPORT HAD BEEN ONLY A PLAN TO BUY AND USE good off-the-shelf hardware—Starboosters, Centurions, a Big Can to replace the U.S. Hab, and Apollo IIs—it wouldn't have aroused nearly the controversy it did. It was the further parts of the plan, the ones that didn't deal with the very near future, that caused all the debate.

As with everything else before about 2010, because I was a child at the time, so much of what I now "remember" is what I have constructed from what people told me, and from the stories of Sig and my mother, and from watching video of the actual events years later. And because I owe my profession—in fact, the whole course of my life—to decisions made back at that time, I am not objective, I cannot be objective, and I don't try.

Even with Starbooster/Centurions and Apollo IIs to take up some of the slack, there was going to be a shortage of ways to get people into space for a few years. But there was very little hope of finding additional money in the federal budget to take the next logical step: build a follow-on to the shuttle, something that could use the flyback Zenit as its first stage and then go on to orbit, carrying a crew.

The X-33 had dead-ended on the way to a true SSTO—single stage to orbit—spacecraft because no material suitable for its hydrogen tanks existed, or was likely to for a while. Eventually, the commission said, there would be SSTOs, and recommended the establishment of a long-range research program to solve the tank material problem. As a friendly gesture to very disappointed SSTO advocates, they suggested that the United States commit to have the material, and begin the design, for an SSTO in 2013, ten years from that date. They suggested dubbing the development effort Project Yankee Clipper, pointing out that the great trading vessels that had carried the American flag all over the globe had also been brilliant designs pushing materials far beyond their limits—and unofficially, as Lori observed, the original clippers could have performed far better if nylon and fiberglass had only been available at the time. "Yankee Clipper" was the perfect name for the ship that would outdo everything else—if only the materials problem could be solved.

Meanwhile, the conservative low-risk approach to getting people into orbit would remain the way everyone had used so far: the staged rocket. You didn't have to meet that so-far-impossible 90 percent fuel ratio if you launched not from the stationary ground but from the top of another rocket. Hence, in the almost sixty years of human spaceflight, rockets always flew in stages: a big rocket (the "booster") lifted a smaller rocket onto a high, fast-moving trajectory, or a group of rockets began the upward journey, all lifting each other, and the rockets that burned out first dropped off. The Saturn V that sent Apollo to the Moon worked on the first principle (the second and third stages were lifted off the Earth and set in motion by the first, the third stage was thrown most of the way to orbit by the second, and the third stage was then already high enough and moving fast enough to head for the Moon). The space shuttle worked on the second principle; it began with all three main engines and the two solid rocket boosters firing, accelerated rapidly upward under all that thrust, then dropped the weight of the solid boosters when they burned out.

In effect, it had another stage as well, the external tank; when the fuel in that big tank was burned, the tank was dropped. Doing this instead of mounting the fuel tanks inside the vehicle meant, among other things, a much more compact body to return from orbit (which was much easier to work with) and less mass to pull around for operations in orbit.

Ultimately, better performance would come with better upper stages; as long as two stages were necessary to get to orbit, rather than build a complete new system each time, it made more sense to alternate—first improve the boosters, since they were clearly a major problem, then build a new upper stage to fly on that booster, then return again to improving the booster—a process familiar to anyone who has ever rehabbed a house or rebuilt a car on a tight budget, of fixing whatever is most wrong first and improving other things later, and always returning to redo the weak spot.

And since to design a new craft took years, if there were to be a follow-on upper stage in a few years, the process would have to begin now—but in the tightly strapped year of 2002, there was practically no money for it.

There was a solution available to the problem, but there were many people who thought the solution was worse than the problem. To such people, it was a deal with the devil—even if the devil came to them in the form of a man as pleasant and charming as the one who would eventually become my stepfather, Sig Jarlsbourg.

At the time he was just thirty-two, but his sandy red hair was already graying, and though he was strong and fit, he moved so quietly and precisely that he gave the impression of someone twenty years older. Four years later, when I first met him, he amazed me the first time he stepped onto a tennis court and seemed to abruptly shrug off his years and play like a teenager.

By the time he was testifying in front of the Congressional Joint Committee, and his picture was on the cover of *Business Week*, it had already appeared there four times—the last time with the caption "CAN THEY STOP HIM? DO THEY WANT TO?"

He was living proof that the best way to get rich is to start that way; his father had been a major player in a large number of oil ventures, and Sig had grown up all over the world. Always adventurous, and with the money to pursue it, he had been a passionate diver by the age of fifteen, with more than twenty technical dives before he enrolled at Stanford. He had gotten his sailplane license a few months after his fourteenth birthday and had begun seriously trying for records before he was twenty.

Given that he was remarkably handsome and well-groomed, he could have become one of the more successful playboys of the decade, but he had his mind on other things. In his first couple years of college he had joined a number of environmental and "green" groups, only to realize, as he put it later, that "the only way to keep crap out of the air and water, and preserve the beautiful places, is to fix it so that it pays to do that; otherwise you're always just chasing down the next oil company."

His father had sent him a short letter telling him that Stanford tuition cost a lot and that the money was coming from oil companies. The next summer, Sig got together a small group of friends who had a wide variety of outdoor skills and some experience with remote areas, secured a start-up loan, took out ads as Planet Vision Adventure Tours in the highest-end travel publications, skipped classes for a week to go to a travel agents' convention and buttonhole people, and sold "two-month planetary tours" at $29,000 a shot. With 250 clients over the summer, he shuffled them from one friend to another, taking them climbing the Andes, fly fishing in Patagonia, on camera safari in Kruger National Park, diving off Sri Lanka, and thus eventually around the world. Meanwhile he and his friends got to spend the summer doing things they loved, as guides to the small group of the extremely well-off that he had managed to charm into the experience. As a side benefit, he extracted donations from many of his clients for various "green causes."

At the end of the summer, he paid the remaining two years of his Stanford tuition in cash, sent his father a check for the past two years, and, after covering the loan and taxes, had $8500 left.

The next summer, he talked a private foundation into a highly irregular grant that let him wander the earth for three months managing PVAT via modem while writing a report on "A Sustainable Planet" in a clear, literate style that made it salable to a commercial publisher. (To the surprise of the foundation, it turned out that Sig had drafted a contract that gave him all the earnings from this, leaving them with the report but no legal right to publish it.) Some people thought it was the equivalent of Paine's *Common Sense*; others tended to compare it to Lenin's *What Is to Be Done?* or Hitler's *Mein Kampf.*

As the business magazines summarized it, Sig Jarlsbourg had concluded that at least half of the most respected industries, ones that could be counted on in any portfolio, had to be shut down within the next century, and proposed a radical plan for putting them out of business. To the environmentalists, he had proposed that all the wild and beautiful places of the Earth, the common heritage of mankind, should be reserved as playgrounds for the rich. And, as he told me years later, "Actually, the only person I cared about what I looked like to was the one in the mirror. Though it didn't hurt that people like Ted Turner and Richard Branson kind of liked me, too."

A fairer summary of the idea was this: the earth's population was so large and the number of people who were either still in childbearing years, or had yet to enter them, so big a percentage of it, that only the most advanced technologies available could supply food, medicine, housing, and heat to keep them alive (and even then there was bound to be some starvation). Yet those technologies, in turn, were extraordinarily energy intensive, and every known large-scale method of producing energy had severe ecological drawbacks: relied on rare metals that were chemically active, and thus would have highly unpredictable effects when released into the biosphere; depended on complex molecules that were so similar to those found in living things that these, too, were bound to have disastrous effects; and so forth.

Furthermore, these interacted; to avoid the hazards of gross pollution associated with coal, one might turn to uranium, only to discover more complex problems associated with radiation, from which one might turn to solar power, only to find that manufacturing solar cells required processing industrial quantities of a witch's brew of heavy elements.

To return to nineteenth-century or earlier technology would insure famine and plague; to try to keep going with advanced technology on the face of the Earth would insure a series of worsening environmental catastrophes. The escape hatch, then, was not to do it on the face of the Earth.

After all, even if you were trying to, you couldn't significantly pollute the quadrillions of cubic miles of space that lie within the orbit of the Moon; and that's only the nearest and most convenient space. A hundred and twenty miles straight up was inexhaustible solar energy—and if you didn't build the solar cells on Earth, from Earth-based materials, no worries about releasing biologically active metals. The asteroids and Moon contained every raw material needed, and when you were done processing you could leave the slag there and it would never hurt anyone. Eventually you could grow food up there—with no need, ever, for pesticides, since all you had to do was not take the bugs with you, and if by chance you did, you need only quarantine the infected crop—and open the door to hard vacuum and hard radiation to exterminate the bugs. The whole Earth could be supplied from space, at least in principle, with no need left for a smokestack or a chemical vat anywhere on its face, and virtually unlimited material goods for everyone.

Or in short, Earthbound resources could not support the Earth's population for more than another couple of generations, unless large parts of what made the Earth beautiful were destroyed, or a much higher percentage of the global population died young. Neither was acceptable. Therefore within fifty years—somewhere around the end of Sig's lifetime—there would need to be an outside source for energy and minerals from either the seabeds or space. The seabeds were hooked to the global ecology in ways that were poorly understood, and there was little point in replacing ruining the land with ruining the oceans. So it would have to be space, and for the space source of resources to work at all, it must be cheaper than the terrestrial source. If it were, then much of the Earth would become too valuable to "waste" on agriculture and industry, and the planet would "re-green" as he called it.

The key was cheap exploitable resources from space. But when Sig looked at the numbers of the time, "cheap" seemed like a very strange word to use. With technologies available at the time, it cost a thousand times as much to generate electricity in Low Earth Orbit (LEO) as it did on Earth, ten thousand times as much to move a passenger into LEO as it did to fly the same passenger across the Atlantic, and a hundred thousand times as much to create work or living space for a person in LEO as it did to create the equivalent in Chicago.

By themselves those numbers did not intimidate Sig. When he had been out of college for two years, his Planetary Vision Adventure Tours had swelled, by acquisition and merger, into Share-the-Planet Tours, which had already become a giant in the burgeoning industry of low-impact high-priced ecotourism. Acquiring a dozen specialized firms to do it, Sig had built hotels offshore in deep water, flown comfortable living quarters into and out of Antarctica, put up independent, solar-powered buildings on Pacific reefs, and in every case filled them with people who wanted to see the wild world—as untouched as possible—without leaving any creature comforts behind. He knew that you could still make a profit in places that were very expensive to operate.

Yet although you can get tourists to pay for all kinds of bizarre things—consider the number of ski lodges that are built in places where concrete costs six times the normal price and labor costs are double—tourism and other very high cost-per-weight industries can only be the beginning of getting people there. The first Western and Chinese traders to Borneo went for spices that were literally worth their weight in gold, but there wasn't much traffic until it became a cheap place for tin and rubber at pennies per pound, and development didn't take off there until it was possible to make computer components at pennies per ton. From a business standpoint, space could begin with tourism, but tourism would have to finance the research and technical improvements that could eventually lead to moving energy production, then mining, and finally industrial production itself, up to orbit.

Chances were it would take a lifetime. That was okay with Sig, because—as he told me years later—"Well, I had a lifetime and I wasn't planning to do anything else with it anyway."

Just as importantly, in the short run, his high-end ecotourism had given him an extraordinarily valuable set of contacts, for obviously the people his business served were mainly those who could afford thousands or tens of thousands of dollars for vacations of a month or more. Furthermore, though his relations with his father were poor, the family contacts he had inherited served him well. And many of his employees and consultants were necessarily experts in high-risk and extreme-conditions sports, and through them he met more adventurers.

Thus, when he was twenty-nine, knowing the vacation habits of a dozen of the world's wealthiest people well—and in contact with hundreds of adventurers from high-altitude balloonists to technical divers and extreme skiers—Sig Jarlsbourg was able to call together one of the most remarkable meetings of the twentieth century. Many of the people in the room—Ted Turner, Bill Gates, Michael Eisner, and Steve Forbes, for example—were nominally on vacation, attending the "free retreat" that Sig had offered them at his new Greenland Glacier Lodge, supposedly to both celebrate the opening of the new facility and also, because the conference began on Friday, July 16, 1999, and would conclude on Tuesday, July 20, to celebrate the thirtieth anniversary of the Apollo 11 Moon landing. J.F.K., Jr., was there, ostensibly to celebrate his father's legacy, actually because Sig had been quietly exploiting political contacts through that channel ever since Kennedy had taken his submarine tour of the Great Barrier Reef; and because Kennedy was there, several other people whose names were household words were there. Perot himself wasn't, but four people from his national organization were, all quietly referring to themselves as "employees of a major national corporation and friends of Mr. Jarlsbourg." Also in the group were members of the small elite of wealthy adventurers, including Richard Branson, just returned from yet another ballooning expedition. The bankers, perhaps, carried more weight, but they would follow the lead of the entrepreneurs and adventurers; the people with political connections mattered a great deal, but again, no one mattered so much as the dozen or so people in the room, most of them men, most in their late fifties or early sixties, each of whom commanded large fortunes without being answerable to boards of directors or other conservative forces.

If Sig's business had taught him nothing else (and of course he had learned an enormous amount from it), it would have taught him how to show people a good time and get them in a relaxed frame of mind, enjoying themselves while becoming alert and receptive. For the first three days the group mostly mingled, trying various kinds of remote skiing, taking excursions to observe rare wildlife along the seacoast and carefully planned no-impact visits to mountain valleys. Always, as they did this, they were reminded of how essential space operations had become to environmental and conservation projects; how fragile the Earth was and how many people needed a share of it now; and somehow—strange that a tourism mogul would do such a thing—they were constantly reminded that nowadays the number of high-adventure experiences available on Earth, while still very large, could be exhausted by a wealthy thrill-seeker before the age of thirty. By Monday at dinnertime—

the last big meal of the vacation and the general gathering for the "special program" about which they had all been whispering to each other for three days now—they were all glad that they had come, happy to be there, reasonably fond of each other and of Sig . . . and vaguely uneasy, troubled by a sense that things could be much better.

As the lights dimmed, Sig drew a deep breath, stepped to the podium, and began. Behind him a large high-definition screen sprang to life.

"I think," Sig Jarlsbourg began, "that we all understand each other here. We know how good life can be, and we know quite a bit about building for the future, about thinking of a few generations into the future. We know that our wealth is secure only as long as others do well enough, and we aren't foolish enough to think that we can stay in our enviable position either by sheer force or merely by tradition. No, I think all of us here understand that if we wish to preserve our success, we must move on to other successes—and we must take the rest of the human race with us. Now, I want you to imagine something."

An image began to swim before them on the screen, not quite defining itself yet. "What I want you to imagine is this. All of us here know that the Earth is hitting its limits, and sooner or later—through exhaustion of fossil fuels, global warming, ozone loss, accidental release of nuclear wastes, or a dozen other possible scenarios—the world is going to take a disastrous turn, and no matter how much wealth and power we have, we will not be immune.

"Not immune when it happens, anyway. You might say I am offering us a long-term vaccination."

The image on the screen swam into shape. It was clearly an aircraft, long and thin, with delta wings at its rear and a canard wing just behind the pilot's cabin.

"You of all people have sampled the pleasures of the Earth. Imagine, then, that you could sample pleasures beyond the Earth—"

For the next few hours he took them back and forth, from what was possible and could be done tomorrow, to a vision of life a century further on when their grandchildren would hang glide off Olympus Mons on Mars and climb mountains on the back side of the Moon. He sketched out pleasures they had never thought of—and at the same time stressed how many hard and practical reasons there were for each step on the way. He pointed out that it would cost a great deal and involve great risks, and at the same time made them feel like they were the few, special people who could afford to take those risks and might well be the ones to lead humanity into its spacefaring future.

Then he got more concrete. Space tourism, in the kind of long run that the super-wealthy families must deal with, could lead to space industrialization, which could lead to a cleaner, richer, safer world for everyone. Once private industry was operating freely in space on a big scale, the rest could follow quickly, because there were abundant resources of many kinds on the Moon and in the asteroids. But no one would go after those resources directly. Earth-based sources were invariably cheaper—"unless," Sig said, "thousands of people are already going there anyway and there's a known, cheap, easy-to-use technology for doing it. And that's the point. If you want that better world, we need to see space tourism take off right away, and it can't be as a plaything of a tiny group of super-rich people. It's got to have broad-based public support and enthusiasm right from the start. And for that, ladies and gentleman, I propose—ShareSpace Global."

Sig had spent a decade learning to be a superb salesman, and he had spent almost as long learning how money worked. He knew what would titillate his audience and what would flatter them. And with careful timing, he had just announced the name of his company to be as the clock chimed midnight, making it the official thirtieth anniversary of the first landing on the Moon.

The plan was breathtakingly simple: build up space-based tourism by beginning with simple earthly activities (trips to see space launches, tours of scientific facilities, high-altitude flights with zero-gravity experience guided by ex-astronauts); move rapidly into suborbital ballistic flights above the atmosphere; from there to orbital adventure trips and to luxury Hilton hotels in orbit; then low-altitude circumnavigations of the Moon—"and as far after that as anyone cares to go!"

"So who's going to go on these and how much are you charging for tickets?" a voice asked in a Southern drawl, out of the darkness.

Sig knew the voice, pointed himself toward the speaker, and said, "Two classes of people. One, we have tickets available that you just buy, at a healthy markup. So you and your kids might just do it for a special occasion. Two—and here's what's important—we sell shares."

"Not like timeshare condos?" a voice asked from another corner.

"Not much. Figure it's a little like a church raffle, where the top prize is really great, the other prizes make you feel like the ticket was worthwhile, and the many people who don't get anything are encouraged to think that they're doing something good for the world as a whole. Now obviously only some of the people who buy shares get the big prizes, whatever those are as we develop—eventually, of course, the big prizes are the rides to space. Thousands more get consolation prizes of one kind or another intended to get them more interested and make them more space-crazy. And for those who don't win anything, we discount your number of chances some percentage, and then put you back into the pool next time with that reduced number of chances. So nobody ever loses all at once, but there's always a strong incentive to buy more."

"You didn't say how much you'll charge either for a flat-rate ticket or for a share."

"There'll be a board of adjusters that changes that constantly; it'll need adjustment all the time. But figure the first flat-rate tickets in each new class of service will be in the tens of thousands of dollars—which means, by the way, we don't do it till our lift cost per pound is less than five percent of what the shuttle is currently running—and shares might be around ten dollars."

An older, white-haired man—whose face had been well known on television before he had gained and kept sixty pounds—put up his hand and asked, "Uh, I hate to mention this, but I do believe people like me could die from high acceleration, and that is just what I would encounter if I did this."

Sig grinned. "Well, we'd need to put you in front of a doctor and have him check you out. Some people can't even handle excitement. And there are people with bad backs and brittle bones. But the numbers are like this: for a suborbital flight, the most you'd have to handle is 1.6 g's—and 1.4 is more typical. So if you weigh 230, you'd have maybe five minutes of weighing ninety-two more pounds, which isn't so bad if you're lying flat on a couch. Even many people with heart disease can handle that, especially if we give them pure oxygen through a breathing tube.

"For orbital flights we'd have to go up to about three g's, and that is a lot compared to normal gravity at Earth surface—that 230-pound person would weigh in at almost 700—but what it really excludes is only people with severe osteoporosis, arterial plaques, or emphysema.

"None of which are at all common in people with a passion for thrill sports. It's true we'd be shutting out the lifelong overeating, heavy-smoking couch potato, but most of them aren't out for a thrill ride anyway—if they were, they'd have been skiing or mountain biking or hang gliding on Earth, and they wouldn't be in that shape."

The older man chuckled. "Well, it sounds like I'd be marginal. And at least I'd have ten years to lose some weight. I don't suppose you know offhand what the acceleration for a Moon trip would be like? One thing you're forgetting is that some of your passengers won't be there for the ride, but for the view."

Sig nodded. "Of course. As long as you don't go all the way out to the Moon—as long as you just go up, and make a few elliptical orbits out to a thousand kilometers—then the acceleration at peak is about the same as it is for a simple low Earth orbit trip. Peak acceleration comes from reentry, you see, not from launch. If you were to go to a lunar distance, then you'd be up at six g's or so, which is rough—because you just can't take enough fuel along to allow you to come back, decelerate into low Earth orbit, and then descend. From a lunar return you'd have to plunge right into the atmosphere and use the air to slow you down, same as the old Apollo capsules did. That's why we're not planning to offer flights to the Moon for a long, long time—not until we can think about decelerating people in stages to hold down peak acceleration."

The heavy man nodded. The woman beside him tentatively put up her hand and said, "Didn't you mean hold down deceleration? You're slowing down—"

Sig smiled. "Deceleration is an English teacher word."

"I was an English teacher. At least until this actor led me astray."

"Well, if you'd taken a walk down the hall to science class, you'd have found out that physicists define acceleration as change in speed or direction of motion, because it all has the same effect. Your body doesn't care whether you're experiencing one g because you're in a centrifuge that's constantly changing your direction of motion, or because you're speeding up or slowing down, or because you're in a one-g gravitational field. It's all the same thing and it's all called acceleration." He stretched and smiled at them all. "And, of course, recreationists have known for many years that acceleration, at least in reasonable doses, is what's known as fun—or how do you explain skyboarding, extreme skiing, roller coasters, and aerobatics?"

Salesman that he was, he knew it was time to set the hook, so he put the questions to them then—would they want to take this step? Was this the time?

Some, of course, resisted it; no salesman is perfect. But enough had stepped forward to shake Sig's hand and make arrangements for further discussions. Within weeks papers were drawn up, large loans at long terms were extended, and a board of directors for the new company was in place (though in reality Sig had control of everything). As of August 4, 1999, ShareSpace Global was underway.

From the beginning it was attacked by government and media. After two years of running tours to Canaveral, Baikonur, Hainan, and JPL, plus "Meet the Astronauts" luncheons and expanded Space Camps, ShareSpace Global had begun to sell shares and tickets for suborbital flights, though they did not yet have a vehicle.

Just as the beginnings of investigations were underway, ShareSpace Global rolled out plans for their first project: Skygrazer, a modified version of a Starbooster shell. The forward engine was there, but where the Zenit rocket itself had been, there was a comfortable space for a dozen passengers, pilot, copilot, and attendant. The Skygrazer could then be attached, belly-to-belly, with a Starbooster, and launched vertically.

It didn't have nearly enough thrust to get to orbit, but it didn't need it to provide people with the ride of their lives. When the Zenit burned the last of its fuel and the stages separated, the Skygrazer would continue on upward until it reached an altitude of just over 50,000 meters. At this point it would be moving at nearly Mach 4 (four times the speed of sound—orbit is about Mach 25) as it plunged over and dove back into the lower atmosphere. At its tremendous speed, the pilot could then bring it to almost level flight, and it would glide for many hundreds of miles, far higher and faster than any airliner ever conceived. This suborbital ride would include almost ten minutes of weightlessness, a view of the Earth from well above the atmosphere, and of course the amazingly fast and silent glide across the better part of a continent. Flights were arranged to various resorts that Sig owned, where runways were to be specially lengthened for Skygrazer landings; passengers would be whisked from the Skygrazer to a large, comfortable cruise ship, taken on a tour of some of the more interesting areas they had overflown, and finally flown home first-class from wherever the cruise ship took them. Or, if they wished, they could spend a long, leisurely shipboard vacation, eventually reaching one of Sig's remote sites, and then return in less than an hour on a Skygrazer. Sig could sell both the adventure of a space ride and the ability to enjoy your vacation until almost the very last minute before being whisked home in comfortable luxury.

As for when Skygrazer would actually be built, Sig had another simple answer: it would take about forty flights to pay off the cost of one Skygrazer plus the Zenit boosters for it; as soon as enough people had paid in, either with full-price tickets or with shares, ShareSpace Global would contract with Boeing (which was ready to go whenever given the go-ahead), build and test Skygrazer, and have it flying its first passengers within six months of the magic number being reached.

Federal safety officials were appalled at a suborbital craft carrying human cargo—much of it well-connected influential human cargo whose heirs would have access to the best lawyers on Earth—with so brief a test period. Financial officials did not like what looked either like extensive no-interest loans from customers, legalized gambling, or perhaps a Ponzi scheme; some of the tickets on the first few flights were now being scalped for more than $60,000.

But neither could do much about it; Sig's base of operations was in Brazil, and Brazilian authorities seemed to think nothing of the irregularities. The Brazilians had had a small-to-medium launch base for a decade, and they were happy to provide the space for long runways as well. Conveniently, too, as Sig always pointed out, they had land along the equator, where added velocity from the Earth's rotation made getting to orbit easier. The fact that they hardly ever inspected anything or asked any questions was the unmentioned additional advantage.

As of 2002, ShareSpace Global had filled thirty-six flights and eight of the full-price seats were now being taken up by heirs of the original purchasers. It looked very much as if by the end of the year people would finally know whether Sig was a visionary or a con man; if so, then the first flights would be in 2004, and about one out of every three seats would be assigned by the Encounter Space Raffle.

And in the middle of all these doubts, with the world about to find out whether Sig was the "entrepreneur for the twenty-first century" (as *Forbes* had called him), or "a plain old-fashioned con man straight out of the nineteenth century" (as *The Wall Street Journal* would have it), he walked into Congress and revealed that Skygrazer was a mere first step—if you believed him—in a much bigger scheme. The next step, which physically bore a remarkable resemblance to the graceful spacecraft that had appeared on the screen at the meeting that launched ShareSpace Global, was Starbird, which, mounted on the next generation boosters, would be able to reach orbit.

Sig's offer was simple: the designs were essentially complete. He had bought them from a retired engineer, Hubert Davis, and provided Davis with enough qualified people and sophisticated computers to make it possible for Starbird to be flying as early as August 2005. By that time ShareSpace Global would have at least a year of experience with the Skygrazer, and furthermore would have acquired sufficient public confidence to begin expanding the Encounter Space Raffle for orbital trips.

The Starbird had been designed to take advantage of existing technology at every turn. A simple rocket plane, its first stage would be the reliable Starbooster. On top of its sharply sloped delta wings, it would carry two DTs—drop tanks—using exactly the same disposable-tank technology that had worked so well on the shuttle. Further, Sig proposed that the drop tanks would have cutouts for easily installed hatches, which meant that every one of them could potentially be used as a habitat or for other purposes in orbit.

Moreover, for building and operating the Starbird/Starbooster system, Sig was not asking for any direct federal money up front. Thus it wouldn't involve spending one dime in the tight-budget year of 2003.

All that was needed was enough of a guaranteed market so that the Starbird could be built right away, instead of having to undergo the "unfortunate delays that the necessity of proceeding cautiously had imposed" on Skygrazer. And Sig's idea was that since Starbird would be perfectly capable of reaching the ISS, and equipped with standard docking equipment, if NASA would simply guarantee that it would buy 100 seats to either orbit or to ISS per year, at a discounted rate from Share-Space Global, that would suffice to get him the loans he needed to put Starbird on-line much sooner. The idea was not new—it had been known as "anchor tenancy," the idea that a guaranteed market could call a service into being, and indeed the most famous example, encouraging aviation by paying any air carrier to carry the mail, had been a great success in the 1920s and 1930s.

Furthermore, he suggested, they could improve matters even further by not making it a special deal for ShareSpace Global, but allowing anyone, worldwide, public or private, to do the same thing: at the price set by NASA, NASA would be obligated to buy 100 seats to orbit per year from any vendor willing to offer them at that price. "In return for this," he said in his prepared testimony, "I propose only this: that NASA be allowed only to require that its engineers evaluate the safety and reliability of the launch system. They may not in any way specify how the system achieves its goals, who builds what, where parts or fuel are acquired from, or anything else concerned with normal operations." Here Sig paused and looked over his glasses at them. "Senators and Congressmen, let's make sure we understand each other. The Conestoga wagons that settled this country were built with no specifications of any kind, except that they be able to go a long way without breaking down. The first airliners had fewer than ten pages of specifications each—generally only saying that they be able to carry a specified number of people a given distance, inside a fixed time, without killing them. If there is anything that this new frontier desperately needs, it is flexibility. If you treat this as an opportunity to parcel out goodies to Boston, South California, Texas, Seattle, and Georgia, you will quickly run the cost and the time taken through the ceiling, and you will have to pay the entire cost of the program, because no businessman in his right mind is going to touch a project in which he can neither control what he can charge nor how much it will cost him. But if you merely want to buy the results of such a project, then if it is possible to sell them at that price, someone will sell it to you. The choice is yours."

The controversy the commission triggered was to first bring Sig before the Congressional Joint Committee—and then to recommend that the federal government take the deal, without changes or modifications.

There was an uproar about that which dwarfed everything else connected with the commission's report. Congressmen from the states with large aerospace industries (except, of course, for Washington State) were appalled at the idea that the federal government might buy flights into space without spreading the expenditures around to the appropriate districts. Free-marketers declared that the millennium was at hand and soon everyone would be able to fly into space whenever they wanted. Safety officials, and the insurance companies, urged that no regulation be compromised in any way and that control of safety issues remain firmly where it belonged. Interviewed in retirement, Newt Gingrich said that this had been his idea all along and that he was sure no one in Washington now could touch it without screwing it up.

Rockwell and Aerospatiale jointly announced that they would be happy to build and conduct an extra seven Ariane/Apollo II launches per year at that rate, and were immediately denounced for price gouging despite their claims that they were getting more per launch under their monopoly arrangement with NASA.

Lockheed-Martin brought out a beautiful design by Bert Rutan for a gigantic airplane, the Condor, which would carry aloft an orbital vehicle, the Peregrine. A Peregrine would be carried aloft with its fuel tanks empty, because in aerodynamic flight (flying with wings) it takes much more energy to lift a weight than it does to keep it in the air; the two craft, still joined, would rendezvous with a tanker to fill the Peregrine's fuel tanks in midair, and then the Peregrine would be pushed into an upward trajectory by the Condor and released. It would then fire its engines and continue on to orbit.

Starbird/Starbooster, Condor/Peregrine, and the improved Apollo II/Starbooster/Centurion were all perfectly workable choices; Congress, to its bewilderment, was not being asked to choose, but only to permit.

In the middle of all of this, my father managed to place himself in a position that no one else had thought of. When a reporter asked him, he declared firmly that he was opposed to it, because if space began to pay its own way, then "commercial and not scientific considerations will decide the nature and character of our space flights," he said, very firmly. "The great tragedy of space is that what matters out there, finally, is the ultimate chance to find out what the universe is all about, but no one ever goes there for what really matters. The scientists gave us the potential to get there, raised the questions that could only be answered by going there, but they were shoved aside, first by the warriors and now by the businessmen, who have made space the arena for violence and greed. I'd be happy to see a space program only half as big if it could be free of the taint of blood and the sleaze of commerce."

That got a lot of airplay; Mom, sitting next to me on the couch, watched the statement and said, "Well, that's two ways your father is in trouble."

"Dad's in trouble?" I asked, always worried about him since the accident the year before.

"Yep. He's in trouble with his bosses for taking a position like that without clearing it—I'm sure he is. And he's in bigger trouble with me, for saying that on somebody else's show."

I don't know whether my mother actually went after him for having given such a great quote to someone else, but she was certainly right about trouble with his bosses at NASA.

It was the biggest fiasco since one of the talk show hosts had asked Aunt Lori to share her fear and let out all the stress of her job on television, and Aunt Lori had said, "I wasn't afraid because I was too busy. Stress is what you get when your job is worthwhile and interesting, and if you can't handle fear and stress you ought to eliminate yourself from the breeding pool and spare us all the burden of caring for your worthless offspring." After that one she had been relegated to talking to carefully selected audiences, generally where no reporters could be expected.

But Dad was always competitive, and maybe he just had to outdo Aunt Lori. They pulled him out of the "Presidential Commission Roadshow" for a couple of weeks, and he stomped angrily around the house, calling NASA or taking calls from them several times a day, not liking what he heard, clearly not pleasing them with what he said. He seemed to be particularly angry and disgusted at Sig Jarlsbourg; I asked him once why he was so mad and what upset him so much about Sig, and he said, "Because the SOB is going to make space just like everywhere else, where money counts for everything, when it could have been the one place where you could really just do science without having money people crap all over it."

As an astronaut's son, even at five I knew that acronyms were often the most important part of communication, so I asked him what "SOB" meant and he wouldn't tell me. Neither would Mom.

In my memory, anyway, it was only a few days later that the first big fight between them happened; she came home and said, "I have to do something extremely important for my career and you're not going to like it but I need to do it anyway because opportunities like this don't come along very often." Just like that, without any pauses, as if she had been rehearsing it all the way home, an hour on the freeway.

Dad prided himself on his reasonableness, so he sat down and looked at her in a very reasonable way, and said, "Well, okay, Amber, tell me."

"I've got an interview and tour with Sig Jarlsbourg for tomorrow."

"Just ask him reasonable questions and report what he says," Dad said.

"I don't think you're going to think my questions are reasonable," she said, a little sadly. "I can't storm in and demand that he tell me why he's spoiling space for the real scientists."

"Why not?"

"I've got to give him the chance to tell his own story in his own words, Chris; it's part of my job. And that includes giving him questions he *can* answer that way."

Right around then was when Grandma abruptly came in and whisked me off to a movie. I knew something was wrong, but they sure weren't going to let me see what, not just yet anyway.

Mom's interview with Sig solidified her growing rep... regarded as a masterpiece, revealing the human, interes... was complex and brilliant man. It greatly enhanced his pop... of a there's little doubt that it also aided in the passage of the... and Space Initiative (the legislative embodiment of the commissi... nt's mendations) later that week, which carried by two votes in th... and about twenty in the House.

Another way to tell that something was wrong was that we... party to celebrate the passage of the bill at our house, and althoug... were plenty of astronauts and scientists around Dad, none of the N... administrators did more than say "Hi." And even I, at five years... could see that for a guy who had worked so hard to get the bill pass... Dad didn't look happy at all. He spent a lot of time at the punch b... and kind of scowled; later, when I wandered outside I found him sitti... on the chaise longue, just looking up at the Moon, and sat down next... him. He didn't look at me, but he put his arm around my shoulders; w... stayed out there till practically everyone had left the party, and I kep... hearing my mother's nervous laugh as she explained, over and over, that her husband seemed to have disappeared but she knew he really appreci- ated that they had come to the party. Finally he fell asleep, and then I climbed up next to him and fell asleep, too; I only sort of woke up when Mom and Grandma came out and got us. By that time, the full Moon had almost set.

4

I GUESS YOU COULD SAY THE NEXT FEW YEARS KIND OF FLEW BY. I DON'T remember much about them. I try not to.

I remember my parents yelling at each other a lot, but I suppose lots of people have similar memories. There was a story or two I heard later;

tioned that she completed her on-camera interview with Sig,
eleven in the morning—he was extremely efficient and cov-
it was needed quickly—and then found herself having lunch
h. By that time there weren't cameramen, per se; for interviews
d the double-track, a digital recorder that kept a camera focused
h of the people involved and recorded a complete sound track. So
low or other at lunch, he canceled the rest of the day's appoint-
s, and she told the network she would be going long—

And I have the tape of the afternoon interview. Sig talked a long
e about his vision of the future, including quoting the Brautigan
m about machines of loving grace and all that. He went on about the
ntial for a world where everything dangerous or dirty was done "out
in he safe vacuum." He talked about what he called the Planetary Park.

Mom always said that she thinks she fell in love with him that after-
non. There's not one romantic word on that tape, nor anything about
love or home or family, nothing that isn't about space industrialization. I
never did quite get around to asking Mom how she fell in love with him
that afternoon; it's just one of those mysterious things, I guess.

Anyway, Mom also says they had no more contact except for three
more interviews, and they all were like that—until the day she and Dad
announced their divorce, and it was in the press. Then Sig waited *exactly*
six months, to the day, and called her. They met for coffee, then they
took off someplace for a weekend, then—less than a year after her
divorce from Dad—they got married. It lasted right up to 2058, when
Sig died, a fifty-three-year marriage, and even now I don't really understand much about it except that the minute they met, they seemed to
have been destined for each other. Stuff like that still happens, even
nowadays, I guess.

Probably it was a good thing, all things considered. Dad wasn't
somebody to stay married to. Understand me, I loved my father, and
there were some things I got from him that are absolutely precious to
me, but the truth was he wasn't such a great husband, and he never really
did understand people very well.

I didn't have much of a handle on what all the yelling was about,
and then later, when I was twelve and he had died and all the scandals
started coming out, I understood that the basic problem was that as Dad
became more famous, he got all kinds of attention, and being the basically arrogant guy he was, he felt he deserved that. I think my mother

always respected him—at least his abilities and intelligence—but what he wanted, or at least what he got used to on the road, was more the kind of admiration that you only get from strangers, when you're famous. Most especially the kind you get from young women.

By then Dad had sort of graduated from the NASA speaking circuit; he was still an active astronaut getting ready for missions, but NASA was no longer putting him on the road. Partly this was because the President's Space Initiative had already passed, and mostly it was because his attack on commercialization and the military had offended a lot of people. NASA certainly knew who paid the bills and why there was interest, and the "pure science" views he was espousing were embarrassing.

That was probably the *reason* so many college campuses invited him; he pretty well assured them of controversy, which meant that his speech would get covered by the press—and every college speaker series wants that. And it was really a something-for-everyone show, because he'd talk at great length about the scientific wonders that were possible to discover out there, then ferociously attack the whole idea of commercialization and privatization, and then, because some student always would ask the setup question, he would get to explain why even though he had some deep disagreements he was still staying with NASA and he was still proud to be an astronaut—and that strong expression of loyalty would be a real tear-jerker. I have no doubt he meant every word, too. I don't think Chris Terence ever spoke a sentence that he didn't mean.

It just happened that old-fashioned loyalty plus complete sincerity was a formula that would appeal to almost anyone, and especially to college students.

After the lectures, for which he was well paid, would come the receptions, and at the reception there would usually be a couple of pretty, polite young women who talked to Chris—or rather listened to him talk—with deep, intense sincerity, as if they found him fascinating. He would ask them questions about themselves, and they would stammer out very simple replies, usually adding that they didn't think they were very interesting people, and after a while there would be just one of them left. Dad would keep circulating, and the young woman would stay close to him as he chatted with faculty and allowed administrators to say things to him that (they would later claim to others) "impressed him very much." Finally there would be just a few people left, and they would all go to a bar for a couple of drinks, and then Dad would go back to his hotel... from the bar with the young woman, who would be the sole survivor of the process.

By the time that the divorce happened, Dad had managed to make himself fairly famous (while never admitting that he enjoyed the fame and attention, and always telling Mom and me that he wished he could spend more time with us), so naturally the tabloids had a field day, and more so because, as everyone noticed after a while, the young women he was taking back to his room looked a lot like college pictures of his wife. I have always been a little glad that I was too young to understand how humiliating the whole thing was for Mom, and I truly have to give both her and Sig credit; neither of them ever really said a harsh word about Dad in my presence.

Anyway, there was a minor custody problem, but nobody ever forced me to take sides; both of them wanted me, neither of them had as much time to spend on me as they would have liked, and therefore they were each trying to insure that I got enough time with the other. Nonetheless it was confusing and upsetting; eventually I ended up with Dad for a while because Mom was off on her honeymoon with Sig.

It was perfectly clear that Dad hated Sig, but he wouldn't let me say anything bad about the stranger who, as far as I could tell, had bewitched and kidnapped my mother. Dad spent a lot of time just sitting outside and staring up at the sky; now and then he'd have a date with somebody way too young to ever be my mother, who always talked to me as if I were three even though I was almost eight. I hated those nights a lot; many times I thought that if Dad had any sense he'd have taken the baby-sitter, who was often my Aunt Lori, out for a date, and left the girl he was dating here to take care of me.

I mentioned it to him once, and he said that nothing between him and Lori would ever have worked out, but that was all he said. All I knew was, he often came back from his dates very depressed and sometimes angry, and sat outside and stared at the sky; usually I had a great time with Lori playing games with me and reading me stories until bedtime. Even then I guess I knew the world got more complicated for adults.

After a while Mom and Sig got back, but since they were going to be moving to Washington, D.C., in a year or so, I stayed with Dad and visited over there. I understood that there was a lot of excitement going on because now the Skygrazers were flying regularly, and people were pouring in to buy chances for them and for the later Starbirds and Starbird/ Luna trips.

Christmas of 2005 was almost okay. By that time I'd gotten sort of adjusted, and I was used to my room in Dad's apartment; I sort of had three sets of parents, because Dad had me during the week, Mom and Sig had me on weekends, and a lot of times if there was any problem with handing me over—like Dad being out of town on Friday and Mom not getting in till Saturday—I would just stay with Aunt Lori. It wasn't as nice as if everyone had been getting along, but I was pretty sure there would always be somebody around if I needed anything.

For the holiday, I got up Christmas morning at Dad's, and Aunt Lori dropped by with a couple of her friends, which pretty much made up for Dad having Allison over (she was a college student with bright red hair; she wore way too much lipstick and began every sentence with "like"; that's all I remember of that one). Allison gave me the kind of stuffed animal that a girl, or a much smaller boy, would get, Dad gave me some books and some science kits, and Aunt Lori gave me an incredibly wonderful kit for building a flying scale model of a Starbird. Dad looked kind of surprised, but since I was so thrilled, he was happy, too. Aunt Lori promised that sometime soon she and I would put it together, and there was a big lot out behind her house where we could try flying it.

Then I went over to Mom and Sig's place in the afternoon, and Dad agreed to come in and have a drink with Sig when he dropped me off, and they were both very polite to each other, which was nice. After a while Dad left and they got out the presents.

Mom had given me a lot of clothes, some music, and some videos of classic movies; I think she was trying to make me cultured.

For a minute as I was unwrapping Sig's gift to me, my heart sank— the box looked just like the one from the Starbird model Aunt Lori had given me, and I was trying to think of how I could be polite. But then I saw that it wasn't a flying Starbird model—it was a Starbooster/Skygrazer combination. Better still, the Starbooster was designed to go with the Starbird I already had, so that I could fly the booster with either the Starbird or Skygrazer.

I looked up at Sig and he winked. "I didn't know what would be cool enough," he said, "so I called up your Aunt Lori and asked her. Was I right?"

"Oh, yeah. Or Aunt Lori was. I think she's always right."

"I'll keep that in mind," Sig said gravely.

The next week, between Christmas and New Year's, Mom and Sig were off skiing and Dad had a conference he was addressing someplace, so I stayed with Lori, and we put the models together—she was one of those rare grownups that can let you do it while still helping you do it right. Both the Skygrazer and the Starbird flew beautifully with the Starbooster, and I realized that I now had something really impressive to show off when I got back to school in a few days.

While Aunt Lori and I were sitting and watching the news, the phone rang; I could tell from the way she answered that it was Dad, and that the news was mixed. She came back and sat down next to me, putting an arm around me. I knew right then that something was up, and even if Aunt Lori was there with me, it was still going to be some kind of bad news. I asked her, "What is it? And why didn't Dad talk to me?"

"Well, he only had a minute," she said, "and he will talk to you tomorrow, and he didn't think I should tell you until he was sure, tomorrow. But I think this is something you should know about, and pretty soon. So will you not tell your Dad I told you?"

I nodded solemnly and leaned closer to her.

"Well," she said, "it looks like your Dad, and probably me, are going to get another mission. He was at a big meeting of the University Space Research Associates, who are the people who have a special experiment they want him to do for them, and if NASA agrees then your dad will go up to the ISS to do that. That means you'll probably have to go stay with Sig and your mother in D.C., at least for a while, because they're moving there real soon. And if your Dad goes, it's a three-month mission, so with training time and everything he won't be back till school's out."

"Will you be back sooner?"

"Unh-hunh. Probably I'll just be at training for a while, about as long as your dad, and then I'll come back ten days or so after we fly. When I get back I'll come and visit you in Washington, if you want me to."

"Sure." I was holding onto her hard, but she didn't try to make me release my grip. "It'll be great if you can come and see me."

Like I said, Christmas that year was *almost* okay.

The funny thing is the longer I spend going over the family records, getting things in order for Clio, the more confusing some things get.

There was the Chris Terence who I knew as "Dad," and he was kind of inconsistent, moody and a little scatterbrained; there was the Chris Terence who was Mom's first husband, brilliant and fascinating but arrogant and sometimes a plain old jerk; there was the Chris Terence of the nightly news and of dozens of academic conferences, a powerful, clear, articulate voice for space science; and there was the Chris Terence of the NASA records, which I finally got on the fiftieth anniversary of his death—an efficient, dedicated, highly regarded astronaut whom other astronauts liked to work with. But for what it was like to *be* him . . . well, that's one of those questions sons never know about fathers.

He had been active for a long time in the University Space Research Associates. It was an outgrowth of half a dozen older projects and cooperative organizations, and he'd been part of those, too. Everyone knew that if there was ever going to be a voice for pure science in the space program, it would have to come from the university research community. The idea was simply that the various large college departments of space science, astronautics, astronautical engineering, planetary science, and astronomy—where so much of the real basic research into space-related subjects was done—should get together in a consortium, pooling part of their funds, raising some for the consortium itself directly, and come up with a long-term program of pure scientific research which they could do cooperatively with NASA, ESA, and any other space agency that would let them. One of the first fruits of this was the Far Side Radio Telescope (FSRT), the experiment that Dad would be working with up at ISS.

The basic idea of the FSRT was simple. What we can know of objects out in space is what comes to us as electromagnetic radiation: radio waves, microwaves, infrared, visible light, ultraviolet, X-rays, and cosmic rays. Several of these had really only become available for study once there were platforms in space—ultraviolet and infrared don't penetrate the atmosphere well, and X-rays and cosmic rays scatter so much in the atmosphere that it's all but impossible to tell, from a ground-based station, where they came from. Thus it was not until orbiting satellites were able to get above Earth's atmosphere that we even began to have any idea where most of these kinds of radiation came from, or how much any given object in the sky was putting out.

Visible light, of course, had been one of the basic tools for studying the cosmos since people first looked up into the night sky, more so since the invention of the telescope in the seventeenth century. But here, too, space had made a major improvement, because air blurred the light coming in (the same phenomenon that made stars twinkle) and dimmed it as well; hence, with a mirror only a fraction the size of the large telescope mirrors on Earth, the Hubble Telescope had been able to see very far, deep, and accurately into the universe.

At first glance, since radio waves are relatively unaffected by passage through ordinary air, it might seem that radio astronomy would suffer far fewer problems from the Earth's blanket of air, and thus radio astronomers would benefit far less from space exploration than any other kind of astronomer. So far that had been true, but the University Space Research Associates was out to change that, in their first big project together.

The problem was not that the air blocked, scattered, or distorted radio waves; it did those things only to a minor extent. The problem was that about the time that radio astronomy was developing in the 1920s— as scientists came to realize that the hiss and crackle of "static," which could be heard over any radio, partly originated from sources not on this planet—the world had begun to fill up with radio broadcasting stations. (It was natural enough; radio had to be invented before anyone would know about radio telescopes, but once radio was invented there were bound to be stations on the air.) The Heaviside layer in the upper atmosphere bounced radio waves around the world; if an astronomer wanted to listen for a given frequency from some star, no matter how carefully he might point his antenna at that star and no other, the more sensitive his detector, the more likely he was to get a college station from Fargo or the farm report from Chile. Further, the Earth's atmosphere is alive with electrical storms, and our strong magnetic field creates vivid auroras at the poles, and both of these are also powerful sources of radio waves, creating vast amounts of noise through which the astronomer must try to hear the faint signals from beyond. In fact, coming in only behind the Sun (a blazing nuclear fusion reactor) and mighty Jupiter (with the solar system's most intense magnetic field), the Earth is the third largest source of radio noise in the solar system.

Merely to have put a radio telescope in orbit would not have done much good. It not only would remain close to the noisy Earth, but it would be in a straight line from many of the noise sources; the only advantage was that since it would be far above the Heaviside layer, fewer stray signals might scatter into its directional antenna. Thus there had been relatively little work with radio telescopy above the atmosphere, because the advantage to be gained was slight compared with what could be gained in most of the rest of the electromagnetic spectrum.

However, better launch vehicles and tools had come along, and now there was a new possibility, one that the University Space Research Associates wanted to exploit. The Moon, with only a very weak magnetic field, does not put out much radio, and one side of the Moon is forever turned away from the Earth. Furthermore, 50 percent of the time the side that is turned away from the Earth also faces away from the Sun. And finally, because Jupiter goes around the Sun in about twelve years, matters worked out so that 5/12ths of that fifty percent— or 5/24ths in all, just over a fifth—of the time, the Moon would also shield a radio telescope on its far side from Jupiter.

At such times, with almost all the noise of the solar system screened out, a very delicate detector could be used. It meant a real possibility of seeing deeper into the universe in the radio spectrum than we had ever done before, and of getting back results with far greater certainty.

There was no way of simply constructing a radio telescope on the Moon as we would do on the Earth, however. Earthbound radio telescopes are gigantic dishes, like radar dishes or television satellite antennas, but much larger. The ones that are small enough to move, move on gigantic pieces of machinery; crews of dozens staff them. To build something on that scale on the Moon—let alone on the back side—was far beyond our capabilities in 2006, and we weren't about to try.

Rather, we took advantage of some naturally occurring phenomena. The Moon has plenty of craters of all sizes, even on the far side (though the very largest, for unknown reasons, are concentrated on the near side). The craters themselves are far from being perfectly parabolic, as an ideal radio dish would be, but they are certainly large and they make adequate reflectors. If they could be corrected to reflect waves from a particular point toward a central antenna, the radio telescope could even be aimed with a fair degree of precision. The natural lunar soil offered some radio reflectivity; a point fifty meters or so above the bottom of a half-kilometer-wide crater should have a fairly strong signal.

The Far Side Radio Telescope was an ultrasensitive radio receiver with enough computer memory to store a very accurate digitized recording of whatever signal it received. It was to be mounted atop a small robot lander, which would fly to a preselected crater on the far side, land near its center, and then put up an antenna, a thin piece of aluminum pipe. Three small robot carts would depart automatically from the lander, crawling out about 100 meters from the landing site, at 120 degrees from each other; each would be dragging several long wires attached at various points to the antenna. When the carts were in position, a small tank of helium would be used to pressurize the inside of the telescoping antenna, causing it to extend upward very slowly; in radio communication with each other, the guy wire robots would continually adjust line tensions to keep the slender aluminum rod perfectly vertical. As the helium pressed each section into its final place, a snap lock would keep it there. At last, after a couple of hours, the aluminum pipe would reach fifty meters into the empty sky of the far side of the Moon, vertical and well-guyed, somewhere near where the crater would reflect radio waves. The computer on the FSRT would work out what were the "quiet times" when Earth, Jupiter, and Sun were all out of line-of-sight from the radio; two thousand kilometers of lunar rock would block and attenuate the radio signals from those strong noise sources—and the FSRT would be able to hear and record fainter signals, from more distant places, more accurately than any instrument ever before.

Two additional features were needed to make it work. The first of these was the most urgent. Unfortunately, a robotic research station that is placed in an area where radio waves from Earth cannot penetrate also cannot receive orders telling it what to look at, nor can it send data back. A relay station was needed, and because the relay station itself was potentially a source of noise, it needed to be a very quiet one.

The solution was the "halo satellite," which took advantage of an odd phenomenon in orbital mechanics, one of those cases where the mathematics of physical equations predicted something that then turned out to be true in the real world. Prior to computers, most many-body problems in orbital mechanics—that is, problems that involved more than two bodies attracting each other gravitationally—were not soluble by any means available; the solutions had to be approximated by treating them as a set of separate two-body problems.

Around the turn of the nineteenth century, Lagrange had pointed out that there were a few places in orbit around a two-body system (like the Earth and the Moon, Mars and Phobos, or the Sun and Jupiter—any system where you could ignore the other bodies temporarily) that did have solutions, stable places that would behave very much as if there were an attracting body there, even though they were just empty space. In those five spots, called "libration points" because they were places where the gravity and motion of the system balanced, a satellite could stay indefinitely, with no need for fuel or energy to "station keep"—i.e., to maintain its position.

Those places were a midpoint where gravity balanced between the two bodies so that neither of them ever tugged the satellite one way or another; two places in line with the two bodies but on the outside, so that the satellite orbited the combined center of mass of both bodies with exactly the same period with which the two went around each other; and the places which formed an equilateral triangle with the two bodies, one ahead and the other behind the smaller body in orbit, where any motion toward one body would result in a stronger attraction by the other and pull the satellite back into place.

Thus the Earth-Moon system (and any other case of one body orbiting around another) has five "Lagrange libration points": places where a spacecraft can sit without expending fuel to keep itself in a constant relationship with the Earth and Moon. These are almost always referred to by L plus a digit. L1, L2, and L3 all lie in a line with the Moon and the Earth; L1 between them, L2 beyond the Moon, and L3 on the opposite side of the Earth from the Moon. L4 is 60 degrees ahead of the Moon in orbit; L5 is 60 degrees behind. The Lagrange libration points had been of great interest since the late 1960s, because they are the most energy-efficient places to put a space station, and when it cost $100,000 to move a pound of fuel into orbit, energy savings were vital.

The Lagrange points have another odd feature. Because they are attractors (things near them tend to fall toward them), it is possible for a satellite to orbit them, even though they are just points in empty space.

This was the birth of the idea of the halo satellite. A satellite orbiting L2, in about a two-week orbit, will always have both the entire far side of the Moon, and the facing side of the Earth, in direct line of sight. It was called a halo satellite because from the Earth it appeared to be making a circle around the orb of the Moon—and thus was never out of sight of either the Earth or the far side. The relay transceiver on the halo satellite, in turn, could be turned entirely off whenever the FSRT was working, so that the only thing running on board was a small clock set to turn the halo satellite back on at a prearranged time, then receive data from the FSRT and relay it back to Earth during the "noisy" periods. For technical reasons a pair of halo satellites worked slightly better, giving more complete coverage of the Moon's back side. No one made much of a point of it, but a halo satellite in place would also mean that if humans ever ventured to the far side of the Moon, they would be able to radio home—a drastic improvement from the days of Apollo.

The other device was a simple, incremental improvement that would allow the FSRT to become a steadily better tool for decades to come. Weighing just forty pounds, the Self-Propelled Ultralight Microantenna (SPUM) was designed to be launched to the Moon using any convenient system; it would find the FSRT by radio beacon during a noisy time and descend into the crater, avoiding the guy wire robots and the previously arrived SPUMs by receiving information from the FSRT computer. Once down, it would unfold a simple wire-frame antenna, not much different from an old-fashioned umbrella, about fifteen meters across—an easy enough size to handle in the light lunar gravity.

Coordinated by the FSRT, the SPUM would run a series of test radio beeps so that the FSRT would know its exact location, plus how to translate what the SPUM said about its position into the FSRT's more general coordinate system. Each added SPUM would increase both the signal strength and the ability of the FSRT to focus; a few hundred of them would make the FSRT into an extraordinarily powerful and effective instrument.

The FSRT, halo satellite, and SPUMs were all to be powered by bat-

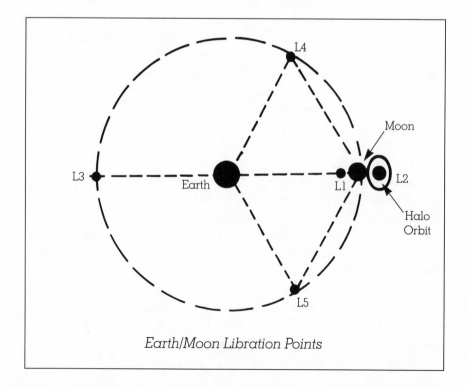

Earth/Moon Libration Points

teries recharged by solar cells. Since by definition when there was sunlight it was a noisy period, the charging process should create little interference with the work of the FSRT.

The system was elegant and cheap; it took advantage of enormous improvements in computers to minimize expensive mass being sent to such a difficult location.

But everyone had learned the bitter lesson of the Hubble Telescope, which had originally gone up with a warped mirror, unable to focus properly. Though it had been successfully repaired, the damage it had done to NASA's public image had been incalculable. The University Space Research Associates, with a far smaller budget and much less public visibility than NASA, needed this first bold mission to be a complete success, and so they had determined that they would thoroughly test each component before sending it on its way. In late 2005, the halo satellite had checked out perfectly, and a Centurion/Starbooster combination had carried it into halo orbit, from which it was reporting that results thus far were perfect.

Next would come testing the FSRT's receiver in Earth orbit, to make sure that it would work properly in vacuum and in the alternating tremendous heat and cold of sunshine and shadow in space. Chris had been assigned to do the full checkout of the FSRT at the ISS, following which, if time permitted, he could use extra time on the ISS for astronomical observations for his own projects and assist the rest of the crew with assignments coming up from the ground.

This was the seventh American flight of an Apollo II on top of a Centurion/Starbooster combination, the temporary configuration to augment the three remaining shuttles until Starbird would replace them later in the decade.

Lori Kirsten was to be the pilot for the mission that would take them up; she had trained with the astro-Fs in France and knew Apollo IIs thoroughly, but she hadn't actually flown one before. The mission's principal functions were Chris's FSRT mission, and getting another escape module (and better still, one that was neither Russian nor French) up to the ISS.

It was really a good thing that Chris and Lori were the only crew; the FSRT took up a great deal of room in the Apollo II so the other four crew seats had been removed.

"Ever feel like a museum reenactment?" Chris muttered to Lori as they strapped in for launch.

"Don't you like the Pigeon?"

"The what?"

"When I went down and trained with the astro-Fs, we started calling it that to annoy the French. It's called a Pigeon because it goes somewhere and roosts for a while, but it's always supposed to come back home."

"Well, it's a better name than Apollo II. Less of a phony sound to it. And these things don't look much like Apollos to me, anyway—too steep-sided and too big."

"Yep, I've seen the original Apollos in the Smithsonian. They're really tiny. By comparison a Pigeon is huge." She wriggled and stretched as much as she could, confined to the acceleration Couch. "Geez, first mission since we lost *Endeavour*. I hope we have better luck with this one—I don't think it'll glide real far."

"Yeah, but these, uh, Pigeons are designed to float."

"Apollo II, this is Control," a voice said through their earphones.

"Roger, Launch Control, Pigeon is here and ready," Lori said.

"Excellent, Apollo II, we anticipate no delays, and we'll be commencing countdown shortly. Please confirm the following checklist—"

They did—everything was perfectly normal—and then watched and listened as the countdown proceeded. Aunt Lori always said the Pigeons were the beginning of the end for the "real" pilots because they were the first ships really designed to do everything either by remote control or by robotics; not even docking was to be manual. She grumbled that from the Pigeon forward, American astronauts were "passengers more than pilots."

Years later, when I began flying Pigeons, I disliked them intensely because it seemed to me that their computer system needed manual overriding much too often. No doubt someday the captains of later starships will wonder how anyone could put up with the living human pilots of the earlier starships.

Chris and Lori endured the high-acceleration ride as first the Starbooster engine plus the upper stage carried them aloft, then the Starbooster peeled off to fly back to the Cape. A while later, they shut down the upper stage.

"Made it to orbit this time," Lori said. "That's a bit more dignified."

Two more burns put them on course for the ISS. As they approached it, Chris whistled. "They've done a lot with the old joint since I was up here six years ago. The truss is done, the solar collectors are deployed . . . and so that's the Big Can."

"We're supposed to call it an HT."

"I bet you're supposed to call this Pigeon an Apollo II, too."

"Maybe so, but if you were a woman you'd get tired of the number of male ground controllers who want to tell you that your Big Can is moving strangely, or that a couple of guys will be docking with your Big Can shortly, or to make sure I put my Big Can up high where people can see it."

Chris snorted. "I imagine those jokes do get old."

"Unh-hunh. Anyway, rumor has it that it's pretty nice in there."

The Pigeon nosed gently into the docking module without Lori's having to touch the controls. "Great system, but I'm not sure the union's gonna like it," she muttered. "Well, let's get inside."

They had unshipped the FSRT and were just in process of getting to know the rest of the crew—two cosmonauts, a Japanese astronaut, and an astro-F—when the chime that indicated a high-priority message sounded.

"Probably something that will prevent dinner," Peter Denisov grumbled, going to the radio. "Preventing dinner seems to be their highest priority down there." Between Mir and ISS, Denisov had almost four years in space; doctors were constantly poking at the pudgy red-haired man to see how many things differed between him and the rest of the human race.

He talked with them for a long time, earphone clapped to his ear. Mostly what he said was "No," and "It can't be," and "I don't believe it." Once he asked if this was some kind of prank. Finally he hung up, still denying everything—whatever everything was.

By that time the room had fallen silent. Tatiana Haldin, the ranking officer on board, finally asked, "Peter Mikhailovich, what are they telling you on the radio?"

"It's a prank. It must be a prank."

She shrugged. "Unless they ordered us to do something dangerous, I think we should comply."

He wouldn't respond at all, staring at the wall, just floating there; afterwards Chris learned that no one had ever really seen him upset before.

Jiro said, quietly, "You should let the rest of us in on it. It won't be a prank on you personally, anyway, even if that's what it is."

Peter Denisov looked up and saw everyone—Chris, Lori, Jiro, Tatiana, and François—nodding. Finally, he blurted out, "They claim that they are getting radio messages from Alpha Centauri."

5

WHAT DAD TOLD ME LATER WAS THAT WHAT DENISOV HAD SAID PRO-
duced an "astonishing silence." Finally, after a long time, Haldin, floating at the other end of the Big Can, pulled her pale blonde hair back
and smoothed her stubby ponytail. Visibly, she composed herself and
said, "Peter Mikhailovich, you will embarrass us. If the message is real we
need to acknowledge it; if it is a prank we need to report it."

Denisov nodded, very unhappily. François said, "If you like, I can
call CNRS directly—we are line-of-sight from France—and see what
they know about it. A back channel approach, so that if it is a joke no
one needs to know that we took it seriously."

"What's CNRS?" Chris said, feeling a little dumb.

"*Centre nationale pour le recherche scientifique*," François explained.
"It's our umbrella science organization; any unclassified problem will go
there first. And this is about as unclassified a problem as anyone has ever
seen, so I'm sure my friend there will know as much as anyone. Shall I
call him?"

"Do it," Haldin agreed. She turned to Chris and Lori. "Well, this is
going to be a memorable first day at the station for you. How did the
flight up go? An American crew riding a French capsule on a Russian
rocket must be a complex job."

"Well, Starbooster engines have been built in the U.S.A. for three
years now, and thank heaven the software and control systems are
American," Lori said, "and that's all I need to talk to." She had recognized Haldin's dig at them, but her orders were to not escalate any arguments; as much as Americans might resent their temporary junior status
at ISS and in space, after all it was of their own making, and given that
the ugly situation with China seemed to be getting worse, and we needed our traditional Russian, Japanese, and French alliances in the event
of trouble, it paid Americans to be nice even when others weren't.

Haldin nodded and said, "An uneventful flight is always to be hoped for."

By that time François had gotten through to a ground station and
was contacting his old friend at CNRS by voice Internet. The small,
muscular astro-F gestured for silence, muttering, "It's a terrible connection, it always is—*Allo, Michel?*"

Chris had only a little bit of French, enough to get him around town at conferences; it had only been very recently that American astronauts had had much reason to learn the language, and Russian was still by far the most common second language in the astronaut corps.

But Lori had spent part of last year training with the astro-Fs in Toulouse, and she had a knack for languages anyway. Chris watched her reactions closely to gauge what was going on. At first she listened patiently; clearly François was making small talk with his friend for a minute, laughing politely and working his way around to the question. Then suddenly François fell silent, and when he spoke again it was fast, loud, and very excited. Then he put the conversation up on the speakers so that everyone could hear both sides. Lori leaned forward eagerly, and slowly, as she listened, her mouth fell open and she breathed in great sighs. By the time the call was over, everyone in the Big Can knew, whether they spoke French or not, from the excitement in the voices.

"It's not a prank," Jiro said, very quietly. "At least for the moment it looks real."

François nodded, gulping for air. "Peter, I think you're going to have to apologize to whoever called." He pushed his unruly dark hair back and stretched in the low gravity. "Practically every antenna in the Southern Hemisphere has been getting it."

"I think probably everyone will want to talk with their home countries and institutions," Tatiana said. "And this time was allocated as down time, for the arrival of the Pigeon, so for the next hour and ten minutes, none of us has anything much we are supposed to be doing. If you don't mind cutting the welcoming party short, we could all get onto communications links and see how much we can learn about this whole situation."

"I feel as welcome as I need to," Lori said. "And Chris will explode if he has to sit here and make small talk while anything like this is happening. Let's do it."

Haldin grinned. "Chris is not the only one who would explode. Well, at the least, let's take this time and let everyone talk to home. The next thing after that is supposed to be dinner and rest, so let's make dinner a general meeting where we pool our information."

Chris found that it was easy enough to find people who knew the basics, but seemingly impossible to find anyone who knew more than that, by phone. And the basics were scanty: sometime within the last twenty-four hours, on a wavelength of about 96 meters, a signal had begun to come in strongly from the direction of Alpha Centauri, the triple star, which is the closest star to the Earth. Bits and pieces of the signal seemed to be strangely ordered—it appeared to be a sequence of tones, two different pitches stuttered at an enormous rate—but unfortunately the Earth's atmosphere is nearly opaque to radio at that wavelength, because it cannot penetrate the ionosphere. Thus it was impossible to catch more than brief snatches of it on even the most sensitive radio telescopes on the ground.

Theories abounded. The media, naturally, was already claiming that it was messages from aliens; other hypotheses included various strange events in the stellar atmosphere of Alpha Centauri A or Alpha Centauri B, somehow causing one star or the other to act as a giant laser at that wavelength; a huge electrical storm in the atmosphere of a planet circling those stars; the gravity of Alpha Centauri A acting as a lens and focusing radio at that wavelength from a distant source, thus making it seem louder; and many more. The idea that it might be aliens was discounted by many, not just because of the sheer improbability, but also because it didn't seem likely that an intelligent species would try to contact others using radio on a wavelength that would be mostly blocked by the water-vapor-rich atmosphere of any planet with life.

All of these theories suffered mainly from the problem that little could really be known directly about Alpha Centauri. Alpha Centauri is the nearest star, but "near" is a relative term; it's like saying that Key West is the nearest part of the United States to the South Pole. At the speed at which the Apollo astronauts went to the Moon, it would take a little less than 110,000 years—time enough for the last four Ice Ages— for a spaceship to get from Earth to Alpha Centauri. A radio signal, which is 26,500 times faster, takes about four years.

Physically Alpha Centauri is not one star but three: Alpha Centauri A, a star very slightly larger than our Sun; Alpha Centauri B, a smaller star that is only a few astronomical units from A; and Proxima Centauri, a very dim, cool, small star which is so far away from A and B that astronomers debate whether it is really in orbit around them or just moving around the galactic center in an almost identical orbit.

A and B orbit around their common center of mass—a point in empty space where the average of their masses would be if they were one single body—about every eighty years. In their endless slow waltz, A and B sometimes get as close as eleven AU to each other (ten percent farther than the distance from the Sun to Saturn) and sometimes swing out as far as thirty-five AU (sixteen percent farther than the distance from the Sun to Neptune).

Chris called a dozen colleagues before it was time for the scheduled dinner on ISS; most of the people he called knew no more than he did. An hour on the phone produced only a list of people to call for the next day.

Other people had had better luck. When they all gathered for sandwiches and squeeze bags of soup an hour later, there were a few other pieces of information which people had extracted.

First of all, there were occasional long repetitive strings in the signal, sometimes with only small variations, sometimes with no variations at all. It was believed that it might be repeating on a cycle of hours or days in length, but there was so much noise that it might take months to get a copy of the whole signal—if it stayed on that long and if it was indeed repeating. It was clearly not the product of static discharges in an atmosphere anywhere—unless somehow a gas giant planet in that system had a lasable atmosphere that had spontaneously tuned itself to that frequency. The best guess was that the power level at which it was coming in was actually remarkably uniform.

Everyone was enjoying throwing in theories when the chime sounded for the phone. Tatiana, as commander, picked it up; a moment later she put it up on speakers.

"No doubt you've heard," said a voice with a Midwestern drawl that Chris recognized at once as the chairman of the University Space Research Associates, "about the noise from Alpha Centauri. Is Dr. Terence there?"

"Yes, I am, Bob."

"Well, in the last few hours some big changes have happened. When the radio noise from Alpha Centauri began, several observatories in the Southern Hemisphere contacted the Center for Short-Lived Phenomena, and they called the USRA, and NASA, with a suggestion. You have the FSRT, which is the most sensitive radio detector ever constructed. Moreover, you are sitting above the Earth's atmosphere, which is to say you can get clear reception of the radio signal now emanating from Alpha Centauri. Of course it would be best if the FSRT were already in place on the Moon, since that would allow us to take advantage of the conditions there, but the fact is that conditions at ISS are better for radio observations in the millimeter wavelength than they are anywhere on Earth, ever. And we don't know how long the signal will last. Thus NASA has authorized us to modify our test for the FSRT; we are asking that you immediately mount a loop antenna, running the length of the truss, and connect that to the FSRT, then attempt to record the signal now coming from Alpha Centauri. A full set of directions and specifications, plus orders from everyone's national governments, will follow immediately by datalink. You're going to go out there and get a good copy of that signal for us."

"I—thank you," Chris said. "I'm looking forward to it."

"We're very fortunate that you happened to be there with the appropriate tool," the chairman said. "Orders follow, as they say; good luck." With a sharp click, the call was disconnected.

"So all we have to do is make a 90-meter loop antenna," Lori said, "out of whatever we just happen to have brought along."

"And rig it overnight," Chris added. "And have the FSRT work perfectly during its tryout—"

"Besides," Denisov added, "you may not recall this, but due to budget cutbacks years ago in your country, there is nowhere on the outward-facing part of the truss to mount any equipment whatsoever—we can't do any kind of real astronomy here on the station."

"I had forgotten that there aren't any brackets or places to attach things on that side of the station," Chris admitted.

Haldin seemed to think for the space of three long breaths, and then she shrugged. "Well, it will do all our careers some good if it works, and hurt nothing if it doesn't."

Denisov nodded. "And we do have a small stock of supplies. We have some large clamps and some insulated wire, probably enough to mount a loop on the outward-facing surface of the truss. Do you have any way of connecting to such a loop?"

"Some of the test circuit stuff takes standard plugs," Chris said. "Yeah, I think so."

"Then let's get to work on it," Haldin said. "We need to work out the technical details now."

After a six-hour nap, Chris found himself going out for an EVA with Peter Denisov. Despite the apparent grumpiness of the heavyset Russian, Chris was getting to like him; he'd come to realize that the cosmonaut was intolerant of nonsense and convinced of his own judgment, but more than willing to adopt a good idea once he was convinced of it. (I sometimes have odd memories of him—he used to come and visit my father, and the two of them would go out on the town, usually with women my father had found from wherever it was that he turned them up; I can remember my mother claiming that he must be subscribing to the Bimbo of the Month club. Then the next day Peter would be down in the basement at the workbench with me, helping me put together a model, or we'd be out in the woods riding minibikes, or a thousand other things—for an old grouch, Peter Denisov was pretty good at acting like a teenager.)

The airlock was tiny, really just a small attachment onto a hatch, and the two men had to go through it separately, each tucking himself and his bulky spacesuit into the small, closet-sized space, half-squatting, waiting for the air to be pumped out of the lock and back into the Big Can, then opening the outer door and climbing out with a bag of supplies and closing the outer door behind himself. Denisov, as the more experienced of the two, went first, and when Chris emerged and closed the hatch, he was already set up and ready to go. "Before we start," Denisov said, his voice crackling through the radio in Chris's helmet, "is this your first EVA?"

"First one," Chris agreed. "We've all had the training, but I'm sure that—"

"I'm sure you'll be fine, too," Peter replied. "Tatiana, cut the floodlights please."

"Roger," her voice crackled in their headsets.

"Now, Chris," Peter said, "I just wanted to suggest that you look up away from the Earth for a moment or two. It's a view every astronomer should have."

I know what he saw, now, and can understand a little of how it must have struck him; when I was a kid and Dad would describe being outside in space for the first time, I didn't understand why he was so excited about there being "so many stars" when after all he was an astronomer and he should have known how many of them there were anyway. Now I have a little more idea that when you have imagined something but never really seen it directly, for your whole life, just possibly the first time you see it may strike you dumb.

They spent the ten minutes, while they waited to come around to the day side of the orbit, looking up into the stars, many times as many as you can see from Earth, the bright ones brighter by far than earthly eyes are used to. They had something pretty important to do, and no doubt they were strongly reminded of that by the brilliant beacon of Alpha Centauri—so close that even though it's just a run-of-the-mill double star with a combined brightness only about one and a half times our own Sun, it's still the third brightest star in our sky.

Chris waited, floating with one hand to hold him in place, till the Sun emerged over the Earth; in less than a minute, the glare on his visor erased the swarm of stars, leaving the sky black. The job was simple—or it would have been simple, on Earth. Nothing is simple in orbit, where the rules wired into your nerves by half a billion years of evolution stop working, and you're encumbered by a thick, heavy pressure suit. The HT-based habitat was attached to the center node, aft of the truss (a long, thin structure on which the immense bank of solar panels that powered the station was mounted). The truss itself had a hexagonal cross section as wide as a hallway in an ordinary house; normally if one had to get to either end of it, one either climbed from strut to strut, along the structural members, inside the truss, or worked tethered to one of the structural members and crawled along the "bottom" (Earth-facing) side, when there were Earth-monitoring or space-science experiments to be conducted.

As the Russians had pointed out, one of the many budget cuts the American Congress had imposed on the ISS had involved planning for a truss that was only "half useful," in that there were no built-in places to attach experiments or equipment that faced out toward space. The United States, having successfully lured other nations into the cooperative enterprise, had almost at once begun to limit its capabilities, like a used car salesman who shows you something too good to be true and then tries to talk you into taking something grossly inferior for the same price. I can remember Dad growling to himself, after the mission was over, that a few hundred ex-lawyers in Washington had decided that everything interesting in the universe had to be in the same direction, the one that allowed orbiting astronauts to take photographs of their districts.

As a result, Chris's first EVA was an interesting exercise in improvisation. Station supplies had included a few dozen Clancy clamps, toothed clamps on a piece of pipe that tightened their grip when a small disk on the pipe was spun to the right, and a large roll of vacuum-proof silver bell wire. (To work in space, bell wire couldn't have just an ordinary plastic jacket, because many plastics in a vacuum outgas the volatiles that keep them soft; hence, the insulation on the wire was a special fiberglass. And because the expense of getting the wire into orbit and the special insulation was already so high, it only added a small fraction to the cost to make the conductor out of extremely pure silver, which was both a better conductor and more flexible than copper or aluminum.) A small committee of experienced engineers and machinists had spent a long time figuring out what ought to be in the ISS's tool and supply kits; so far their record was holding up.

If the truss had been on the ground, it might have taken Chris alone only a few minutes to accomplish the basic job of putting a loop of bell wire onto its space-facing side with the Clancy clamps—he would only need to stretch a few meters of the wire along the girder, put a clamp over it, spin the disk, and move on to repeat the process.

But on the ISS, that required a whole set of other actions. First of all, attached to the structure itself by their tethers, Chris and Denisov were effectively coorbiting with the station—that is, they were bodies occupying their own separate orbits around the Earth that happened to coincide, mostly, with that of the station. Thus there was a tendency, because coorbiting is never perfect, for things to slowly drift to different positions. Everything, including Peter and Chris, had to be on a tether all the time, and tended to drift to the end of the tether, or to wrap around the girders.

Then there was the matter of having something to push against. If you twist on the disk of a Clancy clamp on Earth, the disk turns easily and the clamp fastens, because the force of your hand turning the disk encounters very little resistance, and the equal and opposite force twisting the soles of your feet in the opposite direction is easily overcome by the friction of your shoes. But in space there's nothing to control that opposite force; as you turn the disk, the disk turns you, unless you hold yourself in place with your other hand.

Thus as Chris and Denisov worked their way out to one end of the truss, back to the other end, and then back to the habitat, they had to perform many more tasks than they would have had to do to accomplish the equivalent job on Earth. First, they would move forward to tether themselves, the bag of Clancy clamps, and the coil of bell wire into position. Then they would move back to detach the tethers from their previous positions, and then forward again so that finally after several minutes they were in position to accomplish any progress.

Then Denisov would take the coil of bell wire and stretch about five meters of wire along the girder, using the previously attached clamps to anchor it behind him and holding onto the girder with his outspread arms wrapping around up toward his shoulders, putting his hands on the "top" so that the wire was held in place where it could be clamped. Then Chris would tow the bag of clamps over, fish out one (with one hand, while hanging on with the other), clip the clamp to his own suit for a moment, close the bag and release it, take the clamp off its clip, fit it over the wire Denisov was holding, brace himself with his other hand, and spin the disk to tighten the clamp.

After that they would repeat the process again. It took them about six hours in all—plus an extra twenty minutes or so spent in fetching more supplies.

When Chris climbed back in, he ached in an amazing array of places from the use of so many muscles in such unfamiliar ways, and his coverall under his pressure suit was drenched with sweat. By universal agreement, Chris and Peter got an extra shower that day; theoretically they should then have napped, but within minutes of getting into a fresh coverall, Chris had swallowed some freeze-dried coffee and aspirin, and was on the job of getting the FSRT plugged into the external contact system that Tatiana Haldin and Lori had set up to use the big-loop antenna. In less than an hour, fiddling and scanning, François and Chris had managed to bring in the signal from Alpha Centauri.

When they were sure that the signal was coming in clear, the data were being recorded, the datalink to groundside was working, and that the FSRT was behaving as it should, Chris stretched and said, "Well, now, finally, I'm going to use some of that flexibility they say we have, and take that nap."

By the time Chris arose, the hypothesis that it was an alien signal had gone from the least likely (at least to the well-informed and scientifically literate) to the most likely. François briefed him as he gobbled a quick breakfast.

"They say it is coming in in a high tone/low tone/blank pattern; if we assume the blanks are spaces, then since it is coming as triple beeps, it looks very much like a transmission in base eight."

Base eight, Chris thought; there's the first clear evidence that it's really aliens—or at least that if it's a hoax, someone has really thought the hoax through. The most common numbering system on Earth is base ten. That is we have ten digits, zero through nine, and each place in a number (counting left from the decimal point) represents a power of ten—5280 is $5 \times 10^3 + 2 \times 10^2 + 8 \times 10^1 + 0 \times 10^0$, or as we say it out loud, "Five thousand two hundred eighty"—so casually that we don't tend to remember there's multiplication and addition in there, five thousands *plus* two hundreds *plus* eighty (which is the swallowed English pronunciation of the original "eight tens"). More recently the computer industry has taught many people to work in "hexadecimal"—base sixteen, in which there are sixteen digits (1–9 plus A–E, representing

10–15 respectively), or in bytes, which are base 256 numbers for practical purposes. (16 and 256 are both powers of two, and because the basic machinery of computers, down at the microscopic level, works on binary [base 2] numbers, this makes for compact information storage; if they were not powers of two, some combinations of symbols would have to be meaningless within the system, thus "wasting" some of the potential information it could carry.)

Almost every schoolchild has used the simple code in which A = 1, B = 2, and so forth, and most people know that newspaper and computer pictures are transmitted in pixels: two numbers to specify a position on the screen or in the picture, and another number to specify brightness (or for a color picture, three numbers to specify the brightness of the red, blue, and green components that mix to produce color). Indeed, in the 1930s Kurt Gödel and Alan Turing demonstrated that any information we can understand can be sent as a string of numbers. Thus, a message from another civilization—if that was what this was—ought to arrive in a string of numbers. But since the base of a number system is arbitrary (there's no particular reason why it should be ten rather than twelve or five), it would be extremely unlikely that such a message would arrive in base ten numbers.

Apparently what was coming in was groups of three high and low tones, or, as the Earth-based scientists were shortly to call them, beeps and honks. A group of three beep-or-honk choices could have eight different arrangements:

beep beep beep
beep beep honk
beep honk beep
beep honk honk
honk beep beep
honk beep honk
honk honk beep
honk honk honk

And on some system or other, those probably represented the digits 0–7, which were the digits for a base eight system. The strings of digits would represent pictures or text.

"Base eight," Chris said. "So maybe they've only got a thumb and three fingers?"

"Or eight tentacles," François said. "Or one thumb and one finger on each of their four arms, or they're all Buddhists and it's terribly important to them to express things in terms of the Eightfold Way. Or they have three heads and those are all the combinations of nodding and shaking that are possible. It seems to me that for a while here we will be theorizing in advance of data."

"Just because it doesn't have much foundation in fact doesn't mean we can't enjoy it," Chris said. "I wonder if the USRA has anything they can tell me. I can get them by voice relay through the Internet."

But he wasn't able to look into that possibility for three full days. Time in space is terribly precious, cannot be wasted, and if lost, must be replaced. Thus time is planned to the utmost and only the bare minimum needed for rest is left to individual initiative. Normally, because the hardware is expensive, and the equipment needed for making decisions is bulky, heavy, and better located on the ground, people on space missions don't so much make decisions as execute them. Even (or especially) in emergencies, what ought to happen next is worked out on the ground, right down to how many times to turn a bolt, and the crew in space then carry out the directions with constant monitoring by radio. That doesn't mean that no one ever does anything on their own initiative, but it's rare, it's not supposed to happen, and most of the time when it does happen it's something brief.

One reason why this is so is that time in orbit is unspeakably expensive. Just to get an astronaut, cosmonaut, or astro-F into orbit is expensive enough, but after that everything needed to keep him or her alive, for as long as the mission lasts, has to be gotten up to orbit as well. This is true whether the crew is working on an assigned project, resting, eating, or playing cards. The maximum possible work has to be squeezed out of a space crew, and it's more likely that careful planning from the ground will result in more efficiency than the astronaut's mere following of whim.

But this was different; the mystery signal from Alpha Centauri had been a crisis, because no one knew what it was or how long it might last at the start. Now that the FSRT was running automatically, however, no matter how interesting the crew of the ISS might find the signal to be, they had to make up for dozens of lost person-hours on dozens of other important experiments, and everyone had to pitch in and get that work done before there would be any leisure to look at the serendipitous discovery.

Lori had volunteered to stay an extra week to take up the slack, and even then they did not really have enough hands. Still, NASA understands that people must have rest, and after three days Chris found himself with a blessed four hours, not allocated to sleep, all his own.

He promptly used it to do more work. "Jiro," he asked, "I don't suppose that there's any way I can access the recorded data from the Alpha Centauri transmission?"

"Of course there is," Jiro said, grinning at him. "Join the club. We all spend our recreation time analyzing it. What's your project?"

"Well," Chris said, "I have this idea that the source probably isn't on either of the stars. That would be insanely unlikely. So I think it's in orbit around them; and since I have several days worth of data now, I bet if I analyze it for Doppler shift, I can at least figure out which of the two stars it's orbiting, and maybe even plot a rough orbit for it."

The Doppler shift is the change in frequency that occurs for waves originating from a moving object; the familiar example is the way that the sound of a car's engine, as the car passes you, sounds at first like it's rising in pitch, then like it's falling. It happens because when the waves are coming from an object approaching you, each successive wave starts out a little closer to you, and thus has a shorter distance to travel and gets there sooner. And as the waves seem to "pile up" on top of each other, more of them arrive in a given time—and the number of waves arriving in a given time is the frequency.

Similarly, if the object emitting the waves is moving away, each wave starts further away than its predecessor and takes longer to reach you; thus fewer and fewer of them arrive per second, and the frequency seems to decrease. High frequency sound is high pitched; low frequency sound is low pitched; and thus as the car passes you the sound seems first to rise and then to fall in pitch.

The same phenomenon also happens with light, radio, X-rays, or any other form of electromagnetic radiation; high frequency light is violet, low frequency light is red. Thus by measuring changes in the apparent frequency of radio or light emitted by an object, you can measure whether an object is moving toward you or away from you, and how fast.

For an orbiting body, this is enough, usually, to figure out a great deal about its orbit. The frequency will rise while the object is on the side of its orbit that has it approaching you; it will fall on the other side. If you know its speed at any point in the orbit, or better still over some part of the orbit, then since the speed with which a body moves in an orbit depends only on the shape of the orbit and the distance from the body it orbits around, the exact pattern of variation of frequency will give you an idea of the orbit's shape, and from that you have a good guess at its distance. (Because Alpha Centauri is a double star, furthermore, Chris was able to know *which* of the two stars the body must be orbiting; the orbit of the two stars around each other revealed their masses, and the relation between orbital speed, shape, and distance depends on the mass of the star; the calculated orbit could only be consistent with *one* of the two stars.)

The problem was complex and tricky in a way Chris liked, because before he could study Doppler effects in the frequency of the 0.96 mm radio signals from Alpha Centauri, he first had to factor out several known sources of Doppler effects: the motion of the ISS around the Earth (which created a 90-minute cycle), the motion of the Earth around the Sun, and the motion of Alpha Centauri A and Alpha Centauri B with respect to the Sun. His four hours of recreation were almost up before he finally began to see satisfactory results.

Meanwhile he caught up on his reading about the mysterious signal. The message was repeating, starting over again about every eleven hours and twenty minutes. Each group of 16,769,021 base-eight numbers was taking about two and a half seconds to come in, so that there were 16,384 such groups in all. That was as much as anyone was saying in public.

It was bizarre in many ways. For decades, dedicated amateur radio astronomers, and interested professionals who could squeeze in the time on the big dishes, had been trying to find something, anything, that might look like a signal from another civilization. The prevalent idea had been that most likely, if we found it, it would not be a direct attempt to communicate with us, but a general announcement to the universe, perhaps as a beacon aimed at likely stars. Since they wouldn't be trying to reach us in particular, all the astronomers who had thought about the problem had thought that we would need extremely sensitive detectors and big antennas to hear an alien civilization at all.

Now, years after many of the SETI (Search for Extraterrestrial Intelligence) projects had been shut down for lack of funds, and the rest had struggled to get equipment sensitive enough to pick up faint signals from planets that might be hundreds of light-years away, suddenly here was a loud, clear signal coming in from the nearest star, something that almost anyone could get with even the crudest backyard receivers—and yet transmitted on the least convenient, most noise-prone wavelength imaginable.

At last the analysis program passed its checkouts, and Chris told it to try the data. The program opened the file that contained the signal strengths and antenna positions, loaded the data into the appropriate internal matrix, and began processing. Various short messages indicating that the program had completed another step popped up on the screen; the program was executing properly.

It finished, and displayed a set of equations plus the message "UNIQUE SOLUTION, 95% CERTAIN"—indicating that there was only one mathematically possible result to explain the data, and that the odds were nineteen to one or better that the solution was right.

"Now, *that's* weird," François said, peering over Chris's shoulder. "That looks like—er—"

"It looks like it can't possibly be an orbit around either star, or around their combined center of mass, or around any of their Lagrange points," Chris finished for him. "Yes, I know."

"But the curve is beautifully smooth," François pointed out. "It doesn't *look* like garbage or error, it looks like—"

Jiro too came over to kibbitz. "Hmm. Suppose you're not dealing with one mass but two," he said. "Suppose it's a small body orbiting a larger body orbiting one of the stars. If you figure that—"

"You're right," Chris said, and rapidly keyed in a test sequence. The program ran for several long minutes as it tried and discarded dozens of alternatives. Then quite suddenly, an animated display popped up on the screen, showing dots labeled A and B circling each other like wary boxers—and a strange lozenge-shaped spiral circling B.

"Yep," Chris said. "That's a body in a highly elliptical orbit around another much larger body, which is orbiting B. Seems like a strange place for life, but that's too good a picture not to be right." He tapped the keys a few times, and said, "Well, if you figure that the planet is a gas giant, like Jupiter or Saturn, then an Earthlike planet in that kind of orbit around it would be marginally habitable—usually. It would get mighty cold on the long swings outward, and pretty hot whenever it swung in toward Alpha Centauri B. The real problem is, just guessing at it, I don't think a moon around a gas giant could be stable in that position over a period of billions of years."

Jiro's hands went to the keys. "Want to see if we can modify it to estimate a position and mass for the gas giant, and then check long-term stability on that elliptical orbit?"

"Absolutely," Chris said. "Funny thing, but that's gravity for you—

we can figure out exactly the mass of the planet, but we have no way of knowing whether what's orbiting it is the size of a Volkswagen or the size of the Earth. The mass of the orbiting body doesn't affect the period of the orbit, only the mass of the central body."

Jiro shrugged. "Just the way it works out. Well, our results do seem to be consistent. That central body seems to be about one hundred forty Earth masses—or one and a half times as big as Saturn, or less than half as big as Jupiter. Call it either a super-Saturn or a mini-Jupiter, eh?"

Mission Control, seeing the importance of the results, authorized Jiro, François, and Chris to spend another two hours on the problem of the stability of the orbiting body, from which the broadcast was coming.

At one time it was thought that all the planets in the solar system must be moving in exactly the same fashion every year, because it was assumed that even a slight annual change would accumulate until the planet was in a drastically different orbit, and sooner or later would accumulate so far that the planet would fall into the Sun, or swing far enough out to be lost forever, or eventually drift into an orbit that did repeat over time.

But in the late 1980s, chaos theory—the mathematics that governs situations where a small difference at the beginning could have large and unpredictable effects at the end—brought astronomers to the realization that although each planet's orbit was *generally* similar to the one from the year before, some of the planets and moons—especially in the more eccentric orbits, or in orbits far from the Sun (like Pluto's)—could have chaotic orbits that never replicated perfectly but nevertheless kept the body in orbit for hundreds of millions of years. An orbit was "stable," therefore, if the equations that described it would regularly return to the same sequence of values, so that the motion of the body would repeat, over and over. It was "unstable" if that never happened, and in that latter case, the more unstable (that is, the farther away from ever returning to the same place at the same speed moving in the same direction), the less likely it was to have lasted in its orbit for very long.

The answer checked out but was highly unsatisfactory. "Well," Chris said, "I guess what we've done is solved half the mystery. It couldn't have been there much longer than forty million years. Therefore life didn't evolve there; whoever and whatever they are, they aren't from that moon. That's almost reassuring, since a body with that orbit would be a hell of a place for habitability on a long-term basis. We must be getting transmissions from a beacon or something. Maybe it's a distress call from an alien ship that was forced to land there, or a scientific probe reporting back what it's found, or—"

François looked up from the neighboring screen and said, "Not likely."

Chris stopped and said, "Why not?"

"Because if you remember, one assumption we had to start with was that the signal was of constant strength; so I was rechecking that assumption against the computed orbit. And in one sense it is of constant strength—it's all coming at the same power. But there's been a very slow secular increase in signal strength going on, which is perfectly explained if you assume that we're moving into the center of a beam. Which makes sense—even with a very large aperture, and a highly collimated beam, at that wavelength beam spread should work out to six or seven astronomical units either way from the Sun. You couldn't point it directly at the Earth, perhaps, or there was no point in it—but if you pointed it at the Sun, the Earth would never be outside the beam."

Jiro and Chris gaped at him, and then Chris said what was obvious. "So they aren't broadcasting to the whole universe. Whoever or whatever they are, they aimed that message right at us."

6

AT THE END OF THE NEXT WORK PERIOD, WHEN A GROUP MEAL WAS SCHEDuled, Tatiana Haldin said, "Well, congratulations; thanks to publication on the Internet, the three of you are now famous, and the rest of us will be wanting your autographs. You might be interested to know that the International Astronomical Union has already scheduled a meeting to name the gas giant that Dr. Terence has identified orbiting Alpha Centauri B."

"We don't even know that it's a gas giant," Chris said, "and you can call me Chris. All we know is that it masses about a hundred and forty times what the Earth does. That's not a lot to go on."

Denisov snorted. "And what else is a planet that big going to be made of? It's big enough to have retained almost all its primordial hydrogen and helium, and since they make up the majority of matter in the universe, what else do you think it might be made of? Chocolate ice cream? And you should tell him, Tatiana, about the campaign back in his country."

"I didn't wish to embarrass him," Haldin said mildly.

"Well, I've always enjoyed embarrassing him," Lori said, grinning. "Chris, there's a bunch of nuts back home writing to Congress who want to name that gas giant after you. They're calling themselves the Beta Centauri Terence Society."

Chris groaned. "How many different ways can the same people be dumb? In the first place, all of us had a hand in the discovery. And secondly, the star is Alpha Centauri B—the second largest star in the double star Alpha Centauri. Beta Centauri is a completely different star, in a different part of the constellation Centaurus, a lot farther away, just in sort of the same direction. And anyway, naming that planet, if that's what it is, is the job of the International Astronomical Union. God, if you leave that kind of thing to the vote of the people, someday we'll have planets named after Elvis and Cher."

Everyone laughed; Tatiana said, "I'm sure the new planet won't have a name for a long time. The IAU is at least as political as any other scientific body; they'll have to argue about whether to continue naming planets after gods, and if so, whose gods, and if whose, which of their gods, and so forth indefinitely."

François nodded. "If anyone asks me, I shall suggest 'Marianne.'"

"Is there something especially French about a gas giant around Alpha Centauri B?" Lori asked, curiously.

"No, I don't mean after the spirit of the Republic. I like it because that's my daughter's name. It's as good a reason as any other. But I do think our station commander is right; unless we suddenly have a way of finding thousands or millions of planets, everyone will want the new planet to be named after their particular god or cause, and the IAU probably won't get to talk about much else until it's finally settled—if it ever is. Meanwhile, I do believe Jiro has something to show us."

The Japanese astronaut smiled shyly. "I'd like François to begin. His insight led me to my results."

François, who had gotten that information from his friends at CNRS, began, "First of all, the burst of base eight numbers are coming in groups of 16,769,021, with a longer break between each group. And what makes that interesting is that some bright people ran it through a simple factoring program and discovered that it's equal to 4093 times 4097—two prime numbers."

"Uh, excuse my being dumb, but this means . . . ?" Lori asked.

"Since a prime number isn't evenly divisible by any other number, if you're transmitting a grid-type pattern—say a picture or a chart—and its size is the product of two primes, then there are only a couple of possible arrangements for the numbers in the grid. If either number were not prime, there'd be a very large number of possible arrangements, and that would mean you wouldn't be able to figure out what the picture was a picture of."

Chris jumped in. "Like, suppose you know that you're getting a list of the cells of an individual grid, but you don't know what shape the grid is—only that they sent you sixty cells. Well, sixty could be the number of cells in a five-by-twelve, or a six-by-ten, or fifteen-by-four, or for that matter a two-by-thirty or a three-by-twenty grid. And if the number were much larger, and the product of many different numbers, you could spend a long time looking for a way to arrange the grid that made sense. But suppose they sent you seventy-seven cells; that can only be a seven-by-eleven grid, or an eleven-by-seven that's the same grid lying on its side. So what this means is that they're sending us pictures, tables, charts, something like that—and every picture is four thousand ninety-three by four thousand ninety-seven dots or pixels or whatever."

Denisov nodded and said, "And it's more evidence of their alienness. That's the first prime greater than four thousand ninety-six times the first prime smaller than four thousand ninety-six—and if you write four thousand ninety-six in base eight, it's a one followed by four zeros. So it looks like when they laid out their grid, they set it up to come out close to what they would think of as 'round' numbers."

"Has anyone tried to assemble the pictures yet?" Lori asked.

"I thought you'd never ask," Jiro said. "I have a feeling that everywhere on Earth people are showing this to each other, but they don't quite have the nerve to display it publicly. My guess is that at least a hundred people have tried the same thing I have. After all, the only reason we have a copy of the signal is because we happen to be sitting at the receiving antenna and we sort-of-accidentally happen to be recording it; the ground stations we're transmitting it to not only have copies, they also have a lot of people who are paid to analyze it—whereas I'm just doing it in my spare time. So I'm sure other people have hit on the solution I have, which is this: suppose we assume that the beeps and honks, as they're calling them, really do represent binary one and zero, and that therefore the groups of three are base eight numbers. There are really only four possibilities as I see it: either you read the group of three left to right, or right to left, and either you read beep as zero and honk as one, or vice versa. On that basis, for example; 'beep beep honk' could mean one, four, six, or three. What occurred to me was this: what if we just make a guess that the numbers represent values of bright and dark on a 4093 by 4097 grid? Then there are actually only eight possible images that each frame might be, and furthermore half of them are black-for-white negatives of the others. Well, then, it wasn't all that difficult to set up a program to compute an appearance for all 16,384 frames eight times—they do things much more complicated than that in a matter of a few minutes in the new virtual reality games in the arcades, you know, and we have a good deal more computational power available than they do. And then one further idea struck me—now I have these eight sets of frames . . . what could they be? Photographs? A photographic image of a book page, perhaps?

"The first thing I noted was that quite a few of them in this group" —he clicked on the shared screen and showed the group—"look like kind of an oddly notated star map."

"That's what it is, all right," Chris said. "Those are the principal pulsars near us, with lines proportional in length to distances to us—or more likely to Alpha Centauri. Unless we have a precise tool for measuring the length of those lines on the screen, the differences aren't going to matter much in this scale of a picture."

Everyone turned to look at him, and he said, "I had something like that on my bedroom wall as a kid—the poster version of the plate that went on our Pioneer spacecraft, way back in the seventies. I fell asleep looking at it, a lot of the time. And that's so close to the same pattern, that, since in astronomical terms we aren't very far from Alpha Centauri—"

"I see," Jiro said. "Well, then, no doubt a lot of people have figured that one out, too. And perhaps from that we'll be able to crack their system of numbers and measurements. Certainly there's something that looks a lot like writing, right next to lines that look like they ought to be dimensions. Anyway, it occurred to me that since several consecutive pictures were pretty similar to each other, there might be a reason for what seemed like a lot of redundancy—I think this is a movie."

"A movie?" Lori said. "So each of those sixteen-million-or-so-number sets is a description of a frame?"

"That was the idea I had," Jiro said. "And here's the result: we can only guess at the intended projection speed, at least until we figure something out about their writing, but this looks convincing to me."

The screen popped into focus, and they saw eight creatures climbing into what had to be a spacecraft. Two of them seemed to be very tall and thin, covered with fine fur, with big ears like a bat's. Two others, of the same body shape, were smaller. Two were square-built and strong looking, like gorillas, with strange high ridges that stuck straight up from their shoulders and a high, hair-covered crest that rose from the top of their head like a mohawk. Their fur seemed to be thicker, longer, and coarser than that of the taller ones, and very dark; they had thick beards under their jaws, almost like manes. Two others had the same dark and heavy fur and were also squat in build like an ape, though they stood as erect as any human; they were quite short and had no crests or beards.

As the ISS crew watched, the creatures waved and got into an odd, thick-bodied rocket ship that lay on its side; the rocket floated straight up a long way, and then they saw the engines fire.

The image cut to a rendezvous with something that looked like a space station in orbit: a torus or ring shape impaled on the end of a column sticking through its center. The little craft docked at the tip near the torus, a quick interior shot showed the alien crew getting into the bigger ship, and then the little craft undocked and went away. Abruptly, on the big structure, the end away from the torus fired a great stream of white-hot stuff into space.

The first of the crew to speak was Haldin; she said only, "Jiro, I would have to say that if your interpretation isn't right, it's the damnedest coincidence in history."

The rest of the first forty seconds or so showed them deploying a light sail, sailing away from Alpha Centauri with a couple of gravity assists, making their way to the solar system, and descending to Earth. "That map is Suez and the Eastern Med," Lori exclaimed. "Even though it seems to be upside down, anyone would recognize it!"

"Yes," Jiro said, "and if the blinking dot is the landing site, then I guess they landed somewhere in the Jordan Valley."

An abrupt cut showed another spacecraft also departing Alpha Centauri. "What do you suppose that one is?" François said. "It just streaked off the screen."

The image showing the landing site was repeated; then there were pictures of yet another type of spacecraft departing Earth, and abruptly it cut to three arrows: one pointing straight down at an image of the Moon; the second at a spot on the surface of Mars, near the bottom but at an angle; and the last pointing to the faster-moving inner moon of Mars, Phobos.

"What do you suppose that means?" Lori said. "It looked like the Moon was upside down, and Phobos was going backward, so I guess they use the bottom of the map for north and the top for south. So they're saying they went to the south pole of the Moon, to Phobos, and to somewhere near the north pole of Mars?"

"If an arrow means the same thing to them it does to us," Chris pointed out. "Maybe they're talking about something that came from there, or it's their symbol for where everyone is buried, or where they put the biggest cathedral or their equivalent of the prime meridian."

The camera cut again. It showed what appeared to be a simple, squat box with a cylindrical plug in the corner of one side, and a square plug in the center of an adjoining side. Then the screen filled with text—"That really does look like it has to be alien writing," Peter said. "Directions for how to operate something that's shaped like that box?"

"Or how to pray to the sacred box, or how to build the alien version of the clothes washer," Lori said. "The anthropologists and linguistics people are going to have a great century or two working on all this."

The camera cut again to show, one more time, arrows pointing to somewhere on Mars and probably to the south pole of the Moon. Then it showed a sequence of spaceship departures, one after another, nine in all, each followed by a quick designation of a star from pulsar positions, an image of the star's planetary system in which one planet was marked with an odd symbol, and an arrow pointing to somewhere on a planet. Finally it showed thousands of aliens, some like the ones in the first pictures, descending through huge corridors. Then it showed a flock of spacecraft leaving orbit and repeated the picture of the box.

"Notice that their world is in orbit around a gas giant?" Jiro said. "My first thought was that that confirmed it, but watch the last shot here."

The last shot showed eleven solar systems, ten of them arranged around a central one. Ours was one of them; the central one had a double star, with gas giants circling both of the two stars.

The larger gas giant circled the larger star, and around that gas giant there was a single moon, marked with a strange twinkling symbol. The smaller gas giant, orbiting the smaller star, was circled by three moons, two in roughly circular orbits and one in a highly elliptical orbit; this last moon was marked with another, different twinkling symbol.

"Looks like they agree with you, Chris," François said. "They show a moon in a highly elliptical orbit, around a gas giant, circling Alpha Centauri B." The picture stopped as abruptly as it had begun.

"Well, that makes sense," Lori said. "They put their home system in the center."

"Well, if nothing else, that'll get all the astronomers busy," Chris said. "And there must be a hundred or more planets and moons between all the systems they depict there. Once we figure out how to read their notation, there's going to be plenty of names for everyone to put on things."

"Hah," Haldin said gloomily. "There are any number of people out there who can come up with a list of a hundred things they want honored. Their countrymen, their gods, probably their crops. I rescind my previous claim. It's not going to be decades for the IAU to sort things out, it's going to be centuries."

"Why do you suppose this, uh, alien cartoon isn't all over the airwaves already?" François asked.

"Probably because everyone who has thought of doing this with it—which means undoubtedly someone almost everywhere—is hoping to break the alien code before announcing," Jiro said. "Figuring out that it's a movie will get you on the air for twenty minutes. Figuring out what the movie says—well, that will put you in the history books for a long, long time."

The rest of that last work shift was uneventful, but when everyone arose the next morning, the news from Earth was a mixture of the astonishing and the silly.

Suddenly every television reporter on Earth wanted to interview every astronomer. And since the preliminary results had overthrown the ideas of so many of them, many astronomers, receiving public attention for the first time in their lives, gasped, stammered, or simply refused to talk.

Just the existence of planets in the Alpha Centauri system at all had been enough of a shock to many of them, Chris thought. Since the distances between the two stars varied by a factor of three, tidal forces varied by a factor of twenty-seven; debate had swung back and forth for decades about whether this would sweep the system clear of the primordial planetesimals out of which planets accrete (so that there would be nothing there) or prevent them from accreting at all (so that there would be thousands of very small bodies), or cause them to accrete more readily (so that there might be a small number of very large planets). *Well*, Chris thought, *here's where all the astronomers and planetary scientists get to find out who guessed right.* It sure didn't look good for the two "no planets" theories.

All that attention focused on the astronomical community had also meant that no action by an astronomer was going to be overlooked. Taking advantage of this, an Italian astronomer, Vincente Auricchio, had published via the Internet, and then called a press conference just twenty minutes later. Everyone on the ISS took the extra few minutes to watch this one. Auricchio spoke English (the language of the international media ever since BBC Overseas TV and CNN divided the world between them) with just a trace of an accent; it was as if he had spent all his life preparing for a media event.

"Well," Auricchio was saying, "I see no reason to pretend to a wholly inappropriate modesty, or to beat around the bush, as you say in English. Western civilization is the greatest civilization the Earth has ever seen, and the West learned to be civilized from Italy, and the Italians learned it from Rome. It is thus no accident that I, a life-long citizen of Rome, have found the key to the alien message; I simply compared the orbits figured by the crew on the International Space Station with the orbits described in the animated message from the Tiberians, and by assuming one was a translation of the other, broke the code of their system of representation. Then I turned to—"

"Excuse me," the reporter from the *New York Times* asked. "You said the message from the—"

"The Tiberians. The inhabitants of Tiber. Which is the inhabited moon that circles Juno, which circles Alpha Centauri A. As I was saying, by comparing the orbits that were calculated by Terence, Raymond, and Kawaguchi—and I might note that Terence and Raymond each have Italian ancestors, according to their biographies—"

"And I like Italian food," Jiro said. Everyone shushed him.

"—I was able to figure out their system of time notation, hence where those new planets should be and should have been for thousands of years into the past. Now as it happens, the university here at Rome has a quite good system—in my opinion, the best in the world—that preserves a digitized version of virtually all the astronomical photographs taken in the last century and a half. It was therefore very little trouble to call up into my computer all those photos which ought to show those planets and their moons, if the resolution was high enough; select those with high enough resolution; and by combining these several thousand photos, especially those from the American Hubble Telescope, I was able to show that these few dim white dots, which were always mistaken before for very faint stars at very great distances, were in exactly the right places to be those planets and moons—and here is my list of what I have extracted the sightings of from the record, ladies and gentleman, the first confirmed observations of planets around Alpha Centauri A and B:

"Alpha Centauri A's planet Juno—which seems to be of a mass about two hundred and fifty times that of the Earth, or three-quarters of Jupiter, and orbits its primary at a distance somewhat greater than one astronomical unit;

"Juno's moon Tiber, which is in a twenty-six-hour orbit around the giant planet, is just slightly more massive than the Earth, and is clearly designated in the message as the place from which our alien visitors came or intend to come;

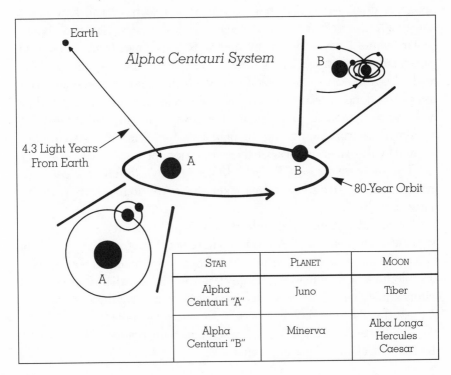

Star	Planet	Moon
Alpha Centauri "A"	Juno	Tiber
Alpha Centauri "B"	Minerva	Alba Longa Hercules Caesar

"Minerva, the gas giant circling Alpha Centauri B at a distance a bit less than an astronomical unit, with a mass of one hundred thirty-eight Earths;

"Alba Longa, the moon of Minerva on which the transmitter is mounted, about one and a half times as big as Mars, in a highly elliptical orbit;

"Hercules, a moon of Minerva about the size of Io in our own solar system, in a fairly wide but nearly circular orbit;

"And Minerva's nearest moon, the hardest one to see, which I have only about a dozen images of—but more than enough to confirm its existence. This moon I have named Caesar.

"My assistants will pass out complete packets of information on these new worlds—discovered like so many other new worlds, by a proud Italian—and of course I shall be delighted to answer any questions you may have about my deciphering of the alien message or about the little we can know so far about these new worlds."

The *Times* reporter, a tall, thin man, stepped forward and raised his arm again. With an impatient sigh, Auricchio pointed at him, and the reporter said, "If I may ask, the names you have given these celestial bodies—"

"Are entirely my right as discoverer. I will not make the mistake of my great compatriot, Columbus, who failed to have the new lands named after himself; it was only sheerest luck that 'America' was also an Italian name. I have chosen my names as grand ones from Italian and particularly Roman traditions; that is as it should be. Western science made this discovery possible, and Italy leads the West intellectually, as it has always done. If other nations wish to have planets of their own, they had best hurry and discover them—but I warn you, my assistants and I are already at work on finding the planets of the other solar systems designated by the Tiberian message. Next question, please?"

The man who rose asked, "It looks like two different species, or maybe three, getting into that rocket ship. Are you sure they are all native to Tiber?"

"It would not be impossible for one starfaring race to already be acquainted with another," Auricchio pointed out. "But it's really too early to tell. For all we know, Tiber was settled from elsewhere and both species are colonists; or they may be one species—after all, an alien visitor would hardly know that a Chihuahua and a Saint Bernard were the same species. Perhaps these are just different races of Tiberians. Next question?"

The *Times* reporter raised his voice and half-shouted, "What about the IAU's declaration yesterday that—"

"The IAU may go to the devil, and undoubtedly they have the address," Auricchio said. "I found it, I named it. No gaggle of fuzzy-minded internationalists is going to call my discovery after some stone idol or swaggering dictator. Now let's have an interesting question."

It went on like that, and when it became clear there wouldn't be much more real news, they turned the television off and got on with the busy routine of the station. Every so often, though, Chris and François, working together on a set of precise gravimetric measurements, would catch each other's eye, and one or the other would mutter, "If we'd just named it Marianne when we had the chance. . . ."

"Or Nero or Caligula," Peter would add. "To provide a more balanced view of Rome, you know."

The names given by Auricchio stuck; they were easy to remember and pronounce, some version of the names already existed in most of the world's major languages, and—as Americans and Europeans usually said when they were polled about it—"they just sounded more like names for planets."

The IAU put out many press releases reminding people that the new names were unofficial; only the *New York Times* continued the IAU's temporary nomenclature of calling the new worlds Alpha Centauri A–I, Alpha Centauri A–I–1, Alpha Centauri B–I, Alpha Centauri B–I–1, Alpha Centauri B–I–2, and Alpha Centauri B–I–3; everyone else said Juno, Tiber, Minerva, Alba Longa, Hercules, and Caesar, just as Auricchio had, and the aliens immediately were dubbed the "Tiberians."

Auricchio did not entirely have things his own way, however. About a year later, a diligent Japanese astronomer at Tsukuba demonstrated that there weren't any pictures from the Hubble Telescope that had little white dots in the places where Auricchio had shown them. Further investigation showed that, stymied by the limits of precision that even the powerful Hubble had to contend with, Auricchio had altered the pictures, adding the images, in order to get "Caesar" into his list of discoveries. He lost his university job, and from then on was only heard of on "where are they now?" programs on television. The single time one of those programs came on in our house, a few years later, my father said a couple of things that he'd have washed my mouth out with soap for, and turned the set off. But even he still called the new worlds by Auricchio's names. They were just too convenient not to, and besides, everyone else did.

*　　　*　　　*

The message kept coming for seven more months before shutting off for good. During that time it was recorded and rerecorded many times, but it was always the same 16,384 frames—a number which, it was quickly realized, was equal to 2^{14}, or 4×8^4—perhaps the equivalent of our 50,000. Teams of experts confirmed Dad's speculation about the location in terms of pulsars, and the pictures of the aliens themselves were gone over extensively as well. Slowly, though there were still many mysteries, a consensus as to the meaning of the message began to form.

One way or another it seemed to be addressed to Tiberian colonies. A change of symbol on Alba Longa (the moon orbiting Alpha Centauri B) in the animation, apparently denoted the point in the orbit at which the message had been sent. This turned out to be the time when the four most radio-noisy objects in the Alpha Centauri System—the two stars and the two gas giants—were at maximum separation from Alba Longa (if you looked from the viewpoint of the Earth). A symbol at the bottom of the screen appeared to be a counter that increased from 112 to 113 (assuming we were reading their numbers correctly) when the symbol popped up; the same counter was at zero when the animation depicted the launching of the mystery boxes. Thus it seemed to most people to say that the broadcast had been made 112 times since the launching of the boxes to the colonies, and that this was the 113th broadcast.

The periods of maximum separation occurred irregularly, and some were better than others from a standpoint of radio broadcasting, but the biggest factor in when they occurred was the eighty-year elliptical orbit of A around B. The second biggest factor was the highly elliptical two-and-a-half-year orbit of Alba Longa around Minerva; times of maximum separation could be anywhere from seventy-two to ninety-one years apart when that was factored in, but on the average they would be just over eighty years. Thus if this broadcast was the 113th from that transmitter, it must be about 112 times eighty years since the first broadcast. That put the inception somewhere around 7000 B.C. As more data became available a more exact date would be possible, but "nine thousand years ago" worked pretty well. Apparently the events depicted in the message had been a century or two before the date of the message.

They had come here, in more than one ship, probably at more than one time, and then for some unaccountable reason, instead of returning home they had gone to the South Pole of the Moon, and to Crater Korolev on Mars. The arrow pointing to Mars clearly designated 73 degrees north latitude; the short flash of a picture that followed it showed a large crater. The only large crater on that line of latitude was Korolev, though it appeared from their picture that Korolev had been less ice-filled at the time of the Tiberian visit than it was now—another mystery as to what had happened on Mars in the intervening years.

But the mysterious box that had been inexplicable to Chris and the other astronauts on the ISS had become the greatest focus of attention. The first clue as to what it was about had been the strange picture at the lower left, which showed a coil of ten black and ten white dots in a tight spiral, surrounded by ten circles, with an arrow indicating one of them. It had taken only a few days for someone to think of the idea that this might denote an atom; the most common form of the neon atom has a nucleus of ten neutrons and ten protons and is surrounded by shells containing ten electrons. The particular spot marked was one of the outer electrons, and again it did not take long to realize this was the way of specifying a wavelength of light. Electron orbits are quantized, meaning they can only occur at particular energy levels and no others; when an electron is kicked into a higher orbit than its "ground" state, it will eventually return to that ground state by giving up the exact difference in energies between the two orbits; this will be the same for every electron in the same orbit around the same type of nucleus in the universe. And because the energy of the photon it gives off to get rid of the energy is directly proportional to its frequency, to specify a given electron transition within the electron shells of a given atom is to exactly specify the kind of light to be produced (and incidentally to give directions on how to make it).

The arrows clearly specified that the viewer was supposed to produce light of that wavelength, pulsed according to another set of directions where the unit of time seemed to be based on how long it took 4096 wavelengths of that light to go by a fixed point in a vacuum. That light should be directed onto the square plug in the box; light at one 128 different frequencies, specified by more pictures of atoms, would emerge from the round plug, stuttered so as to form streams of base-eight numbers. (In effect, it was like having a television getting 128 channels at once; we would just have to pick which channel we wanted to "watch" and which to "tape" first.) The first tiny fraction of that would be a copy of this message (or so everyone interpreted it to say), apparently for calibration; then there would be sixteen days of data coming through apparently at ten gigabaud rates on all the channels.

This was confirmed by what appeared to be a sign showing that there would be ten million times as much information in the message that came out of the box as there would be in the message we had received by radio. Now that we had deciphered enough of the message to know the intended play speed, we knew the message was supposed to be seven minutes and forty seconds long; ergo, the information contained in that box was the equivalent of a movie one hundred forty-six thousand twelve years long—or of perhaps half a million average-length books, the equivalent of a small college library.

So what the box appeared to be was the record—poems, paintings, music, literature, science, engineering, jokes, whatever—of a civilization about 200 years in advance of our own, assuming that their technological progress had taken a roughly equivalent path. Within days of the message being decoded, nearly everyone, all at once, had taken to calling it the Encyclopedia; no one knew where that term had come from.

Probably the message hadn't been addressed to us, but intended to tell Tiberian colonies at the lunar south pole and at Crater Korolev on Mars where to find the box with all the information. Why they hadn't sent one to Phobos, even though their little map seemed to say they had gone there, was another puzzle—I remember Dad, Peter Denisov, and Aunt Lori arguing about that one out on the back porch when I was trying to sleep. Had the Tiberians lost or abandoned their Phobos colony? Had it been just a temporary stop on the way to Mars? To annoy the other two, Peter sometimes maintained that the colony on Phobos had been bad, and that was why they didn't get any Encyclopedia.

The name "Encyclopedia" for the box that contained so much Tiberian information had stuck early and thoroughly. So had the most fundamental idea of all on the subject—that the human race ought to go and get the Encyclopedia, returning to the moon after more than thirty years since Apollo 17.

The question was, which part of the human race, and how? At first, since the Chinese had the only actual plan to get to the Moon, they had simply declared that they would accelerate their efforts, go get the Encyclopedia, and "share" with other nations "according to their needs." This had led to an emergency Four Power Space Conference, comprised of the U.S., Russia, Japan, and France (hastily rejoined by ESA, because the other nations of Europe had abruptly realized they might be left out entirely). With a combination of proven Russian and European technology, plus American and Japanese manufacturing capability and materials, it should be possible to "beat the Chinese from a standing start," as the president of the United States put it.

This was growing more urgent, because the Cold Peace was threatening to get hot at any moment. American vessels were shadowed by Chinese submarines everywhere from Pusan to Haiphong, Russian forces were moving up to the line for "border incidents" every few weeks, and the Chinese were issuing not-very-veiled threats to begin shooting down communications satellites if direct satellite broadcasts into China did not cease. Since many of those satellites were now privately operated by companies in flag-of-convenience countries, and most of the offensive broadcasts were originating with private Chinese émigré groups, even if they had wanted to, the four powers could not have shut them down. Meanwhile the Chinese burned more coal per capita every year, and as dark clouds of soot rolled across Japan, Korea, Formosa, and the Philippines, the Pacific Rim nations, using Japanese money and Korean military expertise, began to rapidly rearm. Confronted with the real possibility of nuclear missile attack for the first time in a generation, Russia and the United States began to seriously plan for and build missile defenses for the first time in either of their histories; China's ICBMs were still few in number, and there was still the possibility that being able to shoot some of them down might make a difference.

In the context of such a competition, the possibility of the Chinese getting the Encyclopedia, and with it a two-hundred-year leap in technology, was completely unacceptable. The Speaker of the House put it succinctly: "We can't let them have the only library card in the solar system."

Yet a race for the Encyclopedia was extremely risky for both sides. First there was the possibility of losing; then there was the prospect that one side or other, in its haste, might take too many risks and destroy the Encyclopedia; finally and worst was the prospect of knowledge from the Encyclopedia being deployed hastily and without forethought—"What if you'd given Napoleon the atom bomb? What if the Civil War had been fought with airplanes dropping poison gas on cities?" It seemed to many of the decision-makers involved that not only did the Encyclopedia need to be secured for everyone, it also needed to be used thoughtfully, with some idea about what we were and weren't ready to tackle at this point in our history.

It was the Third World nations that truly brought China to the conference table, however. Just as in the previous Cold War, the militarily and economically weaker power had to look for cheap ways to harass the enemy, and financing revolutionary movements around the world, particularly in resource-rich areas, had been the obvious way. But the Third World leadership had learned from the squabbles over the Law of the Sea Treaty and the Moon Treaty that if they left the big nations that could get the resources to their own devices, the likely rule for the exploitation of distant resources was "finders keepers"—a process in which the rich nations could get richer while the poor nations lost markets for raw materials. As poor nations, they could hardly approve of that.

The Four Power Plan was not perfect from the Third World standpoint, but it did require that the contents of the Encyclopedia be downloaded into a readily accessible form and made available to everyone. The Chinese plan—that China would decide what everyone else needed to know—was much more threatening. And because Chinese operations in the Third World required great numbers of sympathetic governments there, when a dozen usually pro-Chinese leaders began to complain about the Chinese position, China was forced to sit up and take notice.

Thus, reluctantly, and jealous of its rights, a Chinese delegation joined the Four Power planning session, and within a year a plan had been worked out for a mission to the lunar south pole to retrieve the Encyclopedia. The most important thing to everyone involved seemed to be to get access to the Encyclopedia. To set up a task force to go to the Moon and download it onto other media there, without moving it, was obviously time-consuming and judged to be impractical. Thus the Encyclopedia would have to be found and flown back to Earth.

The plan, therefore, was built around the simple question, "How can we get the Encyclopedia from wherever it is around the lunar pole back to the Earth's surface, where our experts can study it?" First robot explorers would go, to search the area and find the place where the Encyclopedia lay. When the robots found the Encyclopedia, they would plant a radio transponder to mark out a landing site within a short distance. Then an unmanned lunar lander—equipped to haul a heavy cargo, because the description of the Encyclopedia had not specified a mass and for all anyone knew it might be made out of lead, gold, or depleted uranium—would land near it. A team of four would fly in in a second lander, with spare fuel, and set down nearby; the team would then load the Encyclopedia into the first lander and refuel it to capacity. Two of the team would then fly the full lander directly back to Earth for a splashdown landing like the first Moon missions; the other two would return in their lander, or continue their stayover, depending on what seemed to be the most effective use of them.

The plan lasted only until the first robots got to the south pole and found not an Encyclopedia but a complete Tiberian base, including one of their spacecraft parked in a deep crater, a vast bank of solar collectors high up on the inside of a crater wall, clear evidence of habitations for many Tiberians, and something that looked too much like a graveyard— neat rows of stone cairns, roughly of human body length—to be anything else. Within days almost everyone in the world had seen the pictures, and two equal and opposite effects had happened.

On the one hand, "Tiber Base" as it had been dubbed, was seen as a fascinating place that everyone wanted to know more about. On the other hand, it enormously complicated the search for the Encyclopedia, for there were two possibilities: either the Tiberians had moved the Encyclopedia into some part of Tiber Base, in which case human explorers would have to go there and open the doors and peer into the storage spaces, or else the Encyclopedia had arrived after Tiber Base was dead or abandoned and might have come down at a considerable distance. The public, never particularly logical in their approach to the world, concluded that since Tiber Base was the best evidence so far that the Tiberian message had told the truth, then people would need to go to Tiber Base, and in at least the democratic nations of Russia, the United States, Japan, and France, that swung a great deal of weight.

Thus the plan was hastily rewritten and rescheduled. An unmanned lander, equipped to bring a crew back, would go to Tiber Base first. Then a first manned mission would land at Tiber Base to look for the Encyclopedia; meanwhile, the robots would continue to look for it everywhere else around the base. The first mission would also do some simple construction to create a better base for the second expedition, which would arrive after them as the first "stay over" mission (i.e., only two of them would return; two others would remain to work with the third mission when it arrived). The second expedition, among other things, would set up a power plant to process the ice in the deep craters at the south pole (where sunlight has never reached since the craters were formed).

The Moon, where water never flowed and there is no air for any practical purpose, might seem to be a strange place to find ice, but the lunar south pole was a special case. Most of the Moon undergoes a two-week-long day followed by a two-week-long night, for as the Moon swings

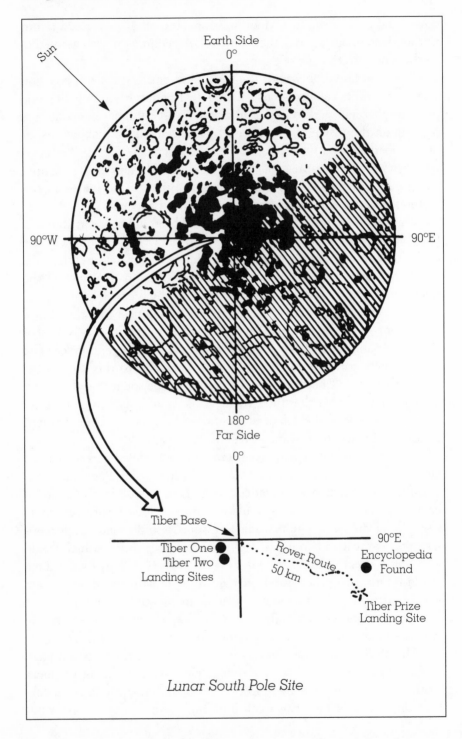

Lunar South Pole Site

around the Earth, always facing the Earth, it rotates with respect to the Sun. (Imagine that you are the Sun, a tree at a distance is the Earth, and a friend of yours is the Moon. If he walks around the tree, keeping his face to the tree the whole time, then when he is nearest you, his back is toward you; when he is farthest away, his face is toward you. In the same way, every point on the Moon's equator must eventually face the Sun.)

During the two weeks of dark, lunar rocks become so cold that any water molecule that hits them will stick to them; if there is any water around it will freeze to those rocks, forming frost. During the two weeks of light, the same rocks grow hot enough to throw the water molecules off, with speeds high enough so that the water molecules don't quite go into orbit, but do bound for hundreds of kilometers. If it happens that they come down and hit a lighted, hot rock, they will gain still more energy, and bounce higher the next time; after anywhere from four to ten bounces off rocks in daylight, the water molecules will bounce right off the Moon and be lost forever.

But if they hit a dark rock, they will stick. Usually they only stick until the sun comes up on that part of the Moon, and then begin the process of bouncing again, until they either hit and stick on the dark side, or bounce off the Moon from the light side. As years go by and lunar day follows lunar night, less and less water is left at the end of each lunar day, and the Moon becomes bone dry.

But that is only what usually happens. The deep craters at the south pole never receive sunlight; the rocks in them are always dark. Thus when a water molecule bounces into one of those craters, it hits, sticks, and stays—forever.

And though such events are rare, water does come to the Moon—often in the form of a comet. Comets, in Fred Hoyle's immortal phrase, are "dirty snowballs"—a scattering of big rocks in a mountain-sized ball of water ice. As millennia pass, now and again a comet strikes the Moon, bursting apart as it digs a new crater and sets millions or billions of tons of water loose on the surface. Most of it disappears quickly in the eternal game of freeze and bounce—but some happens into the craters at the south pole, and it remains there to this day. As the millions of years slide by, eventually it gets to be an immense amount of water.

There were many tons of ice there; ice is made of hydrogen and oxygen—and oxygen is heavy stuff, eighty-nine percent of the weight of water. Not only would it provide water for various uses on Tiber Base, but it would also provide a source of oxygen that didn't involve hauling it a quarter of a million miles into the sky, and later might well provide liquid hydrogen and liquid oxygen fuel for the Pigeons as well. Oxygen gotten in that fashion was dubbed "lunox" to differentiate it from the stuff hauled up from Earth.

With enough stayovers, there would be a substantial base there, using pressurized rovers—big slow-moving land vehicles that looked a bit like milk trucks with room enough for crews to sleep and eat in them—to carry on a search.

Whenever the Encyclopedia was found, the next lander coming out would be sent unmanned to the Encyclopedia site, a crew would go out from the base at Tiber Base (unless, of course, the Encyclopedia was already there), and that crew would bring the Encyclopedia home.

The primary crew cabin for the missions would be the Aerospatiale/Rockwell Pigeon. (By now everyone was calling it that, and "Apollo II" survived only in official company literature.) Habitats and other construction would be built around Big Cans and Starbird drop tanks, since both were already proven-successful pressure vessels. The Japanese undertook to develop the rover; as was rapidly becoming traditional, it was the big Russian boosters, primarily the Energiya, that would supply the thrust to get to the Moon.

The Chinese contribution, more than anything else, was to not try for the Encyclopedia on their own. In exchange for that they got one half of the crew slots; the Four Powers knew which way things went and put up with it, despite the grumbling of the space crews themselves.

"There's another part of the deal," Dad said to me, as we sat outside having ice cream that warm summer night in late 2008. "Not yet made public. Your, uh, mother's husband—" that was usually how he designated Sig to me "—well, he's got an idea. An old idea, really, but he's going to try to make it work. And if he does, then we might be on better terms with the Chinese. It was part of what got them to take the deal."

"So what's the idea?" I asked.

"Well, hmm. It's like this. A lot of China's problems would be solved if they got a decent cheap source of energy, because then they could stop burning coal and making the air over Japan dirty, and they could also raise the standard of living for their people by quite a lot. So one idea that's been around since the 1960s is that if you put a solar power plant in space—where the Sun shines all the time and there's never any clouds—you can beam the power down to Earth using microwaves in a tight beam. You catch the microwaves on an antenna, which converts them back to electricity, and presto, you have cheap power. Much more efficient than ground-based solar."

"What happens if the beam gets pointed in the wrong direction?" I asked.

"If the antenna detects the beam moving at all, it sends a signal up to the satellite to shut off until the problem is fixed. Anyway, uh, Sig, has a contract with the Chinese to build them a power station like that, since his Starbirds are going to make space travel cheaper and he's been able to hire different contractors with a lot of experience building in space. Basically he's doing it for a lot less than cost, and we and the Japanese are picking up the tab and labeling it research—but what it is, is a disguised bribe to the Chinese to get them aboard on this. And since the bribe is flowing through Sig's hands, I guess he'll make a pretty good chunk of money on it.

"Another thing it does is delay the issue of helium-3 mining on the Moon; the Encyclopedia is a bad enough tangle without putting that in."

"Helium-3 is the stuff they run the new fusion reactors on?" I asked. I knew, but I hadn't been seeing much of Dad lately, and I wanted him to keep talking.

He looked up at the darkening cloudless sky, set down his empty ice cream bowl, and said, "Yeah. Once they figured out that you needed the colliding-beam technology to make it work—the only way to get a high enough effective temperature in the stuff you were fusing was to run atoms of it head-on into each other—they were able to figure out what the maximum collision velocities they could get were, and from that they knew that only the light isotope of helium was workable in it. If you remember, Sig's research division was the one that figured out there's enough of it in deep ocean vents so that going to the Moon to extract it from the soil wasn't viable. But now that we're going to have regular traffic, at least for a while, between Earth and Moon—" He sighed. "We just get a frontier opened up again, and already people are figuring out how to make it cluttered and corrupt and a mess. We've never learned a thing, you know?"

I had no idea what he meant, but I was glad to have him there, so I said, "Maybe I don't understand."

"Well, like, think about the American West, in, oh, say, 1848, right after we'd grabbed it from Mexico. Neither the Spanish nor the Mexicans had been able to do much of anything with any parts of it except Texas and California. So you have this whole huge area, the Great Basin and all the surrounding mountain ranges, full of all kinds of species in abundance, and with all kinds of different people for the anthropologists to talk to, and an immense array of interesting things for geologists—and what did we do with it? Dammed the rivers, grazed cattle all over it, killed off most of the big predators, destroyed all the cultures that weren't ours, and covered it with trashy places for trashy people—whole towns full of hoodlums like Tombstone and Deadwood, get-rich-quick places for bums and dreamers like Bozeman and Cripple Creek, and later on, of course, tourist traps like Vegas and Aspen. We had this whole big beautiful place for discovery, and all we could think of to do with it was wipe out everything that made it worth discovering.

"Well, I look at the way space is going, and I find myself thinking, it's pretty similar. More than half the Starbirds that have flown so far have been for your mother's husband's ShareSpace Global, taking people up joyriding. Most of them don't do a lick of real science. Now we're going to make electricity in space, but you can't get a dime for the Hubble III or Hubble IV to see deeper into the universe. We're going to the Moon, but only to go treasure hunting, and once we're there it probably won't be long before we're taking soil that hasn't been disturbed for four billion years, bulldozing it up in carloads, and pumping it through helium extractors. I wonder when they'll open the first casino up there. Probably within my lifetime."

He sat there in the dark so quietly for so long that I started just looking around at the summer stars, something he'd taught me to do. Vega, overhead, seemed very bright tonight. As I often did, I pretended I was on my way to the star directly above me and imagined myself to be falling toward it in the last part of the journey . . . any moment now the point of light would expand to a tiny disk, and then the disk would swell as I fell into the new solar system. . . .

"No one wants to go to space for any important reason," my father said, "but that's not what I needed to talk to you about. I've got another mission coming up, Jason."

"Will I be staying with Mom or with Aunt Lori?"

"With your mother. This could be a long one, longer than the time I went to ISS three years ago, when the message came in." He stretched and then slapped himself. "Houston, the perfect place to relax if you're a mosquito. Not that you'll see any fewer of them in D.C. Here's the story: they've put me on the second manned mission, along with a Chinese woman pilot who's supposed to be kind of a hotshot. Her name is X-I-A-O

B-E, and they pronounce that 'showe bay,' like to rhyme with 'cow day' or 'now pay.' I talked to her on the phone just yesterday and she seemed like an okay person. Peter Denisov is going, too, so at least I'll have a friend on the mission, and François Raymond's in the backup team. Lori's a pilot for mission nine, if they ever get that high."

"Isn't there a fourth on your mission?"

"Another Chinese. Jiang Wu. He doesn't have any real obvious specialties or skills that they've told us about, so we think he's with the secret police, deadheading on this ride so that even on the Moon they'll always have someone watching every PRC citizen." He yawned. "Hope he doesn't distract Xiao Be in all this; there's a lot to get done, and since we won't get much work out of him, she's going to have to pick up the slack. Anyway, it'll be nice to fly with that Russian grump again. But the important thing is, Xiao Be and I are the stayovers—which means I might not be back for months, maybe not till after Lori leaves. So you're going up to stay with Sig and your mother for a while. I guess I should say the usual stuff—behave yourself and don't let me hear that you were any trouble."

7

MOM AND SIG'S PLACE WAS LARGE AND COMFORTABLE, AND THERE WAS A room already set up for me there; the biggest problem I'd had with going up to Washington for sixth and seventh grade was that I wouldn't have as many friends on my Little League or Pop Warner teams. Times before, when I had stayed with Mom and Sig in Reston, I had sometimes attended school there, so I did know some kids from Aldrin Elementary, and I liked them well enough. On the other hand, where I was in Texas, you had to be in seventh grade before you got out of elementary school and into junior high; in Washington there was a middle school, and I would be going to sixth grade there. So I never did get a year of being a "big kid."

The biggest difference, I discovered, was that what was cool and what was passé changed drastically. Around Houston, there were plenty of astronaut brats, and plenty of kids whose parents worked at NASA. So my dad being who he was was no big deal. In Sig's neighborhood there were plenty of congressional brats and kids of rich people, but an astronaut's son was a rarity. It meant a certain amount of teasing and a certain amount of strange second-hand hero worship; I ignored both. I had already learned that there were a lot of occasions when the best thing to do was to shut up and excel other people.

That got more useful, because where in the Houston area the rumor mill revolves around the personal lives of people in the astronaut corps, in Washington it turns around power, who has it and who gets to keep it—and around the art of the deal, who gave up what for what. Consequently, trying to come up with some way or other to relate to me, a surprising number of kids went out of their way to pass on whatever they heard from their parents, who tended to be congresspeople, Washington lawyers, and top-level bureaucrats.

The favorite one seemed to be that there was a lot of tension with the Chinese about the expedition to recover the Encyclopedia. They were said to be hard to deal with and constantly making demands, and every so often there was a rumor that safety was being compromised over this or that Chinese demand.

I could have told them more about it than they were telling me; Sig was up to his neck in dealing with the Chinese, and not happy about any of it. There seemed to be an infinite number of additional nice things to which the Chinese were entitled without further payment, because they were "implied" in the contract. Since the U.S. government was making up the difference between what Sig was losing in building orbiting solar power stations for China and what he could have been making with the same resources used as he normally would, NASA officials didn't hesitate to get involved in deciding which of these demands was valid and which wasn't, thus which ones they would pay for and which they wouldn't. The trouble was that when the Chinese didn't get their way, it was Sig's crews and equipment rather than NASA's that tended to get held (discreetly, of course) as hostages. So every couple of days I'd hear Sig snarling into the phone as he tried to disentangle some problem or other and get one more step farther toward completion.

The whole system at the new house took a little bit of getting used to, too; Sig was home almost every evening, and Mom worked regular hours as well. That meant I was subject to a lot more routine adult supervision than I was used to; besides, the woods were too far away and the parks were kind of scary. I turned into a somewhat better student, just out of boredom.

About once a month Dad would get enough time off to come up and visit. Sig and Mom would have been perfectly happy to have him stay in the house, but he stayed at a hotel anyway. We'd go to a ball game or take a couple of long walks or something. Every now and then he'd bring along Grandma, and that was fun, too.

Even so, I was perfectly happy going back to school on Monday. I had heard plenty of horror stories from other kids about their divorced parents, and I knew Dad and Sig weren't crazy about each other, but the fact was that everybody involved did a pretty decent job of taking care of me and I didn't have to worry much about who was going to look after me. That let me concentrate on important issues, like model rocketry, sports, and my gradually increasing awareness that there was another gender out there and that I approved of the fact. Probably the biggest trauma I can remember from the time when Dad was away in training (first learning the Starbird at Sig's launch site near Edwards AFB, then learning the modified Pigeon lunar lander, and finally off to China to cross-train with Xiao Be, Peter, and Jiang Wu) was that I couldn't quite get up the nerve to ask a girl to the seventh-grade Valentine dance, and I didn't make the starting team in cadet basketball—too many other guys were getting their growth ahead of me. On the whole, it was a quiet time of life—and speaking as a quiet guy, I was already learning to appreciate that.

I don't know when it happened—it must have been one of the times my father got to Washington while I was still in school and therefore had an afternoon in the city—but I know it did, partly by what happened later and mostly because, when I was much older, Sig told me about it. I think he thought I would feel good knowing about it, and I guess he was right.

Anyway, my father got off the plane, made his way to Sig's office, and met Sig for lunch, a "special appointment" that neither Mom nor I knew anything about at the time. They sat on a sunny balcony at a pricey place, where no one would be so gauche as to recognize a celebrity, and chatted politely until the food came; then, after some silent eating, my father said, abruptly, "This is going to sound very strange, but I just don't feel lucky about this trip."

"Oh?" Sig said, setting down his fork and looking intently at Dad. He was good at just letting people say what they were thinking.

"Well, it's going to be my fifth trip up. It *is* the first trip on one of your Starbirds, but I don't think that's what I'm nervous about. And Xiao Be's a good sort and I'd trust her with anything. And we're using a good old proven-out Pigeon to go there. I'm sure I shouldn't feel this way, but for some strange reason I do; I'm just plain convinced that I'm not coming back. It's dumb and I want a chance to laugh about it later, but there it is. I never felt this way before, certainly not before the *Endeavour* mission, and I'm hoping it's just some weird phase."

Sig nodded and said, "Go on."

"Well, it's something for Jason. I took out an additional life insurance policy—just a cheap term life policy that will pay enough, in the event of my death, for one ride into orbit on a Starbird, so that he can go see what it's like up there. I don't want him to think of space as that black void that killed his old man, if you see what I mean. I don't want him to be unnecessarily afraid of anything, and if I were to die on this trip . . . well. A kid could get ideas. He might not realize at his age that crossing the street is dangerous, too, and you can't let fear run your life. So I'd like to have him have that ride . . . and I'm all paid up on the policy, and put all that in the will, but I wanted you to know about it so that if anything happens, you can tell Jason and explain it to him." Then Chris looked down at his plate and took a couple of large bites; this was probably as near to being embarrassed as he ever came in his life.

Sig nodded. "Of course I'll carry out your wishes in this matter. I'm sure you know Jason's college and so forth are taken care of, too—one of the advantages of my having this pile of money is that I can use it for things like that. But let's not bury you before you're dead; perhaps your premonition is only a premonition, without any foundation at all."

"I can hope so," Chris said. "And to tell you the truth, it's a bizarre experience for me; I've never felt anything like it before and I've always prided myself on my rationality."

Sig nodded, topped up the wineglass for both of them, and said, "Well, if I may venture a thought—?"

"Sure."

"I think you know I'm about as cold-blooded a businessman as they make. I have to be—if you're in a visionary game like space exploitation, you have to think in terms of justifying each little step. The thing that used to kill a lot of start-up space ventures was that they were trying to launch some kind of 'Universal Space Lines with Service to Six Planets Daily,' right off the bat, or they had figured out something that they were sure people would pay for and they thought all they'd have to do was offer it. But figuring out how to stay in business once you've got decent suppliers and an adequate customer base—that's always the easy part. Once a business is taking in more than it has to pay out, week to week or year to year, all you have to do is maintain. What's hard is to get to that point.

"And speaking of getting to the point, listen to me. Babbling on. All I meant to say was, I have to be very rational and think pretty hard about the micro-level things, what we have to do this week to be where we want to be in a year, that sort of stuff. And I have hunches all the time and I never ignore them. I don't always follow them—a lot of times I dismiss them—but I never ignore them. I give them my thought and attention and *decide* to follow them or dismiss them. Figure it this way, Dr. Terence: maybe you don't always remember everything you know. Maybe there's a thing or two bothering the back of your head that you won't or can't say to yourself. So since it can't come to you in words, it sends you a hunch. That can be like an inside tip from your subconscious. You have to at least look at it. So, no, I don't think there's anything silly about your taking your hunches seriously."

Chris sipped the wine and said, "Uh—and these hunches of yours—how often are they right?"

"Oh, about what you'd expect from chance," Sig said, grinning. "But the ones I follow are right more often. Seriously, I think you're wise to pay attention to it, and I think if this is important to you, then by god I'll make sure that Jason gets that opportunity. You could have just asked, you know, and I might've just done it anyway, no charge and so forth. Any son of any wife of mine who needs a ride into space to get his confidence back . . ."

Chris looked down and said, "Um, well, you can imagine I wouldn't have liked coming here cap in hand. And besides it's a cheap thing to do—fifty grand of coverage for a couple of years, just to cover an unlikely accident in space, isn't all *that* expensive. I could probably have gotten it cheaper by taking out a bet with a bookie that I was going to die."

"And bookies are less hassle than insurance companies," Sig agreed, "not to mention that when *they* don't pay, they lose business, unlike the insurance companies. Still and all, I'd have to say that . . . hmm. Tell you what. I'll make you a bet: if you come back alive, you let me chip in toward Jason's maintenance while he's with you, like I've always wanted to do. Not to spoil him, but if he wants to try a sport or take lessons in something, a little extra so it doesn't come out of your life. And if you don't, I'll not only send Jason to space to get a taste of it, I'll also start insuring all our astronauts on the same terms: if they die out there, a free ride for their kids."

Chris laughed. "Kind of a Gomez Addams bet, isn't it? If you win, you pay more money, and if you lose, you pay more money."

"Ah, but it's a bet because I'd a lot rather buy Jason a hockey stick or piano lessons than I would help him get over your death. I still have one side that I hope wins."

Chris nodded. "Well, call it a bet, then. I'll take the terms. How's he doing up here, anyway? His grades are looking better."

"We don't have as many distractions—or rather, we don't have any we can safely let him get into. The poor kid is probably bored. Unfortunately, the kind of excitement we have up here is not what I want for him."

"Me either," Chris agreed. "Is he making friends?"

"In his own way. Not like you or his mother would make friends, a roomful at a time. But enough for Jason."

They chatted about me for a couple of hours, according to Sig, but he never talked much about the particulars. I've had a life full of miracles, I guess you could say, but there's one that few people would notice: my father, who thought business was dirty and grubby when it wasn't just plain crooked, and my mother's husband, who thought of science as an amusing hobby for people who couldn't do anything serious, were perfectly capable of sitting down with each other over lunch and a couple of drinks and making sure that I was getting what I needed. I guess things like that aren't in most people's definition of love. They're in mine, though.

It's been a strange feature of the age of spaceflight that two successful crewed launches in a row seems to make everyone assume that space-flight is perfectly safe and routine—until the next disaster. The crew for the Tiber Base stayover expedition (officially called "Tiber Two") was in danger for a long time before the accident actually happened, just because they were in space and riding on rockets, but because things went so smoothly, there was little news coverage. I have watched the little bit of film of my smiling father getting into the Starbird, as mission commander; I have seen the way that he and Xiao Be worked together, and it looks flawless to me.

Whatever the reality, the Starbird, assisted off the pad by a Starbooster, made a perfectly uneventful journey to ISS, which was being used as a marshaling point because with its highly inclined orbit it was relatively easy to work into a polar approach to the Moon.

The Pigeons for this mission were known universally as Pigeon Racks, because they flew lying on their sides, supported in a steel framework which was fitted with thrusters, with a Starbird drop tank filled with hydrogen in the same framework directly behind them. It made them ungainly looking, but it also gave them a major advantage for this mission: unmanned versions could be parked permanently on the Moon's surface, and once their liquid hydrogen was drained off, they could easily be modified into surface habitats, living quarters for the Moon. They were awkward and ungainly to watch in flight—like metal squids shooting backward through space—but they did the job.

The transfer to the Pigeon Rack at ISS took only a few hours; a returning pilot from ISS would then take the Starbird back to base. Less than ten hours after the launch from Earth, the Tiber Two crew were given the go-ahead for translunar injection, and with a burst of fire from the main engine that squatted between the steel legs of the platform, sticking sideways from the HT, the Pigeon Rack was on its way to the Moon.

It took about three days, just as it always did; as long as we were using chemical rockets, the efficient thing to do was a hard boost to get out of Earth orbit at a point where instead of falling on around the curve of the Earth, as it had been doing in LEO, the ship would instead be on a high trajectory, rising away from the Earth until, as it slowed from Earth's pull behind it, it reached a point where it would fall toward the Moon and another deceleration thrust would slow it into orbit around the Moon. The time taken for those long falls would be three days in all, and until you had an engine that could boost you the whole way—a solar-electric or nuclear-electric rocket—the length of those falls would determine your schedule.

There were occasional news reports featuring interviews with the crew of the Pigeon Rack, but not many, and they played only on the more obscure channels. There had been a great deal of excitement, of course, when Tiber One had explored the South Pole Base, but now that everyone had seen all the pictures of dead Tiberians and of the still, silent equipment that had sat there for millennia, and then of the crew crawling all over the site looking for the Encyclopedia, the viewers, in their usual way, had decided that enough was enough. We could call them again when we brought back the Encyclopedia and held the parade.

So I don't know a great deal about how Dad spent those days; the official reports were kind of terse and dry, the news reports scanty, and nothing much got said in them. Peter said it was a fairly happy crew, "as much as could be expected given that our pilot, while a great person, was constantly being spied on by a fellow who never talked," he added. "Chris and I had gotten to like Xiao Be a lot, you know, while we were in China—her approach to things worked so well with our own—but as soon as Jiang was around she'd clam up."

So I imagine that on the long trip out they mostly did what the mission plan called for them to do: conducted a few small-scale experiments that one agency or another had dreamed up, ran some drills, and practiced their maneuvers on simulators.

Chris and Xiao Be would be on the moon for some months. Peter and Jiang were to return on the next ship, but there was already another Chinese astronaut, suspiciously short on technical qualifications or duties, slated to arrive on that one. The other powers might fume, but it was the deal they had been able to get. As far as they could tell, the Chinese intention was only to maintain one political officer at all times on the Moon, keeping an eye on their nationals and making sure that their allies didn't steal anything. If you looked at it that way, at least the percentage of deadheaders would go down over time.

At last, after taking one setting-up orbit for position that incidentally let them sail over both poles of the Moon, Xiao Be fired the main engine and brought the Pigeon Rack slowly down to the landing site, in a broken crater two kilometers from Tiber Base. On the airless world, the descent was simply a fall until it was time to power up the engine, and then a slow, gentle ride down on the rocket until finally they hovered for a split instant on their exhaust before the metal feet settled onto the Moon, only about sixty meters from the scoured-bare spot where the first expedition had landed and departed.

That triggered a real flurry of activity; as soon as they had landed, they suited up, drained the air from the Pigeon capsule into storage, opened the EVA hatch on its upper surface, and climbed out onto the steel skeleton that surrounded the ship, and from there down to the lunar surface.

In one of his calls to me, Dad told me there was a funny sense of completion he got at that moment. The place where they had landed was invisible forever to the Earth, down in the crater, and thus they could not see Earth, either. For the first time, what he had dreamed of since he was a small boy had happened: his boots were planted on the soil of another world, and when he looked up he saw, not home, but only stars. He might have been anywhere in the universe at that moment, for every galaxy must be full of small, stony, airless worlds, and for some reason I never really understood, that was important to him.

They found that the four other steel frameworks that dotted the small plain had landed as they were supposed to and contained the appropriate things in their cargo pods, which were simply Pigeons with the life-support systems pulled out to make more room for cargo. (Because they were never intended to fly back, these were "double Pigeon Racks"—two Pigeons with a DT tank between them graced each steel frame.) The slightly more distant fifth framework, which was the emergency return lander that had been brought there under robot control before anything else came, also checked out as it was supposed to, as the first expedition had confirmed. "Well," Chris said, "We've still got two hours left on our EVA time, and we've accomplished everything we were supposed to do—confirming that it's all here. Would anyone like to return to the Pigeon via Tiber Base?"

Jiang spoke, which was so rare that everyone jumped a little when they heard his voice in their helmet radios. "We are not authorized for such an expedition."

"I can get us authorized in about ten, I think," Chris pointed out. "It'll get them a little news coverage which they haven't had for a while, and it will give us the chance to do some exploring before we settle into routine."

"I would like to see Tiber Base myself," Peter said, backing Chris.

"You won't get authorization if I protest, and I will," Jiang said. "We are here to find the Encyclopedia, and then get off this godforsaken rock. If we are ahead of schedule at the moment, then we need to use that time to drain the HT on robot lander two and move the racks into it to create a habitat. It's clearly stated in the manual of procedures and policies that time gained against the schedule should always be maintained and used to accelerate the working process—not for sight-seeing."

Chris shrugged—not that anyone could tell, he knew, in his pressure suit, but old habits are hard to break. He looked from one space traveler to another: Peter standing with his arms wrapped in front of himself, Xiao Be carefully neutral, and Jiang with arms slightly akimbo and feet wide and planted, as if daring Chris to defy him.

The International Commission had ordered them to cooperate. NASA had ordered Chris not to let the Chinese run the show. And Chris had long ago decided that he didn't like Jiang. So he said, very calmly, "Well, if we've invoked the rules and procedures, it would seem to me that the EVA mission is completed, and we need to radio home for further instructions. And I am required not to compromise your rest. The obvious thing to do is to return to the Pigeon, get a meal and a scrub, and radio Mission Control for further instructions."

"But—" Jiang's protest died in his ears as Chris turned and headed back toward their lander. He didn't listen for more, but kept moving in light, easy bounds, something like a kangaroo and a bit like a squirrel. Around him the lunar surface was a dim gray, lit only by starlight and by reflected Earthshine and sunlight from the bright distant peaks. He knew without looking that Peter would be right behind him, but he was pleased to see Xiao Be come up on his right; Jiang would have no choice but to follow.

The next work period was mostly spent outside. They opened the DT space and let the little puff of hydrogen vanish from it, leaving it clean and dry inside. Next they unloaded the pressurized rover, with its awkward-looking crane on the back end for construction work and various other jobs (most importantly, getting the Encyclopedia into a lander). It had to come out via the nose hatch in one of the cargo Pigeons, and that meant it came out in several large pieces which they then had to assemble, working with thick-gloved hands that, despite all their practice, fumbled the tools and often struggled to get things into their right places.

With the crane they could start moving the racks—the internal structures—into the DT that was to become their permanent home at moonbase. As they shoved a load of material in through the side hatch that they had opened, Peter said to Chris, "You start to wonder if the whole universe is going to be covered with DTs. This one, four more on the other robot landers, one on ours, one at the International Space Station, your country is putting up another one next year in orbit, and then one at the L1 point, and . . . well, there will be a lot of them."

"Mobile homes of space," Chris agreed. "It's even about the same size as a single-wide mobile home with one extra room. Not elegant, but we can afford them—even if they do kind of make everywhere look alike after a while."

"Still," Xiao Be pointed out, "this one will have a genuine bathroom. I don't suppose you gentlemen will refuse to use that for aesthetic reasons?"

As each rack was loaded in and bolted into place, the interior looked less and less like an old pressure tank and more and more like home. When they had gotten all the racks into place and all the materials that were to be unpacked inside, they finally replaced the three hatches with Plexiglas windows, attached the airlock, and filled it with air. It was at full pressure in ten minutes, and when it had held pressure for twenty, they gingerly removed their pressure suits and got to work on the job of unpacking. After five hours outside, the first thing they wanted to unpack was the food, and the second thing they wanted was to get the bathroom working. It was late in the shift when they had finally made sure that they would be able to stay in the newly-equipped habitat for the duration of their stay; only then, despite occasional grumbling from Jiang, did Peter get around to setting up the radio and trying to raise Mission Control.

They came in loud and clear, almost at once. "Tiber Base, we have great news for you. One of our robot rovers has identified a site as the Encyclopedia landing site. And a camera on a polar orbiter satellite has confirmed it. We will be dispatching the Tiber Prize lander under robot control within a few days; as soon as it arrives, we'll send you after the Encyclopedia." Then the voice of Mission Control—an old friend who was temporarily out of the astronaut rotation due to minor surgery— added, "Hope you weren't getting to like the Moon too much, Chris, because chances are you'll be back here within two weeks."

Chris looked out one of the windows they had installed at the sharp, ragged edge of the crater illuminated by brilliant sunlight. Its lines uneroded by air or water, and able to stand at a steeper angle than you ever saw on Earth, lit in the harsh glare of the Sun in perfect relief in that vacuum, the crater wall looked as if it had been made that morning, but it was billions of years old. Beyond it the stars shone with a light steadier than any ever seen on Earth. "To tell you the truth, I *was* kind of getting to like it up here," Chris said. "Well, I hope it's a nice day for a drive when the lander finally gets here."

8

THE MAPS CAME THROUGH THE NEXT DAY, SCROLLING SLOWLY OUT OF THE small fax in the main lunar habitat. Chris and Xiao Be sat down to pore over it. "Well," he said, "we certainly get to see Tiber Base—we'll have to drive through there anyway. After that . . . well, I'm not sure I like doing this with just the radar and optical maps."

"I don't either," Xiao Be said. "But I don't know how we can possibly get any more information than this."

"Here's a helpful note," Peter said, looking up from the computer screen. "They want you to drive slowly."

"How very helpful," Chris muttered.

Jiang glanced up and then looked down; whatever he was working on, on his terminal, he didn't talk about it much.

The lander would not arrive at the Encyclopedia site for almost a week, so they continued to develop the base, getting things unpacked in the habitat and the unmanned cargo landers, and setting up the permanent observation instruments. As the days crept by, the Sun shone on different parts of the crater rim above them, working its way around the Moon's 656-hour day. "And when it gets all the way around it will start over," Chris pointed out. "You never think of the Moon as having a summer and winter, but it does, because its orbit is at an angle to the Earth's orbit, and the Earth carries it around the Sun; in six months you won't see the Sun on the crater wall at all, for many weeks."

Peter sighed. "I'm not sure how much people think of the Moon at all. And I suppose from a small-scale perspective they're right; most of the time it's just a pretty light in the sky. But I'm sort of glad that Tiber One didn't find the Encyclopedia right away. If they had, I have a feeling they might have just canceled our mission entirely and left exploring Tiber Base for, oh, some other time. It seems to me that we haven't changed much in the last fifty years or so; we're still always looking for a reason to just give up."

Chris shrugged and passed his friend a sandwich; they were sitting at what they had nicknamed the "observation terrace," the one tiny spot in the lunar habitat where there were two places to sit down, a surface to eat from, and a view out the window. "Oh, I'm sure nothing's changed. And at the same time the world is full of people who would love to be where we are, but will never have the chance, not to mention people who still don't believe you can land on a light in the sky anyway. Well, do you want to get an early start on our EV so we can catch it?"

"As long as we're here we might as well see the sights," Peter agreed. "And besides, there's a lot to get done before you and Xiao drive off with the crane and leave it out in the woods to find its own way back."

"It's a big robot and it's time it started looking out for itself," Chris said. "Let's suit up."

Twenty minutes later, outside, as they loaded a set of solar panels onto the back of the pressurized rover, Xiao Be's voice broke in over their suit radios. "Just about time now," she said.

"Right," Chris said. "Well, let's get to where we can see."

The two of them bounded across the dusty plain to an open space they had chosen; Xiao Be bounced along from the other side. All of them looked like pale ghosts in the eternal dark of the crater, lighted only by the reflecting walls above. The dust flew out from their feet in straight lines, forming no roiling clouds, just glimmering once in the dim light, dispersing, and falling back to the surface where it had lain for billions of years.

The three met together, almost at the center of the crater, where they would have the maximum view of the sky. "Jiang didn't want to leave the habitat," Xiao Be explained. "I think he has a long message from home, or maybe a report to file, or maybe he just wants some time to himself." Neither Peter nor Chris answered. They had both decided that they didn't want to run the risk of anything they said to Xiao Be getting her into trouble, and it was obvious that nobody was supposed to notice that Jiang had very few duties and seemed to have been trained for very little. Long afterwards, Peter used to say that the one thing a secret policeman can't stand is people acting like he isn't secret.

High above them, the Southern Cross shone brilliantly, amid a blaze of stars.

"How many more stars are there?" Peter asked, as the three stood together and looked up. "Than we could see from Earth, I mean?"

Chris chuckled. "Well, that would be a great question for an undergrad astronomy course. And I thought I was never going to teach another one. Part of it depends on what you mean by 'from Earth,' because on some very clear nights in some very high, dry places on the Earth you can see a lot more stars than you can in the swampier parts. But putting it roughly; well, since the brightest stars have a magnitude of one, and the next brightest of two, and so forth, and each represents a tenfold decrease in brightness . . . and since there are always more dim than bright stars and that's roughly proportional . . . heck, I don't know. But I'd figure we can see three more magnitudes, at least, even allowing for the visors on the suits, and if you figure there's about ten times as many more stars per order of magnitude, that would come to something over a thousand times as many."

"It's still easy to pick out Alpha Centauri," Xiao Be said. "With a magnitude of a bit less than zero it ought to be. I wonder why they came all this way and then never came back again."

"Maybe in a few weeks—or a few years, depending on how long the linguistics people take to crack the Encyclopedia—we'll know. It certainly is a bright one," Chris added.

They had run out of anything to say, but that had always happened to Chris when he looked up at the night sky anyway, ever since he'd been a child. High above them the bright stars shone with the steady brilliance that never happened on Earth; all around them the airless plain, silent in a way that nowhere on Earth ever could be, stretched far and wide. The only sound Chris could hear was his own breathing; better life-support packs had reached the point where air blew softly through the suit without noise of any kind.

He thought, this is one of the best parts; just to get the real calm, for an instant now and then, of not having anyone playing music or running machines in your ears. Not even the brush of a wind or the crash of a wave; just a quiet like the one that's been there since the rocks of the heavy bombardment stopped falling, broken only every few thousand years. Just the soft fall of light from above, light that started on its way centuries or millennia in the past. Though it was only a short time to wait, and they were each within a meter of the other two; nonetheless they stood all by themselves, in eternity.

Far away above the crater rim, a dim star moved, and the radios crackled to life "There it is!"

"Where—oh, I see!"

"Here it comes!"

As they watched, a Pigeon Rack seemed to jump over the horizon, up into the Southern Cross itself, shooting fire in front of it as it went. The Tiber Prize lander, operating at the moment only under robot control, was passing over them, far up enough to reflect sunlight, finishing the last third of its descent.

"I thought you might want to know," Jiang's voice said in their headphones, startling them. "Everything's nominal on the lander."

As the brilliant oval crossed the middle of the sky and fell toward the horizon, it grew longer and seemed to go slower.

The now brighter, bigger dot, not much bigger than a period in type, which was the DT of the lander itself, sank slowly on a twisting, glowing white-hot pillar ten times its size, like an upside-down white exclamation point on the black of night. They watched till it passed behind the dark gray shadowed peaks on the other side of the crater.

"You know there are going to be people, someday, who won't bother to look up when something like that goes overhead?" Peter said.

"Don't blame me," Chris said. "I still look up when I hear an airplane."

"I'd certainly look up if I saw one here," Xiao added. "I guess Jiang will let us know if it gets down all right, or—"

Jiang's voice crackled to them. "The report from Earth is that it's making a perfectly fine descent and they expect it to touch down shortly. Mission Control says they've got the Encyclopedia on visual and they're quite sure they'll manage to land without hitting it."

"Now, that would be an anticlimax," Peter said.

They spent the rest of the day getting the solar panels up to where they could get some sun; in part this was a chance for Xiao Be and Chris to practice scaling lunar cliffs, in case that should prove necessary on their journey. It was harder than it looked, because, although it was much easier to haul themselves upwards in the low gravity, many of the spires and cliffs were fragile. Early on they realized that the important safety rules were not to try to grab or rope anything directly overhead, and especially not to get directly under each other. It took an hour to get up the first cliff, even though they could stick to it like flies, but once they found a sound spot to put the pulley, and threaded the cable through it so that Peter could use the crane's winch, the job of getting all the panels up into place went quickly enough. Two hours later a row of them hung on the cliff face, and the cables snaked down to the pressurized rover below. Chris and Xiao Be found that going down a lunar mountain was much more fun, because leaps of twenty feet or so weren't particularly difficult, and the descent took much less time than they had expected. "All right," Peter said, "we're getting power this far anyway; let's see if we can string the cable to the habitat."

A short time later, because they were no longer forced to run on fuel cells, there was a great deal more power at the habitat. Peter and Jiang took the pressurized rover to a deep hole in the crater wall that had been spotted by a robot; sure enough, there was a deposit of ice in there the size of a large house. The pressurized rover could only bring back four tons, but with the added power, they could melt it, run it through a purifier, and heat it—so that late during the following work shift, they were all able to take the first showers on the Moon, with water that had lain undisturbed for more than three billion years. "It isn't the biggest event in space technology," Chris wrote in his diary later, "and it certainly isn't going to revolutionize anything, but still, it's nice to know we'll all find it that much easier to get along."

The next day, with Xiao Be driving, the pressurized rover rolled off toward the Encyclopedia. Its fuel cell power system, supplemented by solar cells later on, would allow them to cover ground at a steady eight kilometers per hour—and since the Encyclopedia was about ninety kilometers distant, by the winding path that had been picked out as safe for them, this would mean more than eleven hours of travel time. The pressurized rover was good for twenty, so they could get quite close to the Encyclopedia site before they would no longer have the option of turning around. But during the last dozen kilometers, if anything went wrong, they would *have* to reach the lander at the Encyclopedia site—there would be no option of returning to this base.

After his experience with *Endeavour*, and the sort of things that can happen when an area is left between the last safe place to turn back and the first place from which a safe destination can be reached, Chris was less than pleased. He had tried to hold out for waiting a few weeks, until Tiber Three could be positioned somewhere in the middle, to provide them with a fallback base, cache of supplies, and alternate escape from the Moon, but it had fallen on deaf ears; neither the four-power consortium nor the Chinese wanted to wait any longer for the Encyclopedia, and it was much too easy to just tell Chris and Xiao Be to go out there and get it. After all, if everything went according to plan, there should be plenty of safety margin.

Their route took them by Tiber Base, within the first hour of the journey. They had seen many pictures before, of course, both on the news and in training films, but little could have prepared them for the sight of it as they made their way over the broken rock that separated their older crater from the newer one where Tiber Base lay. The first moment of seeing something so clearly built by aliens was nothing so much as disorienting; the lander was oddly shaped and proportioned, though clearly streamlined, and although it rested on metal legs as their landers did, the legs seemed to reach out from underneath in a way that seemed vaguely spidery.

The Tiber One crew had discovered, using ultrasound, that most of the lander was hollow; apparently liftoffs and landings had been assisted by pumping all the air out of the tanks, which were made of something fairly similar to the aerogels that had been developed on Earth only about twenty years before. This stuff was clearly far superior to most aerogels in strength and durability, but like any aerogel it weighed almost nothing, was completely transparent, and had an enormous ratio of weight to strength. The SSTO people were already fascinated—it seemed like it must be the perfect material for their hydrogen tanks. The best guess was that the lander had originally been intended for a world with air, probably the Earth. It must have descended on rocket thrust, probably supplied by the strange object that looked like it had to be the engine. Probably when it got close enough to the ground, by putting a hard vacuum in the tanks, at its lower density it had floated, or almost floated, in air, allowing it to move quietly and efficiently. Physically it looked a bit like someone had tried to run a computer morphing program between a rocket, a dirigible, and a submarine, and then stopped when half-finished, leaving various parts of all three sticking out here and there.

Beyond the lander lay the graveyard, a patch of broken ground with many pits and holes, where the Tiberians had placed their dead and covered them with piles of stones. No one knew if the dead were all buried naked because that was their custom or because they had nothing with which to make grave clothes or a casket; but since the Moon had no animals that might disturb a body, nor anything that would allow it to decay (for every practical purpose the Tiberian corpses in the graveyard were freeze dried), it seemed very likely that burial under a cairn of loose stones was some part of their customs, or at least derived from a custom modified for lunar conditions.

Beyond that, they couldn't quite see the huge heaps of melted and fused rock that covered the entrances to the lava tubes that the Tiberians had pressurized, obviously for use as habitats, and those looked like nothing so much as blobs of glass with small round doors. As yet no one had any idea how that could have been done; the common theory due to the geometry of the melt marks was that the Tiberians had some sort of laser that was far more capable than anything we had developed yet, but if so, which of the dozens of inexplicable pieces of hardware it was—if any—was not yet known.

Tiber station fell behind them as the little pressurized rover continued to pick its way across the lunar surface. On Earth it would barely have been able to move at all, but here it could climb steep hills almost easily, though with the protruding crane tower, Xiao Be had to be very careful not to tilt it too far to one side or the other and thus risk a tipover.

Chris was supposed to drive the second shift, so he stretched out and did his best to go to sleep, since they were also supposed to arrive rested and capable. It wasn't easy, with the wild country of the Moon all around him—the sharp edged scarps, high pillars, and all the wild and broken land out the window were fascinating. And because there were so many meter-sized boulders to steer around, miniature avalanches under the wheels, and occasional body-slamming potholes, his reclining chair was not the best of places for getting a nap. But he managed to doze for two or three hours out of the five he was supposed to be resting.

When Xiao Be officially summoned him to take over, he checked the distance gauge. They had covered only forty kilometers, not the fifty-five that were scheduled. "Damn, what happened?"

"What you might guess." She shrugged. "It takes a lot of careful steering and picking to get there without smashing up or tipping over. We're still covering enough ground so that we'll make it with some reserves."

"I hate narrow margins."

"I can understand that, but that's what's available, Chris. Now drive carefully, and try not to wake me up; this has been pretty exhausting." With that, she transferred control of the pressurized rover from her panel to his; as he took control and ran a checkout to see what his status was, she reclined her seat and stretched out, pulling her visor halfway down over her face so that in the event of the cabin's depressurizing, it would snap closed automatically and her suit would pressurize.

Chris sighed for a moment, tasting the stale air of the cabin. According to the computer-generated map in front of him, they were within five meters of the trail it had picked out; he looked five meters to the right and saw a house-sized boulder there. Probably the computer had liked it because it had a flat top, and for some reason radar and optical hadn't quite picked up on the problem of its towering over their heads.

He put the pressurized rover in motion and picked his way forward, at first going very slowly, then gaining some speed as he got more practice and thus more confidence. After a while he checked and discovered he was making only slightly worse time than Xiao Be had been; growling to himself, he pressed on harder.

Supposedly he had been scheduled to drive for four hours before they would get there, after sleeping for seven; then he and Xiao Be would transfer to the lander, she would finish her rest, he would do the preparatory scouting, and finally the two of them would load the Encyclopedia in and take off for a direct return to Earth. Now at the current speed he would get there in just under nine hours (leaving them four hours of pressurized rover operation to spare) and they would have to rearrange everything drastically. As he drove between boulders he reviewed Xiao Be's voicemail file and discovered that she had kept Mission Control fully appraised via the polar satellite relays.

Well, if Xiao Be was reporting, he should too, and here was a stretch of more or less bare rock to pick up some time over, during which he would have time to record a message. He made it short—just confirming that Xiao Be's decisions had all been perfectly correct and that no one else could have done differently, that they still expected to complete the mission successfully, and that there wasn't much of anything to report except that the radar and optical maps were just not as good as might have been hoped for.

He clicked off, setting the message to upload at convenience, and settled in to the difficult job of driving; it was a lot like taking a four-wheeler out in the desert back home, except in extremely slow motion and with the added hazard that if he broke an axle or got them into a spot they couldn't get out of, they would die.

He was so intent on working his way down a slippery, loose landslide into the next crater that he actually jumped when he heard the crackle in his headphones. "Tiber Two Mobile, this is Mission Control."

"Go ahead, Mission Control," he said.

There was a long pause; it takes almost one and one half seconds for radio to travel from Earth to Moon, and of course it would then take one and a half seconds for the return message to arrive; with reaction time, the delay was quite noticeable. "Tiber Two Mobile, we've assessed your situation and we concur that you can reach the Encyclopedia site with adequate reserves. We believe from corrections to the radar map that we can give you an alternate improved route; information gathered by the earlier part of your expedition has been incorporated into our interpreting software and the pathway corrected. Upload is underway through the data channel. You are cleared to proceed to the Encyclopedia site."

"Thanks, Mission Control, will do. Next time put a gas station on the highway, dammit."

Again the time crept by before the reply came through. "Roger, Tiber Two Mobile, we'll do that for your next alien contact mission. Good luck!"

"Thanks, Mission Control." He clicked the heads-up display, which projected a ghostly green image of a computer screen onto the windshield so that he could see what had come over in the data transmission. Positioning the cursor on "IMPROVED MAP—SELF INSTALLING," he selected it. A moment later, it flashed up "INSTALLED—USE?" He selected YES and clicked to use the new map; it showed a slightly higher position on the slope. He turned a little left and climbed up toward it; he didn't notice much difference, but maybe that would come later. "Thanks, Mission Control, I'm on the new map now."

There was no other real news; a short recorded message from Jason that only said hi and I love you and that sort of thing; an equally short one from Lori Kirsten that told him not to speed and to wear his seat belt; and one from his mother that said she was proud of him. Nobody ever knows what to say to anyone who's being watched by several million people, in an environment where they might die at any instant if something goes wrong. Especially since usually nothing goes wrong, and it would seem hopelessly morbid to dwell on the danger; and because so much of the time spent in space is dull and routine, and thus almost everything you can say about it sounds melodramatic.

Chris uploaded short reply messages, all of which said he was thinking of them and he liked hearing from them. True enough, and if anything did go wrong it wouldn't be a bad set of last words. . . .

He wondered again why he was getting so morbid; the premonition before the mission and now he was worrying about whether those might be his last words. Maybe he was just getting tired, or maybe it was the sheer difficulty and frustration of getting the pressurized rover through this shattered terrain. Whatever the cause, he didn't need it. He took a squeeze bag of coffee, set it in the little warmer, and waited for it to heat up as he worked his way over the ridge top.

Just at the top, he found that his route lay around the high parapet of a crater, the flattish ring of debris that lay around some of them, through sunlight. Well, this at least would give him a chance to recharge some batteries and run on something besides fuel cell power for a while, and it seemed like more even territory. He wasn't sure he wanted more time to think.

With just three hours and fifteen minutes of reserve power left, the pressurized rover rolled up to the parked Tiber Prize lander. "Xiao, time to wake up, we're here," Chris said.

She sat up, pushing her visor up for a moment, blinking at the bright light; almost half of this crater was in sunlight. "Great," she said. "Where's the hotel? Order me a Caesar salad and a large spaghetti from room service."

Chris snorted. "It was quite a drive. And I'm ahead of you now for time spent driving this damned disgrace of a vehicle. But we are here. How about we get inside and get some rest and a somewhat more comfortable place to use the bathroom? Mission Control has okayed me to sleep for a few hours before we get into this, and I'd like to get started."

"Suits me," she said, reaching to pull her visor down, but he stopped her for an instant. "Probably, though," he added, "we ought to park this thing in the daylight and then hop our way back here. With the electrolysis rig it can get itself recharged in a few hours."

"Sure." They drove over into the broad patch of bright sunlight; it would be days before the shadow of the crater reached this far. After shutting down the fuel cell system and putting its recovered water into the electrolysis system, they deployed the solar cell banks to their fullest extent. Now the electricity made from the sunlight would break the water that was the byproduct of fuel cell operation back into its component hydrogen and oxygen, for reuse; the many batteries on the pressurized rover would recharge as well.

They lowered their visors, secured them, and popped the canopy on the pressurized rover, stepping out onto the lunar surface. Fifty long bounds had carried them about halfway back to the Pigeon Rack when Xiao Be suddenly cried out over the suit radio. "Hey—there it is!"

They stopped and approached it slowly. The rectangular box, about the size of a large office desk, sat on a metal truss, about a meter tall, extending for more than a meter beyond the box in all directions. The truss had a little device underneath it that looked for all the world like a cheap lamp. Beneath the device, on the landing site, there was a dark mass of glass, as if the stone itself had melted there.

"Don't tell me that's their whole propulsion system," Chris said, in awe. "Where the hell are the fuel tanks?"

Xiao Be gestured as well as she could in the pressure suit, raising her arms and dropping them. "Maybe by the time you're ready to go to the stars, you're ready to get over silly ideas like needing fuel. Or maybe whatever it runs on only requires a liter of juice to get from Alpha Centauri to here. Or maybe they just left it here and that's the ritual ground melter that produces the religiously required fused soil. Our job is to get this thing home; it's the science guys who have to do something about it."

They experimented for a moment with seeing if they could lift it off the frame, which was far too large to put into the Pigeon for return to Earth. They discovered some simple hand screws that seemed to attach it, and though they turned to the right rather than the left to loosen, they turned easily enough. Experimentally they tried to pick the whole thing up; it was at least as heavy as an average-sized automobile, Chris judged, and they couldn't budge it. "Well," he said, "it's not going to be as easy as we could have hoped for, then. I'm dead on my feet; let's get back to the Pigeon Rack so I can stretch out."

This Pigeon Rack was different from the others Chris and Xiao Be had dealt with to this point. Pigeons actually had three doors, but normally only two of them were enabled on the Pigeon Rack—the nose hatch, for docking so that the crew could get in and out in space; and the underside hatch, which went through the lower cargo bay, for exit by ladder onto the lunar surface. The door that, on most Pigeons, was used for direct entry into the crew compartment before leaving Earth, and for EVA in earth orbit, was on the upper surface of the Pigeon when it lay in a Pigeon Rack, and so was normally not enabled for that configuration. But for this job, most of the seats had been removed to make room, and the upper hatch was enabled, to allow the Encyclopedia to go in with the help of a crane. On the sloping lower surface inside the Pigeon there were special tie-down points so that the Encyclopedia could be webbed into place; since in that position it would be hanging directly over Chris and Xiao Be during reentry, Chris had to hope the webbing would do its job.

Aside from the seats, webbing, controls, and basic set of supplies to keep them alive on their way back, everything else had been stripped from this Pigeon to allow more room for the Encyclopedia and more spare mass for a larger fuel tank; it was all right as a place to take a nap, but they didn't dawdle over its comforts, because there weren't any.

Hours later, when he arose and took a quick sponge bath, Xiao Be had a short list of accomplishments and a slightly longer list of orders from Mission Control. She had removed the screws that seemed to hold the Encyclopedia to the frame and after careful examination had determined that there were no other connections; it should now lift off easily. Using the hook of a force gauge to try to lift up each leg of the frame, she had arrived at an estimate that the Encyclopedia massed at least six metric tons—"so it's about as dense as solid aluminum," she said. "Difficult but not impossible, I guess you'd have to say. The weight is only that of a metric ton on Earth, around the weight of a small car, but we'll have to be very careful with that much mass and make sure we remember that once we get it up on the crane and swing it, it will be very hard to stop—especially because the bigger a thing is here, the worse the discrepancy between weight and the mass we're expecting, and the more likely we are to screw up. It's well within what the Pigeon can take back to Earth, anyway."

Further, she had laid out the lifting slings so that they would be ready to slide between the Encyclopedia and the frame as soon as Chris was available to help lift with a crowbar. "And the most annoying thing is that after measuring it, it turns out that its smallest diagonal won't quite go through the hatch on top of this Pigeon. It will go through the nose hatch, though, as long as we're careful, but we're going to have to swing it in like longshoremen rather than just lower it in from overhead."

Mission Control had deliberated all of a minute and a half before telling her that they were to go through with the mission. She added, in a low voice, before they put on helmets that might be monitored, that her home government had made a particular point of sending her a private message telling her that they were putting as much pressure as possible on the Four Powers to deliver the Encyclopedia as soon as possible; a few short months would mark the hundredth anniversary of the beginning of the Chinese Revolution, and they wanted enough of the Encyclopedia decoded by then to be used in some of the commemorative ceremonies.

"Well, then," Chris said, "I guess we'd better get to it."

The first part of the job was simple enough: Chris lifted each corner of the Encyclopedia with a crowbar, and Xiao Be slid a strap underneath it and then around it. When they had completed that part of the job, they tied the straps at the top—this involved Chris boosting Xiao Be up onto it, but it seemed sturdy enough and, as she pointed out, the aliens couldn't possibly have built something that would break apart at the first thump and then sent it all this way. In any case, it seemed none the worse after she finished and lightly jumped down, sinking slowly to the lunar surface. "Time for lunch," she said. "I negotiated that into our schedule."

After a break and some rest in the Pigeon, they got ready for the actual loading. After getting back into their pressure suits they pumped the air out of the Pigeon into storage, then opened and braced the nose hatch. They climbed out through the regular EV hatch and bounded across the floor of the crater, racing to get to the pressurized rover. Xiao Be won, both of them laughing at the silliness of it all, and as they checked on the recharge—which appeared to be a bit ahead of schedule—Chris said, "It will be nice when the work's over and we're on our way home."

She clicked off her radio; he saw the gesture and did the same. Without radios on, the recording instruments in the Pigeon couldn't pick up anything they said. They touched helmets, letting physical conduction carry the sound between them (though it required some shouting). "Nicer still when we land," she said. "Since we'll be landing right off your state of Hawaii, assuming it's an American ship that picks us up, I'm planning to request political asylum. I can't stand the thought of another trip with someone looking over my shoulder the whole way. Are you willing to help me if it comes up?"

Chris swallowed hard and said, "Yeah. One hundred percent. Now let's get this thing done." They turned their radios back on.

But as he turned back to his work, he could hardly help thinking about how the decisions had shaped up. Normally a Pigeon landed on a parafoil, a cross between a wing and a parachute that allowed it to glide fairly gently down to land. This time, however, with such a heavy cargo on board, their margins were tight. They didn't have enough available energy to make a plane change into the orbital plane of *Star Cluster*, and hence they could not take the Encyclopedia back to orbit for transfer down by a Starbird or shuttle; they would have to take it down to the surface themselves. And the extra mass was too much to permit using a parafoil. Instead they would have to descend on an oversized parachute, at the mercy of the winds, and splash down in the ocean, as the early astronauts had, an expensive and occasionally dangerous way to do things.

Of course the whole problem could be avoided by waiting another year to retrieve the Encyclopedia, until adequate equipment was on line to do the job in a more conservative and careful way, but no politician wanted to tell the voters that we had to wait a year to do it right. Thus, Chris thought, because no one has the wit or guts to explain it to the voters, we are going to take the most precious cargo in human history and subject it to six g's, after which we will dunk it in the ocean.

Oh, well, it wasn't his job to worry about that. He turned back to his work. The pressurized rover was fully recharged, with all the water reconverted, so they folded up the solar panels, put it in a driving config- uration, and headed back toward the Encyclopedia. The crane swung around, its hook caught the ring on the straps, and they lifted the object—thousands of years old, from light-years away—into the vacuum, and swung it inboard, setting it down on the rear platform of the pressur- ized rover, as simply as if it were a crate going onto any ship on Earth. "Got it," Xiao Be said, nodding.

The pressurized rover handled oddly with such a heavy weight over the rear axle, but it still took only a couple of minutes to drive all the way back to the Pigeon. "You know, twenty centimeters less, and we could have brought it in the top hatch—just lowered it right in," Chris remarked.

"It still would have been a nuisance," she pointed out. "The place we have to secure it to isn't in a direct line from either hatch. I guess nobody that designed this ever moved into a small apartment up a nar- row flight of stairs. So we'll just have to swing it in through the hatch."

"Are we going to be able to pull it in?"

"Not a prayer," she said. "We can't possibly get it in except by using its momentum. It'll be fine. All you have to do is have a good light hand on the controls."

"All *I* have to do?"

Xiao Be sighed. "I know I've got a better hand on the controls from more practice, Chris, but in case you haven't noticed, you're a head taller and a lot thicker than I am. When the Encyclopedia swings through the nose hatch, someone has to be there to give it a hard shove to the side so that it lands more or less where we're supposed to tie it down. That someone has to be standing along the side to do it."

"What if it swings in toward you?"

"No problem—the cable will be carrying it upward, and anyway, if you hit the hole right it'll move in a straight line. The thing that worries me more is that after I get it shoved into the right direction, you need to hit the cable release so it doesn't just fly back out of the hatch. When I yell 'now'—not before—is when you do that. If you were to release it too early, it would keep moving in a straight line and could either smash something important in the Pigeon, or maybe break, or just possibly get me. On the other hand, if you release too late, or don't release—all that happens is that it swings back out and we have to try again. So release when I yell 'now,' but don't be early. Got it?"

"Got it. You're sure there isn't room for me in there?"

"Wish there were. I'd rather have someone with your bulk doing it. But if anything goes wrong, being smaller, I'm going to be a lot better at ducking than you are. Now let me get into place; let's take a couple of practice swings to make sure we understand how it works."

She climbed down out of the pressurized rover—they hadn't bothered to close the canopy for the short time they would be using it—and scrambled up the frame onto the side of the Pigeon Rack, then in through its open EVA hatch. "Okay," her voice said over the radio, though Chris could not see her anymore. "Pick it up and bring it up to the hatch, real slow."

Using the control panel easily—he had done this in any number of practice runs back in Houston, then at Edwards, then in China—he lifted the Encyclopedia, turned and extended the crane to get it to the nose hatch, and winched the dull black box, wrapped with straps, up to parallel with the nose hatch. "Great," she said. "You're right on the line. Now, very slowly, swing it back."

He did.

"Okay, now, give it a quick swing in the door," she said. "I'm not going to try to catch it this time, I'm just going to see exactly how it comes in, so it'll swing right back out; let it swing back, bring it to stationary, and if it looks good then we'll try it for real. Okay?"

"Roger," Chris said. "Ready for it?"

"In place and ready to go. Start it up."

He whipped the crane around quickly on its pivot, hoping that the centrifugal force wouldn't bring it far enough out to hit the side. The Encyclopedia, glowing in the reflected light from the bright side of the crater, flew through space swiftly, following the bending cable. He started to release a sigh of relief as it went into the nose hatch cleanly, without touching anything, and the cable snubbed on the edge of the hatch.

A shuddering lurch ran through the pressurized rover as the crane broke at the upper pivot; at the same instant a hideous scream rang in Chris's helmet, coming through his suit radio.

He bounded to the top of the framework in one hard leap, and was inside the Pigeon, through the EVA, in another instant.

The Encyclopedia lay in a sideways diagonal in the nose hatch, where it had slid as the breaking crane released it. Under one corner of it was Xiao Be's left leg, and an edge pushed deep into her abdomen, her rib cage all but hanging over it; the pressure suit was stretched tighter than any he had ever seen before. He could hear the harsh, bubbling rasp of her breathing through the suit radio.

9

CHRIS DIDN'T THINK AT ALL; HE RUSHED FORWARD AND JAMMED HIS SHOULder against the Encyclopedia, trying to push it back through the hatch. It wouldn't move at all; he saw that it had wedged, with Xiao Be as one point of the wedge. He shoved again as hard as he could. Still he had no luck.

"Cut it loose, push it in, get me home," she gasped suddenly.

"What?"

"Crane broke, didn't it? I saw it."

"Yeah, it did."

"Get the cable off it. Don't try to get it out of here. Use the crowbars to lift it, drag me out, drag it in, close the hatch. Fly home." She was breathing hard and he could hear the agony in her voice. "Don't know what it did but it doesn't feel good. Some kind of injuries inside. Jiang's a medic, but he can't do surgery or treat a broken back. Have to get home for that. Without the crane you can't get it out. So get it in and let's go home, fast."

Chris stood. It made sense, but it wasn't going to be easy. He leaped back out of the EVA hatch and climbed forward on the top surface of the craft to the Pigeon's nose. With the emergency knife from his suit he slashed through the straps, so that the crane hook suddenly fell away; then he swore and flattened himself as the crane tower, which had been leaning over sideways, held up by the cable, fell over and crashed past him, kicking up dust and sending a reverberating thud through the ship. Xiao Be had started to breathe harder.

He jumped down to the pressurized rover. In falling over the crane had bounced off the side of the main fuel tank, there was a dent there that he might have checked if there were time, or anything he could do about it, but there was neither. Chris grabbed up the crowbars and was back in the Pigeon in three short bounds.

At first he could find no angle that wouldn't push the huge object harder onto Xiao Be. Then he realized that if he could at least force the edge out of her abdomen, though it might drag the corner across her leg and do more damage, at least it would relieve the terrible pressure on her internal organs and let her breathe easier. He jammed the tip of the crow in and heaved as hard as he could; the Encyclopedia bucked a foot inward and up, and with his foot he swept Xiao Be's body in toward himself. With a silent crash he felt through his boots, the Encylopedia hit the deck, two inches from the tip of his boot. He looked at how it had landed; it seemed to be braced at a steeper angle than before, with more of a corner sticking outside.

He turned to Xiao Be and she was whispering into the radio, "Close the hatch and let's go home. Close the hatch and let's go home."

Risk of a broken back or not, she wouldn't survive if she were just lying on the bare deck when they took off; he carried her to her acceleration couch, the low lunar gravity making the job easy, belted her in, plugged in her hoses, and turned on the life support. Then he returned to the Encyclopedia.

Ten more minutes convinced him of the grim truth: he couldn't move it at all. When it had fallen into its new position, one corner had slammed into an upper surface, making a deep dent that it stuck into. To get it out of there would take more than the strength he had. And another corner still stuck out the hatch.

At that moment his suit radio crackled, and a very deliberate voice said "Tiber Prize, this is Mission Control. Please report your status. Can you explain what's happening?"

Quickly Chris explained the situation. He was expecting a long three-second delay, but another voice spoke at once. "Chris, this is Peter. Bring the ship back here. It's a short ballistic hop. Three of us should be able to get it into order, and there ought to be enough fuel left with a little bit of margin for you to make it back to Earth's surface. After all, this Pigeon Rack was configured with a lot of extra fuel. I'm sending over the coordinates for the flight right now—should be in your computer. And while you're doing the hop we can recheck. Just program the hop and jump for it with the door open; you've got some time left in your suit, don't you?"

Chris checked. "Nearly an hour. I'll have to jump soon if I do that."

He turned to the control panels and began the power-up for liftoff, doing things much faster than he ever had before, doing all kinds of quick shortcuts and changes, rarely looking at instruments to confirm that anything was coming on-line. The voice of Mission Control crackled in his ears again. "Tiber Prize you are go for abort to Tiber Base— Chris, it's the only plan we've got at the moment. Good luck. We'll be back in touch as soon as you've lifted off."

"Right." Chris's hands slammed at the computer keys, the thick gloves forcing him to type with two fingers. The coordinates from the base had come through just fine; he plugged them in and told the Pigeon to get him there. "I'm no pilot," he muttered to himself, "not for one of these things, so I sure hope this software knows what it's doing."

Six times it demanded to know whether he was aware the doors were open; six times he told it to override, that the situation was an emergency. At last it told him to stand by for emergency procedure, and he leaned back into his acceleration couch, plugging in his life support and comm connections to conserve what was left in his suit.

A great vibration thundered through the ship, and when Chris leaned back so that his helmet touched the couch, he could hear the low sound reverberating. With a wash of flame that flipped over the wrecked pressurized rover once again, the Pigeon Rack rose into the lunar sky on a hard engine burst, taking off at half a g. Beside him he could hear Xiao Be crying out in pain as the acceleration crushed down on her internal injuries; a moment later he heard Mission Control again. "We have downloaded your flight plan from your computer," a voice said, "and we have confirmed that you have enough fuel for both a hop to base and for a return to Earth. You are go for your plan. Godspeed."

"Thanks, Mission Control," Chris said, not sure what else to say. A moment later the engine shut off; now the Pigeon Rack soared upward in a ballistic arc, like an artillery shell, headed over and down toward where Peter and Jiang waited for them. It fell for long moments of weightlessness.

"Xiao?"

"Still sort of here. Passing out a lot. Get me home, Chris. I'm scared."

"I'll get you home," he said.

"Don't leave me alone on the Moon."

"I won't. Do you want an injection of painkiller? I've got it right here."

She said nothing; her voice rasped and groaned. According to the first aid training, you couldn't use a painkiller on someone who was unconscious; he just hoped she wasn't feeling anything right now.

The attitude jets cut in and the ship rolled over slowly, end for end, until it was falling toward the Moon with its engine pointed downward again. Then the engine fired and Xiao Be woke up again with another scream; deceleration force rose steadily and Chris heard her labored breathing in his headphones getting rougher and harsher with each gasp. At last, with a final burst, it stopped, and again he felt normal lunar gravity.

Peter climbed in through the EVA door, Jiang right behind him. Chris unstrapped and he and Peter crawled forward to the Encyclopedia, heaving and pulling on it; Jiang stayed back with Xiao Be, working feverishly as he ran through all the through-the-suit diagnostics.

With two people to balance and coordinate, it took only a few hard heaves to get the Encyclopedia out of the nose and to slide it down onto the place that had been set up for strapping it in; after all the drills together, Peter and Chris had it lashed into place almost at once. Behind them they heard Jiang dogging the nose hatch closed, and a moment later he said, "Stand by to pressurize."

Air pressure returned to the cabin almost instantly, and Chris unfastened his visor and pulled it up. He had had fifteen minutes of suit life support left.

There was a terrible smell, and they looked back to see Jiang lifting the helmet off of Xiao Be. "She's bleeding, she's vomited, and I think she lost her bowels as well," he said. He lifted the phone and spoke into it.

"Mission Control, this is Jiang Wu. I have examined Xiao Be. Blood pressure has taken a big drop which may be due to a hemorrhage, but it's currently stable. Breathing is strong but irregular. She's fighting for air. No evidence of chest punctures or any problem with the pleura, but we can't rule out broken ribs given where she was hit. Tiber Prize, out."

"I can move my feet," Xiao Be said, very softly. "Wiggle my toes."

Jiang grunted. "That's the first good news so far. Probably no serious spinal injury." He looked at the graphs and said, "Most likely we have injuries consistent with one very severe blow to the abdomen. Impossible to diagnose further under these conditions. She's got to get back to Earth. No possibility of treatment here, nor do I think she's likely to recover without treatment. Well, that's one issue. Is there any way we can transfer the Encyclopedia to the other lander?"

"Not a prayer," Peter said. "It would be like the three of us trying to carry a small car from one third-floor apartment to another, back home."

Jiang sighed. "I was afraid of that. All right, then, what I'm recommending to my government is that we get Xiao Be home on the other lander as quickly as possible and leave the Encyclopedia here until a larger crew can move it safely to a lander for return to Earth. If you didn't notice before now, the main fuel tank is not only dented, but there's a little bit of hydrogen snow around the dent—you've got a slow leak there. I don't think this ship is fit for the Earth return." His fingers clattered over the keys as he filed his report.

"I concur," Chris said, "and I'd figure as mission commander it's my call. Okay, let's send in that report."

There was a crackle in the intercom. "Sending the report," Jiang said.

They waited for three seconds, and then Mission Control said, "You are go for a return to Earth with the injured crewperson and the Encyclopedia both."

"Mission Control, that's got to be a negative," Chris said. "We have reason to doubt the functioning of the lander and we are unable to transfer the Encyclopedia. We have urgent need to return with Xiao Be at once, please reference Jiang's medical report."

The three-second delay came and went; finally another voice came over the intercom, a different one from what they had ever heard before. "This is Liu Wan Xi, representing the People's Republic of China. We do not accept this analysis of the situation. We emphasize that we have a right both to the return of our national heroine and to immediate access to the Encyclopedia. Pressure loss has not been substantial in the main fuel tank and we believe this is an unnecessary delay being inflicted to increase the pain to our citizen and to deprive China of its rightful place, as the place where civilization began and has reached its highest level, to be first to receive the information contained in the Encyclopedia. We demand that if this proposal be accepted that both the People's Heroine Xiao Be and the Encyclopedia be returned by the first available all-Chinese crew directly to China."

"Bastards," Jiang said very softly. "Liu is a political hack. He thinks he can turn this to his advantage—"

Mission Control broke in and said, "We're not happy with this, Chris, but as we see it the best of possible solutions is immediate return. Even if you have a leak, you still have a large fuel reserve, and besides the pressure record shows only a momentary loss right when the crane hit it; there's probably no hole but just a bit of overpressure forced some hydrogen out through a safety valve—"

"*Idiots!*" Denisov shouted, "There is hydrogen snow right around—"

The voice said, "This is an order; you are go for immediate return to Earth with both Xiao Be and the Encyclopedia. And the very best of luck to you."

"Mission Control, we strongly advise against that," Chris said. "Mission Control, I repeat, we have reason to believe that may be dangerous."

Three seconds went by, then ten, and Denisov shook his head. "Well, do we try to restart the debate, do we follow orders, or do we do what we think is best?"

Jiang groaned. He had spoken more in the last hour than he had in all the time Chris had known him, and for the first time Chris was beginning to feel some liking and respect for the Chinese astronaut. "It's a direct order. And they may be right. And if they are right it really is the best thing for Xiao Be. All of those things are true. But I feel in the pit of my stomach that they are making a terrible mistake . . . and yet . . . well, I can't disobey orders."

Reluctantly, Chris nodded. "We can't second-guess Mission Control. They've still got more information than we do, like it or not."

"You never heard them respond to anything I said about hydrogen snow!" Peter said, urgently. "You don't know that they have all the facts. All they have is the complete telemetry—"

"Which is many more instruments than we can read in the time we have," Chris pointed out, firmly. "Peter, they *do* have more information. And your guy Liu might be a bastard, but I can't believe that everyone would just roll over for him," he added to Jiang. "I don't think he could be exerting much influence, not if he's just gotten in on the situation. We shouldn't let ourselves be distracted by that. If they say go, we have to go—we're never going to know enough to second-guess them. On the other hand, you two *are* supposed to stay over, and I'm the mission commander. So I'm going, Xiao Be's going, and the Encyclopedia is going. You're staying. And I'm taking off as soon as we can get a trajectory and get you guys clear."

"But—"

"Sorry, Peter, I don't see any other way. And if I do have a slow leak, the situation is getting worse every second, so get out of here before I lose any more fuel."

Jiang and Denisov glanced at each other and began to suit up; in a moment they were gone, and Chris looked out to see them trudging back to the parked habitat. He thought with longing of his bunk, a shower, and a hot meal there; he watched them walk away in the ghost light and wished he hadn't had to order them to go.

He told the computer to calculate and carry out a fastest-trajectory return to Earth; he knew that might well mean even higher g forces for Xiao Be, but the one thing he most had to have was time. As the computer began its countdown, he stretched out on his acceleration couch, hooked up his life support, and looked over at Xiao Be; only her life-support equipment readings told him she was still alive. "I'm right with you," he said, in case she could hear. "You're not going to get left on the Moon."

The engine fired and they rose from the lunar surface; he had just a glimpse of Tiber Base again, with its silent lander and rows of cairns, and then they were arcing up high and far above the lunar surface, the engine roaring for all it was worth. He breathed deeply from the suit air supply; this would be an eight-minute burn, direct to Earth orbit injection, not even taking a setting up orbit around the Moon because even though it would take them three days to fall back into orbit around the friendly old Earth, every second of delay at this end translated into a second at the other, and who knew how many seconds Xiao might have left? He could only hope that she could last through this acceleration;

after that at least the weightlessness would not force more hemorrhaging, though of course it might well cause blood to pool in unusual places and create more nightmares for the surgeons back home.

Two minutes under acceleration, and they were now far above the surface; the radio crackled and Mission Control said, "Tiber Prize, we've got you now, loud and clear. You are go for TransEarth Injection per your flight plan. Looks like you're going—"

He felt a thud through his feet. Abruptly, he was weightless. Alarms sounded, but Chris knew what it must be:, a tank had breeched and the computer had shut down the engines. So rather than check the instruments, he twisted around to peer out the window. A great billow of white was pouring out of the side of the DT, from right where the dent had been.

Unperturbed, still on the other side of the three-second delay, Mission Control went on, cheerfully talking about a "successful completion even with some rough spots, and . . ." There was a long silence.

The screen flashed a message: INADEQUATE FUEL. ABORT TO GROUND (YIN)? Chris's gloved finger pounded the Y key, giving the simplest of instructions to the computer—get them back down onto the Moon, for a soft landing, anywhere it could. He started his and Xiao Be's life-support packages onto fast, emergency recharge; there was some risk of damaging batteries doing this, but if he had to walk back carrying her, he wanted both of them able to breathe.

He tried not to estimate how far that walk might be, or how far he could go.

The computer let the ship ride out its upward ballistic trajectory and begin to fall back toward the Moon. The voice of Mission Control said, "Chris, our estimates of your fuel are extremely unreliable at this point."

He was looking out the window again; back along the Pigeon Rack he could see white wisps and flows eddying around the ship. "I'm not surprised," he said softly.

"We're guessing it's about fifty-fifty whether your landing is soft or not. No prediction on whether you'll find a spot that's fit to land on, either," Mission Control went on. "And you have no fuel to hover or search. This will be a blind landing for all practical purposes."

Chris looked out at the Moon, which was becoming less round and more a flat swath of land every moment as they fell toward it at an ever-rising speed. "Good luck to you, Chris, and we hope it works out. Set off your radio beacon as soon as you're down. And we've got someone here to say something."

He heard Jason's voice. "Dad, I'm at NASA. They came and got me out of school when things started to go wrong. I'm really proud of you. I love you. Make it back if you can. I love you."

There was a long pause, and Chris said firmly, "Jason, I love you, too. Don't know how this will work out, but if I can't live I'll die trying. And listen, I want you to have space for yourself; I gave you a gift that Sig will explain to you when—"

The rocket fired under him; Chris glanced out the window to see the razor-sharp edges of the mountains, the dark hollows of the craters. They looked close, the number on the altimeter looked low, the speed indicator terribly high.

The engines thundered against the fall, and the craft fell more and more slowly, ever downward toward the wild jumble of peaks and craters. Chris sat and waited; radar showed speed relative to the ground falling, falling, falling, till they were moving at less than 50 kilometers per hour—already he was below the peaks of the tallest mountains he could see, less than half a kilometer off the lunar surface. About a minute more, and his craft would touch down somewhere; he could only hope it wouldn't land on a cliff edge or giant boulder.

Then the Pigeon Rack shook violently as the engine began to chug out the last gasps of fuel. The floor pounded against Chris's feet for a scant few seconds as the final bits of fuel burned erratically in the combustion chamber; then there was only the eerie silence and weightlessness of free fall.

Chris spoke quickly. "Ah, hell, Jason, all I wanted to say is I love you and have a great life."

Then Chris turned up the volume on his headphones so that he could hear anything that might come up from Earth, and stood and listened for those words that might come after the three-second delay, watching the altitude and speed indicators. The engine had burned out at 470 meters, and his speed relative to the ground had been 50 km/hour or about 14 meters per second. His speed tripled, as the altitude indicator whirled down toward zero. He waited quietly for the zeros, listening for the long seconds as his family and friends called out to him across the quarter-million-mile gulf, knowing that he wouldn't have time to see the zeros. In fact the "152.8" of the digital speed indicator was the last number he ever saw, as the rocky cliffs abruptly whizzed into view past his window, the frame of the Pigeon Rack broke against the ancient rockfall, and the stone face of the Moon tore into the Pigeon Rack as it smashed its way down the slope. Chris had a moment to see the world turn upside down, to see rocks pouring in through the breach in the hull, and just one last glimpse of the brilliant, steady, eternal stars before, with crunching finality, the ship slammed against a cliff face and fell sideways down into the crater, breaking apart as it went. He was almost certainly already dead when the Encyclopedia broke from its mooring and fell out onto the slope, crashing separately down to its resting place.

I think I still believed Dad might make it until he said "I love you" for the second time; something about his tone told me this was it, and no mistake. They lost radio contact a second or two after, so I don't think he heard me blurt out "I'll miss you so much!" or Aunt Lori saying "Go with God, Chris," and of course even if he did he had no way of knowing that I hung onto Aunt Lori for half an hour afterwards, sobbing. When Sig and Mom finally came around to the NASA building to collect me, they had a counselor already sitting at the house, waiting to take care of me. It didn't make much difference at all; a counselor can only work if you talk, and for a couple of days I wouldn't.

It was almost two months later, after I'd begun to eat and was back in school again, that Sig and Aunt Lori sat down and told me about Dad's life insurance policy. I would be going to space—if I wanted to, when I was ready.

That night I spent a long time sitting at my bedroom window. It was a clear night, for D.C., and the Moon shone very bright and clear. The newspapers had made a big deal of pointing out exactly how to find the crash site, though even the best telescopes on Earth couldn't actually see the wreckage; it was a little dark spot almost at the bottom of the Moon that marked the place, not a spot made by the wreck of course, but just a place that had been there for all of eternity. I looked at that, and at all the bright stars, and now and then at Dad's picture. Every so often the tears would get too thick and I couldn't see any of them. I guess I was up about half the night and I didn't sleep well in the little time I spent in bed.

That next morning I told Sig I was ready. He asked if I was sure and I said I was. That afternoon when I got home from school he was home early and on the phone putting some kind of deal together. I didn't pay much attention at the time.

But a few months later, there I was in the world's first "extra-small" spacesuit—I still hadn't gotten my growth, and it looked like I'd be cut from the team for eighth-grade football, too. Aunt Lori, beside me, rested her hand on my shoulder and said, "Stop playing with your visor, it annoys the telemetry people."

"Yes, ma'am."

"And if you don't stop being so polite you'll annoy me."

I smiled at that, a little, and said, "Well, you know, there's this thing about making a good impression. I don't want to be the first brat in space."

I couldn't feel her hug through the heavy layers of the pressure suit, but I knew it was there. "Well, I don't think you have to worry about that. Really. And besides, all you have to do is be a passenger. This is my first time flying one of these things."

The new ship was called a Peregrine, and it was sort of descended from Orbital Science's air-launch rocket, derived from the X-34 program, a mid-1990s plan for putting small satellites into orbit. The Starbird, plus the rush to get the Encyclopedia, had created such a huge market for manned launches that Lockheed-Martin had designed this beautiful ship, getting Burt Rutan out of retirement to create the giant Condor subsonic first stage, and the world now had its first real take-off-anywhere spacecraft—or almost anywhere. You still needed runways long enough for a tanker or a heavy bomber.

The other thing the world had now, thanks to this private venture, was its first really beautiful spacecraft. The Peregrine was sleek and trim, its delta wing and fuselage forming a shape like a long, gracefully curved needle. As it sat there gleaming in the sun, I thought I had never seen anything so beautiful. "Are you looking forward to flying it?" I asked Lori.

"Are you kidding? Look at it, it's gorgeous," she said. "I can see why your stepdad is planning to buy a fleet of them; heck, I'd *pay* for a ticket just to *ride* in something like that. The thought of taking one to orbit—well, six people have so far, and every one of them has come back swearing it's the only ship worth taking to space. I don't know if they'll ever get the Yankee Clipper project started, what with all the politics, but I'll tell you this, the Yankee Clipper will have to be a hell of an act to compete with this thing. But the most amazing thing to me is this: it's so reliable that you can really schedule the flights. I mean, a ticket to space that means something more than 'we're going to try to do it sometime after this day.' Now *that's* a plain miracle, Jason."

We got the signal and walked forward through the gauntlet of video cameras; there were eight of us on this flight, each with our separate purposes. I was on the flight so that they could schedule an early return for me—there's not much use for a kid in a space station, and even a quiet kid like me was apt to make administrators nervous. And since Peter Denisov would be bringing this Peregrine back down just a few hours after we arrived, they would return me to Earth as soon as they could while still making good on my father and Sig's promises.

Aunt Lori had a very different job. When Denisov and Jiang in Tiber Two had lifted off from the lunar south pole, the lander they had been flying had been the one that had brought them; having carried in a heavier mass, it had used up more of its fuel, and so there was no prospect of being able to hop over to the crash site, most especially because the crash site was a mountainside. Still, they'd been able to go first to lunar orbit, and passing over the site five times, radar, video cameras, and binoculars had revealed only that whatever was left there, it was in a lot of pieces and they were scattered all over the scree-covered mountain slope. Nothing quite had the distinct shape of the Encyclopedia, but there was so much torn rubble it was impossible to say.

Now Lori was leading the expedition that would land at a site about twenty kilometers away, three Pigeon Racks going together as a group: one to carry crew, one to carry a pressurized rover, and one for the return—it was hoped—of the bodies and the Encyclopedia. A lot was hanging on this; if the Encyclopedia had survived the crash (and lots of things could survive 150 km/hour crashes, the argument ran, why, that wasn't even 100 mph and think of all the things on Earth that survived that speed in a car crash), then once it was finally retrieved, there would be decades of work in interpreting it. Many people said that would be the time to take a pause in space exploration, to work on making it safer and more profitable, especially now that the Moon was really open for our exploitation and held such a promising archeological site (not to mention abundant water in the polar craters that would allow large bases to be built there eventually). But if the Encyclopedia were gone, our next best hope was Mars—either its moon Phobos or Crater Korolev in its arc-

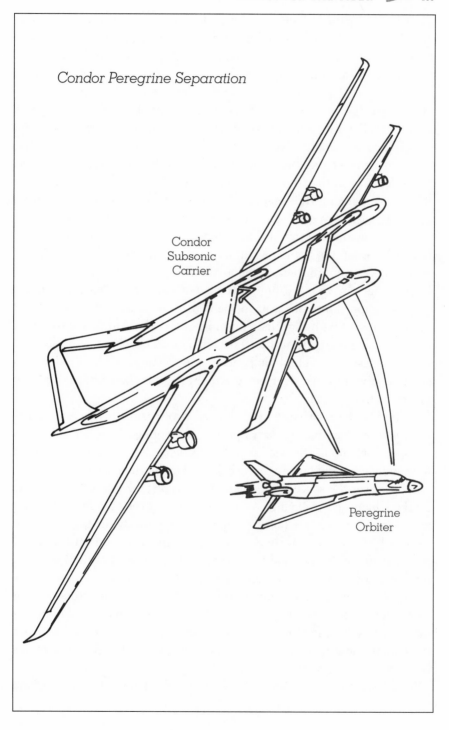

Condor Peregrine Separation

Condor
Subsonic
Carrier

Peregrine
Orbiter

tic, whichever the message had intended us to take as the search site. And Mars was always at least 140 times as far away as the Moon; it would be a long journey, and no one would go there, rationally, just to visit for a day and turn around. Chances were that crews would stay there for months or years, with all the attendant expenditure and difficulty.

The stingy and the short-horizoned prayed that the Encyclopedia would be all right, that we could find it, get an immense return, and stop. Those with more adventure in their souls couldn't help hoping that we'd have to go to Korolev first. And though there was no way of making a decision until it was recovered, that didn't stop Congress, or the Russian Parliament, the Japanese Diet, the French Chamber of Deputies, or anyone else from arguing loudly about exactly what we should do.

Me, I just missed my Dad and hoped that wherever he was he was happy. I was kind of hoping a burial service might put a close to this terrible time in my life. If they found the Encyclopedia, or they went to Mars, either way, that was fine with me, but I didn't feel much part in it.

We strapped into our seats in the Peregrine—Lori said it had a lot of room compared with Pigeons, Starbirds, or shuttles, but it was still a lot more crowded than any airliner. Lori ran a quick checkout, and then one of the coolest things of all happened. I was looking out the window as a great shadow reached over our craft: the Condor was pulling up over Peregrine to connect to it.

The Condor had a vast wingspan and two separate fuselages; it squatted over our Peregrine and firmly gripped the connector on top of us with the special clamp in the middle of its huge wing. The Peregrine retracted its landing gear, and now we hung balanced under the bigger ship.

As late as the space shuttle, countdowns had taken several days; the Starbird managed to count down in just a bit over one day. But Peregrine/Condor was a true quick-turn-around system, the first, and as soon as they had connection, the Condor pilot talked to Lori on the radio, and then to the tower, and the moment they were authorized we were rumbling down the runway, taking off into the clear desert air.

At first it wasn't much different from a regular airplane ride—except that after a while another airplane showed up, a great big lumbering tanker. I watched, fascinated, as the tanker came in above us; I couldn't see exactly how it made the fuel connection, but I had seen pictures before so I had a general idea.

At last, after almost an hour of loading the Peregrine with fuel and oxidizer the tanker flew away, and the Condor carrying us started to climb and accelerate again, laboring against the heavy load. The sky got deeper, clearer, and bluer.

Finally, the Condor could do no more. The Condor, despite its slender appearance, was so huge that it carried nearly as much fuel as a big tanker, but it burned almost all of it on the way up, returning to base in a gentle glide. As we reached peak altitude and velocity, Lori exchanged a few phrases with the Condor pilot, then ignited our Peregrine engine. We dropped away from the Condor, which turned away to begin its return; the Peregrine's jet engines fired hard enough to hold me down into my seat. We accelerated to supersonic, then hypersonic speeds as we continued up through the tropopause into the darkening sky of the stratosphere. The sun had an actinic glare off the Peregrine's wings, now, and when I looked below I could see all of Florida spread out, and still we climbed farther. Then, as the air grew too thin for the jet engines, Lori ignited the rocket engines and we roared on up toward space, the curvature of the Earth and the blackness of the sky seeming to increase with every heartbeat.

10

I'M NOT SURE HOW MUCH THERE REALLY IS TO SAY ABOUT THAT STRANGE day just a few weeks before my thirteenth birthday. Even as we accelerated up into orbit it was already beginning to write itself into my mind as a highlight, as something that I would have to remember forever no matter what. Somehow I felt that the important thing about it was going to be remembering it afterwards, and so there was very little time when I just saw, when I was just there. Most of the time I seemed to be looking at things hard, forcing my attention into them.

And yet, for all that, it was still an astonishing experience, and for decades afterwards I would have dreams about it. The Peregrine roared on as the sky became velvet black and the Earth sank below into a huge round face; when the engine cut out, we were abruptly weightless, and though I couldn't unstrap yet—there was still some maneuvering required—I could feel it.

The sight of the Star Cluster was another amazing thing. The family of space stations that had grown up, in the years since the alien message had come, were so numerous that now each major spacefaring nation except China had one or two Big Cans on some sort of a truss with solar panels slowly drifting in their coorbit with the old ISS in the space of a few miles; often there were many Starbird DTs attached as well. The total population of the nine stations—the old ISS, the French *De Gaulle* and *Verne*, Russia's two *SuperMirs*, the Chinese *Spirit of Mao*, Japan's *Blossom of the Sky*, and the new American *John Glenn Station* and *Star Port* (where we were going)—was clear up to thirty-five, as opposed to six when Dad had first gone there.

Metal doesn't oxidize in space, and the paints they were using didn't peel or fade much, so you couldn't tell the new from the old parts of Star Cluster at a glance, but still anyone looking at it got a strong sensation that this had been thrown together very quickly, completely ad hoc.

People called it "the flying junkyard" and "that trailer park in space," but whatever it might lack in aesthetics, it was still an amazing thing to see, and more amazing from the window of the Peregrine; there were three suited figures working outside who took a moment to wave. The huge array of metal and glass shining in the brilliant sunlight above the atmosphere has stayed alive in my memory ever since, even though I have been there myself many times, now, and was there the day they celebrated getting their hundredth permanent resident.

The Peregrine drifted gently sideways, Lori jockeying it with its attitude jets, until it bumped against the docking port and locked in. There followed a series of bumps and mechanical noises that probably meant things to the astronauts but not to me. Then Lori turned around and said, "Okay, people, unstrap and let's go in."

My first impression of *Star Port*, the new international mission staging orbital base, was that it was like the airport when you're little (and when I was little I went through a lot of airports)—that is, there were several extremely solicitous people hovering around trying to make sure I was in the right place and not too unhappy. I didn't even get everyone's name, but luckily it didn't matter, because suddenly I heard a voice. "Jason?"

I turned and saw a tall, dark-haired man floating toward me. "François Raymond, the station commander for this month," he said, with a very slight accent. "I flew with your father once." He extended his hand and I shook it, but he was already looking at everyone else in the room. "Slight change of plans, people. I've gotten two people to volunteer to take over for Peter Denisov and prep the Peregrine for return. So consequently Peter has the time free, and I'm authorizing him to serve as Jason's guide."

A moment later Peter came around the corner, moving like the big kid he always seemed to be. We grabbed each other in a tight hug, and he murmured in my ear, "I'm so sorry about your father, Jason, but this is something he wanted you to have. Come with me and let me show you some things."

I had not seen Peter since Dad's death, and I had only seen Lori briefly. All the spacefaring nations had accelerated their efforts at Tiber Base, trying to get as much information from the archeology as possible. But to get scientists to the south pole of the Moon, you needed pilots to fly them there and engineers to keep the equipment running. Hence Lori, Peter, and every other operational astronaut, astro-F, and cosmonaut had been getting into space more often in the past few months than most of them had in several years before.

Peter was finishing up an assignment at *Star Port*, where he was engineer in charge of readying spacecraft for their return flights to Earth. He would have just a few days on the ground with his family, and then be headed back to the Moon, where he would be part of the surveying expedition to lay out the new Russian base at Crater Tsiolkovsky, on the far side.

When the time had come for my flight up to space, purchased with Dad's life insurance, Sig had scouted through the manifests until he found the one time this year when Lori and Peter would be at *Star Port* at the same time—my father's two best friends, to show me space, to help me see why my father had devoted—and lost—his life.

Peter whisked me into a little space to get out of the pressure suit and into a comfortable suit coverall—changing clothes in space is challenging and fun the first time you try it, since your clothes have a tendency to want to leave the dressing booth without you. In five minutes we each had a squeeze container of hot chocolate and were floating in space by the window, looking down on the vast expanse of the Earth.

"It's so . . . immense," I found myself saying.

"And it's just one of a lot of planets," Peter said, grinning at me. "There's at least one more that we could get on our way to, today, if we had the nerve and will to do it."

"Mars," I said. "And after that Mercury and maybe some of the Jovian moons. Dad used to tell me about the order things could happen in, that you had to forget about Venus for the time being because the equipment to keep someone alive there would be so difficult to develop. I know, he used to give me whole guided tours of the solar system."

As we came around to the night side, I saw the strands of cities, like brilliant gems peeking through the gray-blue clouds whose tops glowed in the broad bright moonlight. "Hard to believe from here," I said, "that it's really a very small planet circling an ordinary star out toward the edge of an undistinguished galaxy."

"Chris used to say that," Peter said.

"I know. I wondered what it felt like to say that while you're looking at it."

"How did it?"

"Well, it didn't make me feel like my father," I said, and took another sip of the chocolate. "Peter, can I tell you something?"

"Sure."

"Well, I always knew this could happen. Space travel is dangerous. Dad told me about how maybe he might not come back, some time, years ago, I think before I was six, about as soon as I could get any grasp of the subject at all. I miss him a lot, but it's not like this is a big surprise to me. It's a shock but not a surprise, if you see what I mean. But everyone keeps acting like I'm going to die or something, rather than just be sad for a while, and then get over it. And I keep wondering why that is. I'm not that fragile, I know I've got Mom and Sig to take care of me, and all of Dad's friends still look in on me, you and Aunt Lori and everyone . . . so why does everyone act like I'll break?"

Peter smiled a little sadly. "You may just be a long way ahead of the rest of us," he said. "But I guess that doesn't answer the question. Now that the Sun has set, want to change windows and go look outward for a while?"

"Sure."

Swimming through the air to the other window was a lot of fun, and

Peter said we'd do more of that in a bit. I sat down and looked out the viewing port; he pulled a curtain behind us, to mask the station's internal lights from glaring off the windows, and then we looked out into the vast fields of stars. "I asked your father once, on the Moon, about how many more stars we can see up here than down there," Peter said, and told me the whole story about standing outside with my father and Xiao Be, watching the lander come in.

I listened eagerly and asked questions for the next few hours as he took me around the recently added third American Big Can hab, down the tunnels into labs, and over to the European hab where we visited some astro-Fs. Along the way, we played an odd game the Japanese had devised, Ping-Pong inside a Plexiglas cylinder that they had shipped up for some now-forgotten reason (to get the ball "over the net" you had to get it through the central hole), got a couple of people to explain their experiments, and used the new Terence Telescope to get a good look at Mars. It was just in its dust season and thus relatively featureless, but you could still see the poles plainly and the black smear across it that marked the Valles Marineris.

And all the while we did that, we talked about Dad. Mom and Sig had seemed afraid to, the NASA people hadn't been willing to, all the expensive counselors had just kept tiptoeing around the issue, all of them afraid to do or say something wrong. Even Aunt Lori had evaded the issue most of the time. But plain old straight-from-the-heart Peter Denisov wasn't devious enough for that; I had said I was ready to start talking about Dad, and he had taken me at my word, so we talked about everything either of us remembered. Sometimes it hurt a little, but mostly it felt good, like having him back, like now it was okay to remember him.

Lori joined us for our first meal and showed me a couple of tricks for getting around in weightlessness. "As soon as there's enough room up here," I said, "there's going to be a *real* tourist trade. This is more fun than skiing and skydiving at the same time. If there were just room enough, think of what you could do."

Lori grinned. "Now you're talking like Sig. And you may get your wish sooner rather than later on that one. I understand that now that they've finally come up with standard Big Can racks, so that they can put up space stations about as fast as they can get equipment built into HTs and get them launched into orbit, your stepdad has already started the process of buying four of them to be linked together into a 'space hotel'—and he says one Big Can is going to be just an empty padded space that people can use as a gym. If you've ever seen the old Skylab films of people playing in weightlessness—well, lots of people will be, and soon. You'll probably be to orbit ten times before you're an astronaut."

I was a little startled. "Me, an astronaut? I mean, I *have* been thinking about it, but . . . well, how'd you know?"

She ticked it off. "Smart. Natural athlete. Not too tall. More inside connections than anyone could count. You don't *have* to be, of course, but do you know how many kids have the same dream and don't have a tenth of the chance you do? Why throw it away?"

I shrugged. "I guess I hadn't had anyone add it up that way to me, before. But you know, Dad really seems to have decided when he was only two years older than I am now—or maybe even before that." I told them about the college guide with his careful pencil notations on the nearest flying bases.

They listened, shaking their heads. "That was Chris, all the way," Lori said, wiping her eyes a little. "The first time I met him it was because we were the only two people still awake studying, I was desperate for coffee, and I smelled his. I was up late because the math was a struggle; he was up because he wanted to make sure he came in first."

We shared stories for a while, and then Peter said, "Well, did you get it authorized?"

"François told me that if we lose him, he's going to lock the doors and we'll have to walk home, but otherwise yes."

That was how I found out that aside from being "the first kid in orbit" (as one of the annoying cable channels had dubbed me) I was also going to be the first kid on an EVA. It wasn't much—they just took me out and tethered me to the truss, letting me float in space for a few minutes, while I looked down at the immense dark Earth decorated with cities, out at the huge numbers of distant stars, and occasionally up at the nearly full Moon, cold and shining with a clarity you never see on Earth.

I guess it was then that I knew, before my ride back down with Peter. Something made me say, deep inside myself, *This is not something you can turn your back on, Jason.* I felt like a lot of the adults in my life would be very pleased at that decision, but that wasn't why or how I made it; no, it was just the moment of realizing that if I wanted to come back here, if

I wanted to live out here between the stars and set my boots on worlds that no one had visited since the Sun began to shine, the opportunity was there and I could get about as much help as I wanted. And knowing that, I felt, somewhere inside me, that I could finally let go of Dad's death, that after all everyone dies somewhere, many people on the job, and that there was no meaning in where and how he had died, only in how he had lived.

When we went back inside, Peter apologized because we had spent a little bit of extra time on the EVA and now would have to hurry to be ready for the Peregrine return window. "That won't bother me," I said, "I'll just hurry."

"Well, there really wasn't time for you to see much," Lori said sympathetically.

"It's okay," I said. "I'll be back."

I liked the way my father's friends smiled at each other.

The ride back had its astonishments, too; for two-thirds of the distance we were still in space for all practical purposes, and to fly in space is an amazing sensation. The Peregrine carried only me, Peter, and the pilot; I sat close to the front so I could see from the pilot's viewpoint, but I didn't look out the window as much as I had thought I would—I was too interested in all the things Peter was doing to steer the ship.

I had been home a week when Lori's expedition finally reached and searched the lander wreckage. They found Xiao Be still on her couch, her visor, oddly, open; one theory was that she might have released it in the last instants, to make sure that, badly injured as she was, she would not have to spend minutes or hours dying alone on the Moon. Dad's body had been pierced by a torn piece of metal from the hull; freeze-dried blood had dotted the lunar soil, and the best guess was that he had died all but instantly from the combination of blood loss and explosive decompression. A long time afterwards Lori told me that he had had a strange, warm smile, as if somehow he were laughing at a little, private joke.

And the Encyclopedia had broken into a dozen pieces as it rolled down the slope, and each piece, when it finally hit a rock or fell to a resting place in the deep pits below, had splintered into many smaller pieces. The little bits of silver-colored metal and glass, speckled with gold and black, were lovely but useless; microscopic examination over the next few years revealed that it was an immensely sophisticated optical switching system which could undoubtedly have held as much information as they said it had, and—if it were in one piece, or if it could have been put back together—would have been quite readable. Physicists learned immense numbers of things about optical microswitches, tunable lasers, and a dozen other things from examining the bits and pieces of the Encyclopedia.

But all this was like learning neurology by examining the cut-up brains of a dead genius; you might eventually understand a great deal about how a brain worked, but the thoughts that had been there, wandering from neuron to neuron, were lost to you forever.

Or perhaps not quite so lost. Within a few months I found myself going to the White House—I took the bus because Sig was in New York about some deal or other, buying out a couple of old partners, and Mom was covering a volcanic eruption in Celebes. There were a lot of us standing there on the Rose Garden lawn. I was the youngest, of course; the three Apollo 11 astronauts, now into their eighties, surprised everyone by the presence of all of them. The president got to the point pretty fast; she said that China had joined the four powers, that the five space powers were now committed to exploration and to recovery of the Tiberian artifacts, and that we would be moving ahead rapidly, expanding the Moon base at Tiber Base, establishing a separate American base at Tranquillity, expanding *John Glenn Station* at *Star Cluster*, adding a separate LEO station to be named *Shepherd*, building a new space port to be called *Armstrong* at the lunar libration point L1—and, most importantly, moving ahead with plans for Mars ships and for the new single-stage-to-orbit Yankee Clipper. "We have demonstrated, time and again, that we lead the world in hardware for space; we are going to devote ourselves to continuing to be the best at it," she said.

She ended by committing us to a landing on Phobos before the end of the decade—fifty years after the first American Moon flights.

I liked the speech, but then, considering what I wanted to do for a living, you'd have to expect me to. Afterwards, in the receiving line, she shook my hand and told me how much everyone had admired Dad (that seemed to be something everyone had to do several times), and then said, "And the Secret Service detail tells me you just came here on the bus? They say you just walked up to the gates and presented your ID. We could have gotten someone to drive you, you know."

When you're thirteen, talking to adults is bad enough; famous adults you don't know at all is even worse. So I stood as straight as I could, and said, "It's okay, Madam President, I like going to places I've never been before. It's fun to see how far you can go."

Clio Trigorin:
April 2075

THERE ARE NO BOUNDARY LINES IN SPACE, OF COURSE; NOT EVEN A ROAD sign to tell you when you cross from one imaginary place to another, nothing that says "leaving Sol System" or "entering Alpha Centauri." But according to the astrogation people, 100,000 AU was about as close to an outer boundary of the Sol System as there was, and so the crew of *Tenacity* had elected to have a party on the day that they crossed it. One hundred thousand AU, a little over one and a half light-years, was the outermost boundary of the Oort Cloud, the great cloud of cometoids (frozen balls of ice and gases that, if they ever fell into the center, would become comets) that surrounded the solar system in all directions, so far away from the sun that it looked like nothing more than a very bright star, and the outermost of them had only completed two journeys around the sun since the extinction of the dinosaurs.

Out here in the freezing dark, the last of the cometoids was past—not that *Tenacity* had come within any significant distance of them, for space is so vast that even a huge number of objects can leave it mostly empty. Hollywood has always loved to depict "asteroid belts" of floating rocks, all apparently within a mile or so of each other, but any such group of bodies, so close to each other, would long ago have fallen together into a single one. The fact is that you could point a ship through the "thick" part of the asteroid belt and zoom through at peak velocity with almost no risk at all. And the Oort Cloud is even emptier—it is only its immense size that allows it to contain so many cometoids, for all of the planets whirl around the sun in a volume that takes up only about a trillionth of the space taken up by the Oort Cloud.

So the boundary between the Oort Cloud and empty space is mostly a philosopher's game, if it is anything. But the ship needed a celebration, and besides, crossing out of the Oort Cloud represented just a little less than one third of the distance between Sol and Alpha Centauri, and very nearly half the time. So Captain Olshavsky had proclaimed a party for that work shift and told everyone to attend with something to celebrate.

Clio had no problem finding something to celebrate: she had finally completed the first part of *From the Moon to the Stars*, covering the career of Chris Terence, and she had promised herself she would take a year or so off of that project to work on something else: a college translation of *The Account of Zahmekoses* and *The Account of Diehrenn*. It was a strange thing to think about; Uncle Jason had actually been there when humanity finally retrieved the Encyclopedia and got its connection to Tiberian culture, after his father's death in that horrible bungle. And that had happened less than five years before she and Chris II had been born.

Yet the knowledge from the Encyclopedia had become pervasive almost overnight. For her, the Encyclopedia had always been there, and she had started taking Tiberian in her freshman year in college; by that time every Harvard instructor in the language had a Ph.D. in it and there was increasingly a standard reading list that anyone was expected to know if they were a serious student of the Tiberian culture. A few years after their discovery, they were a basic part of our culture.

So she smiled and nodded to the other people at the party—the same people who had been there at dinner every night, whom she would see every night for seven more years—and gave them very little attention. Instead she thought about the whole problem of doing a college translation; you had to be accurate enough for faculty to assign it and interesting enough for students to read it, not easy with a language so different from her own. Her publisher had insisted that this be a book for undergrads who would never take Tiberian; thus, it had to introduce them to the two great accounts of the Tiberian voyages to Earth, and yet not be so alien as to put them off. In vain, Clio had pointed out that when you deal with material this alien, there is bound to be something truly alien about it.

Her job, then, was to give something of the flavor of Zahmekoses's and Diehrenn's stories, even though she was also supposed to keep from making beings who *were* completely strange *appear to be* completely strange. How did you begin, expressing to adolescents the views of a species that had no adolescents—for with Tiberians the age of reason came so early, and sexual maturity so late, that they spent decades as sexless adults with reason and emotion but no sexual feeling of any kind? How did you deal with the problem of subspecies differences? All human beings are racially the same in every way that is important. We are all fully interfertile and not much more different genetically than fiftieth cousins could be expected to be. Inuit and Bantu, Andean Indian and Ainu, Swede and Maori, are far more alike genetically than any two breeds of dog, horse, or cat are, despite millennia of genetic isolation from each other. How to explain a species where the races were as distinct as dogs and coyotes, or horses and donkeys, so that it took so much more than ordinary common sense and courtesy to overcome bigotry? Or to explain the actual differences between Shulathian, Palathian, and Hybrid without mirroring any of their ancient prejudices? And what about a culture in which every sentence you spoke was addressed by gender, social class, and age? How to get across to them that the Tiberians had managed to be free and joyous, to have fun and explore, even while following a code of conduct that—

A voice beside her said, "Excuse me, do you mind if I get drunk and act silly while you muse?"

Looking up in some surprise, she saw Sanetomo Kawamura, the expedition's astronomer, grinning at her. "Here," he said, handing her a glass of wine. "Musing assistance. What are you celebrating today?"

"Oh, I finished part of a large book project. And I'm just starting into something that I think will be fun; I've got a contract to do a translation of *Zahmekoses* and of *Diehrenn*. For undergrads, supposedly to make it easy and entertaining reading."

He shuddered. "Tiberian was my dead worst subject in school. I can't wait till we catch up to them so that I won't have to study so much stuff out of their books."

Clio grinned sadistically. "You mean you can't still recite the four forms for subject-verb agreement—"

"In my sleep, I just don't understand them." He smiled. "And yet I owe those guys a debt, I guess, since that's what I'm celebrating. Using their slow-imaging technique and our very long baseline, I was able to show the spectroscopic lines for free oxygen coming from a point orbiting Tau Ceti, in the habitable zone."

Clio almost dropped her drink. "So there may still be live Tiberians?"

"Well, live things somewhere the Tiberians went, yes. Free oxygen in spectroscopic lines, not from the sun but around it, means a planetary atmosphere with free oxygen. And free oxygen shouldn't be possible, at least not over geologic time, without the presence of life. So, yes. Life elsewhere in the universe, and in the present. Or sort of in the present. Fourteen and a half light-years away, so up till fourteen and a half years ago, at least. Can't vouch for what's happened since."

She noticed that they had been slowly walking toward the row of seats; you always walked slowly carrying a drink on *Tenacity* because every other week or so, some of the bank of thirty zero-point-energy lasers that propelled the ship would unexpectedly lock up, or one of the ones that had locked up would come back on line, so that the nominal 0.06 g sideways force caused by the ship's acceleration was forever fluctuating unpredictably between 0.052 and 0.062. The main gravitational component, produced by rotating the cylindrical living quarters that joined the bulbous life support system to the zero-point-energy laser "engines," had a fierce Coriolis component as well.

So on *Tenacity*, liquids in open containers never quite behaved themselves. It might have made more sense to serve the wine in squeeze bottles, as liquids usually were, but none of the crew would have heard of that. A party should feel like a party, and that meant "real" wine glasses, even if the wine was synthesized and the glasses were plastic. When they had sat down with a minimum of slopping, he said, "Now tell me what's so fascinating about the two Accounts. They were the thing everyone in my school dreaded."

She started to tell him, and sipped some wine, and then the conversation became more and more of a blur for a few hours; they ended up being among the last people at the party, which was bound to start some gossip, but they both agreed that neither of them cared at all about gossip. They had agreed to meet for breakfast, Clio realized, as she sat brushing her hair, and reached for her portable terminal, where she carefully marked her calendar.

Still, wine and excitement aside, as she drifted off to sleep, she found herself thinking of Zahmekoses again, and he seemed to stand in front of her in her dreams: almost seven feet tall, big ears like a bat's and face elongated like a dog's, eyes two dark pools like those of a horse, soft amber fur rippling . . . saying to her, *Now, explain a thing like me.*

And the next morning, before breakfast, she had begun her introduction, tapping it out on her keyboard as she sipped her first coffee:

"There is hardly a more relevant document from the Tiberian exploration of Earth than the *Account of Zahmekoses*. First and most astonishingly, he actually lived through the whole period of Tiberian exploration in the Sol System, coming as a child on the first ship, playing a role in the affairs of the second ship during his later years, and finally writing his account as a very old being on the Moon. . . ."

PART II
LIGHT OF DAWN
7328–7299 B.C.E.

1

"HEY, POINTY-EARS!" MEJOX SHOUTED, POUNDING AT MY DOOR. "YOU ready to go?"

"Hey, yourself, fossil-man." I opened the door. "I've been ready for ages. Just sitting here thinking."

Mejox was my best friend, had *always* been my best friend, because we were five years old now, fully conscious and capable of reasoning, and we had first met when we were three and barely verbal. I didn't really remember the Public Orphanage at Atherebof; we had always lived here, in the crew training quarters on the Windward Islands. Mejox said he didn't really remember his parents' house, either.

Mejox was Palathian, so he was shorter and squatter than I was, with a flat nose, round ears, and a lot of body hair. I was Shulathian—tall, thin, long-nosed and long-eared, and all but hairless. Though we were only dimly aware of it, we were probably among the few people on Nisu to whom that made no difference at all. Not that either of us knew many other people. Mejox, along with the girls, Priekahm and Otuz, were the only other children I had ever known.

Mejox held up his bag proudly. "Got all of my clothes and stuff into one bag, just like Kekox said I should. How'd you do, Zahmekoses?"

"In one but just barely," I said. I'd had no trouble, but Mejox tended to make everything into a contest, and he was a sore loser.

"Hey! Kekox and Poiparesis say to get moving!" Otuz shouted from the hall. "They say if you boys don't come right now they'll make you ride outside on the liftsail!"

We were used to terrible threats that the adults thought were funny,

Palathian

but we both grabbed our bags and ran down the hall anyway because we *were* eager to go.

As usual, the adults had reserved window seats for the Palathian kids, and it would never have occurred to Otuz or Mejox to offer to share with Priekahm or me. Fortunately Soikenn, my favorite among our teachers, had saved a spot next to her, and Priekahm and I wedged into it together, so that we could both see. Sort of.

It was a long flight from the Windward Islands to Palath, mostly over water. Priekahm and I stayed glued to the window anyway, as the aircraft flew ever westward. Just behind and above us, we could see a dozen escorts ready to move in for a rescue if anything looked even a little wrong. It was always that way whenever we flew.

The sun set ahead of us, and an hour later Zoiroy set as well. "I guess it's getting close to the last time we will ever see a star that bright," I said, suddenly. For the last few eightdays they had been telling us to be sure to look hard at everything, because after the voyage, when we came home, we would be old, two-thirds of our lives gone. "There's no second star in the new system, so there won't be a star that bright."

Soikenn hugged me. "Not bright enough to read by, like Zoiroy, but there will be other things to see. There are many more planets in the night sky of Setepos, and some of them will be very bright. What you'll *really* miss will be the sight of Sosahy. The new world has a big moon and there will be some light from that, but there won't be anything like Sosahy in the sky."

"What's a moon?" Priekahm asked. I could never tell if she asked a lot of questions because she didn't pay attention, or she knew the answers but she wanted the attention. Whatever the reason, she got away with it. She was pretty, and lively, and even if you thought about strangling her, somehow you were laughing before you got around to it.

Soikenn said, "A moon is what we are to Sosahy. A little body that goes around a big one. So the moon of our new planet won't be as big as Sosahy—it will be a little circle in the sky not much bigger than the sun, and much dimmer. But look, now, we're going to be coming over the Line soon, and then you'll see Sosahy—you don't want to miss that."

Shulathian

After a long wait, the great pale wedge reared above the horizon, and swelled to cover one-sixth of the sky. It always hung over Palath. If the scientists were right, Palathians and Shulathians alike had originated in the mountain valleys at the heart of Palath, directly under Sosahy; there were people who said this was why the sight of Sosahy always lifted our souls.

I just thought it was beautiful.

Once, I had heard an old Shulathian shouting, to a crowd on a street corner, that Mother Sea made the Shulathians but Palathians were descended from animals of Palath, and that was why Palathians looked like animals. I heard no more, for Poiparesis grabbed me up and carried me away, so I had only a glimpse of Imperial Guards moving in to disperse the crowd.

Afterwards, Poiparesis had talked with me about it. "We are all the same species," he said, "no matter what the old fanatics say. There are differences in our appearances—hair and nose shape and all that—but we are the same species, Zahmekoses, and don't forget it. Even though you're Shulathian, you are as good as any Palathian—and as bad. Though I wouldn't say that around Mejox—he's sensitive. Anyway, whatever may have happened in the past, there are many very decent Palathians now—you know we on the crew are all friends, and look at what the Palathians did for us after the First Bombardment. We'd never have gotten through without them."

I said I understood all that, and that anyway Mejox was my best friend and he was Palathian. Poiparesis got a funny expression for just a moment. I hadn't been sure about what. I knew there were Shulathians who hated Palathians, and vice versa, and it wasn't something you talked about. After all, even though the crew was supposed to be very equal, Priekahm and I had learned to be careful, especially around older Palathians.

Maybe I remembered that conversation, so many eightdays ago, because it had been the first time that I had really been aware of how different things were for Priekahm and me than they were for the Palathians. We were the pick of the Shulathian orphanages—supposedly the brightest, "most stable" (whatever that was), and "most talented" children they could find. Otuz and Mejox had been chosen based on family, the way Palathians did everything—their parents were active and important members of two of Palath's five royal families. When we returned Mejox or Otuz might even be selected as emperor or for one of the hereditary ministries. After all, Mejox was high on the list in his generation of the Roupox family, and the last three emperors had been Roupox.

But of course anything might happen before then; we would be returning as adults of long standing. Right now I was really more concerned with the problems of sharing a window with Priekahm as we watched the immense bulk of Sosahy rear up out of the sea in front of our aircraft, the way a tall building does when you approach it from far away. By the time the aircraft landed, at Battle Gorges, Sosahy would be straight overhead.

Priekahm had no patience, so after a bit of uncomfortable squirming, she gave up on the window and turned to whining at Soikenn for attention, which she could always get. That left me with the window to myself. I watched the dark waves roll far below in the warm light of the giant planet overhead until I fell asleep.

When they woke me, as we drew near to Palath, the skies were crowded with aircraft of all kinds: big passenger liners moving slowly across the sky at high altitude, huge freighters that skimmed just above the sea, little racing yachts like the one we rode in that dashed and darted in all directions, and of course the menacing black police craft and blue rescue units that hovered everywhere or prowled slowly up and down the air lanes.

Mejox and Otuz had gotten into some kind of game of counting how many police craft carried their respective family insignia, and Otuz was apparently winning, which is why there was getting to be an unpleasant edge in Mejox's voice. That didn't seem to bother Otuz—she was the only person who really stood up to him. She had a knack for picking just the thing he was most vulnerable about and teasing him—like right now, as she kept saying that some other family crest, neither his nor hers, was actually in the lead and that maybe her mother would have to marry into that family just to preserve her chances of being empress someday.

Otuz's remarks kept getting louder and Mejox's whining tone was getting dangerously nasty. Beside me, I could feel Priekahm tensing. When things got noisy, she and I got punished, no matter where the noise was actually coming from.

"I think we should count the Zowakou family crests for my side, because they're allied with my family, and we should start counting over. That way it will be fair."

"Oh, nonsense," Otuz said, very loudly. "You know we're passing over the Zowakou family's territory. Almost all the police craft we see will be theirs. When you say 'fair,' what you mean is 'that way Mejox will win.' "

Mejox jumped out of his seat, straight at her, but before he could get to her, the captain, Osepok Tarov, had grabbed Mejox by the hair on his back and bellowed, "Sit!"

He did. Osepok was officially just another teacher, right now, but we all thought of her as "the captain," even though it would be some time before we left. Osepok was the only person who could consistently make Mejox behave when he really didn't want to. Unfortunately, usually she just ignored him.

"We can all do with some silence," the captain said. "Think about the fact that you're looking at home for the last time, at least for many years. Is that clear, Zahmekoses, Priekahm?"

"Yes, Captain, sorry," we said. We always apologized, especially when we hadn't actually been doing anything.

"Otuz?"

"Yes, Captain."

"Mejox?"

"Everyone else already *said* it was clear," he said.

"Is it clear to *you*, Mejox?"

"Yes, Captain." Mejox was just respectful enough not to be overtly rude, but if the captain heard his tone, she chose to ignore it.

The quiet lasted until we were near Battle Gorges, far into the interior of Palath. As we approached the air harbor, the pilot brought the impellers up to full power—I liked the way the air swirled coming out the back. Then she extended the liftsail, increasing our drag, and engaged the compressor, filling the ballast tanks and reducing the aircraft's buoyancy. We sank into aerodynamic flight and glided down toward the field.

Soikenn had assigned me to make a report about aircraft and how they worked a couple of weeks before, and I was quite impressed with myself for remembering. We glided in over the runway, already moving slowly, and the pilot reversed the compressor to drain ballast tanks, so that we became a little more buoyant and began to be more affected by wind resistance. With a little jump, rise, and gentle drop, the aircraft came to a stop and settled onto its metal feet; ground crews ran to secure the liftsail and tie down the feet as the pilot ran the compressors flat out, filling our tanks with compressed air and making us sit firmly on the ground.

The airfield we were using for this trip was a private one, belonging to Otuz's family, but there was no one here to greet her. Priekahm had whispered to me once that Otuz's family were all very old-fashioned and didn't want to associate with her because she had been seen in public with Shulathians so often. Whether this was true or not, I didn't know. Priekahm inclined to very dramatic explanations.

But I didn't think Otuz's feelings would have been hurt much even if her family *were* snubbing her. Like all Palathian royalty, she had been raised by nurses and nannies and, if she had stayed home, would not have really gotten to know her parents until she was past puberty and of an age to be engaged—and nobody even entered puberty until they were at least twenty-six. Many royalty didn't meet their parents until they were past thirty and married, with children of their own—though their parents had probably arranged the marriage.

The flight had taken most of a day, so we would make our official visit tomorrow. They gave us an evening meal. Afterwards, Soikenn talked to us about what we would see at Battle Gorges tomorrow, and Kekox told us a couple of stories about the expedition he had been on to Kahrekeif—the farthest voyage in space so far, though the one we were about to go on would dwarf it by far.

"It's a terrifying place," he said. "The only thing you can say for Kahrekeif is that the other moons are worse." Toupox and Poumox, the other two moons of Sahmahkouy, were worlds of tidal volcanoes, blanketed with thick poisonous atmospheres with a huge greenhouse effect, so that molten lead lay in pools on their surfaces and exposed steel or aluminum burned and smoked; I had seen the pictures.

"But you weren't afraid," Mejox asserted, firmly, "no matter how dangerous Kahrekeif was." Kekox was his hero.

Kekox laughed. I liked it when he did that; though he was an old-style warrior, and had been an Imperial Guard, there was something kind and warm about his eyes. "I was scared out of my mind, Mejox. Anyone with any sense would be. You could easily die there; four of our crew did, and which four died was all a matter of luck. We had no idea how dangerous conditions actually were until we got there long enough to take a good look."

"How far away is it?" Priekahm asked, breathlessly. She was doing her usual routine on Kekox, making her eyes get big and looking cute.

It always worked, too. "Well," he said, and his voice got warm and he talked as if we were all still preconscious, "Zoiroy is a smaller star that goes around our sun every seventy-one years. Sahmahkouy is a planet that circles Zoiroy, just as Sosahy circles our own sun. And Toupox, Poumox, and Kahrekeif all go around Sahmahkouy, just as we go around Sosahy. But how far away it is . . . well, that depends. Sometimes it's three times as far as at others. Anyway, it took us several years to get there and return during the nearest approach."

As he warmed to the subject he stopped talking baby-talk and began to look more at Otuz and me. "We didn't have time to wait for the next time there would be a close approach, and the next approach wasn't going to be as good as this one, anyway. So the situation was very unfavorable for getting a probe there any time much before we went ourselves. We had to leave before we really had gotten much data back. We had sent a few fast flybys, probes that went by Sahmahkouy and Kahrekeif so fast that they didn't take up an orbit around them—too fast to take a good look. The trajectories for an orbital probe would have required so much energy that we decided to just go and take our chances."

"Nobody understands that energy stuff," Mejox said. "We want to hear the adventure."

"I understand it," Otuz said, "and so does Zahmekoses, but he's afraid to admit it."

Kekox moved to sit between Otuz and me, and then asked, very gently, "So, Otuz, what was the energy problem, if you understand it?"

She sighed in the big dramatic way she always did when some grownup asked her to prove she understood something. "Our world, and Kahrekeif, are both going around planets that go around stars that go around each other. That's a lot of motion. To go from here to Kahrekeif you have to change your speed and direction—and your position—by enough so that you go from moving like one of them to moving like the other. That's a huge difference in speed, and it's a very long distance, and changing speed, position, and direction that much takes a lot of energy."

"Not bad at all," Kekox said, grinning at her, and then did the thing I was dreading—he looked at me and said, "So what's the energy associated with a trajectory?"

"Some ways of getting from one place to another require you to speed up more or slow down more at one end or the other, and like that," I said. I was babbling; if I pretended not to know, Kekox would pick on me and Poiparesis and Soikenn would be shamed, but if I admitted that I did know, Mejox might sulk, or even give me a beating later.

For the moment my trust in Kekox won out over my fear of Mejox, so I went right on babbling. "When Zoiroy and the Sun are close together, *and* Sosahy and Sahmahkouy are between them, that's called a close approach, and at that time there are a bunch of low-energy trajectories, because the two gas giant planets are close together and moving pretty much in the same direction at the same speed. But during most of the orbit the directions and speeds are very different and the distances are much bigger."

Kekox's eyes were warm and friendly, and I felt better than I usually did when I was forced to excel Mejox in public. Then he turned to Mejox and said, "Now, see, you *do* understand all about the energy for trajectories, and you understand that it's an important part of the story, right?"

"Oh, yes, sure," Mejox said, looking at the floor.

"Well, as I was saying," Kekox went on, "we had no idea what we'd find, and we didn't realize that Kahrekeif's inclined, highly elliptical orbit meant trouble. We didn't even realize until we were on our way and got data from the last few fast flybys that Kahrekeif had been captured by Sahmahkouy so recently that it was still spinning."

"Recently?" Priekahm asked. "Like the year before?"

"Like ten million years before," Kekox said, smiling at her as if he were going to pat her on the head. "A short time in astronomy and geology."

"And wasn't it very hard to land on it if it was spinning?" she asked. Every so often I wanted to pinch or slap her; she wasn't nearly as dumb as she acted, but she loved the attention she got from our teachers by playing stupid.

"The spin is not a big problem for landing—coming down from orbit you're moving so much faster than the surface is that the little bit of motion of the surface doesn't really matter. It had better not be a problem, Priekahm, because Setepos is rotating." Setepos was the new world we were going to; we all leaned in to hear better, because whenever an adult would talk about it, it was the most interesting possible subject to us.

But Kekox didn't take the hint, and continued his story. "We had landed on Kahrekeif near its equator, still knowing nothing. Pretty clearly at one time it had had liquid water—there were channels, dry riverbeds, and lake basins filled with icy slush. Kahrekeif still had enormous deposits of ice, some just below the surface or covered with dust. There was a lot of frozen carbon dioxide at the poles, but the air was very thin, only about five percent as thick as what we need to breathe, and since it was almost all carbon dioxide, even if it had been thick enough we couldn't have breathed there. And the strangest thing of all was that Kahrekeif—they think this is because it was spinning—was one big magnet."

"Why didn't the ship stick to it?" Priekahm asked.

"One big, *not very strong* magnet," Kekox said, sounding amused. If I had asked such a question, he'd have glared at me for being silly; if Otuz had, he'd have told her he was disappointed in her.

"All those were clues to what was going to happen. Another clue that we really should have noticed was that although the air was very thin, there were no impact craters anywhere; that should have told us something was resurfacing Kahrekeif regularly. Maybe if we'd managed to get an orbiting probe there first we'd have realized.

"But we didn't, and we wouldn't find out how all of the clues fit together until much later. We were climbing over a raw basalt scarp, about a day's hike from the lander—"

"What's a scarp?" Otuz asked.

"A long straight cliff wall, between one plain and another," he said. "Like the Great Barrier Cliff of Palath, though that's much more eroded than this was. Scarps are made when a world shrinks as it cools—they're like cracks in a cooling pastry—and since these were new and raw they were pretty good evidence that Kahrekeif was a relatively new world. Anyway, we had climbed halfway up the cliff face and were resting on a wide flat spot. We had wanted to get up onto the higher plain to take some observations as Kahrekeif began its close approach to Sahmahkouy.

"Because its orbit was so highly elliptical, Kahrekeif's orbit around Sahmahkouy was more like a comet's than anything else—it swung in much closer than we ever get to Sosahy, and swung back out to fifty times as far. And because, you know, the speed in orbit depends on the mass of the central body, Kahrekeif actually takes longer to go around Sahmahkouy than Sahmahkouy takes to go around Zoiroy; the planet goes around the sun in two years, but the moon goes around the planet in about two and four-fifths years. So once every fourteen years, it happens that Kahrekeif first makes a close pass at Sahmahkouy—it seems like it almost grazes the cloud tops—and then swings way, way in toward Zoiroy, toward its star.

"What we didn't know was that the huge electric charges in Sahmahkouy's cloud tops actually discharge to Kahrekeif; the little moon gets hit by lightning for about half a day at its nearest approach. Fortunately for us—or I wouldn't be here to tell you the story—the magnetic field of Kahrekeif guides those gigantic lightning bolts down to the poles, so that none were hitting where we were, or through the orbit of our ship. But it was a near enough thing anyway.

"The first part happened in less than a twentieth of a day. We had pitched a normal camp up there on the ledge, halfway up the scarp, and we were getting ready for bed. The next day we were to go up to the top to observe the eclipse that happens at that point in the orbit.

"Just at sunset, the northern sky flashed bright blinding white, over and over, and the radios stopped working. We couldn't raise the ship or the base on the radio. Even the helmet sets were unreliable within a few armslengths of each other, so we had no idea what was going on. Electric shocks came right through the ground, not enough to burn, but enough to make your legs kick, and all the freestanding metal was suddenly a shock hazard.

"We had barely begun to figure out what must be causing it when the air pressure started to rise, fast. Tutretz, the expedition's meteorologist, made a brilliant guess, which is why we're alive. He realized that the big electric currents caused by the lightning strikes must be flowing through the slurry of water ice and frozen carbon dioxide that made up the polar caps, and in the low pressure it was heating them enough to vaporize them. The whole atmosphere was re-forming around us, and as Kahrekeif swung in toward the sun for the next half-year, it would cause a rapid greenhouse effect; there was going to be a lot more air, and liquid water, and it would be a lot warmer. So even though the winds were rising with every breath, he made us strike camp, pile all the gear we could onto our packs, strap on respirator packs, rope ourselves together, and start climbing, up and off that shelf, to a place he'd spotted earlier that day.

"So much dust had been whipped into the air that it was black as Shulathian night. We climbed by the light of our helmet lamps, staggering, falling, dragging each other, but by the Creator, with Tutretz pushing us, we *climbed*, even as the winds rose to hurricane force. We got up to the small place he'd spotted—a long, long way above, and it would have been a hard climb even in daylight. It was really no more than a deep overhang, and how he found it in the pitch dark and the howling wind, I have no idea.

"We set up and sealed shelters in there. So many radio parts had burned out that there was no hope of contacting base, or the ship, that night—between fifteen personal radios we weren't sure we had the parts to make one working radio. We were all hopelessly exhausted, so as soon as the shelters were up we all went to sleep—it wasn't completely safe and it violated a lot of tradition, but there wasn't much point in setting a watch—the alarms would wake us if anything went wrong, and besides no one could have stayed awake. We'd had a day's climb before the storm started, and the better part of a day afterwards in the dark and the wind.

"We had reached the overhang far into the night, with a dark storm howling outside, dark enough to hide the giant lightning flashes from our direct view, though some light did flicker through the thick clouds of dust and water, lighting the shelter walls with sudden bright flashes. If there was dawn, none of us saw it; shortly after, the eclipse started, and that lasted for many hours, so it was dark and stormy for a long time. I have memories of looking out the viewport of my sleeping bag—we were in the shelters, but we all pressurized our bags that night because we weren't sure the shelters would hold—and seeing the wall of the shelter shaking in the howling wind, even in the protection of the overhang, and lights flashing on the shelter walls, probably more reflected light from where the bolts of lightning were entering the upper atmosphere, over the poles, half a world away. At least we were on reasonably insulating rock now, and the electric currents flowing through the soil didn't bother us.

"We all slept more than half a day by the clock.

"Most of us seemed to wake at the same moment in mid-afternoon, or maybe the first people to get up made so much noise when they saw all the light shining through the shelter walls that they woke the rest of us up. The shelters hadn't breached, so we were able to get out of the sleeping bags to put on pressure suits. As soon as we could we ran out of the shelter airlocks to see what had happened.

"We looked from the lip of the overhang back down toward the broad shelf where we'd been before the chaos started. Falling down onto it was the biggest waterfall I've ever seen in my life, and where our camp had been there was a big cold blue mountain lake shining in the sunlight—yes, the sunlight. The sky was blue and held big fluffy clouds, and out beyond the scarp we could see lakes and rivers. Tutretz checked his instruments and found that we had gone from a pressure of five percent of what is normal here on our world to just about twice normal—forty times as much air as there had been the day before. The air was almost entirely carbon dioxide and water vapor—greenhouse gases—so that as we swung inward toward the sun for the next ten eightdays or so, temperature and pressure would continue to rise rapidly.

"We tore apart four radios to make one working one, and then hailed the ship with no problem at all; their electronics had taken hits the previous day, but they were all right. There was no trace of the base. We never even found any remains of the four crewmen who died there.

"For another eightday, while the orbiting ship's crew got the uncrewed cargo lander modified so that it could haul us up, we explored the high plateau. The sudden injection of all that CO_2 had created a runaway greenhouse, and so much of the ice was bound in weak structures that there had been a lot of explosive melting and sublimation. The ship photographed all kinds of places where wet soil was erupting upward in cold mud volcanoes.

"Tutretz worked it all out later: during the times when Kahrekeif is swinging outward from Sahmahkouy, and away from its sun, there's not enough greenhouse effect to keep the atmosphere unfrozen. So it slowly freezes into a slush of water and CO_2 mixed with dust—we called it 'fizzy frozen mud' so often that that became the recognized scientific term. Every two and four-fifths years, Kahrekeif makes a close pass at Sahmahkouy and is blasted with lightning, and the ground currents evaporate the fizzy frozen mud explosively, but usually the cold mud volcanoes just erupt for an eightday or so, and then freeze again, and the bulk of the fizzy frozen mud stays solid. But every fourteen years it happens that the orbital positions line up so that Kahrekeif gets a long period of warming, then gets zapped, and then gets another long period of warming—so that the ices are much more ready-to-go when the lightning hits, and then the thicker atmosphere goes right into runaway greenhouse. Five years later there's another period of sustained cold, and the process starts over again. So it wasn't surprising that so much of the surface looked new; it was getting resurfaced every fourteen years.

"The expedition wasn't wasted at all. We learned a great deal about geology—but we also learned that Kahrekeif was a terribly dangerous place, and one where the dangers would change all the time. Probably someone will try to settle there, but it isn't likely to be the place that saves our civilization." He sighed. "And here I just meant to tell you about the adventure on the scarp. Well, bedtime, all of you, tomorrow you start your history tour."

2

AS I WAS PUTTING MY CLOTHES INTO MY BOX THAT NIGHT, I HEARD VOICES from Mejox's chamber next door. I put my ear to the wall and listened.

Kekox was saying, "Mejox, I don't want to hear one more word from anyone about your bullying Zahmekoses. Especially not when he does something better than you do. He's the most loyal friend you could want. More than you deserve. Do you understand that? He is worth five thousand times as much to you as your loyal friend than whatever satisfaction you get out of making up games that you win against him. He's not going to complain, but *I'll* know and you'll be sorry."

Mejox's voice was whiny in a way I hated. "I just like it to be fair. And I like to win."

"Learn to like *people*," Kekox said bluntly. "People are what an emperor has to know and like. When you're rich and powerful—*if* you last that long and we don't all die on this trip—the only friends you will be able to trust are the ones you make now. And a brilliant kid like Zahmekoses is the kind of friend you should be making. Now, treat him like an equal and remember that your friend's success is your own—or answer to me."

Mejox said something I didn't quite hear; his tone was whiny and unpleasant. There was a sharp, flat crack and a shriek through clenched teeth. The old Guard had slapped Mejox, who cried out in pain. My blood froze.

"Now listen here," Kekox said. "I know you're a Roupox and I know your family has a lock on the Imperium. But for the next twenty-four years, you're my charge, and you're going to grow up decent. You have to *lead*, Mejox, and if you don't *know* the difference between leading and throwing your weight around, or getting someone's loyalty and bullying him into submission, *learn* it. Or I'll hit you again." His voice became gentler. "Don't you see? Isn't Zahmekoses your best friend? Don't you want him to be happy?"

Mejox was crying—I could hear the low, keening noise. He must have said yes, because then Kekox added, "Then *be* his friend. He adores you, Mejox, he'd do anything for you. That won't last if you keep making him take second place. He's Shulathian, for the Creator's sake, it's in his nature to be smart and creative and artistic, but of course he's also flighty and irresponsible. It's just the way those people are. Now, a lot of the Shulathians I know are wonderful people and some of them are great friends of mine, people I'm always glad to see. We had three Shulathians on Kahrekeif with us and I have nothing but good to say about them. I've said for years we ought to let them into the Imperial Guard. Shulathians will do things out of personal loyalty that us practical Palathians would never dream of. If you make him your good friend, you'll always have someone smart and loyal at your back, ready to die for you if he has to. But if you keep hurting his feelings and bullying him, he'll fester and brood until you won't be able to get a thing out of him. Never forget that the Shulathians did govern themselves—even if they did it very badly—for thousands of years before we conquered them, and as much as they need us, we have to *earn* their loyalty."

"Zahmekoses *is* my best friend," Mejox said. I felt a small glow of happiness inside. Mejox went on to demand, "Why do you say those things about Shulathians? If they're so bad—"

"Not bad," Kekox said emphatically. "Don't even let yourself start thinking that. We have enough bigots and troublemakers out there as it is. But they are flighty, excitable, and irresponsible. That's why they make great scientists and lousy engineers, and great lawyers but they're terrible leaders. But you *need* everyone's skills, Mejox. On this expedition we had to have a couple of first-rate scientists, for one thing, which is why we have Soikenn and Poiparesis. And then . . . well, you're not too young to know there was political pressure, too. There's been a lot of pressure ever since your grandfather's uncle gave Shulath home rule. There was pressure on us from all those Egalitarian maniacs.

"But that's neither here nor there; these are the people you have to work with, and Zahmekoses is the best friend you'll ever have. I'm telling you how to make sure he *stays* your best friend. I suppose I can't make you listen—but I know you'll listen to this. If you abuse or exploit that boy again, or force him to lose at things where he's better than you—wham. You get hit. Learning to bear pain is another part of leadership, and I don't think I've taught you enough about it."

"Zahmekoses *is* my best friend, and I like him better than anybody," Mejox insisted.

"Good, then it won't be hard for you. Now get some sleep. Tomorrow is going to be a very long day." I heard the door close on Mejox's room, and slipped silently onto the bed and made myself relax and become still.

Kekox came in and made sure that the cover was over me; he very lightly touched the top of my head with two fingers, the little gesture for "sleep" that mothers make to their children. I don't know where an Imperial Guard learned to do something like that, but a mother's touch couldn't have worked better; I was asleep instantly.

The next morning they took us out to Battle Gorges, a set of braided badlands canyons falling away from the Creation Mountains of Palath. The canyons led up from the plains into the breaks of the Alpiax River and then into a wide pass through the mountains, forming a natural set of roads between the dry plains to the east and the hilly, brushy country of the west. The most natural invasion route through the middle of Palath, they had been busy places for millennia. It was said that if you dug anywhere here, you would find the bones from battle after battle, going back way before written history.

But in modern times Battle Gorges had become famous for something else. In the old Palathian religion, Sosahy was the Creator, and in their tradition Battle Gorges, directly under Sosahy, was where people had come into existence. Then a century ago scientists had discovered the oldest known remains of people in caves, sealed with clay, all over the Battle Gorges—a hundred times older than any remains found elsewhere, a window into life a million years ago.

The people they had found here, mummified in the cold anoxic clay, had not quite looked like Palathians, but more like them than like us— the cave people were even shorter and hairier than Palathians, but with long pointed ears and faces like Shulathians. "This is where we began," Soikenn was saying, "all of us."

The sunlight was bright—the sun had climbed most of the way up the sky and was drawing on toward Sosahy, which formed a great lighted bow, its center bent outward toward the sun. Within the arms of the bow lay the dark bulk of the huge planet, the part not lit by the sun at that moment. I looked around, blinking at the bright light. I imagined the people who had lived in the caves up there . . . before there were Shulathians or Palathians, making their spears, cooking meat over fires, the children running and playing. If they could see this place now, I wondered, would they recognize it? Would it be the same place as before, or completely unfamiliar?

By my side Mejox was listening, eagerly, like me. Otuz too was rapt in Soikenn's stories, about how scientists had found drawings on the walls, and stones laid in elaborate geometries on the cave floors, and the tallies of different kinds of animals taken at different seasons of the year.

"Why do you suppose they ended up here?" Otuz asked.

"They had to be somewhere," Mejox said.

"They did indeed," Soikenn agreed. "They may simply have begun here and stayed here. If they wandered in from anywhere else, probably they picked here because of the caves—somewhere to live without the trouble of building—and for pretty much the same reason that the area later became a battleground. It sits right where several different ecosystems come together, so there were many kinds of food available. Of course, also, because conditions were so perfect for preserving their bodies, whether or not this place was important to them, this was where we were likely to find them. And they *might* really have originated right here, anyway. The fossil record shows all kinds of things that might have been our ancestors or our cousins, all right around here. The old legends just might be true. I suppose that's why we call these the Creation Mountains."

Usually the captain didn't speak much except when she taught math and science, so we were all startled when Osepok suddenly added, "And there's another lesson here. They found forest fire ashes, evidence of earthquake collapses, layers of volcanic ash, all kinds of things in this area. We might have started here, but it was a tough place to stay alive. So we spread out—down the rivers, up into the hills, across the plains, eventually over the seas to Shulath—and now out into space. There's not a place in the universe that's safe forever; the universe is telling us, 'Spread out, or wait around and die.' "

We were all so surprised Osepok had spoken that we said nothing for a long minute. Smiling, she added, "I'm sorry. I don't suppose that lesson needed driving home right now. Hey, look, the eclipse is about to start."

The noon eclipse in Palath was the only time you could see the stars, because Sosahy, hanging over us in the sky, was bright enough to turn the sky blue most of the time. But right during the daily eclipse, Sosahy blocked the sun, and we faced the part of it that was having night, and then the stars would pop out.

We glanced up and saw that the sun was near Sosahy, almost touching its huge disk; Sosahy takes up about fifty-five times the width of the Sun in the sky, a number everyone learns early. It was no more than the time of two long breaths before the sun disappeared behind our big mother planet, and we were plunged into darkness. "There it is," Captain Osepok said softly, pointing up into the sky, off to the west. "We are standing where we began, and there's the thing that's going to put an end to us. Or it's going to try, but we won't let it."

The white smear in space might have been mistaken for a tiny cloud or a puff of smoke, but none of us had any trouble identifying it; we'd been shown it almost every night since we were small. The first time I could remember seeing it, it had been smaller than the tip of my smallest finger held at arm's length; now I needed almost two fingers to cover it. "The Intruder," Mejox said softly, beside me.

"The Intruder," the captain agreed. "This is why we brought you to this place at this hour. Because you are standing where our species began to climb up toward the stars, and you are looking at the greatest threat to our existence."

It was ninety-five years since the Intruder, the great ball of dark matter one third the size of our world itself, had been captured into our system by our double star, then had looped in close to the Sun and been torn apart by tidal forces. It had fractured into billions of chunks, ranging in size from pieces no bigger than your fist, all the way up to pieces as big as mountains. The devastation it had left in its wake had started the long struggle that had led to our building *Wahkopem Zomos*, the first starship—and the ship on which I, the other three children, and our four teachers would soon leave for a distant star, to see if we could find a new home for our people.

"The only reason we can see it is because it's spread out half as wide as the distance from here to the sun, and so it's such a big reflector. If it had all stayed in one piece, we wouldn't be able to see it at all," Soikenn said. "Not until it was almost on top of us, like the last time."

"It's going to miss this time?" Priekahm said, sounding a little fearful—but then, I think we were all a little fearful, just because we knew plenty about what was coming. From the training base on the Windward Islands, on a clear day we could see the Ring, a string of high mountains forming a circle wider than the biggest city in the world, reared up above the sea by one of the impacts.

"Of course it will miss," Soikenn said. "And besides, we'll have left by then. We'll be getting close to halfway to Setepos."

We watched the Intruder, but after all it was just a smear in the sky, not to do anything for the next fifteen years. After a while I looked around. In the opposite direction, just above the horizon, distant Zoiroy gleamed. I wondered how it must feel for Kekox, who had been there, to see it in the sky. Our Sun and Zoiroy circled each other in the sky; by the time that the Intruder passed through our orbit again, we would be on the other side of our circle with Zoiroy. Most likely nothing at all would strike Nisu, and only a few detectable pieces would hit Sosahy.

The time after would be our turn again. And the Second Bombardment was predicted to be much the worst: Sosahy, and Nisu with it, would pass directly through the center of the cloud of rocks formed by that Intruder.

We stayed till the sun came back out from behind Sosahy and Battle Gorges was flooded with light again. Then we had to go to a public presentation; it was very boring because we'd all been through it so many times before. A group of leaders, mostly Palathian, made speeches, and the speeches mostly said that unless we found a new world to start civilization on, our species would be dead. Then one Shulathian got up and talked about how important it was that Palathians and Shulathians were working together.

Meanwhile we stood there in the hot sun, being as dignified as we could. I stood a little behind Mejox, so that older Palathians who didn't like the equality idea could sort of think I looked like his servant, but Shulathians could still see me and feel equal. Priekahm stood the same way behind Otuz. We had all learned to make our minds go blank and smile whenever the crowd applauded.

The next day we flew to East Island. No one knew for sure, but it was the farthest east bit of Palath, almost a four-day sail from the mainland, and it was thought that probably the ancestors of the Shulathians had been people blown off course from here, maybe in canoes or rafts, and carried all the way to the Windward Islands. That was where the oldest evidence of settlement in Shulath was, and as you went on east through Shulath, you found newer and newer settlements. There had been a long pause when the early Shulathians ran into the long, thin, snaking continent that stretched between the poles; it had taken centuries to settle and explore there, for the land was not hospitable, the high coastal range made a passage across very difficult, and the deep desert to the east of the coastal range made it difficult to reach the sea at all, and once you did, the coast you reached offered no materials for building ships.

But eventually the great trading kingdoms had spread out from the islands and planted large colonies on the continent, forced roads across the desert, and dug a couple of canals through the continent. By that time people were writing history, and so the settlement of the Eastern Ocean, right out to the little rocky island dots of the Leeward Islands in the Far East, had come fairly quickly and we knew the names of all the explorers for that area.

If we had been following history in chronological order, we would have flown next to visit the Windwards, but that was where our training base was, and we had seen, almost every day, the Dawn Stone, the big rock on which Shulathian legend claimed that Mother Sea placed the first people. So instead we made a tour of Palath, visiting mostly ruined cities near the center and thriving ports around the edges. Palath was like a big lumpy oval, cut into quarters by an east-west mountain range and a north-south row of scarps, with a big, deep arc of lakes curling around the middle.

The histories of the two sides of our world were very different. For long centuries the Shulathians had flung themselves into trading and exploring, with a certain amount of piracy and conquest on the side. The League of Ports had barely been a government at all. Its General Court was really just a committee of representatives from the larger trading cities, mostly interested in suppressing piracy, blockading ports that endangered business and quarreling over religion and philosophy. The League Judges had always been slow to act and spent a lot of time arguing and deliberating.

Meanwhile in Palath great empires had been built, flourished, torn apart, built up again, replaced, reconquered, and so forth in a dizzying whirl. It had taken a very long time to establish the Imperium, and then a thousand years of fighting until the Imperium finally ruled all of Palath, until rebellion was impossible. Then Palath had "settled down to finally develop the fruits of peace"—that was what our history book said. They built roads and temples, monuments and statues everywhere, destroyed old run-down cities to build bright shining ones in their places, and, under the first nineteen emperors, built a government strong enough to rule Palath effectively.

There were still rebellions, of course, during that time. The Imperial Guards still had to march out and put down trouble on a regular basis. Many Palathians, apparently, didn't want to pay their taxes when harvests were bad, or didn't want to contribute their fair share of labor to building temples. The history books said it was more or less what you had to expect.

I always felt, secretly, a little bad about it all, because I had a lot of trouble understanding the "government" and "leadership" parts of the book. Every so often I liked to imagine myself as an old-time Shulathian pirate, out terrorizing the seas. (I never understood why it said that, either—all of the money was in the ports, so why terrorize the seas?) I knew it was probably a good thing that the Palathians, once they conquered Shulath and gave it a real government and leadership, had wiped out the pirates; but it was fun to dream about them, not least because it gave me a chance to imagine being really bad. I suppose any child who is usually very well behaved and studies hard, every so often, likes to feel that he has the potential to go bad.

We spent a whole eightday standing on famous battlefields and among ruins all over Palath, trying to keep the names of all the kings and republics straight. They made still and moving pictures of Mejox in front of every statue, war memorial, and ruin in Palath, or so it seemed to Priekahm and me. They kept trying to get Otuz to do it, too, but she would scowl or make faces and they finally gave up.

On the last day in Palath, we went out to Kaleps, which was now a great city, but we didn't go right away to its huge civic center, or the grand Municipal Mausoleum, or any of its halls of art or science. They chased away all the picture-makers and news-tellers so that the eight crew members could be alone in the quiet of the little park by the waterfront.

I suppose if anywhere is sacred, on the whole round world, it's that place. The little park had been there for well over four hundred years, and in that time there had been many different monuments there: the first one had showed Palathian soldiers conducting a line of chained, head-bowed Shulathians, and General Gurix standing with his foot on Captain Wahkopem's throat, but that had been long ago. Now there was a simple statue of the two men, facing each other, hands open and empty, standing on their single common pedestal together. The inscription below read:

On this place, in the eighth
year of the reign of
the Empress Rumaz, Family of Roupox,
and the 28th Year of the League of Ports 92nd General Court,
Captain Wahkopem Zomos
arrived here after a voyage of six eightdays.
He submitted to the authority of
General Gurix Zowakou.
Through the courage and bold action of both,
peace and law were secured throughout the world.

The place was eerily quiet. General Gurix had a hard, flat face, like Kekox, but much more so; he didn't look like he was thinking anything or doing anything, more like he was just waiting. Wahkopem looked like he was about to smile; there was a faraway look in his eyes that I guess is the way you look after fifty days at sea watching an empty horizon.

After we had looked at it, in silence, for a very long time, they brought in one picture-maker, and a couple of officials. They made pictures of all of us laying big bunches of flowers and baskets of fruit at the base, several times. Then they asked Mejox and me to climb up and stand next to the statues and take some poses, holding the hands of the two leaders, standing between them with our arms around each other, and so forth. I wasn't sure why I was involved in this. Usually they only wanted to take pictures of Mejox.

That night Kekox sat down and very quietly told us the true story. At least he said it was true and at that time I trusted all four adults completely. He started out by saying to Mejox and Otuz, "Understand that I've decided to tell you all this myself because I want you all to understand that this is not Egalitarian propaganda, and it's not Shulathians making up stories. As far as we can tell, this is what happened. Is that clear?"

They nodded that it was.

Then he turned and said, "Priekahm, Zahmekoses, the other side of the issue is that although a great wrong was done to Shulathians a long time ago, and many wrong things are still being done to them, this is not grounds for any sort of grudge or feeling of superiority. Do you understand that?"

We both said we did.

"All right, then, and a question for all of you: do you understand that tonight, and tomorrow, and from then on, you will be exactly the same people you were before? That what you learn changes nothing about who you are or what our mission is?"

He must have felt satisfied with what he saw among us, because he began to tell the story. Kekox was good at telling a story, and soon we were caught up in it, just as if it had been any adventure tale before bed.

Wahkopem had already been the greatest captain in all Shulath, an explorer credited with charting dozens of islands, for years before he had finally put together the financing from a dozen banks for his dream—a voyage to settle the argument between the Big Worlders and the Small Worlders.

The argument was this: by observing the position of the sun, and the way shadows moved on the ground, it was possible to work out how big a curve the world moved through as it turned around. The number was huge; it suggested that there must be hundreds of thousands of times the width of the known world of open ocean out there, or perhaps that there might be many, many archipelagos and continents. That was the position of the Big Worlders.

And yet, when surveyors measured the curvature of the world, by studying how far away the horizons were, they found that the other side of the world couldn't be much bigger than Shulath itself. That was the position of the Small Worlders, who turned out to be right—or mostly right, since they argued that it must be all empty ocean, because surely if there were people over there, we'd have found each other.

Of course, looking backward, we know that what the Big Worlders were actually measuring was the width of Nisu's orbit around Sosahy—but Sosahy is not visible from anywhere in Shulath, so the Shulathian astronomers had no idea that they were circling a gas giant. They might have found out if anyone had managed to reach either pole, but the great barrier of the glaciers, the high mountains, and the bitter cold—especially because the glaciers were so thick that the air was too thin to breathe on top of them—had made that impossible.

The debate had raged for centuries, and might have gone on for many more. Kekox tried to keep the amusement out of his voice in telling us about this, but I could tell he was thinking, how typical of Shulathians to spend forever debating an issue. Privately I thought, how like Palathians not to notice that there *was* an issue.

Finally, Wahkopem had put together the necessary money and permissions for his voyage; that took a long time, for the old General Court of Shulath did nothing fast and debated everything very thoroughly. At last his new ship, *Sunseeker*—an improved design he had arrived at with the help of the new calculus, just developed by his half-sister—set sail eastward from the Leewards for the unknown. *Sunseeker* had been designed to cross the whole ocean if need be, to run all the way around the world and come back to the Windward Islands. To have a chance to do that, and leave a safety margin, Wahkopem had optimized his ship for greatest speed, largest capacity, and smallest crew, so that they could go as far as possible before food and water ran out.

The Small Worlders had always argued that if there were anyone else anywhere on the ocean, they would already have found Shulath or been found, because after all, the wind blew west to east and sooner or later ships would go right around the world. The Big Worlders, on the other hand, said that the distances were so immense that there might be no land for twice the width of Shulath, and there could still be forty worlds like Shulath over the sea. The reason that no ship ever returned when it was blown far to the east was, if you were a Small Worlder, that there was never enough food for them to survive so many eightdays on an empty ocean before coming back into Shulath from the east; for the Big Worlders, it was proof that the distance to the next islands, if any, was huge.

No one knew enough meteorology to understand that the spurs off the polar continents made the sea a few days west of Shulath savage beyond belief. Nor could anyone imagine that since Palath was one vast expanse of land, with just a scattering of nearby islands, there was so little reason to make ocean voyages there that it had never occurred to anyone to explore the easy, eastward direction from East Island, which they could have done even in their few crude coastal freighters.

Most of all, no one knew that in a hundred years about a dozen ships, blown off course from the Leeward Islands, *had* wrecked on the coast of Palath.

That is, no one in Shulath did. General Gurix was a disgraced son of the Zowakou family, one of the most unpopular nobles in Palath, but he was also too well connected to execute and he had inherited the right to his command. The miserable West Country to which he had been assigned as governor hadn't produced a decent load of taxes, ever, and no one there had the energy for a rebellion. The general had a great deal of time on his hands, and he spent much of it reading old records and going through the museum.

Slowly, he became convinced that there was land on the other side of the ocean. His predecessors had simply seized the ships coming in, sold any surviving crew into slavery, and kept the more interesting objects as curios. Each time, they had simply confirmed that this wasn't the first time a mystery ship had washed up, and then, since it was not unprecedented, done more or less what the district officer had done the time before—written up a report and forgotten about it.

But General Gurix was a different sort of person. He had not become disliked because he was incompetent, but because he tended to do and say what he thought was right, and he was usually right. Worse yet, he had a tendency to say, "I told you so."

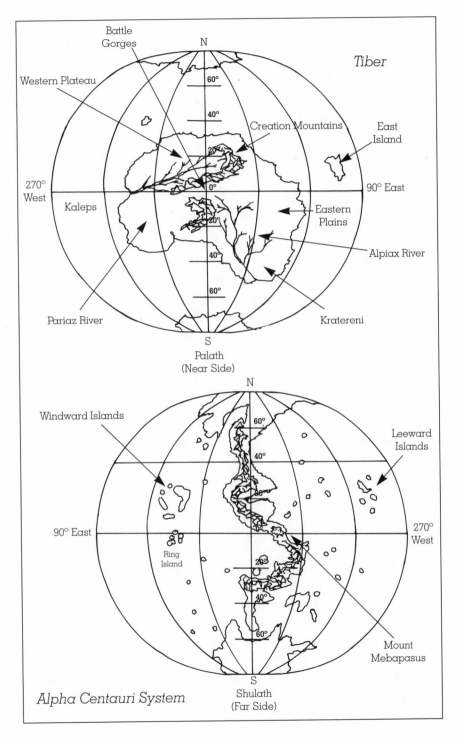

Tiber

Battle Gorges

Western Plateau

Creation Mountains

East Island

270° West

90° East

Kaleps

Eastern Plains

Alpiax River

Pariaz River

Kratereni

Palath
(Near Side)

Windward Islands

Leeward Islands

90° East

270° West

Ring Island

Mount Mebapasus

Alpha Centauri System

Shulath
(Far Side)

Now he bent all the power of his mind to the problem of where those ships came from, and what kind of place it might be. He had made a lengthy list of facts: there were seldom many weapons aboard the ships, and they were not built to fight, if the drawings and preserved parts could be trusted. Conclusion: the people to the west must be unskilled in war.

It took him a very long time to figure out the workings of the nine clocks, and a bit longer to decipher the purpose of the four sextants in the Governor's Museum. But the most interesting thing came to him only after ten years of study. He realized that the *oldest ones were inferior to the newest ones.* And once he realized that, studying the drawings, he could see there had been improvements in the ships themselves. A hundred twenty years before his time, these people to the west had been making things as good as the best workmanship in Palath, and they had gotten steadily better ever since. And there had been very little progress or change in Palath in the last few reigns; it was widely believed that everything worthwhile had been invented long ago, during the Ages of War, and that nothing important remained to be found. Conclusion: Palath was falling behind these people, possibly very rapidly.

He had written a long letter about this to the empress, still keeping his old bad habit of saying what he thought. Somewhere out west were people who had more and better things than anyone in Palath, but weren't much as fighters. If they could be located and conquered—the sooner the better—there might be great wealth and advantage for everyone. If the situation were ignored long enough, the civilization over the seas would be far in advance of Palath—and fighters or not, they might well conquer. Given the constant improvement in ships, contact was inevitable.

After almost a year of waiting, Gurix received a short note from one of the empress's anonymous underlings, suggesting that General Gurix didn't have enough to do (which was true) and that he was crazy (which wasn't). Gurix barely read the note; he had finally found two survivors of the last shipwreck, twenty-two years before, both of whom had been sold as slaves. He had confiscated those two survivors from their owners and spent a long time talking to them, slowly beginning to piece together their language and a little idea of what Shulath must be like. He was confused for a while by the fact that their accents were different, because they were from different islands; baffled briefly by the apparent absence of a government in Shulath (it sounded like the whole area was ruled by lawyers); puzzled by the whole idea of "astronomy" and that over on the other side of the world apparently there was an "eclipse" that lasted half a day. But he liked puzzles and mysteries, and he went on learning.

And as he went on learning, he moved his headquarters to Kaleps, because it was the best port on the coast (even if it harbored only a fishing fleet and a few coastal freighters) and that was where the next mystery ship would come, when it came. He gave strict orders about how a mystery ship was to be dealt with. And he waited.

Four years later, having successfully made it through the worst storms anyone in the crew had ever seen, *Sunseeker*, the best ship in the world, commanded by Wahkopem Zomos, sailed into the harbor at Kaleps. *Sunseeker* was greeted with appropriate signals and directed to an anchorage; meanwhile, General Gurix called together his personal bodyguard and instructed them, then summoned his two Shulathian slaves to act as interpreters.

Most of the Shulathians didn't know there was a fight until it was over, and Gurix had command of the ship. Kekox was visibly uncomfortable, but forced himself to tell us children about what Gurix had done, sparing the details but making it clear that he had tortured and enslaved the crew and that Wahkopem Zomos had gone to meet the empress as a bound prisoner.

Proven right, Gurix rose rapidly at court, especially because he was not only proven right but had a scheme for making Palath—and all its royalty and nobility—wealthier than they had ever been. He had achieved all-important popularity, and now mobs flocked wherever he went to cheer wildly for him. The Palathian mob was notoriously fickle; when it took Gurix to its heart, suddenly his blunt, abrasive personal style became the reason they trusted him and the measure of his honesty. Within a year he had married a member of the imperial family, and the alliance between the Roupox and Zowakou was formed; his direct descendants would include three emperors and four empresses—not to mention Mejox.

In one way Gurix badly overestimated the Shulathians; he hadn't been able to believe their complete lack of organization, or that their legal procedures were so complicated, and hence he expected them to organize a counterattack quickly and thought there would be a lot of hard fighting, especially with so many places to take—there were dozens of cities on the charts that Wahkopem had brought with him. Thus he overprepared, taking Wahkopem's ship as a basis for his design and producing a hundred warships and a thousand troop transports, equipping his new army with an improved version of the rifles he had found on board the ship.

That mighty fleet struck at the Windward Islands without warning, and in less than a day, the whole archipelago was in their hands, and no ship had escaped to tell the tale. In less than a year, Gurix had overrun all of Shulath, and the world was under the Imperium for the first time. The ships ran back and forth at a great rate, and at times it seemed they would need all of the ships of Shulath just to carry all the loot back to Palath: art finer than anyone had ever seen before, beautiful furniture from a thousand palaces, slaves, whole libraries, gems and precious metals.

Wahkopem Zomos died three floors beneath the Imperial Palace, still in chains, twenty-four years later. It was said that he never bowed to any empress or emperor, refused to swear loyalty to the Imperium, and kept faith with the General Court that had sent him—though it had long been replaced by a General Court appointed by the empress—until he died.

"You see, that's why our ship is named after him," Kekox said. "He's the real founder of our world civilization, and a hero to both our peoples, both for his boldness and his steadfastness. Never forget that we would not have a whole-world civilization now if he had not had the skill and courage to make that voyage, and that when everyone else had consented to the new order, or been silenced, he remained the one person who demanded justice. But never forget either that all of this happened because he didn't know what he was going to find. We can honor his courage, faith, and skill, but we must understand that the unexpected happens to everyone. I don't know if more foresight or caution by Captain Wahkopem might have meant a happier result for him personally, or might have meant that Shulathian and Palathian would have met on more equal terms. Perhaps not—on the day the General Court was seized, eight months after the Windward Islands fell, there was still a debate raging in there between Big Worlders and Small Worlders, and no one had been able to get a discussion of defense onto the floor. We'll never know what use Shulath might have made of more foresight—but we do know this: they never got to try. So as we set out, keep asking yourselves, *What are we overlooking? What are we blind to? What do we take for granted here that isn't true at all where we're going?* Remember how much went wrong with the expedition to Kahrekeif, for that matter. *Never* economize on information or forethought.

"The only other thought I have is this. You children have been under our care, and that will continue. But years from now, sooner or later, you will be in direct contact with the base back here. And I have no doubt at all that someone will try to stir up trouble, whether it's a Shulathian agitator or a Palathian bigot. That's why we were all very careful to tell you the truth about the relations between the races and about past history. Now some of you might feel a little tempted to think of yourselves as special—or as having been wronged—because of some of what you've been learning. I want you to remember this . . . look around the room and look at your friends. *These* are your people. Someday, maybe, the whole world will be as good as you kids are at getting along. Not yet, I'm sorry to say. But you're our hope for the future—in more ways than just the expedition. We can hope the world will be a little better place when you get back—not only from the advances we'll make, but from your example. Never forget the whole world is watching you, and you need to act like what is *best* about our people. *All* our people."

3

THAT NIGHT, BECAUSE WE DIDN'T HAVE TO BE UP EARLY THE NEXT MORN-ing and we were getting a few days' break before doing the Shulath part of our world tour, Mejox and I were awake late together in his room. It never seemed to cause any trouble, even when one of us fell asleep in the other's room, probably because the adults wanted us to be friends so much.

After Poiparesis had come through and said goodnight, I slipped out of my bed, gently opened the door, and slid into the hallway without making a sound, carefully closing the door behind me. A moment later Mejox welcomed me into his room.

Not much happens in the lives of children, especially happy children, but still they find a great deal to talk about. For a while we just chatted about all the times we'd had to stand on parade; the crowds were always the same, because Mejox's family, the Roupoxes, had so much power and influence that they were able to turn out big, enthusiastic crowds on cue. Furthermore, the Roupoxes controlled some of the major news-teller groups, and those had been saying really good things about all of us too.

"It's all the same, though," Mejox said. "The news-tellers only do it because they're told to. Next week they'll do it for a singer or an athlete, or a policeman with a bunch of arrests, or a salesperson who set a record. Everything is always about the cheering, nothing's about the doing."

"Yeah. Some of the uniforms are fun to look at, but we have to stand so still, we miss half of what there is to see."

Mejox gestured agreement. "Sometimes I wish I could watch the parade instead of be in it."

There was a very soft knock on the door. "C'mon, boys, let us in," Otuz whispered. "We know you're in there."

I lurched to my feet, but Mejox beat me to it, opening the door with a sweeping bow. "Enter, ladies. We have just decided to admit female members in the Can't Sleep Club."

"Hah. We just came down the hall to accept you into the Bedtime Is Too Early Association," Otuz said.

The only furniture in the place was a chair and bed. Mejox took the chair, which left me sitting on the bed between the two girls.

"Now," Mejox said, "what's the occasion?"

"Same one it is for you," Otuz said. "At least I think so. We couldn't sleep. The things Kekox told us. I feel like crying; I never knew what had happened to Wahkopem—isn't it funny how they just stop talking about him, in the history lessons, after the voyage?—and now I'm upset."

"He's been dead a long time," I said.

Priekahm said softly, "I tried to tell her that already. *You* two didn't steal anything from *us*. You're our friends. And Zahmekoses and I would never have had this chance—"

Mejox sighed, a heavy sound. "I've been doing a lot of thinking, too," he said. "The trouble is, you know, I *am* a Roupox. What General Gurix stole—half the world!—is a big part of what I'm going to inherit—*if* I inherit, don't forget that the Senate has to ask my family for a candidate, and the family has to pick me, and then all the other cousins they could have picked have to agree—so I really wish people wouldn't keep talking about me being emperor, I wish I'd never heard of the idea, it just makes me think funny and throw my weight around . . ." He sounded more unhappy than I had ever heard him. "I don't like being this way, I don't, but whenever I want something . . . it just kind of . . . pops out and I start acting that way. And it'll be even worse if I get to be emperor—"

I reached forward and took his hands. "You're not as bad as you think you are."

"You're not even as bad as *I* think you are," Otuz assured him. "I mean, it's not like we really did anything bad ourselves, but I found myself thinking about all kinds of things I've seen and heard, the way people talk about Shulathians when there aren't any around—"

"Not Kekox," Mejox said, ever loyal.

"No, I guess not him. Not everybody. But I guess I never realized before today how terrible that all was. I guess I never realized how much of society is built around the Conquest."

It was on the tip of my tongue to say something, but Priekahm, who had been sitting very quietly, beat me to it. "Well," she said, "we aren't going to hold any personal grudges. Really. And you couldn't pay us back even if you tried and we wanted you to, and we don't want you to. Right?"

"Right." I agreed.

"So it's just what Kekox said, is all. We are not going to live the way grownups did before. We're going to make a new society, our way, and it's going to be equal. We're all in this together."

In the dim light, I saw Otuz stick her hand out, into the center of the group. Priekahm reached for it, and then before I knew what I was doing, I had grasped their hands and Mejox had taken all of our hands. We sat there, not sure what to do, and then very softly Otuz said, "We promise that we will make a world where Palathian and Shulathian are equal, and where everyone has a fair chance. We will use our influence to make the world a better place."

We all said we promised, and I looked from face to face in the dark and thought, these are the best friends I could have had. I cleared my throat and said, "And we will stick together, with each other, no matter what."

"No matter what," everyone echoed.

"We will do what seems right to us and we won't do anything stupid just because it's traditional," Priekahm said, and we all agreed to that.

We hadn't exactly planned to swear oaths when we started out, let alone that each of us would come up with one, so I felt a little twinge of sympathy for my friend; Mejox would have to come up with something for all of us, and we'd sort of said all the easy things first.

I felt his hand tremble for a second, and then he said, "You know what's important to me? You know how sometimes they make Otuz and me go spend a day or two with other kids from royal families?"

Priekahm and I nodded.

"Otuz," he said, "aren't you always glad to come back? Do you feel like you're 'royal'?"

"Now that you mention it, no, I don't feel like one of my family, and of course I'm glad to come back to you all. I thought that was just because I didn't see much of my family. They don't seem to want me to visit as much as the Roupoxes want you to, Mejox, so I just wasn't very attached to them—but when I listen to you, I don't think that it's just that my family doesn't want to see me; I think it's that you all make me feel so welcome. You're my *home*, all of you."

"That's what I meant," Mejox said, "and I guess I do have something for us all to promise, too. From now on we promise that what comes first is our group; the group is our family, our home, everything to us. Nothing is more important, not being emperor, not being Palathian or Shulathian, *nothing*. Friends, home, and family to each other, now and always, no matter what."

"Now and always, no matter what," I said, and squeezed his hand; Otuz and Priekahm muttered the words, too, and we all sat a long time, not letting the magic of the circle break. Through the window, the light of Sosahy, now almost full since it was close to midnight, shone down clear, bright, and cool, making the sky glow beautifully; only the gleam of distant Zoiroy marked the deep blue sky. We all got up, went to Mejox's window, and stood looking out for a long time.

With Priekahm on one side of me, Mejox on the other, Otuz only a breath or two away, I said to myself, *These are my friends. I really have a home now.* And I thought how we would voyage all the way to Setepos, and come back, and raise children and grow old with each other. And nothing would come between us. Nothing.

The tour of Shulath was very different. Geography and history didn't make that big a difference—monuments to battles and monuments to "first settlements" and "unknown colonies" and so forth all look pretty much alike.

The difference was Shulathian crowds. Palathians stared and ooohed and aahed, and they applauded wildly whenever Otuz or Mejox was called on to say anything. Palathians prided themselves on their ability to agree with each other and all do the same thing; they thought of it as having common sense. It didn't seem to be in the nature of Shulathians to agree about anything.

Wherever we went in Shulath there would be protests, some from the Egalitarians, some from religious groups, many from philosophical groups whose positions nobody could understand. All the Shulathians would shout and holler until the Imperial Guard would move quietly forward, and then most of them would get quiet and a few would get arrested.

We stood there quietly and nodded at the right times, and we made sure that we only answered questions that our adult teachers repeated to us, because there were a lot of people shouting questions and comments, and if we appeared to pay attention to them it might accidentally have political effects, or even cause a court case. I remember that once as we were getting back into the aircraft, Kekox muttered that he'd never seen so many people trying to get children to say something inappropriate. Poiparesis muttered back, "Don't forget, we have twenty-seven percent of the population and ninety-eight percent of the lawyers over here."

The last three days in Shulath were different. We had finally looked at all the important monuments of the exploration, settlement, and Conquest; now we flew to Mount Mebapasus, a high mountain near the equator, to visit the observatory complex. The pressurized buildings, where they kept the computers and the radio telescope controls, were huge. Hundreds of astronomers worked there. Most of them tracked stray bodies kicked loose by the Intruder; we would be meeting with a very special group that did something else—it was a meeting that we were all looking forward to.

First, however, we put on squeeze suits and oxygen masks and climbed the long stone stairway, all the way up to the Old Observatory, the 220-year-old building with its great telescope chamber. The old-fashioned telescope, with its oxygen hood surrounding the base so that the astronomers could breathe and work without wearing masks, stood gleaming and silent. It was no longer used, but its brass case was polished, its mountings were kept perfectly lubricated, and had there been occasion, it might have been put back into service at any time. "This is where it all started," Poiparesis said to us, as we all crowded into the oxygen hood. "Right on this site, right through this eyepiece. The Observatory was first proposed hundreds of years before, at the time the telescope was invented, because even then everyone understood that if you could get above most of the air, you could see much better. But it took them a very long time to get around to building here—there were so many scientific questions and so many questions about who should pay so much, and of course technology kept improving, and every time it did the whole Observatory had to be replanned.

"They did build it. They had to use pack animals in oxygen masks to haul things up, but they managed. The first oxygen systems up here were electrolysis systems—they'd bring ice up on a rope, thaw it out, and decompose it with electricity. The whole operation was powered by the big windmill you can see down the slope."

Mejox, sitting beside me, made a little noise of impatience. "But we know all that."

Poiparesis laughed. "True. I'm just always astonished to know that they built this before they had workable aircraft or decent engines. But the important thing, of course, is that almost exactly a hundred years ago, three astronomers—a Palathian and two Shulathians—announced that they had seen the incoming rogue planet, as big as Sosahy, and that they expected it to have a close encounter with Zoiroy."

I knew the story well from the history books, so I listened with only half an ear. Instead I put my imagination into thinking about this place in those days. The Observatory had almost been closed down; a telescope simply couldn't see far enough to see anything very interesting, at least not in the immediate neighborhood. After a hundred years there had been little to examine once the surveys were completed of Zoiroy, its planet Sahmahkouy, and the moons Poumox, Toupox, and Kahrekeif. Twice they had observed large comets, and of course they had established that many stars were double, like our own, and that the nearest star, Kousapex, was almost a twin for our sun, though it was thought at the time that there could be no life there, since most of the theories said a single star would never develop planets big enough to support life. But all of this had been in the early decades; then the paucity of things to look at or search for had begun to make the enormous expense of the Observatory, up here beyond ninety-five percent of the atmosphere, seem like a waste of money. There had been many suits in the General Court to have the Observatory funds allocated to other purposes.

So on the night of the great discovery, the three astronomers, in their awkward old-fashioned heavy squeeze suits, had been gathered around under the oxygen hood, where the pressure was brought up to just a comfortable level for breathing the pure oxygen without a mask. They had been conducting a search for cometoids, balls of ice that might someday fall into our solar system to become comets, in the wide belt far beyond our double stars. They had found two, and already been denounced in the General Court for "coming up with two snowballs in all the vast reaches of space." One of them wrote in his diary that if they had two more successes like those, the Mount Mebapasus Observatory would be closed down for certain.

I often wondered, because it never said in the history books, how many times they rechecked their work before reporting it. The comparison photos must have told the tale the first time they pointed their telescope in that direction; how many times did they check before they got the nerve to report the results? Did they debate among themselves what the best way to publish it would be, how to make the most modest claims without causing their work to be ignored?

They must have known that no matter how many times they rechecked or how careful they were, there would be a storm of protest, and sure enough, they were right. Debate raged in the General Court for three years, until the incoming body became visible to the naked eye. Then, by order of the emperor, the three astronomers were given the funds they needed to build a second observatory on the peak, from which they would be able to obtain a more precise notion of what the Intruder, as it was now known, would do.

There were more delays because in those days there were no aircraft that could reach the top of the mountain, so an electric monorail had to be built first, and no one had ever built generators or motors so powerful before. By the time that they were ready, it was less than half a year until the Intruder's encounter with Zoiroy was due.

The uproar they had caused by finding the Intruder was nothing compared to the uproar they caused when they arrived at their conclusion: the Intruder's interaction with Zoiroy would cause it to swing by close to the Sun, losing energy at both passes and ending up in permanent orbit around the double system. Moreover, it would make a very close pass by Sosahy—and our world—before climbing back out to aphelion.

There was more uproar, but by now there were many observatories and astronomers ready to confirm their work. At first it was thought that there might be a spectacular display in the sky, then that the Intruder might crash into the sun and then briefly the concern that the Intruder would actually collide with Sosahy.

None of that happened, exactly.

They had all been surprised at the effect when the Intruder passed close to the Sun; it was only years afterwards, well into Reconstruction, that the mathematics was worked out. The closer a body comes to a large mass, like the Sun, the stronger the tidal effects—and the more difference in tidal effect there is from one side of the body to the other. In a close pass at the Sun, the Intruder was subjected to tremendous and differing tidal forces on near and far parts of it. More than that, the Intruder itself had formed in the dark and cold between the stars, at low temperatures for the most part and without much centrifugal force, and thus it had no metal core like Sosahy. There were rocks, and chunks of nickel iron, all the way through its scarred body, and the whole thing was very loosely held together by water and ammonia ice, which broke down rapidly as soon as the outer layers began to strip away.

The Intruder shattered into billions of pieces of all sizes, scattering into a great cloud. Thus, although the dense central part of the cloud missed our world by a wide margin, the debris—abundant even in the thin edges of the cloud, the biggest pieces the size of mountains, most boulder-sized or smaller—had sprayed our world, and Sosahy, in what the history books called the First Bombardment.

The First Bombardment had been bad enough; one out of eight people worldwide killed, and Shulath wrecked. The Second Bombardment would finish off Nisu. One hundred and forty-some years in the future, there would be nothing left of us—unless some of us, somehow, could be somewhere else.

I couldn't help wondering, as we stood there in the Old Observatory, in our squeeze suits, under the old oxygen hood, just as the astronomers had once stood, if the scientists up here that night so long ago had had any inkling, or even the faintest suspicion, that they might be finding the end of the world. For a class project I had read all about them, and looked at old motion images of them, now grainy and off-color, and no one had mentioned any doubts they might have had. Perhaps they had not had any, but I doubted that very much.

In the next three days, we would be visiting all the places where the First Bombardment had torn into our world. Though Sosahy, with its bigger disk and much greater gravity, had taken the brunt—astronomers in Palath observed five thousand huge explosions on the gas giant in a matter of hours—there had still been plenty left for Nisu, and almost all of that had hit outward-facing Shulath. More than a hundred sizable bodies had struck Shulath, some of them leaving craters bigger than small islands.

Shulath had been wrecked, more than if we had been conquered all over again. Nineteen populated islands were wiped from the face of the world, by direct hits, by the volcanoes that followed in the wake of some impacts, or by erosion from huge tsunami; in those nineteen places nothing stood above water anymore. Fully a hundred islands remained above the water (at least in part), but lost their entire populations. Seven new islands—including the great Ring Island south of the Windwards—formed in the aftermath.

The First Bombardment had been just a glancing blow. Most of the Intruder was still out there, now expanded into a huge cloud of rocks, dust, balls of ice, and all sorts of junk, in a 108-year orbit that we had now measured with the greatest precision.

The Second Bombardment would be a direct hit. The positions of the sun, Sosahy, and the world in their orbits would put us squarely in the center of the path of the Intruder's dense middle. The best estimate was that our world would take seven hundred times the number of hits we had taken the last time—between seven and eight thousand blows. At least twenty of them would be bigger than the one that had thrown up the Ring Island. Moreover, with around 40,000 impacts on the gas giant we circled, so much material would spray out of Sosahy that new rings and moons might form, some of which would fall onto our world later.

Even if there had been a hope of surviving the catastrophe of the Second Bombardment at all, every 216 years afterward, for at least five thousand years, the Intruder would strike again. Civilization was doomed, even in Palath; nothing could survive under the icy clouds, or in an atmosphere poisoned by huge volcanic eruptions, or under any of the thousands of other possible consequences.

The First Bombardment had been the most revolutionary event at least since the voyage of Wahkopem. It had led to the Great Rescue and to Reconstruction, as millions of Palathians had volunteered years of time and effort to save what was left of Shulath. Indirectly the First Bombardment had led to the abolition of slavery, home rule for Shulath, and at least some measure of equality. And the scientific effort to understand what had happened—and to do something about it—had brought about the scientific renaissance that had taken us from the crude aircraft, computers, radios, and electric monorails of that time to voyages into deep space and antimatter energy.

But no matter how big it had all been, it was dwarfed by what was coming. Colossal as the effects had been, the First Bombardment had been no more than a little warning tap, a little shake to get us to wake up, get out of bed, get moving. Whole lands thrown under the ocean, chains of islands reared up, great volcanoes that still thundered a hundred years later, smashed cities and scoured coasts—all that was not the main blow, but the merest touch of the Intruder's finger.

But for all that, it was part of Nisu's future, not mine. I would be dead before the Second Bombardment. And thus I was a lot more interested in what waited for us later that afternoon, in the screening room of the Mount Mebapasus Observatory—the newly compiled, first up-close images from a near flyby of Setepos, the new world we would be traveling to.

I don't know if the adults also felt the same way, or realized that we were bored, or perhaps the schedule was just that way anyway. After a while of having us all fidget around the old telescope, we were allowed to go down the mountain and into the main building, get out of squeeze suits, and sit down to wait for the presentation.

They took a long time in setting up, and we had to listen to several people talk about how they had gotten the flyby probe up to speed, about the poor quality of some of the pictures—about everything, except showing us pictures of where we were going. I fidgeted and squirmed, trying to behave myself, and Mejox—who wasn't trying at all—practically bounced out of his seat.

The adults weren't trying to control us, either, which meant they were just as impatient as we were.

Finally the astronomers admitted they might be ready, dimmed the lights, and began to show the pictures. The first pictures were familiar ones, from the long-distance fast flybys that had gone through the system just a few years before, showing us the basic information: eight planets, one double cometoid, and one belt of asteroids circling a single lone sun. Two of the planets had some potential for our survival there: the third and the fourth from the sun. The third one from the sun, which they had named Setepos, was one-fifth closer to Kousapex than we were to our own sun, but because that sun was cooler than ours, they actually got fourteen percent less light than Shulath did, or two percent less than Palath did.

Setepos had considerably more surface area, with a surface gravity somewhat less than ours. The atmosphere instruments on that first probe had detected water vapor, a temperature not too different from our own, a surface pressure like ours—and, most importantly, free nitrogen and oxygen. "Nitrogen and oxygen, at those temperatures, in the presence of water, would react with any number of things in the rocks and soil, and quickly leave the atmosphere," the science lecturer said, quite unnecessarily, since all of us had been over this many times. I thought Otuz would interrupt to tell him so, but Osepok put her hand on Otuz's shoulder before she could speak.

The science lecturer went on: "—so the only possible conclusion is that something is continuously liberating the oxygen and nitrogen, and that something is almost certainly living things. It's a living world, at least a little like our own.

"The fourth planet, on the other hand, showed mostly a very thin atmosphere of carbon dioxide, with some water; it seems a bit similar to Kahrekeif, except, of course, that there would never be anything to thaw it out. Still, in a crisis, some of us could survive there, and if we managed to take enough of our industrial plant with us, even live on it for generations, building a civilization with the materials there. But that would be a scheme of desperation, like certain very eccentric proposals that involve using captured parts of the shattered Intruder as raw materials for habitats entirely in space. I might note here that one of my more reckless colleagues—"

"Oh, come off that," a tall, thin, older Shulathian in the front row said. "It's merely my argument that if we *have* to build a habitat in space, we might as well build it where there's a lot of free solar power and materials are concentrated. Nobody's saying life in space would be better than on the surface of a planet, and I really hope the third planet works out, but if we were to decide it hadn't, we might as well build in the orbiting rocks and iron bodies, rather than go to all the bother of moving onto a planetary surface just to be pelted with sandstorms, wind, and hail. Once you have to make your own air, what's the advantage of being on a planet?"

Another three Shulathians seemed eager to argue with him, but then Osepok said, "I know you are all fine scientists, but it does occur to me that I have four children who are doing their best to behave patiently while you talk about all this, and it's the third planet we are interested in. Is it a suitable home or not—from what you can tell, I mean?"

Everyone sat down except for the chief lecturer. They all looked embarrassed. With a glare around the room, he said, "Well, I suppose . . . for the sake of the children . . . we could temporarily pass up some of the material about the fourth planet, since it is in fact not a terribly hospitable place. And since the results from the third planet are *quite* encouraging. We have a total of one hundred optical pictures, a radar map of all but the polar areas, and a large number of instrument readings, including results from twenty impact microprobes. To talk about that, we have Teacher Verkisus."

Verkisus was Shulathian, of course, and very elegant looking. He brushed down the long fluffs of hair below his pointed ears, thoughtfully stroked his long nose, and began by asking, "Would it perhaps be better if I just conducted this as a tour, rather than discussing all the fine points of theory and evidence?"

"Much better," Kekox said firmly.

"Not just for the children but for us," Soikenn added. "We will be the ones who will live out the rest of our lives there, after all. I can learn the pressure gradient and viscosity of the atmosphere on the way, if that's important; for right now, tell me about the place where I will live my last years."

Verkisus beamed at us. "That's really how I'd rather teach," he said. "I like a good story myself. Pull your seats up close to the screen, then, and I'll show you things as they come up in the story."

From then until the evening meal, we were enthralled. Teacher Verkisus was a natural storyteller, and as he warmed to his subject, it felt as if we were standing on the tiny probe that, just four and a half years before (it had taken that long for the radio signal to get back to us) had raced through the distant solar system.

There was no question now that Setepos was a living world, even though the probe had passed between the planet and its moon at such great speed that it crossed the diameter of that moon's orbit in less than a day. The probe's fifty-year voyage had, as its final purpose, one eightday of approach, one eightday moving away—and that single day close to Setepos.

But such an astonishing day.

It was a very different world from ours, it seemed to us. Where our world was a little under one-fifth dry land—and almost half of that was under the polar ice—Setepos was one-third dry land, and it looked like much more because there were large parts of the sea covered with ice. At first we were all a little horrified at how much ice there was, but Verkisus hastened to assure us that there was plenty of warm, comfortable land around the equator. "The best evidence is that they may have a very long cycle—30,000 years or more—of ice ages and warming periods, and it looks like they are just coming out of an ice age. The south pole there is very much like our polar continents, except that because of the smaller pressure gradient, the air would be breathable—though it's still terribly cold. In fact, where we have several volcanoes that stick out almost into space, none of Setepos's highest mountains even clear the troposphere. The gravity is eight-ninths of ours, and there's almost a third again as much area, but most of it is ocean—the ocean area is very nearly as large as our whole world. But that still leaves room for more than three times as much land as we have. That hook-shaped land mass is about the size of Palath—and as you notice, it's much smaller than the big land mass north and east of it. We've given the continents names, temporarily, but we certainly hope you'll eventually come up with names of your own. The huge one that stretches most of the way around the northern hemisphere, we call simply Big. The one south of it, just touching it, below that long irregular peninsula, we call the Hook, because it has those big bulges that make it look hook-shaped. West of the Hook, across the narrow ocean, is the Triangle. We had a hard time thinking of what the continent north of the Triangle should be, but finally someone pointed out that it had so many thin peninsulas and things jutting out that it looked sort of like a crushed insect—you know, legs sticking out in all directions—so we named it the Bug. And finally, southeast of Big, there's this flat piece of continent; since it's the only one entirely in the southern hemisphere, except at the pole, we called it Southland. Rename them any way you like, though."

After settling us into the basic geography, he produced the ten pictures that counted the most. The tiny probe weighed only about as much as a full-grown adult, but it had been blasted away toward Setepos with one hundred times its weight in fuel for its fusion drive. It had slowed down on a magnetic brake, just as we would, but because it was so important to get some kind of look before our ship departed, in the interests of getting it there in time they had still left it moving at enormous velocity.

As it whizzed by the planet, it had thrown out hundreds of optical sensors on long cables, each shooting twenty pictures per second and also recording its exact angle and position relative to the probe. Twenty microprobes had shot toward the planet, snapping pictures until they exploded in its upper atmosphere. The data had been compiled and recompiled to form as many accurate images as possible.

And the images were the kind of thing that could burn in your brain. Here, roaming the plains of the Bug, was a herd of animals, many tens of millions of them. There, on Big, was a sweep of forest as big as all Palath. There were easily twenty islands larger than the largest ones on our world. On the other hand, Setepos had no mountains as high as ours. It looked like there were very few volcanoes compared to our world, and where ours were scattered in long straight slashes across the oceans on the Shulath side, most of their volcanoes seemed to sit on the edges of their giant continents. "There's also a strange belt of hot spots running down the middle of the oceans," Verkisus said. "Everywhere we turn, more mysteries. But of course twenty-three years is a long time, and the probes we are launching now will get there much faster than you will. By the time you land, all sorts of mysteries will have been cleared up—which, in the nature of science, means you will have a *different* set of mysteries to work on."

One microprobe picture showed some kind of gigantic sea animals swimming with their backs exposed in warm waters off the Hook; an infrared photo showed a strange kind of forest, unknown on our world, that seemed to be extremely humid and very dense, appearing on the Triangle, the Hook, and the southern part of Big—all land masses near the equator. There was a huge desert drier than eastern Palath on the Hook, and the land masses themselves were scarred with deep canyons, and mountains that ran in long, twisted ridges utterly unlike the geometric lines of Shulath or the rough parallel streaks of Palath. "There's actually a theory," Verkisus said, "if you look at the way that the Hook fits into the Triangle, for example, that perhaps the land masses there are very slowly moving around. Something a little like that does happen on Toupox, in our own system; maybe Setepos is a more extreme case."

Setepos seemed to be endlessly varied—great fields of ice, warm seas, wide deserts, vast forests and plains, immense rivers, lower mountains but so many of them—all teeming with life.

I can't speak for anyone else, but that night I was so excited that I didn't sleep at all. I lay in my bed trying to imagine how there could be so many long rivers—a hundred or more that were longer than our Alpiax—or what it might be like under the tall trees of those hot, wet forests, or trying to picture the big, slow, low-energy waves that rolled over the ocean.

Verkisus had told us, too, that the faraway moon that hung in their sky induced tides at least six times as large as what we were used to. "If there were any sailors there," he said, "they'd have to really think about tides. If you look at these pictures of river mouths, you'll see how there are huge areas that look very green; we think that's because such big rivers deposit vast amounts of material at their mouths, and then the tides wash back and forth over that soil, feeding life there. Those areas must be swarming with life."

Something about that phrase—"swarming with life"—stayed with me. I thought of what a huge world it was, and how much more varied than ours it seemed to be. I made up strange forests and fields, and animals of hundreds of kinds.

When the sun came up I was very tired, but I think my eyes were still shining with excitement. Before that night I had not dreamed of Setepos as anything other than a sort of distant, "when-I-grow-up" kind of place, not unlike Mejox's palace or a seat on the General Court or any of those other dreams children had. Now—even though it would be a quarter year, fifteen eightdays, before we departed, and I would be a full adult for a long time before I got there—I was burning with eagerness to see the new world.

Soikenn noticed how excited I was and asked if I had a fever. When I tried to stammer out an explanation, she looked worried until Kekox said, "I felt the same way, once, about Kahrekeif." He looked sad when he said it.

In the long years after, I would often wonder if there had been any clue as to how differently things would turn out. Always I would arrive at the same conclusion. My thoughts had all been of joy and excitement. I had had no premonitions at all.

4

WE CHILDREN HAD BEEN TO SPACE TOGETHER FOUR TIMES BEFORE, SO weightlessness was no stranger to us. It wasn't even our first time aboard *Wahkopem Zomos*—just a few months before we had come up for an orbital shakedown, spending three eightdays swinging out into a big elliptical orbit around Sosahy to test the reaction engines. So we knew our way around the ship and what it would be like to live in it.

What we didn't know was that on the day of our departure from Nisuan orbit, we would find ourselves *bored*, sitting around in the common dining area, making up arguments to pass the time.

"I'd rather watch from the *rear*," Mejox said firmly. "The exhaust is really going to be the big show for the first part, and then the booster separation—"

Priekahm said, "That's where I'm going to watch from, too. Besides, won't that be the best place to catch our last view of home?"

"There aren't any adults around, so you don't have to play dumb," Otuz said crossly. Lately she had been angry all the time. "Who are you going to make big eyes at, anyway?"

Priekahm tensed, but then softly said, "Otuz, I know that Nisu will be visible as a disk for six days after we start, and that Sosahy is going to be visible to the naked eye for more than a year, and so forth. That's not what I meant. I mean it's the last time, until we're old, that we'll see Nisu filling the sky, that it will be something more than just a bright light in the dark. That's what I want to say good-bye to."

Otuz seemed about to jump on her again, so to keep the peace I stepped into the middle. "Orbits aren't at all simple. Just because we're leaving Nisu doesn't mean that it will be behind us all the time, or even most of the time. We'll be moving in big, looping curves, and Nisu will be on different sides of the ship at different times. Besides, once we drop the booster, they're going to spin the ship to give us gravity, so unless Nisu is directly behind us or dead ahead, you'll just get glimpses as the window spins by it."

Priekahm turned her big, warm smile on me, and once again I knew why she could always get her way with the adults. "Thank you, Zahmekoses. That was what I wanted to know."

"Sorry, Priekahm," Otuz muttered. The Palathian girl sighed. "I was taking my bad mood out on you. It wasn't a nice thing to say. We're all on edge, I guess. I wonder what happened to all of the 'too busy' that they said we'd be once we were onboard?"

We were all floating around in the common dining area, the place on the outer deck where we would eat, hold classes, and hang around with each other during free time—once they spun the ship to give us gravity. It was almost a big room, six bodylengths cubic, and was designed so that it was open to both the inner and outer decks, with spiral stairs descending from the inner deck entrances, so that the ceiling was twice as high above our heads. Supposedly this room would help us keep from becoming claustrophobic.

There were chairs on the floor below us, but because the ship's gravity would not start till after boost and spin-up, there was little point in sitting in them, or even in being near the floor. Instead, we floated in a loose clump in midair, about at the height of the inner deck entrances. We could see into the inner deck hallways, but not very far because they curved away from us.

Theoretically we should already have left, but all the important people in Palath's five royal families had to be recorded talking to the crew just before launch, and the more important ones had to go last, and among Palathian royalty you showed your stature by being late. While all this was going on there was plenty of time for a lot of last-minute suits, bills, motions, and petitions in the Shulathian General Court, a few of them trying to stop *Wahkopem Zomos* from leaving, but most just trying to delay it till the next launch window, thirty-two eightdays away, so that somebody's favorite sentence could be added to the mission's statement of principles. At least half of those motions and suits were not actually intended to work, but were strictly to impress some constituency or other.

Meanwhile we sat in orbit, watching the clock roll down on our launch window, while Kekox and Soikenn, in the conference room, talked with ground control and tried to find a moment when it was legally and politically possible for us to start, and Captain Osepok in the cockpit and Poiparesis in the observatory kept the ship's computers and general status updated and ready-to-go, so that when we got a chance we could take off right away. Absolutely nothing coming up from the ground made any real difference to the mission, since we would be in constant radio contact anyway for many years afterwards. But they all wanted to get their words, or motions, or whatever, into the history books as part of the departure of *Wahkopem Zomos*.

"At least we're not the adult crew," Mejox said. "They're all trying to fly the ship, answer stupid questions and orders from the ground, and argue with each other at the same time. It doesn't leave them much time for us."

We had been banished from everywhere that anything interesting was going on because we "might" make noise or get into trouble, or perhaps do something inappropriate in front of a recording device. (As if we hadn't been in front of recording devices all the time for the past few years!) So we were exactly where nothing was happening, left to amuse ourselves without actually doing anything. It was enough to make you wish for homework.

"So what window do *you* want, Zahmekoses?" Otuz asked. "You've been the only one that hasn't had an opinion."

"That's because I really don't have an opinion," I said. "I haven't decided. Probably I'll just take any old window. I guess I'm not fussy."

"I guess," Otuz said. She reached over and scratched my back gently, as she often did when she was feeling affectionate toward me. "Zahmekoses, if there were three bowls of stew and a bowl of rocks at dinner, you'd volunteer to choose last."

Mejox protested, "That's because Zahmekoses is such a good friend to all of us!"

"True," Otuz said. She scratched lower on my back, right where it felt best. "But he'd still end up with the bowl of rocks."

"Probably," I said. I think I was agreeing with her because I didn't want her to stop scratching. "But in this case I really don't have any preference, *really*. I can't imagine there's going to be a dull window anywhere on—"

A chime sounded, and then we heard Kekox's voice. "Are all you kids in the common dining area?"

"Yes, sir," we all said, almost in unison.

"All right, good. The clever people down on the ground seem to be about to let us go, and Captain Osepok informs me that we're ready to boost any minute. Get to an acceleration-protection spot, strap in, and stay there. If you need to get a drink or visit the head, do it *now*. Get moving."

We all said, "Yes, sir" again, and the intercom clicked off.

"Rear study room, outer deck?" Mejox asked.

"Sure," Priekahm answered. The two of them shot out the door into the passageway together, his squat Palathian body framed by her tall, slim Shulathian one.

"Were you thinking of anywhere in particular to watch from?" I asked Otuz. "I really *hadn't* made up my mind."

"Let's go to the computer lab."

I laughed. "That's the other area with a good rear view. So you just argued with Mejox to annoy him?"

"Can you think of a better reason to argue with Mejox? Besides, if he needs somebody to agree with him, there's always Priekahm. Come on, let's get strapped in—I'd rather not start out by splatting against a bulkhead."

Since they had gone out to the right, along the outer deck, we went left, along the inner deck.

Our little private chambers all had windows, but those were small, and besides, by unspoken agreement, we all wanted to share the departure—the beginning, really, of everything that would be important in our lives—with our friends.

Otuz and I swam above the inner deck through the narrow passageway to the computer lab, which had the two things we needed: acceleration webbing and a big rearview port.

Wahkopem Zomos was a stubby cylinder, wider than it was long and about as tall as a four-story building, inside a wide ring that surrounded its base and extended about one fourth as high as the cylinder. We lived in the ring—once we were on our way, the ship would be spun along its axis, so that the outer edge of the ring formed the outer deck, with the gravity we were used to, and an interior deck formed the inner deck, with about four-fifths of Nisuan gravity, a little less than the gravity would be on Setepos when we got there.

Yet despite the apparent size from the outside, quarters were fairly cramped inside. The entire central cylinder was devoted to the ship's farm, sail room, power plant, and lander storage; life support, waste recycling, general storage, and everything else took up more than half of the ring. So we actually only lived in the outermost part of the ring, on a double deck that barely had head clearance for Poiparesis. And many parts of the living space were things like the cockpit and the biological laboratory that couldn't be used for much of anything else and weren't used most of the time. Even with all that space in the ship, at the time, as a child, I could already span my compartment with my outstretched hands.

Inside the central cylinder were the power plant, the reaction engines, the recycling system, the ship's farm, and the squat, dark forms of the two landers, *Gurix* and *Rumaz*. Though it would be almost twenty-four years until we used them, they were always there, reminding us of what we were intending to do. The forward third of the cylinder was taken up with the sail, brakeloop, shrouds, and winches to operate them.

Otuz and I climbed into the acceleration webbing, checked each other's fastenings, and settled in to wait. Probably there would be another delay or two before we got started.

There were acceleration webs nearly everywhere on the ship—light-weight, closed-top hammocks of strong webbing that would distribute the load, secured to a pole by a rotating cuff so that they could swing freely with the acceleration. It had been necessary because preliminary surveys had indicated that we would need to do a few rapid course corrections on the way out—at peak velocity, one-third of lightspeed, even a grain of sand striking the ship could be a disaster, and radar might not see it till we were within minutes of a hit. Thus there had to be some way to quickly and safely tie ourselves down when the collision alarm sounded.

From the standpoint of us kids, this had meant that during the ship's early boost phase, we had a wide variety of places where we could safely be.

We strapped in with our faces pointed into the webbing, so that we could see through the gaps, because we knew that with the boost coming from the rear, the hammocks would swing so that their bottoms pointed toward the rear viewport. Now we floated next to each other, peering through the webbing, waiting for the big rocket behind us to fire.

"You wouldn't really have splatted against the bulkhead, you know," I told Otuz. "The acceleration on this thing isn't all that high. They just don't want us twisting an ankle or getting hit by falling junk that someone forgot to put away. It won't even get over one gravity of acceleration till the last half hour. It's not like a regular rocket at all."

Otuz nodded. "I know. I was exaggerating for effect, Zahmekoses. You're always so serious."

"It sort of comes naturally."

I must have sounded defensive, because she reached through the webbing and grabbed my hand. "I kind of like it. You really like the lessons and studying, don't you?"

"Yeah. So do you."

"Mejox and Priekahm—" she said, and hesitated.

"I know, they'd be just as glad if we never had to learn a thing more. It's okay, it's not that I can't see things about people, you know; it's just that I kind of know how delicate things are and I have to watch myself, so I don't usually say anything," I explained.

"It doesn't seem fair," Otuz said. "Just because I'm a princess I can say anything I want about anybody. But you have to watch out for Mejox because he's royalty, and you have to stick together with Priekahm because she's the other Shulathian, and—"

"It's all right, really," I said. "I *could* still be back at the orphanage, hoping to qualify someday for a job as a mechanic or a dentist. And I really do like all of you, so it's not that hard to be polite and watch out for what I say. Don't worry about it too much."

"It's still not fair," she said.

"Boost imminent," Osepok's voice said from the intercom.

We turned to look out the big view port. Behind the ship, connected by a long, thin pole, was a big structure of struts and tanks, a third as wide as the ship and five times as long: the booster. It filled most of the window, shining silver in the harsh light of space. For a long breath or two nothing happened. Then a glow appeared behind the booster and spread to fill the rest of the window.

There was no sound, of course, with no air to carry it; just the purplish-white glow. We sank into the webbing, and the hammocks swung around so that our faces were pointed down toward the view port as the ship began to accelerate. Moment by moment, we felt ourselves gaining weight, sinking deeper into the hammocks.

Ordinary spacecraft had to take off from Nisu's surface, starting with no velocity and fighting directly against gravity; they had to accelerate at about one and a half times the acceleration of gravity, increasing to three gravities, for periods of a thirty-second of a day or more, to leap up to orbit. But *Wahkopem Zomos* was already in orbit around Nisu, and Nisu was orbiting Sosahy; we could begin with a gentler thrust and let it run for a third of a day.

At first the thrust was pushing *Wahkopem Zomos*, plus all those tanks and struts in the booster, *plus* the immense weight of fuel, thirteen times the weight of the ship itself. The ship and booster sped up very slowly. But with each passing instant, more of the fuel was gone, and yet the engines pushed just as hard. Acceleration increased, and the webs pressed harder against our faces.

The glare we saw was hydrogen plasma, heated far beyond the point where its electrons and protons stayed together, so that it was a mere thin wisp of atomic particles. By weight the booster was almost all liquid hydrogen, and the rest was the assembly of girders, tanks, and pipes that held it together—but a tiny fraction of the total mass, held in one small compartment that any of us could have picked up and carried with one hand, was the key to the whole thing: antimatter. Mix liquid hydrogen just above absolute zero with one millionth of its weight in antimatter, and it became hydrogen plasma hotter than the core of the sun.

Had we been outside, looking directly at the glow instead of seeing it through a shielded viewport, we would have been blinded; on Nisu below us, people had to be warned not to look directly at our boost out of orbit, and we briefly lit up the sky so brightly that night animals went back to their dens and plants opened their leaves to what they thought was sunrise.

We hung there in the webbing for a long time, getting steadily heavier as the acceleration increased. The glare that danced around and behind the booster flickered and wavered in colored sheets, endlessly fascinating against the black of space, as occasional stars shone through it and now and then a glimpse of Nisu or Sosahy would appear as we swung outward in our escape orbit.

It was always changing and yet always there, like a flame, and in the same way that after you watch a campfire for a while with an old, close friend, you begin to talk seriously, Otuz and I eventually slipped back into conversation. "Thank you for inviting me," I said. "I'm glad to have someone to see this with."

"Well, I didn't want you just moping in your compartment, with no friends," she said. She was still holding my hand; I looked at the thick brown fur on her heavy forearm, next to the soft tan-yellow skin on my long slim one. "You've seemed kind of lost these last couple of eightdays, since Mejox and Priekahm have gotten so tight with each other. I mean, ever since you started standing up for yourself—"

I was surprised. "I didn't know that I *was* standing up for myself. Or that I wasn't before." A great cascading pink sheet rippled across the plasma outside, and we paused to watch it rip into pieces and vanish in little dark blue pulses.

"Really?" Otuz said. "You don't notice a difference? Priekahm and I certainly do. A few eightdays ago when we were on the last big tour of Nisu, just before we crossed over to visit Shulath, all of a sudden you stopped pacing yourself to hang just behind Mejox and started setting

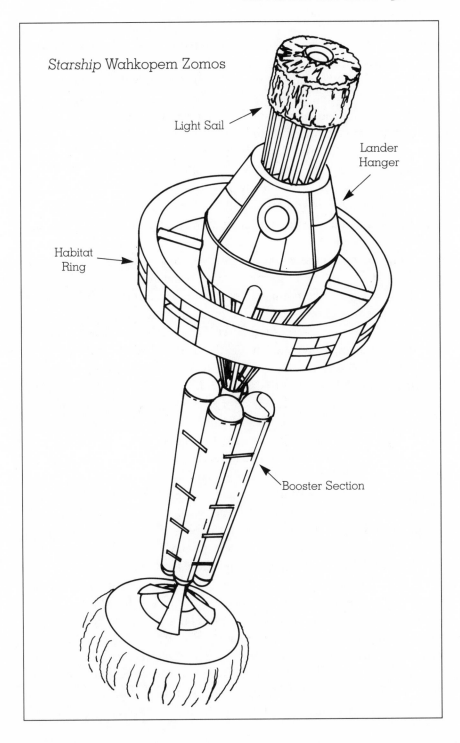

Starship Wahkopem Zomos

Light Sail

Lander Hanger

Habitat Ring

Booster Section

the pace for the rest of us. It was like overnight you just stopped being afraid of him. I guess he must not have liked that—he doesn't deal very well with people disagreeing with him or showing him up, you know. I mean he's very loyal and he doesn't mean to be that way, but he gets angry and mean when he comes out behind. And then you just stopped worrying about it and let him sulk. I thought it was great."

"I didn't even notice," I said. "Maybe I just got some more confidence or something. You don't think he's still mad at me or anything? He *is* my friend and I don't want bad feelings between us."

"He'll get over it, if he's really your friend. Anyway, it's no big surprise that Priekahm is around him all the time now. He likes people to suck up to him, and she doesn't know what to do with herself if she isn't sucking up to somebody."

"That's nasty," I pointed out. A great streamer of orange swayed across the viewport for a moment, seeming to curl around the crescent of Sosahy.

"It's also true. I like them, believe it or not. I just don't think I have to lie to myself—or you—about what my friends are like."

I didn't answer because I was watching another green sheet shimmer and twist. Besides, I had suddenly realized what had caused what Otuz thought was my "sudden change." After Kekox had warned Mejox not to beat me up for doing better than he did, I had been afraid Mejox would be punished again just for doing better than me. So I had been careful to stay well ahead of him wherever I could. I'd even shown Mejox up in front of adults now and then, just to be on the safe side.

But I had thought he would be relieved not to be punished. It hadn't occurred to me that he wouldn't know that I knew . . .

Were we still friends? With most of our lifetimes ahead of us, I hoped so.

A great red and orange ball, silent like all the others, big as a large mountain, billowed out of the booster exhaust, then abruptly vanished as if it had been turned off. Otuz made a gulping noise in her throat.

"Beautiful," I agreed. "What a way to say good-bye."

We watched the dark, and felt our increasing weight sink into the webbing, but she didn't say anything more and I drifted back into my thoughts. It was true, now that I thought about it, that Mejox had been spending a lot of time with Priekahm. But after all, our friendships waxed and waned all the time. Ever since we had become fully conscious and articulate, around the age of four, we had been together, constantly discovering each other, clashing over this and banding together over that. Mejox and I had been close for almost a year, but still, when we had first arrived at the training base, Priekahm had been my closest friend. If Mejox was fading, well, Otuz and I now had more in common, since we both liked school much better than the others did. There would be a lot of years, I thought, and we would all be friends of one kind or another for a long time.

I hoped. I couldn't help thinking that Mejox *did* hold grudges a long time.

Had I offended him by not lagging behind him, as I'd done before? But if I hadn't, Kekox would have surely hit him again.

Or was this whole thing Otuz's imagination? Priekahm often saw things between people that weren't there—usually very dramatic things . . . was Otuz the same way, was it something all girls did? I suddenly missed my closeness with Mejox; he had been rude and pushy but comprehensible. I wondered if I would have to wait for twenty years or more, till puberty hit, before I would understand girls.

Otuz was staring at me. "I didn't mean to upset you," she said. "Are you all right?"

"Just thinking."

The last part of the acceleration seemed like the longest; there were just as many bright colors and interesting effects, but by now most of the fuel mass was gone, and the acceleration was much greater, so we sank deep into the webbing face-first. It wasn't terribly uncomfortable, and because the mesh was wide we could breathe and see, but it wasn't as pleasant as it had been.

Finally, the weight ceased all at once. "Remain in your webbing," Osepok reminded us over the intercom. "Engine shutdown is complete, but we're preparing to jettison the booster."

A long minute crawled by, and then a bright light flashed far out on the long spar connecting us to the booster. The explosive retaining ring had blown, and the now useless assemblage of tanks and engines was falling away from us. Briefly, a small rocket motor on it flared to life, to kick it safely into an orbit that would crash it into the Sun—since there would be so many operations in space in the next century, it was vital to keep space junk to a minimum. With a slight thud, the ship expelled the spar from its rear attachment, and that too whirled off into space.

The explosive separation, the falling away, and the boost of the small motor all happened in complete silence. The only sound I could hear was Otuz breathing softly beside me. The acceleration webbing hung loosely, and we floated freely on the tethering lines.

As the booster fell away behind us, there, hanging in the sky, was Sosahy, cut neatly into a dark and a light side by the terminator line. The gas giant was strangely shrunken, as much as it had been during the shakedown cruise, and as we watched, suddenly a crescent wedge formed on the curved side of the great bow of light that the day side of Sosahy made in the sky. Rapidly the much smaller curve grew to a half-circle, and if we squinted we could just see a few dark dots peeping through the clouds and water—a little bit of the Windward Islands or the Ring. By the naked eye at this distance it was hard to tell.

"Priekahm will be insufferable," Otuz said. "It's right where she thought it would be."

The intercom crackled again. "All right, everyone stay in place for one more thing."

There was a faint rumble through *Wahkopem Zomos*, and the ship began to vibrate; we could feel it even through the web. Then Sosahy and Nisu began to roll over in the view port, faster and faster. Captain Osepok was using the attitude jets to spin the ship up to speed for the voyage. Our acceleration webs stretched and settled toward the deck. A few moments later, the captain gave permission, and we unfastened ourselves. We slipped out of the webbing and put our feet on the inner deck, standing up carefully. Outside the view port, Sosahy and Nisu looped crazily around each other, but the ship was big enough so that we did not feel ourselves spinning—rather, it was the sky outside the viewport that spun.

We were on our way.

5

IT TOOK TWENTY-EIGHT DAYS FOR US TO FALL INTO OUR CLOSE APPROACH to the Sun. In a sense, those twenty-eight days were the first "normal" ones in our lives—if "normal" means "the way things are supposed to be for most of your life." Seventy years in all—twenty-four on the outward voyage, five exploring Setepos, and forty-one on the return trip—would be spent in the ship, with only ourselves for company. This was the first taste of our daily routine.

Not surprisingly, Otuz and I adapted to it better than Mejox and Priekahm. We tended to like studying and reading anyway, so now that we didn't have to stand in front of people and cameras all the time, and could spend a whole day concentrating, we were at no loss for amusement. Often, after a brief conversation with whichever adult was relevant to the subject, Otuz and I would simply tackle something we both wanted to learn, and would spend most of the rest of the day in companionable silence, working in the labs, running computer simulations, or assembling and reading a group of documents. Usually, late in the day, Kekox would have to remind us that we needed to put in our time in the gym and then get dressed for the short presentation that we radioed back to Nisu every day.

Meanwhile Mejox and Priekahm worked out extra sessions in the gym, played make-believe games, and did assigned homework under the supervision of one or more adults. They didn't seem to be able to take off for a day and work on something just because it was interesting. More and more, Mejox spent his time studying history with Kekox, doing the bare minimum in science, math, and arts; I could hardly have condemned him for it since I spent most of my time in math and science, only doing enough history to stay out of trouble. Once, I overheard Kekox and Soikenn discussing it; as always, I listened in—adults got very weird about being overheard, so I was careful to stay out of sight, but after all, those four people ran our universe, and we tried to know what they were thinking whenever we could.

I didn't know why they thought our specialization was so interesting, but after worrying about it for several minutes, they both seemed to agree that we would outgrow this phase, and take a "more balanced" approach later. "It doesn't matter much what the order is as long as they learn," Soikenn said.

Kekox sighed. "I guess it's not so much the over-concentration that worries me as it's the reasons for it," he said. "I wish I could get Mejox to quit thinking about what he'll need when he's emperor, or about all this romantic adventure stuff he's going to do on Setepos and how it will look to the people at home. We had an expression in the Imperial Guard about not planning the victory parade until you've been to the battle, and it seems to me that's just what he's doing."

Soikenn laughed. "Where I come from we call that 'accepting the prize before you do the experiment.' He's young, Kekox; it's still more than twenty years before he even hits puberty. No doubt he'll have other annoying habits in the future, and lose some of the ones he has now. You have to let kids be kids."

Kekox grunted. "Yeah. The trouble is some people have let the last couple of emperors be kids. It would be a great joke on everybody if Otuz ended up as empress."

"She's brilliant," Soikenn pointed out, "and she does her work. She'd probably be as good at that as she is at everything else."

"She'd get all the decisions made before noon so she could have the afternoon to read. And they'd be good decisions. Oh, well, all of us will be dead before we see any of it happen."

"Now there's a cheerful thought," Poiparesis said, joining them.

"Kekox is trying to stop the crumbling of civilization," Soikenn said. "Practically all by himself."

"So the subject is Mejox," Poiparesis said.

Both of them laughed, and the subject changed to trivia, and then to those inscrutable jokes about sex that adults liked. It sounded like the interesting part was over, so I got up and casually walked past the door. Kekox was muttering something in hushed tones.

I was almost out of earshot when I heard Poiparesis say, "Well, it's a risk that no one thought of. But they're all twenty years from mating. For right now there's no harm in their all just being friends. And it happens that our two serious students are Otuz and Zahmekoses, which sort of leaves the other two at loose ends."

I froze and leaned back against the wall. It had never occurred to me that things might be that way, that Otuz and I might be excluding Mejox, but as soon as it was mentioned I could see a dozen ways I had done it—I was interested in things that he wasn't, I pushed on in academic stuff faster than he could go, and I was often off by myself.

Well, I could fix some of that. I had gotten to enjoy my freedom to learn as fast as I could, and I wasn't going to pretend anymore that he was the smarter one—he himself wouldn't have believed it—but I could make some time for him, be a better friend . . . I turned, headed the other way, and nearly collided with the captain.

Very softly, she said, "What are they talking about in there?"

"Mejox," I said. I couldn't have lied to the captain to save my life, and just then that was what I thought was at stake.

She gave me a strange little smile. "Of course. It would be. Has it occurred to you that if you do anything about what you hear, they will know you listened?"

I gulped. "I wasn't going to—"

"That's right, you're not going to. Mejox Roupox is your friend. He's not your job. He needs to find his own way through life. You've done nothing wrong and you've consistently been a better friend to him than he deserves. Keep being his friend—but if we catch you making yourself his slave, both of you will be sorry."

That made me so angry, I actually talked back to the captain. "I'm not *anyone's* slave," I said.

Her hands landed lightly on my shoulders. She drew a long breath. "No," she said at last, "you're right. There are no slaves anymore." Then she smiled very slightly and added, "But it's very clear to me that you're Poiparesis's student."

I didn't know what she meant by that, but she let me go, so I tried not to worry about it—I already had enough to worry about.

All the training in the world could not have prepared us for what it was like to round the Sun. This time we had no choice about where to be—acceleration webbing couldn't possibly have held us against the accelerations we would be taking. Furthermore, passing so close to the Sun, most of the ship itself was going to be uninhabitable; only life support, the ship's farm, some delicate scientific equipment, and the crew shelter on the inner deck could be kept at a comfortable temperature. The rest would get hot enough to sear flesh, and was being filled with an inert-gas atmosphere to keep flammable objects from exploding.

As Poiparesis was strapping us in, he went over his explanation again. "Understand this is the most danger we will all ever be in, at least until it's time for the return flight. And—" he turned to Priekahm, who seemed about to complain again "—we do have to make this close pass at the Sun, and then another one at Zoiroy. Almost one-fifth of our total speed is going to come from doing this, and the only way to get such a big boost is to go in very close, where our light sail can do the most good. So we have to do this, and it is going to be very uncomfortable, and if anything goes wrong with the cooling and energy dissipation systems, we are all going to burn. That's just the way it is."

I imagined Priekahm was still pouting, but I couldn't see her. I had stretched out and was snugged far down in my own acceleration couch.

The couches had been designed to fit our bodies exactly and to support specific bones and internal organs; we had all just had an incredibly uncomfortable procedure to fill our bowels and body cavities with support liquid, a nasty gelatinous goo. The fact that Soikenn had administered it, and had been very gentle and sympathetic, hardly compensated for having needles jabbed into us and being squirted full of the heavy liquid while another needle sucked out air.

Once we were all in position on the couches, the mouthpieces that would protect our teeth and tongues went in next. If anyone was going to whine or complain, the chance had gone by.

"Bite down hard," Soikenn said. I did, and that triggered the mechanism; tiny clamps grabbed my teeth and a lever slid out of the mouthpiece to push my tongue flat against the floor of my mouth. Soikenn bent over the indicators as she pushed the button to take me to full IV. A moment later I felt the needle slide between my ribs and into the thick clump of veins behind my blood mixer, deep in my back.

"Looks good," Poiparesis said, joining Soikenn at the monitor stand, and triggered the support system; from now until it was time to release me, the needle sticking into my circulatory system would supply oxygen and sugar, and carry away carbon dioxide. I no longer needed to breathe through my lungs.

The two of them watched the dial for what seemed a long time, until they were satisfied that they could trigger the next step. Finally they gestured agreement, and started the process.

Until you've experienced it there's no sensation anywhere like having your lungs filled with fluid. The suction pulled the air out abruptly, and I felt my reflexes try to stop it. Then the suppressor, a tiny electrode wired into the back of my brain, kicked in, and my diving and asphyxiation reflexes were suppressed.

This meant I wasn't in a panic anymore, but it did nothing for comfort. Cool glop flowed out of the tube and down into my lungs as the air was gradually taken up; it felt like a hideous chest cold.

I lay there listening while they did it to all of the others. A peculiar sob/scream noise for a few seconds must have been Priekahm; it sounded like her suppressor wasn't quite working and fluid had started to flow into her lungs without it, so that she was panicking and choking. There were quick, hasty footsteps, Poiparesis's soothing voice, Soikenn's low murmur, and then I heard Soikenn say "I think I have it working now" and Poiparesis add "Looks good, she'll be fine."

That completed getting us into the bunks. "Now," Poiparesis said, "last review. The ship will be running robotically for about a fifth of a day. The worst will be over after the first twelfth of a day, but do *not* try to get out of your couches until you're allowed to. Remember that although you can lift several times your body weight with your thigh and hip muscles, most of your body is too delicate to take so much force.

"I'm afraid the only amusement we can offer you is the screen over your couches, which will be showing you some scenes from outside. You'll miss the most dramatic part anyway, first of all because you'll probably black out—I hope so, because that's about the most comfortable thing that can happen—and secondly because even if you do manage to stay awake, your eyes will distort under the force of the acceleration.

"I'm afraid during the high acceleration you will be just about as alone as you'll ever be—even though the rest of us are only a body-length away, no one will be able to reach you.

"I know you'll all be brave about it, and if it's any consolation, the pass at Zoiroy will be much more gentle than this one. And remember that everyone back on Nisu is holding their breath right now; if billions of prayers to the Creator and to Mother Sea can do us any good, we have them. Now I have to get to work on securing the adult crew and myself; I'm sorry I can't be with you right up to when the acceleration starts. If I have any advice at all, it's to try to sleep through the whole thing. Think about squeezing that anesthesia button! See you for our next meal."

Then he passed out of sight from my acceleration couch. The support liquid felt like the worst case of constipation I'd ever had in my life and I couldn't imagine how Poiparesis was enduring having to walk and move, filled with it, while he got the adults secured.

He had told us many times that we ought to just sleep through it. Even now I had only to extend one finger toward the anesthesia button by my left side, and I would be knocked unconscious within a minute or so. At peak acceleration, the brief period when we would be pulling more than twenty times the force of gravity, I would not be able to move that finger, so if I found I really couldn't stand it, it would be too late then.

But none of us had had any patience for the idea of going through the most dangerous part of the voyage—and the part that only two people, Steraz and Baibarenes, the test crew, had been through before—asleep in bed. Or at least that's what we all said. It suddenly occurred to me that Poiparesis had rigged things so that if one of us decided to be unconscious, none of the others need ever know.

The balance organ in my forehead was hurting, so I snorted hard to clear it. That drew more liquid into my lungs, and though the IV oxygenator was working fine, it still triggered a spasm in my chest. I could feel all of my hearts pounding, and there was an unpleasant gurgle from my blood mixer; I shook myself and the sloshy gurgle subsided. I could hear the others snorting and sloshing, and the sound was so funny I began to giggle, snort, and slosh as loudly as I could. Pretty soon we were all giving a whole concert with our internal organs, and then Poiparesis said, "All right, everyone, we all know what noises you can make, now stop that!"

We subsided into occasional giggles, and now and then Mejox would softly snort, which would send us all off into laughter again—a sound that grew higher in pitch as the liquid slowly filled our lungs. I don't know if Poiparesis was too busy to do anything about it, or had decided to let us get our high spirits out of our systems.

At last we heard the captain's voice, from her couch. "All right, everyone, let me just remind you all that I expect everyone to bear up well, but courage has nothing to do with this—it's out of our control—and all we have to do is survive. I know you'll bear it with patience. I have complete confidence in you, as does everyone back home on Nisu. And now I'll put in my mouthpiece before Poiparesis comes around and makes me do it. Good luck!" Before she switched off her microphone, we heard the gurgle of liquid into her lungs. It set us all giggling—or rather sloshing—again.

Long ages crept by and I watched my screen. I itched in a couple of places and quickly scratched those, always watching the clock on the screen to make sure that it wasn't too close to sail deployment. Poiparesis had told us that if we got a hand trapped under ourselves, very likely we would break every bone in that hand and in our wrists, and give ourselves deep bruises in whatever flesh lay across the hand.

Time crawled by slowly. The screen showed the sun bloated and swollen, almost as large as Sosahy seen from Nisu's surface; the filters over the cameras meant we were seeing less than one ten-millionth of the actual brightness outside, and yet the screen was becoming uncomfortably bright to look at.

If we had tried to use a rocket, to have made the trip to Setepos and returned within our lifetime would have taken a vastly larger ship that would have had to be almost all antimatter. As it was we had burned virtually all the antimatter of Nisu, nine years of production, in our booster at takeoff, and the speed it had gotten us up to would have taken tens of thousands of years to get us to Setepos. We needed more power than all of Nisu produced in a year, and we needed it early in the trip so that we could travel as much of it as possible at high speed.

The solution was a light sail: a huge, flat parachute made of a super-thin weave of beryllium and boron, only about three hundred atoms thick.

Light exerts pressure. Ordinarily the pressure is so slight we don't feel it, but if it's exerted by a really bright light on a really large surface, it adds up.

The sail for *Wahkopem Zomos* was wider across than the Ring Island, and all the billions of people on Nisu lying down on it wouldn't have covered a twentieth of its surface area. But I had held scraps of the sail material in my hand, and they were so light that they couldn't be felt. In essence the sail was one big beryllium-boron molecule, the individual atoms woven in an intricate matrix that was stronger than any other material (except for the spun-diamond shroud lines that held it to our ship) and yet so thin that if you put a sheet of it next to the ceiling in an ordinary room and let it drop, its air resistance was so much greater than its weight that it might spend an eightday spiraling down to the floor.

We would use this wisp of a sail first to catch the fury of the sun, kicking us up to fourteen times our current speed, and then to pick up another kick in our close pass by Zoiroy, so that as we left the system we would be moving at over twenty times our present speed. Then we would move onto the beam of the giant laser that had been built in solar orbit, and that would speed us up until at peak we were moving at two-fifths the speed of light, just about eighteen years from now. All of the energy required to reach such a tremendous speed—ninety times what the whole world of Nisu used in a year—would be caught and handled by that thin film of woven atoms.

The clock crawled downward. The outside temperature on the ship was just below the point where we would have begun to glow cherry red, and the antenna of our reradiation system, which carried heat from the ship surface into a high-temperature collection system and then got rid of the energy as short-wavelength electromagnetic radiation, was glowing a strange deep violet color whenever the camera looked at it; most of the energy was now radiating away as ultraviolet light.

Still the compartment was growing warmer and warmer, even though we were in one of the coolest parts of the ship.

I was afraid to scratch, and one of my legs was itching fiercely. I watched the last thin wedge of remaining time, a mere thousandth of a day, vanish from the dial.

The view shifted to the forward camera. A streak shot out in front of the ship—the rocket to deploy our sail. Then a long silvery strand, pointing straight ahead, became visible—this was the sail itself, not yet unfolded, looking like an ultrafine wire reaching into infinity. A forty-eighth of a day crept by as it spun out from the spool. The distant glare of the rocket motor dwindled to nothing, and still the sail kept streaking out in front of us.

Finally a large white lump—the nuclear-fusion charge at the base of the furled sail—shot out into space, taking only an 8192nd of a day to zip out farther than we could see and reminding us just how fast the rocket still pulling the sail was going. After the charge, the shroud lines—hundreds of strings of spun diamond—followed the same line out into space. These were transparent, so that rather than shining in the sun like the sail, they glimmered and flickered. The shroud lines were so fine, yet so strong, that they would cut right through steel with a touch—the winches on which they were wound had to be jacketed with woven spun diamond. All of this took a long time. I could probably have scratched, I told myself, if I had realized how long the sail would take to deploy, but it was certainly too late now.

I thought I couldn't endure watching the glistening stream pour into black space for one instant longer. It went on, flickering white-hot once it cleared the ship's shadow and moved into the three-million-times normal sunlight, far out in front of the ship so that we seemed to be on a thin line to infinity. Time crawled by. A brilliant white silent flash, like a sudden star, announced that the little nuclear-fusion charge had been set off to deploy the sail.

The bright star in the viewscreen widened into a circle, swelling quickly. The nuclear-fusion charge had been reflected from the inside mirror surface of the sail, and the pressure of its light shoved the sail open at enormous speed. As I stared up at the viewscreen, the sail spread across it, over and over, a dozen times in the space of a single breath as the view kept scaling up to get the whole sail onto the screen. Each time it scaled up it darkened, as the filters compensated for more and more intense light being reflected back toward us.

The couch swung on its pivot and settled with my back pointing toward the rear of the ship, as "down" changed all but instantly from outward to rearward. The screen scaled up twice more and became stable. I felt a low vibration through my back as the blast of sunlight caught the open sail and flung it wide open, the shroud lines yanking the ship closer to it.

I thought of squeezing the button for anesthesia, but I wanted to know what this would be like—

Acceleration rammed me deep into the couch and kept increasing. Too late. I could no longer lift my hand. The force pulled my face backward, my lips sliding over my mouth guard. The liquid in my lungs was no longer uncomfortable, but welcome, as it held my chest open against the fierce pressure.

I felt as if I were pressed between blocks of stone. I fought for breath; even with the added pressure it took great effort to force my chest to expand. My eyes began to ache, I had trouble blinking to relieve their dryness, and it was getting dark around the edges of my vision. The mouthpiece felt like a giant piece of lead jammed into my jaws. I thought about how hard I was being pressed into the couch and then couldn't focus enough attention even for that.

The world became dark gray, and then sank to black.

At first all I knew was that I was beginning to dream again. I dreamed I lay on my back, and Mejox was piling rocks on top of my chest. I couldn't breathe and I couldn't cry out to him to stop. I looked up at his face and saw that he seemed to be in agony himself, that he didn't want to do this to me, that it was all a mistake—

First dim gray. Then shapes. I began to be able to think, a little, and though my eyes ached and I was troubled by abrupt flashes of light (they said those would happen from the stresses on the vision center in the brain), I was able to see the screen and its clock a little. I had been unconscious for more than a sixteenth of a day. I was still almost nine times as heavy as normal, and it wouldn't be safe to move, but I seemed to be all right, though I felt as if I had been beaten all over with a heavy stick and then rolled under a huge wheel.

Finally the indicator lights showed that I could expel the liquid from my lungs. I clicked the control button to tell the machinery yes, do it, by all means.

Instantly the suction through my mouthpiece began to take up liquid; I felt my chest spasming and struggling as it collapsed, but the pain was welcome as the liquid was pulled out of me. Then the tongue depressor and tooth grips released, and the mouthpiece lay inert on my face, still intrusive, but no longer forcing its way in.

The suction had only removed most of the support liquid; the rest came up in a savage fit of coughing, hard gutwrenching coughs followed by deep painful whoops for the hot, foul air. It was still, comparatively, wonderful.

At last my coughing subsided into occasional hard hacks, and I could pay a little more attention to my surroundings. The others around me were also just coming out of their coughing.

My lungs felt as if I had just had severe pneumonia, or been rescued from a near-drowning. But much as they burned and stung, it was a wonderful relief. At last I could breathe, and think.

The velocity gauge showed that we had multiplied our speed by a factor of ten, and it was still rising. I lay back and thought, *The worst is over.* Now all it would take would be patience.

It took a lot of patience. For the next twelfth of a day, there was nothing to see but the pictures of the sail and the sun behind us. The sun, mercifully, was shrinking, and the sail was growing less bright, but though that was good, it was hardly enough to keep a person amused for the long time I lay there, still weighing too much to safely move.

When acceleration was down to four times normal gravity, Poiparesis's voice said, "Do *not* try to sit up, but you can now remove your mouthpieces if you like."

My arm, four times its normal weight, at first seemed impossible to lift, but with an effort I raised it, gripped my mouthpiece, and pushed it upward away from me.

"Don't forget," Poiparesis added, "the relation between weight and inertia is different. Things are hard to lift, but they still have the same momentum you're used to."

I let my arm sink beside me and breathed the comfortable cabin air; outside temperature had dropped almost back to normal, internal cooling had taken hold, and from the other numbers crawling across the screen it appeared that the ship had come through unharmed. "All right," Poiparesis said, "now that we've all breathed—how is everyone?"

"Fine here," the Captain said.

"Fine," Poiparesis said, and Soikenn said, "Sore, but nothing serious."

"I'm all right," I said.

"Me, too," Priekahm added, and then Otuz asked, "Does being really bored count as damage?"

Poiparesis laughed. "If it does, we're all dead. Mejox, are you all right?"

The answer was just slow enough in coming so that I dreaded it before I heard it. "Uh, uh . . . "

"Are you all right?" Poiparesis repeated.

Mejox's voice was strained and unhappy. "I got, uh, caught, trying to scratch, just when the charge went off. I thought I could do it and my leg itched so much—"

"Mother Sea's blood," Poiparesis said, softly. I had never heard him swear before. "Is there any bleeding?"

"Not that I can tell. Can I try to raise my head and look?"

"*Very* slowly," Poiparesis said. "Come up slowly, take one look, *gently* bring your head back to the couch, and then tell us what you saw."

There was a long moment while we all worried, and then Mejox said, "I am not bleeding, but there's a great big lump on the side of my thigh, and it hurts too much to try to move my hand out from under myself. I'm sorry, Poiparesis, I didn't mean to break the rules but I thought—"

Poiparesis sighed. "I'm not worried about the rules, I'm worried about your condition. I bet it must hurt a lot."

"Yeah," Mejox said. There was a trace of a sniffle in his voice.

"I'm going over to him," Kekox said.

"No, you're not." Captain Osepok's voice was absolutely firm. "You could easily break your spine doing that."

"But—"

"No buts," Soikenn said. "Mejox is a big kid and he's hurt, but he's not dying. Mejox, it's going to be at least a twenty-fourth of a day before we can get to you, and a lot longer than that before we can do much for you. That's a long time to lie there in pain. I think you'd better just give yourself a shot of anesthesia. Can you reach the button?"

"Yeah. It's the other hand that got hurt." There was a long pause, and when he spoke again it was slurred. "I didn't mean to break the rules!"

"That doesn't matter now," Poiparesis said gently. "Is the anesthesia helping?"

"Some. I still hurt."

"If you want to give yourself a double shot, the control system won't let you overdose. Go ahead and do that. It really would be common sense."

Mejox sighed. "I know, but I'm scared, and I hate to quit talking to all of you and be all alone again. It was really scary before I could take out the mouthpiece."

"It must have been," Poiparesis said, sympathetically. "Really, just give it two good squeezes and I'll keep talking to you till you fall asleep. Then when you wake up your hand will be splinted, that internal hemorrhage in your leg will be drained, and you'll have all that uncomfortable support liquid out of you. Just give it two more squeezes, and keep talking to us, and it'll be just like falling asleep after you're tucked in."

"That is, if we tucked you in by piling rocks on your chest," Otuz added.

Mejox made a little noise that might have been a laugh. "All right, I guess that's common sense. Squeezing the button now . . . it really does hurt."

"Of course it does," Poiparesis said. "Having your hand crushed hurts. So does internal bleeding. You're dealing with it really well."

"Yeah," Mejox said. "Kekox, what do they do about these in the Imperial Guard?"

"We saw off the leg and use it to beat the patient to death," Kekox said.

It was so unexpected that we all laughed, even Mejox. The old Imperial Guard added, "Mejox, you don't have to prove how brave you are to all of us. Save being brave for when you have to use it. For right now just make yourself comfortable and we'll have you mostly fixed when you wake up."

"Is it going to be safe for me to make the pass by Zoiroy?" Mejox asked.

"The cast will be stronger than the bone, so it should be," Poiparesis said.

"Besides, it's not like you can get out and walk," Otuz added.

"Guess not." We heard a long sigh from him. "I'm getting really sleepy now. I really was scared, you know, when I first came out of blackout and started to feel the pain. And I'm still really sorry about breaking a rule."

"Anybody would be scared," Poiparesis assured him. "And you can stop worrying about the rules. Now go to sleep."

He didn't answer. We lay on our couches for another third of a day; Kekox told a couple of stories, and Poiparesis sang for us, and we made up games in our heads, but it was still a long dull time, and we were all worried about Mejox.

Finally, when the acceleration was down to little more than double normal gravity, and the sun in the screens was still huge but no longer the all-devouring ball of fire it had been, Soikenn and Kekox very carefully climbed from their couches and moved over to look at Mejox. "Crushed hand and a hematoma, just as we thought," Soikenn said.

"Will he be all right?" Kekox asked.

"He's going to be fine. And he's a brave kid. That must have hurt a lot more than he was letting us know."

"He did directly do what we told him not to do."

"Yeah, that's Mejox. But I bet he's acquired a new respect for rules and advice."

When the acceleration had come down still further, they moved him onto a cart and took him down to the outer deck. With only eight people, none of whom were expected to be sick very often, we didn't have a sick bay or infirmary, but three of the rooms could be converted to emergency surgical spaces. The gravity was still too high for Soikenn to do any surgery on Mejox, but they could get the room set up.

Meanwhile the rest of us were left with just our thoughts for company. "You all can sit up," Poiparesis said, "but we don't need any more injuries, so I suggest you *just* sit. Your portable terminals are by your couches, so you can read, do homework, or play games, but I really don't think anyone should get up and walk who doesn't have to. I'm going down to the outer deck also, to see if I can help. I'm afraid we may have to wait till we're back to much lower accelerations before we can do anything much for Mejox. One more failure of planning—we never thought we might need to do surgery while accelerating. It's a good thing his hemorrhage wasn't worse. Anyway, *don't* add to our troubles by moving around and getting hurt."

"I'll keep an eye on them," Captain Osepok said. "There's not really any use for me in the cockpit till it's time for course correction and furling the sail."

"Thanks," Poiparesis said. He climbed slowly and carefully to the door—the direction of down was still almost ninety degrees from what we were used to—and went out.

"Is Mejox really going to be all right?" Priekahm asked.

"Well, Soikenn is about as good a doctor as you can be without doing it full time," the captain said, "and Kekox has seen a lot of injuries. And they both seemed worried, but they didn't act like it was anything that they couldn't handle. It should be all right. Would you all like to get that foam out of yourselves? You won't need it anymore, not till we make our close pass at Zoiroy."

She wasn't as gentle as Soikenn, maybe because of the high gravity, so the needles and tubes hurt more going in, but she was efficient, and it felt good to have all that filler removed. As soon as it was out, we all noticed that we were exhausted, and ended up stretching back out on the couches to sleep. Priekahm and I slept right through Mejox's operation, three-eighths of a day, and only heard about it over the first meal after we were allowed to move around again. But Otuz said that even though she was awake, they wouldn't let her watch. "They said it might upset me and I said how can anyone get upset watching people stick knives into Mejox."

"That isn't funny," I said. "He was really hurt." We were sitting in the common dining area, still working on that huge meal. Not having eaten for a full day gives you an appetite.

"That's what Soikenn said. Nobody has a sense of humor anymore. But I gave him a lot of my blood to replace what he lost, so I figure if he's going to get the blood, the jokes come with it."

"I just hope he's all right," Priekahm said.

"I do, too," Otuz said. "But all the adults say that—"

Poiparesis leaned in the doorway and said, "You all have a friend who'd like to see you." It took only a couple of breaths before we were gathered around Mejox in the improvised surgery.

"Hi," Mejox said. "Hope I didn't scare anybody too badly. I feel really stupid, but I'm glad to be here. And thanks for your blood, Otuz."

She was so startled at his being polite that she barely gasped out a "You're welcome."

Five days later we were all piled together at the entry to the cockpit to watch Captain Osepok furl the sail. By now we were almost four times as far from the Sun as Sosahy and Nisu were, plunging on toward Zoiroy. The acceleration from the sail fell off with the cube of our distance, so it was now only one one-thousandth of a normal gravity; we would need to have the sail furled again when we passed by the smaller star, so that we could unfurl it as we were moving away and thus receive another big kick along our trajectory.

It turned out to be just about the dullest thing we had ever watched.

The robot winches slowly wound in the cable, and since the sail they were winding up was the area of a large island back in Shulath, or of a province in Palath, that took a very long time. Nor could we escape from watching the process. Captain Osepok pointed out that we would next get to see this several years from now—then many years after that—and finally we would have to do it ourselves. "If you're only going to get to see it three times," she said, "and the whole success of the mission depends on you doing it right as long as seventy years from now, I think just maybe you had better not miss chances to watch."

So we watched cable strain on readouts, and looked at what radar was showing us about how the sail folded in front of us, and spent a long, boring day before finally the ship was ballistic again and we were headed for our close approach to Zoiroy. It wasn't till shortly before bedtime that Otuz muttered to me, "Did you notice Mejox?"

"What about him?"

"When have you ever seen him sit still for so much boredom?"

"He has to sit still—his hand's in a cast and his leg's sore."

"You know what I mean. He didn't make any trouble."

"I'd think you'd be glad."

"Oh, I am. And when I spied on the adults earlier this evening, they were all really happy about it, too. But it sure isn't much like him. I suppose getting hurt and not being able to do anything about it must have made an impression on him."

Something about the incident did seem to change Mejox for the better. Certainly he became quieter and politer. I spent a lot of time coaching him on math, and within a day or two I felt that we were as good a pair of friends as ever.

About fifty days later we were in final approach to Zoiroy. I don't know what the others did, but I squeezed the button for anesthesia. Zoiroy was a much smaller star than the Sun, so it was only going to be eight gravities. We wouldn't need support liquid in the lungs. Still, I had seen everything of close approaches that I wanted to see.

By the time I was out of anesthesia, Captain Osepok had jettisoned the extra part of the sail that we would not need, maneuvered us onto the laser beam that we would ride for the next few years, and headed us out into the dark reaches of interstellar space. We had raced across our solar system, from the Sun to Zoiroy, in just sixty days—a distance that the first expedition to Kahrekeif, the one Kekox had been on, had taken two years, just under a thousand days, to cross.

With the laser pushing us, we would reach the great cloud of cometoids which marked the outer boundary of our solar system in just about a year—and beyond them, then, we would voyage for more than twenty more years.

I made a game of it to myself: going around the equator of Nisu was a long way—we had spent days doing it on the final tour. And Nisu's orbit around Sosahy was forty times that far. And the distance from Nisu to the Sun was one hundred times as far as *that*. And the distance from the Sun to Zoiroy was about thirteen times as far as *that*, at the time we went. So we had already gone 52,000 times as far as it was around Nisu, and we had done it in only sixty days, and with the push from the laser beam we would eventually be moving at seven times our present speed. . . .

And it would still take twenty-three and one quarter years, nine eightdays, and three and two-fifths days, in all, from the moment of our launch until we entered orbit around Setepos, to get there. When I thought about how fast we were moving and yet how immense the distances were, I would end up staring out a viewport at the endless blackness between the stars, until one of the other children would sneak up on me and startle me. After a while I lost the habit of looking out viewports at all, or even of thinking of us as moving. Our world was our little metal torus, in the middle of a void dark, huge, and empty beyond imagining, chasing after a vast, dimly glowing disk.

6

A LONG TIME LATER, WHEN I HAD TOO MUCH TIME TO THINK ABOUT THE past, I would think of the first twenty years of the voyage, before any of us entered puberty and while things were still on the plan, as the "happy time." I know it wasn't perfect. I squabbled with the other children, and I remember many hurt feelings and apologies. Once I broke my wrist in the gym and had to wear a cast, and once Otuz got angry at Priekahm and beat her badly. There was a period of more than a year when Soikenn and Osepok would not speak to each other and none of us children knew why.

But for all that, time went by pleasantly. Automatic machinery ran the ship's functions, and it was so reliable that after the first few eightweeks, Captain Osepok visited the cockpit once per day only to make sure that things were functioning normally; years went by and nothing unusual ever happened. Every few eightdays, she would spend a couple of days practicing with the simulators, to keep her skills current, and now and again she would have me or Otuz practice the same maneuvers. Really, however, the controls were much simpler than they were for the lander simulations that we worked every few days, and steering and navigating *Wahkopem Zomos* was much simpler than operating an ordinary aircraft.

That left us a great deal of time to occupy, and with our immense library, including all sorts of visual and auditory recordings, we probably became the eight most educated people ever. We studied literature, music, history, dead languages, all the sciences, a dozen games of skill and strategy. We all worked out in the gym frequently.

And of course there was an immense amount of research to be done. Though dozens of unmanned probes were passing through interstellar space ahead of us, they could only relay back what they had been programmed to report; if there was an interesting anomaly in the data, it took years for the data itself to reach Nisu, then more years for any radio message changing the program to get back to the probe. By that time, the probe, moving at half the speed of light or more, would be far away from the anomaly, so a new probe would have to be dispatched—in the hope that it could find the same spot in the vast reaches of empty space, and that the phenomenon would still be going on a decade or more later.

But we were right there with our instruments. When any of the thousands of readings we took per second started to show something interesting, one or more of us could take additional observations; experiment with laser, radar, or particle beam probing; compare it with all the data up to the present—in short, we could really do science, interacting directly with our environment, in the way that people back home could not. That advantage, plus having so much time available, made us some of the most productive research scientists in history.

Traditionally very good students are allowed to put their names on some scientific works in their last couple of years before puberty, but

Otuz and I both had credits before we were ten, and more than a hundred each before we were twenty.

But though we were understanding so much about where we were, and where we were going, it was getting harder and harder to understand news coming from home. We received the major broadcast channels over the relay continuously, along with any books and recordings we wanted, but somehow, Nisu and we seemed to be growing apart from each other.

Part of it was the time lag caused by our increasing distance. After we had been four and a half years on the voyage, it took a full year from the time we sent the message to get a reply from Nisu. Twelve and a half years into the voyage, when we received word that the old emperor had died, it was two and a half years after the fact, and though Mejox endured the quarter-year of the selection period just as if it had been happening right then, the new empress had been on her throne for that same two-and-a-half-year radio lag by the time he knew her name. "It drives me crazy," Mejox said to me once. "Somewhere back behind us, slowly catching up with us, is a radio signal that would tell me what I want to know. It's so weird to know it's already settled and there is no way at all that we can hear it any sooner."

"You could get out and wait for it," Otuz said.

He probably would have been just as glad if the message never reached us. The new empress was not a Roupox, and moreover she already had a child. Hence—though Mejox was by no means ruled out, since the council of the ruling families could choose anyone they wanted from within their own ranks—he was no longer nearly the candidate for emperor he had been.

In the eighteenth year, as we reached peak velocity, we were about ninety percent of the way to Setepos, but it would take us a quarter of the total time to cover the last tenth of the voyage, for we were now moving at two-fifths of light speed and it would take us years to slow down safely. By now we children were old enough and experienced enough to participate in the deceleration maneuver, so Otuz was in the second seat in the cockpit, Priekahm watching instruments with Poiparesis in the observatory, and the rest of us working at terminals in the computer lab, making sure that the sail stayed straight and intact.

The first part of the maneuver took the better part of a day, slowly furling the sail, taking in the diamond cable, tracking it to make sure it didn't twist, tangle, or worst of all strike any other part of the sail or the ship, since the microscopically fine, spun diamond would slice through any other material. It was interesting, but it was also very much like all the practices we had been running for the past twenty-two eightdays.

At last the screens showed that the great circle of the sail—which had been as big as Sosahy for so many years—filled the sky completely. A few glimpses of dark showed where, now and again over our eighteen years on the voyage, a particle as big as a snowflake had struck that vast sheet, instantly vaporizing a tiny part of it. Then, ever so slowly, that huge circle began to distort and fold in toward us. The last of the cable was winding onto the spool.

The sail itself came in next, the rollers running smoothly to every-one's relief. We had spent days checking all of them and making sure they were perfect, but a machine being used for the first time in eighteen years is not a comfortable thought no matter how careful you've been with it. There were anxious moments, now and then, as we cleared wrin-kles, and though the collision alarm had sounded only six times since we started out—and none at all in the last five years—the thought kept crossing my mind that if we had to dodge sideways to avoid a stone smaller than my thumb, it might be an eightday before we straightened out the sail again.

But the sail came in smoothly as well, and then we were ready for reaction maneuvering. The small rockets we used for positioning and maneuvering *Wahkopem Zomos* were liquid hydrogen–antimatter, like the booster that had pushed us out of Nisu orbit. The silent flicker of their jets licked out from the ship in another display of auroras, but we had much less time to watch them. In less than a fifth of a day, we had moved out of the beam of the laser.

Captain Osepok's voice came over the intercom. "All right, every-one, get ready; this will probably feel very strange."

Years aboard the ship had accustomed us to the notion that outward toward the rim of the torus was "down," inward toward the core cylinder was "up." The acceleration from the laser acting on the sail was so small a fraction of the "gravity" from spin that we never noticed it.

Then the tiny attitude-adjustment jets began to fire, and the whole ship swung slowly end over end, to face the opposite direction. It was disorienting because we were so used to the ship's centrifugal "gravity" never changing; the effect was small but felt subtly wrong.

The jets cut out, letting the rotating torus act as a gyroscope to stabi-lize us in our new position. "Down" resumed its normality.

"Position?" Osepok called into the intercom.

A moment later we heard Priekahm's voice. "It's all correct. Attitude is accurate and we're on trajectory. Nice work, Captain."

"You can thank Otuz. I just sat here and watched her drive."

We all looked a little startled, though my second thought after my initial surprise was, *Well, why in the Creator's name not? She'll have to, eventually.*

Otuz spoke on the intercom. "Ready for sail deployment into magnetic configuration?"

"Ready in the observatory," Poiparesis replied.

"Ready in the computer lab," Kekox added, but then said, "But if our pilot will permit, since it's going to take a third of a day, perhaps we could get some food and rest first?"

"Good idea," Otuz said, "pending approval of the captain—"

We heard Osepok laughing. "Keep it up and anyone would think this was a real ship. All right, let's take a couple of hours to eat and nap."

After the break, we deployed the brakeloop. Physically it seemed simple enough—a thread barely thick enough to be visible to the naked eye. We spent an eighth of a day paying it out, and a bit longer getting the spun-diamond shroudlines on which it was hung unwound.

We couldn't see the next step, and that was unnerving, but there was nothing to be done about it. To "see" it we would have needed a very high resolution electron microscope, even though it was happening along an immense distance.

The "thread" was actually tightly coiled fibers much thinner than the naked eye could see. Once out in space, we gently applied a charge through the spun-diamond cables, which had been surface-doped with a conductor for the purpose. The thread began to repel itself, and the coils pushed open; shortly, it had formed an immense loop behind us, bigger in circumference than the East Island back on Nisu. As the charge was applied we had begun to spin the ship back up to rotational speed, so that in short order there was gravity again.

Now we bled off the charge from the loop; centrifugal force would hold it open. Slowly Otuz and Osepok applied a current through two of the conducting shrouds.

Like the spun-diamond shrouds or the light sail, the braking loop was effectively one immense molecule, in the shape of a tube formed into that immense ring. Within the tube was a microscopic ribbon of a superconductor—or rather of a material that when cooled enough would become superconductive. The tube itself, when a mild current was applied, became cold on the inside and hot on the outside, carrying away heat to maintain superconductivity. Otuz watched in the cockpit as the temperature of the loop fell steadily until it was well within the range for superconductivity.

Now that the thin inner ribbon was superconductive, we began to apply current to it, so that shortly an electric current was flowing through that infinitesimally thin wire around that huge distance.

"Watch your viewport for a show," Osepok said.

There was a low thrumming through the body of the ship. All the long eighteen years of the outward voyage, we had been capturing a very small portion of the laser energy to drive antimatter converters; now the antimatter we had saved up, so little of it that if you could make it into a lump it would balance on a fingertip, would provide power for most of the rest of the journey.

And it wasn't just the ship's life-support and electric systems that needed energy. In the central cylinder, well away from us and in a sealed, insulated space, there was a great generator. It was the vibration from that which we now felt through our feet as the generator built up that huge current in the loop.

Across the next twentieth of a day, we felt the brakeloop begin to drag us, and our weight moved a little away from the "floor" we had been used to, toward what had been the "rear window" and now was the front of the ship. Interstellar space is a hard vacuum, better than any that can be made in a laboratory, but not an absolute one. There are about 50,000 atoms of hydrogen in a body-volume of space, which sounds like a lot until you remember that there are about 500,000,000,000,000,000,000,000,000 atoms in a body-volume of ordinary air. When the loop swept through that thin hydrogen, carrying such an immense current at our tremendous velocity, it simply tore those hydrogen atoms apart, even at immense distances from the loop itself. A current flowing through a conductor produces a magnetic field, and the bigger the current, the stronger the field. A magnetic field exerts a force on a charged particle; the direction of the force depends on the charge on the particle. Since a hydrogen atom is made up of a single electron (with a −1 charge) orbiting a single proton (with a +1 charge), the magnetic field of the loop would literally tear the atoms in its path apart, pushing the electron one way, and proton the other.

But to change the motion of anything requires energy; separating the electron and proton took some energy, and then as the charged particles were whipped around in the magnetic field, they absorbed yet more energy. And the source of that energy was the motion of the loop. As the kinetic energy of the loop became the thermal energy of the thin interstellar gas, the loop slowed down, and since we were tied to it, so did we. Or look at it this way—every push or pull the loop exerted on a charged particle had to be matched, by the laws of motion, with an equal and opposite push or pull on the loop, and the sum of all those tiny forces, added up across the immense length of the loop, was a force big enough to slow us.

"Now that we're running normally," Poiparesis said over the intercom, "let me show you something on the screen."

Behind us, a deep blue, almost violet, glow blazed in a huge ring. "What—" I asked, not quite able to form the question.

"Braking photons," Soikenn said. "The same thing we see in a cyclotron. When you accelerate a charged particle it gives off photons—that's why electricity running through a coil creates a magnetic field, because photons are the carriers of magnetism, among other things. And in this case what you're seeing is all those protons and electrons changing direction and speed within a tiny fraction of a second. That's a lot of acceleration, and they're giving off a lot of fairly high-energy photons, high enough energy to be visible light and ultraviolet."

"Shield's up," Poiparesis said.

He set the screen to show the forward view and now there was nothing to see. Though there wasn't much of it, and we needed an area the size of a big island to catch enough hydrogen to slow down a vessel that wasn't much bigger than a medium-sized house, still our ship was running into intersteller hydrogen, smashing it into high-energy protons and electrons, which were radiation and over time could be deadly. While we had been accelerating, the sail had sheltered us; now that the sail was furled, and the brakeloop was hanging behind us, Poiparesis had deployed two cone-shaped pieces of sail material, one in front of the ship and one in back, and given them large positive charges. They would trap the electrons, and guide incoming protons around our ship.

Unfortunately they also blocked the view, but one couldn't have everything. Cameras on long poles let us keep looking through the screens, even though the ports showed only the dark insides of the shields. Looking to the rear we saw only the stars shining through the faint blue glowing ring of accelerated protons around the ship.

We plunged on toward our new home, the drag of the loop pulling at us constantly, and as the older and older news from Nisu seemed daily stranger and more irrelevant to us, new things began to take up our interests. We didn't know it yet, but the happy time was coming to an end.

7

TWO YEARS LATER, OUR VELOCITY WAS DOWN TO ABOUT ONE SIXTIETH OF lightspeed, and though Kousapex was still just a star to the naked eye, already our telescopes were beginning to resolve Setepos into a disk. It was more than six and a half years between request and reply, and the news we were getting was over three years old. Back on Nisu, the big news—as far as we were concerned—was that work was being delayed on *Imperial Hope*, the immense ship that was to move several million people to Setepos a hundred years from now. Yet though the Intruder's close pass, just five years ago, had missed Nisu as the astronomers had said it would, surely all of Nisu had seen the Intruder stretch as a hot white streak a hundred times as wide as the Sun. You would think anyone who had been of conscious age at a time to look up at the night sky would be able to figure out that a hundred years was really too short for the job to be done.

The reason *Imperial Hope* was not being completed on schedule baffled the children and disgusted the adults on *Wahkopem Zomos*. It had started just before the emperor died—in fact, the last message we got from him before we heard of his death had been his congratulations and best wishes for having reached the outer edge of the new solar system.

We had long since gotten used to watching news and public information broadcasts and hearing almost no mention of ourselves or *Wahkopem Zomos*, since after all we hadn't been doing anything very interesting to ordinary people for the last few years—our scientific work was important but you could hardly expect the average Nisuan to appreciate it. Still, at least once a month there was a progress report on *Imperial Hope*.

Because the huge ship would have to move millions of people, and the Intruder was bound to destroy any set of laser boosters and the para-lenses needed to focus them, the big ship would have to take several life-times on its journey. It would make close passes at the Sun and Zoiroy, just as we had, and there would be a few years of laser boost before the rain of rocks and ice destroyed the laser boost stations, but a ship that size could not go as near the suns because the tidal effects were stronger on a big ship than they were on our tiny one, and with its far greater mass, the lasers would be unable to push it up to anything like our peak velocity of two-fifths lightspeed. It would take a few hundred years to cross to Setepos, during which time *Imperial Hope* would be the only world our people would know.

When the emperor died, it was the right of his successor to appoint a new General Court of Shulath. Traditionally the new emperor or empress would hold an election in Shulath to decide who to appoint; in addition, many of the Imperial positions reserved for Palathians turned on popularity, so for both sides of the planet it was a grand occasion for public debate.

The politicians were telling people what they wanted to hear. That had changed a great deal in the twenty-seven years since the last general election. The old generation who remembered the First Bombardment were all dead now, along with the ones who had spent their youth work-ing frantically on Reconstruction.

Nowadays everyone seemed to favor slowing down on *Imperial Hope*. At root its argument was only that everyone alive now would be long dead before the catastrophic Second Bombardment, and since, out of Nisu's billions, only a few million could go, it was very unlikely even that any individual's descendants would actually go to Setepos.

If you stated the case that baldly, according to popularity studies and referenda on Nisu, people rejected it. They still wanted *Imperial Hope* to be designed and built, and they still wanted the Migration Project to go on. But if you phrased the issue as one of "balance" or a "measured slow-down," the Migration Project lost, because Nisuans wanted more for themselves, in the here and now. It didn't seem as if it should be so difficult to "strike a balance," as the new Chief Judge of the General Court said, "between the needs of the future and those of the present." And the new empress clearly agreed with him.

Besides, the argument ran, if they waited, *Imperial Hope* would benefit from more advanced technology. And there would still be many decades in which to get it built, so why not slow down just a little and gain the advantages of improved technology, the security of more forethought—and the chance to spend a little of the wealth that the Reconstruction had brought to Nisu?

"Why is it I don't trust anyone I see on a broadcast anymore?" Osepok said, one night, as we watched a debate in the General Court, three and a half years old.

"Because they're not the people who sent us," Kekox said. "Especially the new empress is not the person who sent us. And even though if we were there, we could make all kinds of arguments—I mean, it's just common sense—"

Poiparesis groaned. "Yes. If we were there. But not only are we not there, what they're getting is our reports from years ago. Back when we were being really bland and dull and treating reporting back as a pointless task that we just had to do now and then. They haven't even seen the flipover and deceleration yet. No matter how well we argue our case now, it will be years before they start to get our side of things."

"There are still plenty of politicians on our side," Kekox pointed out. "And though the new empress isn't all she could be, she still says the project must go on. And there really *is* plenty of time, though I wish they wouldn't use it to play around doing endless redesigns. According to the master schedule the plan should have been set and construction started by the time we land. Now I'll be dead, and these kids will be halfway back, before that happens."

"Shhh," Soikenn said. "This sounds important." We all leaned forward to listen in.

No one could remember ever having heard of this speaker before. His name was Fereg Yorock, and he was one of ten Palathian members in the General Court—back during the Emancipation, ten representative seats for Palathians had been created on the General Court, and ten posts in the imperial bureaucracy had been reserved for Shulathians. Nowadays, theoretically, all the posts except emperor were open to either race; in reality it didn't happen.

"I don't remember any Yorock family," Osepok muttered.

"They couldn't be that important or he wouldn't be in a ceremonial slot like that," Kekox added. "Normally it's bad form for one of us even to talk in General Court. What's he up to?"

Soikenn shushed them again; the introductory speaker had finally gotten done with reading all the credentials for Fereg, most of them minor posts in provincial bureaucracies.

"My friends and equals," he began. Kekox muttered; that was the way Egalitarians began speeches. Soikenn shushed him, and meanwhile Fereg went on, "—no one can doubt that the efforts of the Reconstruction agencies and of the Migration Project have been heroic and have been carried out with the utmost spirit of intelligence and cooperation. Nisu is a better world because of their efforts, and indeed our whole civilization is not only richer, but far more equal and free than it was a scant hundred and fifty years ago.

"I argue only that the time has come to consider not only our duty to our honored ancestors, and what must be done for future generations, but also what can be done for we, the living. The unprecedented advances of science and technology which we have made—moving from crude aircraft and steamships to our first starflight in only a century—is itself a rich inheritance, and I believe that without jeopardizing any of our accomplishments, we can still draw upon it for everyone's benefit."

"Words, words, words," Poiparesis said. "Come on, tell us what you want to do."

The image of Fereg on the screen smiled and said, "I have examined budgets and plans exhaustively for the last half-year, and what I have found is that we have considerable room for the improvement of life here on Nisu, for this generation. I call this the Planetary Improvement Program, and what I propose is . . . "

It was a long list. Public parks, beaches free to everyone, two extra eightdays of paid vacation each year, retirement two years early for most people, a complete reequipping of the Imperial Guard with more modern aircraft and ships, two new legions of Imperial Guard to be raised in Shulath . . .

"Something for everybody," Osepok muttered. "Right. Now just what do you suppose he plans to use to pay for it?"

It took some time, because the number of things he was promising was so large, but after a while he got around to talking about paying for it. His plan had just three parts: step one, stretch out planning and design studies for an extra eleven years on *Imperial Hope*, "to take advantage of technical advances and so that the large capital expenditures of the early years of the Planetary Improvement Program will not come at the same time as the start-up costs of construction."

"Right, stretch it out, make it cost more, and get more snouts into the trough," Kekox said.

Step two, put the missions to the five other systems known to have habitable planets on hold, since Setepos was so clearly promising, and if it should prove unsuitable, there would be time to refit *Wahkopem Zomos* again and send it to the next most promising system.

Soikenn groaned. "Right. Bet the whole future on this ship."

Step three: Delay by twelve years the power-up of the next-generation boost laser, so that the solar power satellites intended for it could be diverted to lowering energy cost on Nisu and thus "enhancing the climate for our neglected private enterprise sector."

"What!?" Captain Osepok stood up in shock.

None of the rest of us could speak at all. Our entire plan for returning home depended on that laser, and even though it was twice as powerful as the one pushing us now, it would still take us forty-one years to get back.

The reasons for that were simple and unavoidable. At Setepos, we would have no antimatter–liquid hydrogen booster to start us falling toward Kousapex, the sun of that world. We would take well over a year to maneuver ourselves into an elongated elliptical orbit that would bring us in close enough to Kousapex, in the proper position, to get a solar boost to start us on our journey.

But that boost, too, would be smaller; Kousapex was only three-quarters as bright as our Sun, and it had no companion star to give us another boost. We would leave moving at less than one-thirty-second of light-speed—as opposed to the more than one-twentieth at which we had left our home system.

So we would be delayed in starting, and we would leave more slowly. But the last of all the problems was the biggest: we would have to "swim upstream" in the laser beam. We could do this because once we had received enough of the beam to carry us to Setepos, an enormous light-weight mirror, five times the diameter of our sail and made of the same material, was being sent out on the beam after us. By the time we finished our mission on Setepos and were on our way home, the mirror would pass us and continue on into space, reflecting almost all of the light back toward our home system.

Our sail was beryllium on the side that faced us, and boron on the side that faced out into space. The bright beryllium reflected light; the dark boron absorbed it. Reflected light gives twice as much push as absorbed light; thus the light reflected from the mirror would push twice as hard on the beryllium surface as the light coming directly from the laser would on the boron, and we would move toward the laser at half the acceleration with which we could move away from it—*if* the mirrors and sail had been perfect. However, the mirror, like our sail, reflected only about nine-tenths of what fell onto it, and further, the dark boron "outside" surface of the sail did reflect about one-twentieth of the light falling on it. Thus the effective push on us for our return trip, when all the countervailing forces were added up, would be only nine-twentieths what it had been on the way out.

The only advantage in speed that the return trip would have over the outbound was that instead of electrostatic braking using interstellar protons, we would be able to simply turn the ship around and use the laser itself to brake. Because of this, we could accelerate (though slowly) almost the whole way home. Even so, with the new laser power station, twice as powerful as the one now driving us to Setepos, the return journey would still take forty-one years. Now they were talking about not bringing the new station in on schedule—which meant we would be forced to make the first part of the return trip at much lower acceleration.

"How long?" Kekox asked.

"Figuring it," Soikenn said, tapping at a wall terminal. Poiparesis had pulled out his portable terminal, and for a long moment we all watched the two Shulathian scientists as they worked, hoping to hear a different answer from the one we knew we would hear.

"I get sixty-nine years," Soikenn said.

"Same here. Mother Sea's blood, you kids will just get home in time to die of old age," Poiparesis said.

"Shh," Osepok said, "I think somebody else figured that out and now Fereg is explaining."

Fereg was answering a shouted question from a news-teller; he said, "No, not at all. The point is that by canceling the other missions, we can eventually add the power stations planned for them to the *Wahkopem Zomos* mission, which will give them much more acceleration toward the end of the trip. My experts can show you that they'll be back in just about twenty percent more time than planned. Which will cost nothing extra—"

"Twenty percent?" Osepok said. "So even with his plan that's still about forty-eight years. Assuming they don't find reasons to cancel or divert that power production later. Which I certainly wouldn't assume."

"You know what I'm afraid of?" Otuz said. "That they'll give up entirely, and the way we'll find out is that all of a sudden the sail will just stop glowing, because a few years ago they turned off the laser boost, and the last of it will bounce off our sails and we'll be on our own, somewhere in the void."

Soikenn shuddered. "You're going to scare yourselves to death," she said. "Look, we're all worried, and we're angry, but it's not necessarily anything to be afraid of. Politicians usually don't mean anything, when you come right down to it. Pretty soon someone will make a fuss about how *Imperial Hope* isn't getting built fast enough, and accuse these people of destroying the Migration Project, and the same people who voted for 'striking a balance' will throw Fereg and his crowd out on their ears to 'save the future' or some slogan like that."

But the newscast went on and on, showing more and more public protests in Shulath and even big rallies in Palath itself. It looked like the Planetary Improvement Program was very popular.

And though the politicians were always careful to talk about "balance" and "of course we don't want to lose a century of progress," many of the ordinary people interviewed said bluntly that they didn't see any reason to save their great-grandchildren.

One old Palathian appeared on the screen and said, "I don't call it no century of progress. We got all this new stuff but nobody can use it, and you just know where all the jobs and money are going, don't you? Right over to Shulath, for those tall skinny long-ears to play with. Shulath is getting rich off all this go-to-Setepos nonsense, and once they get money, all those long-ears go around acting just like they're equal, just like they're something special, and they forget their place—"

"Turn it off," Kekox said. "We can always play that recording some other time if anyone really needs to see it."

During the next few eightweeks, the news was bad every night. The Planetary Improvement Program carried easily in the General Court and the empress adopted it virtually as her own.

"The trouble is, all our constituency is either dead or not born yet,"

Otuz said, as we children shared a late meal after a day of studying. We often met together as a group in the evening, to talk about our research and ongoing projects.

"That never stopped anyone from voting in Shulath, if the history books are telling the truth," Mejox said.

Priekahm looked around wide-eyed at us, and said, "Well, you know . . . I mean, I don't agree with them, but I can understand them. Of course hanging out here in the middle of light-years of vacuum, *we* see that we need the support, and *we* understand that the thing has to go forward. But if you look at it from their viewpoint—"

"I'd rather not," I said. "I mean, I understand wanting to just toss away the future and have fun now. But I also understand that *we* can't do that. Nobody asked us, either, and we're all giving up a lot more than any taxpayer back home. All of us have given up most of our lives to this. The adults are going to *die* on Setepos. We're going to be old before we ever see Nisu again, and after just a few years of going outside again and exploring big, beautiful Setepos, we'll have to get back inside this metal box and put in a fifty-two-year return trip—assuming Fereg Yorock and the empress keep even that much faith."

Priekahm shuddered and touched Mejox's arm. "Let's not talk about that."

"Sure, of course you're right," Mejox said. "Zahmekoses, I have an idea I'd like to talk with you about, later."

One of the odder things about Mejox in the last year had been his protectiveness of Priekahm; he acted as if he couldn't bear for her to hear anything that might upset her. Odder still was that she not only accepted it, but seemed to like it. So it was no surprise that he dropped in on Otuz and me the next day, while we were working in the lab—and while Priekahm was doing remedial math with Osepok.

"I guess what I wanted to talk about," Mejox said, "is this whole stupid business of leaving Setepos once we're there."

Otuz sighed. "It will be hard on all of us, but I'm sure it will be hardest on you. You're practically living there already."

Mejox, who had never seemed to care much for study, though he was certainly bright enough, had flung himself into the study of the probe data with surprising enthusiasm. We had been getting a steady stream of information as successive generations of probes from Tiber, launched with better and better technology (so that they were lighter) and more power available for boost, had been getting to Setepos more and more quickly and reliably. Moreover, as we got closer to Setepos, radio lag grew shorter; we were now receiving signal from the probes years before scientists back home got them. Some of the gossamer probes had descended to Setepos's surface and relayed back some pictures, and Mejox's private chamber was literally lined with copies of those pictures, particularly the three that showed largish animals.

"I wish that were true," he said. "It's so beautiful. I don't see how I'll even have time to look at the hundred or so places I most want to see: those strange boglands at the mouths of rivers, those wide plains, all those wet hot forests—so many strange places. And I'd like to float down one of those rivers in a boat, and take a year to do it . . . but after we've only been there five years, we've got to start back. And get old before we breathe open air again!"

He seemed to be gasping for breath, and I think we were all about to ask what was wrong, when he suddenly jumped up and ran into the passageway. A moment later we heard his door slam.

"What was that about? Did I hurt his feelings?" Otuz asked.

"I have no idea," I admitted.

"Me either," Otuz said.

The next day he apologized, saying he was sorry if he had offended us, and then in the middle of apologizing he started to cry. When we tried to comfort him he ran down the corridor and slammed his door again. We went to find somebody to tell us what was going on, and we found Poiparesis in the observatory.

"This is either a habit or a disease," Otuz said.

"Close but not quite right," Poiparesis said. "He's going into puberty. He's a little ahead of the rest of you, but you'll all be acting like that soon."

"Did *you* act like that?" I demanded.

"Er, yes."

"And I was worse," Kekox added, coming in. "You'll all have to try to be nice to Mejox, and that won't be at all easy because he's going to be rude and unpleasant, and once puberty hits you, you'll be just as bad."

Otuz was next oldest, but Priekahm was the next to go into puberty. If anything, she was worse about it, and she and Mejox seemed to rotate between rudely ignoring each other, sobbing in each other's arms, screaming at each other, and cuddling up and talking baby-talk.

Otuz and I couldn't stand them, in any of their phases, and we started spending even more of our time together. Our friendship had grown so deep that it often seemed that when one of us spoke, it was to finish the other's thought.

We knew the adults were unhappy about Priekahm and Mejox, but, being still children ourselves, just *why* the adults were upset didn't occur to us for a while. But as it happened the day that Soikenn decided to take Priekahm aside for a talk in the computer lab, we were in the rear study room, right next to it. We crept over to the door to hear what Soikenn was saying so softly and urgently to Priekahm.

"You're not an adult yet," she hissed, "and you don't have my experience. And I can tell you've forgotten who you are and who he is. You're a Shulathian, Priekahm. You can't marry him, and if he takes you as consort it will destroy his future. And the way Palathian males treat females—"

"Mejox is not—"

"I'm not a bigot, and I've worked with Palathians all my life and I like many of them, but there's a certain amount of truth in the old saying about them being half animals. He'll get what he wants and after that he'll think you're his whore, that he can have you for sex whenever he wants it. We've got to protect ourselves against—"

"Like you did?" I had never heard such anger or aggression in Priekahm's voice; she had always been the gentle, timid one among us. Now I cringed just to hear her tone.

Soikenn gasped slightly, and then, choking with fury, she said, "Who told you?"

"Mejox said he saw you once, and he heard the captain saying—"

"That's *enough*." Soikenn's voice was tight and cold with anger, but she kept her tone even. "But I'm the case that proves it, Priekahm. Poiparesis and I had been no more than colleagues to each other for a long time. Kekox gave me the impression the same was true for him and Osepok. It didn't seem wrong, and it was certainly a relief. But in the first place, Kekox was lying to me—and even though he'd deceived me, it was me that Osepok was angry with. And ever since then—well, it's hard to explain. Let's say Kekox will probably never take anything I think, do, or say seriously again. *And he's about as decent as Palathians get.* Most of them would have been much worse about it; at least he's careful of everyone's feelings. Or everyone's except mine, anyway. And he's never said a word in front of you children. But that's the best you can hope for from Mejox—when he's done he'll treat you like a toy that used to be interesting. Is that all you want?"

There was a crack and a soft moan; it took me an instant to realize that Priekahm had hit Soikenn. Then I heard Priekahm running down the inner deck to her room, and the door slamming.

After a long time Soikenn sighed. The door opened, then closed very softly behind her. Finally we could stir from our hiding place.

"Never," Otuz said, "absolutely never."

"Never what?"

"I'm never going to let them marry me to Mejox. He was always greedy and pushy, and I'm not as dumb and docile as Priekahm. They aren't going to turn him loose on me."

"But then," I stammered, "I mean, we're going to hit puberty, too—"

"Zahmekoses, you're my best friend. That's usually who people end up with, back on Nisu. If they didn't want us to feel that way, they shouldn't have let us spend so much time together—"

"There isn't much choice in a spaceship," I pointed out. "And look, the whole idea scares me a lot. I've seen how crazy Mejox is and I'm not looking forward to it. And even if he is headstrong and willful, he's my friend."

Strange intense feelings were surging through me and my breath seemed to catch in my throat. I wanted to punch Otuz. I wanted to gather her into my arms. I wanted her to shut up and I wanted her to say—I didn't know what.

"He's my *friend*!" I screamed. "He's not going to act that way! And I don't know what you're thinking, but I know this—back home they *kill* Shulathian males for things like what you're thinking about!" My breath was jammed in my throat, big as someone's foot rammed down there, and then my feet seemed to throw me out the door and down the corridor.

I heard Otuz calling "Zahmekoses!" after me, but I didn't care and kept running. My room seemed like such a welcoming, friendly place, and when I flung myself into it and slammed the door, I was suddenly limp with relief. I stretched out on the bed and cried for a long time.

After a while, Poiparesis knocked and called "Zahmekoses," very gently and softly. I didn't answer. He came in anyway, closed the door, and sat down on the bed beside me.

"I didn't ask you to come in," I said.

"I didn't ask you to go into puberty," he said. "You do know that's what's happening?"

"Yes." I lay there, trying to feel calmer, sinking facedown into my bed. "Two years of this?"

"Around two years. Maybe you'll come out sooner."

I groaned. "Well, I read all the stuff you told us to, and I think I understand it all." I hoped he would go away.

He didn't. "Ah. Hard thing to bring up, you know. All of us—the adults, I mean—have been talking about, well, things. Uh . . ."

"Otuz told you," I said.

"She's sort of jealous, you know, because she's second oldest, but she's getting puberty late."

"She can have mine if she wants it."

Poiparesis chuckled. "The worst thing is, it doesn't kill your sense of humor. You're still acutely aware when you're being ridiculous."

"Do *you* think—"

"Not right now. And I hope to the Creator that I don't laugh at you myself; I remember what it was like to be laughed at when I was going through it. Anyway, let me tell you what I came to tell you. Otuz told me your whole conversation, as much as she remembered, and I thought maybe a few things ought to be explained. All right?"

"I'm listening."

"Good. To begin at the beginning, we aren't under Nisuan law here. The Creator alone knows what it's going to be like when you get back—maybe there will be more tolerance, maybe less. It would really have been better for everyone if you kids had paired off the way it was planned, but there's nothing we can do about it now, I suppose. Except hope you all outgrow it."

"Sure, but when I get back—"

"You know there's not a death penalty anymore?" he asked, as if he hadn't been listening to me.

"Yes, I do, but—"

"Let me tell you something every biologist learns but nobody will say in public. Shulathians were slaves for hundreds of years. Supposedly all mixed-parent offspring were aborted or killed right after birth, right?"

I nodded. I was suddenly realizing that Poiparesis seemed to be almost as upset as I was, and I didn't know how to feel about that, or what was going on.

"Well," he said, "in all those centuries, do you suppose every baby born came out with a tag that said 'one hundred percent pure'? Of course the two races are different in appearance, but we blend into each other—I'm sure you've heard Kekox mention that his older brother was called 'Long-ears' by everyone in the family, and that there were jokes about his mother and the family tutor? Well, chances are that he *wasn't* a crossbreed—and I certainly would never suggest that he was around Kekox—but there's a good chance that there was some crossbreeding in the family. In most families, in fact. Especially the older Palathian aristocracy, which had so many slaves for so long. It's pretty well established that one emperor was a substitute baby."

"I'd heard of substitute babies, but I don't know what they are," I said.

He grunted. "Simple. In the old days sometimes a Palathian line couldn't produce an heir for one reason or another, so the male would impregnate a female slave, preferably one they thought was crossbred anyway. Then the female would go into confinement and pretend to be too ill to see people. When the baby was born they'd present it in public as their own."

"What happened to the female slave?"

Poiparesis stared at me, his face hard and flat. "What do you think?"

I shuddered. "That's what scares me so much."

"It should. Never forget that even though Kekox and Osepok are just about the most kind, decent, loyal people you'll ever meet, not every Palathian is like them. And even they—well, that doesn't matter at the moment. The point is that yes, you have to watch out for yourself, and you have to keep your position in mind. But it's a long time till you get back. Anything could happen in that time. And you won't be getting sterility reversals until you're en route back. So after a lot of *extremely* candid discussion among the adults—at the strong suggestion of Captain Osepok—we've decided to try to put our feelings aside and let you do what you think best. We won't conceal from you that we would like to see everything settle out as it should have, and if that happens there won't be a word of any of this back to Nisu—it will be just as if it had never happened. But if not . . . well, I think you should all do what seems best to you. It will be better, though, if we're all allowed to pretend that we don't know." He got up from my bed, and I rolled over to look at him. From the way his shoulders sagged, he looked really old. He glanced back. "You're all right?"

"Except for being insane for the next two years, and having to worry about getting hanged when I get home, sure." I rolled over and lay facedown on my bed. After a little while the door closed and I knew he was gone.

8

OTUZ ENTERED PUBERTY AN EIGHTH OF A YEAR LATER. BY THAT TIME IT was a great relief to me; there was someone else I could stand to be around some of the time, and she seemed to feel for me a lot of what I felt for her.

Within days of the first time Otuz and I touched each other sexually, I could tell that Kekox hated me, but since I was mad at the world that year, it didn't make much difference. I kind of enjoyed it. I did remember Poiparesis's warning, though, and I tried not to do anything very physical with Otuz in front of the old Imperial Guard, especially since it seemed to me very likely that if anyone on board was going to hurt anyone else, it would be Kekox attacking a Shulathian. He had the training and it was clear he wasn't as open-minded as he was trying to act.

Otuz, on the other hand, seemed to want to do *everything* in front of Kekox all the time. After a while Osepok took her aside and pointed out that she could get me killed. We both resented Osepok for it.

Meanwhile, although we each spent more time with the girls, Mejox and I became good friends again, because we finally had a common interest: Setepos. We spent most of our working hours in the computer lab, extracting images from the data now pouring in from all the probes ahead of us.

Picking a landing site was getting to be more and more difficult; if you didn't count the one at the south pole that was under ice, this new world had five continents to Nisu's two. All of the continents had a larger area than Shulath, and the biggest—the one we called simply "Big"—dwarfed Palath. The Hook was somewhat bigger, and Bug wasn't much smaller. There was also an enormous number of islands, and they varied much more than those of Nisu did—we guessed that there must be at least a dozen island formation processes at work, where on Nisu only two were known.

Furthermore, because there were so many land masses separated by water, and so many wide deserts and steep mountain ranges (though none of them high by our standards), Setepos had a much larger number of semiisolated local ecologies, and thus a far greater variety of animal life than we were used to.

This made it all the more complicated, for our soft-landing robot probes had actually touched down at only eight sites, and unfortunately none of them were anywhere that animals passed by frequently. The two in the hot, wet, equatorial forests were hanging from the shroud lines of their parachutes, high up in the dim gloom, and saw little of the life around them except when something climbed or slithered over branches near them, or when the flying animals tried to perch on them. The probes in the deserts and mountains had simply set down too far from anything an animal would be interested in. The only exception was one that had landed on a broad plain near a riverbank in the center of the Bug; it was fine as far as it went, except that the only species of any significance around it seemed to be the immense brown-and-black horned animals who came down to the river to drink twice a day.

"There are five more four-probe packages on their way," Soikenn said. "We'll get twenty more looks before we land. And we still have more than a year of deceleration and maneuvering. Plenty of time."

"Oh, sure, yes," Mejox said. "But for right now if I see one more big furry coat—"

"It ought to make you feel at home, fossil-boy," I said. As our friendship had renewed, so had the teasing.

"Somewhere out there on that planet," Mejox said, "there is an animal with long ears. Preferably a smelly animal with unpleasant habits and long ears. And I think it's a priority to find one, so that I won't be at a conversational disadvantage."

I laughed; Soikenn sighed. "When you two are on your way back to Nisu, promise me you'll both spend the last ten years practicing *not* talking that way. I know it's all a game to you, you've grown up equal and comfortable with each other all your lives, but—"

" 'It could get us killed back home,' " we said in unison.

She laughed and put an arm around both of us, "I *have* said that pretty often, haven't I? I'm sorry. Anyway, we have a hundred more images to process, if you aren't tired."

"Never," Mejox said. "Insane but not tired, that's us." We worked over the pictures silently for a long time; again there was nothing but desert, rock, ice, and the limb of one tall tree. In one picture from a tree, we did find one small animal being swallowed by a long, thin, legless one. At first we thought the thin, legless one was just another tree limb. "I've never seen anything like that no-legger before, but it's creepy," Mejox said. "I hope there's nothing big enough to do that to us."

"Oh, if there is, you have four expendable old people to try it out on," Soikenn said.

Mejox snorted. "Osepok is too tough to swallow, Poiparesis isn't enough meat, Kekox is bitter, and I like you. Let's get the last images done—"

I was about to leave them to finish the set out together—I usually did, since Soikenn and Mejox had a lot more patience for the fiddling process of imaging than I did—when I saw something forming in one image and stuck around.

The picture came from a probe that had landed in the desert in the north part of the Hook. Where we had collected days and days of pictures of sand, rock, and sky, suddenly here was a big animal—almost a bodylength and a half long, probably more than a bodylength tall at the shoulder, and the ugliest, most graceless beast that had ever gone on four legs. It had an apparent huge upward crook in its spine, a strange swaying neck, a long head with thick lips, and ridiculously big feet on silly long thin legs. It seemed to be covered with long matted brown hair. It was staring at the probe with an expression of such vacant stupidity that all of us burst out laughing.

"You're in luck, Zahmekoses," Mejox said, "this one has short ears, too."

More probes landed on Setepos. It was still more than half a year until we got there, but now we were entering the inner part of Kousapex's surrounding cloud of cometoids; we even took a look at one through our telescopes and radars once, but it looked exactly like every other cometoid, a soft ball of snow with rocks and chunks of iron in it.

Shortly after that, one of our probes came down in an open meadow in the middle of a forest, near a stream, in the eastern part of the Bug. We cataloged dozens more animals in a short time. To Mejox's delight, one smallish animal that hopped on its hind legs turned out to have long ears; he promptly named it a "zahmekoses" in my honor. A few days later a probe in the equatorial part of the Triangle, hanging from the tree where its parachute had caught, sent us a picture of a hair-covered, flat-faced creature which looked for all the world like a freeze-dried half-scale Palathian except that it hung by its long tail from the branch; I named it the "mejox," returning the favor. The girls told us that if we ever named anything after them, we'd be sorry.

We were now mostly past the worst of puberty; it was no worse than being occasionally irritable and depressed. Mejox and Otuz's dark adult fur had come in, and Mejox had a really rather splendid top crest. My adult muscles (such as they were—even for a Shulathian I was always going to be thin) were coming in, and Priekahm's hips had widened. By the time we landed, if we hadn't been given reversible sterilizations, we'd have been ready to have children; as it was Priekahm and Mejox did a lot of "practicing," making a lot of noise about it, and Otuz and I very quietly were doing the same.

Both the Palathian adults were outraged by Otuz and me, but only annoyed by Priekahm and Mejox, however much they believed in equality in principle. If Priekahm was willing to be a concubine (or less than one, since there would be no ceremony), it was after all just "part of the nature of Shulathian females, they've got to have all the sex they can and their own males can't keep up" as we heard Osepok say—timing it so that Soikenn would hear it. So although they wished Mejox would "get serious" and form a couple with Otuz, they generally just regarded the situation as a typical young Palathian male having fun before settling down. What it might mean to Priekahm, I think, never occurred to them.

Poiparesis and Soikenn were humiliated by it all, of course, since from their view Priekahm was behaving like the stereotype. And Mejox and Priekahm seemed to go out of their way to be noisy and public about their affection.

The situation was very different for Otuz and me. I don't know what arguments were used or who was on what side, but it was clear that all of the adults were very uncomfortable about a Shulathian male paired off with a Palathian female. Kekox barely spoke to me at all. Osepok remained close to Otuz and was always very carefully polite to me, but I could feel her anger.

Soikenn tried so hard to be friendly and accepting that she made all four of us children uncomfortable, but at least we could get along with her whenever we weren't in couples; one on one, or with just the girls or just the boys, she was usually fine, but when we were in couples—which was almost always—in some ways she was worse than any of the other adults *because* she tried, which let us find out what she was actually thinking.

She never tried to speak to either Otuz or to Mejox about the cross-racial connections, which told us more plainly than words that she didn't think our Palathian friends could be trusted. That alone would have been enough to alienate me and Priekahm, but worse yet was that whenever Soikenn spoke to us it was in two voices. She would keep telling us that the idea of mating across racial lines didn't bother her (when obviously it did) and that she was only concerned with what people on Nisu would say or might do after we got back—as if fifty-seven years into the future was even really worth thinking about. And when she said "People on Nisu will say that . . ." she might as well have said "I think . . ." because that's how it seemed to us—with her constant talk of Priekahm being regarded as a slut and as having disappointed all of Shulath by becoming a concubine, and her equally frequent reminding me that I was apt to be killed by a mob of angry Palathians on my return.

In many ways it was easier to endure Captain Osepok's reaction to it all—which was to pretend that she heard and saw nothing, even when she would sometimes catch Otuz and me fooling around in the lab. Still, even the barest acknowledgment would have helped us feel like we were still accepted, and we never saw any acknowledgment from Osepok.

Kekox stayed silent, glaring, and angry, for many eightdays, speaking to none of the younger generation. After a time we almost forgot he had ever talked to us, for if at all possible he left any chamber we entered and seemed to be spending as much time as he could in his own chamber.

Then during one second work shift, he went into the gym when Priekahm was in there, working out by herself. Later she said she was surprised to see him at all, but even more surprised when he spoke to her; her first thought was that perhaps he wanted to make amends and be friends.

Then he pushed her against the wall, said, "Let's see what Mejox sees in you," and reached between her legs.

"Stop it!"

"I know you like it. I hear the noises you make with Mejox every day. I'm just getting a share for myself—"

"I like it *with Mejox! Not with you! Stop it!*"

"You just have romantic notions because he's your first, so you think it's him, and not what you're doing." Kekox's voice was calm, warm, and friendly, Priekahm said later, even as he pinned her hands over her head and began to stroke her copulatory organ. "You and I both know you like it. You just relax now and —"

Priekahm screamed, bit him on the shoulder, and got a hand free to smash into his face. He fell backward, clutching his bitten shoulder. "Creator burn out your womb, I only wanted some fun—"

Soikenn burst in, saw everything at once, and ran to get between them. "Leave her alone!" Her shout was even louder than Priekahm's scream, and that brought the rest of us.

Kekox was panting and angry, so much so that my first thought was that he was going to spring on Soikenn. "I just want some of what Mejox has been getting all the time. And if it was such a big deal to you, Soikenn, you'd still be taking care of my needs—"

Soikenn all but spat on him. "Is that what we are to you? Slaves? Breeding animals?" She turned to face the rest of the crew. "Well, you've all guessed it I'm sure. Kekox just tried to force Priekahm. He seems to think that Shulathian females should all be at his service all the time."

Kekox seemed about to reply, but Poiparesis grabbed him by the elbow and said, "You'd do better not to say anything right now." There was something about his tone—not angry, not challenging, but completely firm—that seemed to take all the fight out of Kekox, and he left with Poiparesis. They were in Poiparesis's chamber for a tenth of a day; occasionally we could hear Kekox's raised, angry voice coming from there, but mostly we heard the endless reasonable drone of Poiparesis, sounding the way he always did when he was trying to find a way to peace.

But that was later. While the rest of us were still trying to figure out what was happening, Soikenn dragged Priekahm off to her chamber, and the captain took Mejox up to the cockpit.

Priekahm said afterwards that Soikenn gave her an endless lecture of the familiar—about how she had brought this attack on herself by her carrying on with Mejox, that if she couldn't see that Palathian males were just animals from Mejox's behavior, surely this would convince her. She used a lot of old Shulathian standard phrases like "living up to our freedom" and "working through an unjust world to a better one" and the old "maybe in a hundred years" phrase.

After a while she seemed to run out of energy, and Priekahm said, "I'm ready to live free *now*. And I can. There are just four of you in my way. That's all. Why don't you get out of it and let me live the way you *say* you believe in?"

Soikenn's voice was flat and bitter. "You got to where you are today because you stood on the shoulders of generations past—Shulathians who were conquered, robbed, enslaved, and fought their way to equality. You owe it to your race—"

"And do you suppose Kekox owes it to *his* race to keep me in my place?"

Soikenn didn't speak for a long time, then finally said, "Look. Don't take this wrong. We know people are equal. But like and equal are not the same thing. Palathians aren't like us. And one way they aren't is that when it comes to sex they are animals, and *mean* animals at that. What you just saw is typical Palathian male behavior—"

"Is that how Kekox took you?" Priekahm asked. Soikenn swung a hard slap at her, but Priekahm caught the blow before it landed and forced the older female's arm back to her side. "No more of that, either. You'd better get used to the idea that I'm grown up now. If you had so little respect for him, if you always thought he was a dangerous animal, why did you have sex with Kekox for so many years?"

Soikenn was silent; Priekahm said later that it was at that moment that she knew that she had won, but not what she had won. Nevertheless she pressed her advantage. "Now understand me. By the time we return to Nisu—*if* we ever do—everything may have changed anyway. You won't be there to see it. And we'll be old. And we are not going to live our whole lives to fit the judgment of people who will see us when our lives are almost over. And especially we are not going to drag your old stupid ideas about how the races should relate into our lives!"

"I'm sorry I tried to slap you," Soikenn said.

Priekahm said that even though she knew Soikenn hadn't really listened to a word, she choked down her rage and said, "I don't like the way this makes me feel, Soikenn, but I can't let you or the other adults treat us this way anymore. You wanted to make new, better people. Well, that's what I am. That's what my friends are. Kekox's response is more honest—at least he just hates us and tries to hurt us, which means he sees us. But we don't exist to be what you want us to be. We just exist. We are what we are. You worked hard to make us without prejudices— now you'll just have to live with people who won't put up with your prejudices. Is that clear?"

Soikenn gestured assent. It looked like she might cry, so Priekahm left then. When she was telling us about it later, Otuz asked what Soikenn was crying about, and Priekahm just made a noncommittal gesture and said, "Probably everything. People do cry, you know, when the whole world turns upside down. Even when it *needs* to be turned upside down."

I have no idea what Poiparesis said to Kekox in his chamber while all this was going on. Otuz and I just did our work in the lab and avoided conversation of any kind. Mejox spent the time doing piloting drills with Captain Osepok in the cockpit; he said, "She kept running me through all the standard drills the ship's computer had, trying to get my deviation from perfect down to zero, but when I would miss, she'd just say 'better next time' or 'that's all right, it's the stumble before the big leap' or things like that."

Toward the end of the practice, with the last meal of the day drawing near, Mejox said, Osepok had said, "A lot of times when you just don't want to think about something, when there is nothing you can do and the waiting is just unbearable, it helps to demand a lot from yourself, to do or learn more than you thought you could, and just let your concentration get you through the bad time. It's how I've lived for years." Then—and his voice had a tone of awe in it—she had ripped off a perfect simulated landing, right down to a touchdown with zero force.

"And she said," Mejox added, " 'See what enough unhappiness can do for you—I hope you never have to develop this much skill.' You know, I think she has probably been practicing toward perfection ever since Kekox started with Soikenn, all those years ago. Captain Osepok is probably the only person in the universe who can do perfect landings. . . ."

We had been sitting in Mejox's chamber—a tiny space, but at least we could close the door—and comparing notes, trying to figure out what we would do now. But now the bell sounded for the last meal of the day, and we all looked at each other uneasily.

Someone tapped on the door. Otuz opened it—it was Poiparesis. Without being asked, he stepped inside and closed the door. "I think we've had the last incident of that kind," he said without preliminaries. "Of course things are still very tense. And I know that you were entirely in the right and Kekox was entirely in the wrong, Priekahm, but I don't think you'll get an apology from him immediately. I thought you should all know that all the adults are planning to behave themselves at dinner."

"We're not going to cause an uproar," I said. "As long as it's understood that Kekox was the cause of all the trouble."

"Understood by me, and I think by the captain, anyway," Poiparesis said. "Maybe even by Kekox, and I'm working on that." We noticed he didn't mention Soikenn, but no one brought it up. "And *everyone* has agreed that we'll keep a lid on it. I was hoping you would be willing to do the same."

"Zahmekoses already said so," Mejox said.

Poiparesis gestured agreement. "So he did. All right, then. Thank you."

At evening meal all the adults were very subdued, and all of us were very nervous, but speaking.

That evening, I was studying some distant-star gravimetrics in the smaller computer lab when Kekox came in. He sat down, looked at me, and said, "Well."

"Hello," I said. I kept working. If he had anything to say, I should probably let him say it, but I wasn't expecting anything worth hearing.

He sat a long moment, then said, "I just want to ask you something. Poiparesis has assured me that it's something I have no business asking and that you will take offense, but it is something I badly want to know." His voice was too quiet and reasonable—he must have been extremely upset. The computer lab was dead still. The only motion was the pale blue curves on the screen, marking the rise and fall of distant star gravity as the ship traversed the space between the stars.

Every curve was as smooth as theory predicted it should be. All the animations showed smooth rise and fall. I let the moments click away, watched the distant stars roll over and over through the pale blue curtain of braking photons, and listened to Kekox shifting in his seat. Probably I had some hope he wouldn't talk at all.

It was so long before he spoke that I almost jumped when he did. "I just want to know . . . This, uh, involvement between you and Otuz. Is it a serious one? I mean, since Priekahm and Mejox are so protective about her . . . being exclusive . . . Poiparesis insists on calling it her 'chastity' . . . well, is your reason for all this you have been doing with Otuz, perhaps, that you don't have a normal sexual outlet with your own kind? Or are you perhaps being deliberately offensive, either to me or to Mejox? Or is it some kind of . . . well, some kind of perverse attraction for . . . well, I just wanted to know why."

I recorded a graph I thought they would want to see back on Nisu. "Actually I'd say it's more that we just like each other. We always have. We're interested in the same things, we do the same work, we were close for more than a decade before puberty . . . you could hardly expect it to be otherwise, could you? Of course, all of us younger generation are friends, but it's not the same. Otuz and I are more like each other than either of them. So . . . well, it just seems very natural to me. I'm much more attracted to Otuz than I ever could be to Priekahm, and—"

"She feels the same way about you," Kekox said, his voice flat and dull. "I already talked to her." He groaned and rubbed his crisp, bushy top crest, now beginning to go gray. "I understand everything I guess except why sex has to get into it."

"Well, you've had sex, or tried to, with every female on board except Otuz. *You* tell *me* why it has to get into it."

From the way his back hair bristled I thought I was about to get a beating, but then he said, softly, "I wish I knew. My father used to say I must have Shulathian blood from somewhere. Seems like it's been all my life that it was the most important thing there was, that it's what I thought about whenever I wasn't on a mission. Especially what I thought about tended to be the next one, who I was going to copulate with next . . . it's hard to explain. We've been on this voyage for so long now, twenty years, and . . . I'd literally kill for a chance at a new female. I never thought that could be an issue, but it is. I guess I can't fault you or Mejox for being interested in sex, either . . . but still. When I was growing up, what you kids do in front of everyone was the kind of dirty joke that could get you into a fight. It's just hard for me to . . ." He let the sentence trail off and sat, squirming uncomfortably, for a long time before he said, "Well, I guess I look like an idiot?"

"Well, not an idiot, maybe, but you know, none of what you're saying is *our* problem. We're on the ship. On the ship everyone is equal. So why shouldn't we love who we love?"

Kekox sighed. "The strange thing is that there was a time when I would have agreed completely. I used to use my opinions to start brawls with guys I wanted to fight. But now I find . . . I'm not as big as my principles. Funny." He looked over my shoulder at the screen. "Is that anything interesting?"

I took his invitation. "Oh, it looks like a few more stars may have dark companions than we thought," I said. "And most stars have a lot more planets than we'd thought. If anyone back home was the least bit concerned with finding habitable worlds anymore, we would have a list of at least three hundred possibles for them—all the places with enough mass in their habitable zones. A few fast probes could settle the question and then we could scatter our people to a thousand worlds, instead of betting everything on the poor old *Imperial Hope*. If they ever finish her, that is." I pointed to the comparison graphs. "See? We measure the microgravity at every fourth eightday—we've been doing that since we started—and then we do a mathematical decomposition to pinpoint the sources. Way down in the fine grain of the noise, we find things that have moved and resolve those into masses and positions.

"Gravity is a lot weaker signal than light is, but they don't attenuate or block nearly as easily, so we can find the right places farther away. The biggest thing we needed to do this kind of astronomy is to be able to take measurements at points far enough apart—and we've certainly had the chance to do that across these past twenty years."

Kekox asked me to show him how to do the basic solutions, and he and I worked together silently for the sixteenth of a day until bed. After that we were almost friends again, speaking to each other anyway, but now and then I would see him staring at me and Otuz and I would know it could never be entirely over. And though he didn't try anything again, Priekahm was afraid of him till the day he died.

And so for three more years we decelerated into the Kousapex System. Kekox was civil but distant, Soikenn alternated between sullen silence and false heartiness, and except for her turns in the cockpit, the captain tended to stay in her chamber, listening to music, watching performances, and reading old books. The only adult that all of the younger generation were able to talk to was Poiparesis, and that was strange because he was the only one who spoke to us openly about the way we had paired off. He accepted that Mejox was being reasonably decent to Priekahm and did not seem likely to drop her abruptly, as Soikenn feared. He even conceded that the way we had arranged things was a better fit to our personalities.

But, he would add, always, love and marriage were two different things, both difficult enough, and he didn't see why we had to make things so much harder by rebelling against the old ways. And now and then when Mejox and Priekahm would sit with arms draped around each other near him, or when Otuz and I might brush hands or whisper to each other, we would catch a glimpse of Poiparesis wincing.

Yet despite all that, we liked and trusted him, and we were all around Poiparesis a great deal for another reason: he was doing the most interesting work on the ship. We had many probes down on Setepos now, and a sizable number of orbiters, and Poiparesis was trying to process all the pictures and data into a single decision: where we would land and build our base.

It mattered a great deal: we children would live there for five years (or five and a half years of Setepos—we would have to get used to a new calendar). And the adults would live out their lives and finally die there, while doing the long-term research needed for *Imperial Hope*'s millions of settlers.

"Always assuming they ever build *Imperial Hope*," Poiparesis said. Two days before we had gotten a news update: the design phase was not only to be stretched out, but to be stretched out seventeen rather than eleven additional years. "Sometimes I think that all the evolutionary advantages of being able to think about the future are canceled out by the ability to figure out how far away the future is. We don't seem to be able to balance things out between understanding that we still have time to act, and that the future is always going to get here."

"You're being philosophic today," Priekahm teased. "It's what you get for watching the news."

"It would make a philosopher out of you," Otuz said, "or a suicide, depending on how seriously you took it. Didn't you check it, Priekahm? Seventeen-year stretch-out now. At least they're still letting us have the new power station on schedule, and the mirror is on its way. Hey, look at these pictures! Look at the size of those animals!"

We all bent around what Otuz had pulled up on the screen; she worked image enhancement on it and added a measuring stick.

"They're at least twice a body-length high at the shoulder," Mejox breathed. "And look at those snouts—that is their nose, isn't it?"

"I'd say so, but for all I know their spine folds around and that's their tail," Poiparesis said. "Can't tell till we get there and cut one up. Or unless we move one of the moving-picture probes over to the eastern Hook, which is where we found this one—and we've pretty well ruled it out. Big predators, not enough water, no good river transport . . ."

"Oh, of course, I know," Otuz said, "but aren't they wonderful?"

"It's an amazing planet, based on a sample of two," Poiparesis agreed.

"You're so lucky, Poiparesis," Mejox said. "There will be time for you to explore a lot more—"

"If it were up to me," he said quietly, "we'd all stay. I think there's something crazy about sending you back."

The room was perfectly still. We had never heard any adult voice a thought like that, not even privately to each other when they thought we weren't listening.

He sighed. "I suppose I shouldn't have said that. Everyone seems to have strong opinions about what opinions I should have. But the only reason for you all to go back is to be living examples, symbols, people they can trot out to make the case for the Migration Project. We all know Mejox and Otuz are pretty much out of the running for Emperor now; the empress has had four children we know about, and I would bet that somewhere out there in space behind us there're radio messages announcing two more. As celebrities you'd have a great deal of influence, but I'm sure that if you stayed here, there would be decades more of exploration and setup completed, and the colonists are going to need that data so much . . . it seems so insane to spend all the time, money, so much of your lives to get you here, and then to send you back so you can shake hands and lead parades." He looked around. "Am I depressing all of you?"

"I'm depressed enough as it is," Mejox said. "It's hard for me to remember that when I was little, I used to think the parades and ceremonies and so forth were the greatest things in life. I guess because I thought they were all for me, and I thought that they had something to do with being powerful and getting my way. Nowadays . . . well, even before I left I guess I had figured out that the one they hold the parade for might as well be a prisoner. All he can do is walk where he's supposed to."

I always liked to tease Mejox when he went into self-pity, so I said, "Of course, scientifically speaking, we'll want to test that by holding parades for some prisoners, and then maybe imprisoning some celebrities—"

Mejox made a sour face. "All right, I'm exaggerating. I'm still not happy about—"

Priekahm cried out as if something had bitten her.

"Look!" she said. Her fingers were stabbing frantically at the keys on the controls. "Let me play this part back. It's from one of the roving probes, the last-wave ones . . ."

"What part of Setepos?"

"That big peninsula off the southwest corner of Big. Near where it joins to the Hook. It's one of the list of a hundred possible base sites— nice weather, forests, mountains." She popped up an inset screen and showed us the glowing spot, then turned back to relocating the short burst of moving picture that had excited her. "Here, now watch—"

We had gotten used to several of the basic groups of Seteposian animals, and we already knew there was one whole family that looked quite a bit like us—indeed, the ones I had named mejoxes looked like miniature Palathians with prehensile tails. There were big ones and little ones, some that lived in trees and some that lived on grasslands; the little bit of moving pictures that we had gotten of them seemed to indicate that they were unusually intelligent for animals.

This band of them that crossed in front of the camera looked much less like us than the mejoxes did. They were even more hairless than Shulathians, though shorter; they had small curved ears and flat faces like Palathians, and they were intermediate in build, with broader shoulders than a Shulathian but without the thick, heavy knot of back muscles of a Palathian.

"They're walking upright," I said, staring stupidly, feeling even as I said it that somehow I was missing everything important.

"Let me get image enhancement—" Priekahm said.

Otuz was making a strangled noise, and Priekahm added, "So you see it, too. Let's just see if we're both crazy—"

The brief section of moving picture, no longer in time than it takes to draw three breaths, ran backward, enlarged, clarified—and began to run forward again. We all bent to look—and then we were all shouting at once, louder than Priekahm had.

Clutched in the hands of most of the animals were sticks fitted with shaped-stone blades—unmistakably sickles. Each of them was wearing a long vest of animal skin over a shift of woven fabric. And the meadow in which they stood in a long, ragged line, was all of one kind of grass—tall stuff with bunches of seeds on slender stalks, like the *retraphesis* from which we made bread and porridge at home.

The other adults came running to see what the shouting was about, Kekox in the lead. It was at least a forty-eighth of a day before everyone stopped gabbling at once and we began to talk about it intelligibly. The first thing everyone actually heard was Poiparesis's comment: "Well, if nothing else, this means that the mission is finally going to get some attention from the news services back home. Too bad we'll have to wait to hear what they think until *Wahkopem Zomos* is already on its way back."

"Fascinating," Kekox said. "It's like something out of the early pictures taken by Wahkopem, after he discovered the Leeward Islands."

We all crowded still closer to the screen as the short clip of motion picture ran over and over again. "Think of what they'll have to say to us," Soikenn breathed. "How different they'll be, how wonderfully different the world will look to them."

As I looked at them, I found myself thinking that I had never seen any creatures quite so ugly before in my life; the humpbacked thing we had seen some time before was nothing compared to these hideous beings clad in crude rags. Their faces were flatter than any Palathian's; their heads seemed to be nearly spherical underneath the wads of filthy matted fur that grew above, and in some cases down onto, the face; their bodies had neither a Palathian's confident power nor a Shulathian's grace, but something between the two that might be called sickly clumsiness. They looked like nothing so much as the unfortunate result of an illegal medical experiment.

I could tell Otuz was revolted, too. She leaned back against me, as she usually would, any time in the lab, and unconsciously, looking at these distressing creatures, we took each other's hands.

Kekox was babbling on. "Unbelieveable. A living world so close was a small miracle, but these are actual *people*; they must have poetry, and religion, and music, and—" He saw that Otuz and I were holding hands and touching, and for a moment I thought he might turn and strike me, but he swallowed hard and contented himself with glaring at me.

The sudden interruption had made everyone turn and look; I saw Soikenn and Osepok glance away, in some pain, and Poiparesis sigh. Otuz leaned back harder and I extended my arm further around her.

Mejox finally saw—he had been watching the screen more intently than any of us. His face set flat and hard; he glared back at Kekox. Priekahm slid into his arm, flashing a thin smile at us. There was an ugly set to Kekox's eyes at that.

Poiparesis, too suddenly and too brightly, said, "Isn't it amazing? We had thought the biggest thing this expedition would have to deal with would be octades of loneliness, and now we see that the problem is going to be an excess of company. Just think of what will happen when we start to talk with them!"

Kekox turned back to the screen. "Amazing," he said. I could see him forcing himself to relax, making himself deal with what was on the screen and not with what was in the room. "The most wonderful thing we've seen so far."

As he said that, Mejox, jockeying the image, got us an up-close look at one of the creatures; it was more hideous in detail than it had been in general.

We all spent a while longer looking at the pictures, but shortly we of the younger generation started to find ways to drift out, heading down to the common dining area. The adults were still burbling at the picture and I'm not sure they even noticed our going.

I was last to join the others; they were sitting at the table, untouched cups of warm drink in front of them, and it didn't look like anyone had said anything in a long time.

"What do *you* think, Zahmekoses?" Priekahm asked, not looking at me.

"I think they're thrilled out of their minds to find what's probably a very dangerous kind of vermin all over one of the best colony sites—and they can't wait to make friends with it—but if any of them saw a cross-bred child, *especially* one they were related to, they would stomp it to death without compunction."

"I think you're right," Mejox said. "Isn't it funny that they're all *so* thrilled with finding another intelligent species, they want to go cuddle right up to it, and just love the Creation out of every one of those smelly savages, but they can't bring themselves to accept love between a Shulathian and a Palathian?"

"Unless the Shulathian is a whore-oh-sorry-I-mean-consort," Priekahm added.

I sat down. Thoughts were whirling through my mind. "Well, be fair, Soikenn and Poiparesis are scientists. They just think this is remarkable. They haven't thought about the implications yet and probably never will until someone makes them."

Mejox groaned. "Yeah. Like, one beautiful planet down the drain. No chance to talk about just staying there and having kids. At least not unless we want our kids to grow up always having to watch out for a big, smart, dangerous animal like those. I guess we didn't realize how lucky we were to live on a world where most of the dangerous animals were killed off long, long ago. Isn't there one decently safe part of Setepos?"

Otuz shrugged. "Well, where's your spirit of adventure? Didn't you want to wander all over an untamed world?"

Mejox laughed ruefully. "I sure did. A nice, safe, *tame*, untamed world."

I had finally pulled out a thought that might be useful. "Remember our vow, way back on Nisu?"

They all gestured assent.

"Well," I said, "here's the thing. We pledged to be united. We pledged to belong to each other first, Nisu next, and not at all to our individual races. And it seems to me the time has come to start thinking as a group of friends—and as Nisuans. What's the biggest problem on our homeworld? Don't answer the rhetorical question . . . just think about how Kekox just reacted, and that poor stupid old bastard is trying *not* to be a bigot. And why is the prejudice so deep? Because the races are so different, right? Now right now we know nothing of these things on the planet's surface—or almost nothing. But don't we all agree they're hideous? And clearly they're crude and stupid . . . look at the way they live. And . . . well. Here's my guess. As soon as we have a 256th of a day's real acquaintance with them, we'll hate them to the bone. So will the adults, for that matter. The Seteposians sure aren't attractive, and if there's anything that our own history teaches us, it's that race hatred is natural and normal. They won't like us either. So I say . . . if it's going to be hatred, and it's us or them, we should get the jump on them."

Otuz gestured her agreement. "And think about this too. Before the Conquest, all the little principalities of Shulath, even though they had sworn allegiance to the same General Court in principle, were constant-ly at war with each other. There were traditional hatreds between differ-ent islands and cities and branches of Mother-Sea-Worship that went back too far for anyone to know how they'd started. But after the Con-quest . . . well, all that disappeared in a hurry. Everybody who was tall, crestless, and long-eared learned that there was only one enemy worth hating—the one who had conquered them. In a couple of generations all Shulathians were brothers. Nowadays no one even knows which of the many original nations any one Shulathian is descended from." She ges-tured at us all. "Well, compared to our differences with those intelligent Seteposian animals, we're all identical twins."

Priekahm was gesturing eager assent. "You're right," she said, "on both counts. First the difference it might make in our culture to find real aliens to hate, and secondly that we don't really have any basis for call-ing the Seteposians people. There are pets on Nisu that could be taught to build a hut or even to till a garden. Until we know that they're any-thing more than smart animals, we shouldn't be calling them people."

"I hope you're not talking about us adults," Poiparesis said, coming in. "There you all are. Well, as you might have guessed, we have a sud-den emergency research project. Get a snack if you need one and meet me in the rear computer lab in a sixty-fourth of a day. I've got a long list of tasks for all of you; we have a meeting at the end of the eightday to decide what to do, and we'll need to get every piece of information we can together by then." He turned and went.

I guess I was still angry; I turned to the others and said, "Well, there you have it. As soon as anything important comes up they drop all this silly pretense about discussing with us as equals." It came out in a nasty, sarcastic tone that I disliked as I said it, but perhaps only I heard the tone, for everyone else was gesturing assent.

"How about we hold a meeting of our own, real soon?" Mejox said. "Maybe after evening meal tonight?"

9

AT THE END OF THE EIGHTDAY, WAHKOPEM'S WHOLE CREW MET IN THE common dining area. "Let's begin by facing facts," Osepok said. "The decision has to be entirely ours. No matter what we decide, a lot of Nisuans won't like it. Right?"

We all gestured agreement. "All right, then," she said. "It seems to me then that what we do is decide, plan what we're going to do, and then radio back the plan with the news. That way we don't give anyone back on Nisu a chance to argue about what we ought to do before they know what it is. At least they can't get mad about being made irrelevant."

Again everyone agreed.

"So much for the easy part," she said. "Now what do we do? Let's turn this over to Mejox, who operated the two mobile probes we used for looking into this."

Mejox got up and dimmed the lights. "Here's highlights from motion pictures taken by probe one, which I sent to a high hill that overlooks a settlement site."

The first picture dashed any hope we might have had that the whole thing was somehow our misunderstanding. The village was surrounded by a wooden palisade with stones piled around its base, and fields around it were planted with grain and various other plants. "Let me bring up some details," Mejox said. "If you look here, you'll see what's pretty clearly a crude irrigation system, and when we enlarged and enhanced this part, we found this gadget: the long lever raises the animal skin bag full of water out of the river, as you see, and then they swing it around to the trough and set it down. The bag empties into the trough, the trough spills into the ditch, and the ditch carries it out to the field."

Poiparesis grunted. "And is that smoke?"

"Oh, yes," Mejox said. "They have fire. The tools are stone, but some of the ornaments on their necks and wrists look like metal, maybe gold or copper, something easy to smelt in a cellulose fire."

"Cellulose?"

"Yep. Amazing, isn't it? Something we only know as a synthetic is basic to life here. Thanks to their habit of burning trees for fuel, we were able to get a spectroscope shot of the flames, and cellulose is what Seteposian trees are made out of. Which is why Seteposian forests grow a lot taller than ours, I suspect—Seteposian trees aren't limited by the water pressure needed to hold them up. Probably the core of the tree is just deposited cellulose and isn't even alive. I bet they don't have to bake the wood before using it to build with. But anyway, it looks like a thousand of the animals probably live in that village. Now here's the clip from probe two, which I sent in after the first probe disappeared."

"Disappeared? You mean it stopped transmitting—" Osepok said.

"No, disappeared. A satellite overhead saw it on one pass and didn't see it on the next. This made me suspect that the animals in the village had something to do with it. So I sent the next probe to a hilltop farther away, got the pictures, and told it to fly out into the desert when it was done. That drained the last of the batteries and it had to sit and soak up desert sunshine for two full days to get operational again. But it was definitely the way I had to do it—let me show you. Now in the earlier clip you noticed this big building I'm sure—" He popped a still picture onto the screen. "I thought it was a granary, or maybe the boss male's den. But look here—"

They had pulled off large parts of one side of the building. Inside there was a statue, probably of stone, of one of their females sitting cross-legged; in front of it were the remains of the probe, solar panels torn off, sections missing from its wings, thrusters gone, instrument package ripped open. I looked closer. "Did it get covered with all that mud when—"

"That's not mud," Mejox said. "Watch."

The clip changed. One of them, in a long robe, a strange mask over its face, raised a small struggling animal—not the same species, this one was covered with thick hair—over his head, then forced it down onto the flat upper surface of the probe's right wing. With a gleaming stone knife, he cut its throat and let it bleed over the probe.

"Oh, no," Poiparesis said. "No. This just keeps getting worse."

"Exactly," Osepok said. "I'd be pretty surprised if that's anything other than what it looks like. A religious ritual. Not too different from the ones the sacrifice cults did when Wahkopem found their islands, assuming his description was accurate. Either they think the probe is a god, or they think it was sent by one, and they're giving it gifts."

"My guess is that they don't think at all," Mejox said. "They're interesting animals, but let's not get carried away."

The next shot was a slow pan. Nearly half the crude log-and-mud buildings in the village had wing sections or chunks of solar panel over the door, and several close-ups of individuals showed that they were wearing thrusters or instruments on thongs around their necks.

"So far, not only are they there first, but they seem to be outwitting us," Kekox commented.

"Otuz will have the next section, about the problem of the distribution of these things," Mejox said.

She got up and brought up the lights. "I wish I had Mejox's flair for the dramatic, but I don't. So I'll just say that I've got everything documented and I can show you the detail if you need more proof. But here's the gist of it: we used all the pictures we had of these animals to set up a program that processed through every satellite and probe picture we had, looking for evidence of them elsewhere on the planet. And the quick answer is that these animals are the kind of vermin that spreads everywhere. We found them on all the large land masses except the ice-covered one, in desert, grassland, mountains, swamps. Almost certainly they're in the forest areas, too, but we can't see them under the tree canopy. The biggest parts of the planet where there aren't any, as far as we can tell, are some islands here and there. Some of the islands are quite decent places—these two southeast of Southland, this one by the Hook, and many of these small chains in mid-ocean, all have nice enough climates, but any island we picked might become infested with them before the colony got here, a few hundred years from now." She scratched her ear fiercely, something she did when she had to tell you bad news. "It's not clear that they've gotten anywhere by sea yet—they may have walked on land bridges ten thousand years ago when there was much more ice and the oceans were lower—but if you look at this satellite picture, it wouldn't quite resolve, but it does look like a log raft traveling across this strait here. We'll probably know more later, but for right now I'm not sure we can say any part of the planet is secure against them, except perhaps the ice continent."

"So conflict is bound to come," Mejox said.

"So, *if* we settle there, conflict is *absolutely* bound to come," Soikenn agreed, emphatically. "They're already living in towns, possibly doing some metalwork, and growing crops, and it looks like their population dispersal has been rapid and recent because they don't differ physically nearly as much as Shulathian and Palathian—it looks like except for minor pigmentation differences they're still all one race."

Otuz agreed emphatically. "Right. We really can't avoid these animals. Like it or not we're going to be moving into their way."

Poiparesis winced and said, "These 'animals,' as you call them, show every sign of being as bright as we are—"

Mejox asked impatiently, "So where's their spaceship?"

"Where was ours a hundred years ago?" Soikenn demanded. "As I see it, the only thing we can do is land as far from their settlements as we can—probably on islands in the big ocean—and try not to let them see too much more of us. We can capture huge amounts of scientific information here—both about the huge variety of ecosystems this planet has, and about the development and deployment of the intelligent species here. The information is absolutely priceless. But once we've done that, we need to remove whatever traces our base has left. I'd suggest building it close to a coastline and simply blowing it up after we leave with one of the spare sail-deployment fusion charges, so that whatever isn't blasted or burned can wash into the sea. The little bit of residual radioactivity won't have any effects you could detect after a couple of decades.

"Then we take all that data we've acquired, and *all eight* of us head back to Nisu. I know we older ones will die on the way, and the idea of being buried in the cold dark between the stars gives me chills, but we don't dare leave our bodies or camp behind for those people to find. We've got to leave them free to find their own road to civilization, first of all because they have a right to it just as we did, and secondly because we'll be able to study them while they do it. When we radio our reports back to Nisu, I have no doubt they'll dispatch a small permanent colony to observe these people as they develop—probably a main base on the moon of this world, and then various surface bases anywhere where they can operate without interfering. And in a few thousand years, probably, we'll be ready to talk.

"Meanwhile, though, this ought to get those idiots back home off their self-satisfied rumps and get the five other scouting missions restarted. Intelligence is obviously not as rare as we thought it would be, but living worlds are still very common and we can find a more suitable one. Better yet, several suitable ones, with a big ship going to each one. Do you see it, everyone? If we treat these people fairly, learn from them and study them—well, then. It can be a model for our whole new civilization, for a future when Nisuan ships sail between ten different stars, and when we bring them in as our partners, maybe twenty thousand years from now."

There was a long pause before Captain Osepok spoke. "I'm not sure I'm so optimistic about the people back home doing the right thing. This Fereg Yorock isn't likely to want to do anything that doesn't pay off in two eightdays, preferably at two hundred percent. But at least it will get them to dispatch one or two more scoutships, and maybe to think a little about the future. And we can follow the course of action that's right . . . and just hope that the people back home and in the next generations will follow through." Her voice seemed to gain confidence as she thought about it. "And I don't suppose we're responsible for what people will do in the future." She smiled at Soikenn. "That's a great solution to the problem."

Soikenn seemed to relax.

Poiparesis drew a deep breath and let it out. He was sitting with his arms folded across his chest. "Well, I'm not sure that it's the best course."

I felt a deep relief and I noticed Otuz relax as well. At least *all* the adults weren't going to be irrational.

"It seems to me," Poiparesis said, "that there's no special reason why these people should have to fall over the same bumps in the road as we did. Sooner or later, just to mention the most obvious example, one of their civilizations will get ahead of the others militarily, and will probably conquer and enslave everyone else—and they'll have the same kind of horrible relations within their species that we have between Shulathian and Palathian.

"I mean, we didn't train the children by letting them touch hot stoves or leaving out sharp knives to play with. We didn't force them to repeat every experiment in the history of physics or chemistry, especially not the poisonous or explosive ones. Why should we let this younger species make the same mistakes we did, the ones we're all still paying for? I say we should study them—and then make contact, tell them who we are and why we're coming, perhaps even make a point of asking their permission to land." He smiled warmly and looked from face to face; it was clear that somehow he thought he had found a compromise position, or the best of all possible ones. Perhaps if we had all heard his argument first, things might have been different—I thought that often, many years later. But probably not; however kind and gentle Poiparesis's words often were, the actions of the other adults shouted them down. "But," Poiparesis added, "we old ones have been doing all the talking. Perhaps we should hear from the younger generation."

We had prepared for this carefully; Otuz, Priekahm, and I all turned to Mejox as one, making it clear that we expected him to speak for all of us.

Mejox drew a slow, deep breath, and said, "All right, then. Let me make this as simple and as clear as I can.

"No doubt if the people back on Nisu had kept the Migration Project on track, we would be able to reserve this planet as a scientific preserve, send probes to lots of others, and find somewhere that was more comfortable. And I'm sure many Nisuans, scientists particularly, would greatly prefer that. I suppose the animals down there would prefer it if we just went away.

"But we have to think of Nisu. That's what this mission is about. And from that standpoint, I think that the discovery of intelligent animals on Setepos is not a drawback but a tremendous advantage. I propose that we land right where the most advanced groups of the animals live, attack and subjugate their civilization, domesticate the survivors, and establish an economic basis for a colony that will exploit these animals to the fullest, for the benefit of all our people. Then I propose that we simply radio back to Nisu, explain what we have done, and tell them to come join us. We undo our sterilizations, settle down to run the plantation, and our great-grandchildren will be there to greet the colony— with a vast economic base set up so that everyone can live in comfort.

"Now, obviously it's better for us because we don't have to spend the rest of our lives in this metal box. Just as obviously it's better for the settlers to come, because they arrive on a planet that's ready to accommodate them. But what it's really—"

"You aren't going to try to claim it's better for those people?" Poiparesis broke in sarcastically.

"What people?"

"The ones on Setepos."

"There aren't any, yet. There are some unusually smart animals," Mejox said firmly. "And that's the point I'm getting to. What has been the great disaster in Nisuan history? The split between Palathian and Shulathian, the failure to see that we're united by being Nisuan. So here we have animals smart enough to have a kind of primitive religion and government, and do all kinds of work, but not smart enough to have ascended from living the way our remotest ancestors did.

"They are not Nisuan, nor can they ever hope to become Nisuan. And though we'll need their labor, the most important thing they will do for us is they make it clear that *we're all Nisuan*. The differences among ourselves are nothing compared to the difference between us and these animals—"

"If you consider them animals—" Poiparesis began.

Otuz glared at him. "What else are they? They aren't people. We couldn't possibly have a common ancestor. We came here to claim Setepos, and it's ours, and just because some of the animals are building fires and using pointed sticks—"

Poiparesis seemed to be struggling for self-control. Finally he managed to squeak out, "So to give equality to Shulathians, you'll make slaves out of a whole other intelligent species? One thing—"

"A domestic animal is not a slave," Priekahm said, firmly.

A glance passed among the adults. After a long pause, Osepok spoke. "This sounds very much as if all of you have decided something, together, and we are just now being told what it is." She looked directly at me. "Zahmekoses, do you agree with this?"

"Yes," I said flatly. "And yes, we did discuss it before. A lot of you won't talk to us anymore, remember? So don't be surprised if we arrived at some agreement."

They all looked angry; Poiparesis in particular seemed furious. "I would think a Shulathian might *object* to slavery," he said, staring directly at me. "Not *plan* for it."

I ignored that, as it deserved, and started to explain. "If we use these animals—"

"People," Soikenn said.

"Animals," I said firmly. "And I'm a little tired of hearing all this ranting about rights, and insisting that we have to treat them like people, when all of you act like we're criminals for mating with a different race."

Kekox stood up and glared at me; for a moment I thought he was going to lunge and attack me, but then he deliberately crossed the room so he could speak only to Mejox, with his back to the rest of us. "I see what you're after. I should have seen what it was leading to when you were a little snot-nosed brat—which of course you still are. *Emperor Mejox!* And if not Emperor Mejox of Nisu, then Emperor Mejox of Setepos. Oh, better yet, Emperor Mejox of Setepos, the first emperor in more than a century to *own slaves.* Oh, yes. You can probably get the poor superstitious bastards to worship you as a god. With a Shulathian whore for an empress, of course, and by the time the colony ship gets here a whole bunch of mixed-race mongrels to be the aristocracy, and millions of slaves, so that decent people—"

"That's enough," Mejox said. It was strange—I had expected him to scream or shout, but his voice was low, even, and angrier than I had ever heard before. It chilled me to the bone, even knowing he was on my side.

Kekox's eyes narrowed. "Oh. The Emperor of Three Brats objects to what I'm saying. Well, just listen to this, because I will only point it out to you once. For most of our history, *we* made do with pointed sticks and fire. You have *no* evidence that they are less bright or capable than we are. In fact, from what I have seen, they seem to be a lot smarter than you kids. So think about this. You may be products of a much more advanced civilization, but you have *no* experience with fighting. *None.* You've got three steam rifles and nowhere on the ship where you can practice using them. *You'll* have to use them right the first time. *They've* been practicing all their lives with stone-tipped spears. And at their stage of civilization I would bet warfare happens every summer. It's probably a whole tribe of combat veterans. They know what it's like to see their friends die beside them. They know how to keep fighting when they're hurt. They know their weapons so well that they're like extensions of their bodies. You may have twenty thousand years of technology on them, but they've got all the skill and experience that really matters. So before we talk about the fact that your plan is disgusting—and that *you're* disgusting, Emperor Mejox, Consort of Her Majesty the Long-Eared Whore—let's just make sure you know that *it won't work.* The Seteposians are the ones with all the advantages. Do you understand that?" As he said it, he stabbed his finger into Mejox's chest. Mejox, glaring, slapped Kekox's hand away.

Poiparesis stepped between them, pushing them apart. "Stop it!"

"Oh, yes, hide behind daddy," Kekox said, reaching around Poiparesis to flick Mejox under the nose.

"Stop it right now," Poiparesis said. "We *can't* fight in here, and you know it. We are only disagreeing about where to land and what to do on Setepos. We don't have to talk about everything else in the universe."

"Sit down, Kekox," Osepok said. "Please sit down. We will talk it out. Please."

Kekox took a step back. Mejox was backing away, too, and Poiparesis had stepped out of the way, when Kekox drew a knife and struck at Mejox, a hard, sharp, underhanded blow. But Mejox had been training in combat sports for twenty years now, more seriously than any of the rest of us, and he had been training mostly against Kekox. His hands slapped closed over Kekox's wrist in a fast, hard disarm; with a crunch, the old guard's wrist shattered, and the knife fell to the deck.

Mejox snatched it up, his eyes burning at Kekox, and struck upward. Poiparesis turned and lunged into the fight, trying to stop Mejox, I think, or to keep him from using the knife. I'm not sure whether he slipped and fell, or misjudged the distance, but the blade sank deep under his ribcage, into his blood mixer; a great gout of dark purplish blood washed over Mejox's arm, and, as he and Kekox stared in horror, Poiparesis fell dead on the deck.

Kekox, still clutching his wrist, stared down for a long moment, and then said softly to Mejox, "See what you've done."

None of the rest of us could move. Mejox turned him over, but from the sheer volume of dark blood we knew what had happened: the blood mixer is up inside the rib cage, usually a safe spot, but if it is pierced, since it's where the body's whole blood supply returns to the hearts, the loss of blood pressure alone is fatal in moments. Probably he had been dead before he struck the deck.

The puddle of dark blood spread across the floor, huge and thick, and Mejox stood in the middle, his arm drenched with blood and the rest of him spattered with it.

"See what you've done," Kekox repeated.

Mejox looked up at us, face distorted with grief, as if he hadn't heard Kekox, and said, "Let's move him up onto this table." Looking sick, he drew the knife from Poiparesis's abdomen and dropped it into a waste slot.

"That's evidence," Osepok said dully.

"It's all right, I confess. And you're all witnesses. Help me move him onto the table, and let's compose his body and cover it." Mejox's voice was very soft and gentle. Though if anyone had really killed Poiparesis it had been Kekox, it was clear then that Mejox would take the blame to keep the peace.

He was talking to all of us, and I stood up; so did Captain Osepok, and the two of us lifted the still warm, heavy body up onto the table. We laid his arms gently across his chest, stretched out his legs to lie flat, and then—surprising myself—I closed the lids of his eyes and pressed his jaw shut. I was having trouble seeing, and my stomach was rolling over. The down on his face was as soft as I remembered from childhood. I gently brushed his long ears out as well, so that they lay straight on the table. Suddenly unable to bear it any longer, I turned away, and found myself huddled against the captain, who was beginning to sob.

After a long while, hanging onto each other, we both looked up. Mejox and Priekahm were standing side by side, holding hands, still looking down at Poiparesis's body; Soikenn still hadn't moved; Kekox stood with his hand dangling from its broken wrist.

No one had heard Otuz go out, but in a moment she came back with the medical kit. She murmured something to Kekox. He sat down and let her work on his wrist; after she got it stabilized enough, they went down the hall together to where Otuz had already changed one of the convertible chambers to an infirmary, so that she could splint his wrist and sedate him.

Mejox and Priekahm left silently, quickly, going somewhere to comfort each other. Captain Osepok and I stood for another long moment, and then she said, "I need time alone."

"So do I," I said, feeling heavy and dull. I needed to cry or to sit and stare at a wall for hours, it didn't matter much which. "Soikenn, do you—"

She had not even raised her head; her ears had not twitched at the sound of her name.

"Soikenn," I said again. She might as well have been carved out of stone.

"Let her be," Osepok said. "She has a lot to think about. Soikenn, do you just want to be here alone?"

Slowly, she worked her mouth a couple of times and finally said, "Yes."

"All right, then," Osepok said. She pulled a blanket down from a locker and I helped her put it around Soikenn's shoulders. Then the two of us went down the corridor to our separate chambers without speaking again. The last glimpse I had of the common dining area was of Soikenn, still staring at Poiparesis's body, the blanket wrapped around her, shuddering as if she were terribly cold.

I spent a long time, perhaps a fifth of a day, lying on my bunk and staring at the ceiling, sometimes drifting into brief sleep.

Three thoughts chased each other around in my mind. Impossibly, feeling foolish even for thinking it, I wanted Poiparesis back. On another level, I wanted someone to tell me what would happen next, and I wanted it to involve no effort or decisions from me. Most of all I remembered the touch of his two fingers on my forehead when he would tuck me in, long ago.

Mejox must be devastated, but knowing him, he would pull into himself emotionally; only Priekahm could talk to him right now. The captain had always been solitary; I doubted she would have anything to say. Kekox was knocked out at the moment, but when he woke up, I thought it was fairly likely that he would be busy blaming Mejox and too full of anger to talk to any of us; the captain or Soikenn would have to deal with him.

Soikenn. With a guilty start I remembered how we'd left her. I got up, washed my face, and hurried down to the common dining area to check on her.

I realized I would have to see the body again and braced myself for that. It was not quite as awful this time; I suppose I was beginning to accept that Poiparesis was dead. I looked at the body again, its face a clotted mess, and felt my heart sink, then turned my attention to Soikenn.

She had moved a little, pulling up a seat so that she could sit close to Poiparesis. She had not acknowledged my coming into the room. It seemed worse because she did not sob, cry, or keen over Poiparesis—she just stared, seeming to ponder, as if she were trying to decide whether or not to wake him.

She shivered again, and I went to move more of the wrap onto her shoulders. "Thank you," she whispered.

"I'm here if you need me," I said, rubbing her thin bony shoulders and sinking my thumbs into the hard muscles of her back. "Is there anything I can do for you?"

"Don't go away," she said. "I might need to talk." It was strange; she might as well have been the child, and I the adult. She felt as cold as a block of ice. She didn't speak at all.

As I looked at the hideous matting of blood all over Poiparesis, I thought how distressed he would be to be out in public and looking such a mess. As soon as I could I was going to get a wet cloth and clean all that up.

Finally Soikenn spoke. "Poiparesis was different from the rest of us. Osepok likes it out here, she'd have sailed the ship, all by herself, to wherever they told her to, and been happy to have it all to herself. I like getting papers written and doing science. And Kekox—well, you understand, don't you, that he's from a minor house? His family isn't very high in the Palathian order of things . . . so what he has been doing is serving out a difficult, boring duty, so that his nephews and nieces can rise in the world. But Poiparesis wanted to go there and see. He wanted to actually go to another world.

"How strangely it's all turned out! There was one thing that we all thought we were united about—that we were going to put an end to the deep split between the races, somehow we were going to be the first really fair and just society Nisu ever produced. Maybe not enough people ever tried before, or maybe we didn't listen to the ones who had. Eight people can't undo hundreds of years of history in just twenty years. Not even within themselves. I try so hard to accept the cross-mating and I just make a fool of myself. Kekox turns out to have principles better than his feelings. And Poiparesis . . . well, that was where he was different, too, a little."

"We always felt welcome around him." I pressed the knotted muscles behind Soikenn's ears; she must be giving herself a headache.

"He used to have arguments with all the rest of us, trying to get all of you a fair shake. He thought it mattered, I guess, that all you kids felt welcomed and accepted. More than the rest of us thought about it, anyway." She groaned and I thought now maybe she would cry, but instead she said, "I guess I need to get some sleep."

I walked her to her chamber; we didn't speak. She looked down at the deck the whole way.

Afterwards I realized I was so tired that I might as well just go back to bed myself, but then I remembered that I had wanted to clean Poiparesis's body. I got the things to do it with and went back to the room; when I got there I found Otuz already doing it. We didn't speak at all, but we cleaned him up together and arranged the body more carefully than the hasty job the captain and I had done. After that we cleaned the floor, so that when we were done it looked as if Poiparesis had just gone to sleep on the dining table.

Still without talking, Otuz and I went back to my chamber, holding hands. The bunk was really too small for both of us, but we curled against each other tightly. It was the first time we had ever dared to share a bunk for the whole night.

10

THE FUNERAL WAS THE FIRST TIME SINCE POIPARESIS'S DEATH THAT WE HAD all been gathered together. Soikenn was chief mourner and sat closest to the body; she shuddered through the whole service. When her time came to give the first eulogy, she merely got up, stood behind his body, raised his hand between hers, and stammered that we had loved him and would remember him. Captain Osepok had enough composure to stand still; her eulogy was delivered in neat, crisp, military sentences, a brief summary of Poiparesis's career, but as she gave it her face became wet with tears, and we could see that she clutched Poiparesis's hand hard.

The funeral lots may choose wisely but never kindly. Tradition was that after the chief mourner and the captain, the rest of the order of speakers was determined by lot, and though we had no reason to maintain any particular tradition, we had no cause to change this one. The lots decreed that the other three children spoke, then me, then Kekox. Mejox, Priekahm, and Otuz said essentially the same thing: that we had always relied on Poiparesis and looked up to him, and we would miss him terribly.

I had spent most of the past day thinking about what I would say, and now, as I stood before the others, holding Poiparesis's dead hand in both of mine, I had a sinking feeling that it was a terrible idea and a terrible speech, but it was too late to think of anything else to say. His hand was so cold, his dead face so empty . . . I swallowed hard and began. "This is our first parting. When they sent us, they assumed that if we were not directly linked by family ties, we would have none of the problems of a family. But they were wrong. . . . As we gather here to say good-bye to Poiparesis we discover that this *is* our family." I worked from there to what I really wanted to say—that somehow we all needed to come back together again, even if it meant some of us would have to give in on any number of issues. I was really talking to Mejox and Kekox, of course, but I tried to address it to everyone. I finished by saying something that I knew was true—that Poiparesis would not have wanted us to quarrel.

Then I set the heavy weight of his arm down, looked at his face one more time—thought of ten thousand little things from childhood and my education—and sat down. Kekox rose and walked to the speaker's position behind the body.

He looked down for a long time before picking up Poiparesis's hand with his good one; the other, in its splint, reminded us all of what had happened. Then he looked out and said, "I had thought I had a speech. I had thought I had three speeches or so. And now I find I don't want to deliver any of those." Kekox seemed to stare at his face. "Now I find that what Zahmekoses said is so bitterly true.

"We are a family; we are joined more intimately than most families of either Palath or Shulath, and nothing matters more than that, nothing can matter more. As Nisu has receded behind us, it has ceased to be our home; now it is merely where we are from. We don't feel much kinship with the ones who sent us anymore. Poiparesis mattered more to us than our whole home planet and all the generations yet to be born." He gasped, choked, and broke down a little, looking at that cold hand in his own, struggling to get enough control of himself to go on. After a moment Otuz got up and stood beside Kekox, resting her hand in his elbow.

He breathed deeply a couple of times and then at last spoke again. "I've struggled not to see it, and I've deluded myself that as an Imperial Guard I had a stronger loyalty to home than all of you. But this place has been my home as long as it has been all of yours, and I could bear that all of Nisu had been blown apart far easier than I could bear this." He drew a deep breath and said, "I've lost my dearest friend and I never told him that that's what he was. I've spent years struggling to make everyone behave according to rules that didn't really even matter to *me* anymore. I've behaved shamefully toward several of you. Well, now, too late, I can at least do what he'd have wanted me to do—forgive, forget, join with the rest of you. I will. Let that be my monument to my best friend." He set Poiparesis's hand down tenderly and gently pressed his fingers down on his forehead, the same gesture of putting a child to sleep that we all remembered so well. Then he looked up. "And I love all of you. You are all my family."

So far we had been following the tradition for a burial at sea, the analogy they had suggested in our standing orders. Now we did something new; we stood in a circle as we watched the little cargo elevator carry Poiparesis up into the central services core. A moment later, as we stood quietly with each other, in a linked circle of hands, there was a hard, shuddering thud through the ship; our probe catapult had hurled Poiparesis out and away, ahead of us, into the dark of space. We were still above escape velocity for our new sun. He would make a fast hyperbolic orbit around it, then continue on out into the depths of space forever.

For two days after the funeral, we went by "sick rules," the provisions that had been made in case the whole crew fell ill at once; no one felt like working or attempting the simplest things. The third day, we held a meeting of the whole crew, and at least for me, Poiparesis was only absent physically. In most senses his was the biggest presence there.

The first question was what, if anything, to tell them back on Nisu. Despite orders we had not been reporting daily for many years. In fact we had come to realize, by comparing timing of responses, that the messages we did send were being spooled and sometimes not read for several eightdays. It would be at least another eightday before we *had* to transmit.

"You know what they would make of it," Otuz said. "It would become entertainment. By the time we got back, if we decided to do anything as foolish as go back, we'd be nothing more than a set of freaks for exhibition, the survivors of 'the most famous murder case in history' or something. And long before we get any message from them we're going to have to settle everything anyway. So why tell them? Why even talk to them at all?"

We all must have appeared a little surprised, because she looked around impatiently, as if wondering why we could not see it. "If we're never going back and we want no more to do with them—and those are at least the positions I'm in favor of—then why do we have to shame ourselves in front of them? You know that they're never going to understand anyway, because they won't *want* to understand. They'll do what Nisuans always do: make a big flap, do a lot of talking, throw around all kinds of feelings and expressions and make sure everyone gets heard—and upset, and then arrive at the conclusion that we should have consulted them and that it was a terrible thing. Probably it will be an excuse for just turning off the laser, canceling everything, and partying till the rocks fall."

After a pause, Soikenn said, "I don't see what purpose it could serve to tell them what's happened, either. If Poiparesis just disappears from the story, it will occur to someone to wonder and there will be all kinds of wild speculation. If we tell them the truth, we'll end up as material for sensational news-telling. Nothing we can do will get them to think about species survival, that's plain. Nisu sent us out and then forgot about us. So your idea is that we just stop transmitting?"

Otuz nodded. "Or even better, we make our landing and leave behind a message that breaks off, as if we had crashed on landing. Maybe if we can't get them to come out here to save civilization, a news-teller company might finance an expedition to find out what happened to us. And by the time they get here, our great-grandchildren will have nothing to be ashamed of."

"There are other advantages, too," Mejox said. "Back on Nisu there's bound to be a lot of controversy about these intelligent animals. Look at how we all reacted here. So whatever solution we arrive at will already be in place—for generations—before they ever hear about it. And I trust us, and our descendants, a lot more than I trust Nisuans."

"Not only that," Priekahm pointed out, "but if we just vanish, they have to build *two* more starships. One to find out what happened to us and one to get a backup destination in case whatever killed us might prevent their using Setepos. Nisu gets two refuge worlds and two chances to survive. And they'll afford it if they have to—let's not forget that the total mission cost for putting another ship on its way out here, now that the big laser is built, is only about the budget of one big entertainment show."

Kekox nodded. "So we might be more valuable as a silence than as a presence."

I thought about it and decided not to speak. It seemed to me that we didn't actually know what was going on back on Nisu, and especially we didn't know what effect the data coming from the last two years of probes had had on Nisuan public opinion. For all we knew the Nisuans had thrown out Fereg Yorock and the Planetary Improvement Program, the empress was dead in childbirth, and the new emperor had ordered the whole Migration Project sped up. Indeed for all we knew there were four ships being launched behind us at this very moment, and they would all arrive within our lifetime. There were a *lot* of uncertainties.

And everyone seemed to be rationalizing going off the air and not telling Nisu what had happened, sparing us vast amounts of shame. That seemed to be our unspoken first priority.

I wasn't about to say that, and I kept my peace. For many long years in the future I would wonder whether that had made any difference; I always concluded that if I had spoken up, it would have made no difference at all.

We didn't really even take a vote; everyone favored sending routine reports back for the twenty eightdays until we entered deceleration. Chances were that no one would pay much attention to the routine reports—more likely if anything got attention it would be the data coming back from the probes. The report from our close pass at the new sun, Kousapex, could be mainly technical, as could the maneuvers to get us into orbit around Setepos. And then we need only begin our landing in the usual fashion, and click off the required channel at the right moment—a robot circuit on *Wahkopem Zomos* could do that.

With almost no discussion, we decided to make the real commitment to staying; Soikenn undid everyone's sterilizations, because by now even if all four females got pregnant immediately, we should be safely down on the ground and settled before any of them began to be inconvenienced. Long before we rounded the sun, it was no surprise to discover that Otuz and Priekahm were both pregnant; a bit more surprising when it turned out that the Captain was as well, but at least it gave Mejox and me something to tease Kekox about.

Our plan for staying and settling got more and more advanced as we brought more probes to bear on the little settlements in the southwest corner of Big. We had ascertained a great deal about them, but we still weren't sure whether they were smart animals or stupid people, so we developed plans for either case. Both plans were simple enough so that it was hard to see how anything could go wrong with them. And if our reasons for not returning and starting a colony of our own weren't quite what we pretended they were, still, the effect back on Nisu might well do more good than not.

As we fell into the new solar system we gave Poiparesis a kind of last tribute: we took thousands of observations and measurements of the Kousapex system's eight planets, working at a frantic pace to make sure that all those observations got back to Nisu under his name before we had to cut off transmissions. Naturally it also helped to conceal that he was no longer with us, but speaking for myself, anyway, knowing how much his scientific career had mattered to Poiparesis, I don't think that's why we did it; I think we just wanted his name remembered. During that same time, as Mejox and Priekahm worked the probes exploring Setepos, they often signed his name to that work as well.

We multiplied our knowledge of the system manyfold as we steadily closed in on Kousapex. We jettisoned the magnetic drag loop, which we would not need again, and let it tumble on into space ahead of us; almost surely it would pass close enough to Kousapex to be annihilated, but it was such thin stuff, spread across such an immense distance, that our best instruments would be hard pressed to see it. We unfurled the sail and spun it up to full extension, facing the ever-brightening new star.

There was another period of a day's miserable high acceleration as we used the solar sail for braking, making a close pass at Kousapex; it reminded us far too much of twenty-three years before, when Poiparesis had been there to take care of us, and though there were no injuries this time, and indeed we were all adults and could take care of ourselves, still we were all quiet and withdrawn for a day or so afterwards.

We came out of the blazing light of our new star in a highly elliptical retrograde orbit and made a near pass by the second planet of the system, using its gravity to brake us further. Visually it was about the least interesting planet in the system, covered with a dense carbon dioxide atmosphere with an all-but-featureless cloud layer so that it merely looked like a shiny ball. Still, we all spent as much time as possible at the viewports as we swung by it. After twenty-three years en route, it was strange to see a planet, unmagnified, hanging in space. Its gravitation dragged at us as we made our near pass, and now we were just rising in Kousapex's gravity fast enough so that when we intercepted Setepos, on the prograde side, we would fall into the right orbit—more or less. There were still a thousand tiny adjustments to be made.

More eightdays went by as we closed in on Setepos. Once we had moved at a speed so great that we would have crossed this solar system in about a day and a quarter; now we were taking ten eightdays to get between two of its closer planets. When *Wahkopem Zomos* was within a hundred planetary radii of Setepos, we spent a day furling the sail, just as if we were going to use it again.

Six days after furling the sail, we fired the rocket motors to bring us into orbit around our new world, and Osepok spent all of that day in her cabin, having been assured by the rest of us that we could handle the very small amount of manual work necessary. She was listening to music, we realized later, because this would be her last chance to lie in the comfort of her bunk, just listening. Kekox sat and gazed out the view port, and Soikenn sat beside him, both silent and motionless as statues, watching Setepos grow from a dot until it filled the view port. With Otuz at the helm, Priekahm monitoring engines, and Mejox and me reading instruments and verifying astrogation, we slipped into our new orbit. That evening at the last meal of the day, all three of the older generation congratulated us on doing it so neatly.

The next thing we did had been a matter of some discussion. About a third of the central cylinder of the ship had been taken up with the furled sail, which we now, at least theoretically, were not going to need. We had now all gone off birth control, which meant after the children were born we would rapidly reach a point where we could no longer take everyone back with us. We had resolved to fake the accident. In every way we had committed to this system, and the sail that was to take us back was taking up a great bulk of room that we needed for *Wahkopem Zomos* in its new capacity as the space station that would provide technical support for our civilization down on the surface. Thus the sensible thing to do was to get rid of the sail.

And yet we hesitated, a little, because it was our only way to go anywhere else if this didn't work out. Once we jettisoned the sail, the maneuvering engines on *Wahkopem Zomos* were so low-powered that we couldn't even get out of orbit around Setepos; their primary intention was for station keeping. "But," Mejox pointed out, "if we dock one of the landers at the back of this thing—well, then we can use it to push us up to escape velocity. We'd have to go to wherever else by ballistic flight, and that could take a few years, but so what? We're used to living in this thing for years at a time, and anyway there really isn't anywhere else worth going in this solar system. My vote is we jettison it."

His had been the last speech on the subject; we managed to overcome some premonitions and foreboding, and the next day we pointed the ship so that the sail would jettison behind us in orbit, and triggered jettison.

Though the sail and its cables weighed many tons, because they were virtually single-molecule materials they had folded into tiny spaces. Now, as we watched it go, the great black-and-silver fabric began to unfurl in orbit as the sunlight caught it, and the diamond cables, one eightieth of the circumference of this planet, started to stretch out from it. Then, far below, we saw a spray of bright red lines as the spun-diamond cables began to drop into the atmosphere; the added drag yanked the sail open, so that for one instant it was immense in the sky, and then as the drag grew more intense, it billowed, folded, and fell at its awesome velocity into the upper atmosphere of Setepos. Only about three hundred atoms thick, it vaporized and burned in a sudden great flash, like a piece of tissue paper tossed into a hot chimney flue. It must have been quite a show, down below.

Soikenn and the captain spent the next day frantically getting a set of up-close pictures of Setepos and its moon. That left Kekox plus the younger generation to ready the *Gurix*, the lander that would take us down to the surface. We had chosen it partly because of its name—General Gurix, after all, had conquered a world, whereas Rumaz, the empress after whom the other lander was named, had merely been on the throne when he had done it for her.

We spent one long, nervous, frustrating day getting decades-old power and data systems up and running, and there were times when we all struggled not to voice the thought to each other: *What if, after coming all this way, we can't get one of our landers working, and we're never able to touch the world that fills our viewports?*

At the end of that day of struggle, we finally seemed to have electric power everywhere we were supposed to, the containment on the antimatter mixing had held for a full tenth of a day, and all sensors were at last responding intelligibly. We set it to run a self-diagnostic while we slept, and then all but staggered through the narrow tunnels to the main body of *Wahkopem Zomos* and fell into our bunks. Tomorrow we would do the final checkout, then move on to outfitting the *Rumaz*.

After we arose, and ate a long, relaxed meal, we went back into the central core to do the checkout. The lander had leaked most of the air in its cabin, and the computer had eventually shut off the air supply to avoid losing all of it into space.

The *Gurix*'s seals and gaskets had deteriorated, whether from cryonic temperatures, vacuum, interstellar radiation flux, or aging, we had no way of knowing. There was nothing for it but to make a fresh batch of the plastics, cut new parts, and install them. The ship's computer had all the specifications, but more days went by while we did that, and as we replaced parts, we often had to redo things we had done on the first day. Then, of course, we repeated the process on the *Rumaz*, and finally we had two working landers.

"It's a good thing we brought along tools and materials to make every part for the lander," Mejox commented at dinner that night. "Someone back on Nisu knew what they were doing, amazing as that seems."

"What it makes me wonder about is whether everything would have held together on *Wahkopem Zomos* if we had tried to voyage back to Nisu," Priekahm said. "After all, we're only about a third of the way into the voyage they planned for us. A fifth of the way with Fereg Yorock's revised schedule. If there's that much deterioration on the *Gurix*, who knows what parts of *Wahkopem Zomos* might be about to go?"

I shuddered, but I pointed out, "Well, we *have* been working with and monitoring everything on the main ship, replacing parts from time to time. I suppose if we had the raw materials we could build just about everything with the material fabricators and machine tools on board, except the sail, the shrouds, and the brakeloop. It's not quite the same thing as leaving the landers in storage for all that time."

"Storage," Kekox said. "We still haven't even started to work out the logistics. Which stuff should go down on which lander flight?"

That sent everyone scrambling for all the reports we had on the site, and then put us all to arguing about what we might need first—other than the steam rifles and the incendiary throwers needed to establish ourselves as the species in charge on Setepos. Everything had to change now that we were no longer planning a slow exploration followed by departure.

It took several days, even after we had our lists in order. Much of the gear had been stowed with an eye to its convenience during the voyage, some things had been moved without the information being recorded, and of course among the things that had been stored for twenty years there was some deterioration and breakage that had to be dealt with, and things that had to be remanufactured. Furthermore, though no one talked about it, our feet dragged a little as we went about our tasks, because we were planning to begin moving out of home forever.

11

WE WENT THROUGH THE FINAL CHECKOUT THREE TIMES, AND EVEN THEN our stomachs turned over a little as the *Gurix* lurched away from *Wahkopem Zomos*. We had discussed this many times—going down in one versus going down in two landers—but Kekox's military sense had won out over pleas from Soikenn and me for engineering, and we would not be dividing our forces (though it meant running the risk of a single equipment failure for this first mission). Later, of course, we would be flying both landers routinely.

Otuz was still our best pilot by far, and she had never crashed on a simulation run, so she was at the helm. I called off numbers for her from the navigation computer, and everyone else, I suppose, just sat there and worried.

Antimatter is a compact fuel—it has such a high specific impulse that you don't have to use much of it to get where you're going. We fired the main rocket to slow the *Gurix* down and start it on its drop into the atmosphere, and the fuel indicator barely showed a fraction of a percent consumed. The glowing stream of plasma whipped out ahead of us, distorting in the planet's bizarre magnetic field, and we sank toward our destination, weight pushing against our feet.

It was very different from the space flights I remembered from my childhood. There was enough surplus power so that rather than using the air to slow us, for the most part we simply rode down on the engine. As we hit the outermost tenuous atmosphere there was a brief, dull red glow from some of the *Gurix*'s exposed parts, because our speed was still very high relative to the air, but it cooled and darkened. By the time the sky above us had turned to deep blue and the stars had vanished, the outside of the ship was cool. We watched the air over the lands below grow from a thin film to a thick smear, and then merge into the world around us. The lands around our landing site went from blotches on a globe to smears on a map, and then to sharply detailed relief, until finally we found ourselves hanging above land, descending past a few white, fluffy clouds. The great inland sea to our west vanished from our viewports, and then the salt lake north of us likewise disappeared; the thick forests below began to take on traces of individual detail.

We hovered as Otuz corrected our position slightly, moving us some distance south and a little east. We had decided we would land within sight of the largest village. If they turned out to be more intelligent than we thought they were, then our descent from the sky on a pillar of flame would surely help to produce the awe we would need to subjugate them.

The village became individual buildings, and then we could see the animals running and scrambling around inside its palisade. We sank slowly onto one of their grain fields, the *Gurix* now just balancing on its exhaust. We could see individuals clearly, as they raced about, gesturing frantically at each other, flinging themselves on the ground or leaping up to see us.

Our engine exhaust lashed into the field of rain-damp grain, setting a wide ring of it smoldering, scorching a spot below us into a great black circle. Otuz slowed us still further, and as gently as the flying insects of Setepos settle onto its flowers, the *Gurix* put its feet down onto the freshly charred field of grain.

"Well," she said, turning to us, "was that satisfactory?"

"It was brilliant," Kekox said. "As you know. All right, everyone, get ready. It's time to put on our little show."

We had spent some effort on planning just what we would do when we stepped out of the ship. The problem, of course, was that we were dealing with animals (or just possibly thinking beings) of a type we had never met. Would they recognize a weapon if we threatened them with it? How would they respond if we killed a few of them? And since we didn't want to feed them or have to tend them—the idea was to have them do those things for us—how could we avoid having them all sit down and wait for us to tell them what to do?

The three steam rifles we had been supplied with were hunting weapons, intended for killing fresh game and repelling large predators, not for any sort of military use. They held thirty-two shots per magazine, each delivering enough momentum to knock a quadruped four times our mass off its feet. Magazines could be reloaded using a little gadget that drew electricity from the *Gurix*'s power plant; plain sand was all the raw material needed. They were nice weapons, but there were only three of them, and we had no way to make them more potent than they were. We had already figured out, from the wildlife observations, that the steam rifles wouldn't be adequate for large areas of Setepos; Soikenn's theory was that the lower gravity here had allowed animals as a whole to be bigger, and this included predators much larger than the steam rifle had been designed to deal with. We just hoped that we were right in thinking that if the smart animals could live in this area, and they were about our size, then there wasn't much around here that would kill or eat them routinely.

Otuz, Kekox, and Mejox had practiced a lot with the steam rifles in simulation, enough so that we were fairly confident that they could make them work when we needed them to. The plans we had settled on—one for if the Seteposians turned out to be smart animals and one for if they were stupid people—weren't so much plans as first steps, to be followed by a lot of contingencies and improvisations.

The first step went perfectly. We looked out the viewports to see that the animals from the village were approaching the *Gurix* in a great, incoherent mass. "One right guess," Mejox said with satisfaction. "They're not in any kind of order or under any kind of leadership."

"That's not much to evaluate them on," Kekox said. "I'd imagine they were taken by surprise, even if every one of them is a genius."

We formed up, facing the door. Kekox took the point position, his steam rifle at ready. Behind Kekox, I stepped into place, with the improvised incendiary launcher that we had come up with: a simple tube with a hydrogen-oxygen capsule at its closed end, and a thin plastic can full of methanol blocking its open end. With luck, anyway, when I pressed the button on its side, the capsule would explode and throw the can out the end of the open tube. The explosion should also set fire to a wick in the can, and when it hit, if we were right, the lightweight can would break, the wick would ignite the methanol, and we'd set whatever building we pointed it at on fire.

At my side was Priekahm, with another incendiary launcher. Then behind us, with recording gear, were Osepok and Soikenn, with cameras to record our first encounter with these animals—if they had some sort of rudimentary language, we needed to start learning it. Finally, behind us, came Mejox and Otuz, steam rifles ready.

Even if worse came to worst, and they attacked us straight off, we knew that between what was already loaded into the steam rifles and what was in the magazines we were carrying, we had three slugs for every inhabitant of the village. Against that, they had a collection of pointed sticks—big thick ones to stab with and little thin ones they propelled with a bent stick, in some way we had not yet figured out from watching moving pictures of them. And of course they could throw rocks or hit us with sticks.

So when we had planned all this, we had been about as sure as we could possibly be that this next part would go well. We had been more worried about seals holding and navigation gear working on the *Gurix* than we had about this first contact. The difference now was that we knew the *Gurix* had landed and we didn't know how this was going to come out.

"Our public awaits," Mejox said. "Let's go." Kekox pressed the button and the door slid open; beyond it, the stairway extended down to the wet ground.

They were close to us, now, but they seemed to freeze in fear when the stairs came down. Kekox walked slowly down the steps, his head moving quickly from side to side as he scanned for any threat. We came down the steps after him, as quickly as we all could without falling, since if trouble started we didn't want to be bunched together. As soon as we were off the stairs we fanned out into a rough triangle, with Osepok and Soikenn at the center, and Mejox and Otuz forming the back corners. At Kekox's command we moved slowly forward.

One of them approached Kekox. They were an ugly species, flatter in the face than Palathians, with less fur than even a Shulathian, and head fur that grew in great messy profusion, not in a neat crest like a Palathian's but on top of the head (and all over the face as well, in the males), so that the whole effect was of a blank wall with eyes behind a curtain of hair.

They were shorter than Shulathians and taller than Palathians, narrower in the shoulder than Palathians and broader than Shulathians. They had small rounded ears like a Palathian but the tops of their heads were crestless like a Shulathian's.

Yet though they were in some ways intermediate between our races, they did not look like the crossbred Nisuans I had seen in biology textbooks, or exhibited stuffed in museums. Those had been curiously attractive; these creatures were simply hideous.

The tall one approaching us was only half a head shorter than I, and I was the tallest of our crew. He was dressed in a long tunic—really not more than a shirt that extended to his knees—into which had been stuck hundreds of soft, rustling objects. Later I was to learn that these were the "feathers"—flexible scales—of "birds"—those flying creatures we had seen in such great numbers in the probe pictures.

He drew close to us. His eyes were strange—only a small area around the lens was colored, so that instead of a smooth swath of red, yellow, or green like ours, their eyes were white with a small colored circle. I did not know at the time that one reason why the white part was so large was because he was terrified.

At last he spoke. There was no question that he was using words.

"Anyone have any idea what he's saying?" Priekahm asked.

"Forgot to bring my dictionary," I said.

This started all of them gabbling at each other, so that the tall one turned around and spoke very loudly. Their voices were very odd; Otuz and I figured out later that it was because in normal speech they emitted a large number of tones all together, rather than the single pure tone that we usually spoke in. We had no idea of it then, but they had just named us the "Singing Ones."

"People or animals?" Kekox asked us. "Anyone got an opinion?"

"People," I said. "Not necessarily smart ones."

"People," Otuz and Priekahm concurred.

"I agree," Kekox said. "Anyone think differently?"

There was a long pause. I was slowly beginning to notice things around me: the burnt smell from the charred grain, the warmth of the air, the more distant faint odor of the forest. So many different colors, so many different smells, the sounds of what must be hundreds of kinds of living things; I had just a moment to think I might like it here.

"Then we're gods," Kekox said. "We go with Plan Two. Remember to stay bunched up. If any of them moves between us, shoot it; we've got to stay compact."

As we neared the village, the crowd began to pack in closer. There must have been a hundred fifty or more inhabitants, counting only those old enough to walk by themselves. And to judge by the number of infants being carried by mothers, the population was growing rapidly.

The press of people gave me a chance to sneak a look at their tools. "Shaped stone, as we thought," I said. "Looks like they grind or polish it. Heavy, but it probably does what they want it to. Copper ornaments, maybe some tin and silver. And of course the stuff they tore off the probe."

"They do some kind of weaving," Priekahm observed on my other side. "Very coarse. They probably hand-plait the thread and then just lay it crisscross to make the cloth. Probably keeps the worst of the rain off them, and assuming the adult males have genitals that protrude as much as the juveniles near us do, I'd guess that it's for comfort as well."

Osepok noted, "I can't make any kind of sense of it yet, but it feels like all the ornamentation falls into some kind of pattern. Probably a very complicated system of ranking and relations."

We walked on toward the village; it was a short distance away, but the crowd around us was thick, so it took a long time. So far none of them had tried to get between us, and I was certainly glad about that because the ones that seemed most apt to get into the middle were the young ones, and Kekox's orders or not, I didn't think any of us could shoot a little one.

As we entered the open gate in the palisade, I noticed a plate of lashed-together logs sitting beside the opening, and two upright logs set behind the main walls. "Probably they slide that across the opening at night," Priekahm said. "Which means either they've got big predators or they've got warfare."

"Bad news either way," Soikenn said. "Have you noticed how much they talk and argue with each other? I'm afraid they'll never make well-behaved slaves."

"It's a little late to change plans now," Kekox said, curtly. "Unless you all want to take a vote in the middle of this mob?"

We didn't, of course. I was going to wonder a lot later what might have happened if we had. But I know my heart was starting to sink; there's only so much you can see on a probe camera, and the one thing you can't see is the way they look at you, the way they clearly want to communicate. I wanted nothing so much as time to think, and time to think was the one thing we did not have—unless, as Kekox said, we wanted to stop, right there in that dusty public courtyard, and conduct a debate. The Creator alone knew what they might make of that—*But then*, a little voice in the back of my mind said, *the Creator alone knows what they will make of the next thing we're going to do, anyway. I hope this works the way we thought it would.*

Too late now. Kekox had gone through the open gate, and we followed him toward the temple at the center of the compound.

It was a two-story building, of a sort, made of logs with a mud-brick facing on the vertical walls. The first story was short and had no windows or doors; a broad flight of mud-brick steps ran up to a sort of porch that stuck out of the second story, and a doorway opened onto that porch. On the porch itself there was a simple mud-block table, on which we had seen them sacrifice animals, and on top of which now lay the remains of the first probe that we had sent on ahead of us. Behind it was a large clay statue of a Seteposian female sitting cross-legged.

We halted. There was no one between us and the temple. Priekahm and I nodded to each other and raised our incendiary throwers, when abruptly one of the Seteposians came out the door of the temple.

The thick thatch of hair surrounding his head was a deep gray, and his face was lined and brown. Perhaps because it was a common color change everywhere—as animals get older they make less pigment—or perhaps because of the slow, shuffling way he walked, we knew at once that he was old.

He raised his hands over his head and started shouting at us. We didn't know if it was greeting, or exorcism, or what. "Anyone got any ideas?" Kekox said.

"He's got to be the priest of the old god," Mejox said. "Who we're getting rid of."

"So do we recruit him or make him a martyr?" Otuz said.

"This is turning into a debate," Kekox said.

All of them were staring expectantly at us. Clearly it had been some kind of challenge, or at least they were trying to see what would happen. There wasn't a breath of air, and no sound but the drone of distant insects; every Seteposian was motionless. "We have no idea how to recruit him," I pointed out, "and *I* think he just called *us* out. So if he's the old god's priest, he gets to be the old god's martyr."

"Makes sense," Kekox said, raised his steam rifle, and fired.

The steam rifle made a little *phht!* A gush of blood, red like ours, sprayed out of the old Seteposian's back, and he fell over on his face, dead. We had loaded the steam rifles with expanding slugs, intended originally for maximum stopping power against big, fast predators, and the result was that when they hit the Seteposian in the chest, they tore whatever internal organs were nearby to jelly.

There were murmurs and cries among the crowd. I raised my incendiary thrower and fired it, sending the little fire-starter canister in through the temple door. By sheer good luck it hit the female statue and caused flames to leap up from it; the Seteposians screamed and fell to their bellies around us.

Priekahm's shot arced higher, landing in the heavy thatch of the roof, and burst against a rafter there, setting the whole roof on fire. Flames leaped up, billowing bodylengths tall within the span of two breaths.

There were screams and cries from the crowd around us, and the more distant of them turned and ran.

"The tall ones that greeted us at the ship are right over there," Priekahm said, pointing. "And whatever they're chanting, others seem to be picking it up."

"More martyrs for the old faith," Otuz remarked; and shot the three leaders and several Seteposians around them.

"Get the ones with spears," Kekox said. "Spare anyone who doesn't have a weapon." He and Mejox shot with a steady, even rhythm, raising steam rifles and killing Seteposians who had their hands on spears or axes, about one per breath; one more way to tell that these people were smart enough was that before ten more of them died, the rest were throwing away their spears and axes, and then prostrating themselves.

By now Priekahm and I had reloaded, and we fired again, this time hitting the outside walls of the temple, down low, and sending fire licking up the wall. "Cover me, I'm going to finish it," I said to Kekox. I set down my incendiary thrower, pulled the construction blasting charge from my pack, set the timer for a hundred-twenty-eighth of a day, and dashed forward to the temple. One of the small spears they threw with the bent stick hissed by me, a wild shot, and I heard several shots from the steam rifles behind me.

Then I was close enough to the temple to feel the blazing heat singeing my skin; I wanted to get close enough to make sure I got the charge well inside. I armed it as I looked for the right place to toss it—saw the trapdoor with its ladder right behind the porch—and lightly lobbed it in there. Probably I had just tossed the charge down into the center of the secret rites; so much the better for what we were trying to do.

I turned and ran zigzagging back to them, not taking any chances this time. Now that I had done what I was supposed to, I had time to remember the evil hiss of that little spear and to think what a nasty hole it could have made in me—or I suppose, if it had somehow gotten through the weak ribs by the lower spine, when I was bending over, and into my blood mixer, it might have even killed me.

When I was back between my companions I grabbed up my incendiary thrower. Priekahm had already reloaded it. "Let's start something on the other side of the compound," she said, aiming hers in a high arc. I did, too, and we fired simultaneously, sending the cans arcing over the temple and into the back of the compound. To judge from the shrieks there, we had probably splashed at least one of them with burning methanol, and from the way smoke and flames leapt up, their construction had been no more fireproof on their palisade and houses.

"Okay, we've done the job," Kekox said. "Back to the *Gurix*. Nice and slow, but keep moving. We've only got about a two-hundred-fifty-sixth left till that charge blows."

We all backed up slowly, keeping an eye on the crowd. "The one with the little spear-launcher just popped up out of one of the houses," Priekahm said, "and he was fitting another little spear onto the string when Mejox got him. And we had two more pop out with spears; they're pretty brave, or some of them are, anyway."

We had backed about 256 bodylengths, a third of the way back to the *Gurix*, when the charge I had tossed into the temple blew. We saw the blazing thatch and timbers fly up above the walls of the little settlement, some of it landing all the way outside, and an instant later felt the shock in our feet and heard the boom of the concussion. Many more of the Seteposians ran out the gate, turning so as not to run in our direction, and fled off across the fields. Mejox raised his steam rifle and shot three times; two females and a small child fell.

"Why did you—" Kekox started to ask.

"Gods get more respect if they're capricious," Mejox said. There was something unpleasant about the way he was smiling; I had a sudden sense that he might be enjoying all this.

When it became clear there would be no pursuit, we turned and walked back toward the *Gurix* more quickly, Otuz leading, with Mejox and Kekox keeping watch behind. "Well, that's that," Soikenn said suddenly. "You've made sure we can't be friends for a long time. Did you see how excited they were, how much they wanted to meet us? And then when you were done how frightened they looked? We've *chosen* to be enemies."

"Oh, shut up," Priekahm said. "Our grandchildren can debate the morality. Right now it's time to be practical. You're not going to complain when we've got a nice big town going here, with hundreds of us building up a place for all of Nisu to settle, are you? We've got a lot to do and this is the way to get it done."

"Shut up back there, both of you, until we're on the *Gurix*," Otuz said. "We don't know that there won't be six of them waiting in ambush. As you said, Priekahm, they're smart and they're brave."

I'm sure she said it only to quiet the annoying argument, because to judge from the screams and shouting coming from behind us, the Seteposians had many other things on their minds. Finally, we reached the *Gurix* and climbed inside, Mejox and Kekox last. The door closed and the air cycled once to capture, on filter, anything interesting that might have come in on us.

"Check the long-distance viewer," Mejox said, and I jumped to do it.

"Well, looks like fifty or so of them are still on their faces in the burning village. Fifty or so live ones, I mean. The rest have all run off into the fields. Looks like mostly they're heading for the woods and the hills."

"That's evolution for you," Soikenn commented. "The smartest ones are up there surviving. And just possibly figuring out better ways to fight us than face-to-face."

Kekox snorted agreement. "Selecting their smartest ones for them is probably the last favor we'll ever do the poor bastards, and even if they think we're gods right now, in a generation they're going to know how much we're not their friends. We'll have to watch our backs right from the start, just to get the habit, but that's the way it goes. Let's get on with it."

Mejox brought up the engine; a pool of flame roiled across the burnt field around us, and we lifted gently. He opened the throttle more and we climbed upward until our tail of flame was well above the ground. Then he brought us to hover and fired the side jets, just barely, so that we moved sideways, drifting as slowly as anyone might walk across the fields toward the burning village.

The plan had been that if the Seteposians turned out to be people, and we were displacing the old gods, we would take their place physically, by parking the *Gurix* where the temple had stood. With nothing else to do, Otuz and I watched the screens; now that we were up high we had a much better view. There were now many of them lying prostrate out in the fields, too, all facing the *Gurix*. Some were running madly about in the burning village, dashing in and out of the burning houses, some carrying small bodies. "I think when we fired the houses we killed a lot of infants," Otuz said. "Bad idea if we want breeding stock. They must be more afraid than any of us has ever been."

"Wasn't that the idea?" I asked.

"Sure," she said. "I didn't say I disapproved, or even that we had any other choices. I just said they must be frightened."

The *Gurix* swept in over the walls, still far up in the sky from the perspective of those poor creatures cowering in the burning wreckage. The temple, directly below us, was already a scattered pile of burning timbers and ashes. "You know," Mejox said, "it's really no danger to the lander—we're proof against temperatures a lot higher than what's down there—but if we were to set a foot down on a burning log or something, that could give us a nasty bump. I'd rather err on the side of caution. I think I'll try to blow that area clear before we touch down on it."

"There are still quite a few of them inside the village," Otuz said.

"Their bad luck," Priekahm replied impatiently. "The whole idea is to give them such a taste of death and terror that they can never even consider disobeying—isn't it?"

Mejox gestured agreement but added, "Still, I can come down in bursts. That ought to get at least some of them running. The survivors *are* going to be valuable, so we might as well have as many of them as we can."

He popped the throttle three times, so that we would lurch downward in free fall and then slow to a stop before rising again at about two gravities. It was sickening and dizzying, but it did what he wanted it to: many of the villagers, startled out of their paralysis by the motion, the noise, and the great bursts of flame, got up and ran out through the gate, leaving behind the burning log palisade of their village. A few remained prostrate, because they were too stubborn, too scared, or perhaps just too determined to placate the new gods.

One of them seemed to split the difference, getting up and running around aimlessly within the compound. Soikenn popped her viewer up to look more closely, and we saw that it was a female chasing a little one who was running back toward one of the burning houses. She was getting closer to the little one, but it looked like the child would reach the burning house before she could catch it.

"Here we go," Mejox said. He gave us a big drop and then hit boost at two gravities to bring us to a landing. It shoved us all hard, but we were braced. We were so close to the ground now that the blast of flame shot down into the glowing embers of the temple, washed in a white-hot flood across the village, and knocked down whatever houses were still standing, along with most of the palisade wall; the flood of fire was encircled by a dark billow of blowing gray ash and dust. I saw the child ignite and roll like a paper doll in a fireplace, and the mother, diving for the child, flipped end over end, then ignited, herself, in the instant before the black curtain of dirt and smoke whisked across them and they vanished in the white blast.

The burning houses and palisades tumbled out into the fields around, like toys in a high wind. Then Mejox throttled us back to eight-ninths of a gravity, just enough so that we drifted toward the ground, the flames retreating from the village they had eaten. I saw the dark spots where the ashes of the mother reached toward the burnt child, and shuddered. Some things were necessary, but—

I didn't have time to finish the thought. The lander bumped to a stop in the middle of the cleared, burnt-black area, right where the temple had stood. The thunder beneath our feet stopped. All around us, at a distance of fifty bodylengths or more, lay a ring of smoldering rubble that was all that was left of the Seteposian village. The outside temperature gauge showed that we were sitting in air hot enough to boil water, but the *Gurix*'s cooling system would have allowed us to land and take off in a puddle of liquid lead, so we did not feel it inside.

"Well, we're home," Captain Osepok said. "This should add to the awe—not only do we come from the sky, destroy their temple, kill them at a distance—we come living out of fire. I'd say our godhood is well established and that it's high time to get a meal and some sleep. We're going to be busy little gods tomorrow."

12

THE *GURIX* HAD BEEN DESIGNED TO SERVE AS OUR HOME FOR UP TO A YEAR after landing, so though its bunk room was small, it wasn't uncomfortable. Still, I had a restless night. It was the first time in more than twenty years I had slept for the night in a room other than my chamber on

Wahkopem Zomos. I missed the way my bunk felt, the background sounds of the ship in normal operation, the wheel of stars by my viewport. I missed Poiparesis terribly, as well, and wished these little bunks were big enough for two so I could curl up with Otuz.

Eventually I drifted into a doze, but I didn't sleep well. Nobody seemed to, to judge by the tossing and turning. As soon as I woke to see the chronometer display showing it was near local sunrise, I got up and started to put breakfast together. I found Priekahm and Otuz sitting at a viewport; they had gotten up a twenty-fourth of a day earlier.

"They haven't come back yet," Priekahm whispered. "I thought a few of them might. With the infrared scan I've been checking the woods; there's a few campfires up in the hills, a few Seteposians around each fire. A lot more are in huddles out in the brush."

"If we were serious about improving the breed, we'd bomb the camp-fires," Otuz said, "leaving the ones smart enough not to show a light at night."

The joke fell flat. I don't know about Priekahm, but for me it was the thought that two nights before I had been snug in the only world I had ever known, and now I was on a hostile planet with a whole new life to make, missing that old world terribly—it was too much like what the Seteposians had just gone through, and I imagined being huddled in terror in the cold, wet dark, and it seemed to me that I would have built a fire, danger or not. I didn't like identifying with terrorized savages, but I did.

Priekahm spoke softly. "You know, I have a thought, but I don't know if it's a good one. But I wanted to say . . . well, we could just give it all up as a bad deal. If we hate doing this, I mean. We could just fly right out of here, back to *Wahkopem Zomos.* Then they'd just decide the gods were mad at them for smashing up the probe, or whatever it's appropriace for a Seteposian god to be angry about, and in twenty years we'd be purely legend, and that would be the end of us as far as they were concerned. Then meanwhile we'd reoutfit and go to one of the big islands, like we talked about. There are several that are beautiful and probably have undergone ecological détente—nothing big, aggres-sive, or venomous on them. There's really nothing to stop us from doing it."

"Except that our grandchildren would live like we found these sav-ages living," Kekox said, coming out of the sleeping cabin. "No doubt with cleaner habits and a bigger and better library, but still like that.

Maybe by the time *Imperial Hope* got here they'd have a city a bit like Sixth Dynasty Kratareni—wide stone streets, comfortable passive solar buildings, running water, public sewers, some electricity. But could they even *hope* to have room for an added two million people? And just think about how different the two groups of Nisuans would be. There's going to be trouble enough when they come here and find we've hybridized, I'm sure." He sighed. "I know I was opposed to the idea of slavery before, but now that I've seen what they live like—and smelled that town of theirs, and seen what an ugly bunch of brutes they are—"

"So *you* think they're animals now?" I asked. "I was just realizing how shocked I was that they turned out to be people."

Kekox gestured impatience. "Oh, they're *people*, Zahmekoses. No animal would keep a nest as foul as this one. For that matter look at the blood sacrifice and the crude way they do things when better alternatives are obvious. The kind of failure of evolution and refusal to pay attention to their surroundings is what you get when you have people, who can be ruled by their thoughts, instead of animals, who are ruled by the real world. Though I grant you that with a good costume, some of them might make politicians back home.

"The thing is, the Seteposians have helped me see that the difference between people and animals is that animals always live up to their potentials and people never do. The Seteposians had a lot of science and math to learn and technology to invent, but still . . . well, why wasn't Sixth Dynasty Kratareni waiting here already? Surely it's not too much to expect intelligent beings to build a space that's pleasant to live in and to at least move their own shit and garbage away from themselves?"

I thought about that and gestured agreement. "So you think—?"

"I think we may be doing them a favor after all, in the long run. In two years the survivors of this village will be cleaner and healthier than any of their species ever has been before. And they'll be the nobility of the biggest and richest empire their planet has ever seen. In twenty years Setepos will have a dozen real cities, with decent roads connecting them, and by the time *Imperial Hope* gets here, this world will be rich, peaceful, and *civilized*. Every Nisuan who arrives here will step onto a beautiful estate, ready and running for him or her.

"And I'll admit it, in a few thousand years, probably, Seteposians and Nisuans will sit at the same table, share the same language, and rule a hundred more species that need civilizing. Because when I look at this squalid little town and its smelly people, and think about what they could be like with some thought and work on their part . . . well, I see that Poiparesis was right. We can't just keep civilization to ourselves. We need to lift these people up. And it only takes a look—or a sniff!—to tell us they aren't going to *ask* to improve, or do it willingly. So for the next few generations, we supply brains, discipline, and know-how; they supply blood and sweat; and we all advance together."

Otuz sighed. "Everything you say makes perfect sense. It's just very hard not to feel sorry for them."

"Of course it is, but be rational about it." Kekox looked around at all of us and seemed to find agreement. "A little pain for a few generations, in exchange for a glorious future later. I'm sure they won't like being slaves—but could we really have left them the way we found them?"

Priekahm's gesture was noncommittal. "Well, we can't now. They're going to be very different thanks to the experience we've just handed them, anyway. And even if we took off right now, we couldn't put them back the way they were. So I guess it's just a matter of deciding what's best for them in the long run. And we might as well get on with it. Zah-mekoses, is breakfast ready?"

"Whenever people want it," I said, checking the pan.

"Then we might as well see if everyone else is ready to get up, and—"

"I am," Soikenn said, staggering in, "and Mejox is just dressing. To judge from the noises Osepok is making, she'll be along soon, too."

Over breakfast we set the two large screens for a full surround view. The village had finished burning during the night, and now it lay in ashes around us. A few charred logs poking up from the low ridge of dirt were all that remained of the palisade. Rims of black timber showed where houses had been attached to the surrounding wall.

"Stupid," Kekox said.

"What is?" I asked.

"Stupid of them to put their huts right against their defensive wall. And even stupider to roof it all with cut grass and tree branches. At the least they should have laid flat stones or split logs on top of the thatch. Even an army of their own kind, with just spears, could easily drive them out of here—just set the roofs on fire with thrown torches, or break a part of the palisade down and come in through one of those huts."

"Maybe they don't fight that way," I suggested.

"They're people, aren't they?"

"Well," Osepok said, "if you go by Wahkopem's accounts of the Lee-ward Islanders—which is the last time before this a civilized person met real savages—then warfare might be ritual for them. They come out to the battlefield—the same one every summer—wave magic sticks at each other, run down the hill and slash at each other a little, then run back home and brag about it. Probably almost no deaths, and no loss of valuable buildings or crops."

Kekox chewed a large bite for a long moment, and then said, "That makes sense. They can't be fighting seriously. If they were, a surprise night attack and a massacre would take care of any of these towns—and we know that the rivers and lakesides in this part of Big are crawling with these little towns. If they were fighting real wars, either they'd have real fortifications, or this would already be part of an empire—and then it would still be fortified, it's too logical a strategic strong point." He cut another bite of food and added, "This is even easier. We teach these people how to conquer and enslave their neighbors for us . . . that creates an inner ring of vassal villages . . . and then the inner ring conquers the outer ring for us . . . and so forth. We might have this whole part of Setepos under our domination with only a few people ever having seen us. Like a pyramid sales scheme."

I laughed at that. "And of course, like any pyramid scheme, the best time to get in is at the beginning. The people who do the best are the ones who start them."

Kekox laughed in response. "So we came all this way to set up a franchise-distributor system like an illegal sales promoter. Well, let's get going. Have any Seteposians come back yet?"

"Not yet," Otuz said. She sat down to operate one of the remote cameras. "But—yes, I saw them before we started eating and they're more than halfway here now. Eight of them, adults to judge by their size, and something else warm-blooded with them, maybe a child or a domestic animal. I would guess they'll be here in a thirty-second of a day or so. Everyone might as well just relax for a while."

Relaxing wasn't easy. We had no reason to fear them, but we did have to hope they were coming here to beg mercy from the new gods, rather than to exorcise demons—because if that were the case, the demons would have to prove *again* that the old magic wouldn't work on us. That would mean more killing and suffering, needlessly this time since all the Seteposians had to do was settle down and behave. I hoped they would have the sense to see that.

The time crawled by. We watched each other, the wall, the viewports, or whatever, not having much to say.

Finally, Otuz checked the amplified viewport for what seemed like the hundredth time and said, "All right, at least they're in view now." She clicked the image over to one of the main screens.

As she had said, there were eight Seteposians, and they were leading or dragging, mostly dragging, a small animal by a rope tied around its neck. The animal was covered by black and white hair in irregular splotches and walked on four hard little feet. Short horns sprouted from the top of its head, and they had draped its neck with several garlands of flowers. As we watched the little animal bent forward, clearly trying to eat the flowers. They pulled its head back up, but the animal balked and braced its feet; it took four of them to kick and drag it into moving again, and in the process several flowers were knocked off and gobbled up.

"I hope sacrificing it to the new gods involves killing it," Kekox said, "because as a live sample it would be too valuable to kill, and I don't think I want to cope with having it in here."

Another sixty-fourth of a day brought them down into the burned-out village. The animal must have sensed something—the smell of ashes and death, or perhaps the fear of the Seteposians—for he began to struggle and kick until finally he had to be dragged by the rope and half-strangled to get him into the clear space in front of the *Gurix*'s main hatch.

"One more way to see how smart they are," Soikenn said. "They remembered where the door is. It's not obvious from the outside, especially if you've never seen anything like it before. But I guess most of the evidence is irrelevant now, anyway."

"Not irrelevant," Otuz said. "We have to use Seteposians as slaves for the time being, but we probably should remember they're people, and that the things we have to do are as much for their good as ours. If we remember how smart they are, maybe our great-grandchildren will be more willing to let them be our full partners once the time comes."

"It if comes that soon," Kekox said. "Meanwhile, if we remember how smart they are it could keep us from underestimating them, which is probably more important."

Otuz had turned back to the view port, and now she said, "Well, it looks to me like they're going to kill it." The Seteposians bound the animal's feet together and turned it over. It was obviously completely terrified, arching its back, turning its head, and crying out. Otuz brought up the external audio and we heard the cry, a weird flat bleat alternating with a horrible bawl.

Over that sound we could hear the Seteposians chanting and singing. Slowly they drew together into a tight circle around the bucking, screaming animal and began to whirl, feet moving in a distinct rhythm, bodies swaying. "What in the Creator's name are they doing?" Mejox asked.

Priekahm scratched behind one ear. "I doubt they could explain it either. I mean, try to explain *any* religious ritual. And these people are ten thousand years or more behind us; they probably believe a lot of strange stuff, *really* believe it, I mean."

"At least it works that way on Nisu," Osepok said. "The farther back you go in time, and the lower the technical level, the more complex the religion gets and the fewer explanations people give for it."

The circle of Seteposians whirled faster, slapping their hands together and stamping. It rose to a crescendo, then stopped abruptly. The ring of Seteposians closed around the animal; all of them knelt, pressing their faces into the ground so that they formed a huddle of bodies around the animal. Then the one facing the hatch, a squat, heavily muscled male with thick facial hair, rose to his feet and pointed a knife at our hatch.

"Polished stone," Osepok said. "The very oldest tools on Nisu, or at least the very oldest ones anyone is willing to agree are tools, are almost exactly like that. The ones in the museums in Palath look just like it except for the shorter handles—I guess because they've got one more finger than we do."

The Seteposian was holding the knife over his head and chanting so loudly that, aside from the external audio, we could hear it faintly, directly, through the *Gurix*'s walls. After a while he stopped chanting, and the rest began to chant, a few notes over and over, rising into a scream. Then the muscular Seteposian struck savagely downward, with the full force of his body, nearly severing the neck of the small animal. He struck again, disemboweling it with a single neat stroke, and as blood and viscera poured onto the ground, they spread the gory mess out onto the ground, arranging the guts in a rough pattern.

"What are they doing now?" Otuz asked.

Osepok gestured noncommittally. "Maybe that's how you make flesh acceptable to the gods. Or it's how you foretell the future. Or how you find out if the spirits are angry. Or maybe it's the sacred signal for 'please don't kill us,' or 'demons go away.' We'll have to learn their language before we even know what question would be appropriate."

The little sacrifice party was backing up. "What do you think? Should we go out and accept the sacrifice?"

"Might as well," Kekox said. He tossed me a disposable environment suit, then put one on himself as I wriggled into mine. "Let's go see just how acceptable to the gods this one is going to be."

The dead animal was a lot heavier than it had appeared. Moreover, because its neck was nearly severed, it was very awkward to lift up, and since the ground was covered with blood and guts, the footing was slippery as well. Helpfully, Soikenn reminded us that she needed the guts, too.

We ended up stuffing the entrails back into the gaping empty belly, getting blood and unspeakable other things all over our environment suits, and dragging it over to the biosample hatch by its legs. At least the biosample capsule was big enough for it, so we dumped it in, sealed it, and pushed the button to send it into the *Gurix*. Then we moved around to the decontaminater and let it spray the suits with superheated steam for a couple of minutes. That made a lot of the blood clot in a very unpleasant way, making the suits stiff and hard to move in, and the heating load made the respirators hard to breathe through, too.

When we got into the airlock, the sampler said there was nothing alive floating in the air, so we gingerly detached the arms of the suits, slipped on the gloves that hung in waiting for us, and peeled off the rest of the suits, throwing them into the hopper to be melted down and reformed. By the time we got inside, Soikenn was already down in the utility compartment, dissecting the thing with Otuz.

As Kekox and I scrubbed the dank sweat off ourselves, he muttered, "As new god around here, my first commandment is going to be that all sacrifices will be by non-messy techniques."

"Completely agreed," I said. "At least I don't think I'll have any trouble waiting for lunch."

There were a lot of exclamations from down in the utility compartment, but not nearly enough room for anyone to stand in there and watch what Soikenn and Otuz were doing, so we waited and amused ourselves with long-range scans. The villagers seemed to be gathering up in the hills, in one large clearing.

"Could be massing for an attack," Kekox said.

"Yes, or they could just be getting the story from the animal chopper himself," Priekahm pointed out. "If they head this way with weapons, we'll know in plenty of time. But most likely what they're getting is the short report: the new gods found the gift acceptable. Which is even true as far as it goes."

By time for the midday meal, Soikenn had her report ready to go, and our appetites were back. Partly it was that the day here was one fifth longer than Nisuan standard, and thus meals were farther apart and the waking time tended to be longer; partly it was that we were realizing how dull it was to sit in this little metal box waiting to find out whether we could do anything else.

"Well," Soikenn said, "I'll refrain from showing photographs and give you the highlights. First of all, it's built on the same basic plan as we are: muscles and bones surrounding a digestive system, so the digestive system can get near food and the muscles can get fed. It has a brain inside a protective skull, with all the specialized sense organs located close to the brain.

"The biggest difference is the heart and circulatory system. They have two big lungs, instead of our hundreds of small ones, and one huge heart instead of our eleven small ones. No blood mixer; the heart just has four chambers, in and out to the lungs, in and out to the body. The body-side receiving chamber does more or less what our blood mixer does, but it's part of the heart, and it only contains a small quantity of blood at a time."

"So if we assume the Seteposians are built on a similar plan, then up close they'd be a lot harder to kill in a fight than we are," Kekox said.

Soikenn gestured noncommittally. "Don't be so sure. Whatever they gain by not having a soft target like the blood mixer, they lose by lack of redundancy. Remember we can live with three hearts gone, or as many as twenty lungs punctured; I think even one lung—and certainly that big heart—would be enough to kill them. And the chest is a pretty big target for a steam rifle."

"That's good to know," Kekox grunted.

"Here's something even better to know," Otuz said. "This animal, anyway, has a ninety-six percent match to our amino acid mix. He'd be nutritious if we ate him. And in about two hours the toxicology simulator should be done, and the cell exposure tests; if both of those say he's okay, we can have him grilled tonight."

Actually, it was stew—it seemed like a good idea to make sure the animal was thoroughly cooked—and it was astonishingly tasty. We all gorged on it and agreed the gods were pleased. "And it's harmless?" I asked Soikenn, as everyone had, repeatedly.

"Three of us are pregnant," Osepok pointed out, "and we all read the full report. As nearly as we can know anything, it's harmless."

"There are a lot of long-chain proteins that don't interact with our proteins at all," Otuz amplified, taking seconds. "Almost all of them break down into something we can digest when they're heated. The rest will probably just pass through. That's also why it would be hard to get a local infection—most of the germs aren't going to find much in us they can eat—our body proteins are just different enough to frustrate them, and they're so different from us that they'll really be obvious to our immune systems. It should be generations before any of us really has to worry about getting sick."

The next morning, the same male who had sacrificed the animal to us was waiting outside the hatch, patiently kneeling with his face on the ground.

13

OSEPOK WANTED TO GO OUT, COMMUNICATE WITH THE SETEPOSIAN, AND get the process going right away, but she had to wait a while, along with the rest of us and the Seteposian himself. Like it or not, we were all part of an experiment.

"Are you sure you don't want to do an autopsy to find out why I'm still alive?" Kekox grumbled. "I've given you my blood, my mucus, and my urine. What more do you want?"

"Everyone else's," Soikenn said, impassively. "Behave yourself and cooperate. I need to get the samples right now because we don't know how long we'll be talking to that Seteposian. Now, is everyone feeling well?"

"Never better," Osepok said. "Can we go outside now?"

"Not till Mommy has your blood," Soikenn said. "For what it's worth, so far the analyzer is turning you all up as perfectly normal."

"Then it's defective," Mejox said.

We were probably all just a little silly at the prospect of actually getting outside and beginning to really live on our new world. All the tests were showing that our protein compatibility was ideal—just compatible enough so that we could eat the local fauna (if we cooked it long enough), but not so compatible that the local germs were apt to get us. Of course we'd have to test each new food, and there were bound to be some local things poisonous to us, but it looked like this place could be our home, and we were all eager to get the process underway.

At last, after rechecking everyone and listening to the fetuses growing inside the other females, Soikenn declared she was satisfied. "And look at it this way. Now we know that our visitor is probably edible, should the need arise. Let's go out and see what he thinks of the idea of teaching the gods how to talk."

We had worried about that point. Gods ought to be all-knowing. But there was no cure for it—you have to interact to learn to speak a language well, and we thought gods who spoke ungrammatically with a terrible accent would be even less credible. Furthermore, we wanted to keep as much of our language as possible for ourselves, to give us one more edge in dealing with the slaves.

When the door opened he went from kneeling to prostrate in one thud. We advanced on him in a group, but he remained facedown. After a long pause, Mejox said, "It's very respectful but it's not the easiest position to communicate to or from."

He bent, grasped the Seteposian by the long hair of his head, and yanked him to his knees. The Seteposian looked around, gasped, and fell over sideways.

"You don't suppose that killed him?" Mejox asked anxiously.

"Well, at least his weird heart and lungs are still working," Soikenn said, pointing to where his throat was moving. "So I'd say he's probably okay. Maybe they're just knocked unconscious by strong emotions. It doesn't have to make any more sense than anything else evolution does. Possibly with just one heart his blood pressure can fall very fast."

"Assuming you're right," Osepok asked, "how do we wake him up?"

"Well, if it's caused by a blood pressure drop, then probably his brain was getting either too much or too little blood. So we move his blood around."

"All right," Mejox said. He rolled the Seteposian over, lifted him by his armpits so that his head hung down, and shook him hard. "Let's see if—"

The Seteposian gasped and made a horrid ululating cry which started Mejox so much that he dropped him onto his face. The Seteposian pulled himself back into his starting position, prostrate with respect.

"Well, we've gotten back to where we started from," Osepok said. "Now what?"

"Well, we could try being a bit politer," I said. I crouched by the Seteposian, slid my hands under his shoulders, and gently lifted. He sat up. This was the closest I had seen one, and familiarity was not improving his looks any.

I pointed to myself and said, "Zahmekoses. Zahmekoses. Zahmekoses. Zah. Meh. Koh. Seez."

Then I pointed to the Seteposian's mouth. He continued to stare.

"Zah," I said, pointing at his mouth.

He drew a breath and said, "Shah."

"Zahmekoses."

"Shahmekotheesh."

"Not bad," I said.

"Not bad," he replied.

Everyone laughed, and he threw himself back into the prostrate position. It took some time to get him to sit up again. Much later I learned that our laughter sounded like a mixture of growling and screaming to them. (Their laughter is a strange barking or bleating sound.) When we all made that noise he thought he must have spoken a word reserved for the gods themselves, and that he was about to pay the penalty such a blasphemy warranted.

Right then, of course, I didn't know any such thing. But I could see we had lost some ground, so I got him through "Zahmekoses" a few more times. Then we proceeded through "Mejokth" and "Otush" and so forth, until he could name us all. Finally I pointed to him and learned he was "Rar."

By now it was time for midday meal, so we decided to break for that. "Do we feed him?" Priekahm asked.

"Better reserve god-food for us, till we find out how powerful a magic it seems to be to them," Osepok said. "They're very much like the Leeward Islanders in some ways, and of course drastically different in others, but the food of powerful beings was supposed to have a lot of power in all our primitive cultures. Might as well play it safe and not give him any till we know how he'll interpret it."

I picked up a stick and thrust it into the ground. The Seteposian stared at me. I put a smaller stick into the ground at the tip of the shadow of the bigger stick. Then I put in another a small angle away from the first, carefully making sure it was eastward so that the shadow would move in that direction. (I certainly wanted to see him before tomorrow morning.) Then I said "Rar" and pointed at the ground, then at the stick the shadow would reach in about a twentieth of a day. I indicated, I hoped, "Rar here" for each short stick, and then indicated the angle between them and pointed out at the open spaces around.

He gestured agreement and prostrated himself, chanted our names, and crawled backward away from us. When he had reached the ashes of the palisade, he turned, rose, and ran for the hills. "Do you suppose he actually got that?" Otuz asked.

"I don't know, but he acted like he did. I guess we go eat, then wait till the shadow hits the second stick and see if he turns up again. I kind of think he will, though. He seemed to be getting it," I said, playing at being more confident than I really was.

"Well," Osepok said, "at the very least, Rar has some ability to understand from context. He used the assent gesture, and we didn't teach him that one. He must have figured it out by watching us."

Rar was back right on time, prostrating himself by the crude sundial. We went out and raised him up. The long afternoon, and the next eight-day, were spent learning a few hundred of his words and a rudimentary grammar of his language.

The grammar was extremely complex and difficult, which according to Osepok, as we talked it over at one evening meal, was "pretty much what we'd expect. Primitive people's languages tend to be more complex and specific because they don't have the diversity of things to talk about that technically advanced people do. So they build the specificity they need right into the words, instead of constructing it at the sentence level. So it will take a while to learn, and we'll probably always feel it's a very stiff and formal way of saying a very limited variety of things.

"Chances are that once we get an empire going, their language will rapidly become simpler in grammar and more general in vocabulary— but I'm afraid that will take a few generations."

She returned her attention to her food. After a pause, Kekox said,

"Er, Captain, I'm curious. You've been remarkably good at all these, uh, matters of relating to primitive peoples, and we've been very glad that one of us is—but we were wondering . . . where did you learn it?"

She looked sad. "Well," she said, "after Poiparesis . . . died, I missed him terribly. I think you know that he and I . . . well, we spent a lot of our time in each other's chambers."

None of us had even had a suspicion.

"Anyway," she went on, "all of a sudden I had a lot of time to spend by myself, and as the proverb says, you can't mourn forever. At first I listened to favorite music or watched old performances, but you know, that doesn't give much stimulus to the mind after a while. So naturally, since—please forgive my saying this—I really didn't want to see or talk to any of you for a while, I started to look for some study or interest to keep myself amused and sane with, something I could work on all by myself that might be useful. Well, the one thing nobody had thought of sending on the trip was an expert in cross-cultural study, and even if they had . . . well, after all, it's been a long time since we had the chance to do it, really, and there's no one with any meaningful experiences. After all, the last primitives were found in Wahkopem's time, and then Palath took over and most of the primitives were carried off as slaves. So no one had done what they used to call 'field work' in centuries.

"Now since *I* was sure they were people, I thought techniques for studying primitive people would be a good thing to know. So I learned what I could from books, which turned out to be quite a bit. On the way I had to master Early Modern Shulathian and learn a little bit about twenty or so extinct languages. But it was worth it, both as a distraction and now that we have some use for it all. More useful than astrogation and subnucleonics, anyway."

In the days that followed we found out just how much her new skills were worth to us, as we made rapid progress in understanding the situation. We had indeed wiped out both the hereditary governing family and the hereditary priesthood. Without quite meaning to, we had created a new priest-king, for as the only one who spoke to us, Rar had ascended to the height of his society. Before our coming he had been nobody special, an ordinary hunter and farmer among the bachelor males, but now, in just the two eightdays we had been there, he had acquired four wives ("three widows and a fresh one," he told us proudly), and a picked band of loyal retainers from among his group, which called themselves the Real People.

"Well, I don't think we meant to create him as our all-powerful representative," Otuz commented, "but he's certainly working out well." We were watching the Real People till, weed, and irrigate their fields. When we had noticed the crops dying, we had told Rar we were no longer angry with his people for worshipping the false Mother God, and that they could save their crops and—*if* they continued to please and obey us, and stayed away from false gods—we would show them how to rebuild their town and make them the greatest people in the world. But if they fell away or disobeyed, we would strike them all down.

Not surprisingly they had taken the deal. They were working hard, now, and only occasionally glancing our way. We had promised them a bumper harvest, and we were making good on that; Soikenn had studied the metabolism of "wheat," the stuff they grew in their fields, and found that the local soil was a bit too acid and a little deficient in nitrogen, and we had prepared appropriate supplements and ordered them to spread them on the fields.

I hadn't had much of a chance to be alone with Otuz lately, and of course with a hundred pairs of eyes on us, including Rar's, we weren't quite alone anyway. It didn't matter as much as it might have, for she was now quite swollen with her pregnancy, and I doubted very much that she would be in the mood. Still, we could stand on the hill and speak Nisuan and talk about all that had happened. "I think Kekox is right," she said. "We should wait till next spring before beginning the conquest. All things in due time, and so forth."

"That seems to be Kekox's principle," I said.

She swatted my arm. "Now, if Osepok and Soikenn are both happy about it, who's to condemn them? And at least Osepok got pregnant by him first." She turned to look over the field and said, "I could almost admire the old rascal."

There was a distant thunder high above us, and we turned to watch the *Gurix* coming in. With Mejox at the controls, it was moving swiftly and smoothly down to the landing pad by the big, comfortable log house we had built for ourselves with power tools from the ship. "Want to hear whatever the news is?"

"Sure." We walked down the hill hand in hand. I looked around, felt the warm amber sun Kousapex on my back, saw our slaves tending the grain with Rar standing over them, and then looked down to our house. "*Gurix* and *Rumaz* only have one more trip each to make for supplies," I said. "Then no more trips to space . . . or if we go, it'll be just for fun."

"Nothing wrong with fun," she pointed out. "There's enough anti-matter in their tanks to make a trip every eightday for as long as we live. But yes, an era is coming to an end, I guess. We'll have to content ourselves with being all-powerful gods."

"And parents," I pointed out. "Which I'm told is quite a bit different."

When we got there, Mejox, Osepok, and Kekox had all come down, leaving Priekahm and Soikenn up on the ship. Usually everyone came down with the supply ferry, but, Mejox explained, "There's some kind of problem with Priekahm's pregnancy and Soikenn wanted to use the better gear on *Wahkopem* to diagnose it."

We had just gotten the supplies unloaded, and were about to settle onto our porch to watch the sun set over the wooded hills, when the radio called for our attention. We keyed up the visual in the *Gurix* and crowded in to hear what Soikenn had to say. "Well, it's messy, but we can deal with it," she said. "It turns out that protein incompatibility is a mixed blessing. There are several things that we're not excreting—I've tested my blood and Priekahm's, and we're crawling with a number of foreign proteins. We had thought that they were functionally inert, but it turns out that they're putting a terrible strain on Priekahm's child's kidney."

"Is there a way of getting them out of the bloodstream?" Mejox asked.

"Well, yes, two ways. I can set up dialysis in the short run, and clean us and our unborn children up in a matter of an eightday. It's already working in a lab version, and it's really not a complicated job because what we're screening for is so different. But that's not a permanent solution. I can't make a dialysis rig that we can take down to the surface, and if I could, we'd all be dependent on it forever. So that brings up solution two . . ."

"Which is?" Kekox asked.

"A tailored virus to do a genetic modification. It could work while we were doing dialysis every four eightdays or so. After a year, it will have regenerated enough kidney tissue so that we'll be able to process the alien proteins ourselves. And we'll also pass the trait on to our children."

"What's the catch?" Osepok asked. "You don't sound happy."

"It's a vector, potentially, isn't it?" Otuz asked.

Soikenn gestured assent. Her expression was grim. "While it's in our bloodstreams, it's a kind of code translator. Just possibly it will hook up with some local virus or bacterium; organisms like that trade DNA very easily. In effect it might tell some local bug how to dial into our receptor sites, or how to look less weird to our immune systems. We run a big risk of throwing away that perfect immunity we've had since we got here."

"But if we don't," Kekox said, "then everyone dies a few years after the last dialysis machine breaks?"

"Well, they could stave it off by only eating Nisuan food—I'm going to suggest that we do that till we're all gene-treated—but yes. Without the modification, as soon as we lose the ability to do dialysis or to live entirely on Nisuan food, our whole species dies, after a few years, probably from kidney failure. If something else doesn't turn out to fail faster than the kidney. And I really see no way that we can count on keeping the ship's farm, the *Gurix*, or a dialysis rig running for three hundred years. We're going to have to do the genetic modification."

"Well, you've persuaded me we have to," Osepok said. "And I think you've persuaded all of us, actually."

"I was hoping one of you would have a brilliant idea for a way to avoid this," she said, a little sadly. "We thought Setepos might be paradise. It's still pretty good, but I'm afraid there's one way in which it will be less perfect than I had hoped—we'll be able to get sick."

That fall we discovered that the gods were going to have to do some taking care of their faithful people. We had showed them how to raise a good mud-and-stone wall, but they had to harvest crops as well. We had demonstrated to them why they would want a stone tower to serve both as granary and observation deck, but there was too much for them to build before the rains came again, and with the crop losses we had inflicted upon them, there was a real risk of famine. If we wanted a healthy army for the spring conquest, we would need to lend them a hand.

We used the *Rumaz* to bring down a small treaded tractor; with that, we excavated a foundation in a day, when it would have taken them several eightdays. The tractor plus a log sledge let us move twenty times as much stone per day as all of them working together could have done, and we needed only Rar and a few helpers. And with the aid of a few blasting charges, we made a local cliff supply us with more stone than an army of them could have found or cut.

The stone walls enclosed a large area, most especially including our log house and the field for the landers. With the machine tools and Rar's now quite skillful interpretation of our directions, our little community was safely behind its walls, with all the grain into the tower, well before the first rain fell. Kekox and Mejox went out with Rar and a party of bearers for several days and shot a large number of wild goats, deer, pigs, and aurochs—animals which had become almost as familiar to us as to the Seteposians—and we introduced them to the basic techniques of smoking and salting meat.

When the first rains fell, the Seteposians threw a "thanksgiving," in which they presented us with quite a lot of food (which we put into the cooler we had installed in our house). In return, we presented them with a few thousand fired mud bricks and a lot of planks we had made with power tools; it seemed like a small gift, but two days hard work put them all into more or less dry houses with much less flammable roofs.

After the houses were all up, they "danced" (that strange rhythmic motion we had seen around the animal sacrifice) and later all got intoxicated on a fermented mash of the local fruit. There were some not-serious fights that Rar put down with his loyal assistants, and after that people settled into making their houses more snug and comfortable.

Soikenn had finished tailoring and testing the virus, so with considerable nervousness, she gave it to Kekox. When he seemed to be fine after two eightdays, and his kidneys began to regenerate with the capability of handling the foreign proteins, she gave the rest of us doses of it as well.

And still the rain fell, turning the fields to mud and bringing the river to flood. We were well above it, and we and our Seteposians were snug indoors, but there was something intolerably dreary about it. We had not gotten around to making window glass yet, so we spent most of our time behind wooden shutters, in glaring artificial light. We ate, we studied, and we met regularly with Rar. It took a great deal of effort to explain to him what kind of war we would have in the spring, that the Real People, who were now our slaves, would have all the neighbors as slaves. At first he could not see why they had to burn villages, or attack at night, or destroy the idols in their temples. But with time he came to understand, and he was invaluable as Kekox began to drill the fighting-age males in the new way of fighting.

The other great news of that autumn was that Otuz and I won the sweepstakes: our daughter, Diehrenn, was born about a week before Mejox and Priekahm's Weruz. The first son—and the only nonhybrid—among our second generation showed up two eightdays later, when Captain Osepok gave birth to Prirox. All the births went without trouble, but just to be on the safe side, Soikenn flew each mother up to *Wahkopem Zomos* when her time was due. The babies were healthy, and they too could process Seteposian proteins. They gained weight and got strong.

The winter was mild and a little dryer, but only a little. Still, it was chilly enough so that there was not much pleasure in being outside. There was nothing to do but play with the babies (a limited amount of fun; it was hard to believe that on the time scale of this planet, with its faster orbit, it would be six more winters, not five, before they were fully conscious) and prepare the spring campaign (which took little preparation, really; it was after all a project for forty Seteposian males with axes, torches, and spears).

Whenever the thin sun would work its way through the clouds, I would usually sit outside with Kekox or Mejox, just to have something to do and not to have to talk about babies. After Soikenn had delivered Osekahm, she too had focused most of her attention in the nursery. It was true that babies needed a lot of attention; it was also true that our females really enjoyed giving it.

On one unusually fine but quite cold day, Kekox, Mejox, and I sat watching Rar drill the troops. Locally battles were a matter of one-on-one duels, which was a good way to settle who was bravest, but a poor way to win. We had introduced the idea of using spears as a unit, overwhelming the individual fighters on the other side. Today they were practicing with untipped spear shafts, and doing pretty well. "Not the best troops I've ever seen, but they should cut through the neighborhood pretty fast all the same," Kekox said. "With luck the first wave of conquest can be over before the second planting of wheat. And I've got an idea; if we penned up goats and pigs regularly, instead of the occasional way they do it now, I would bet we can add a lot more meat to our side's diet. Make them bigger and stronger in another generation."

Mejox yawned. "The number of things we have to do for the next generation. You know, every so often I think we're not quite the impressive gods we used to be. They've really seen a lot of us, and we've really been very fair and nice. I don't think they have quite the same . . . uh . . ."

"Terror," I said. "I think I prefer it this way."

Mejox started to answer, but then he had the strangest expression I had ever seen, and quite suddenly he made a hideously unpleasant noise and spat blobs of mucus all over the ground, some of them narrowly missing me. Without even apologizing, he did it twice more. As he sat back up his eyes were filled with panic. "What—"

Kekox groaned. "I see Soikenn was right. Mejox, what you just had—" and he made the same hideous noise and mess. "Oh, wonderful. What we're having is a cough, my young raised-in-sanitary-conditions friend. I predict that very shortly we will all feel perfectly lousy. I am going to go to bed—after I tie a cloth over my face, so I don't spread this, as if we don't probably all have it already." He got up and went inside.

I had watched in some amazement, and was about to ask what it felt like, when abruptly there was a horrible pain in my upper chest, I felt a sharp spasm around my blood mixer, and I erupted with the same awful noise and results. "Sorry about your foot," I said to Mejox.

Two eightdays later, all of us, the babies especially, were coughing constantly. Every one of us had a headache and fever as well. Soikenn, face wet with mucus most of the time, was working frantically on a specific to kill the new virus, with very little luck. Mejox, drugged almost silly with painkillers and fever suppressants, had taken the *Rumaz* to *Wahkopem Zomos* and gotten some drugs that seemed to be helping the babies, but when he returned he went to bed and stayed there for two full days. Hardly any of us could move much without acute pain in the chest.

One morning much like the others, the babies were coughing softly, and there were occasional groans from everyone else. Kekox was up getting water for us. Rather than deal with whatever might be living in the local water, we were using the water system of the *Rumaz*, pouring local water into its sanitary system and letting the lander's still produce potable water. As we had gotten worse, Otuz and I had rigged a connection so that a hose carried water from the *Rumaz* into our cabin; this meant that it was only necessary every couple of days for someone to carry chamber pots over to the *Rumaz* and dump them into the sanitary system.

Kekox went to the pitcher, which should have been full of water dribbled in over the night, only to find it was as empty as when it had been set there. He was so weak that I saw him stumble and catch himself on the table. I thought of volunteering to go out and fix it, but when I tried to push myself up from my sweat-soaked bed, I became too dizzy even to speak.

Still, I saw what happened next. Kekox opened the door to go outside and see what was wrong with the water line. At once the door flew open, and Rar stepped in, pushing Kekox back, and swung a small ax up. Any of the rest of us would have died right there, unaware we were attacked, but Kekox was still the old Imperial Guard. He deflected Rar's ax arm, swept his foot, and hurled him back through the door, ramming it closed with his shoulder and latching it as the Seteposians outside began to beat on it.

Mejox and Priekahm fell out of their beds, going for the steam rifles beside the door. As axes began to thump on the door, Mejox, Priekahm, and Kekox fired through it; there were screams from the other side, and then it got very quiet.

We had no window, so we could not see what was happening outside, but the appalling din suggested that they had turned their attention to the *Rumaz*. There was a rhythmic chant like they used when they dealt with heavy objects, and then a long, savage crash that told us they had tipped it over, followed by the crash of more stone axes against its door. "It's not built to take that," I said, and Osepok added—"If they force the door with it lying like that, they're likely to trigger the antimatter safety jettison, and then—"

There was a wild roar, the walls shook, and we had just time to realize that the *Rumaz*'s computer, sensing breach everywhere and immense damage, had fired the little package that took the antimatter containment right out through the hull and far off into space before the antimatter container could breach. Somewhere very high above us there was a great fireworks display; down here the power of the takeoff meant our house had been washed in flames, and though many Seteposians were dead or badly burned outside, to judge by the crackling sound and the thickening smoke, we had just a minute or so to get out.

We formed up as best we could, sick, coughing, almost passing out, many of us cradling babies. Kekox kicked the door open and we rushed, trying to get off the porch and head for the *Gurix*, but we had staggered only a few feet, spraying those near us with our steam rifles, when a thrown ax took Kekox from behind, and then the rush of them was on us. I started to shout something, began to cough in the icy outside air, and then either the coughing—or a blow from the fist of one of the soldiers—knocked me unconscious; I barely kept Diehrenn cradled in my arms as I fell.

14

"HE'S COMING AROUND, I THINK," OTUZ SAID. "COME ON, ZAHMEKOSES, wake up."

I blinked hard, trying to see, realized it was dark, opened my eyes wider, and slipped back into unconsciousness. A while later—I'm not sure how long—I stirred again, tried cautiously opening my eyes. I could feel Soikenn's hand on my arm. "Zahmekoses? Zahmekoses, can you hear me?"

"I—" My throat was parched. "Water," I managed to croak.

"We don't have any right now," Soikenn whispered. "I'm sorry. They took all our things and they haven't given us food or water yet."

Memory was coming back—not that I wanted it to—through the fog of pain. "Kekox?"

"Dead."

"I . . . thought so." It was hard to focus, hard to think, and then when I had something to say, it was hard to make my lips and throat form the sounds. "The others—"

"Mejox has a broken leg from when they wrestled him down. A compound fracture; it looks pretty bad. Otuz and I are just bruised and shaken up. And . . ." Even through the fog of pain I could tell that Soikenn was worried—"Priekahm's fever is so high that I'm afraid she'll get brain damage from it. And Osepok doesn't seem to be hurt physically, but she doesn't seem to know where she is or what is going on. Maybe she's just in shock—or maybe she's lost her mind, Zahmekoses. She just sits there and won't respond when we say anything, except once she asked about the regular shipboard duties and whether we'd done those."

"My head . . ."

"You got hit hard from behind—one of them clubbed you. I think that's all. Do you hurt anywhere else?"

"No. But my head hurts." Then I fell back asleep again.

The next time I woke up, the world wasn't spinning as badly, and the first things I noticed were that I must have vomited and urinated where I lay. Probably if they had no water no one had been able to clean me. The second thing I noticed was that there was light, though it didn't quite resolve into an image just yet. There seemed to be several bars of light too brilliant to look at, surrounded by complete blackness, occasionally crossed by shifting shadows. Finally I realized that one other thing was strange: I had no fever and I could breathe.

I made a croaking noise—I was terribly thirsty—and this time Otuz came over to me. "Zahmekoses? Are you awake?"

"Kind of."

"What do you remember?"

"Everything, I think. Have I been out long this time?"

"All night. It's morning. They just brought us water, from the external port on the *Gurix*—that's how they tricked us, they cut the water hose on the *Rumaz*, but they understand that we can't drink their water—and a little food—would you like a drink?"

"Yes."

She made me take small, careful sips. The water was warm and tasted flat, but if she had let me I would have gulped it all down.

"The others?" I asked, after a while.

"Soikenn is asleep. She and I have been taking watches to take care of the rest of you. Priekahm's fever broke. Soikenn is . . . she's not good, Zahmekoses, even though she's holding it inside. We lost her child; the baby died earlier today, maybe from the cough or disease, Diehrenn and Weruz seem to be better, and Prirox isn't any worse. We've done what we can for Mejox—everything wrong, by the standards back home—pushed the bone back into the wound and set it as best we could. It seemed to pop together, and the strange thing is there's no sign of infection, so just possibly none of the Seteposian bacteria that infect wounds have learned any new tricks yet. Did Soikenn tell you about Osepok?"

"Yes."

"Well, she's more alert, and she doesn't want to talk, but she does say she remembers what happened. She nurses Prirox and cuddles him, so we think she's coming out of the shock of Kekox's death."

"And Diehrenn is getting better?"

"She's fine, really. In fact she seems to have stopped coughing and be on the mend."

"I think I'm the same way," I said.

Otuz sighed. "If we'd all just gotten a little better a little faster . . . well, nothing for it. I guess we have to see what they'll do with us. Unfortunately we've already taught them a lot of things . . . like slavery and control by terror."

I sighed, and then winced because the change in breathing hurt my head. "I think I have a concussion."

"I'm sure you do. Your reflexes were a mess last night, but they're much better this morning. I'm glad to see you getting better."

"Do you know what they're going to do with us?"

"Not yet, but I think we'll learn. Rar, by the way, is now called Nim Rar. Nim is a title, I think—I get the impression a Nim is like a king or a priest, but a bit better than either. I guess in a while when we can talk, he can tell us what he's planning to do. If they haven't already done it by then."

"At least if they didn't do it right away they probably aren't planning to kill us. What would be the point?" I said. My head still hurt terribly, but it felt good to be able to form an idea again.

"At least they aren't planning to kill all of us, or not all at once. I've been doing a little watching through the door, Zahmekoses—have you been able to see at all yet?"

"It's coming back," I said. I had figured out that the bars of bright light were daylight showing between the logs, and now I knew that the shadow bending over me was Otuz, but I still really couldn't make out her face, though I was sure it was light enough in our little prison.

"Well, they're rebuilding the temple. They dragged the burned out shell of the *Rumaz* to it and set it back up on its two legs, with a log propping the third corner; that seems to be acting as the back wall. In front of that they're putting together a log and stone two-story thing, with a statue of the Mother Goddess in it, not too different from what we saw when we came here. So I'd say it's a conservative movement to restore traditional values. . . . Anyway, if you want my guess, I think that what's in store for us is slavery at best and being sacrificed at worst. I don't know what good we'll be as slaves, but I suppose they'll find something to do with us. Though Mejox—well, he's still mostly unconscious. It could be a long time before he's well. I guess what happens to him depends on how fast he gets better and how much patience they have."

There wasn't much to say after that. Otuz sat by me and held my hand until I fell back asleep.

I woke again toward late afternoon, feeling much better. They had left more water, and I tried a little of the food: boiled mashed grain, the sort of thing we fed to infants. It wasn't wonderful, but it was edible, and since Otuz and Soikenn and our three surviving infants seemed to be doing fine on it, probably it wouldn't kill me.

Nim Rar looked in briefly. He had a swagger about him I had never seen before, and there was something about the practical, simple way he lifted my chin, stared into my eyes, and poked at my abdomen that told me he did not have the slightest concern with how I felt about anything—he was going to do what was best for him, as he saw it, and it would be a bad idea to get in his way.

He left abruptly. "Maybe he had a full calendar of appointments," I said to Otuz.

"You're feeling better," she said. "Can you stand up?"

I tried; I was weak but not dizzy. "I seem to be okay."

"Good thing. I want you to take a look at Mejox's leg. Soikenn is still grieving for poor little Osekahm, and I'm not sure she's always paying the best attention to what she's doing."

Soikenn had been my teacher. But that thought didn't bear examining, so I asked the immediate question instead. "They took our medical kit?"

"They took everything. And I wouldn't count on getting anything back in good condition. One of our guards is wearing one of the land navigation units around his neck, on a string, driven right through the center. Probably our communicators have all been pulled apart for jewelry."

"Doesn't sound good," I said, "but chances are that anything the computer told me to do, I wouldn't have the stuff for anyway. Let's have a look at Mejox. Has he been conscious?"

"Just muttering now and then. Usually calling for Soikenn or Priekahm, even though they're right there. Sometimes for Kekox, which is pretty hard to take. I don't think he knows where he is or what's happened."

My eyes were focusing fine now, and although I thought a few of my teeth might be a little loose and one ear seemed to be crushed and a bit bloody, I was in pretty good shape, considering. "Well, then let's look." I glanced around and saw Osepok sitting in her corner and Soikenn curled asleep on the floor.

Mejox was lying on his back. Priekahm, still coughing slightly, was sitting beside him, holding his hand; her other arm cradled Weruz.

His breathing was shallow and his heartbeat elevated; his skin was cool to the touch, his nose was dry, and most alarmingly part of his crest was crushed. "I think they hit him on the head at one time or other," I said. "Hope his crest took up enough of the shock, because that's going to add to the problem. He seems to have lost a lot of blood, but if that was going to kill him it would have done it by now." I drew a breath and let it out slowly; memory was rushing back. I did have some considerable abstract knowledge about crushing injuries and compound fractures.

The trouble was, it was mainly useless. I couldn't do a brain scan, give him a transfusion, or administer a mild electric shock between his lower jaw and crest to revive him, all standard therapies in this case. I didn't even have a stick to splint his leg with.

I bent to examine the leg. "You all did right," I said, looking at it. At least the bone was no longer exposed to the air, and the guide membrane that allows new flesh to grow beneath it had formed normally—always assuming I remembered what "normally" was accurately. As Otuz had said, there was no sign of infection; given what it smelled like around here, I figured that was a good sign that most of their normal septic germs couldn't touch us yet.

I put a hand where I judged the bone break might be.

"Is it safe to touch his wound with your hands?" Otuz asked.

"Usually, yes. The guide membrane seals it. And we need to find out if his leg is set right before the permanent matrix starts to regenerate. And we really hope it is, because breaking the temporary matrix to reset it is a nasty, dangerous job." I put my other hand under the sole of his foot and said, "Mejox, my friend, I'm glad you're unconscious, because this would hurt a lot if you weren't."

Very gently, I pressed my hand against the break, through the guide membrane. Then I pushed upward firmly on his foot, ready to snatch my hand back if the bone broke under the pressure. It held; I pushed harder, and it barely bowed. "He's forming the temporary matrix, and pretty quickly. It'll be hard in another couple of days, and after that if he wakes up he might be able to walk on it, though it won't be very strong. And Soikenn did as good a job as anyone could of setting it. There's a splinter underneath that will probably make him limp a little for some years until it's reabsorbed, and he might never run very well again, but for field conditions this was brilliant."

I peeled back one of his outer eyelids and whistled sharply in his ear; the inner lid flipped down and up, in the Teravorsis Reflex. Otuz asked, "Was that good?"

"As far as it goes. He's got some higher brain function. Let's check the other side." He had the Teravorsis Reflex on that side as well. I probed gently at his crest; it was bound to be sore. The thick, heavy tufts of hair that make up the crest in a mature Palathian are supported by a dense network of blood vessels, and those in turn run in and out of the skull through a thick piece of bone networked with thousands of tiny holes, the Urdebok Structure, that helps in temperature regulation. If the Urdebok Structure is crushed hard enough, even though the skull is not fractured, bleeding within the structure can cause blood clots to form and circulate into the brain, with all kinds of disastrous consequences.

I didn't want to dislodge anything that might have already formed and be rattling around loose in there, but at the same time I badly wanted to know whether his Urdebok Structure had been crushed, or whether it was only the stiff short hair at the base of the crest that had taken the damage. So at first I probed very gingerly, and then I searched around systematically. "I don't find any soft spots," I said. "So he's hardheaded, I guess."

"Just as we always knew."

"Unh hunh. Probably just a bad concussion, compounded by blood loss and shock. If he and I got hit about equally hard, he'd be in worse shape—that's a major difference between Shulathian and Palathian. He probably didn't form any clots, but he almost certainly took a pressure wave in the brain from the Urdebok being compressed. And given what his leg and head would feel like right now, in a way he's lucky to be unconscious. Have you been able to get any water into him?"

"It takes some effort, but yes. We sort of brush it onto his mouth until that gets wet, then he reflexively licks it off. We get a couple handvolumes into him that way, over the course of maybe an eighth of a day."

"That's good. It's keeping him alive. If we can keep him alive long enough, and if they don't run out of patience or hurt him further, then he'll probably recover."

"Will it be a full recovery?"

"Well, he'll be a lot better off than this. After that, the Creator only knows."

Soikenn woke up then, and we reviewed Mejox together. She was upset at having failed to notice the concussion, but since the news was at least sort of good—Mejox might be all right and I probably would be—it was at least not a *miserable* conversation. As I finished giving the news, I noted that for the first time in a long time my head wasn't actually hurting. About that time the guards brought us more boiled grain, this time a thick paste of it with bits of cooked animal flesh. We weren't sure if the taste of the animal or the way it was seasoned was what was so peculiar, but we were hungry and the flavor wasn't enough to keep us from eating.

"Well, the food's improving," Otuz said, when we were done. "Or maybe that's the standard evening meal. Either way, we apparently won't starve or die of thirst."

Priekahm sighed. "I suppose comparatively speaking things are looking up."

There was a distant booming thud, in a regular rhythm, which rapidly grew louder. We all rose and moved toward the door.

Our little prison faced one side of the new temple; they had rebuilt it almost overnight, but then it was a fairly simple construction in any case, and they had learned a lot about building from us. The mud statue of Mother Goddess was uglier than the one before, which was going some. The altar, where the probe had been in the old temple, was bare, and there was a long row of people kneeling on the "front porch" with their backs to the new wall.

In front of the row of Seteposians, between the temple wall and the new, bare altar, was a tall chair, and in that chair sat Nim Rar. He was wearing a tall feathered hat and all sorts of jewelry, much of it obviously from the probe or from our personal gear. The hat, I realized, was in the shape of a lander, echoing the shadowy burned-out bulk of the *Rumaz* behind him.

In his right hand he clutched an ax. Soikenn stared for a long moment, then shuddered and whispered to us, "I bet that's the ax that killed Kekox."

The deep thudding noise grew louder, and the crowd parted. I caught a glimpse of a huge pile of wood down in front of the porch; then I saw that the rhythmic thudding was coming from a group of Seteposian drummers, who marched in and gathered around the porch. They were followed by a group of torchbearers, who planted their long-handled torches around the group; then the last of the torch bearers dipped his torch to set the piled wood on fire. It blazed up quickly—a dense odor came to our nostrils.

As the fire blazed up brightly, the drumming became more rapid. Nim Rar stood up. Something draped around his shoulders, and he spread it wide behind him—

Otuz began to vomit beside me before I had quite realized what Nim Rar was wearing.

Kekox's skin, with his head still attached.

Soikenn was crying and groaning beside me; Priekahm simply kept whispering, "No." I hoped Osepok was too far gone, still, to look.

Then they carried in his body, dressed the way they dress game. I was numb with shock and rage, wanting to look away, unable to do so.

The pounding grew faster still, and then Nim Rar, still wearing Kekox's skin, cut up the corpse. His assistants roasted it, and all of the assembled Real People ate it. It must have taken an eighth of a day in all.

It was not until I smelled my lifelong friend cooking that finally I vomited, wept, crawled back into the hut, and let myself faint. I don't know what they did with the bones when they were done, but Kekox's skin hung in that hideous temple for many long years.

"Get up, Zahmekoses, I think they're moving us," Otuz whispered in my ear. I was awake instantly, every horrible memory of the night before still vivid. There were Seteposian voices outside, a great confusing gabble of them, and our guards seemed to be talking with everyone at once.

Soikenn was groaning as she got to her feet. "Let's try to wake Mejox if we can," she said. "We can always carry him between Priekahm and Otuz. Osepok, me, and Zahmekoses can at least carry the babies."

But as Soikenn and Priekahm lifted Mejox up by his shoulders, he coughed, loudly, several times, and looked up at me. "Zahmekoses?"

"I'm here, Mejox. Can you move any part of your body?"

Ever so slowly, he stood erect, or as close to it as he could manage just then. "I seem to be all here," he said. "My shin feels like it's on fire."

"You had a compound fracture. It's healing. The Seteposians have captured us," I said. "We're prisoners."

"Weruz?"

"She's all right, Mejox," Priekahm said. "And now that you're awake, so am I. Do you remember what happened to Kekox?"

"They killed him," Mejox said. "I don't really remember, but that's the only way we could have ended up like this. Did we lose anyone else?"

"Osekahm," Soikenn said. It was the first time she had pronounced her daughter's name since the child had died.

No one quite knew what to say, but then Nim Rar strode in, surrounded by half a dozen guards. He looked around the room with apparent satisfaction. "Well," he said, "I should thank you." It took me a moment to realize he was speaking quite clear Nisuan; he had undoubt-edly listened to us long enough to pick it up. How many ways had we given it away that we were not gods? How many ways had he found out we were vulnerable? Perhaps it was better not to know.

"If you want to know what will happen," the Nim said, now in Seteposian, "I very much like this *empire* idea of yours. And your won-derful devices. The only thing wrong with it all was that you were in charge of it. Now that has been corrected. I am assuming that, as I was a pleasant and cooperative slave, so will you be.

"Now, you've never met my entire family; I had a son by a woman whom you burned alive with your *Gurix* the first day. It happens that he survives. Let me introduce him now that I know you have no power to harm him." He clapped his hands. "Inok!"

The Seteposian who entered was young, though well-muscled for his age, and just reaching reproductive age. Rar must have started young, I thought to myself, and then realized that as briefly as they lived—the oldest man in the village had lived no more than forty of their years, or thirty-six of ours—they probably all started as young as they could. "You will teach him Nisuan. You will teach him everything," his proud father said. "He will be Nim after me, and will rule a great empire with many slaves. It is fitting that he know everything you do." With a slight nod of his head, Nim Rar left us alone with the boy.

He did not have his father's gift for languages, but his accent got bet-ter and more understandable as we worked. As the eightdays slid by, it seemed to me I had always been one of Inok's tutors, living in my cell near the great palace of Nim Rar—our old house, which had not burned after all, though the inner walls were now black with soot. The house was the Nim's now, along with the *Gurix* he had captured from the sky gods. It was with polite interest, later that spring, that I heard of the conquest and enslavement of the nearest neighbors to the Real People: the Rat People, the Snake Eaters, and the Ugly Woman People. "I don't suppose we have to worry about introducing any unpleasant tendency toward bigotry into this culture," Otuz muttered to me, after Inok fin-ished telling us the tale.

The first word Diehrenn said, that summer, was "Mama." Not a Nisuan word, but a word in the language of the Real People. We were thrilled anyway.

15

THERE WASN'T MUCH ELSE TO DO, SO WE WORKED HARD AT TEACHING Inok. He seemed to be bright enough, and we got along fairly well, except that he didn't believe a thing we told him, since manifestly the world was not round, it wasn't moving, the sun circled Setepos, you could not see any other worlds beyond the sky, and anyway the stars were tiny and therefore the *Gurix* couldn't have come from them. He had accepted his father's insight that we were flesh and blood, along with Rar's realization that we were more use to him if most of the Real People thought we were gods or demons whom he had subdued.

Inok had already had something of an education from the story-tellers. He knew that there were legends of people along a big river south and west of here, tales passed on by the Snake Eaters, who heard it from their neighbors, the Dog People, who presumably heard it from *their* neighbors. There were even more shadowy stories of "people across the water" that trickled in from the west and the north, along with accounts of "traveling people" who had no place of their own and lived by moving from place to place.

This education—possibly the best in Real People Town—had given Inok the ability to see through our silly story. As far as Inok was concerned, the world had so many kinds of people in it that we were plainly just another kind. Sooner or later we would stop lying and tell him where we were from, and then he and his father would take the *Gurix* and go conquer Nisu, since we were a weak and silly people, but we did have wonderful things. Till then, where we came from was just not terribly important.

Yet though he believed none of the things we told him, he loved stories of our history, and apparently so did the rest of the Real People, because he would repeat whatever we told him to them in the evenings, and it was very popular entertainment. We taught him Nisuan, but we kept back the three major ancient Shulathian languages that all of us had learned in school, speaking them only at night when we could breathe them in each other's ear.

A year went by; Mejox grew stronger, the three surviving children flourished, and Priekahm and Otuz were pregnant again. The Nim made it clear that Soikenn and Osepok should also get pregnant soon, but neither Mejox nor I could quite bring ourselves to take that step yet. We told Inok that they were our mothers, but this only meant that (based on resemblance) I was told to impregnate Osepok, and Mejox was told to impregnate Soikenn. We continued to stall.

Maybe it was just the need for nursing him for so many days, or perhaps there was some kind of a real bond of friendship there, but Inok and Mejox seemed to take to each other. As I had feared, Mejox did end up with a permanent limp. He said it wasn't painful and that we really shouldn't worry about him, but it was clear that though he could walk well enough with a cane, he would never run or jump again, unless we got him back up to the ship and used *Wahkopem Zomos*'s surgical equipment to rebreak and reconstruct his leg. Though Inok spoke to Nim Rar about it, we could not get permission to do that, even with most of us staying below as hostages.

In the evenings, sometimes, when the guards didn't seem to be too close, we would all lie down with our heads close together and murmur to each other in Windward Islands Shulathian. There was one thing that was clear to all six of us adult survivors: that if we could just get ourselves, and our three babies, onto the *Gurix*, we would be safe and free again. The Seteposians had not managed to open the hatch, and the *Gurix* was still sitting there, ready to go.

Unfortunately they knew perfectly well that it was our one means of escape, and no more than two of us were ever allowed out of confinement at a time.

"I've got an idea about all that," Mejox said. "How do you all feel about Inok?"

"Smart kid," Soikenn said.

"If I knew him in other circumstances I think I'd like him," Otuz said.

Priekahm agreed. "He's very considerate and he *is* smart. You must have noticed that he's wonderful at tending Weruz and Diehrenn—but that also means they're becoming attached to him, and if we stay here till they grow up, they'll be his most loyal slaves. He's cunning."

I added, "Well, the only thing I have to add about Inok is that he seems to be more genuinely curious than Rar, and certainly a lot more interested in the wider world than most of the Real People. You could teach that boy just about anything."

Mejox scratched his crest; it had grown back in crooked, after his concussion, and between that and his limp, he now always looked as if he were falling over to the right. "Well, here's the question: do you think he'd like to go to space?"

We all gaped at him.

"Think about it," he said. "We can go places as long as we have him along. He's already said he wants to learn to fly it."

"They'll never let us all get onto it at the same time," Osepok pointed out. "They aren't stupid. We've already found out just how not-stupid they can be."

"Oh, I agree," Mejox said. "But suppose we started lessons, as it were—so that, for example, he learned how to power it up and get it flight ready—with all three of you back here. And then, when it was powered up . . . if I got control and brought it over here to the prison in a short hop—well, you'd still have to find a way to knock out the door here, but then—"

"I think Inok would probably object strongly to being kidnapped or having the lander taken away from him," Priekahm pointed out.

"That's where what you all think of him comes in. What if we told him we were going to take him back to Nisu with us? Do you think he'd go for that?"

"And would we?" Otuz demanded.

"Go back to Nisu with my daughter of mixed race? Are you crazy? Maybe we should just offer to show him *Wahkopem Zomos*. He can come along with us if he wants to, when we build our colony on one of those islands—the ones you were right about, Soikenn, where we should have gone in the first place. We could give him that much of a choice, though I doubt he'd take it. Anyway, after he visits *Wahkopem Zomos*, we could always drop him off a short distance from here, in the middle of the night. If we can get him to help us—most especially if we can make it happen honestly, which is the way I prefer—I think we owe it to him to give him the choice and at least let him see space."

Otuz said, "So the idea is really to win him over if you think you can?"

"That would be best. Failing that, we can kidnap him temporarily, but well—I don't like the thought of betraying a friend."

"Suppose we had to kill him to get away?" I asked.

Mejox sighed. "Then we would. Of course."

"Good. Then it's a plan, or the start of one."

From then on, we worked harder than ever at being Inok's friend. That turned out to be easier than we had thought it might be, for though Inok was accorded a great deal of respect nowadays as the Nim's son, it was clear that he had never had many friends, and better still—from our standpoint—he resented this.

"It seems sort of natural to me," Otuz was saying, as we waited one morning for Inok to finish showing Mejox something. "Rar was a nobody in the village until his initiative and courage—which he only got to display because we turned up—made him the Nim. Inok spent years as nobody's son. And without any other way to win prestige; after all, what makes you important around here is being big and strong, and skilled with weapons. Inok is not large for a male his age, and he doesn't seem to be very gifted athletically. So now that his father got to be the Nim on the strength of having captured us, he's got a lot of prestige, but he's still completely dependent on his father for it, and he knows better than anyone that none of his new friends really cares for him."

Whatever Inok thought of the rest of us, it was clear that Mejox was his particular friend. Now, as Otuz and I waited for our time with the boy, we saw him leading Mejox over to talk to Nim Rar. Mejox now had an odd, rolling gait because his foot wouldn't quite go straight without hurting, and one leg was a tiny bit shorter than the other. He tired quickly, too, when he had to walk any distance; he had told me one evening he was actually looking forward to getting back to *Wahkopem Zomos* to have his leg rebroken and reset. Well, perhaps we could do something about that soon.

Mejox and Inok talked to Nim Rar for what seemed like an unusually long time, and when they turned to join us, Nim Rar came with them. We bowed to the ground, as we had been taught to do when the Nim passed, and then in Nisuan, he said, "You may rise. Come with me to the Lookout Hill. We have much to talk about."

It was a long walk up the hill, and Mejox had to go very slowly, but Rar seemed to be willing to pause for frequent rests. On the way he talked with us about the things we had told Inok—about how far away Nisu was, and how the emperor ruled it, and a great deal of our history. His accent was a bit strange, but he was completely understandable, and he made almost no errors of grammar. Sometimes we'd switch over to the language of the Real People.

He had brought us to the top of the hill because he was the first ruler in memory who actually ruled as far as he could see. But our stories had given him a bigger ambition. "Imagine how clever your emperor seems to me; he rules a whole world," Nim Rar said to us. "Now tell me about—"

He seemed fascinated with what we thought were small details, but it was something to talk about, and it relieved the fear to some extent.

From the top of the hill, we could see that the country around was broken and rugged, so we could see other hilltops a long way away. There was a great deal of exposed stone, and the oak forest was broken and uneven. "It is said in the legends that the oaks once covered this whole area," Rar said. "Now they will not grow even when we plant them; the old ones have deep roots and live on, but there's not enough water to start a young one, except in the valleys. I suppose a day will come when nothing grows here; we can see where the floods once rose on the cliffs, but no one has ever seen the water rise that high, as far back as memory goes. The old priest said that the gods were once angry and drowned most of the world, but I myself think that there is just less water than there used to be."

Otuz said, "That seems a reasonable supposition. Three thousand years ago—"

"What is a thousand?" Inok asked.

Otuz thought for a long moment, and then said, "I know your word hundred. A thousand is a hundred tens."

Inok and Rar exchanged glances. "No one would count that high," Inok said. "Everything we need to measure is smaller than that."

"Nonetheless," Otuz said, "the time I speak of was three thousand years ago. At that time, in the lands north of the Big Salt Sea, the land was covered with ice; the wind blew across the ice and picked up water, and when the wind blew against the hills down here, the water came down as rain, and it filled the rivers, watered the trees, and put water into the . . . aquifers. An aquifer is a river that flows under the ground and feeds the wells," she hastened to explain. "Now, very slowly, this area is losing its water, because what the trees and aquifers capture is never as much as what the rivers carry away and the air picks up. So you *are* right, Nim Rar. There is much less water than there used to be."

Rar sat back with a look we had come to realize meant he had heard exactly what he wanted to hear. Naturally his son decided to argue. "But how could you know what happened so long ago?"

"From high up," I said, "we can see the scars on the land that the ice made, and we can see the little bits of the ice that remain to this day. And we know because of other worlds that we have studied that scars like that are made by ice, and from how much healing the land has had, we can guess how long ago the ice melted away."

Inok seemed to be satisfied as well. "It is good to know these things," he said.

Rar grunted assent. "But enough small talk. We are on this hill for a reason. It seems to me that in a few summers I might rule from the Dead Sea to the Big Salt Sea, north to the mountains and south to the desert, just as your emperor does. From this high place we can see the neighboring lands, and the horizons beyond. I wanted to talk to you, my most valued of slaves, about how we are to proceed."

"Well, then, I can think of one thing," I said, glancing significantly at Mejox. "Just as this hill puts you up high where you can see—"

Mejox caught my point and leaped in. "Exactly what I was going to suggest." I thought he was overplaying the loyal slave routine a little more than necessary. "By using the *Gurix*, you will be able to scout out where the enemy is, take the enemy by surprise, perhaps even use the lander to terrify them into running away, or use its exhaust to set enemy villages on fire—"

"I don't want to burn enemy villages, I want to take all their possessions and their good-looking women," Rar said impatiently. "Your Kekox was much too bloodthirsty. You have much to learn about warfare; I am surprised your emperor is able to rule as much country as you say he does. But except for that silly suggestion, the rest is very well thought of. Perhaps it could even—in some circumstances, say, if we had them trapped on a hill like this—descend to burn most of the opposing fighters alive. It would save us all a great deal of trouble in killing them later. And of course there would still be some survivors that we could make work for us."

"Father," Inok said, "this idea is a very good one. Most especially if we can find the enemy quickly, we can be fresh and rested, while they are tired from a long journey. And we can surprise them, on their way, instead of meeting them at the traditional battlegrounds, and thus there can be a great killing of them."

Rar clapped his hand on his son's shoulder. I think that was the first time I realized that among Seteposians that is a gesture which indicates warm approval. "Very good thought, indeed. Well, then, as I see it, since I must command, it is my son who will fly the *Gurix*. You all must teach him how. But since I know any reasonable slave will run away if he can, I must insist that while my son learns to fly, any of you not teaching him at that moment must stay in your cell, or under my direct observation, as hostages."

That night, when the three of us carried the news to the rest, we all congratulated each other. True, we hadn't escaped *yet*, but we would now have our hands on the lander controls regularly, and it had enough anti-

matter to allow it to make thousands of takeoffs and landings from surface to orbit. The more it flew, the better chance that our supervision
would get lax—and as soon as that happened, somehow or other, using
whatever tricks we could think of, we would all be back on *Wahkopem
Zomos*.

Just before I drifted off to sleep that night, Inok came by and took
me out on the hill to answer questions. He said he wanted to show me
something. After a while, a bright star rose over the horizon and began
to slowly crawl across the face of the heavens.

"I suppose a new, moving star in the sky *would* be a little upsetting,"
I said.

"Can you tell me what it is?" the Nim's son asked.

"It's the ship we came from Nisu in," I said. "So big that it carried
the lander in its belly. It circles the world eight times during one of your
days, which is why you can just see it moving now. And it shines because
it is so high up that it is not shadowed by Setepos, and so it catches the
sunlight."

"My favorite slaves tell wonderful stories," Inok said, but he hung
around while I described *Wahkopem Zomos* in glowing detail, with special emphasis on the beauty of its sail full spread (without mentioning
that we had thrown it away) and on the astonishing voyages it could
undertake and the wonderful things to be seen. Finally when I had run
out of glowing descriptions, he sat beside me, silently, and watched
Wahkopem Zomos sink slowly over the horizon. I hoped he was learning
to look with longing.

Flying lessons began the next day. The trick, we realized early, was to
keep Inok hung up on small details. Since neither he nor any other of
the Real People had any idea how long it *should* take to learn to fly, this
could be dragged out a long time. I spent nearly a whole day "helping"
him master the use of the combination lock for the door. (We thought
about whether that should come later, but he didn't seem to be so foolish
as to play with the controls, and at least the lock itself had very little to
do with making the ship fly.) Otuz taught him to read a long list of readouts, none of which could ever really be expected to be anything other
than "go." Soikenn coached him through extending and retracting landing gear, which of course he could not do while sitting on the ground.
And all the time that we did these things, we encouraged him to talk
about his feelings, who he wanted for a mate, how unfairly the other

boys had treated him, how he would be the Nim someday, everything that might bend his loyalty away from the Real People and toward us.

We also talked a lot about the wonders of Nisu and of *Wahkopem Zomos*. He seemed to find all of it fascinating; some, we realized, because he was gleaning what we told him for military and political information that his father could use in creating an empire of his own, and some because the whole idea of customs being different (as opposed to wrong—the neighboring peoples had *wrong* customs) was so novel to him. But he also seemed to enjoy the many glowing accounts of life on board and life on Nisu. I'm sure those were made much more convincing by the passion with which we wished to be there.

There are only so many controls on even the most complex machine, however, and Inok was a fast learner. The day rapidly approached when we would have to begin teaching him something about how to fly the *Gurix*. That meant we would have to teach him how to do one of three things: power up the engines, work the flight controls, or program a mission into the ship's computer. At least, we thought, until he had all three capabilities, he would not be dangerous.

We thought the flight controls might be the place to start; Inok was clearly getting impatient and wanted to impress his father, so it was about time for him to have a visible success. With luck our giving him this success would tighten his bond to us.

The day came for Inok to try his first flight, with Mejox operating the engines. The "mission" was simply to ascend high enough so that the exhaust would not be a danger, circle the town, and land in the same spot again. They were going to leave the door open the whole time, so that Inok could be seen at the controls by all the chiefs of the conquered villages.

Our group stood a safe distance back, with Nim Rar himself. We didn't think Mejox should try anything this time; Inok was not yet reliably on our side, and getting us away from the Nim's guards would be too hard. So this flight was to be played strictly legitimately.

Behind us was an immense crowd by local standards—village chiefs from all over the Real People's ever-growing empire, everyone from the town, and many people from outlying towns who had made the time to be here. The excitement was so contagious that even we caught it.

Inok was almost shaking. "Everyone's terrified on their first flight," I said to him. "Don't worry."

"I'm trying not to."

Then Nim Rar nodded to Inok and Mejox, and the two of them set out across the open space together. Mejox was hobbling more than usual—he had said his leg was hurting him a great deal that morning. After a few steps we saw Mejox rest a hand on the young Seteposian's shoulder as they went out to the lander. It made an odd picture to us, the possible heir to the imperial throne—and to sixty centuries of civilization—walking with a cane, partly supported by a young barbarian dressed in skins and rough cloth, headed across the town's biggest open space to the gleaming lander.

They climbed in, did the checkout—taking much longer than any of us ever would have, but Inok didn't know that—and then Inok moved to the controls, taking hold of the twin sticks as if he'd always held them.

We had done everything we could to emphasize Inok's place as the pilot. He turned and shouted a crisp order to Mejox to power up the engines, and though the order was in Nisuan, and no one but us and Nim Rar understood it, a cheer went up from the crowd—they must have been reacting to Inok's tone.

Mejox brought the power on line by the book, a particularly slow way—we wanted Nim Rar and his guards to think takeoffs took much longer than they actually did, against the day when we might need to surprise them by doing a takeoff in a hurry.

There was a deep bass rumble through the ground, and a shimmer of heat under the main nozzles. The lander bumped visibly on its landing gear.

And then, without warning, Inok turned, seized Mejox by the collar, and threw him out the door. He fell four times his body length, landed on his back, and rolled over, pushing himself to his feet with his hands. Meanwhile, the ladder retracted abruptly, and the last we saw of Inok was as he reached to slam the door.

"What is he doing?" Otuz shouted, over the wild cries of the crowd. "Mejox!"

Our friend was standing up now, obviously badly shaken, and began to stagger toward us, as fast as he could without his cane.

"He will probably let Mejox get a safe distance," Nim Rar said. "But we have watched you and how you teach. We know you do things slowly and with unnecessary steps. My son Inok is clever; he knew that there were only three controls for the engines. Now he has seen what they do, and he knows how to work the flight controls. He can make it fly, and he is going to. He is going up to this wonderful *Wahkopem Zomos* you say is the bright star over our southern horizon, to bring back good things with which I shall reward my chiefs. You slaves are clever, and I do not fault you for that, but you must learn you are not as clever as the Nim and his son."

We stared at him in horror; how do you explain so many things at once, when there's no time, when the person who needs to know them isn't there anyway? I knew it was hopeless to save either the lander or Inok at that moment, but I turned to see if Mejox would make it. He was staggering and fighting his way across the square, and without thinking that I might get an arrow in the back, I ran out to grab him up and carry him over my shoulders, as fast as I could, back toward the crowd and safety. As I turned with Mejox slung over my back, I saw that all the Nisuans had gone flat to the ground in a bunch, sheltering the babies under them.

Perhaps Inok was impatient, or maybe he didn't realize how far out the exhaust would spread across the square. Surely he didn't know that you couldn't just throw the throttle wide open—and if the computer had been engaged it wouldn't have let him do what he did. But we had never told him there *was* a computer, we thought you couldn't fly the lander without it, but we were wrong—you just couldn't fly the lander anywhere *on purpose* without it.

With a terrible roar behind me, the lander took off. It must have been pulling seven gravities, the maximum the engines could give it. Probably Inok was knocked to the floor, out of reach of the controls, at that moment; I have always hoped he just died, of a fractured skull or any number of other injuries, when the floor leaped up to crush him.

Meanwhile, I had no time to worry about Inok; Mejox and I were caught at the edge of the blast, his fur singed all over his back, and we were thrown rolling across the ground. The pain was horrible and indescribable. The last thing I remember before I lost consciousness was Otuz frantically beating out my smoldering fur with her hands, while Seteposians tossed dirt on me to smother the flames. Mejox didn't remember even that much; he must have been knocked unconscious by the blast itself, and he never recalled the terrible burns that cost him an arm later on, or Soikenn and Osepok throwing him into an irrigation ditch to douse the flames.

In a sense, we were lucky compared to the rest of the Nisuans. When they could spare a moment, they looked up to see the tiny dot of the *Gurix* vanishing into the sky, probably still accelerating at seven gravities. If, as I surmise, Inok was knocked to the floor and unable to change the controls, there was enough antimatter available to keep that engine running at full clip for several days, and the life-support systems could have continued running indefinitely. There were stocks of food aboard, if he figured out how to get to them, and if he survived the high acceleration while lying in a heap on the floor. But somewhere out there, sooner or later, as the *Gurix* plunged out into space at far above the escape velocity for that solar system, if he didn't die of injuries, he starved to death. Unless it fell into the sun or one of the planets, I have no doubt that the *Gurix* is still out there, somewhere deep in space between the stars, serving as the coffin of the first Seteposian to venture into space.

All these thoughts came later. I was unconscious for days, and then when I woke my first concerns were the terrible pain of my burns, and then whether Mejox would survive. But I did eventually think all that through, and work out what might have happened to Inok. A slave has lots of time to think.

Clio Trigorin:
May 2075–December 2076

CLIO DECIDED THAT SANETOMO WAS GOING TO ASK HER TO MARRY HIM after about a month of spending time with him every day. She knew that it was very likely that he had arrived at the same decision by that time. She also wasn't about to spoil it all by even faintly suggesting it for a while.

And truth to tell it wasn't as big a deal as it would have been on Earth, even though the idea of getting married was so much more serious, she thought as she sat and worked at the problem of Zahmekoses's use of the impersonal rude in so much of his private notes. Combining impersonal nouns with rude verb forms had two possible implications in Standard Tiberian: either Zahmekoses had been gently condescending toward his homeworld, or he had wanted them to look down on him slightly. It issued a challenge to the reader to decide who was superior or inferior; there was nothing like it in English at all, and "in Japanese," Sanetomo said, "you can indicate whether someone else is your superior or inferior, but you can't challenge them to decide."

Clio shrugged and, using her chopsticks, pulled out a small piece of fish tempura, dipped it in the sauce, and plopped it into her bowl of rice. That evening, as they did once a week, they were having a private meal in Sanetomo's quarters. He wasn't a great cook, but it was hard to ruin tempura, and Clio didn't come here for the food. "Well," she said, "it's ambiguous to anyone who reads Tiberian, but I have to make it one or the other for those idiot American undergrads who can't be bothered to learn one of the foundational languages of our civilization. Now I know what one crusty old Latinist I knew years ago was complaining about; he always used to say if you want to understand what Seneca says, you should learn to read him, not find someone to make him say something you already understand."

"Were you the type that always got along with teachers?"

"Not with that one. He wasn't even a real historian or a real classicist. He'd come from some other department years before. Looked like a fat, bald monkey."

"Well," Sanetomo said mildly, "from the Tiberian point of view, didn't we all look like bald monkeys?"

"Unkempt ones, anyway," Clio said. "So to shorten the story some more, I'm having to translate *The Account of Zahmekoses* on the assumption that he's being humble and wants to be sneered at a little. Pretty silly assumption when you think about it—he was awfully proud and overbearing in some parts of his own account, and he sure didn't have much respect for the Tiberians back home."

Sanetomo nodded politely. There was a funny surge to the side. "Laser cutout," he said. "Glad it wasn't my shift for maintenance—somebody's going to spend an hour swapping out one of the ZPEs. I'll be glad when we learn to build them as well as the Tiberians did."

"Not me," Clio said. "I like this set-up. I wouldn't want to spend all that time in an acceleration tank, and having all these years of unlimited thinking time—and no committee work!—is about as close to heaven as a historian can get."

"Or an astronomer," Sanetomo added. "Or any other kind of intellectual. This might just be the major effect star travel will have on human life. But then we all repeat that to each other six times a day, don't we? More fish or should I freeze it?"

"I'm stuffed," she confessed. "And maybe it's a cultural failing but I'd just as soon not tuck away much more fish."

"What are you planning to eat for the next seven years, then?"

"Fish," Clio admitted, "but I'd rather not."

The fish on board was tilapia, carp, and bass—freshwater species suited for life in the forward tank, right at the nose of the ship, where the enormous load of water served as an important protection against radiation for the ship's farm and the living quarters beneath that. Moving at just over one third of lightspeed, they were transforming the interstellar atoms they collided with into bursts of radiation, up at the front; but down here they were effectively under thirty feet of water and, if you added up all the little soil banks in the farm, sixteen feet of dirt.

That night, after they had made love, Sanetomo went straight to sleep, and Clio lay awake beside him, happy, drifting, thinking idly about her translation. There was a difference between that first Tiberian voyage to cross this vast lonely gulf of vacuum, and this first human one . . . something she couldn't quite put her finger on. Both had knowingly taken along vast numbers of projects to do . . . both had sent along people smart enough to amuse themselves . . . but there was a difference.

As she drifted off to sleep, she seemed to hear Zahmekoses whispering to her, "When you know what that difference is, you'll really know something."

Weeks rolled together into months, and Clio and Sanetomo spent more time with each other. It was odd, she realized, that here on *Tenacity*, in a way, what they were doing was duplicating that silliest experiment of twentieth-century America: high school. People here had lots of time to do what they needed to do, and no real need to earn a living *per se*—no paychecks, no rent, no bills—and thus they had lots of time for esoteric interests and for relationships. Why weren't they driving each other crazy, and then using up all that excess time dealing with the craziness, the way high school students always had?

She was having that thought as she set up her artificial Christmas tree; she paused a moment to deliberate whether she would put the star or the angel at the top, the only decision there was to make every year, since the tree really only fit into one spot in her quarters, and she always put every one of her home-made ornaments onto it. Christmas of 2075 was not going to be much different from that of 2069, 2070, or any other year since departure.

She knew Sanetomo's knock at her door so well that without looking around she simply said, "Come in." The door opened with a soft thud behind her.

"That's gotta be the ugliest piece of bonsai I've ever seen," he said.

She shrugged. "Hey, I'm a Martian. This was the only kind there was where I grew up. And at least I didn't have to torture it to keep it from growing taller. C'mon in and shut the door; there's soup on the stove, which somebody who isn't me ought to re-season."

She had just settled on the star and put it into place when she heard him slurp a couple of times and say, "Slightly short on salt. Nothing else wrong. You're getting better. Well, today we confirmed another one—there's free oxygen in the atmosphere of the fifth planet of Zeta Tucanae. It looks like they succeeded in terraforming all but two of the nine planets they tried it on."

"All but three of the ten," Clio reminded him. "Their effort on Mars was a legitimate try at terraforming, even if it didn't go very well, and even if they didn't have any equipment intended for the purpose. Let's just look your new one up, though," she said, and clicked on her display screen, checking through the list of colonies. "Well, the folks going to Zeta Tucanae thought they would name that planet Preka Retahrka, which means something like 'New Hope' or 'Another Chance' or 'Better Try.' Sounds like they at least made a good try."

"They certainly generated some hope for us, if not for themselves," Sanetomo said. "And that expands the list a little further, anyway. I wonder what could have gone wrong at the two that didn't work out?"

Clio shrugged. "Maybe nothing their fault. Maybe their collision avoidance system failed and they hit a rock and blew all over the sky. Maybe their ZPE locked up for good and their descendants are still out there somewhere, thousands of light years away, unable to slow down. Bad luck happens, you know."

"Spoken like someone who's been translating ancient Tiberian. How far along are you?"

"Oh, I've almost got them to Setepos. Earth I mean. I kind of decided to at least give the kids a flavor by using Tiberian place names." She took the wine and glasses from him and set them on the table, next to the warm bread and soup. "Dinner's on. Say, let me put a question to you—how come we haven't all gotten involved in complex cliques about who's sleeping with who and who's best friends and who's not and all that stuff? We have a classic setup for it here: lots of time off and no worries about material conditions that we can do anything about. How come we're not all enacting high school for grownups?"

He shrugged. "The psychological screening, maybe?"

"Those silly little tests? I can't believe that they would have—"

"No, I mean the self-screening. Remember that you couldn't get considered for the crew unless you had a big project you wanted to put years into, and they really did judge the quality of the projects. So everyone here has something they'd rather be doing than mooning over each other. Usually, that is. I intend to moon over you for at least ten minutes after dinner. You are sublimely moonworthy. You are the maximally moon-over-able person I know. You—"

She groaned. "All right, let's stop before we get to anti-non-moon-over-able-ous-ness. Did anyone ever tell you your sense of humor is predictable?"

"And you like it."

"In moderate doses," she said. "Which is how you like my cooking. Dinner's on the table, let's eat."

As they sat over the soup, he said, "You know, more seriously, I think we'll get better discoveries out of this than we did out of some of the early explorations."

"Out of what?"

"Out of sending smart people with time on their hands. Idleness is only the devil's plaything if you aren't smart or creative enough to fill it. But the best minds have always flourished on idleness. Here we take all kinds of bright people, send them out to explore another star system and to look at the ruins of an ancient culture far greater than ours—and thanks to the light speed limit, and the huge distances, it's going to be more than a decade till we get there. I mean, at our present speed we could travel from the Earth to the Moon in about four seconds, and the speed is increasing all the time, and yet we've been traveling for years and we still have years to go. And everything we know of physics says that light speed is absolute; we'll never go faster, which means it will always take years to reach the stars.

"Well, those years are the time we need to develop ourselves, get to know ourselves, really grow into something. Which means by the time we arrive we'll be really ready to do the job—which is a lot more than you could say for Columbus's crew, or Magellan's, or Captain Cook's, or even for a lot of the astronauts. It used to be that getting there was such a small fraction of a human lifetime that you could send just about any old kind of human, as long as they were physically and mentally up to the rigors of the voyage. Now you *have* to send someone to grow."

She smiled. "Of course, sure, none of us is the person who left. And mostly we're getting better at living with each other, and certainly more learned and better at the intellectual skills."

"Wiser," he said, "is the word. In fact the one thing I wish they'd let us do on this trip is raise kids. Being a parent seems to deepen people back home, and certainly a kid who grew up here would get a big head start on the world, wouldn't he?"

Clio might have had an answer, but she thought Sanetomo was leading up to a proposal, so she waited for it; clearly he was just waiting for an answer to his idle speculation, and the moment slipped by.

That night, drifting off, it occurred to her that if she had really had the high school mindset, there was no doubt at all that she would have been frustrated by Sanetomo's failure to propose when she thought he would. As it stood, she was almost as frustrated by the failure of their conversation to go on—and that wasn't much. After the holidays, maybe, or after she finished a couple more sections of *The Account of Zahmekoses*, if he still hadn't, she would. "Unless I think of something better," she mumbled, stretching into final position to sleep.

"Think of better what?" he said, his speech slurred.

"Doesn't need to concern you," she said, snuggling in closer. "Yet."

On Halloween 2076, Sanetomo knocked on her door, and when she opened it, he said, "Trick or Treat. Marry me."

"Is that a treat or a trick?" she asked him, her face carefully deadpan. By that time, she had not only gotten used to his sense of humor; she could duplicate it. And by that time, he knew that answer was "yes," without her saying it. The only disappointment for either of them was that when they shared the news at common dinner, everyone on the ship looked up, a bit baffled, and said "But I thought they *were* engaged."

"Are you ready to go through with this?" Sanetomo asked her.

"Well, we're supposed to be bringing terrible luck on ourselves by letting you see me on the wedding day, but otherwise, sure." Clio adjusted her headgear one more time.

"That only applies for Western grooms," Sanetomo said, firmly. "You're marrying a Japanese, you only have to worry about Japanese superstitions. Those are the official rules. And what kind of a wedding is it, anyway, when the bride stays up late the night before to finish her book instead of her dress?"

"The dress was done and the book wasn't. And what kind of wedding is it where the groom knows a thing like that?"

"Five minutes to showtime," Captain Olshavsky said, sticking his head in the door. "Which one of you is going to cry and say it's all off?"

"Must've been some other wedding you heard about," Sanetomo said, smiling broadly. "Clio, you look terrific. Did I mention that?"

"Not often enough. And you do nice things for a dress uniform yourself."

"In that case," the captain said, "I guess we're going through with it. Come on down to the dining hall when you're ready."

"Did you really finish your translation of *The Account of Zahmekoses* last night?" Sanetomo asked.

"Yep. You don't think I'd have stayed up for fun? Anyway, now the honeymoon, then on to *The Account of Diehrenn*. And one of these days, back to the straight history. But I guess before we start the honeymoon, we'd better get the marrying part out of the way."

The ceremony was brief, and of course since no one was going anywhere outside the ship, every guest turned up as expected and the newly-wed couple found their way to the "honeymoon suite"—Sanetomo's room as decorated by his best man—without difficulty. The party went on for a while—it had been a long time since they'd had one—but naturally Sanetomo and Clio slipped away a little early.

Afterwards, they lay snuggled together in the now double-sized chamber. One of Sanetomo's neighbors had already moved into Clio's old one, and they had spent the better part of the previous day taking down the partition. Sanetomo said, "Well, here we are. As of this morning, Olshavsky said we'd covered 142,160 astronomical units. Hard to believe it took us more than a year to reach the first hundred and now we're doing close to a hundred per day; it would only take us about five hours to get from one side of Saturn's orbit to the other, and yet we're still five years from our destination. . . ." His voice was already fading, and as he slipped an arm around Clio he muttered, "I wonder if other couples talk about how much we're all alone in the middle of an unimaginable void on their wedding nights."

"Traditionally," Clio said, "I think that comes later."

"Well, anyway, at least now we're a tiny bit past half way. Only 132,000 AU to go, the captain says. Wake me up when we get there," he murmured, and fell asleep.

Clio lay back and thought about things; it had been a long courtship and a short engagement because in such a tiny community with so little space, moving in with each other was a decision with so many implications that they had to be very sure of themselves before they did it, but once the decision was made it was extremely easy to implement.

During most of that time she'd put off working on *From the Moon to the Stars*, ostensibly to finish her translation of *The Account of Zahmekoses*.

She thought about where she was. *Tenacity* was moving through space at fifty-five percent of the speed of light, fast enough to go around the Earth at the equator four times per second; yet even though they were moving at such a tremendous speed and were now over halfway to Alpha Centauri, the distance was so huge that they would not begin to brake for another two years and one month, by which time they would be moving at almost seventy-five percent of lightspeed. Then they would find out just how good their copy of the Tiberian magnetic loop brake was, for though more than fifty of them had been tested on unmanned probes before this, still one never knew until one tried it whether the particular magnetic loop was working.

In just ten and a half months they would cross the sort-of boundary of the Alpha Centauri System: the orbit of Proxima Centauri, the distant, dim companion that orbited far out in space from where A and B eternally circled each other. (Though of course Proxima itself was nowhere near their trajectory.)

And once they were braking, long after they had flown deep into the Alpha Centauri System, it would still take two years to get the rest of the way into the system and rendezvous with Tiber. So only about five years left till arrival, and since she and Sanetomo had radioed their request for permission to have a child back to Earth from here, that would mean they would be on Tiber for at least a year before they got permission, or were denied it.

I'm not sure, but I kind of think the custom of calling home to get everything approved isn't going to last much longer, Clio thought as she lay drifting, waiting for sleep to come.

She closed her eyes and let herself picture *Tenacity* as a tiny dot of metal hurtling through the black vacuum at hard-to-imagine velocities, no other living thing within light-years . . . and yet, here in one small room in that dot of metal, she and Sanetomo had chosen to begin a life together. It was a pretty big leap of faith.

Not as big as the one Diehrenn had made, she reminded herself. And certainly in terms of plans turning out differently . . . and the impossibility of calling home for directions . . . yes, she was eager to get into the new project.

In some ways she had saved translating *The Account of Diehrenn* because it was the more interesting . . . to be born a slave in the Stone Age and be buried as the president of Mars . . . and because she had seen the frozen, preserved body of Diehrenn, exhibited in the museum on Mars, and thus could picture her. Just as Clio fell asleep, it seemed to her for a moment that the Hybrid female stood before her, asking her something—though whether to tell her story, or to listen to it, Clio didn't figure out before drifting into deeper sleep.

PART III
THE LIGHT THAT FAILED

7254–7208 B.C.E.

1

I WAS FORTY-THREE YEARS OLD, AS TIME WAS RECKONED ON SETEPOS, AND I was now raising my third generation of the Nim's descendants—as close to an elder among the Nisuan slaves as you could be without having arrived on the ship from Nisu.

But seniority cannot override a warm spring day. I could shout all I wanted at the children, but I wasn't going to have their attention for any longer than I could have a butterfly's. Even the younger slaves weren't paying much attention to me today. I was just their mother, big sister, or aunt, and the Seteposian children, whose pets they were, were princes and princesses. I had heard them, often enough, arguing about precedence, based on who owned them and who they cared for. Probably if they had a chance to be free, or to go back to Nisu, tomorrow, they'd turn it down.

That was a gloomy thought; for some reason the fine spring day seemed to be bringing on despair. But since Grandmother Soikenn and Uncle Mejox had died last summer, and Mother had fallen ill with the same strange sickness, there was really no one to talk to and I felt very alone.

"Diehrenn!" Messlah shouted. The Seteposian boy was my favorite in that he was usually polite and a bit quieter than the rest. "Over here! What's this?"

I ran to see what he was shouting about, and was so surprised when I saw it that for a long moment I just gaped at it as it fluttered there in the thornbush. Finally I said, "I had thought that all such things were found long ago, and yet here's one not four long stone-throws from Real People Town. Well, they'll certainly be proud of *you*, Messlah, for finding such a thing."

"But what *is* it?" he asked.

"You haven't seen anything like it?" I prompted him. "Not in the temple?" One way in which Seteposians were strange was that they were often sexually mature before they even began to think like adults, and so they could be quite sizable and still think like children, all wild guesses and enthusiasm.

Menomoum, the young full-blooded Palathian slave who was appointed as Messlah's companion, spoke up. "It's a . . . it's a . . . the thing from the thing, Diehrenn! A piece of the . . . whatever it is that lets the . . . whatchamacallit come down to the ground slowly." He was nearly as excited as Messlah, and with less excuse—he was well past the age for full consciousness even if he was still years short of puberty.

I let it pass. "You're right," I said. "It's a piece of parachute. See where two of the—" I had to struggle for the word myself—"shroud lines are still attached? It's what the probes used to descend from *Wahkopem Zomos*. It's very important—they haven't found any of that since I was little. We should take it back to the palace right away."

"But we just came out to play!" Messlah protested.

I looked around the circle of children in the bright sunlight. The Seteposians, all smaller than Messlah, were making that strange face they did when they were frustrated or about to demand something— their lower lips bulged out and their eyes squinted slightly.

We Nisuans were holding perfectly still and keeping our facial expressions neutral. If the Seteposian children complained to our masters afterwards, *we* were the ones who would be in trouble.

Still, I was in charge, and this sort of thing *did* have to be taken to the Nim at once. It would only interrupt playtime for a little while.

This was frustrating, too, because even a few moons ago, I would still have been out here as Set's companion, and he would have made the other Seteposians mind me. But he had gotten old enough not to need a nurse or companion anymore—he was off with his grandfather's army— and now I was the nurse for Esser, his five-year-old niece, by far the most spoiled of Nim Rar's descendants.

For an instant I hesitated, wishing that I had Set here, wishing that his son—born this year—was in my charge, as his father and grandfather had been. Wishing, however, could not make it so and didn't solve the problem.

The trouble was that there were no good outcomes. They all wanted to play right now. So if I took them all trooping back, with the precious piece of parachute, they would be angry and surely get even later. The older Seteposian children would make up some story or other to get me whipped.

If I took the parachute material back myself, Menomoum might or might not manage the children successfully until I could get back—and if he didn't, which was likely since he tended to let Messlah do whatever he wanted, then I would be whipped.

Or I could take the children, go play, and pick up the parachute material on the way back. The trouble was that Nim Rar, sooner or later, would find out that I hadn't come straight back with it as soon as we'd found it. And he was very protective of any Nisuan artifacts that turned up—so if I had neglected one, I would be whipped.

It wasn't much of a choice.

"Diehrenn!" a voice shouted behind me. I turned around, and there was Set, striding down the hill, mane of brown hair bobbing in the sunlight, soft robe billowing around him. I had never been happier to see him.

"I just got back from the war," he said. "We took thousands of fresh prisoners. It's another great victory, Nim Rar's one-hundred-twelfth, and he named me one of his great warriors for it." As he drew nearer, I could see his teeth; his lips were drawn back in that expression that meant a Seteposian was pleased. "I hope you're very proud of me."

"I am, master," I said, only partly lying. If I had a favorite of all the Nim's descendants, Set was it. He was generous and friendly, and he had never ordered a beating for me, let alone beaten me himself.

But the older generation had raised me to remember that it was sheer bad luck that we were the Nim's slaves, and not vice versa. Set's courtesy and friendliness only made it more clear to me that I was a slave and an alien.

Still he would be useful now. "That's wonderful, Master Set," I said, "and it's a very good omen that we just heard the news at this moment— look what Messlah just found!" I pointed to it.

Set took two steps toward it and then said, "But . . . but that's impossible!"

I was a little disconcerted. "It certainly is possible, master, it's right there."

Set turned back to me with a strange expression in his eyes. "Oh, I know you're not lying, Diehrenn. That's a piece of parachute and I know it's not any of the pieces from the temple, either. But it's still impossible.

This thornbush was always the Snail Eaters' Base when the other boys and I would play 'Real People Against Snail Eaters.' See? You can still see where there are spots worn in the ground by the goal keepers when we played. There've been dozens of boys around this thornbush for years and years. It couldn't have avoided detection for so long."

"Master, maybe it was stuck in a high tree somewhere, and then tore loose and blew here, master?" Menomoum suggested. My nephew was very afraid of Set, perhaps because he was directly in line for the throne.

"That might be," Set said, "though it doesn't show any signs of weathering, or dirt . . . or does this material weather at all, Diehrenn?"

"Not so far as I know," I said, "but I have to admit I've never even touched that material; all the pieces I ever saw were in the temple." *On the wall by Kekox's skin*, I wanted to add. That would hardly be fair to Set; he himself had burst into tears the first time he had seen the skin and head of Kekox on the temple wall, and cried until the Nim himself had promised that no such thing would ever happen to me. "I don't suppose it weathered much in there. But some Nisuan materials are very tough and don't wear out at all as far as we can tell."

Set nodded assent, and moved closer to the thornbush. He reached up to take the fabric in his hands. "It's soft," he said, "and very slick. You can see it was woven out of something or other, but the fibers are finer than spiderweb. And—"

"Diehrenn! Set! Look in the trees over there!" Messlah shouted.

Our heads jerked up at Messlah's excited scream. In one of the old, gnarled cedars, a great swath of fabric hung down farther than the temple was tall. I felt a strange tingling on my spine, and my small crest stood up until it felt as big as Uncle Mejox's.

"Menomoum, Messlah," I said, as casually as I could manage, "I think we need to have you two guard the children. Set and I should get a closer look at this before we let the little ones get too close to it." Sometimes suggesting to older boys that I needed them to act as protectors or seconds-in-command would make them behave for a little while.

Set asked, "Do you think they can handle that?" his tone indicating that he didn't think so.

"I'm sure they can," I said. Set and I headed down the hill, toward the brook, the old cedar, and the parachute. Thanks to Set's comment, they now desperately wanted to prove that I was right, and they would do their best—whatever that might be—to make the other children behave.

"Thanks," I said, as soon as I was sure that we were out of earshot.

"Welcome to it," Set said. "I don't know how many times, on patrol or in battle, I was glad that you were strict with me. Those kids need discipline; it's a shame the old Nim is getting soft."

Maybe toward his grandchildren and great-grandchildren, I thought. I hadn't noticed that he was being any nicer to his slaves. "How do you suppose we could have suddenly gotten a whole parachute, Master Set? Maybe a probe hung up on a tree somewhere upwind of here and couldn't make it down, then got shaken loose and blew here?"

"Except all of the area upwind has been part of the Nim's empire for a decade or more, patrolled by his army—and every soldier knows there are big rewards for bringing in any Nisuan stuff. It would have to have been well-hidden—but in that case, how did the wind get to it?"

By now we were almost in the shade of the cedar, its earth-spicy scent and the cool air under it about to brush over my thin fur. Something else occurred to me. "There hasn't been a storm in several days. Nothing to shake this loose, either. And people are in this area all the time."

"And," he added, glancing sideways at me and lowering his voice to a whisper, "it wasn't possible for probes to get permanently hung up in trees, was it? I mean, they could move themselves around—"

"Grandmother Osepok says there were many kinds of probes, and they launched hundreds of them, master. Some of them were little more than a camera on a parachute."

I could see him struggling with his memory, so I explained the Nisuan word. "A camera is one of those devices that lets you see a thing from far away. It sends the picture to a receiver on *Wahkopem Zomos.*"

"I remember now," he said. We stood before the big cedar, its shade just falling at our feet, and looked up at the great swath of hanging fabric. The glare of the sun was behind the shroud, so that its white iridescence made a play of strange rainbows, and as we looked at it our faces seemed to grow hotter and hotter; the space under the tree seemed dark and cold, and we hesitated a moment before stepping into the cedar-smelling cavern.

Then the two of us stepped forward into the dim, dark green light. I blinked once as my eyes adjusted.

Set gasped. There, under the tree, was a probe, sitting on its twelve metal feet—with a little scorch mark leading to it, presumably from flying the short distance, after cutting off its parachute, to this place under the tree.

I just had time to realize that the smell of burnt mulch must mean it was still active. Then it swiveled the round bulb that sat on its top like a head, and we saw ourselves reflected in the big, clear, dark circle, as wide as my hand, on the top of the bulb. With a slight hum and clicking noise, it lifted three of its six "front" legs up, extended them, and took a slow, graceful step toward us. The round thing on top—its *eye*, I thought, but that was the wrong word for it—tilted up to look at our faces, and swung back and forth between us, as if making sure it could memorize what we both looked like.

"Camera," I said finally. "The round thing on the top that looks like an eye is a camera, Set. It's sending pictures of us to someone, or something. But I don't think it's to *Wahkopem Zomos*."

From the Report of Thetakisus, Captain's Assistant,
Egalitarian Republic

The first time we ran the engines of our starship, *Egalitarian Republic*, at full, and went up close to lightspeed, was as we departed from Nisu, so we had no real idea what we were getting into. We had made short trips in the ship at high acceleration, but never more than half a day at ten gravities.

For our initial boost out of the solar system we were going to be taking off at more than ten gravities for forty days. There were volunteers who had spent that long, at gravity that high, in centrifuges, and the People's Space Exploration Foundation assured us they had all survived and suffered little pain or difficulty. Indeed we were given to understand that after a few days acclimating, the five eightdays' acceleration would be like a long, comfortable vacation. It wasn't until we actually experienced it that we noticed that none of us had ever actually met or talked to any of the volunteers from the centrifuges.

The Nisuan body was just not made to withstand ten gravities of acceleration for five eightdays. And they could preach all they wanted about how much stronger so many of us were, being Hybrids, but even if that were true it only meant we were stronger than purebred Palathians or Shulathians. Yarn is stronger than thread, but neither will hold up a bridge. We Hybrids were still just flesh and blood, and our bodies weren't up to it. Besides, the Palathian and Shulathian members of the crew didn't seem to me to be any more or less miserable under high acceleration than we were.

We spent forty days immersed in the tanks, much of our ten-times-normal weight buoyed up by the special fluid, the pressure equalized by filling our body cavities with the same fluid. We breathed through masks for the entire time, switching them with the backups for cleaning every day.

Hand-operated voice synthesizers and speaker plugs in our ears let us talk; the same goggles that protected our eyes from the terrible pressure also allowed us to read text or watch motion pictures projected on them. Catheters carried off waste, and we "ate," "breathed," and "drank" intravenously.

We survived, but by the sixth day in the tanks we knew that things were not really going according to plan; unfortunately, with the Political Officer right there in Tank One with us, the rest of us in that tank could hardly discuss it or decide to change a mission plan that had been laid out at the highest levels of the state. So we endured it, and we wondered—or I did, anyway, since I didn't dare to find out if anyone else felt the same way—whether they had planned for us to be this uncomfortable, and not cared, or whether they had even done the centrifuge experiments at all as they said they had.

A forty-day stay in the tank was a mixture of ways of being uncomfortable. First of all there is a limit to how much you can talk about, how much you can watch, how much you can read, as anyone who has been bedridden for a while can tell you. The tanks were small, too, so that even if we had been able to get off our couches, there would have been nowhere to go.

Rather than bet on our ability to operate the ship while in the tank, they had automated everything, which meant that nothing we did during those five eightdays *really* mattered. I remember Captain Baegess complaining that he might as well not have come along, since every important maneuver was being done by the machines. So not only were we bored, but for the moment, we were unnecessary.

And everything ached, not so badly that it was agony, but just enough so that we never felt physically well. The engineers and biotechs had kept us from being permanently injured or killed by cushioning and buoying our bodies and the major organs within them. But they could not possibly protect every little corner of the body from every vagary of pressure and acceleration, and they had not tried. Joints tired and became sore from pushing against unaccustomed loads. Little places— our gums, our ears, the pads of fat in our buttocks—seemed to be constantly injured and bruised. Muscles most people hardly know exist—the ones that moved food through our digestive tracts, for example—ached with overwork. The large muscles in our bodies, forced both to be inactive and to carry heavy loads, cramped or felt worn out. Nothing was hurt badly enough to require medical attention, and yet everything hurt.

The day we emerged from high acceleration had been planned as a day of celebration and rest; it ended up being a day of rest, followed by another day of rest. We took our acceleration down to a tenth of a gravity, just enough to keep us comfortably in our bunks, and stayed in bed. It was the first of many times we disobeyed the original flight plan, but if Captain Baegess got any complaints from Streeyeptin, our Political Offi-

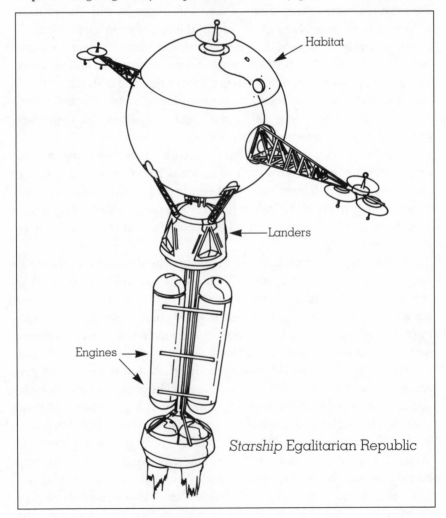

Habitat

Landers

Engines

Starship Egalitarian Republic

cer, he didn't mention them around me. Besides, we were now twenty-two light-days away from them and moving so near the speed of light that any radio message about our getting off the plan would only overtake us after we arrived at Setepos.

Streeyeptin seemed to accept that things would be politically looser on the ship than at home with good grace and kept mostly to himself, making it clear that he was not concerned with any subversive remarks we might make, nor with watching us for deviant or prerevolutionary behavior.

Not that they had much to worry about from the crew of a starship. All of us under thirty—more than half the crew of twenty—were Hybrids. In the old days before the Revolution, we would have been killed at birth. The older ship's officers were mostly veterans of the Revolution. We probably had the best political reliability profiles of anyone Streeyeptin had ever been around.

Besides, anyone who wanted to go into space had to be pro-Revolutionary. Not least among the crimes of the last empress had been the way that, with the Intruder already on its way around for its final, world-wrecking pass, she had squandered precious time and money trying to bribe the people into continuing to support her tyrannical regime. The Revolution had come about in part when we learned that our single remaining hope, *Wahkopem Zomos*, had failed, and that the Imperial Academy had been sitting on the revolutionary discovery of the zero-point energy laser, the engine that could take us to the stars.

So if you supported space, you supported the Revolution—for without the Revolution there would have been no starships. Every member of our crew had spent at least ten years trying to get a berth on the starships, particularly on *Egalitarian Republic*, since it would fly the first real interstellar mission, and I think that if there were anyone on board with any counterrevolutionary tendencies, all the rest of us would turn such a person over to the Political Officer at the first opportunity.

After our rest days, the captain pushed acceleration back up to a comfortable eighty-eight percent of standard gravity, the same gravity we would experience on Setepos. We were already moving at just over ninety-eight percent of lightspeed, so we weren't going to gain very much external-frame time by going faster. At such speeds, acceleration went almost entirely into mass—that is, because as a body approaches the speed of light it gets more massive, accelerating when we were already so close to lightspeed only added slightly to our speed but greatly increased the ship's mass. Not that we felt any such thing on the ship, of course; relative to the inside of the ship, our mass was what it had always been. It was only an outside observer—if anyone could have observed us, far out in the dark between the stars, moving almost as fast as light—who would have seen our greater mass.

But just as mass increased as we approached the speed of light, our internal time slowed down. Each tiny gain in velocity, bringing us a little closer to lightspeed, made time run much slower inside the ship. The trip was thus much shorter for us because we stayed under acceleration.

When we had come out of high acceleration, one day of shiptime had equaled about six and a half days at home; now, as we approached peak velocity, one day of shiptime equaled eight days back home. The strangest thing, in some ways, was that there was no perception of this directly. It was not just the clocks, but our bodies, our heartbeats, the way we blinked, the motion of objects, so that there was nothing against which you could check time and see it running more slowly—nothing except a purely artificial device: the small clock in the cockpit that showed the date and time at home. That kept running faster, but for every other sign we had, the ship might as well have been on a routine training mission. We would go to bed, arise the standard seven-twentieths of a day afterward, and discover that three and three-fifths days had gone by at home. But even that clock did not actually register time at home; it simply displayed the results of a computer program that estimated it.

The acceleration added to our comfort in another way; acceleration feels just like gravity, and gravity is handy stuff. It keeps food on the table, papers where you pile them, calcium in your bones, your body in bed at night, fluids in the tissues where they belong, and your food down. Our zero-point energy drive gave us so much surplus power, especially when hooked up to a small ship like *Egalitarian Republic*, that running the engines at eighty-eight percent of one gravity all the time was easier than spinning the ship, as the old *Wahkopem Zomos* had done decades before.

The eightweeks flew by. It seemed to us that only a little over half a year passed, and yet the clock in the cockpit showed we had flown years into our future. There was so much to get done that there were times when I wished for less time compression; I wondered if we would ever have all the probes in order. In the last couple of days before we went into the tank again, I almost gave up sleeping and eating entirely.

Captain Baegess noticed. "Assistant Thetakisus, you need a rest."

"I do, sir," I agreed, "and I'll sleep a lot in the tank. If the probes aren't ready to fly—"

"Then we'll manage," he said firmly. "How many do you have ready to go?"

"All but eleven, sir, but four of those eleven are the rovers—"

"Then get two rovers working. Tomorrow. After you get a full night's sleep. That's an order."

There wasn't much to do about it, then, so I got the sleep, got back to work, and got the rovers working.

Going back into the tank this time was, if anything, much worse. First of all we knew what we were in for; secondly, we would be spending longer in the tank because we were coming down from a higher velocity than the one we had climbed to at the start. It would only be an extra day and a half, but that was still more than it had been.

This time we knew enough to remain still most of the time, moving only often enough to avoid developing pressure sores and other such ailments. While we were in there, the ship automatically began to launch probes; because they could stand higher deceleration than we could, they would race into the Kousapex System ahead of us, then fire "throw away" zero point energy rockets to slow them down, and finally arrive on magnetic braking, much as *Wahkopem Zomos* had, forty-four years before them.

There were a thousand theories about just what had happened to the crew of *Wahkopem Zomos*, and it was hard to say which was the least plausible. Contact had drifted over time—the Imperial office in charge of staying in touch with them had had its budget cut over and over, and fallen more and more into the hands of political hacks, so that they often omitted to record blocks of whole eightweeks of data coming back. By the time that whatever it was had happened (actually years after, allowing for the time it took a radio signal to get from Setepos back to Nisu), there were huge gaps in the data.

We knew *Wahkopem Zomos* had achieved orbit around Setepos and begun to attempt a landing at one location. Beyond that we had a few other pieces of data, and none of them were of much use. Only three pictures recorded from that landing site had found their way into the database, though it was clear from directories of document titles that the crew of *Wahkopem Zomos* had sent a great deal of data about it. The pictures appeared to show a crude village from a great distance—but the dates and times on the pictures were obviously wrong since they indicated that the pictures were taken before the explorers landed, and they would have built no such thing anyway—they had more than adequate prefabricated shelters available. So why had they chosen to construct a village big enough for a hundred people, out of native materials?

Discounting the crackpot theory that the village was actually built by mythical Seteposians, who shot down the *Gurix* as it tried to land, the most likely explanation was that the pictures were architectural simulations, probably prepared by Priekahm, who was known to have considerable artistic abilities. Probably she had sketched what sort of colony the first settlers might build. Then, of course, the *Gurix* had crashed, and *Wahkopem Zomos* had continued slowly transcribing all of its data back to Nisu, eventually sending along those three cryptic pictures.

The one problem with that theory was that *Wahkopem Zomos* had continued to relay data from its probes, and some of those probes had continued to operate for years. Only one probe had been in the immediate area of the landing site; most of its pictures simply showed stretches of desert, riverbanks, or forest, as it wandered around the edge of the hills that the ill-fated *Gurix* had tried to land in.

But one picture was different; it appeared to show four figures with long sticks crouching in the desert, as if they were stalking the probe itself. Computer enhancement of the picture, it was claimed—though personally I found it just made it fuzzier—marked one of the figures as a Shulathian holding a steam rifle. And since that had been the very last picture from that probe, the crackpots had of course claimed that the crew had survived the crash, that they had joined with the natives, and that for some strange reason they had taken to stalking the probes with steam rifles.

I didn't think that the enhancement had even adequately demonstrated that any of the figures were Nisuans, as opposed to shrubbery.

The other odd piece of data was that the *Wahkopem Zomos* log of the successive positions of the *Gurix* seemed to show it at the landing site, making six round trips back to the ship over a period of almost a full local year, and then abruptly somewhere in space, moving at a highly implausible speed if one plotted the successive positions. This was more evidence, at least, that the date and time recording system had become unreliable.

Our expedition was only the first of many; the People's Space Exploration Foundation was constructing nine more exploratory ships. The last one of those should be just departing when we arrived back at Nisu, a decade after leaving in Nisu's time, less than two years by shiptime. We had to get the possible sites for colonies scouted quickly, before the Intruder returned, and the Second Bombardment pounded our civilization to pieces. And we had to hurry about it, after years of time-wasting by the emperors. Strangely, the *Wahkopem Zomos* expedition might well save our civilization, because en route it had done a series of gravimetric experiments, using the very long baseline made available by being so far out in space, which had revealed three more habitable worlds within our reach.

When the crew emerged from the tank we were just a few eightdays from Setepos, and our probes were already orbiting or had landed. The job fell to me of looking through the visuals to see what I could figure out.

I thought for a moment of being impulsive, getting the first good look by just flipping my viewscreen directly to the view from one of the probes, decided against that, and started the protocol I had written before, a program that would scout through reported probe data and find the most improbable pictures—the ones least like what might have been expected from the data we had from the old *Wahkopem Zomos* probes.

The first picture that popped up made me laugh, perhaps to avoid snarling. It showed a patch of sky between trees from high up, through branches. It was plain that the little camera probe had gotten hung up on branches and pointed the wrong way. I clicked to the next one.

This one showed a flat expanse and distant mountains, taken from a short distance above the flat expanse. It was the only picture that probe had sent after getting under cloud cover. It took me only a moment to realize it had descended into a mountain lake, and since it was another one of the cheap camera probes, it undoubtedly sank to the bottom and was there now, patiently recording whatever swam by, its transmissions not reaching us because of the interference from being underwater.

There was only one significant anomaly left, but that one was from one of the two functioning rovers. I popped it up on the screen.

There was a very long moment while I just stared. Then I checked to make sure that someone could not have put this into the interpreted data as a prank. Finally, summoning my nerve, I clicked on the communicator. "Assistant Thetakisus requests Captain Baegess and Political Officer Streeyeptin to come to my console; I have something you should both see."

They were there almost instantly. "Sirs," I said, gesturing at the screen, "this is one of the anomalies from the probes. I've verified that it's genuine. I request that my superior officers confirm to me what I see here."

On the screen there were two figures, in a brief loop of motion picture. Apparently the rover had been sitting under a tree, in deep shade; halfway through the short motion picture there was a distinct pop as the rover selected another light level, and the two shadowy figures sprang into sharp relief.

The one on the right was indisputably female, Nisuan—and a Hybrid. Furthermore, she was too young to be part of the *Wahkopem Zomos* crew; I wondered for a moment what strange feeling had struck me, and then realized that it was merely the realization that she was pretty.

The figure on the left was impossible to describe; it might have been a severely deformed Nisuan, or some kind of native animal. But around its neck it wore an object that appeared to be an old communicator— the type the *Gurix* might have carried, a museum piece on Nisu— pierced with a leather thong. And as the two of them gabbled, staring at the rover, a few words stood out.

Distinctly, she said "probe," "camera," and *"Wahkopem Zomos."* The rest of her speech was no language I recognized, but her strange companion seemed to respond in the same language.

"I think," Captain Baegess said, "that your place in the history books has just become secure."

Streeyeptin gestured his agreement. "You're in for an extra promotion at the least when we return. Are there more pictures from the same rover?"

There were not. Like the *Wahkopem* probe before it, after taking a single intriguing picture, our rover had shut down completely. "Captain," I said, trying not to smirk, "I request permission to stay up late and get the other rovers working."

He granted it without argument.

2

THE BIGGEST DIFFICULTY WITH BRINGING *EGALITARIAN REPUBLIC* TO REST above Setepos was aiming the exhaust.

As the assistant assigned to the captain, I had seniority over the other two assistants on board, so I was in command of the first step, an honor that would have been nicer if it hadn't been so dangerous.

As we plunged into the Kousapex System, still at many times solar escape velocity, decelerating at eighty-eight percent of gravity, we got to work on the first step, unpacking the disperser from storage. Without the disperser, we would not be able to park *Egalitarian Republic* above Setepos, and though our landers could reach orbital speeds if they had to, it would greatly complicate our operation if they had to orbit and deorbit for every trip up and down. Thus, since our engine could put out many times the thrust needed to counteract Setepos's gravity for periods of years—after all, it had just done so—we would hover on thrust above the planet's surface, outside the atmosphere to avoid the turbulence we would cause by superheating the air below us.

But even with the ship safely out beyond the atmosphere, heat was going to be a big problem. Our engine was a zero-point energy laser, and at the thrust needed to keep us in place, if we just pointed it at the planet's surface and turned it on, its power output was enough to vaporize rock explosively. (After all, we would be literally standing on a beam of light.) Whatever spot we hovered above, if it were dry land, would swiftly turn into a gigantic volcano.

The disperser was a device to make the beam spread out enough so that we could safely point it at the ocean surface, and use the boiling water and steam to carry off its enormous load of energy.

The disperser took three full working days to get to the point where we were ready to begin. Naturally the People's Space Exploration Foundation, back home, hadn't seen fit to provide us with a hatch that a complete disperser could go through, or a disperser that could go completed, through our hatches, so we had to check out components, get the three pieces ready to go together, and then plan to assemble them outside in space. All this, of course, without complaining, since you never knew what Streeyeptin might remember once we returned.

When at last we were sure that all three pieces were working well and could be interfaced to the others, just five days out from Setepos, the captain turned on the antiproton spray and turned off the zero-point energy lasers that had propelled the ship all the way here from Nisu and were now braking us as we came into the Setepos System. Abruptly, the acceleration was zero, and we were weightless.

The three assistants met with the captain just before we went outside to put the disperser into place. Our being chosen for this part of the mission meant we were "about to set the record for the fastest spacewalk in history," Captain Baegess pointed out. "We *think* our system for protecting you will work, but of course this is the time we really find out. At least so far, for the last tenth of a day, nothing big enough to hurt you has hit the ship."

"Except the gamma radiation," Krurix pointed out, voicing what Bepemm and I had been thinking.

"Except the gamma radiation," Captain Baegess agreed, "but that's not nearly the problem that being blown apart would be."

Though we were now far below lightspeed, the velocity of our ship was still so high—about ten thousand times that of a slug coming out of a modern steam rifle—that a dust grain delivered more than enough energy to tear one of us in half, and as we were now entering the new solar system, dust was getting thicker outside the ship.

Inside the ship we had been protected by our deceleration exhaust; any dust that drifted into the zero-point energy laser were either vaporized (if dark), or accelerated away from us at great speed (if reflective). The particles streaming away helped to clear space in front of us as well.

But we couldn't work outside with the laser turned on, and so it would not protect us from the dust we would be running into. Instead, the captain had flipped the ship back over so that its nose pointed in the direction we were going again. We would use the antiproton spray that had protected the ship during the long years of acceleration.

The antiproton spray was simply a long tube running through a magnetic coil, pointing out into space ahead of us. There was a big negative charge on the ship end of the tube, and a big positive charge on the far end.

Because antiprotons have a negative charge, a fine mist of antiprotons sprayed into the tube would accelerate away from the negatively charged ship, follow the lines of the magnetic field down the tube toward the positive charge that attracted them, and shoot out into space at close to lightspeed. When one of them struck a dust speck, a small part of the burst of energy released by the antimatter/matter reaction would be transferred to the speck (like a bomb going off next to a rock) and the speck would shoot off away from us (since the "explosion side" would always be toward us).

The problem was that while a small part of the energy would move the dust speck, a large part of that energy would become hard gamma rays; those of us outside were going to be exposed to some radiation over and above the usual space crew's dosage, even with the whole ship between us and the antiproton spray. "That's why we want you to work fast," Captain Baegess reminded us for the hundredth time. "Your suits provide some protection, but not nearly as much as being inside the hull of the ship. So get done quickly; we don't want to have to treat anyone for cancer on the way back, and we want everyone to come back."

"Yes, sir," I said, along with Astrogator's Assistant Bepemm.

Engineer's Assistant Krurix added, "We feel just the same way."

The captain had a chronic problem with Krurix, who couldn't seem to respond to simple orders without making a joke out of them, and Bepemm rolled her eyes at me as if to say, *Here we go again, punished for whatever Krurix does*, but either the captain was in a good mood or saw the humor in the situation, and said, "Then we're all in agreement. Good, then. Go get it done."

The dispersion coil was simply a big set of superconducting electromagnets forming a lumpy torus; each of us would go outside with one-third of the torus. We would connect the parts together and mount them around the aperture of the laser—all the while taking a certain amount of hard gamma from antiproton reactions that took place far enough out to the sides so that the ship did not shield us from them.

Krurix was occasionally annoying, but he was good in weightlessness and he was quick about his work; Bepemm and I were glad to have him. We got the assembly done in less than the expected time, and then mounted the disperser. A quick run through the checklist showed it was working properly.

"Thetakisus, look at the sky, up toward the ship," Krurix said suddenly, his voice crackling in my helmet radio.

I looked up. For an instant I saw only stars, among which Kousapex, just by the ship, was now much the brightest. There were some brief flickers—then as I realized what I was looking for, I saw the dozens of little dancing streaks of light seeming to form a crown around the nose of the ship.

Bepemm's voice said, "Must be a side effect of dust hitting the antiproton spray. Probably the antimatter reaction heats the dust motes hot enough to glow."

I watched for another instant and said, "I think you're right. The streaks are blue-white at one end and red-orange at the other." Now that my eyes were adjusting, I realized that there were hundreds of streaks. "The bright ones must be the closest, and the dim ones must be the farther-away ones. And when you look at them all as a group, you can see that the blue-white ends are toward the center and the red toward the outside. Just what you'd expect."

"I think it's just beautiful," Krurix said softly.

"You're right," Bepemm said, "and I'm glad we saw it . . . but every streak started from an event that put out a lot of hard radiation. And there are a lot of those events, and we can see the blue ends of quite a few—and if we can see them, they can irradiate us. Not to mention that probably only the dust collisions are showing visibly—there must be millions of collisions with stray atoms for every visible dust streak—and all those are making hard gamma, too. It's beautiful, but I think we'd better go inside."

"Yeah," Krurix said, some disappointment in his voice.

For the first time on the voyage, I felt a little sympathy for him. It *was* beautiful, now that I could see it clearly, like a flower with thousands of hair-fine petals, a blue-white center with red edges. We went in, verified that all the tools had come in with us, and closed the outer airlock door. There was a push against our suits as pressure came back, and then the inner door slid open. Before we were quite out of our suits, there was a strange lurch as the ship flipped, and then the captain put the ship back under deceleration. By the time we made our way to the cockpit for our report, he had already tested the disperser and found it to be working perfectly.

When we were just one day away from Setepos, we were all terribly seasick. An ordinary orbital transfer maneuver is pretty smooth, but we weren't going into orbit around Setepos—we were joining its orbit around Kousapex, so close that Setepos's gravity perturbed our motion severely. Thus our interaction with Setepos (and its moon's) gravity was not the smooth, gradual change of accelerations with which the ship cooperated (so that we were in free fall and didn't experience it at all). We were coming in under acceleration of our own, hopping back and forth so that our laser exhaust did not intersect surfaces where it might cause explosions.

Thus our acceleration varied rapidly and unpredictably from zero to almost a full gravity, shaking us all like a sailboat in heavy chop.

When it finally stopped it was absolutely abrupt; one moment we were still pitching about as *Egalitarian Republic* swung from side to side, thrusting and turning off, thrusting and turning off—and the next moment it felt as if we were already sitting on the planet's surface. I looked up from where I had had my head down in a sickness bag and saw that one viewscreen showed the broad face of Setepos spread out below us. Bepemm and I hastened to wipe our faces, and then hurried up the ladder to the main viewing room. This final approach was to be conducted by the captain, his first officer, and the engineer and engineer's mate, and thus there was nothing for us to do. Krurix had elected to observe from the engine room, so we would not be troubled by his irritating presence either.

The only other person in the main viewing room was Political Officer Streeyeptin; he seemed friendly enough today, and besides there was hardly anything controversial we could have said about it. He motioned us, graciously enough, into seats near his, by the big screens.

It was hard to believe a world could have so much land. We were looking down at one of the most land-rich possible views, hovering over the area where Big and the Hook, the two largest continents, joined.

Streeyeptin gestured at one screen. "You can see you did good work with the disperser."

We had wanted to be as near as possible to the site where the *Gurix* had set down (always assuming our fragmentary record was accurate), near the mysterious village, since this would allow us to use line-of-sight radio to operate one of the rovers directly from the ship and take a good, thorough look around before sending our own landers down. Fortunately, directly to the east of that area there was a sizable sea, with more than deep enough water to let us point our zero-point energy laser into it. Now we could already see the great billow of white clouds, brilliantly illuminated even in daylight by the powerful laser. Slowly a plume of dense clouds was drifting out of the focus of the beam, eastward toward land.

"There are going to be some big rains down there in a few days," I said.

Streeyeptin nodded. "We can only hope that we aren't setting up flash floods upstream of any Nisuan colonists. We're certainly going to fill up some lakes, put some extra snow on mountaintops, and make the rivers run faster while we're here."

When the zero-point energy laser had first been pointed at that area—the size of a large city back home—water had boiled down to a depth of just over sixty bodylengths, but now the dense clouds were dispersing most of the heat before it reached the surface of the water. The sea surface was still boiling, but most of the heat was carried off by the great plume of steam that reached high into the atmosphere, constantly heated by the laser light pouring down on it from above.

"The Creator alone knows what we must be doing to their weather," Bepemm said; she winced at referring to the Old Religion in front of the Political Officer.

If he noticed, he gave no sign. "I wonder if that's visible in the daytime from the colony site—it surely must be at night," he said. "Well, whoever—or whatever—is down there, I suppose they know something is happening, even if they don't know what."

"Assistant Thetakisus, please report to the cockpit," Captain Baegess said over the communicator. "We want to get a rover operational as soon as we can."

"Yes, sir," I responded, and hurried to comply.

When I got there I found an argument in process. Naturally half of the argument was Krurix, but the surprise was that he was arguing with Chief Engineer Azir, and in front of the captain besides. Usually Krurix worshiped Azir, the one officer he obeyed without mouthing off.

I slipped unnoticed into the cockpit—it seated eight when it had to, and there were only five of us present, so I simply took a seat by a utility console and waited.

"—just a day or so," Krurix said. He sounded like he was trying to keep his voice even. He wasn't managing it, quite. "If we just put the ship into orbit—it's a simple maneuver—and spend a day in free fall, we can do the overhaul. It *won't* be too much trouble. Not compared with getting shipwrecked."

"You're willing to go to all that trouble because you don't like the responsiveness graph, although it's well within tolerance?" Azir asked. Her tone was gentle, but it was clear that she was incredulous.

First Officer Beremahm was obviously enjoying the argument and wasn't about to say anything; her quiet gesture to me indicated that as usual she thought Krurix was ridiculous and was going to enjoy watching him make a fool of himself. As always, that gave me mixed feelings. As senior assistant on board, I felt that whatever the other two assistants did reflected on all of us, and Krurix, with his constant arguing and chasing off after any stray idea at all, embarrassed me terribly. Yet at the same time, Krurix was one of us, and if he thought (for whatever unfounded reason) that the ship was in danger of crashing, I wanted his views taken seriously.

So I sat there wondering what I should say, if anything.

Fortunately, Captain Baegess wasn't one to take chances, even if she didn't think much of Krurix either, so she saved me the trouble of thinking about how to draw him out. "Tell us about it, Krurix, please. Why you think it's something to worry about, I mean."

"Well," he said, "it's kind of basic. Zero-point energy gets produced when charged plates that are only about twenty atomic radii apart are pushed down to within a few atomic radii of each other. The space is lasable, so all that energy ends up as laser light and drives the ship."

"Thank you for your tour of the ship, sir, it has been very educational," Beremahm said, so sarcastically that Krurix cringed.

But Azir came to his defense. "I think Krurix was just laying out the basis for his physical reasoning," she said. "He'll get there soon enough."

Krurix gulped and went on. "Well, to get continuous power we have to vibrate those plates really fast. The faster we vibrate them, the closer they get together at the bottom and the more times the laser pulses per unit time. So to increase thrust we cycle the plates faster. Well, this time, as we were executing maneuvers, I was running all the routine checks, and I was surprised to see that when we changed the speed of vibration, the profile of change wasn't what it should be. It was like the plates kept vibrating at the old speed a little too long, and then abruptly jumped or fell to the new speed, with just an instant or two of chaos in between. May I show you on the screen?"

"Please do," Captain Baegess said.

Krurix turned to his console and clicked a few times; two graphs sprang up on the group screen. "You see?" he said. "The smooth one on the left, that looks like an ordinary exponential decay, is the way it's always looked before today. The one that looks like a jagged step function, with that little 'twang' of noise just before it levels off, is what it's been doing today."

First Officer Beremahm stopped smiling and sat much farther forward. "What do you think is causing it?"

"Well, this is where I'm just going by analogy. The vibration of the plates is approximated by a simple harmonic oscillator, right, like a pendulum, a water wave, or a weight bouncing on a spring. And what changes the behavior of other simple harmonic oscillators is changes in *damping*—how sticky the pivot on the pendulum is, how thick the stuff the pendulum moves through, how viscous the water is, how flexible the spring is and how much kinetic energy it returns per potential energy put in. So my guess is, something has changed in the plates, or more likely in the superconducting magnetic levitation we use to keep them in place. And if it's starting to change—after being completely stable for literally years at very high acceleration—since we don't have any lab experience with an engine like this running for this long under such high accelerations, I don't think we can dismiss the possibility that the plates might fall together, or spring apart, and *stop* vibrating. And if that locks up . . ."

"Oh, but then we're fine," Azir said. She was obviously relieved. "We have an emergency backup system to reseparate the plates and start them vibrating again. It might be a long, frightening few moments while we fell, but we'd be fine, once the engine cut back in."

Krurix sighed. "Well, yeah, but then I started to play with the computer simulation. The emergency separator takes some time to cut in. And that time is long enough for us to fall into the outer atmosphere of Setepos. Once we do, we'll need to accelerate a little above one gravity to keep from hitting the surface—but if we turn the engine on with that much power" —he clicked on his console again—"here's what happened when we first put about that same amount of power into the atmosphere—infrared picture."

Before our eyes, we saw a great plume of superheated air leap upward, far above the surface. Captain Baegess made a noise of acknowledgment. "How big is that explosion?"

"Like a good-sized hydrogen-fusion device," Krurix said. "And it doesn't care how close we are to it. Way up here, far above it, it's just interesting to watch. But if we were down there in the atmosphere, it would happen right next to us. Temperatures, pressures, and accelerations far above what the ship was ever designed for."

"It would blow us apart," the First Officer said, her long Shulathian ears pulling back as she thought about it. "I see what you mean, Krurix, and yes, you were right to bring it to our attention."

Captain Baegess said, "And so your suggestion is that we put the ship into a ballistic orbit, so that we can shut down all engines and overhaul all the separators and plates? I have to agree it would fix the problem."

"It would certainly be the safest thing to do," Azir agreed.

I could see the bony plates of Krurix's shoulders relax, and the hair of his crest lie down. He had clearly been scared out of his mind, arguing with the senior officers at a time like this. I had to admit that I couldn't be sure I'd have had his courage, or his perception. Well, maybe he was useful after all, even if he wasn't likable. I resolved to listen to him more.

At least when he wasn't making terrible jokes about orders.

Streeyeptin climbed in and said, "Is there some delay? Everyone below would like to know what we're doing."

Captain Baegess glanced up. "Assistant Krurix has found a major risk to the ship and suggested a fix for it. We're trying to decide what to do about it."

The Political Officer gestured impatiently. "We aren't crashing, are we?"

"Not yet." Baegess's voice was flat. "But it's serious."

"We've got a mission." Streeyeptin pointed out. "Are we starting our investigation yet?"

"We will as soon as I'm sure we've secured our survival," Baegess said. "Self-preservation and safe return is the first priority—that's in the orders, too. And this is that serious."

So naturally it all had to be explained to Streeyeptin all over again, in much simpler terms. Eventually he nodded. "Yes, I see the point. But we will proceed with the original plan. I'm not sure even now, after all that babble, why you give so much weight to that argument—however ingenious, and Assistant Krurix, it does speak well of you that you are constantly thinking—when you consider two obvious points. The People's Space Exploration Foundation built this ship to make the round trip, with a wide margin of error, and thus we are much less than halfway through the distance it was designed to cover. Therefore, the probability of any serious problem is negligible. Moreover, we've just arrived here safely after traveling an enormous distance, and by your own acknowledgment, after the anomalies, the engine is now running normally.

"Therefore the chances that anything is wrong are very slim. That being the case, then our orders are very clear. We are to proceed at once to determine what happened to the crew of *Wahkopem Zomos*. Once that is determined, we are then to make a brief determination about whether the Nisuan Republic should attempt to plant a colony here, and then to return home. That is all that we are authorized to do; since making sure the engine is working properly is clearly a task for the homeward journey, we will do the maneuver you suggest just before our departure, or sooner if a suitable block of time during which we don't need regular access to the ship should come along.

"You see, it's all there in the orders, if you just pay attention to them." He looked around the room, a satisfied expression. With a sinking heart, I realized that he had just resolved the matter, as far as he was concerned.

Captain Baegess sighed. "We are also obligated for self-preservation and safe return. We have no experience with catastrophic failure of a zero-point energy laser. For all we know it could happen anytime. If it happened now, my suspicion is that Krurix is right—we'd all die."

Streeyeptin's expression was cheerful but not pleasant. "It seems to me that this is the first time, in quite a while, that you have been interested in the original orders."

Captain Baegess surely understood the threat, but he didn't let that show. He merely said, "There is no question of *Egalitarian Republic*'s loyalty."

Streeyeptin seemed very pleased. "Obviously." I suppose in his line of work, he'd gotten used to being happy with everyone just quietly acquiescing, with all those expressionless faces that said yes and carefully did not tell him what they thought.

3

BEPEMM'S VOICE CAME OVER THE INTERCOM. "CAPTAIN, I HAVE MADE contact with *Wahkopem Zomos*. It's right in the orbit where it was supposed to be. The access codes all worked, too. I'm ready to start downloading everything from *Wahkopem Zomos*'s main computer."

Before Captain Baegess could reply, Streeyeptin picked up the mouthpiece. "Do it," he said. "Then search all documents from the landing forward, back-referring as you need to, and see if you can establish what happened." Technically he wasn't supposed to be giving orders to Bepemm, or any other crew member, directly, but no doubt he felt that he needed to assert his authority after the dispute that had just ended.

One of the first things a citizen of the Republic learns is that you don't argue with a political officer. "Right away, sir," Bepemm said, her voice suddenly crisply obedient.

"And while we're waiting for Bepemm's report, Captain, I strongly suggest you have your assistant get the rovers down on the ground and operating. We have a mystery to clear up here, and the people who sent us don't like mysteries."

Captain Baegess nodded to me, and I turned around in my seat, powered up the utility console, and configured it to drive the rover. "Krurix," I said, "I can use your help if Azir doesn't need you further—pull up a seat."

"I don't need him for right now," Azir said. "I want to run some routine checkouts on the engine."

"See that they're routine," Streeyeptin said.

"Yes, sir." She went out quickly, as if glad to get away.

Krurix popped out the seat at the utility console next to mine and configured into parallel with me. Streeyeptin and Captain Baegess went to Streeyeptin's cabin to confer—I was glad to be so busy that I didn't have much thought to spare for whatever was going on in there. That left Beremahm as the commanding officer in the cockpit; Tisix, the helmsman for that watch; and us.

Krurix and I had operated robot probes by remote control, together, many times in practice, and as long as I worked fast enough, he wouldn't talk and irritate me, so I put myself to the pleasant task of getting the probe checked out and readied as quickly as possible. I had outfitted this one with a more powerful power plant than usual—an antimatter cell with a heated-gas rocket—so that it could run fast and hard if it needed to.

As a side benefit, we wouldn't need to descend by parachute; I could fly it all the way down on its engine, by remote control. Krurix sat backup on me, ready to take over if something distracted me, or if I asked him to. At least he knew enough not to do anything annoying at a time like this.

"Ready for me to launch you?" he asked.

"Launch on my mark," I said. "Three. Two. One. Launch."

There was a faint shudder through our feet as the tail-end catapult tossed the rover out, dropping toward the planet, and as it all fell away from us, I checked its controls; response was excellent, almost as if we were in it.

The job was nothing like flying down from orbit; *Egalitarian Republic* was hovering on its laser exhaust far above Setepos's atmosphere, stationary relative to the surface, but nowhere near as high as geostationary orbit—Tisix was flying us sideways, using positioning jets, at a pace just enough to keep us above a constant point in the sea between Big and the Hook. So the probe I was operating had almost no velocity parallel to the surface of Setepos—it was more like dropping off an impossibly high building.

I set the probe to fire a burst every time its speed of approach toward Setepos got too high, bringing itself to an all but complete stop each time. Thus, as we looked through the probe's camera, we approached the ground in a series of leisurely jerks until we were almost down into the troposphere, without ever reaching a speed high enough to heat the probe's skin much. "Like operating an elevator," I said.

"Nice flying," Krurix said. "Do you want to try for the desert northwest of the village? I've got a position for you."

"Give it to me," I said, letting the little probe hover where it was, still far above the ground but now well down into the atmosphere. At once a green dot appeared on my down-view camera, far off to the side. "Got it," I said. "I'm going to go almost straight down on it so we don't accidentally draw attention by flying low over anyone." I angled my thrust very slightly, throttled up a bit, and moved the probe toward the green dot, watching the landscape crawl by underneath. I spun the probe around so that the thrust vectored the other way, let it drift to a stop, so that I was back to hovering. The dot was, as nearly as I could tell at the scale, directly under me.

"That *is* nice flying," Krurix repeated, "you got it in one pass." More softly, he added, "And thanks for getting me out of that one. I was afraid the Political Officer was going to give me a full-fledged grilling and all, to see why I was interfering with the mission."

"He praised you," I pointed out.

Krurix looked at his feet and muttered, "Everyone knows that's when they're dangerous."

I had to let that pass because it was true. "Anyway, I wasn't rescuing you, I was keeping the heat off all of us."

"I'll take my rescues any way I can get them," he said. "If you're ready, let's set the probe down and work out our next step."

"Sure," I said, and cut the throttle back just a little. The probe drifted downward, gaining only a little speed before I opened the throttle a bit so that finally it hovered just a finger-thickness above the grainy desert soil. I let the throttle drift down quickly to zero, and the probe settled on the surface of Setepos.

A quick camera scan around us showed low hills and dunes on most sides, with a range of high, rocky, forested hills rising to the east. "Okay," Krurix said, next to me, "I've got a fix on the lander and the village, and I'm getting a decent radar topo of the area between. As you move toward those hills, you'll encounter a series of low ridges, and between the ridges you're going to find a lot of stuff that looks like cultivated fields, with little canals running through them. Those will probably have people working in them, so what we want to do is follow ridgelines, just low enough to not be silhouetted against them, cross from ridge to ridge wherever there's cover, and eventually reach one of the ridges that looks across the river into the town."

"Good plan," I said, because it was. "If you'll jock the extra cameras and the instruments, that will leave me free to fly close and low." We reconfigured for that. I lifted the probe a bodylength off the desert surface, far enough so that the little jet wouldn't be at risk of setting any fires, and we sped off toward the line of ridges, Krurix calling off results as we went. "Temperature, pressure, gravity, humidity, all of that is just what we'd expect from all the other probes. The bio sampler is getting what looks like pollen and bacteria, mostly, plus a couple of insects. Still nothing different from what we've seen on any other probe. Certainly looks like we can walk around without any special suits. That should make the senior officers happy—we can get right into the next phase."

"They've got their orders too," I reminded him, "and getting on with it will make their lives a lot better when they get back."

"What are you two muttering about over there?" Beremahm asked. Maybe she heard enough to know it wasn't completely appropriate—at least not with our political officer acting up—or maybe she just distrusted assistants whose voices got too quiet.

"Just some tricky technical stuff," I said. "We're flying right above the dirt and there's a lot of fussing to do, and besides there's more relevant data at the altitude."

We swept up the first ridge, avoiding staying on the two footpaths that we crossed. The more broken ground and thicker brush meant I had to bounce higher, but Krurix said there was no one to spot us, at least no one he had seen in any camera. We popped up for an instant, and through a distance lens Krurix saw two Seteposians hoeing a field, so we dropped back and glided along till we found a patch of broken woods and country that seemed to be unobserved. Weaving between trees, we made the next ridge, climbed a gully in its side, and began to repeat our little game of creeping along behind the ridge, looking for a suitable place.

It took a good sixteenth of a day to cross the several ridges until Krurix assured me that the town would be over the very next one. "Well," I said, "taking a peek is getting more and more dangerous." As it was, we were sitting in a low depression on one side of the gully, hoping not to be noticed, but since three footpaths ran into the hollow, it seemed unlikely that we could be unnoticed for long. "Let's make sure we take one really good peek, anyway. I'm going to just pop over the ridge—get all the cameras and instruments ready for quick high-resolution shots, in case that's all we can do. As soon as I do this I'm going to have to start improvising."

I made the probe creep forward, a quarter-bodylength off the ground, until we got into a grove of trees that extended almost to the top of the ridge. Then I popped up out of an open spot in the canopy, dove over the ridge, and brought us to a fast hover two bodylengths off the ground on the other side. Beside me at the other console I heard Krurix's little grunt of effort as he shot more pictures in less time than any of us had ever managed in a practice run.

I had just looked around once when a sudden motion caught my eye. It was a Seteposian, and he was throwing a spear at the probe. I slammed the side jet on and lurched out of the way; the Seteposian turned and ran.

"Let's chase him," Krurix said. "Our cover is blown, we have plenty of juice to get out if we need to, and we might learn quite a bit by seeing who, if anybody, he reports to."

It sounded good to me. I vectored thrust and we sailed down the foot trail after the fleeing Seteposian as he charged down the badly eroded path straight down the hillside. Out of the corner of my eye I was aware that Krurix was getting many good shots of the town: the stone-walled inner part with its big buildings and tower, and the outer huddle of huts surrounded by a wooden palisade. In forty years or so it had grown far beyond what the single cryptic picture had shown us; most remarkable of all, right at its center, apparently attached to the largest building, was the burned-out hulk of one of *Wahkopem Zomos*'s landers.

The figure in front of us continued running downhill, and I kept pursuing, trying to keep an eye on my side and rear cameras in case any friends showed up to help him. They wore more clothing than we did, I noticed—the fabric in which he wrapped his body was flapping madly as he ran. Probably this was the fastest he had ever run. I could hardly blame him.

"Don't let me distract you, Thetakisus," Krurix said, "but there's a really astonishing array of things in that town. That's a full-fledged stone-age city, like they found back home on Nisu, twenty years ago, when they finally found First Dynasty Kratareni."

I glanced over at his screen, since we were now chasing our lone spearman across fairly flat planted field and I could trust the collision avoider for a few instants. The picture looked like it had come out of a historic motion picture back home. I went back to chasing my Seteposian.

He was running up on a small wooden palisade by the trail; I didn't know what might be inside it, but I figured I could—

There was a sharp scream on the probe's internal audio. I clicked for a fix on it and switched the cameras to scan the probe's own outside; there was a decorated stick protruding from one external audio pickup. It took me a moment to realize that must be a projectile fired by a Seteposian weapon of some kind.

Two more of the sticks shot by—they were miniature stone-tipped spears with something tied to their backs to make them fly straight. I jigged around to spoil their aim. Now I could see other Seteposians, advancing across the field we had just crossed, fitting the small spears to bent sticks, which they clearly used to launch them somehow. Then twenty more came rushing out of the little fort in front of us; they were carrying spears.

"I suggest we get the probe out of there before we lose it," Krurix said.

I hit the preprogrammed command, and the probe boosted at four gravities. The down-pointing cameras showed a flock of spears, large and small, rising after the probe, then falling back. The field and fort blended into the green around them, then the town and ridges disappeared into the land as well.

"Not completely friendly, are they?" Krurix commented. "I think we want to be pretty careful about approaching them. And I don't like the fact that Seteposians were all there was in that fort. It kind of suggests to me that it wasn't our side that ended up in charge. I'd have expected a Nisuan officer if the *Wahkopem* people had won out."

I logged off from the probe, leaving it to find its own way back up to *Egalitarian Republic*, something it could easily do. Free now to just talk, I grinned at the other assistant. "Would you say we have a good handle on what happened to the robot probes?"

He gestured agreement. "It has to be. I couldn't swear to it from that encounter, but you know, I think they knew what they were doing. Did you see how quickly they moved to surround the probe? The robots are programmed to move away from anything big that moves toward them. I think our friends have worked out how to confuse a probe's program so that it runs out of ideas."

I noted that into our report and said, "So. We'll want to try again soon. I don't think we're going to get much of a look by chasing sentries."

Krurix scratched behind one ear and then rubbed his crest vigorously. "We need to go at night, to begin with. Put all the cameras on infrared, show no lights, do very low-powered hops so we don't show much flame, really use the audio pickups heavily. More or less the way we'd try to sneak in, in person, I guess. We should probably come in straight down, so we don't have to sneak past any guards, and sometime when there's no moon in the sky."

We had just figured out that we were close to a new moon, the best of all times to go, when Beremahm came over and rested a hand on each of our shoulders. "The captain wants all officers to the main conference room—including me, so we're leaving the ship in the hands of the ordinary spacers. Tisix," she added, "you will promise not to crash us?"

"If the ship blows up, you can dock my pay, sir," the helmsman said.

"Anyway," Beremahm said, "given how many standing orders and regs this goes against, there's obviously something big happening. Apparently we're going to hear your friend Bepemm's report, and the captain and the Political Officer would also like it very much if you would please

present something or other as well—he says it doesn't have to be orga-
nized, but he doesn't want to completely surprise you when he asks.
Unofficially I suggest you take a few minutes to pull out a file of pictures
before you go down."

The main conference room was also the dining hall and where recre-
ational games were played and Political Education lectures given. There
was room for everyone there, and since the ship's crew was about half
officers, this meant everyone could have spread out. Instead, we piled
into the front two rows, leaning forward, trying to guess what Captain
Baegess and Political Officer Streeyeptin had heard from Bepemm to
cause this unprecedented meeting.

The last to come in were Proyerin, the engineer's mate, and Depari,
the astrogator, both of whom had been asleep. As soon as they were seated, Captain Baegess began. "Well, after today I am not sure I will ever
believe there can be such a thing as too-wild speculation. As we all
know, some of the most bizarre ideas about what happened to the
Wahkopem Zomos expedition have turned out to be true. It was clear
before now that they landed near a village of intelligent Seteposians and
that at least some of their descendants still live there, so in that sense
the greatest shock is over with. But what Astrogator's Assistant Bepemm
has turned up is not merely surprising—it is shocking, and I don't use
that word lightly in this case. Most of you will be shocked. Therefore I
want you to give her your *full* attention *without* interruption. And you
may find that harder than you think. Still, I want to hold all discussion
until we have heard all the facts—with one exception. I wish to exercise
my captain's privilege of pointing out to you all that Bepemm has done a
superb job, very rapidly finding the relevant documents and compiling
them into the strange and horrifying story you are about to hear, and is
greatly to be commended. So now, give her your full attention.
Bepemm?"

It was certainly unheard of for one of us assistants to address the
whole session of the ship's officers; normally the whole session met only
before and after a voyage, not during one. And for that matter, most of
the time we were invisible as we ran from one duty to the next. It wasn't
surprising, therefore, that Bepemm looked a little frightened. She
glanced toward me and Krurix, and we covertly gestured approval at her;
that seemed to relax her, and she began.

The captain's preface had not been exaggerated. The story was horrifying. It began with the murder of the only morally decent crewmember,

the only one who had advocated equality with the Seteposians and who had not had racist ideas about cross-marriages. Apparently he had dissented from a plan to establish a slave empire on Setepos—Bepemm was still looking for exact evidence on that point.

The "crash" message received on Nisu—the very message that had been the trigger for the Revolution—had been a fraud, intended to keep anyone from coming to see what was going on. For us, the children of the Revolution—and for older officers who had fought in it—this was perhaps the hardest blow.

But not the worst thing we heard. Records uploaded from the *Gurix*'s computer showed that the Nisuans had indeed established a slave empire, overrunning some twenty neighboring settlements.

Finally we got the story of the disease that developed among them. After Mejox made the last run for medical supplies, records came to an abrupt end until almost three years later, when the *Gurix* suddenly took off at maximum acceleration and continued right on out of the solar system, beyond radio range, till finally its engines flamed out at just about the distance that could be explained as running out of fuel. "They took off in no particular direction," Bepemm noted. "The nearest star they *could* have been trying for is a red dwarf more than twenty light-years away, which the *Gurix* still won't reach for decades—about seven gravities for about an eightday only got it up to about thirteen percent of the speed of light. And the *Gurix* was unequipped for a crew to survive that much acceleration. I can't believe that trip was intentional."

Captain Baegess waited a long moment and then said, "You should give us your hypothesis on this one, Bepemm. Political Officer Streeyeptin and I agree that it makes a great deal of sense."

Bepemm looked nervous. "Well, er, the problem is that it happens to have no real evidence. I just thought that the voyages between *Wahkopem Zomos* and the surface probably stopped because they just didn't need anything more from the ship to run their empire. If you look at the plans and lists when they started out, the *Gurix* actually made one more trip than it was supposed to—the one for medical supplies. So I think they had planned that their little empire would be independent of the ship. If it hadn't been for the illness, Mejox Roupox would not have needed to make that last trip.

"Then as for what happened three years later—I think most likely Soikenn, who had been close to Poiparesis, who had frequently dissented, and whose child—the youngest among them—was extremely sick and might well have died, did it as an act of suicide, and also to take away the basis of the Nisuan empire on Setepos. Probably after seeing how things had turned out, she decided to eliminate herself and the access to *Wahkopem Zomos* at the same time. If she was careful about how she did it, she would have been killed on takeoff, and she wouldn't have suffered much."

There was a very long silence.

Then Streeyeptin said, "I would like to hear the probe report."

Krurix and I gave it, as quickly as we could, describing everything we had seen and stressing that no Nisuan appeared to be in charge down there.

Streeyeptin nodded, and said, "Questions?" There were none. Everyone was too stunned. "Very well, then," he continued, "I should draw your attention to the real nature of the prerevolutionary regime and the kind of consciousness it engendered. No sooner did they reach a new world with a new sapient species than they set out to replicate the worst of the old—slavery, monarchy, racism, imperialism, wars of conquest, the whole business. But I'm sure that lesson *can't* have been lost on you. Now we have at least some idea of what we face down there. Even if the Seteposians have taken it over—and I think Krurix and Thetakisus should be able to confirm that with a couple more probe missions, flown, as they suggest, with a little more stealth—even if it is a Seteposian slave empire now, it is unquestionably a slave empire. Therefore our task is twofold: to reeducate the Nisuans living there, whether they are slaves or masters, and to overthrow the present regime and empower the Seteposians to develop into a free and equal republic. If we succeed, we will have new and loyal friends in the universe. Should we fail, well, I need only point to what has already happened." He turned to Captain Baegess and added, "It's clear that we need to begin as soon as we have all information in hand. Get our worthy assistants on the job as soon as they're fed and rested. And I would think a round of applause from the assembled officers is owed to all three assistants."

They gave it to us, and then swarmed out of the room, back to duties or bunks—since it was plain we were going to be busy. On his way out, Streeyeptin leaned over to Krurix and said, very softly, "Well, you've redeemed yourself," then went out the door before Krurix could react. When I looked at the engineer's assistant, he was pale around the eyes with fear.

4

BECAUSE OF THE RAIN AND THE DARK THAT HAD LAIN LIKE A COLD BLANKET over the Nim's empire for ten days now, all the Nisuan slaves who had independent living quarters were allowed fires. My father had built his in front of the one-room hut he shared with my mother, just close enough so that we could sit under the overhang, relatively dry while the fire blazed in front of us and the light misting rain hissed and spatted around its edges.

I had put Esser to bed—no great problem as I'd had her romping outside in the mud all day to tire her out—and gotten permission to spend the evening down here with Father and Mother. It was the first chance, really, to talk alone with Father about what everyone was calling the Pillar of Fire, the strange glowing vertical cloud to the west of us that had appeared the night before it began to rain so unseasonably. I don't suppose I'd have gotten permission if anyone had been thinking about it—the Nisuan probes creeping through town by night and around the outskirts by day, seen by dozens of people now, had made all of Real People Town nervous and fearful. But after a few gloomy gray days and with the Pillar visible whenever an opening appeared in the clouds, with the whole city rife with rumors of avenging Nisuans about to return, of Inok returned from the sky to punish his father for exiling him there, and that the probes themselves seemed to be alive and thinking in a way no one could recall, the nobility of the Real People had become thoroughly demoralized, and when I had asked my mistress's permission, she had simply waved a hand at the door. I didn't stay to discuss her feelings with her.

That evening, Mother was no better; she was still having lucid intervals once or twice a day, but otherwise she either slept or babbled nonsense. Her muscles were terribly weak and visibly wasting away. So far she had no sign of a cough, but both Soikenn and Mejox had finally been killed by pneumonia, as far as we could tell, brought on by being bedridden and perhaps by atrophy of the muscles. We turned her and changed the straw under her, to prevent bedsores, and since she seemed to be unconscious, we left her in what we hoped was a comfortable position and went outside to talk.

"So," Father said, in Nisuan, "it looks very much as if they did send an expedition back to us. Poor old Mejox—he'd have liked to see it, and if he'd lasted just a little longer he might have. Oh, well, it pleases me to see an end come to the Nim, and Osepok will be ecstatic I'm sure. And perhaps they can do something for Otuz as well."

"You're sure it's them and not someone else?" I asked.

He almost laughed at me, then caught himself. "I suppose, growing up here and getting what education you could mostly in secret, it's hard for you to understand. But there is no civilization advanced enough to do any of this on Setepos, and the odds of there being any other civilization nearby—and of its coming here—are vanishingly small. No, it's from Nisu. Another clue is that they appear to be using a zero-point energy laser to hover over the planet's surface—"

"Is that what the Pillar is?"

"Does it help you to know the name of the thing?"

"Sometimes. At least it lets me feel like I'm not one of our savage masters," I said. "But how do you know what it is?"

"While we were en route, as you know, Otuz and I, plus your Grandmother Soikenn and poor Poiparesis, who you never met, all of us did a great deal of scientific work, and we read a great deal of other people's work."

"It's always sounded to me like that was *all* you did."

"Very nearly. Anyway, one of the reports that came in from Nisu was of an energy source called zero-point energy. Essentially it works because throughout the universe there is always energy popping in and out of existence, and, if you will, it's a gadget for trapping energy on this side of existence. Physically it's two vibrating plates very close together, so that when the plates are apart there is just enough time for the energy to come into existence, and when they spring together they trap it before it has enough time to pop back out of existence."

"That doesn't make a lot of sense to me," I confessed.

"Now that I don't have the math ability I once did," Father said, "it doesn't really to me, either. But when you get down to atomic scale—down to things so small that you can hardly imagine them—you really can't visualize things the way you can in our everyday world. So you just have to take what the math tells you and make whatever sense of it you can—and follow the math, not the sense, if you see what I mean. Anyway, it was a tremendously powerful source of energy, and shortly afterwards another report we got said that they had demonstrated it was lasable—meaning you could use it to make laser light, the same kind of light that *Wahkopem Zomos* sailed here on, but even more powerful. At the time we thought perhaps that would allow them to send us more power on the return trip laser, and thus shorten our way home, but by then it was becoming clear that money for science and research and exploration was drying up. Well, clearly the spring started running again sometime in the last forty years, because here they are with a very high-powered laser—much more powerful than *Wahkopem Zomos* used to get here—and one that fits right inside their ship. So besides Nisuans being the only people likely to show up, these people have exactly the right technology to be likely to be Nisuans. If you see what I mean."

"Close enough," I said, though I had understood perhaps half of it. I hated to remind him how little he and Mother had been able to teach even the oldest Nisuan children born here—it always made him terribly sad.

"Anyway," he said, "at the top of the Pillar is a Nisuan ship. It's been sending the probes. They are scouting the ground down here before they commit a party of people, which is exceedingly smart of them in light of what happened to us. The reason the new probes are so hard to catch is that instead of being simple robots that only know how to do a few things, they are being remotely controlled from the ship. So never fear—there will be an invasion. Soon, I think."

"I think," I said, "that the Nim thinks so, too. He's said to have withdrawn into his palace, won't talk to anyone, issues orders suddenly in a blind haste and then countermands them half a day later. . . ."

"He senses what's coming," Father said. "And don't forget that when he first met us, he was quite seriously worshiping us as gods. It's our bad luck that he was smart enough to figure out how weak we were, while we were ill, and brave enough to act on the knowledge. He's a very tough and dangerous opponent, as every village for six days journey around here has learned. But with all that, he is still really only the master of two thousand Seteposians with various kinds of pointed sticks. He is one of the few of the Real People old enough to have seen a steam rifle in action, and the only one old enough to have seen us destroy the original Real People Town in less time than it now takes him to take his bath. So he's very afraid and he's doing his best to find a way to win out again, even though it's probably hopeless. That combination might make anyone mad."

"So you think he's as sure as you are that they are Nisuans, and they are going to land."

"Diehrenn, is your father still so sure of that?" a soft voice said, from the dark. Aunt Priekahm came into the firelight from the dark mist, looking sort of like a bad copy of a Seteposian. The last few years she had complained constantly of being cold, and had taken to wearing shawls and skirts like they did.

"Well, it is what makes sense," Father said.

"Zahmekoses, so far nothing has happened that wouldn't be consistent with an artificially intelligent robot mission," Priekahm said, "and we may well have to wait for many years till anything that can take us home comes out to see if we're still here. I think it's foolish to get your hopes up when—"

I could tell from the tone of their voices that this was one of the eternal arguments they had come to love as they grew older—and worse yet, it was a new one and thus they were still inventing new things to say, so if they got into this one they'd argue all night. I broke in and asked, "Well, *if* there are people on that ship, what do you think they'll do?"

Priekahm thought for a moment and then laughed. "Well, the one thing that probably hasn't changed is that we are a contentious species, Diehrenn. The only guarantee is that they won't approve of what they find, though exactly what they'll disapprove of and why is a good question. And the other thing to trust in is that they will 'fix' whatever they don't like first, and then ask questions later. Assuming they really are Nisuans."

Father gestured agreement. "It's a bitter joke, but you're right," he said. "I suppose a species that all got along perfectly with each other would never make it to the stars, because they'd never argue enough to make their ideas work. And a species that thought everything through first wouldn't get there because they'd never get around to it. So the galaxy will eventually be ruled by impetuous bickerers."

Priekahm laughed again. "This is what comes of following logic too rigorously." It was good to hear the old ones just talking, now that there were so few Seteposians really watching us anymore. If there had been anywhere to go—or if we hadn't wanted to see what was about to happen right here—for the first time I could remember, it would have been easy to run away.

"Well, so they won't be pleased," I said, "I'm not entirely pleased either. Perhaps—"

"Diehrenn?" my mother called softly from inside the little hut. I went in silently; she was lucid so rarely now that we tried not to waste an instant of it.

The hut was small and very dark. "I'm here, Mother."

"Has the new ship arrived?" she asked. Her voice was very soft and weak.

"It's still up there, but they haven't come down," I said, sitting close to her and taking her hand. I could barely make out her shape by the dim firelight coming through the door. "How did you know—"

"Zahmekoses has been telling me about it whenever I'm awake. He's so excited about it, says they must have developed better technology." Her breath hissed in her slack throat as she spoke; I leaned in close to her mouth to hear better. "He adds up the time and says they must have . . . I think he's being optimistic . . . I wanted to see you tonight because . . . oh, look, the water's all pink again." She began to sing in a low, tuneless moan, with occasional words, as she always did after a lucid moment. I pressed my face to hers, and then went back out to Father and Aunt Priekahm. "She's the same," I said, before they could ask. "Clear but weak for a little while, and then nothing."

"I wish Soikenn had lived this long—or that I had paid more attention to my medical studies," Father said glumly. "It's got to be something to do with the modified protein processing, toxins that build up and slowly cause brain damage and muscular atrophy, perhaps a by-product of the process that allows us to eat their food. If only Soikenn hadn't been the first, or pneumonia hadn't come so quickly after, or even if she'd just thought of—"

Aunt Priekahm interrupted to point out that without the equipment of *Wahkopem Zomos* or the *Gurix*, Soikenn's knowledge would probably have been useless anyway. Since Soikenn had died a year and a half ago, they had argued exactly this question in exactly this way many times. What made me shudder was that when the argument had started, Mother and Uncle Mejox had been part of it.

On occasion I had gotten to talk about it with Prirox and Weruz, the Nisuans who had been born in the same year I was (especially Prirox, because every few months the Seteposians tried to breed me to him again; they couldn't seem to believe that apparently the birth of my sixth child had left me sterile). We all saw it the same way: either you got the disease from getting old on Setepos, or you got it from living on Setepos a long time. Since Osepok was so much older than either my mother or Uncle Mejox, that argued all too well that you got it from living on Setepos for a long time—and that meant that all of us were likely candidates, too.

Aside from that, those of us with any knowledge of Nisu at all were dying pretty fast—three in less than two years, plus of course the occasional ones who ran away, were killed by cruel masters, or suffered accidents. There were probably fewer than ten of us who could really speak Nisuan, surely fewer than twenty who knew any Nisuan at all, all of us more than thirty-five. Only the generation that had come in *Wahkopem Zomos* had managed to pass on anything of Nisuan culture to their children; of my own four living, not one spoke the language.

I had drifted quietly into that gloomy stream of thoughts, letting my mind wander away from the new hope from the sky, when suddenly shouting pierced the air.

I looked up and cocked my ears, trying to make out the direction; in a moment we all agreed it was coming from the Palace Square, the blasted area in front of the palace where the *Gurix* had landed, where because the ground had been baked into stone it was impossible to dig a foundation, grow a tree, or indeed do anything much except leave it bare. Beside me, Priekahm and Father were also standing. He looked in for a moment to make sure that Mother was all right and, since there was little enough we could do for her and the Palace Square was a short distance away, hurried there.

What had attracted the attention in the first place was becoming plainer by the moment: there was a light descending from the sky. At first it was just a blue glow; then we heard a low rumble, like thunder, as it got larger and brighter.

The light became several lights: a great blue one on the underside, and many more floating above it. The thunder grew deafening, and still the lander—that was what it *had* to be, though I had never seen one—came closer and closer. Now we could see, dimly, the sides of the ship, a gray-white smear illuminated by the lights it carried; it resolved itself into a great cone, resting on its base, and as it drew nearer I could see lettering on its side.

We had kept the secret of reading and writing from the Seteposians, but at the cost of very little practice for those of us who did learn, so my skills were very rusty. While I was still spelling it out, Father read out loud, " 'Ship's Launch of the People's Space Exploration Foundation Vessel Number One: *Egalitarian Republic*.' So that's just one of its landers.

Amazing—it's got to be bigger than the whole *Wahkopem Zomos* was. The ship must be huge. And if it's named *Egalitarian Republic*, then—"

"Then there've been a lot of changes back home," Aunt Priekahm said. "Which I think we're about to learn about. Maybe even some *good* changes."

The lander was now low enough so that the pale blue flame that boiled from its underside touched the ground, right in the center of the black, hardened area that the *Gurix* had burned out forty years before. Abruptly, brilliant white light blazed from the lander's underside, a hideous hooting scream emerged over the roar of the engines, and the blue flame went out. The lander descended, still hooting loudly.

"Well, they don't have to ride the jet all the way in—some kind of internal aerostat?" Priekahm suggested.

"Probably," Father said, "especially when you look at how *huge* that thing is. And if they can carry that *inside their ship*—well, things *have* changed a lot."

"Wonder how long it took them to get here?" Priekahm said.

"Well, if they can take a straight line—unlike us—the minimum is around four years, at lightspeed. I don't guess modern physics has repealed the speed of light limitation. But we got up to forty percent of lightspeed with a laser that couldn't do a thousandth of what theirs can. They might easily have come here at just barely below lightspeed—"

"I have an idea, Zahmekoses," Aunt Priekahm said. "Let's walk over and ask them."

Father and I both laughed; as long as I could remember, he had been willing to talk theory endlessly—and that was always when she got most practical.

"All right, let's go. With luck Osepok will already be there to do the official representing, and we can just gawk."

As we neared Palace Square, most of the crowd were freeborn Real People, who normally would have shoved us aside. But now they parted around us, and though they were outside to see what would happen, they didn't seem very eager to get any closer. Already the arrival of the lander was changing life beyond recognition.

Aunt Priekahm had noticed, too. "You know, I think they don't want any of us to be angry with them anymore. What a refreshing change."

"I think so, too," Father said, "but let's not get our hopes too high just yet. It sounds very much like there was a revolution, and Nisu is now a republic. It also sounds like the Egalitarians won. And if you look at it one way, we would seem to be employees of the evil previous regime. So we might just find all we've done is gone from Slaves of the Real People to Enemies of the State."

"Diehrenn, have you ever thought that your father might be a pessimist?"

"Constantly," I said.

We came into the Palace Square itself, with the palace on our right and the temple to our left. The palace, I knew, had been the house that my parents and the other Nisuans had built for themselves, taken over by the Nim after he killed Kekox. Nowadays Seteposian children were told that we had built it in a single night under the magic compulsion of Rar, after he captured our souls with his powerful magic. I had never seen it, though that was often a dozen times in a day, without resenting our stolen birthright.

Now it was occurring to me that even though the Nisuans had come for us, that didn't mean, necessarily, that we would be getting the palace back.

Our banter dropped away as we finally saw how huge the lander really was. The temple was two full stories with a roof tall enough to be a third story, and the burned-out hulk of the *Rumaz* towered a story over it. This was three times as tall as the *Rumaz*, at least. Its immense feet were settling very softly onto the hard ground. It seemed to drift for a moment in the light evening breeze, as if its whole bulk were all but weightless. The hooting and screeching stopped abruptly, and we heard a loud hiss; the lander sank onto its legs, compressing them, and settled firmly onto the ground.

Palace Square was almost empty—around its outer edge there was a crush of Seteposians, who probably wanted to see, but not that closely, and in the middle there was a small group of Nisuans. We hurried to join them. "Prirox!" I shouted, seeing him.

He turned. "Diehrenn. So, are you ready for the whole world to change?"

"Yes, as a matter of fact. Preferably for the better."

Osepok was in the group, and Weruz as well, along with several other older Nisuans. It looked like it was about the older half of us. "The rest of the Nisuans are either in the nursery, or the Real People families that own them are keeping them for some reason or other," Weruz explained. "And I can think of one or two who are probably just as frightened as the Seteposians. I think we probably have everyone who can speak Nisuan here, anyway."

"Ha, look at the palace," Father said. "This means getting down to business quickly."

A group of about twenty-five Seteposians came from behind the palace at a dead run. They were the Nim's personal guard, except for their leader—

"Set!" I said, in some shock.

Aunt Priekahm said, "Yes, of course. I'd say the old Nim is as sharp as ever. Well, bad luck and an ugly death to the lot of them."

I must have looked shocked, for Father turned to me and said emphatically, "Now, no sentiment. Rar is going to try to storm the door on that lander as soon as it opens. He remembers what modern weapons can do, so his only hope is to try for surprise. He's no fool. I'm sure right now he's more afraid than he's been in a long time. But there might be a chance, and he's taking it. The only way to beat steam rifles—or whatever it is they carry nowadays—with spears is to not let the steam rifles get into action. So he's going to try to get in before they even know they're attacked. Mother Sea knows it worked once."

"But Set—"

"Is up there because he'll attack like a mad dog till they kill him or he wins," Priekahm said. "And you of all people should know you can't possibly talk him out of it. Before you get terribly sentimental about all of this, just remember that if Nim Rar and Set triumph, we stay slaves. I'm sorry your favorite Seteposian is in line to die, but if it would get me my freedom, I'd be delighted to kill him myself."

I looked back at the lander, not wanting to hear more, hopelessly confused, my eyes filling with tears and my mind with no emotion I could name. From far above the ground—as high as the roof of the temple—a door opened, and a long flight of steps extended down to the ground. A Nisuan stepped onto the steps, his face obscured by a huge mask.

Set lunged forward out of the group of guards and hurled a spear with all his might at the figure. He shouted for his men to follow, and they all rushed toward the flight of steps that led up into the lander.

But the Nisuan, several bodylengths above Set, had plenty of time to see the spear coming. He stepped slightly to the side and slapped hard, and the spear thudded against the wall of the lander, then fell to the ground below.

The Palace Guard, with Set in the lead, had almost gained the foot of the stairs when the Nisuan in the huge mask turned to someone inside, who handed him a heavy object that looked like a cylinder with two protruding stubby bars. Grasping a bar in each hand, he pointed the cylinder down at Set, who was now rushing up the steps with the Nim's guards behind him.

It made a strange whirring scream. Set's body burst apart from his neck to his waist, spraying back onto the men behind him. What remained of him fell sideways off the ladder.

I breathed "no" just once. Then the small insectoid figure took one step forward and looked over the whole Palace Guard, which seemed to have frozen in their tracks. He pointed the cylinder again, this time to one side. Again it made the whirring scream, this time for much longer. The Nisuan swung it back and forth.

All the guards seemed to shriek and fall at once, clutching faces, chests, or bellies. Most lay still. A few still moved, but if they did, the Nisuan pointed the cylinder, it whirred briefly, a body would dance and flop on the ground spraying blood—and then they would lie still. In a few moments they were all dead, or near enough.

The whole thing had taken the time of a couple of long breaths. It took a little longer, perhaps one breath more, before the Seteposians began to scream and flee Palace Square.

Raising their hands above their heads, Father and Priekahm walked slowly toward the Nisuan lander. In a moment they were joined by Ose-pok, still walking proudly erect despite her enormous age.

I might not have followed, but then Weruz and Prirox raised their hands and walked forward, so I followed them with my hands up and then all of the Nisuans in the group did the same.

Now that the fighting was over, Nisuans, all wearing the same enormous masks, were coming down the steps swiftly. The one with the cylinder pushed the mask up off his face and looked around. There was something about the cool, calm way he looked around—*He has never had a master*, I said to myself. Then I noticed that he was of mixed parentage, so at least Father's worry that we might all be executed for miscegenation seemed to be unfounded.

He was also strikingly handsome, but I'm not sure whether I noticed that then or a little later.

He gestured our way and called out in Nisuan, "Please do come closer."

We all sped up a little to get closer to him; even those who didn't understand Nisuan understood how warm and friendly his tone was.

As the first of us drew closer, he peered for a moment and then said, "You must be Captain Osepok Tarov, late of the Imperial Expedition to Setepos?"

"Never heard of her," Osepok said dryly, and everyone in both groups laughed. "Yes, of course, I am. And allow me to present Zahmekoses and Priekahm, of the same expedition. I'm afraid our other survivor, Otuz Kimnabex, is not well enough to come out and greet you. And you are—"

"Thetakisus Gereg, assistant to the captain of *Egalitarian Republic*. As soon as our forces secure a perimeter here, we'll introduce you to our captain and our political officer. A preliminary announcement, however—" He lifted a small black cube to his mouth, and suddenly his voice boomed across the square, louder than he could have shouted. "Political Officer Streeyeptin sends his greetings and announces that there will be a complete amnesty for every person of Nisuan descent, for any act in violation of the laws of the Republic committed up to this time, whether knowingly or not, including crimes against the Intrinsic Laws."

There was a long pause. Then Thetakisus said, "Ah, it would be customary if you all said you accepted the amnesty."

"I think that since our new friends are presumed rational, we will consider the amnesty accepted." The voice that came from the doorway above was cool and dry, and sounded mildly amused. "We can always let them rescind it," he added. A slender but very muscular Shulathian male emerged from the doorway and walked down the steps toward us. "And I would imagine that slaves have had little opportunity to pass their language on to their children, so probably most of them did not understand you. So though protocol has been served, and everyone has received amnesty, I'm afraid we can't quite expect them to thank us for it just yet." His words sounded carefully calculated to be friendly, but he seemed to put nothing behind them.

Thetakisus seemed a little embarrassed. "Political Officer Streeyeptin, may I present . . ." I thought it was amazing that he remembered all the names correctly.

"I am Streeyeptin," he said, when Thetakisus had finished. "No family name, as I'm an orphan like Priekahm or Zahmekoses. Since you didn't have political officers in your day, no doubt you are wondering what I do. I think explanations should wait until we've made you more comfortable." He looked around. "Captain Osepok, would you be willing to translate something for me into the local language? We need to announce it to everyone, Nisuan and Seteposian, as soon as possible."

"Certainly," Osepok said. "But Diehrenn is our best scholar and she speaks Real-People without an accent." She motioned me forward, and I nervously approached the Political Officer. I had already decided it was at least as frightening a title as Nim.

Father added, "She is my daughter, and Otuz's."

Streeyeptin nodded. "I know. Diehrenn is mentioned toward the end of your records, as they are stored in the main computer of *Wahkopem Zomos*."

"Then, ah, you know—"

"A great deal. That was why we declared amnesty as soon as we landed. I didn't want any foolishness about hiding past acts, let alone to have to arrest you for them."

Father seemed to relax all at once.

Streeyeptin turned to me. His eyes ran over me once, not as if he were interested, but just to memorize and file my appearance for future reference. "So, you are a historic figure," he said. "The first Nisuan born offworld. How very appropriate that you are a Hybrid! Many people at home will be pleased by that." Not knowing what to say, I stayed silent. He held the message up to me. "Can you read it aloud?"

"I haven't had much practice, but I'll try," I said, and took the page from him. It was easy enough, I realized with relief, as I turned it toward the lights from the lander. " 'Everyone of Nisuan descent is to be brought to this lander; no one is to harm any of them. Bring all Nisuans to the lander at once,' " I read, in Nisuan. "Ah, there's no Real-People word for 'lander'—why don't I say 'Palace Square,' which is where your lander is sitting?"

"Excellent," he said. "Thetakisus, set her up with a loudspeaker, take a party of the other assistants and a couple of ordinary spacers, arm everyone, and make the announcement all over town. Shoot only if provoked, but once they provoke you, make an example that will make them think twice. We want the Seteposians to understand that they *want* to do what we tell them, and they *don't* want to do anything we disapprove of."

"Yes, sir," Thetakisus said. He turned and shouted orders to someone inside. At once four people ran down the steps to join him. Very formally, he said to them, "May I present Diehrenn? She will be acting as our translator tonight. Diehrenn, this is Assistant to the Astrogator Bepemm." She was a tall female with a friendly smile. "This is Assistant to the Engineer Krurix." He was a squat, muscular male, but he smiled just as nicely as Bepemm. "And this is Itenn and Sereterses, both ordinary spacers, or so their rank says." The two smiled at that. Itenn was older, some gray showing in her fur, a Palathian with a huge crest; Sereterses was another mixed-race male (what was the word Streeyeptin had used? Hybrid, that was it), about my age.

I nodded to all of them, politely, having no idea what else I should do. If I did anything wrong, they didn't let me know.

We walked across Palace Square, away from the lander, into the dark and the rain. I wasn't quite sure where we were going or why. The shock of the massacre I had seen was beginning to settle in, along with one wonderful, burning feeling of joy: *No more masters.*

Even so I winced as I passed the massacred Palace Guard. In the dim light and at the distance from them, I had not seen the horrible gouges, big enough to stick the whole first joint of my thumb into them, dotting the bodies, nor that the ground had been sprayed with a fine mist of blood.

"The holes are made by the slugs exiting," Krurix said. "They're so small and go in so fast that you can't see where they go in. The wounds happen when they burst out the other side and—"

"Krurix," Bepemm said, "we don't know much about the situation. It's possible that Diehrenn has friends among the dead, maybe many friends."

"But—"

"Bepemm was looking for a polite way to say 'shut up,' Krurix," Thetakisus explained. "It may have been a mistake for her to try to be polite."

Krurix sighed. "Probably. I'm sorry, Diehrenn. It was thoughtless of me."

I wasn't quite sure how to respond to being taken so seriously. It seemed wrong, somehow, that I was getting that much attention. "Some of them I knew very well," I said, thinking of Set—how just the day before he and I had worked together when we found the probe, and of the years when he had been whatever protection I had.

It got darker as we reached the edge of the square, and I noticed the cool rain more as it made the clay mud slicker under my feet. I felt bad because I didn't regret Set's death more, I realized. Though I had often benefited from his protection, I had still been his slave, and that was the reason he had protected me. Sometimes he had interceded when I had been very afraid of what some Seteposian might do to me. But I had worked when I was too tired, borne pain and sickness, sweated in the heat and shivered in the cold, just so Set could have trivial pleasures and pointless baubles. I had done what he told me, and I had never told him no, because I could not, and because I was so afraid of being given to a worse master.

I felt a little strange about watching him die. But after twenty years with the best master that I could have hoped for—since I didn't have to fear getting a crueler one anymore—all I could summon up for Set was the feeling that I hadn't liked watching him torn in half. I liked that he was dead.

I suppose, if you're a master, that's about as much as you can expect from your slaves. It occurred to me, too, that many of us had bigger grudges against some Seteposians than I had against Set. I wondered whether these newly arrived Nisuans would let us get our hands on those killing cylinders. I hoped so; we were the ones who knew which Seteposians needed killing.

As I thought this, I walked, with my head down, into the dark at the edge of Palace Square. Away from the lander it was now full night, and the clouds had closed in, so that I looked at my feet, partly not to stumble, partly to sort out my feelings, and mainly to avoid thinking about walking in the streets of Real People Town with beings out of my parents' stories.

5

WHEN WE WERE ALL STANDING AT THE EDGE OF PALACE SQUARE, FACING the street that led by the stone tower to the main gate in the inner, stone wall of the town, I felt Thetakisus's hand on my shoulder. Softly, he said, "I'd like you to get used to the loudspeaker. Let's get you a light so you can see what you're reading."

He took out a thin circlet of some material and fastened it around my forehead, getting it snug but not tight; then he pressed something on it and a beam of light stabbed out from the middle of my forehead, so that it pointed wherever I was looking. "Now," he said, "you can see. Let's equip you to talk." He handed me the same small cube he had used when announcing our amnesty, whatever that was, and said, "Look at the surfaces. The side with the narrow slits is the one you talk into. When you want to be loud you just press down here, on this thing that sticks up. And the sound comes out of the round holes on the other side. Go ahead and try it." He took it back from me for a moment, held down the thing that stuck up, and spoke into the narrow slits. "Like this." His voice boomed across Palace Square.

He handed it back to me, and timidly I copied what he had done. "Like—?" I asked, and was so startled at how loud my voice had become that I almost dropped it.

I saw Krurix and Bepemm fighting smiles and felt ashamed. Thetakisus's face was kind. He said, "Just let the amplifier make things louder; you won't need to shout into it. Try again."

"Like this?" I asked timidly, and this time my voice was loud but not overwhelming.

"Just like that. All right, now you read the text aloud, over and over, just like you and Streeyeptin agreed you would, into the amplifier, and we'll walk with you through the city to protect you and maybe collect some refugees."

The next part of the night came back to me in dreams for years afterwards. I quickly got used to what they were asking me to do, and after a few times through the short message I had my Real-People translation of it memorized, so I no longer needed the page. That left me free to look around me.

Everywhere, Real People Town was falling into confusion and chaos. The only thing that seemed to be certain was that Nisuans were supposed to go to the Palace Square, so there were a number of Nisuan children and house slaves winding through the streets, with everyone giving them a wide berth. Now and then a Seteposian would hurry by, carrying a Nisuan baby that the family had been given by Rar to bring up in slavery; once one of them shouted to me, "Please, Diehrenn, if you will, can you tell them I am taking this child to the square as quickly as I can, and we have been good to him?"

I repeated what they had said in Nisuan, and Bepemm said, "Tell her that if that is true, no harm will come to her or her family." I repeated that to the woman. The Seteposian woman seemed to be almost fainting with fear, but she headed toward the brightly lit lander that towered above Real People Town.

"You looked startled," Thetakisus observed, "when she spoke to you. What surprised you?"

I looked down at the ground. "Well," I said, "I'm really not used to anyone asking me rather than telling me, and she said 'please,' the same thing as the Nisuan request for courtesy—it's only used between equals. No Seteposian ever spoke to me that way before. So even though she used my name, it took me a moment to realize she was speaking to me."

I didn't know quite what the glances the Nisuans exchanged meant. They didn't seem to be disapproval of me, yet I could tell they were not pleased.

"Well," Thetakisus said, "I guess we still have some ground to cover, and we should get that done. Streeyeptin wanted to get the word out before anyone got any stupid ideas about harming Nisuans or taking them hostage."

We had already circled the square, first in the inner ring of streets and then in the outer, and thus covered the territory within the stone wall; as I explained to Thetakisus, this meant that we had reached almost all the Nisuans and their masters within Real People Town, because the people beyond the stone wall gate, in the larger outer part of town, were usually too poor to merit Nisuan slaves. "But there are a few outside," I said, "all close to the stone wall. It will be faster if we just go to their huts."

The Nim was not completely heartless or impractical; some Nisuan slaves were invalids from one injury or another; a few, like Captain Osepok and my father, were really too old to work; and then there were a number of "breeders," very fertile females who were kept constantly pregnant or nursing. There were no more than ten Nisuans in the outer town, counting two not-yet-weaned babies, and most were on the gate side of the stone wall. It was a matter of only a few moments to go to each hut.

Still it took us a long while, because we quickly realized that many of the people we were talking to could not move themselves. Soon our party was burdened: two Nisuans lamed by their cruel masters were leaning on Krurix, as a sort of shared crutch; my younger sister Geremm, disabled with pneumonia, was leaning on me; Itenn was carrying two babies, and we were accompanied by mothers carrying two more, plus several Nisuans who could shuffle along but not carry anything themselves. When we reached my father's hut, our last stop, I was relieved to discover that my mother was not there, and there was a note lettered by my father hanging from the lintel that said he and Priekahm had already gotten her to the Palace Square.

As we moved our little party of invalids through the streets back toward the shining tower of the lander, I used the amplifier to repeat the announcement a few times, just in case there were any stragglers or anyone still holding out or hiding. We were getting near Palace Square when something hissed by my face, so close I felt the cool wind of the arrow before I fully knew what it was.

Thetakisus and Sereterses were thinking faster than I was; I later learned that those huge masks they wore permitted them to see in the dark. At the time all wonders seemed possible; if they had both turned into wolves or walked straight up the wall of a house I would have been no more and no less surprised. From their utility harnesses they pulled cylinders small enough to fit in the palms of their hands, touched their own faces once, and then turned and clicked the cylinders with their thumbs, all in one swift movement. At once, from the surrounding darkness, I heard screams. The two Nisuans dashed into the dark together. There were more screams, and I heard a couple of Seteposian voices begging for their lives, then "not my children," and then more screams. A moment later flames leaped up from a house, and by their light I could see Thetakisus and Sereterses dragging still bodies out of the house to line up in the street in front of it.

They returned to us, and Thetakisus said, "I'm afraid I'll need you as translator. This is going to be unpleasant, but it's highly necessary." He turned to Bepemm and said, "Get everyone back to the square. If you're assaulted, same drill I followed—kill the attackers, everyone near them, and everyone in any building they came out of or fled to. Burn all the buildings connected with them. Display the bodies."

Under his mask Krurix looked a little ill; Thetakisus asked him sharply if there was a problem. "No, sir, I'll follow orders, of course," he said.

I got Geremm set up to be supported by three of the mothers who could walk. They headed out to Palace Square, and I returned with the two males to the burning building. A crowd had gathered around, looking at the bodies. Thetakisus and Sereterses kept the cylinders out where people could see them. "It's a hand maser," Thetakisus said as we approached the crowd. "Shoots an invisible beam that cooks flesh in an instant and will set wood or fabric on fire." He pointed at a part of the roof of the house that was not yet on fire and squeezed his hand maser, making another click. With a soft *whoosh*, flames shot up from where he had pointed. The crowd of Seteposians moaned with fear.

"Okay, now use your amp and tell them what I say to you," he said.

I held it to my mouth and translated as Thetakisus explained that he had killed "this bag of garbage" (pointing to the corpse that still wore a quiver of arrows) for taking a shot at us, four others for being with him, and the rest for allowing them to hide behind their house. "This is what will happen to everyone who raises a hand against us and to everyone who assists them in the smallest way, whether deliberately or not," he said, and I repeated it to the Seteposians. "Furthermore, there is to be no gathering or mourning for these bags of garbage; they are to receive no burial or funeral honors and no one is to gather for any purpose connected with their deaths. This crowd is in violation of that order, but because we are merciful we will only punish a few of you this time, so that the rest of you can explain our rules to the other animals."

They stood stunned, not understanding what was about to happen. Sereterses walked into the crowd and grabbed three of them, dragging them forward into the light of the burning house.

I saw something and darted into the crowd for a moment. I heard Thetakisus cry out in surprise, but I didn't stop to explain—I just grabbed and got her by the hair—Esser, the five-year-old who I had been attending. The little beast had had me whipped many times, for no reason other than that I had frustrated some whim or other. I wrapped my fingers in her hair and dragged her over to join the three others, screaming and crying. To make sure she stayed put, I pushed her down onto the pavement, hard, and treated myself to kicking her in the head. She wailed in fear and pain. It was wonderful. "Her too," I said to the startled Thetakisus.

He gestured agreement, his expression under the mask a little baffled. He had me announce that these would suffer the penalty for having formed a crowd around the site of an execution, as an example to the others, and then he and Sereterses clicked the cylinders at them, pointing at their heads. They died instantly in an odor of roasting meat.

Thetakisus held up the maser and announced, through me and the amplifier, that he would use it on anyone who was still in sight after he counted five. The crowd broke and ran in terror. He turned to me and gestured at Esser's body, asking "Why?"

"Because she was my most recent master," I said, "and because she's of the Nim's family. It helped make it clear that they can expect nothing and that they are to obey." I kicked the little corpse once. "Why did you say this was going to be unpleasant?"

It was our first time back on *Republic* after seven days, local time, on the ground, and Bepemm and I had just finished showering and dressing and were considering what to have for dinner. We decided to have everything.

"What a job," I said, after we had both spent a while stuffing our faces. "I don't think I slept an eighth of a day uninterrupted after we got down there."

She yawned. "That's my big plan for after this. A long nap. Who'd have thought . . . well, any of it?"

During those seven days, we had discovered two things: every Nisuan in Real People Town was hell-bent on taking revenge for the decades of slavery, and the inhabitants of Real People Town both expected to be slaughtered and expected to be fed. When the gods arrive, apparently, there's no need to be responsible anymore. At the direction of Prirox, who had managed a great deal of the agriculture for years, we had had to force them to clear canals, carry water, weed and hoe, and do all the other necessary tasks. Then we had discovered that we also had to manage the granaries and put out fires—in short, do almost everything that they had been doing for themselves before we got there. Just before the lander had shuttled us up here for rest and normal food, a group of Seteposians had come to us wanting us to settle a dispute over land, and another group had come to complain that various surrounding villages were not paying taxes they "owed" to the Real People.

The most popular thing we had done—at least among the Nisuans we had rescued—was killing off Nim Rar and all his heirs. Just to make things extra-clear, we also blew up the stone tower and breached the walls. Real People Town, as an imperial capital, was finished. At times I felt sorry for various terrified Seteposians; but when I did, I thought of what I had learned from talking to Diehrenn and her father.

"So are you going to take your native princess back with you?" Bepemm asked, a strange glint in her eye.

"What?" I said, through a mouthful of food.

"Exactly what do you have in mind for Diehrenn?"

I was startled. "Well, I don't think that's my decision—"

Bepemm snorted. "Right. She follows you around like a pet, you spend hours talking to her, you're even learning Real-People from her, and she happens to have a wonderful body and a beautiful face. And all this is coincidence."

It occurred to me that Bepemm might be jealous, but since she and I had never actually been involved, I could see no graceful way to discuss that, so instead I said, "Well, don't be silly. She is one of our best interpreters. She does like working with me, and yes, she's beautiful, but neither she nor I have talked about anything like that."

"And she just happened to come up on this very lander for her dialysis," Bepemm said.

"Well, her mother had regained consciousness—it was about time she got to see her. She's been worried."

Using Soikenn's work from decades before as a starting point, it had only taken Dr. Lerimarsix a couple of days to track down the slowly accumulating toxins produced by the Nisuan immune system trying to deal with ubiquitous unassimilable Seteposian proteins, and to show that those were what was slowly causing kidney and lung failure, as well as early sterility and half a dozen other complications that the Nisuans in Real People Town had not even known they had. Once the problem was solved, he had constructed dialysis rigs to clean out the toxins, and induced-regeneration drugs could then fix up most Nisuans as good as new. He had started on the Nisuans who had arrived on *Wahkopem Zomos*, because they had accumulated more toxins due to eating adult portions of Seteposian food almost from the day they arrived. Now he was starting on the first generation born on Setepos.

"You know, if we'd been a couple of years later," I said, "there might have been no one who spoke Nisuan at all. A lot of the older 'native' generation were very close to the line, or so Dr. Lerimarsix says."

"Do you suppose if they'd had no memory of a time before slavery, and no memory of adults telling them about it, they'd have been less vengeful?" Bepemm asked.

"Being a slave is being a slave, wherever you came from, I think," I said. "I don't think any of us will ever understand how deeply they all hate Seteposians. I don't think I would want to be able to understand."

Bepemm took a large mouthful and chewed vigorously. "Me either," she said. "But seriously, Thetakisus, even if you don't feel anything for Diehrenn, she's clearly fascinated with you."

That made me even more uncomfortable, because the truth was

she'd been haunting my dreams—when I'd had time to sleep, which wasn't often or much. Her ferocity shocked me, her experiences appalled me (from puberty on, she had copulated with whomever she was ordered to copulate with—and seemed to regard it as the least unpleasant part of her job), and yet . . . there was something about her I found really magnificent. Possibly I was just impressed with what she had survived, or with her fierce curiosity and longing to learn everything new right away. Perhaps Bepemm was right and it was only that Diehrenn was beautiful.

From the way Bepemm was glaring at me, I realized I had probably gotten a faraway look in my eyes, right when the subject of Diehrenn had come up—a bad idea. I was trying to think how to correct the situation when Krurix came in, carrying a pastry that was probably part of finishing off *his* big meal. "Do the two of you have a minute to talk?"

Bepemm looked visibly relieved; maybe she hadn't wanted to have a fight, either. "If we can stuff our faces while *you* talk, that's even better."

He sat down, took a bite of the pastry he had carried in, swallowed, and said, "Well, to start with the embarrassing part, it's about the zero-point energy laser again, and the way the plates are working. When I got back and looked at the recorded graphs, from every time we modulate the laser—which we have to do because every time either of the landers docks or launches, and every time we launch a probe, we have to retune it just a little to maintain station—well, the plate responses have been getting weirder. The periods of chaos are taking longer, less and less of the curves are smooth. I'm really afraid it's deteriorating."

"Uh, isn't this something for you to talk to Azir about?" I asked. What he was saying was alarming, but we weren't the people who could do anything about it.

"Yeah. That's what I want to talk to you about. Azir is so scared of going back to Streeyeptin that she won't even try. It *would* throw the schedule off by quite a bit, you know. The overhaul in ballistic orbit would be about ten days, and with having to fly rendezvous maneuvers instead of just coming up like an elevator, each lander would only be able to make a trip every other day or so, I think, instead of the two per day they're making now. So it would really throw Streeyeptin's plans off. But I think if Streeyeptin understands the risk, he's not going to be completely unreasonable. He wants to get the mission accomplished and get home, too. So I think he needs to know that it looks bad, and what's bad about it, and what I wanted to ask you is if you have any brilliant ideas about how to approach him." He took a large bite, chewed hard, and added, "The thing is, I don't care if he's mad at me as long as the ship is safe, but I know I'm a pretty irritating person, and I don't want to blow the chance to explain the situation. And I'm afraid that's just what would happen. I think that—"

"Pardon me," Streeyeptin said, coming in. We all froze. He looked around and sighed. "No, don't think you're in any trouble. Krurix, I wasn't deliberately listening, but I was passing by when you started your conversation. So it is your judgment that we have less time than you had thought before the main drive fails? And do I remember that, if it fails, the ship could be destroyed?"

"Only if it fails during hover, sir," Krurix said. "If we're in orbit or en route, we'd have all the time in the world to fix it, and it's not hard to fix. It's only if we should drop into the atmosphere while the plates are jammed at the bottom that we could get blown up, once the emergency restart kicks in. But if that happened . . . well, then, yes, the ship would be pretty much gone. That's why I'd rather take us to orbit; that would mean we'd have all the time we needed to do the overhaul."

Streeyeptin seemed to consider, and finally said, "Well, there's a sort of compromise that we can make, but I'm afraid it's bad news for the four of us." He saw that he had our attention and went on. "Here's the situation. No doubt it's occurred to you that the Nim's breeding program has put us in a terrible spot? We had planned to have room to take along ten Nisuans, in case a couple of children had been born to the original expedition. Twelve, with a great deal of squeezing and discomfort, is the limit. We can't take even one-third of the Nisuans off of Setepos and back to Nisu in *Egalitarian Republic*.

"Now, that's bad enough. I've already sent a radio message back to Nisu about all this, and when they get it, four years from now, assuming ships aren't desperately needed for dozens of things they probably *will* be needed for . . . then I would guess it would only take them two years to get a rescue expedition together, which would take about four and a half years to get here—so we're looking at any help being at least a decade away.

"But there's another problem, one that none of you would have had much reason to think about just yet. The Nisuans here are former slaves and they hate Seteposians violently. Ergo, if we arm them and tell them to wait for us here, all we're going to do is recreate the Nim's empire with a Nisuan royal family. Equality, if it means anything, has to extend to everyone—even to Seteposians living in the Stone Age—and we need people here on the spot to make sure that what develops is a fair and free society, to teach these people, both the former slaves and the former masters, how to live together, at least as well as we've managed on Nisu. The most obvious person for such a job is a political officer, and hence I'm volunteering."

"You mean—you're going to stay here for ten more years?" Krurix asked, incredulous.

"One doesn't always get to pick what one's duty is," Streeyeptin said. "There are other implications as well. First of all notice it's ten years until the rescue ship gets here, then another four and a half before it gets back to Nisu. So it will be more nearly fifteen years before I see home again. But secondly, because there will be a permanent team here, there is no special need for *Egalitarian Republic* to remain. As soon as necessary equipment has been delivered to the ground, the ship can leave. So for those who do stay on board the ship, this cuts the mission short by almost a year."

"Lucky them," Krurix said, looking down. "You said a team would be staying with you?"

"Well, what I need are several junior officers with a mix of skills," Streeyeptin said. "I'm purely a social planner and a policeman, you know. Relevant to the job but not capable of doing it all by myself. I need people with technical backgrounds and officer training to help get a functional society going here. Senior officers have to fly the ship, ordinary spacers don't have enough education . . ."

I saw which way it was going and used the same good common sense that had gotten me the job of captain's assistant. "I'll stay," I said. When it's clear that they want you to volunteer, it's a bad idea to drag your feet. And everyone knows you really can't fight a Political Officer. Had I tried to get out of staying, I knew things would go badly for me, and I would still end up staying. By volunteering, I at least got the credit for doing it. Besides, though it probably would not help me make captain, it would give me an important role in a major scientific project, it would establish me as one of the people most experienced on frontier worlds at just the time when they were figuring out who would hold executive positions for the Migration itself—and doing Streeyeptin a big favor would probably set up some political connections. There was more than one way to climb the pyramid of power.

And, a small voice in the back of my head said, there was always Diehrenn.

I never asked Bepemm what her reasons were for volunteering; probably many of them were the same as mine. I was much more surprised when, with a strange shudder, Krurix followed suit. Maybe it was because Bepemm and I were the closest thing he had to friends, or perhaps he had just figured out the situation about the same way I had. There are things it's better not to know about each other, I guess.

And just like that, we were in for a decade more on Setepos, trying to bring the former slaves and former masters together, through a hundred centuries of progress, almost overnight. When I lay down to take my nap, I made sure I slept well and long. I had a feeling it would be a very long time before that happened again.

6

TWO EIGHTDAYS LATER, KRURIX AND I WERE SWEATING OVER THE FOURTH crate of lab supplies that we had wrestled into headquarters—the former palace—that morning. "Quote me some numbers," I said to him.

He grunted and lifted; I grabbed the other side of the crate, and with one big heave we got it onto the table where it was supposed to go. Then he sighed and said, "All right. Current schedule is for seventeen more lander trips to and from *Egalitarian Republic*. Last three trips bring down the dialysis rig. You and I unload all that by ourselves because Bepemm is going to be busy cramming enough medical information to pass as our doctor. One last down and up for our farewell dinner and to get Otuz, Priekahm, Osepok, and Zahmekoses onto *Egalitarian Republic*. Eighteen trips at one per day for two landers means nine days, but they're taking longer and longer to get each fresh trip underway. So my current bet is that we get three more leaves on the ship before it departs. Pick your three favorite meals and think about your three favorite kinds of shower."

I sighed. "Same numbers as before, then."

"Always worth rechecking," he said. "Well, that's all they left on the porch this time. It's half a day till the next lander comes back down, and Bepemm doesn't like to work with either of us on the stuff she's setting up. Want to get some food and rest a little?"

"Suits me completely." I mopped my face with the piece of native cloth that hung down around my head; we had gotten in the habit of wearing the same head covering the Seteposians and the Nisuans born there did. It was one more thing Bepemm was angry at us about. "I think I saw the cooks roasting a couple of goats earlier this morning. Let's go see if those are done."

We walked through the camp that had been Real People Town, saying hello to people who waved and said hello to us. That was mostly Nisuans, but a few Seteposians had learned that as long as they accepted the new order, we weren't going to make life impossible for them. Except for the greetings, we didn't talk much, but it was a friendly, companionable silence.

It occurred to me how strange that was. I wasn't sure how much I had changed, but Krurix surely had, all for the better, and somehow though our forty-four eightweeks subjective aboard ship hadn't made us friends, the short time working together on Setepos had. Some of it, I knew, was that the more accepted he felt, the fewer jokes he made and the easier he was to talk to. He was smart, and very loyal to anyone who was kind to him.

Then too, since Bepemm had decided she was permanently mad at me, he was who I had to hang around with. Perhaps some of my not liking him before had been a matter of seeing him through Bepemm's eyes.

And finally, unlike Bepemm and Streeyeptin, hard as it was to admit, we sort of liked it here. Not enough to look forward to losing our favorite foods, showers, recorded entertainment, and comfortable bunks, but enough so that whenever it was time to "hurry up and wait," we tended to go exploring in town or nearby together, even if it was only to try some Seteposian food or to get the view from a hilltop.

"Streeyeptin seems pretty worried," Krurix commented as we sat down with our sticks of chunks of roasted goat and onions. "I don't think it's just that there's so much to get done and so little time to do it, either. I think his political meetings with the younger Nisuans haven't been going the way he wishes they would. And it's not only because he doesn't speak Real-People very well, or because they haven't learned much Nisuan just yet."

I took a bite and chewed for a moment or two. "Well," I said, "remember it took us a while to find out that he was basically a decent guy, even if he does have kind of a rules-are-rules approach to things. With the language barrier—and the fact that he's trying to talk them into exactly what they don't want to do, establishing a decent relationship with Seteposians—well, there's bound to be a clash, just as you said. I don't see why you have to look for any other causes for the trouble."

Krurix sighed. "I just have a feeling that that's not all of it," he said. "You know, they may have been in the Stone Age a few eightdays ago, but they aren't stupid. And the first thing an intelligent animal learns is to tell other intelligent animals, particularly ones in authority, what they want to hear."

I almost choked on the goat. "Too right," I said, laughing. "Well, when does he get back here to resume political education? He was supposed to be on this last flight—did his note say when he would be back?"

"Apparently it's taking him a while to get arrangements made on *Egalitarian Republic* for Itenn to take over as Acting Political Officer, and that's cutting into the time for writing and transmitting his reports," Krurix said. "He's afraid that if our transmitter here goes down or doesn't work well, it might be a long time before any of his reports get back to Nisu, and they might not realize how urgent the situation is here. But it *is* a nuisance not to have him around. He's the one with the plan and the authority, after all—"

At first I thought the deep rumble was thunder, but then it was much too loud, and went on too long. A great light shone through the clouds.

Krurix leaped to his feet, letting his lunch land wherever, and I followed him as we raced back to the palace. The thunder grew louder, the light from overhead grew brighter, and as we ran we felt a low pulsing rumble through our feet. Suddenly we were knocked from our feet by a savage, hot wind; we rolled, got up, ran again, and were knocked down twice more by further shocks.

By the time we got to headquarters Bepemm was already there, talking frantically into the radio. "Acknowledge contact, please, *Egalitarian Republic*," she was saying. "Please acknowledge contact." She groaned with frustration. Without looking up from the control panel, she added, "Run playback on the communications link, please, Krurix. I want to make sure we don't miss any message that might—"

Krurix was at the other board in an instant and his fingers raced over the keys. "One message, short," he said, "which probably means—"

The played back message crackled through the speaker. The voice was flat and expressionless. "Baegess, *Egalitarian Republic*, reporting. Zero-point energy plates locked up in main ship drive laser. Ship is in free fall toward Setepos. Unable to disable the emergency plate separator, hence engines will reactivate with probable catastrophic results. We are attempting—"

The message broke off.

The rumble through our feet had ceased, and when I looked outside the door, there was no longer a great light shining through the clouds; rather, it was becoming as dark as night, and a high wind was rising rapidly, sucking up dust and ripping thatch from roofs. I felt rather than saw Bepemm and Krurix come up behind me. "You were right," Bepemm said softly to him. "You were completely right."

"It sure doesn't matter now," he responded. "What are we going to do?"

"Well," I said, "first question is what is *it* going to do out there. What I'd say is we try to work that out, then make some plans, and then see how many people we can get to follow the plans."

"Back to basics," Bepemm said. "So first the big laser cut off. What happened then?"

"The sea stopped boiling and the steam above it stopped superheating," Krurix said. "Given how hot that was, it cooled very fast. Probably in almost no time at all you had pretty good vacuum at the center— which might account for the booming noise we heard, just like the way the air rushes back together after a lightning stroke is over. Then the laser came back on when the emergency separator took hold—"

"Wait a minute," I said. "There was an interval there—while it wasn't running—and in that time Setepos rotated. So when the laser came back on, the ship was not only much lower but also some distance to the west."

Bepemm's face grew pale. "That means almost for certain that instead of down into already-formed clouds, the laser fired abruptly with everything it had out of a clear sky and onto the sea. And from much lower down—"

"Probably it had fallen more than halfway to the surface," Krurix said. "So four times the energy intensity at the surface. A lot of seawater blew up into steam, and the column of superheated air killed the ship. So we have a great big vacuum at one point, and an enormous load of steam at high pressure just west of it."

"A hurricane," I said. "It's going to make a huge hurricane, within an eighth of a day at the outside. The wind's about to get very high, and it is really going to *rain*. And we're sitting in a river valley with a lot of high ground around us, and almost all our people are in flimsy shelters that are going to get knocked down by the wind. We've got to get to some solid shelter, on high ground, right away."

"I can take you to a dry cave some distance up one of the mountains, anyway," Diehrenn said, running up to us out of the rain. "What's going on? Does the big thunder mean something happened to your ship? And what does your word 'hurricane' mean?"

"A big storm," I said. "Probably bigger than anyone here can remember." I explained the situation in a few short sentences.

"We probably have only an eighth of a day or so," Krurix added. "Is there room for everyone in that cave?"

"There's room for all the Nisuans," Diehrenn said, "and that's all who're going. If your ship isn't there to back you up anymore, we can't afford to take care of the Seteposians anymore. And they'll manage a lot better than we will in any case; they're native here and we don't belong. So, especially since your political officer isn't here anymore, let's not hear any more about what we 'owe' our Seteposian 'brothers.' "

Rather than start an argument when it would have been pointless, I said, "We need to get going in as short a time as we can manage. Can you get everyone together—"

"Right here, as fast as I can. It won't be long," Diehrenn said, and ran back into the rain.

All of us grabbed our packs and rammed everything we could think of into them; as we were finishing that, the first Nisuans started to arrive. We had spare packs and bags, and all of these we loaded with emergency rations; any spare space in the packs of anyone just arriving got something vital or something edible. That was as much organization as we could manage.

Meanwhile, outside, the rain was picking up and the winds were rising. "We'll need to get moving soon or we won't be able to move," Krurix was saying as Diehrenn returned with Prirox.

"We've gotten everyone who can walk or be carried together," she said. "Prirox, the cave the Nim's children used to play in is what I've got in mind. I think we'll have to take the straight uphill trail because the easier one crosses two streams and that's not going to be possible today."

"Right," Prirox said. "Are we ready to go?"

No one argued so we were. We let Diehrenn and Prirox lead, and we three assistants, weapons drawn, brought up the rear. When we stepped outside the building, the wind was howling and the cold rain blew in sheets; fortunately the high ground was downwind from town, so most of the two hundred and fifty or so refugees had their backs to the weather. Unfortunately for us, as the rearguard, we had to walk backwards and try to keep our eyes clear.

Hand masers are useless in the rain—the microwaves they put out in a tight beam are scattered and absorbed by the water drops—so we were carrying microslug guns. We had not gotten forty steps from headquarters before we saw Seteposians racing for it. Of course, by letting all the Nisuans in town know that we needed to leave, we had also let the Seteposians know that we *were* leaving—Diehrenn had to announce it in Real-People because so few of our people spoke their own language. You would think that might mean Seteposians would also flee to the hills, and for all I know some of them did. Most, however, decided to see what they could loot now that we were leaving.

We had locked the doors behind us, but that wasn't going to keep the mob out for long; they were quite capable of pulling the building down with their bare hands. And since so much of the equipment we would need if we survived the storm was still in there, we couldn't let them loot and burn. Perhaps the winds or the flood would destroy the building—we could do nothing about those—but we could at least try to make sure that the would-be looters didn't.

We fired short bursts into the crowd; the front rank wavered, then broke and ran. In the heavy rain we could barely see what we were firing at, but we could see shapes moving so we kept shooting until we couldn't see any more. Krurix chanced a shot with his hand maser; it couldn't get through the rain, but it did make an impressive rumbling boom as the rain it hit exploded into steam and then recondensed.

"Not a bad trick!" I shouted over the rain. "Bet it scares them!" We all fired a few maser shots, and as the headquarters building faded into the rain, we stopped for a moment, letting the refugees gain a little distance from us, and then sprayed the area with microslugs. The screams were gratifying. "I guess some people just can't grasp an idea," I said. "And at least in this weather they can't get much use out of those bow-and-arrow contraptions. I think we've done all we can and now we might as well catch up with the group."

As we went over the first ridge outside of town, water and wind lashing us further, we looked back; it looked like flames were leaping up from Real People Town. "Probably getting a little carried away about the end of the world," Bepemm shouted. "Nothing we can do about it right now!"

"How far is the cave?" I asked, shouting to Krurix.

"One more ridge and then a mountainside, I think," he shouted back. "At least after this next valley we're up above the flood level—I think."

It wasn't long before we were between the two ridges, but even then water ran over the tops of our feet and we had to go carefully; a dry wash was about to become a raging river and there was an obvious danger of flash flood. Still, we made it to the top of the second ridge without much incident, except of course that almost everyone was tired and cold, and since we were following the ridgeline from there on, we were more exposed to the wind. Rain was falling so thick that I never noticed when the ridge joined the low mountain. It all seemed to be up, up, and more up until finally, staggering and gasping, I found myself stumbling into a dark place where it wasn't raining. "Here we are," Diehrenn said next to me, but it was so dark I couldn't see her. "I think we all made it."

I turned back and looked; very dim gray light came into the cave through curtains of windblown rain. The cave smelled of clay and bodies.

"I think I can make a fire under the overhang," Krurix said, "if we've got any fuel."

There was a big pile of wood that Prirox and Diehrenn had left for the trips up here that the Nim's children and grandchildren liked to make, and that was quickly passed forward to Krurix. He stacked the logs into a neat pile, then stepped back and shot them several times with his hand maser. Flames leaped up from where he pointed, and after about twenty shots he had the beginnings of a comfortable fire. Some of the smoke went into the cave, and because it was acrid, now and then when the wind blew the wrong way it would start people coughing. All the same, we all packed up around it, enjoying the warmth (even though perhaps more of that came from each other), the light, and the sense of being out of immediate danger.

As the day grew dimmer and the wind more fierce, we banked the fire and everyone piled together in groups in the cave to sleep. Outside the wind howled louder and harder and rain came down thicker; the hurricane itself had hit.

It had been an exhausting day. I was sound asleep as soon as I lay down. When I woke in the morning, I was already beginning to understand that we might very well be on this planet for good. Nothing helps the acceptance of hard facts as much as sleeping on them.

When two hundred and fifty people sleep together in about twenty communal piles, it doesn't take much to get everyone awake on a cold summer morning outdoors; for one thing, if you try to remain asleep, your "blankets" get up and walk away, and your "pillows" crawl out from under you. Thus everyone was up and about the next morning at about the same time. Daylight showed us a mountainside redecorated with mudslides and a scoured landscape below partially buried in deep clay mud.

The artificial hurricane, though fierce, had not been long lived. Probably it would have done little damage if it had happened in a normal season. But the rain that fell out from the plume of steam that *Egalitarian Republic* had formed, after forty days, had so saturated the ground that there was no place for any of the water that fell except as runoff. As it had poured fiercely down the mountainside, the weakened and rotting brush, dying from soaked roots and lack of sun, ripped out by howling winds, had not done much to hold it. Water, mud, brush, and all had washed down between the ridges and into the rivers, forming temporary dams of rubble here and there. The lakes behind those dams had filled and spilled within sixteenths of days, sending huge waves cascading down onto the floodplains.

We made our way back slowly, keeping a good guard ahead and behind, because we had no idea how many Seteposians might have survived, but we knew for certain who they would blame for this, and they might well think that with the ship gone our power was gone as well. In fact, we saw only three of them, and they broke and ran as soon as they saw the company of us. Diehrenn said she thought they were escaped slaves, not Real People. Probably they had been afraid that we were still working for the Real People.

We reached Real People Town just after noon, delayed by the problems of mud, flooding, and having to take so many of the old, weak, sick, and very young with us. Still, so far as we could determine, more by luck than by skill, we had gotten the whole surviving Nisuan population of Setepos out of town and back with no deaths or even serious injuries. I mentioned that to Krurix, and he grinned at me. "Well, if I were a review board, I'd give us all medals," he said. "Unfortunately, those wouldn't do us any more good than not getting them, which I think is more likely."

I laughed; maybe I was getting used to his sense of humor. "Well, I'll take anything that'll make me feel better right now," I said. "And there's not much to feel good about."

We had rigged a line from a piece of rubble to a broken tree across the river; now our little band was crossing, clinging to the line, with able bodies between anyone who might have trouble keeping a grip. The water was only waist high on an adult anyway, so it was more a case of being careful than of any great danger. Now the last of our group, escorted by Prirox and Weruz, were coming up on the bank, and we were forming up for a cautious advance into Real People Town. To judge from the mud and rubble in front of us, the flood had been deep enough to sweep right through the town, but probably not to cover it. What we had seen from the ridge had looked like many buildings still standing, but there had been nothing moving and no signs of life.

The main track to the front gate was no longer visible as such; it had been cut through with gullies, buried by rubble in other places, and mostly had just reverted to mud, its deeply worn spots filled in with silt.

We picked our way along carefully, past drowned goats and piles of brush, till we reached the remains of the wooden palisade. Probably the huge holes we had knocked into it had helped keep the rest up; it was in surprisingly good shape where it still stood. Much of the wreckage from the town had washed up against it: logs, thatch, bits of garments. There was a dead infant Seteposian in one pile as well.

"Nothing of use to us, and it's a sanitation hazard," Bepemm said. "Once we've scouted the whole works, probably we should burn the larger piles."

"Looks like someone beat us to it," Krurix said. "There are fire scars on all the standing hut walls."

He was right; a little distance further into the ruins showed us many that were more fire-damaged still. We found more bodies of very young and very old Seteposians, and at least one young female whose body had been battered severely, though whether by other Seteposians or by the water and storm was impossible for us to tell.

"There wasn't much lightning to start a fire—at least not up on the mountain—and it's hard to see how a fire could have spread in all that rain," I said. "And most of it didn't burn much. I think they probably fired every building they could. It looks like at least one of the old ones died of knife wounds, not drowning. I wonder what happened here?"

Diehrenn raised her shoulders and let them drop, a gesture the Nisuans here had learned from the Seteposians. It could mean a lot of things: complete indifference, lack of knowledge, contemptuous dismissal, sometimes only that an answer was too obvious to bother with. Bepemm, who was the best of us at speaking Real-People, had begun to do it as well. When there was no answer for a few more steps, I finally said, "Er, my question was serious. Do you think you know what happened?"

Bepemm answered. "I would guess they were panicked. It looked like something bad had happened which only the gods knew about. Probably they heard Diehrenn and Prirox summoning people to the palace and figured that whatever was going to get us might get them as well. And so . . ."

"But why would they panic and burn their own town down?" Krurix asked.

"Because they're savages," Diehrenn said flatly. "The bulk of the population were slaves who just wanted to go back to their conquered villages, and all they knew was that the Nim's army came and took them and made them work here. So when they got the chance they ran for it; a lot of them set fires to cover their tracks. And besides, many of the Real People themselves were children of mothers taken captive in war, and they didn't have much idea what was going on either. The Nim didn't spread a lot of knowledge around, so they had only a vague knowledge of what was going on. After we took over, they were hanging around here because we fed them and helped them rebuild and they didn't have anywhere else to be anyway. So when it looked like everything was falling apart, there was nothing much to keep them here, and their first thought was that something a lot bigger than themselves was angry. And once someone got the idea that the *town* was what the gods hated, well, in practically every religion around here, you purify things by burning them. They had to get rid of the bad town. The smart ones ran up into the hills and are probably still running. The dumb ones just ran until the flood caught them. And that's the end of the Real People, which is a fine thing if you ask me."

We had come to the ruin of the old stone gate for the inner wall of the city: a crude affair, formed with a lintel with stones piled on top of it, rather than any sort of arch. We had blown it up, along with the tower, because it was a symbol of the old Nim's power. Now it was blocked; the heaps of stones had furnished solid objects for junk to catch on. It took us some time, even with lots of people helping, to clear out the rubble.

The stone part of town showed just as many signs of fire damage, especially inside the buildings; probably, since it was a little higher up, the water had gotten there later. It looked as if the flood had crested about a bodylength high on most walls.

Our headquarters had been burned and most of the furniture smashed. Many small objects were missing, but whether from fire, flood, or theft it was impossible to say. The old plank roof had fallen in at two points.

It looked like a complete loss, but a little more searching revealed that they hadn't bothered to open crates, a lot of things strewn about were merely dirty and muddy, and whatever theft had happened had been extremely hasty. Too, it looked like the rain and flood had extinguished the fire before it destroyed everything. "There's a lot we can salvage," I said, "and I guess what we can do is set up the best camp we can, get everything out of here we can, and then go . . . somewhere. Or stay here and settle. Or something."

"There seems to be a failure in our planning department," Krurix said.

Bepemm turned on him. "Oh, of course. And I suppose you have some plan for making all this work? In two generations we'll be back to the Stone Age like every other savage around here, unless we—"

Krurix raised a hand; I had been trying to get him to apologize rather than defend, so I was happy that he said, "Just a badly placed joke. Look, since yesterday afternoon we've been doing nothing but run. Between all the packs we probably have two days food. With the flood and all, we're going to have to rig up a still or something before we can even think about drinking the water around here. Everyone's tired and there's too much work to do. I was teasing Thetakisus because we just went through this horrible mess, with him leading most of the way, and everyone is safe and alive, and he was about to start blaming himself for not knowing exactly what to do next. It was a joke between friends. I'm sorry I offended you."

Bepemm sat down abruptly on a log. "I'm sorry, too. And I'm very tired. If anyone has any suggestions—"

I shrugged. "We'll have to set a watch, build a couple of fires, and sleep in the open tonight, probably right on Palace Square, since that looks sort of dry. It's a good thing it's summer, I suppose. We can lay some log floors out of driftwood to get ourselves out of the mud—that shouldn't take long. After that I suggest we mostly get food and rest, and then tomorrow morning we start clearing mud out of the usable buildings. Not much of a plan, but it will do for the moment, I think."

At least it gave everyone something to do. We got our little camp together and set some of the younger males on watch, teaching them how to use the hand masers and microslug guns and just sort of hoping that either they would be responsible enough or the Seteposians would be too afraid to approach us.

I couldn't say which was the case, because I was asleep instantly and I was aware of nothing until Diehrenn awoke me the next morning. Breakfast was a ration bar and a drink of water, not any worse than what we'd often had during training years ago, and apparently a party had gone out to see if it could bring in goat, deer, or pig, so there was some hope of a better meal to come by nightfall. "Well," I said, "I guess we pick the stone buildings that aren't too full of mud and junk, and get everyone to work. A couple of days hard labor should get us enough places for everyone to sleep under a roof, and then—"

Suddenly I heard the most wonderful sound I had ever heard in my life: a duet of screeching hoots that went on and on. In a moment, everyone was looking at the sky. There, hardly bigger than the tip of my small finger now, but growing rapidly as they drew nearer, descending slowly using only their aerostats, were both of *Egalitarian Republic*'s landers.

7

THE NEXT FEW MOMENTS WERE LONG; IT WAS BEYOND HOPE THAT ALL THE rest of the crew had been on the lander, and so we knew we would hear bad news mixed with the good. They must already know from our not responding that we had no radio.

"Why would they have gone to aerostat so high up?" Bepemm asked. "That's a tricky landing—they're going to have to come down out in the fields."

"Hmmm." Krurix looked at the descending ship. "Could be they weren't en route when the fall started. If they had to do a quick getaway from the ship, they might have burned a lot of propellant without a chance to take on more—or if they got away really late, the shockwave from the atmospheric explosion might have given them some damage."

"So they might be just as helpless as we are?" Bepemm asked.

"Not quite. They always have their antimatter charge. The propellant is plain old liquid hydrogen, and they can make that from water here. Built in equipment for it. So they might be good as new in twenty-four hours." He sighed. "If that's true, all we need is somewhere to go."

Given that none of us was formally a leader, I suppose you can't really say that discipline fell apart as the lander descended. Everyone rushed out onto the field in front of the ruined wooden palisade to watch the first lander come in. "I think you're right," I noted to Krurix, as we ran with the others. "Look how little he's using the positioning jets—just enough to avoid coming down on rocks and trees or in the big mud pot there. He's trying to conserve propellant, for sure."

We came to a halt in the mud, and Bepemm said, "He?"

"Captain Baegess," I said.

There was a long silence while my two friends looked at each other. Very gently, Krurix said, "Thetakisus, he'd be the last one to leave the ship. There wouldn't have been time. Whoever it is—"

The lander slid downward, moving very slowly sideways in the slight breeze, before settling onto the muddy plain. I had a bad moment when I thought a leg might sink in a soft spot and tip the lander over, but it settled almost straight, a short spray of mud squirting up. There was a loud slurping hiss as the ballast tanks filled with compressed air, and the lander had arrived.

Immediately, without waiting, the next lander came in. It seemed to be flown even more awkwardly, and abruptly I realized—"That one's empty, someone's flying it on remote," I said. It bumped down to the landing field, sending up huge sprays from puddles, but it stayed upright even when the air hissed back in for compression and it settled onto its feet.

The steps of the first lander came down, and First Officer Beremahm stepped out. I was glad to see her—and miserable because I knew it meant Captain Baegess had not gotten away. We approached slowly; Itenn came down the steps, followed by Tisix and Proyerin, still pulling off the remote rig he had used to fly the other lander down. And that was all.

I walked forward, the two other assistants behind me. Beremahm looked as if she expected us to strike her. "These are all we saved," she said. "We were on board doing repairs when the ship started to fall. The captain overrode our doors to seal us, then she punched jettison and we were outside before we knew what she was doing. Then she jettisoned the empty lander and all of a sudden its robot pilot was calling for a signal from us—she must have told it to do that in her last few moments alive. I . . ." She fell forward and I caught her; she was sobbing.

"She's been very . . . not good . . . ever since," Proyerin whispered to us. I nodded, and we got Beremahm back up the steps and into the lander, hustling her over to a temporary bunk. Bepemm had had more medical training than any of the rest of us, so we let her attend to Beremahm. Krurix and Proyerin immediately started jabbering about exactly what shape each lander was in and how much repair it would need—listening with half an ear, it sounded to me like it wouldn't be much. I turned to Itenn and Tisix, two ordinary spacers, both among our best crew, and said, "Well, I guess I should hear from you. If the First Officer's . . . not well, then I guess Proyerin is our senior officer, and I'm theoretically his second. What happened exactly?"

Itenn sighed. She looked exhausted, as if she had been asking herself that question for the whole day since the ship had gone down. "Just what Beremahm said. One moment we were using the ship's vacuum system to clean up junk from the last trip up we'd made, wiping down and greasing and tightening, you know, all the stuff you have to do around a working machine. Proyerin was in the back. He'd just finished flushing out the liquid hydrogen tank and he had it about five percent filled. Beremahm was doing a checklist run through the lander astrogation system . . . and then all of a sudden we were weightless. Just like that."

Tisix picked up the story. "Well, sir, something clicked for me and Beremahm at the same time. We'd been in the cockpit when Krurix was talking about the thing that might go wrong, how the plates might stick together, so we both knew. We were closed but not sealed, so we started for the doors—I don't know, hoping to get to the bridge, I suppose—but when you're suddenly weightless, well, there's not much you can do. We had no footing, nothing to grab onto right away, and while we were getting ready, there's a sudden thump and hiss, and we know we've been sealed from outside. Then there was a huge thud and we fell sideways into a bulkhead, and by the time we got untangled from that there was space and sky and Setepos under us, all whirling around in the viewport. I braced my feet on the bulkhead, jumped to the controls, slammed one fist on the power-up button and the other on the emergency autopilot. In a second we started to get the right attitude, with our tail down, as the side jets kicked in and the autopilot got us righted. Then the autopilot asked me for a course. I saw the *Republic* falling away below us, already starting to glow orange, and felt the lander shaking and rocking. I had about one breath to decide, or I'd never have done it, but I pointed at the first thing on the menu that would work, 'low ballistic orbit,' and then the main engine fired hard enough to knock us all flat and nearly black us out—we must've pulled five gravities instantaneously, and none of us braced for it. But it did throw us up to safety—using more than half our remaining fuel."

Itenn added, "It was brilliant that he did that in such a short time—and brilliant of the captain to remember he could save us and the other lander. I just wish there had been a crew in it; I think they must have been taking a break at that moment.

"Our cameras caught what happened to *Egalitarian Republic* and it was horrible. They must have been well down toward the stratosphere and parts of the ship already burned off—with luck all of them were dead from the heat—before the emergency separator kicked in and the ship's computer fired the engine with everything it had. The blast ate the ship instantly, and we saw waves with the naked eye, a hundred bodylengths high or more, rolling away from the blast. The air and steam was white-hot all the way up into the ionosphere. If Tisix had been two breaths later, we might still have started to climb out of the atmosphere, but that white-hot shock wave would have had us for sure."

Tisix gestured agreement. "I think Proyerin is right. He looked at the motion picture of the end of *Egalitarian Republic* and he says he thinks the disperser was already burnt off—you know nothing on that ship was ever intended to be in the atmosphere, and a thin structure like that would have burned right off it, just like all the little struts and pods and antennae did. So when the zero-point energy laser kicked in, it probably sent a collated beam, not a dispersed one, at full power. It would have punched right through the sea instantly and made the rock on the seabed vaporize; the explosion was even worse than Krurix thought it would be." He clutched himself tightly and added, "Anyway, there we were in orbit, getting any kind of a look at all about every fourteenth of a day, with practically no propellant. Proyerin was going insane—that was pretty rough treatment for an engine that was only about half-worked-on—and he was crawling all over it, swearing and complaining, even before he found out there was another lander he'd have to fly by telemetry, and that the orbit it had been kicked out into was high and elliptical and practically at right angles to ours. And Beremahm . . . Beremahm . . ."

"Was sitting and crying," Itenn finished for him. "It's not her fault," she added defensively. "You knew that she and the captain were lovers?" she asked me.

"I was the captain's assistant. I had to know where to find him, all the time," I said. "Yes. And it had happened very suddenly . . . and that sudden feeling of weightlessness—she must have felt helpless—"

Tisix gestured agreement. "I managed to think of something to do and I still felt helpless. I thought I was going to get blown up any instant, actually. And then for a while we thought we didn't have propellant enough to make a successful reentry—we thought we were stuck up there for good, or that we might have to rendezvous and dock with the other lander to get back down, since it had somewhat more fuel. Fortunately we came up with two good ideas that just barely got us here— have you ever heard of 'aerobraking'?"

"Bouncing off the atmosphere to lose velocity? I studied it in officer training," I said. "It's how they did reentries in the early days of space exploration, centuries ago. And theoretically you can use it to conserve propellant. You mean you *did* that? And you just learned it from the library in the lander's computer?"

"Well, I spent half a day flying it in simulation," Tisix said. "I wasn't about to try to get it right the first time without some kind of practice. Proyerin sort of remembered that there was such a thing, and we looked it up in the computer, and there it was. But it wouldn't have done any good if he hadn't had a brilliant thought. He realized that the lander's drinking water, and the water in the recycler, could be processed through the propellant generator to make hydrogen, same way we're using the water down here to refill the tanks. And to get down to a workable velocity we only needed the hydrogen from nineteen units of water, and we had fourteen."

"You mean you had fourteen in the tank already, so you only needed to use five units of drinking water?"

Tisix grinned, and Itenn did as well. "We really should let you find out from Proyerin," Itenn said. "If we ever get back to Nisu, he'll be bragging about this one to his engineer buddies for the rest of his life."

"We had fourteen units of water," Tisix said. "Eight from the drinking water—it hadn't been refilled. One from a unit I'd been using to clean up a mess at the time that the accident happened. Five from the wastewater system. We needed five more. And then it occurred to Proyerin that the processor could separate out the water and other hydrogen compounds from any fluid. So—" He held his arm up proudly, showing me the bandage; Itenn showed me hers as well.

"Not bad flying, if I do say so myself," he said. "A procedure I'd never done before, in a ship that was only supposed to aerobrake in an emergency . . . and I'd just lost more than a unit of blood. I'm just glad that the lander we were operating as a robot didn't need my blood, too; it had more fuel to start with and a full wastewater tank, and we were able to direct a patch-through from where we were to get that processed."

I realized my mouth was hanging open and managed to stammer out that it was very good indeed. Before I had to think of anything else to say, Bepemm came into the little chamber where we had been talking. "Beremahm is suffering from exhaustion," she said, "and plain old grief, which is going to be hitting all of us soon. The immediate cause of her symptoms, though, is a concussion from when she was thrown against the wall as the lander was ejected. From the look of her brain scan, she was hit hard enough to leave her severely disoriented and dazed for at least a short time, and then while she was still in the earliest phase of the concussion she took five gravities of acceleration. That would disorient and disable anyone. But I think the worst of it is shame. She's had a perfect record and gone through a thousand emergencies before; she didn't think she was a person who would have a breakdown at a critical moment."

"None of us thought so either," Tisix said. "And none of us would have done any different from what she did, if we'd been hit in the head that hard."

"I've given her a sedative, and an IV to bring her blood sugar up. We'll start her on antidepressants in about a halfday, but I want to keep her under for at least a full day, until we can be sure that she's not going to go into a deep depression that we don't have the equipment to deal with here. But I think if I do that—according to what the medical advisor program in the lander's computer says—she has a pretty good chance for a full recovery."

Proyerin and Krurix had leaned in to hear the diagnosis as well, and Proyerin said, "Well, as ranking officer at the moment, I would love to be able to hand the job back to her. Let's do exactly what you just said. Meanwhile I guess we try to get an inventory of people and resources, and get every gadget that we can working."

"Spoken like an engineer," Krurix said, smiling.

"Absolutely," Proyerin agreed. "Making stuff work is something I understand, and I'd rather do what I understand."

Since we had the lander's radio available, we could be fairly sure that the signals we were sending were getting through to Nisu, and that they at least knew we were here and what had happened to us—or rather they *would* know, in a bit over four years. That wasn't any great consolation—it would be still more years before we got even a simple acknowledgment—but it was ever so slightly better than feeling that we were stranded forever.

During the two days while we got things together and hoped Beremahm would recover, Proyerin was awake almost the whole time, digging things out of the palace and seeing if he could get them to work. Krurix shared in that work most of the time. As much as anyone could be under the circumstances, those two were happy, with so much to find, test, and fix. Several of the younger native Nisuans were enlisted as a search team to pick through the rubble and find anything salvageable that might have washed out of the palace and ended up in the mud of the city, or been carried off and dropped by Seteposians. There were plenty of small objects of all kinds, and because they had all been designed as field equipment, a surprising number of them still worked.

The mucking out of the stone houses, and reroofing two of them, had consumed the energies of a large part of the Nisuans as well, under Tisix's supervision. He confessed to me that since they had a much better idea than he did of how to use a wooden spade and a stone ax, whenever our few power tools weren't called for his real function was to "stand around and make people feel like they should keep working." Hunting parties found that their job was easy: a great deal of foliage had been destroyed, and animals coming down to the river to drink had little or no cover, so that we had almost unlimited food, as long as you didn't mind eating nothing but roasted meat for every meal.

Itenn took over sanitation and cleanup; as she said, she was supervising the only work that required fewer brains than the work Tisix was supervising. The parts of Real People Town that we didn't salvage for our own use, or burn for fuel, went into great heaps that we set fire to with hand masers, in order to destroy all the dead animals and Seteposian corpses. Wild dogs were coming out of the hills to eat the abundant carrion in the valleys, and we wanted them to stay away from our camp.

In the middle of all this, Bepemm and I, with Diehrenn and Weruz as assistants, ran around frantically counting, enumerating, and calculating, taking breaks only for Bepemm to look in on Beremahm, whose progress was rapid and encouraging. We wanted to at least have all the answers she could reasonably ask for; it was strange how the effort of getting those answers together, in such a short time, seemed to help us hold off the perception of just how dismal those answers really were.

Beremahm was fine when Bepemm brought her out from under sedation two days later; like all of us she was extremely unhappy at being marooned for at least the next decade, and she woke up terribly hungry, but after three days of Bepemm's putting her through every conceivable medical check, while she had nothing to do but read through the lander's technical library, she finally said, "Enough of this. Absolutely enough of this. I may not be well, but if I am not, you aren't going to find the cause, and the last three things you've checked me for, Bepemm, have been things that you couldn't treat me for anyway. Let's get to business."

We walked into the middle of what was left of Real People Town— not much, because so much had been burned or reused—past the heaps of stones that marked where the wall had been, and into one of the better stone huts. We had agreed that the Nisuans born on Setepos should elect four representatives, since it was clearly impossible for all of them to be part of the decision, so Diehrenn, Prirox, Osepok, and Zahmekoses were there waiting for us. "They had to elect representatives who spoke Nisuan," Osepok explained, an amused grin playing across her face. "Weruz is too shy, and Otuz had only recently recovered consciousness. And besides, who else here has any understanding of what you're going to talk about?"

"And by pure accident," Beremahm said, returning the grin, "it happened that exactly the ones I'd have appointed, if I were dictator, ended up as your representatives. Now that we have everyone together, let's get started and figure out what's what."

We spent a while going over the total resources available. The lander was actually in pretty good shape and had been fully refueled and provisioned; it could haul up to sixty of us at a time to anywhere on Setepos, so one possibility was to go to one of the areas that Seteposians had not yet reached. "If we go to the big island off the Hook, or better still to the ones that are south and east of Southland, it's unlikely that either place will be reached for millennia, not until the Seteposians come up with ways of doing long-ocean voyaging. And there are a lot of smaller islands, some of which have wonderful climates. None of those places is likely to have any big predators or venomous animals, either," I summarized. "We could get everyone there in four lander trips, with one additional trip to get all our stuff from here to there. With the micro-smelters on the landers, we could also make a certain amount of iron or other metals as needed."

"I think we can modify it to make glass as well," Krurix said, "and we have chemical equipment to make some plastics. We've got an industrial plant for at least a while."

"How long?" Beremahm asked.

"Well, that's another problem," Krurix said. "Each lander still has an almost full charge of antimatter—it uses almost none coming down or going up—and we can use them to give us electricity at max output for about five years. For that matter we *could* make more antimatter—the lander is set up to do it—but the process is horribly inefficient and you need the kind of power input that we used to have on *Egalitarian Republic* to do it in a timely way."

"Well," I pointed out, "we can use the solar panels we found intact to give us enough electricity for our little colony, if we don't insist on using electricity for everything. Why don't we use power from them to make more antimatter?"

"Because every bit they've got isn't enough for the minimum energy to make antimatter," Krurix said, "but anyway, there might be a solution to this. I just wanted to make sure the problem was on the table: we need a really large power source. Something on the order of a fusion reactor or a major hydropower project, if we want the lander to last until the rescue effort gets here."

"All right," I said, "a big energy source is nearly a necessity. If we don't have that, we won't have a modern industrial capability after a couple of years, and should we be stranded for longer than we anticipate—or should we have an emergency while waiting—that could be a very serious problem. Bepemm, I think you have the biggest problem to discuss. Can you talk about that?"

She sighed. "I really wish Dr. Lerimarsix were here. But I guess we'll have to go with what I can determine. It looks to me like the terrible protein reaction disease that struck several of the Nisuans who were here for a long time is not at all far off for many of the Nisuans born here. Weruz was extremely close—she already had a few early undiagnosed symptoms—and Prirox and Diehrenn were so close to it that I doubt they'd have lasted out the year. Now, all of you are safe for the moment, because you've had the dialysis and you're good for another twenty or thirty years, local. But if we assume the forty-fourth local year, give or take one, is about when it will strike, then we're going to lose more than thirty Nisuans to the disease in the *minimum* time it takes for a rescue vessel to get here. That's the number of undialyzed people more than thirty-four years old. But it's clear that second-generation natives, probably due to exposure in the womb, form the toxins much faster—and so you can't expect them to last as long. Even if they do, their birth cohorts are much bigger. So if the rescue is delayed even a few years, we could lose fifty, a hundred . . . who knows how many. The thirty or so oldest are merely the ones *certain* to die; there could easily be three times as many deaths."

"Out of less than two hundred and fifty," Beremahm said. "All of us from *Egalitarian Republic* would live, of course—for another forty-four years, barring accidents—but what you're saying is that if we end up as a permanently stranded colony here, the maximum lifespan will always be about forty-four of Setepos's years. Or just about forty of ours. Our females will die with less than a third of their reproductive years available . . . this isn't going to work well."

"Especially not because the toxins also produce fairly early sterility," Bepemm said. "Even the Nim noticed that; ten years after puberty most of the Nisuans were sterile. We'd have to breed the way the Nim forced people to do: baby after baby as soon as puberty hits. Not a good way to live."

Beremahm sighed. "You spoke of some way out, Krurix?" she asked.

I answered quickly, "Well, it was really Zahmekoses who made the suggestion," and gestured for him to speak. Here, if anywhere, was where Beremahm might decide that we were all crazy.

"We do have a source of Nisuan food," he said. "At least there's a good chance that we do. And remember the problem is caused by ingesting Seteposian proteins, even in minute quantities. So since we can't do dialysis, the only way for us to all survive is to eat nothing but Nisuan food. So what I suggest is . . ." he drew a deep breath, his old voice cracking ". . . that we go up to *Wahkopem Zomos*, which is still in orbit—"

"The ship's farm!" Beremahm said. "That solves it, doesn't it?"

"Not quite," Zahmekoses said. "Nisuan plants, animals, and tissue cultures are undoubtedly susceptible to the same kind of slow poisoning-by-immune-reaction as we are. Furthermore, if we raise them down here they'll take up Seteposian proteins, too. So it would slow but not stop the disease, and there's no guarantee that we can raise Nisuan food at all here on a long-term basis. We need a sterile environment in which we can build a much bigger sealed farm."

Beremahm groaned. "This gets worse and worse."

"Or better," Krurix said. "Here's the other part of it. Remember I said we needed a big energy source, like a fusion reactor? Well, Proyerin and I were fiddling around, and we think we can make one, a fairly crude job. It won't run on regular deuterium, unfortunately, that we could get here—but it will run on helium-3."

"And there's a source of that on Setepos?"

"Not *right* on Setepos," Proyerin said, grinning.

Beremahm looked around at the strange smiles in the room and said, "Well, now I know why Captain Baegess said the commanding officer is always the only person who doesn't know what's going on. All right, you've all come up with a way to solve this problem, and you were all afraid I would think it was too crazy, or perhaps too dangerous. Now if I admit that I'm desperate for a solution, would you please tell me what in the Creator's name you've got in mind?"

"Well," I said, "we need a sterile environment with a lot of helium-3 around. And we suddenly realized that there's a perfect place; something I remembered from the nuclear magnetic resonance map that our low-altitude scanning satellite made of the moon. Plenty of helium-3 because it's been accumulating out of the solar wind since the moon cooled from magma. Right there on the surface waiting to be picked up. The solar panels would easily give you enough power to run an extractor and isotope separator, and then the fusion reactor would supply enough power to keep the lander recharged indefinitely. And with surplus power from all that . . ." I permitted myself to grin. "Well, the soil of the moon is a very low-grade aluminum ore, and there's enough silica around that we can make glass as well, and most importantly, there's a lot of water, ammonia, and carbon dioxide, deposited as ice in deep craters at the south pole. We can build a farm on the moon—and live there as well."

"What's the time frame?" Beremahm asked, quietly.

"Two eightdays to get a fusion reactor going; about the same to get the *Wahkopem Zomos* farm back on-line," Bepemm said. "We move the six undialyzed people who are closest to the edge up to *Wahkopem Zomos*, where Otuz and Zahmekoses start teaching them to run the farm. We think it will only be a few eightdays more, after we get the reactor running, before we have the first sealed and pressurized environments on the moon. Then we seed the habitats, move the first group of colonists off *Wahkopem Zomos* to the moon, move the next group up to *Wahkopem Zomos*, and so forth. About twenty in a group—the bottleneck is *Wahkopem Zomos* itself. In half a year we have a trained cadre of farmers and workers on the moon, with room enough for everyone else. Both landers start running as a ferry; we move the last hundred and eighty in three quick swoops. And at that point we've got a base that could last us for centuries if it had to, especially because between the library and factory equipment on *Wahkopem Zomos*, and the computer and microindustry on the lander, we can make just about anything we might need, except good luck. And we'll be completely independent of this planet and its poisons."

"What happens when we run out?" Beremahm said abruptly.

"Run out of what?" I asked, staring stupidly.

"How much ice is there at the south pole?"

"A few centuries' worth, maybe more, assuming we lose one percent per year to leaks," Proyerin said. "That's plenty of time for us to get rescued."

"Is it?" Beremahm asked. "You know, as your commanding officer, I've been doing a bit of thinking, too, and I had a lot of time to sit and read in that lander while Bepemm did all those tests on me. And I had been thinking along pretty much the same lines as you all, but with a few interesting differences. Here's what I came up with.

"Think about the situation back home. The alien-protein-immune-sickness we discovered here is not only going to happen on Setepos, you know. It will happen anywhere where we are immersed in an alien ecosystem, at least until we genetically modify ourselves enough—and it will take decades to find out what must be done in each case, perhaps centuries to produce Nisuans who can live outside a Nisuan biosphere. And perhaps we can never succeed; perhaps we will always need to be under constant medical treatment to live in any other kind of biosphere. Some places the progress of the disease is bound to be more rapid than here, some places less, but it will happen.

"So what does that imply? There are only about sixty Nisuan years left until the Second Bombardment. And we have just demonstrated to them that *any living world is unsuitable to our long-term survival.* Do you see what that means? For almost a century, we have been looking for the wrong planets to emigrate to! Worse yet, the fast zero-point-energy laser-drive scout ships that have departed in the last four years—at least four of them besides us—have all gone to the wrong places.

"By the time they get our message they will have to scramble to find any suitable worlds at all. What they need are planets that can be 'Nisu-formed,' to coin a phrase—places where there is no life, but which could be modified to support Nisuan life. If they can find such planets, they can seed them with Nisuan life and gradually make them habitable for us. That process may take a few hundred years, but the big Migration Project ships are designed to hold crews of millions for centuries anyway; they can simply orbit the new worlds while they work on them. But when they get our message, they are going to figure out that they must find and scout Nisu-formable worlds immediately. Every available scoutship will have to be diverted to that purpose, quite a few of them diverted en route.

"And remember there are far too many of us to move in a single scoutship; they would have to build a special rescue vessel, or send six or seven modified scoutships here. They won't have time. Some of the places where they will be looking for Nisu-formable worlds will have to be twenty light-years and more away. That means twenty years for the scoutship to get there, and, if the place is suitable, twenty more for the radio message to come back, leaving only twenty to build a city in space and get it launched . . . no, they simply can't spare the resources to come and get us. Everything has to go into scoutships and colony ships, flat out as hard as they can do it, right up till the rocks fall.

"We are here for good."

It took a long time for that message to sink in. Finally Krurix said, "You've convinced me, anyway. I guess we can just settle on the moon and hope we think of something else before we run out of ice. Maybe we can improve recycling or find a way to get enough replacements from Setepos or—"

Beremahm looked at us all with a little secret grin—the kind that we had all been giving her—and said, "But you all give up too easily. And so do I. You have half the solution right there—how our people can live for a century or so. And I have the other half—think about the fourth planet from Kousapex, the next one out from here."

"The War Star?" Diehrenn asked, in Real-People.

"That's the one," Beremahm said. "All the stuff life needs, in huge quantities, but the probes found no life. Two small moons—perfect bases with plenty of raw materials. I rather strongly suspect that given a century to work, we can make a pretty good home there. We might or might not ever be able to breathe without a helmet, we might never be able to create a lake and go swimming there, but we can live a long time. Probably we can live for three hundred years, till the Migration Project ship gets there and starts Nisu-forming, with a better set of tools than we and our descendants will have.

"I just hadn't been able to figure out how we'd get that century or so that we needed to make a home there. Especially since I had forgotten that *Wahkopem Zomos* was still around, so I didn't remember that we had crops and animal tissue from the ship's farm, and of course our poor little lander's life-support system would never make it as far as the War Star. I like that name, by the way. What does it mean?"

I told her, and she laughed. "Well, then, what would be Real-People for 'Peace Star'?"

"They don't have a word for peace," Diehrenn said.

"We really do need to leave this planet," Beremahm said firmly. "Let's keep their name for the fourth planet, then, but resolve to forget what it means." She looked from one face to another, and gradually we all began to smile.

"Twice," she said, "expeditions have wrecked here on Setepos. For our people this appears to be the planet of bad luck, and I say, let's leave it for good. But let's not forget that twice we've survived disasters and gone on, through worse things than the people who sent us could ever imagine. I say, we're not dead yet. Let's get moving—we have two more worlds to conquer before we die."

FROM: Diehrenn Zahtuz
TO: the Grand Council on Nisu:

After all the stories that Thetakisus, my mate, and his friend Krurix had told me of Nisu, I was still astonished to find that a message had come in by radio from Nisu. I have grown used to how drastically my circumstances have changed since the day more than ten of Earth's years ago when the Pillar of Fire first blazed in the skies over Real People Town; I was, after all, raised on stories of Nisu by my father Zahmekoses and mother Otuz; and yet, with all that, to actually see that a message transmitted from Nisu has arrived here— the first of many, apparently—fills me with awe.

As was requested in your message, I have sent along my own account, supplemented by my mate Thetakisus, of how the decisions were first made. I do hope you will find room for it in the copier of the Great Volume of Knowledge sent out to the Migration Project ships, on their way to nine worlds.

Ten worlds seems so many; I have only lived on three. But three is plenty for anyone who spent the first part of her life in a Stone-Age kingdom, I suppose, and I have no complaints.

How many wonders can I tell you of? And would they even seem wondrous to you, who grew up among them, who are even now headed to the stars? Within a year I—I, who could barely read and write when *Egalitarian Republic* first made its blazing Pillar in our sky—was assistant operator for a fusion reactor on the moon. I confess it was some four years later before I really knew what a fusion reactor was or what it did, but that power was still there in me, and I dealt with it—very well, if I say so myself.

A decade later I helped astrogate *Wahkopem Zomos* to the War Star, where we built this base on its inner moon—the place from which I now write, looking up at that faithful old ship, built the better part of a Nisuan century ago, now waiting for yet another voyage back to the Moon, sitting a short distance above us here. Beyond it I see the red face of the War Star, now blotchy with the green patches of lichen that we have seeded there.

The genetics team says the lichens are dying, losing ground after an initial surge, and that this attempt was a failure. But we are patient and strong. We will simply try until we either succeed or die.

Our next try will be with the dust that surrounds the south pole of the War Star; it is very fine and dark, and if we scatter it vigorously enough, we can darken the ice as summer comes on, and thus warm it enough to release the frozen carbon dioxide into the atmosphere, which in turn will warm up the rest of the planet, and perhaps give our experimental lichen a new lease on life and get some rivers flowing and lakes forming. But if that fails, we have other options. One way or another, sooner or later, we will warm the War Star and thicken its air.

Even if we can't get anything to grow on its face, we will live there within my lifetime, for I shall move down there in a few years. There is a circular crater near the north pole that has a place suitable for such a city, and construction has already begun there.

On the Moon, they have found more ice than they had thought was there, and that colony has a new lease on life as well, so we need not hurry quite so much to get them all here. They are talking of building spaceships there, so that we no longer must rely on the single operating lander and *Wahkopem Zomos* exclusively.

That remains our greatest fear. Right now one of *Egalitarian Republic's* landers is useless as a spacecraft, because it must supply power and computer control for the life support systems at our base near the south pole of the moon. The other lander must work in tandem with the old *Wahkopem Zomos*, for the lander's life support system cannot operate independently long enough to travel from Setepos to the War Star, and *Wahkopem Zomos*'s engines cannot even get it out of orbit around either planet. Further, the starship cannot land on the face of the War Star or on Setepos's moon; so the remaining lander must supply the propulsion and the ability to land, and *Wahkopem Zomos* must keep the crew alive. If we lose the lander at the lunar south pole base, or the operating lander, or the starship, then we are surely doomed—but so far, years have gone by, and we are still here. They will all keep functioning, because they all must keep functioning.

And from spaceship to starship is a small step, in the great scheme of things. In a century or two, if there is a suitable place within thirty light-years, and if no one has come to visit or join us, perhaps we will pack our bags and come to join *you*, wherever you may have gone.

This account, and Father's account of the first mission, are entrusted to you, now, for the Great Volume of Knowledge that you intend to send to every world. I can only hope that when it arrives here, it is a wonderful historical curiosity rather than an urgent necessity. I quite concur with your decision; since we are to move down to the surface, to the crater filled with ice that seems to have so much potential, it is far better to send the Great Volume there rather than here. And certainly sending one to the Moon, in case any of our people at the south pole there should decide to remain, or perhaps be forced to by circumstances, is wise as a backup. But do not fear; our descendants will be here to receive it and will remember you with gratitude when it arrives, though I understand that it may be a few centuries before it does. I am flattered that you wanted the story of the two expeditions to Setepos included; you honor our family with that request.

I think your plan of setting up a robot radio station on Kahrekeif, from which a recorded message will be beamed to all the known ships and colonies every time that your sun and Zoiroy are widely separated from their perspective, so that all of our scattered people can always be found again, is probably unnecessary. I find it hard to imagine that any of us now would lose our historical or scientific knowledge, or forget the catalog of planets, or where our bases are. I think our victory is already won, even if our colonies here die out tomorrow, even if no Migration Project ship, with its millions of passengers, ever reaches another star system. We have won because, in our own eyes—the only eyes that can ever judge us—we have made ourselves deserve to win, deserve to go on living and expanding as a civilization. We might have become more soft, more fearful, more greedy, and died quietly at home. We have elected to die—or just possibly live—in the stars.

But I had not intended to lecture you about our destiny, and most especially not to lecture whoever may read this in the far future. If this is being read, we have had a destiny, and they know more of it than I do.

Nor am I scolding you about the extensive precautions you are taking to make sure that the Great Volume of Knowledge reaches our people wherever they go. If the effort of making duplicate Great Volumes of Knowledge and of posting the beacon on Kahrekeif should prove useless because it is not needed, it was still worth doing. If there is anything that all of us understand, here in this solar system and wherever our species may go from now on, it is that the universe is still a very dangerous place.

Even now I find myself saying that if the antimatter plant of the lander that now powers our colony on Setepos's moon were to fail, within hours many would die there and nothing could be done to save them. By the time we got there, they would undoubtedly all be dead. And if something were to happen to the lander, or to *Wahkopem Zomos*, here in orbit around the War Star—well, then we could not get back to Setepos's moon, and I suppose both colonies might slowly die. And those thoughts will cross my mind, again and again, for years to come. These are the risks we assume because we must—because to do anything else meant dying for sure, whereas depending on these aging and irreplaceable machines to keep running until we finally do not need them anymore, was a chance to live. We grasped that chance, and so far this is paying off; any other considerations, since we cannot change our circumstances, are irrelevant.

Goodness, I do go on about this! I suppose it's because so many of our younger generation like to talk all the time about how thin our margins are and how great the chances and consequences of failure. But that has been the way for life ever since it started. I don't think matters will actually ever be any different for living things anywhere. From the simplest bacterium up to the Nisuan level, we will just keep going on as long as we can, and the going on will be what makes us what we are.

Warmest regards from the Kousapex System,
Diehrenn, daughter of Otuz and Zahmekoses.

Clio Trigorin:
October 2077

IT WAS ANOTHER ARBITRARY LINE IN SPACE, WHICH MEANT IT WAS TIME FOR another party. At about 100,000 AU from Alpha Centauri, the dim red star Proxima Centauri orbited the double star every 22,000 years. Since the formation of the triple star, Proxima had been sweeping comets out of the Oort Cloud and down into the inner system, which was a major part of the reason that the early bombardment had been so heavy and explained much about the geology of Tiber.

Now they were crossing Proxima Centauri's orbit, passing near enough so that the dim star was just visible to the naked eye as a kind of glowing spot; everyone was gathered in the common area to look at the relayed image of it on the screen, as probes launched months before made their way down into Proxima. Clio supposed it was impressive in its way, but though "any star is huge by comparison with anything human," as Sanetomo said, it was about as ordinary a red dwarf as you could find.

In the third year of the voyage, five years before, they had launched the probe carrier, a small missile with a cluster of ZPE lasers as its propulsion system and a group of probes in the nose, to diverge from their course and head off to the side, toward Proxima. *Tenacity* and the probe carrier had raced along in parallel ever since, like two cars on diverging roads.

The probe carrier had started with greater acceleration, since it weighed far less than *Tenacity* in proportion to its engines' thrust, but there was no one on the probe carrier to swap out bad ZPE lasers, and as one laser after another failed, the probe carrier eventually had gone into purely ballistic flight. As it neared Proxima Centauri, it had extended a magnetic loop like the one on the old *Wahkopem Zomos* and slowed down considerably. When it drew nearer to the red dwarf, the carrier ejected a family of probes, each on its own lightsail, and the probes in turn had slowed down, braking themselves with the dim light of the little cool sun (little and cool by the standards of stars; it was still immensely bigger than even gigantic Jupiter, and hot enough to vaporize iron). Now they were swarming around Proxima Centauri, many light-days away from *Tenacity*, like a flock of metal blue jays attacking a great glowing red owl, sweeping past the red dwarf, swooping over its poles, plunging into its fiery heart, and pouring back data in immense quantities. The crew of *Tenacity* was gathered here to watch the highlights of that historic flyby as they came in; they were seeing the first data to reach humanity from a star other than Sol.

Tenacity herself was also entering the Alpha Centauri system, but it would still be another fifteen months before they deployed the magnetic loop to slow down. Although the distances between the stars are vaster, solar systems themselves are vast, and even though right now they were covering an astronomical unit every twenty-one minutes, still they had more than one and a half light-years to go, 100,000 AU remaining. They would have to travel deep into the Alpha Centauri System before they even began to slow down, and once they did deploy the magnetic loop and start deceleration (still at thirty-five AU from Juno and Tiber, farther than from Neptune to Earth), it would be two more long years before they came into orbit around Tiber.

She and Sanetomo had been married now for more than a year, and it seemed to suit them better each passing day. Their professional lives went on smoothly; one of the great advantages of twelve years aboard a starship, with the combined libraries of Earth and Tiber in its data storage, was that nobody could phone you or ask you to go to a committee meeting, so they both worked steadily and effectively, with plenty of time to think, and still had all the time they wanted with each other.

And their work had gone pretty well, on the whole. Sanetomo's work on free oxygen in distant atmospheres had gained a great deal of approval back home (or so the more-than-three-years-late messages assured them). Her translation of *The Account of Zahmekoses* would still not reach Earth for almost two years, even now; at the moment it was a set of radio signals far out in the void. Now moving along behind it was her translation of *The Account of Diehrenn*, sent out just scant days ago.

At least by the time she was reading any reviews of it, she'd have developed a certain detachment.

She stood, sipping her wine and thinking about what the long delays could mean. It was finally time to write the last part of *From the Moon to the Stars*; she didn't really think she could delay it any longer.

On the screen before them, Proxima Centauri, like the orange ghost of a star, swelled rapidly as the probe closed in. The red dwarf's surface was blackened by huge dark swirls that marked the mighty hurricanes on its glowing face, far bigger than the sunspots of Earth's sun. Sanetomo and three others were sitting close to the screen, watching the little parade of graphs and images that ran across the bottom, gabbling excitedly to each other about what it all meant and whose theories it confirmed or disproved. Proxima was only a minor sideshow on this trip, but still it was the biggest show there would be for months.

She took another sip of wine and asked herself why settling back into writing *From the Moon to the Stars* was so hard. Perhaps it was just a matter of knowing that Uncle Jason and Aunt Olga might yet read it; at least as of about three years ago, allowing for radio lag, they had still been alive and healthy on Mars. She'd had a long video message from them only a few weeks ago, and it had said that after all the hassle and organizational fighting of two elderly people trying to get permission to return to the wild frontier of Mars, once they had finally gotten there, they had found it had been worth every minute. The lighter gravity and familiar faces seemed to have dropped years from them. She was beginning to think Uncle Jason wasn't kidding about being there to welcome her back.

And all that had paralyzed her a little. What if, in her account of the great events they had lived through, she didn't do them justice? What if she had misunderstood some major thing Jason had told her in all of the taped sessions? By the time she found out that she'd gotten it wrong, the book could be in its fifth printing.

Clio laughed at herself soundlessly. Because she tended to be shy and quiet, and everyone knew everyone's habits well, no one was going to ask her what she was laughing about, and that was good, because she wasn't sure she liked explaining that she was frightened of a partially written history book. Especially when you considered the situation around them. At the speeds they were moving, a grain of sand, had one ever gotten through the deflection system, would have hit with the energy of a ton of TNT. For that matter, what was the dread of finishing a history book compared with the terrifying awareness that they were utterly *alone*—suppose Earth were suddenly hit by an asteroid, like the one that had wiped out the dinosaurs? Their only information on this was apt to be that four years later the signal would just stop. Conversely, if anything happened to them, in four years they would just vanish from Earth's radio receivers—

As the First Tiberian Expedition, the one with Zahmekoses, had done.

She thought hard about that for a while. Was there finally any real difference between Tiberian and human? They had exhibited all the human traits, surely—courage and cowardice, greed and vision, spite and compassion—and finally they had failed, leaving some frozen corpses in the soil of Mars and the Moon, some bits and pieces of their technology, and of course the Encyclopedia. . . .

Had they failed? That was another odd question. Deciphering the Encyclopedia had finally explained, at least in large measure, what was going on. After the horrible experience of the failed First Tiberian Expedition, and the panic of getting ready for emigration after wasting most of fifty years between the first and second missions, it had never been far from the mind of any Tiberian planner that civilization was a fragile thing and many things could go wrong, that all sorts of knowledge and skills might be lost. So as a last assurance, they had sent an Encyclopedia to every system to which their people had gone, a backup repository of their civilization. And on Alba Longa, Minerva's eccentric moon (which the Tiberians had called Kahrekeif), they had put a transmitter that sat waiting for the points in the combined orbits when it would have a clear shot at each of those systems and endlessly repeated the message to each of them about where to look for the Encyclopedia.

And as a result, though there might well be no more Tiberians in the universe, they would live as long as human memory did. Moreover, Sanetomo had now detected free oxygen in eight of the nine systems the Tiberians had designated as visited, though on the world they had named Courage, it seemed to be only a seasonal phenomenon. The Tiberians, once they figured out the protein problem, had gone to worlds that were easily terraformed rather than to wild ones, so this argued powerfully that they had at least gotten self-sustaining ecologies going in the places where they had planted colonies. They might well live on there.

No question that individual Tiberians had failed, for all their courage, fortitude, and intelligence. But no question either that as a culture the Tiberians had found at least one way to pass something on, to defy the cosmic oblivion descending on them. As for what had happened to them as a species, we didn't know yet. That would have to wait at least for decades until there was any reply from the radio broadcasts to the visited worlds; and maybe a century until exploration ships reached all of them.

Failure? What a silly way to look at it. In an intelligent species everybody dies, and perhaps most without learning any really new thing, but every generation can push back the ignorance a little farther.

The phrase stuck in her head, and she found herself holding an imaginary conversation with Uncle Jason. He seemed to tell her to just tell the story, get it recorded, and make his story part of humanity's. And something about that, finally, gave her the urge to get to work, and sit down and tell Uncle Jason's story. She set down her wineglass and headed back toward the room she shared with Sanetomo.

But before she reached the door, there was wild cheering. She turned and saw that the Fast Low Altitude Probe had succeeded in making a pass just above the glowing face of Proxima; she stayed to watch that. The deep red marked by black hurricanes bigger than the Earth itself whirled away beneath, often leaping up in great red peaks and sometimes boiling up in orange sheets. Then, as the probe whipped on around the dim little red sun, the hyperbolic orbit carried it away. The eternal stars popped into view, and the probe, having finished the job it was designed to do in less than half an hour, fell away into the eternal dark and cold, to go wherever it might for the next few thousands of millennia. It rotated 180 degrees and looked back as long as it could, but at its tremendous speed it was a very short time before it saw nothing but blackness, and then its radio signal faded.

It was the kind of machine an intelligent species might build, Clio said to herself. She headed back to her desk to start playing through Uncle Jason's tapes one more time.

PART IV
FIRST CLEAR LIGHT
2017–2035

1

I HAD KNOWN LORI KIRSTEN ALMOST MY WHOLE LIFE; MY MOTHER AND SIG had even encouraged me to call her "Aunt Lori." Fate, which seemed to enjoy playing some obscure game with me, had made her the head of the astronaut corps just three days after I was accepted into astronaut training. She had had no influence on my getting in, but since she had been my father's closest friend, and everyone knew who my father was, my arriving at the same time she did was taken as evidence of my legendary "pull" and "influence." I got the usual hassle about it, and I dealt with it the usual way—I tried to do so well that everyone would agree that I had deserved the chance anyway.

It didn't work. It never had. By the time that I became an astronaut and Lori became head of the corps, though, I was twenty-eight, and I'd come to understand how things worked. Plenty of people would take me for what I was: not an extroverted genius like my dad, but just a guy who liked to fly in space and was really good at it. I had made friends at the Air Force Academy, in flight training, in my assignments, and finally in the astronaut corps, even if it was a little more difficult at first because my name was Jason Terence and I was a small part of a famous story.

One thing I had to be careful about, though, was not socializing too much with Aunt Lori when anyone might see. With more than a thousand astronauts in the corps, it would look fishy for a mere rocket jockey to have lunch with the boss. Generally we saw each other at my mother and Sig's place, where we could "coincidentally" bump into each other and catch up. For several years I saw Aunt Lori only at such gatherings, or on the rare occasions when she'd visit my squadron. By now, at age thirty-four, even though Aunt Lori was nominally my boss, I thought of her mainly as an old family friend I didn't see very often.

So I worked hard at my career and flew a lot, mostly taking crews of scientists up or down between the LEO ports *Glenn* or *Shepherd*, or sometimes out to the collection of habitats and trusses at the old *Star Cluster*, to Canaveral or Edwards, on Yankee Clippers, the first true single-stage-to-orbit system.

And I thought of Lori Kirsten as Aunt Lori when I saw her socially and as Chief Kirsten whenever I had to think about the commander of the astronaut corps. Thus it felt very strange when out of nowhere, in October 2032, I got orders to report to her office the next morning at the Johnson Spacecraft Center outside Houston, especially because she had pulled me off a scheduled Clipper flight to do it, and NASA was still a little short of qualified Clipper pilots.

Bill Amundsen, my squadron commander, was as puzzled as I was; he saw me off at the airfield, and while we waited for the early flight, he asked, once again, "And you have no idea what it's about?"

"None at all," I said. "If she'd wanted me to know she'd have phoned. You know how she is; she's still not used to there being such a big organization that there has to be a regular chain of command."

"Oh yeah." He half chuckled. "She didn't phone you, but she phoned me. Just making sure I wouldn't offer any resistance."

"Resistance to what?"

"Well, first of all, to pulling you from the upcoming flight. I think you're right, sometimes she forgets how much space flight goes on these days. If you get back soon enough, you'll still be flying into space, what, eight times this year? She still remembers when getting scrubbed from a mission might mean years before you got a chance again." He paused, and squinted at the transport rolling toward us in the bright Florida sunlight.

I let him have a minute, and then said, "You said 'first of all.' What else was she worried about you resisting?"

"Hmmph." Very softly he said, "You didn't hear this, Jason. But she told me if I cooperated I could have my pick from the replacement pool."

The hair on the back of my neck rose. Whatever she had in mind would involve transferring me out of the First Aerospace Squadron. And I liked it here. I had been flying out of here for almost four years now, and besides handling flights up to orbit, I had made enough trips between the LEO ports (usually just *Shepherd* to *Glenn* or vice versa, but every so often out to the L1 Port *Armstrong*), and enough trips to the Moon to maintain my rating on Pigeons, the workhorse ships for orbital operations. Because I worked a lot, and never turned down a mission, I got used a lot, which was what I wanted. Also, I knew and liked the other astronauts in the First, and they accepted me.

And why was Aunt Lori reaching down into the low levels of the organization like this? If I was wanted in some other squadron, normally that would have been worked out between Bill and whoever the squadron commander was.

"Well," I said, "if worse comes to worst, I'll have to come back to pack. We can get people together for a beer or something before I go. Just to make sure—if I turn whatever it is down, you won't mind if I stay here?"

He shook his head, laughing. "You log more hours per year and you earn higher ratings than anyone else. I'd rather have you here. But when Lori Kirsten tells me this is a bad time to make waves, I don't."

I nodded. "Okay. Just wanted to know I could come back if I want to—and *if* I win the argument with her."

Then they announced that the transport would be boarding, so I shook hands with Bill, lined up, and got aboard. It was a dull flight, so I spent most of it reading.

Every so often I'd put the book down and work through the numbers again, trying to figure out what the devil she had in mind for me. My record was extremely good, I admitted, trying to avoid false modesty, so it might well be a promotion or a transfer to a special mission. NASA had three aerospace squadrons, which mainly flew missions from Earth up to orbit and back, and two orbital squadrons which flew Pigeons, between space stations, moonbases, and various things in orbit. I was qualified on Peregrines, Starbird IIs, Yankee Clippers, and Pigeons, so I could theoretically fly in any of those five squadrons—there would be no good reason to move me over to either of the two engineering squadrons. Crossing off the First Aerospace, since this was a transfer, left me with restationing to Vandenberg (flying Yankee Clippers, out in the California desert) with the Second Aerospace; Malmstrom (Great Falls, Montana) with the Sixth Aerospace (and they were still flying the old Peregrine, which, lovely though it had been in its day, was now distinctly old); *Armstrong* (the Big Can–based L1 port that NASA had built to support other lunar activities) with the Fourth Orbital (Pigeons, reusable landers, and all kinds of odd flying hardware that went into orbital operations); or the Eighth Orbital, at New Tranquillity on the Moon. None of which had the climate advantages of Florida, and all of which would put me a lot farther from my family. This whole situation really didn't look good.

As we touched down in Houston and taxied to the gate, I realized I couldn't remember a word of the book I had theoretically finished. I looked down to remind myself; glanced up and realized I didn't know what the title was, two seconds later. Making sure I remembered my bag, I got off the plane and caught the shuttle to Johnson Spacecraft Center, which we usually just called JSC. I had about two minutes of the pleasantly cool, sunny day—the only time Houston is really bearable is in the autumn—and then I was being whisked to the Blue Pyramid, as everyone called it, the new headquarters building that had been put up only a few years ago. It hadn't made JSC any less remote—it was still a good twenty-five miles from the city—or any more attractive, but I suppose it was easier to find in a small plane.

When I got to Aunt Lori's office, half an hour early, I was shown right in. That made the whole thing that much more mysterious. As soon as the door closed, she grinned and hugged me. I had to admit, that made me feel a lot better. She took a step back to look at me, and I returned the inspection.

Her crewcut hair was iron-gray now, and there were lines around her eyes and mouth, but she still looked like she could take on any three average people half her age and beat the hell out of them, and her blue eyes had the same old sparkle. "You look well," she said.

"So do you."

"Have a seat. Let's start with the social part of things and then I'll tell you all about what a certain computer program told me."

I sat in one of the two chairs in front of her desk; she took the other and dragged it over to sit closer to me. "And how's your mother, and Sig?"

"Mom's the same as always," I said. "Still ten projects going all the time, still phoning from all over the world to make sure I'm eating right and ask when I'm going to find some nice girl who will help me make a grandmother of her. Which is a pretty strange conversation when she's calling from the Amazon and I'm in orbit, but that's Mom. And Sig . . . well, he's the same, too."

Aunt Lori looked sympathetic. "Same old offer?"

"Same old offer. Four times the money if I'll fly one of his new Starliners."

"You could certainly afford a family on that kind of money," she said, "and I don't think there's much question that the Starliners are going to be safer than most of what we fly—they're drawing on more recent technology and they have the benefit of everyone else's experience. Does the idea tempt you?"

I shook my head. "No, ma'am. Not at all. It would be like giving up driving Indy cars to drive a city bus. They both take a lot of skill, but any ten-year-old can figure out which is more interesting." I was exaggerating a little, but only a little. The Starliner was the commercial version of the Yankee Clipper, and its main cargo was not space crew or supplies but people. Consequently everything that could be done to make the ride smoother, gentler, and safer had been done; it just didn't have the performance possibilities that the Clipper did.

She chuckled. "Good boy. I thought I'd judged you right. And you're happy right now in the First Aerospace? Your record there is as close to perfect as any I've seen, and Bill Amundsen thinks the world of you."

"I like it a lot," I said. "I wouldn't mind staying where I am for a long time."

"Good again," she said. "Because I don't want anyone to take the job I'm about to offer you unless it's what you *want* to do, not just to avoid something you don't like or get out of a boring post." Her smile was getting broader, and she said, "Now, I said the computer told us something. We have an important opening coming up, for an important mission, and when we asked it to come up with the optimal pilot in the astronaut corps, it spat out your name."

I must have looked startled, because she held up a finger before I could speak and said, "Don't be so surprised. You're extremely well qualified, you're having a brilliant career with us, and you should damn well know it. I want it firmly in your head that that's why I'm about to suggest an opportunity. Furthermore, when we ran the top five suggestions by the mission commander, he specifically said that you were his favorite." Her smile was downright impish; it was like she used to smile when she'd tease me back in high school, or when she dropped by to visit me at Colorado Springs.

"Uh, can I know who the mission commander is?"

"Sure," she said. "It's Walter Gander."

It was like an electric shock. Walter Gander was the commanding officer of the Seventh Interplanetary, and had been the first American to set foot on Phobos, Mars's inner moon, on the Phobos One mission. I hadn't even thought about the possibility of joining the Seventh; it was a small, elite unit that flew manned missions to Mars, and operations in Martian orbit. "He's going *himself?*" I asked.

"All our other squadron commanders do," she pointed out. "And he's been out there before, which is important, and most of all this is a vital mission. Besides, he remembers you from the class he taught when you were in training. He liked the way you weren't afraid to try something you'd never done before. *And* he says you've got the most important quality—besides being a great pilot—that anyone can have for this one."

I looked puzzled. She held up a finger and said emphatically, "I mean discretion. You can keep your own counsel, and he'll be able to talk freely to you and not worry about where it gets repeated. Which is going to be vital because you two will be the only Americans on this mission." Now she was really beaming. "I'm not only excited for you, Jason, I'm practically jealous. If I could figure out a way to take the job myself, I would. What I mean is that you're to be the pilot for the next Mars surface hab delivery. I trust you understand that everything from here on out is absolutely secret?"

"Sure." I was a little dazed. The crew and surface habitat deliveries were the basic missions to Crater Korolev on Mars. My job would be to fly myself, Gander, an engineer, and a team of scientists all the way to that crater, in the Martian arctic, where the larger Tiberian settlement—and hopefully the second copy of the Encyclopedia—lay frozen below meters of ice. "Why will we be the only Americans? I thought—"

"Politics, of course," she said. "We've always reserved operating American equipment for Americans—which means the Mars Five mission commander and the chief pilot *have* to be Americans. And on this mission, nobody's willing to take an unequal share of seats. We needed full support from the other four members of the International Mars Consortium, so since the MarsHab takes a crew of ten, it's two per agency. The Japanese, the Chinese, the Russians, and ESA."

"But—isn't the engineer supposed to be an operating officer, too?"

She nodded. "That's our biggest compromise. The mission's engineer—which means the first officer, of course, so she'll outrank you—will be Olga Trigorin, a cosmonaut with a lot of flights under her belt. And she'll be staying over, along with the scientists, so two years later

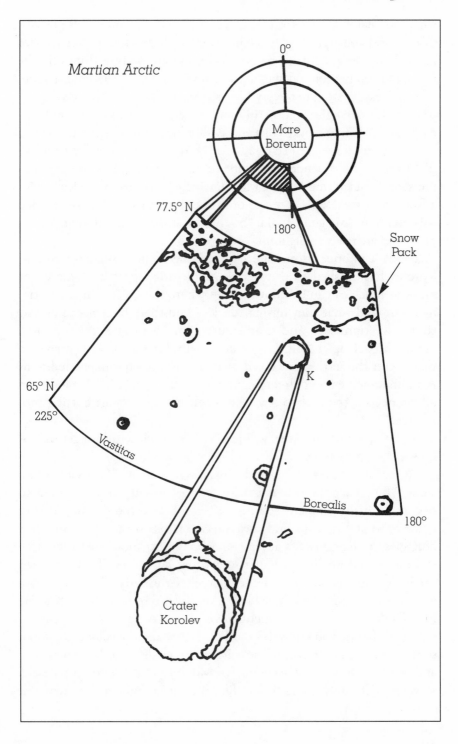

Martian Arctic

0°

Mare
Boreum

77.5° N

180°

Snow
Pack

K

65° N

225°

Vastitas

Borealis

180°

Crater
Korolev

when you catch your return flight on the cycler *Collins*, it will be just Walter and you from your expedition. She's been training for this for more than a year, actually, because there are all kinds of things they're going to need her for and she had to absorb a lot of special information. It wasn't easy getting her everything she needed, either, because we had to keep this mission secret up till now. In fact, the scientists are all being contacted today, too; only Olga and Walter knew this was coming."

"Knew *what* was—" I started to ask, and then I put it all together. A flight that Walter Gander was going to make himself. Extreme political pressure, so much that NASA was allowing a Mars mission to leave with a Russian first officer. There was only one thing that could have created this situation. "My god," I said. "So they must have located the Encyclopedia and are ready to dig it up."

"Got it in one, Jason," she said, smiling. "The permanent crew at Korolev has finished all the seismic and hydrographic work, and they know as much as can be known about where the objects in the settlement are and what they're shaped like. And there happens to be one that's the right size and shape, just about a kilometer away, two meters higher up in the ice—which really suggests that it arrived a while after the settlement was drowned, if that's what happened to it. An unmanned cargo delivery is taking up the special tools, and then all we need is the archeology team itself before we start cutting into the ice."

"So the permanent crew will just leave it in place till we get there?" I asked. "Seems kind of . . ."

"Oh, I'm sure it's boring and frustrating for them," Lori said with a shrug. "But that's the way it is with archeology—if you don't want to risk losing it the moment you find it. Plan before you dig, be ready to preserve what comes up, and always have an expert present so that if it crumbles or breaks there's at least somebody who knew what they were looking at and might remember something important. That has been the basic principle for earth archeology since the early 1900s." Her eyes got a little far away, and she added, "And if we'd stuck to that principle for Tiberian artifacts, you might have been having this conversation with your father, you know. It's our last shot at the Encyclopedia, Jason, so we're taking no chances. The scientists include some Mars veterans, and people with years of accumulated Moon time at the south pole dig, so you're definitely going to feel like the junior guy on the crew. But you're a first-rate pilot, Walter wants you, and you have my complete confidence.

"If you want the job, I should also tell you that after you get to Mars, although your orders give you the right to come back at the next opposition, NASA will hope you *won't* come back—it costs a lot to get anyone there, and once you have some Mars experience they'd rather you stayed, because you'll be valuable there. Now—I'm assuming you'll accept?"

I could see that she was teasing, and for once I didn't mind a bit. "Yes, ma'am," I said. "I accept. Where do I report and when?"

"First you'll need to get moved," she said. "The Seventh is headquartered right here at JSC, and transfer orders are going out as soon as I give my secretary the go-ahead. In anticipation of your accepting, I've arranged for someone to show you some furnished apartments over in Nassau Bay, and then whenever you find something you can stand, you can go back, spend two days packing, and get back here. You'll begin training with Olga and Walter about a week from now. And of course you depart Earth five months before the next opposition, which means you'll be leaving Earth orbit in mid-April of 2033. As of right now, Jason, you're a hundred forty-four days from leaving for Mars."

She stood up, indicating that the interview was over, and grinned. "Jason, the rest of this conversation is with Aunt Lori, not Chief Kirsten. All I can say is, you lucky bastard. And that's what a lot of people will say, you know. I hate to bring it up, but when the Public Affairs Officer for this found out that *you* headed the list, he was beside himself with glee."

"I figured," I said. "It's all right. I certainly don't mind being Chris Terence's son, and I don't think you'd give this job to an idiot based on his ancestry. The reporters are a little aggravating to deal with, though."

"Another way you're a lucky bastard," she said. "In a hundred forty-four days, you'll be going millions of miles away from the press."

The third furnished apartment they showed me looked all right; it wasn't a big problem because nobody lived with me and I had no pets, so I took the first clean and decent-looking furnished place that would let me rent month-to-month and was close enough to work. I gave my mother in D.C. a call to let her know that I had been transferred and would have a new address soon.

"You know, Jason, you're really more like your father all the time.

You don't even complain about being yanked from one place to another. I think you even enjoy it."

"I do like a change of scene," I said, noncommittally. We had this conversation every time I was transferred.

"Well, you're never anywhere long enough to meet anyone, or put down any roots," she said. "I don't think that can be good for you."

I heard Sig in the background saying, "Amber, will you leave the poor kid alone, he's grown up for god's sake," and stifled a laugh as I sat down on the windowsill and looked out over the town. I'd never quite figured out how a guy so different from me had always been able to understand what I needed, but as the years went by I became more and more grateful that Sig had been there when I was a teenager.

"Anyway," she said, "I hope you found a place with decent decor, and not in a high-crime area."

"It's sort of brown-orange," I said. "JSC isn't anywhere near the city, and even if it were, there aren't really any high-crime areas anymore."

"You still don't have to live near them," she said, firmly. We talked for a while about trivial things. She and Sig were coming down to visit Lori next month, and now they would have an excuse to see me as well. Sig's niece had graduated from medical school and was thinking of taking a specialty in microgravity medicine. It was raining more than usual in Washington.

After we said good-bye and hung up, I found myself wandering through the furnished apartment, idly getting used to what views there were, and thinking about the conversation. Older people like my mother still remembered times when there were large parts of every big city where you couldn't go after dark. There were still places I wasn't crazy about, but things were different now; the prisons were slowly emptying.

It wasn't that people were nicer; there were as many jerks as ever, but now they were all jerks with jobs, generally good jobs, which meant they had homes and cars and something to lose, and so they behaved themselves. The world had changed a lot on its way from the disaster on the Moon to this moment, when we were going to take our second chance. I sat in the darkening living room, looking out over the highway full of headlights shooting by, and thought about what had made the changes. It seemed strange that although the world had changed so thoroughly, bringing me to this critical moment in human history, what I remembered most vividly were the things anyone does, the normal changes in my life, growing up and growing older.

It took me a year or so, after I got back from the ShareSpace trip, to really accept and recover from my father's death. During that year, though I didn't pay much attention to it, numerous politicians and pundits made a lot of speeches, did a lot of fingerpointing, and generally demanded that someone do something. Only two things were clear: the first was that space flight was the key if we were to do anything at all about the loss of the vast archive that was now scattered in useless bits of metal and silicon across the far side of the Moon. The second was that now that we knew it existed, we *had* to have that archive. Materials found at the Tiberian base at the lunar south pole indicated that they had been literally centuries ahead of us in materials science; almost everything of theirs, from the four-story-tall lander to their hammers and screwdrivers, was made of stuff stronger, lighter, and more durable than anything we knew how to make. Devices in their small infirmary were quite often compact efficient versions of what we were just barely managing to make at all in our laboratories. The optical computer (unfortunately quite inert) in the lander, and the optical information storage device that had been the Encyclopedia, clearly treated problems that we were only just learning to phrase, let alone to solve, as bits of routine engineering. And of course, as Chris and Xiao Be had noted, the propulsion system that had gotten the Encyclopedia here in a matter of a few decades (if the message was to be believed) was only about half the size of an ordinary garbage can, and had no apparent fuel source at all. By comparison, to get a package of the same mass to Alpha Centauri in one thousand years, we would have had to use the combined thrust of about 100,000 Energiyas, the biggest rocket then in use.

In a way the match was perfect; they were just far enough ahead of us (or had been at the time they stopped visiting) so that we could understand the significance of what they did and realize how much power and potential was in their technology, but not so far ahead that we couldn't eventually understand it—*if* we could get the Encyclopedia. Here was the chance to advance every field of natural science by centuries; here was the chance, for the first time, to compare humanity's art, religion, history, and everything else with that of another species, to gain some insight into what might be unique to our species and what might be common to all intelligence.

Or rather, here had been the chance. With the lunar Encyclopedia smashed to bits, there was only one choice now—get to Mars, get the other one, and do it right this time.

The big five space programs had suddenly had plenty of resources, but they had needed every bit of them. There were a dozen things to do right away: begin preparing for the eventual voyages to Phobos and Crater Korolev, to try to retrieve whatever might be there; return to the Tiberian moonbase and conduct history's most important archeological dig, a quarter of a million miles away, in hard vacuum, in a place where the Sun hadn't shone in billions of years; take hundreds of engineers' daydreams out of the technical literature and turn them into reality; educate the people who could do these things, and get them there.

That last part had been the key. We had to educate more people, better, in less time than ever before, because we needed millions of brilliant and well-trained scientists and engineers for every one of those gigantic tasks. We couldn't even begin until we got every good brain we could find trained as well as it could be.

The first way that I noticed it was two years after the accident, when people with Ph.D.s started turning up to give math tests to my ninth grade class—and if you did well, suddenly you had a scholarship to a superb school where those Ph.D.s would be your teachers. I was relieved, though Sig was disappointed, when I didn't turn out to be quite that brilliant.

It didn't matter anyway, because money and talent were pouring into all the schools, at all levels. For a while, good teachers were so much in demand that many of them were working twelve-hour days and pulling down more pay than corporate middle managers. They had a volunteer program going so that a lot of engineers and professors were "retiring" into teaching in the public schools, at increased pay.

By the time I was in college, the acceleration of education had meant huge expansions of opportunity, so much that even though there were four times as many engineers and scientists as there had been in 2010, the shortage was worse than ever. If you passed a few science classes you could have corporate recruiters beating down your door by the end of your sophomore year—or at least you could if you were at a civilian school. I'd chosen to go to the Air Force Academy.

And it wasn't just the job market that was changing. After decades in which every big project took much longer and cost much more, suddenly things were getting done ahead of time and under budget. Suborbital airliners were being talked about when I was a freshman, but I flew home for Christmas my senior year in one. Six years after the first maglev line between Los Angeles and San Jose, there were 15,000 miles of maglev track in the United States alone. One year after the Japanese pilot project for growing wood into preformed shapes in a tank, Mitsui was shipping whole prefab houses everywhere on the globe. Ocean-floating aquafarms were abolishing hunger; doctors had cured AIDS and Alzheimer's and were talking about human life extension to 150 years.

And all of this was caused merely by the overflow—if you need to recruit and train a thousand superb people, in any field, the best way to do it is to recruit and train a million people, and then pick the best tenth of a percent. Thus to get enough of the very best, the University Space Research Associates had had to produce many times that number of people who were "merely" excellent, and the release of so much highly trained talent into the world had done the rest.

But even while global knowledge and production were taking a leap forward on a scale not seen since the Renaissance, with the news full of one triumph after another, it had all been overshadowed by the archeological dig at the lunar south pole.

That was the hard one to believe. It didn't seem that long since my dad and Xiao Be were going to be the seventeenth and eighteenth people to walk on the Moon, but now, in 2032, the Moon's South Pole Station was a small town with over 200 quasi-permanent residents. A couple of the archeologists and the base operations people had been residents of the Moon for more than five continuous years, and last year a baby girl had been born there.

I got up and got myself a diet Coke from the fridge, drinking it straight from the bottle as I watched the dark settle over the neighborhood and the electric lights blaze to life. I had been in seventh grade at the time of the accident. There had been a swift redesign and replanning, since now they knew that they would have to spend hundreds of person-years studying that site. When I graduated from high school, the first crews to stay over on the Moon, not going back on the same ship that brought them, had been there for just a few weeks, and unmanned probes and supply ships had been going out to Mars on the last few oppositions, a steady stream of material going out and data coming back for the explorers to follow.

During summer training after my junior year at Colorado Springs, they had suddenly loaded us all onto buses to go watch a big-screen TV. We had watched Walter Gander—the man who would now be my commanding officer, I realized, and it still astonished me—step off the Phobos One landing craft, a slightly modified Pigeon the cycler *Aldrin* had carried with them, and carefully plant his boots on the dusty face of the new world. Looking up at the vast ruddy bulk of Mars hanging over his head, he said, "We have come this far, and we're here to stay. And—" suddenly his voice grew emphatic, no longer delivering a dignified public address, but declaring what he really meant "—and next time it won't be another fifty years! Worlds of thanks to Frank Borman, Jim Lovell, and Bill Anders, who paved the way for Neil, Buzz, Mike, and all." NASA had timed the landing carefully; it was December 25, 2018, fifty years to the day since Apollo 8 first reached the Moon.

What we knew about the Tiberians had also increased enormously, but it had a tendency to change drastically every couple of years. My last year at the Air Force Academy, there had been a no-credit class, taught by a history prof who had just returned from the dig on the Moon. The thinking at the time, based on the shelters and equipment they had found, was that the Tiberians had established their main base on Phobos and then set up a secondary base on the Moon. The thousands of broken pieces of everything that the Gander expedition had found all over Phobos tended to confirm this; possibly their base there had exploded, leaving the forward team on the Moon stranded. But then why was there no evidence of an explosion or meteor strike anywhere near their cave habitat on Phobos? And why was there no one inside? Had they all been working at a power plant on the other side of Phobos when the explosion happened? Then why were there no corpses or body parts among the debris? And hadn't anyone been able to abort to Crater Korolev, or anyone from Korolev been able to come up and help?

Whatever stopped the Tiberian base on Phobos from relieving their base on the Moon, it must have happened early on, the archeologists said, because the lunar base seemed half-finished and cobbled together, as if the Tiberians had had to improvise without any external support. Their mission had come to an ignominious end there at the lunar south pole. Their lander, with its strange mixture of aerostatic, aerodynamic, and rocket flight, was clearly capable of reaching the Earth, and the message seemed to say they had done so but then left. Why had they not returned to a world where at least they could breathe? Moreover, the base seemed never to have been fully staffed, because there were twice as many beds as bodies.

The way they had died was a mystery as well. It looked as if they had starved, since the little automatic farm was one of the few Tiberian devices there that didn't seem to have been abandoned in working order. And why had they brought what appeared to be young children with them—in such great numbers? Had they intended to colonize the Earth? "The great mystery," the professor had said with a flourish, "is why, with a working spacecraft and the Earth's surface just hours away, they didn't fly down and collect more than enough to feed themselves—or better still, move to our planet. With their technical superiority over us, given that dust on the shelter surfaces tends to indicate a date around 7000 B.C., which is confirmed by the counter in the Message itself, they could have been our rulers and masters. Why they chose not to . . . or could not . . . well, for the answer to that, we may very well have to wait until we get a look at Crater Korolev, or perhaps something will turn up in the analysis of the debris from Phobos that will be coming back on the special cargo return craft."

I was in flight training in January of 2021 when the Phobos Two expedition landed and set up Phobos Base. A lot of us stayed up late, in an all-night coffeehouse in town, to watch the landing, but due to problems with the transmission, they couldn't show us much of it and we had to be content with interviews with all sorts of people telling us that this was important. We all noticed that the lunar archeologists were already complaining that not enough archeologists were getting to Phobos; it seems to be an early part of pilot training to deal with the complaints of mission specialists. No doubt they feel the same about us.

Meanwhile, everything I had heard at the lecture two years before had fallen into question. Xenobiologists—a field that had come into existence in four years flat and now boasted four monthly journals—had managed to establish that the tissues of all the dead Tiberians had various kinds of damage brought on by the way their immune systems reacted to long-term exposure to Earth proteins, so they not only had to have been to the Earth, they had to have spent years here eating the food. Now the idea was that the Moon was some kind of refugee camp or quarantine area for sick Tiberians being rescued from a failed Earth colony. But then why hadn't they finished the job? And how could a starfaring race not have a big enough ship to just take everyone off the Earth and put them into shipboard quarantine?

Part of the answer came from Walter Gander himself. Some people called him a dinosaur, even then; he had been a rookie astronaut the year my father was killed. He was of the old school, with a doctorate in orbital mechanics and some years as a military test pilot, and there were allegations that he had been picked as mission commander in part just to remind people of NASA's glory days of fifty years before.

On the return trip on the cycler *Aldrin*, with about six months during which the major things the crew had to do were routine course corrections and life-support maintenance, Gander had gotten interested in a problem in orbital mechanics. He later said that what had first gotten his attention was just an idle interest in the complexity of figuring orbits around Phobos; the L1 and L2 points were located about seventeen kilometers from the center of gravity of the Martian moon. As he used up a lot of spare time and computer time figuring orbits, it occurred to him that since they had recorded the exact location on Phobos of each object they picked up, he could write a genetic algorithm in orbital mechanics, to find the minimum number of different places that the thousands of identified scraps of Tiberian material scattered over Phobos could have come from.

The answer was just one—a body orbiting a mere ten kilometers above its surface at closest approach—and suddenly everyone's favorite hypothesis was that the Tiberians had left a starship there, in orbit around the tiny moon. Orbital positions around Phobos are intrinsically unstable; sooner or later the ship had brushed the moon's face and started to break up, first into large pieces. Most of the big pieces had probably bounced into irregular orbits around Phobos, been captured by Mars, and fallen into the atmosphere and burned up; a few had collided with Phobos instead, breaking up further, until finally they had ended up as the scattered, patterned swath of debris we had found.

A couple of years later, as a lieutenant, I had a temporary rotation job in Washington, which meant I was seeing my mother and Sig a lot. That also meant I was constantly trying to deflect Sig's pointed suggestions that someday I might want to come and fly for ShareSpace, since the Starliner was nearing its test phase, and as he pointed out, he could just hire me, whereas NASA might keep my applications dangling forever. By that time it was generally agreed that even if they didn't know much about the Tiberians just yet, the archeologists had at least identified the right questions for whenever it was that we got down to Crater Korolev; in effect, we had a list of known mysteries to solve.

Narihara Nigawa's dissertation, *Anomalies in the Tiberian Technical Matrix*, caused an explosion of controversy, because he reopened a bunch of settled questions and argued that more needed explaining than anyone had tried to explain. According to Nigawa the Tiberian base on the Moon seemed to include several cases of duplicate devices in which one looked like a more advanced version of the other—"The equivalent of finding a Sopwith Camel and a Starbird together, or a crank telephone and a cellular phone," as he put it. And, he said, if we accepted the little indicator at the upper right-hand corner of some of the Great Volume frames as a date, it had been decades between the arrival of the first and second Tiberian ships.

The next year, when I was accepted into training as an astronaut-pilot for the rapidly expanding space program, scientists had finally cracked the operating principle of Tiberian solar power panels; within a few months the price of electricity on Earth was half what it had been. Some of the crew had spent a full year at the lunar south pole.

I had been flying space missions for a year when the famous research group of Ilsa Bierlein, Vassily Chebutykin, and Dong Te-Hua (the "BCD team," as the media dubbed them) had worked out a plausible interpretation of the system of writing from the few pieces of written Tiberian we had, finally confirming that the accordion-folded piece of fabric with symbols on it, found under the pilot's seat, was indeed the operations manual for the lander.

I sort of chuckled as I thought about that one. It all seemed like yesterday to me—I'd been so busy between space flying, advanced training, and a busy-but-never-serious love life—but it had been several years, and unfortunately no one had advanced matters any farther than the BCD team's original work. Though other linguists, cryptologists, and xeno-mathematicians were saying that eventually they expected great things, right now matters stood where they had with BCD's publication: about thirty percent of the common words in the manual were still unreadable, and another ten percent of the manual's vocabulary were unique occurrences: words that were only found once. They had deciphered most of the inscriptions on the lander itself, but they were such informative things as "Be sure to check! Is the (UNKNOWN WORD) turned off? Is the hatch closed?", "To open turn left and lift," and "Check for blue lights on panel before throwing switch."

In 2025, the Mars One Mission, incorporating concepts first proposed by a fellow named Zubrin way back in the 1990s, finally brought human beings to the face of Mars, and to the rim of Crater Korolev, almost twenty years after humanity had first heard the message from Alpha Centauri. The landing was, as scheduled, on July 20, fifty-six years after Neil and Buzz landed *Eagle* at Tranquillity Base. I heard the news while I was bringing a reusable lander up from South Pole Base to the *Armstrong* L1 Port. But that first Mars landing was a bit of a disappointment, for all the pride we took in knowing that humanity's third world beyond the Earth had been reached first by an American—so far we still had all the firsts.

Crater Korolev is roughly circular and about fifty kilometers in diameter—about the area of a midwestern county—and filled with ice as deep as three hundred meters. There was nothing on the surface, and even after the expedition made a traverse following the rim, still nothing showed up. For the first time, we had gone to a place where the message told us to go, and we had found nothing.

The Mars Two expedition of '27 had better success, in part because during the time it was on its way, the researchers operating surface robots on Mars by radio from Phobos had made a couple of interesting discoveries. First and foremost, in many of the ice fields of Mars, including the one in Crater Korolev and the one covering the north pole itself, there was what the seismic researchers called a "discontinuity," a depth at which the ice changed its character and composition. Tentative dating put it around the time the Tiberians should have been active on Mars. It looked as if a large part of the water on Mars had thawed very quickly, then refrozen within a short time and gradually redeposited into the craters and at the poles.

So when the Mars Three expedition of 2029 got to Korolev, it had a highly specific mission in addition to setting up and crewing a permanent Mars base. Using robots and treaded tractors, they installed a network of seismic listening devices all over the deep frozen lake; with sound generators, they probed the whole surface of the discontinuity, anywhere from five to eighty meters deep. The process was slow and the analysis was difficult, but they had time—we were on Mars to stay.

When the Mars Four team was added in 2031, the work went faster, and finally they were rewarded: they had an anomaly lying right on the discontinuity, a few meters under the surface of the ice in the middle of Korolev, and the anomaly was exactly the shape of the Tiberian lander that still sat on our Moon.

Only a few months ago, about the time that my superiors were writing all sorts of nice things about me in reports, making me likely to come to the attention of mission planners, the news had been that the crew at Korolev Base, using microprobes designed to very carefully penetrate the ice, and very low energy ultrasound, had definitely established that it was the second Tiberian lander—under four meters of solid ice, but otherwise unharmed as far as anyone could tell. It seemed to be lying on its side. Near it were the graves of about twenty Tiberians, all frozen solid, which meant that for the first time our scientists would be able to study a Tiberian body that had not dessicated in vacuum. Also there were eight stone buildings, fairly crude affairs, and further keyhole archeology of their interiors seemed to show more frozen Tiberians inside each of them.

Everything we had wanted to know since the message first came, thirty years before, was potentially there at that site. The one thing that wasn't there was the Encyclopedia; like the one on the Moon, it had landed at some considerable distance from the base. Now it had been found, and our team on site thought they knew enough about Martian arctic conditions to know how to get something out of there without destroying it. Our habitat would set down less than five kilometers from the site. Another Terence was going to go after a piece of Tiberian hardware. I hoped, wherever he was, Dad wouldn't mind if I improved on his performance.

It was finally time. I had been preparing for this for most of my life, and on this first day of finding out I would be going, I didn't quite believe it. I sat and sipped the diet Coke as it grew warm and flat, and I fell asleep, fully dressed, on the couch.

2

"OKAY, JASON, WHEN YOU'RE READY." CAPTAIN GANDER HAD THE SAME bland drawl for everything, so there was nothing to indicate that the next step I took would start us moving, and that we wouldn't stop until we were tens of millions of miles away. I picked up the cooling pack beside me and stepped forward onto the metal ramp that led out of the waiting room and into the side of the Yankee Clipper, where it rested on the launching pad next to the gantry. It was a longish walk—more than a city block—and I had the chance to appreciate all over again how huge anything that can get a person into space has to be. The cooling pack hummed a little louder, working harder to compensate for the bright Florida sunlight.

It occurred to me that I was breathing my last natural Earth air for more than two years to come; it was nice that it smelled of the sea, at the moment, for where I was going it might be a long time before I was near a sea again.

"Don't forget to wave," Captain Gander said behind me. "We don't want any Public Affairs Officers to get mad at you."

I was grateful for the reminder. Nowadays, with flights to orbit a few times a day, nobody came out to watch us, let alone television news. I'd flown Yankee Clippers for three years, six or seven flights a year, and the only people who'd ever come out to see me take off were Mom and Sig, and they'd only come out the first time.

But this was different, obviously. We were going to go get the Encyclopedia, and that made us as big a deal as the Phobos One expedition in '18, or the Mars One expedition in '25.

I looked up at the little camera they had mounted over the hatch and, as we had been told to do, smiled at the camera and waved. I took a second to take a good long look off to the side, at the green foliage and the iron-gray sea, locking the memory in place, and then went into the cool dim artificial light of the Yankee Clipper.

I was the first one aboard because the crew cabin in a Yankee Clipper had never been intended for long-term occupancy, there wasn't room to pass, and the ship boarded from the left. Since the pilot sits all the way forward and right, that meant I had to get in before anyone else could. I made my way along the corridor, noting only that what I could see of everyone's gear seemed to be where it was supposed to be, and around the captain's seat to my place.

My pressure suit helmet was in place and tied down; the boards showed that we were getting electric power from the gantry, just as we were supposed to, so, right on schedule, I started the power-up sequence to put us on independent. As the pressurized air came on, I hooked my suit to that and put my cooling pack carefully into seat bin *four*, lower left, the bin that was supposed to hold things we wouldn't be taking. Something felt odd, so I pulled it out, looked, and there was my keepsake box. I clicked off my microphone and said a couple of words Mom wouldn't have approved of, then leaned in and pulled out the box.

"Something wrong?" Captain Gander said, taking the seat next to me.

"The packing crew put my personal possession kit in the return-to-Earth bin," I said.

The captain grunted. "That's not good." He leaned back and shouted down to Olga, who was just coming aboard, "Hey, check to make sure everything that's supposed to go with you is in the right bins. They screwed up Jason's."

I looked around in time to see her make a face. "Packing crews," she said, with disgust. "When are we going to reinvent the sea chest?" She climbed down to her station and opened the bins. "Looks like they got my stuff right."

Though Olga and I had flown two training missions together, I didn't yet know her well. Some bright psychologist had the idea that since planetary manned missions would be years in duration, it might be better if we had to spend some time making friends and forming relationships on the way, rather than knowing each other thoroughly before going. It would give us something to do and help prevent boredom. So though we trained together, we were encouraged to spend most of our time away from the rest of the crew, and our individual studies and practice were often at separate locations. The idea was to have us all comfortable with each other but not too familiar.

It had already occurred to me, anyway, that Olga was fairly attractive and, like me, had no romantic attachments. She was also going to be the first officer while we were in flight, and thus my superior, which might be a considerable problem.

Or not. There were months to sort this out, after all.

I turned back to the checkouts. Every pilot agreed that with the modern big-screen flexible readout, you didn't really need to visually check each individual indicator, but every pilot always checked it anyway. Everything was nominal, so I moved on to the next step of the protocol, clicking my headset to the link channel:

"Control, Mars Five, this is Jason Terence, at my station on the Yankee Clipper. Are you there, Dean?"

The voice crackled in my ear. "Right here, Jason. I show checkout on you is nominal."

"I show the same," I said. "So far it looks just like a training movie."

"Let's hope it stays that way." Dean was an old friend, a guy I'd known at the Air Force Academy, who had made it into the astronaut corps and then turned up with a minor medical problem that might take a few years to get back into order. There had been a number of people like him in space history, going back to Deke Slayton, and it was good to have them around.

Reading all the indicators had taken up about half an hour. In the old days it used to take a lot longer, or so they said, and the switches weren't bright spots on the screen that you touched with a cursor, but little toggles, kind of like old-fashioned light switches. I thought about my dad for a moment; 120 years of aviation and seventy years of space-flight had so standardized cockpits that he'd recognize almost everything here, even though exactly what it controlled and how it controlled it had changed drastically in the last two decades.

I hadn't fulfilled my plan to get away to Arlington and visit his grave, the last time I was in Washington, a few weeks ago for the president's reception. Mostly I hadn't had the time. Once the assignments for the mission, and the fact that we'd be digging up the Encyclopedia, had been announced, there had been reporters following me all the time, and I was sure that if I went out to Dad's grave the media would have a field day shooting pictures and shouting questions.

Well, no doubt, wherever he was, he would forgive me—not having time and being hounded by the press was something he ought to understand.

I had finished rechecking the recheck, and was sitting there reviewing the flight plan for lack of anything more productive to do, by the time that Captain Gander said, "All right, let's get the mission specialists on board." It was exactly the scheduled time; the one thing I knew for sure, after flying with him for the last few months, was that Walter Gander did things by the book.

"Control, Mars Five, we're ready for the rest of crew boarding," I said. They acknowledged, and in a few moments the hatch opened again, and the seven mission specialists, plus the return pilot, came aboard.

Normally eleven people wasn't much of a load for a Yankee Clipper—it seats nineteen besides the pilot and commander—but we had a lot more gear than the average Clipper carries. On most flights, everyone's luggage goes ahead by an air-launched robot package, and all that the Yankee Clipper has to do is haul people.

But we were going to be gone for a long time—those who returned earliest would be starting their journey back at the next opposition, twenty-six months in the future. That was what I was kind of thinking I would do. I liked flying, a lot, and though this mission was too good a career opportunity to pass up, ultimately my career was back here in the Earth system. Mars was a frontier where a pilot was needed perhaps once in twenty or thirty days; Earth and the Moon were where the work was. Probably I'd be eager to get back after a few weeks of assisting the scientists.

But even the thirty-three months that would be my minimum time was long enough so that I was glad to have some family pictures, a couple of favorite books, and a few assorted knickknacks and mementos. It would make my personal compartment a little more like home, and a bit less like a closet or a phone booth.

The scientists might well be at Korolev for six or even ten years. No one knew how long it might be before we could safely move any of the many Tiberian artifacts; we were not going to run the risk of losing anything this time before it had been thoroughly recorded in situ.

"Everyone is aboard, sir," Mark Bene, the return pilot, said, raising his voice to be heard. It was nice to hear a familiar voice. Though we hadn't been close friends, we'd been together in the First Aerospace for some years. He closed the hatch.

"All right, everyone, keep the noise down so we can think," Gander said. The scientists subsided into whispers and got on with business, checking their bins—more things were found packed wrong, but nothing was missing—and rechecking readouts from the ship's systems, as a final backup in case the officers had somehow missed something.

Having finished my checkouts, I watched our scientific team. It was a slightly disorienting way to see them because all of us were almost lying on our backs in the acceleration couches, so it was sort of like looking down the side of a nine-tiered bunk bed.

The first one who caught my eye—because he seemed to command attention from everyone, all the time—was Narihara Nigawa; mostly we just called him Nari. He was a handsome man, just half a centimeter under the maximum height for the mission, muscular and quick. He'd played guard on Waseda University's basketball team and third base on their baseball team, and still found time to learn to fly and finish a Ph.D. before he was twenty-five; he was the one who had raised the question about the mixture of Tiberian technology that no one had an answer for. Supposedly he was engaged to someone back home, but none of us had met her, and the couple of times that he and I had gone out for a beer together, he certainly hadn't acted like he was settled for life.

Right now he was almost laughing to himself with pure excitement, running over the readouts and nodding. He had spent more than a year of his life on the Moon, been part of the Mars One landing, and had briefly visited Phobos, where apparently he'd found confirming evidence—the chunks of metal, plastic, and glass of Phobos, to the extent that they could be identified as anything, seemed to be mostly from his "early generation" of Tiberian technology. Besides being one of fewer than a dozen members so far of the "three-world club" of people who had visited the Moon, Phobos, and Mars, he was the Earth's leading xeno-engineering archeologist—an expert in figuring out Tiberian technology from the remains found on the Moon.

Having just confirmed, as all of us had, that everything was perfect, he turned across the aisle to say something to Paul Fleurant, a veteran astro-F and our computer wizard, a guy who knew more about artificial intelligence and genetic algorithms than just about anyone—and never let you forget how much he knew, either. Paul had been on Phobos Three going out on the *Collins* cycler in '22 and coming back with the Mars One crew in '27, and though he had never set foot on Mars, his place in Martian history was already secure. He had developed the programs that eventually allowed the robots on the Mars surface and the networked computers on Phobos to find the discontinuity and arrive at a date for it. He bent forward to hear what Nari was saying; then Paul's thick eyebrows flew up, and he said something back that had Nari covering his mouth so as not to laugh out loud.

It was probably mildly risqué, because Kireiko, sitting in front of them, blushed and bent over her screen, intensely rechecking things that were already working fine. Kireiko seemed to be shy, and about all I knew about her was that she was a molecular biologist, expert in Tiberian biochemistry, married and had two young kids. There had been a big public outcry about her "deserting her children" to go on this mission; neither she nor her husband had spoken a public word on the subject through the several months of hate mail that had poured in. The other thing, which you couldn't help knowing, was that she was beautiful.

Whatever it was about the joke that had bothered Kireiko apparently was very much to the taste of Tsen Chou-Zung, our doctor and expert on Tiberian anatomy, who was seated next to Kireiko. She snorted and said something that made Paul slap his thigh.

Next to me, Captain Gander took off his headset and said firmly, "It has come to my attention—courtesy of Dean at Control—that the media apparently can listen in to almost everything we say here. This apparently includes some jokes not entirely suitable for a family channel. So if you could all refrain—"

"Sorry," Paul muttered, and everyone went back to the final recheck.

Olga, sitting all the way at the back in the engineer's seat, leaned forward to confer with Mark Bene about something. I figured it was another comment about the whole conversation. Confirming that, Olga caught my eye and nodded, making half a smile. Paul was one of the several things she and I had discovered that we agreed about.

I glanced over the whole group; when you're going to go live on Mars, I thought, a little excitement—especially in the people who don't have to do any flying yet—is pretty natural. Paul and Nari were at least trying to stay focused on their screens; Tsen was conferring with Kireiko about something, both of them talking eagerly, though softly, at the same time.

As always, Vassily, the heavyset, bearded, quiet Russian who was probably the only human being with a triple doctorate in music, linguistics, and orbital mechanics, was keeping his own counsel. I had only heard him speak aloud a few times, but on the other hand the briefings he had written for the officers on the translation problems in analyzing Tiberian text had been fascinating. I had long ago admitted to myself that I found his intelligence intimidating, but admitting it didn't make it any less so.

Next to him, Dong Te-Hua, the oldest and physically smallest member of the crew, had stopped pretending to run rechecks one more time, and was sitting quietly with his hands folded. He and Vassily hung out together because as an anthropologist, his specialty was closest to Vassily's, and perhaps because neither of them liked to talk much. He was a pretty good guy. During the months when we three officers had been desperately trying to get completely caught up on the plans for extracting the Tiberian lander from its resting place under four meters of ice, he had been the one who most often made the time to explain a point of technique or to talk about what they were hoping to find.

That helped me a lot, because it was no easy task to keep track of what our mission specialists were working on. Exactly as Lori Kirsten had told me when I first took the job, the team we were taking to Mars was probably the heaviest concentration of brains per person since the

Manhattan Project. Humanity had spent twenty-four years, since the wreck that killed my father and Xiao Be, getting ready for this mission. We needed brilliant people in fields that had never existed before—and on top of that, they had to be capable of a long-duration space mission, *and* of pioneering in the deadly dangerous wilderness of the Martian arctic. So far only two surface explorers had been killed at Korolev, but fewer than twenty had ever gone there at all.

Dean's voice crackled in my ear. "How you doing up there, Yankee Clipper?"

"Ready here," I said. "As far as I know we're waiting on you."

"Unh-hunh. We're on private channel, Jason; you want the truth?"

"Why not?"

Dean's voice had the tone of sour amusement that it often did; he tended to see the world as living down to his expectations. "The president of Russia is still in the bathroom, and they want to photograph all six presidents watching our departure. They, ah, expect him at any moment. Me, I'd say five out of six presidents is plenty."

I exhaled a half-laugh. "Time and trajectory wait for no man. If he doesn't get out here fast, we'll just have to miss him," I said. "Keep me posted, Dean."

We were flying up to intercept Mars Five in low Earth orbit. The lower a satellite is, the less time it takes to go around the Earth, and the bigger an angle of the sky it cuts out in a given time. The MarsHab was only 300 kilometers up. It went from horizon to horizon in less than an hour, and we could only hit orbital velocity in one small part of the sky, so we had to go when it was time.

"Well, next time maybe he'll remember to pee faster," Dean said. "I'm starting the count." There was a click as he switched the channel over to "open," where everyone on board could hear and the media could listen in. "Yankee Clipper, this is Control. You are go in one minute," Dean added.

"Roger, Control, Mars Five is go," Gander said, beside me.

I took one last glance around the screens in front of me; everything was fine, just as it had been. Then I took advantage of having a seat with a view to get a good last look at Earth up close. The blue ocean in the distance looked soft; I wondered how many shattered rockets and crew compartments lay under it. They had been launching from here for decades.

Dean said. "Yankee Clipper, we are at thirty seconds and holding. Are you ready?"

"Roger," Walter said. "We're go, Dean."

The countdown began, the backwards count every American born since 1960 knew by heart, ending in "Ignition sequence start . . . ignition." There was a thunder under our feet; the big rocket engines were running up to full power. I watched as the computer continued to execute the program, my hands on the manual controls in case of trouble.

We reached thrust for liftoff and the outside camera showed the gantry bridge falling away. In the upper left corner of the screen, I saw us rising majestically on a pillar of white-hot fire even as I felt the acceleration beginning to push me back into the couch. Physically a Yankee Clipper was a winged lifting body; the wings at the rear folded in like French doors, first the stabilizers and then a joint in the middle, flat against the sides, for takeoff and reentry, then deployed for landing. The short canard wing near the nose was also lying flat against the body and would scissor out when it was needed, the two microjets giving the Clipper more maneuverability for landing.

The body looked more like a stretched and squashed pyramid than anything else, coming to a point at the nose, much wider than it was thick, with four big engine nozzles just barely protruding from the back; in the external telecamera view, now, we formed a narrow arrowhead on a great tongue of flame. Acceleration was now steady at 3.2 g, and we were still headed straight up.

I looked through the heads-up display on the windscreen in front of me; it was a copy of the screen. Though only the oldest pilots now bothered looking out the window during launch—the screen was so much easier to read—I liked to see what happened to the color of the sky. The pale blue of Florida April was deepening into the kind of dark blue you get on very clear winter days, much farther north; we were at eighteen kilometers altitude, reaching into the tropopause, and now we were gaining velocity very rapidly.

We were closer to the trajectory line than I could have done manually; that's the way it's supposed to be, but I'd had to do more than enough overrides. I kept my eye on the screen and let the added weight of the acceleration sink me into the couch, rested my hands on the controls (my arms felt like lead) and looked into the sky through the heads-up display. The blue behind the colored graphs and pictures deepened steadily.

We were still hurtling upward at more than three g's. At forty kilometers altitude, the sky was fully black. I let the computer continue to fly the ship as we arced over onto our initial orbital trajectory. They cut out the external telecamera view; by now we were just a bright streak in that view, and there was more useful information in the radar imaging. I watched as the indicators climbed and as the three graphs that showed our pathway all stayed well within the green ranges; we were right on course.

Taking manual control for the first time, I rolled us over for the view; people who weren't going to see Earth again for years were entitled, I thought. Acceleration was still fierce, but because we were so far above the ground there was little sensation of great speed. In the windshield in front of us, and on the front cameras, the Earth came into view, seeming to hang above us because under acceleration "down" is toward the engines. It always got to me every time I saw this view: huge, a shade of blue you saw nowhere else, streaked with white and brown. Europe and Africa lay spread out across the windscreen. "Control, everything is go," I said. "We are two minutes fourteen seconds from cutout."

We thundered on into the sky. Now I could see the sunset line that stretched across India and on up into Siberia. As the computer counted down, we waited until the moment when suddenly the vibration ceased, the acceleration was lifted from us, and there was an instant of feeling as if we were falling before we settled into the familiar sensation of weightlessness. All the indicators showed that we were where we were supposed to be. "Control," I said, "this is Yankee Clipper. We have achieved our designated orbit. Checking all systems before rendezvous with the MarsHab."

"Looking good, Yankee Clipper. Check things out and get back to us. Special message for the pilot."

I had just an instant to wonder what that could be before I heard Lori Kirsten.

"Jason," she said, "this is Aunt Lori. Your mother said to tell you to be careful out there, and to write."

There were not-very-suppressed giggles from the rest of the cabin behind me. I had a feeling that I could probably be doing this until I was seventy, and Aunt Lori—who would be about a hundred at that time—would still be teasing me. "Roger, Aunt Lori. My love to Mom and Sig."

As we all stretched out the kinks you get from acceleration, Captain Gander said, "It can't be entirely easy having Lori as both boss and family."

"I wouldn't trade it for anything," I said, "but sometimes it's easier than others."

He nodded. "Back when the world was young, she was the mission commander twice when I was piloting. I do believe it was then that I learned the importance of shutting up and letting the pilot fly." He touched my elbow. "Nice job; no unnecessary action and you let things go right. Keep it smooth." He unbuckled and pushed off, drifting back to confer with the scientists. Mark Bene came forward to take the second seat, and we put on headsets so we could talk to Olga, in the rear, without being bothered by the chatter.

For the next hour and a half, Olga, Mark, and I, assisted by everyone else, read and reread every output the Yankee Clipper could produce. Now, while we were still in low Earth orbit, and before we attempted rendezvous and docking with the MarsHab, was the time to make sure that absolutely everything was perfect with our craft, because if it wasn't, this would be our easiest time to abort. The human race had struggled mightily to produce the seven brilliant minds for this expedition; we weren't going to risk them on a faulty three-dollar part, if there was one.

There wasn't. Everything was absolutely, perfectly right. As we finished the checkout, I looked back at Olga and found her looking forward at me, holding her thumb up, grinning. She brushed her short black hair from her face. "Well," she said, "apparently we are perfect."

Gander looked at me and raised an eyebrow. "The most thorough checkout in history has found no bugs, sir," I said. I felt like whooping myself; it had been hammered at all of us, constantly, that if anything was even slightly wrong, we were to do the safest possible thing, whatever that might be. Too much could be lost too easily, and what we were doing, and would be doing later, was more than dangerous enough. *No unnecessary risks* was supposed to be our motto.

But difficult as that might be to achieve, it was our way to Mars— and we all wanted, desperately, to go to Mars *now*. If passing the safety check was the way to do it, we would pass it—and now we had, with flying colors.

Gander lifted his headset and slipped it back on. "Houston, this is Mars Five, on the Yankee Clipper. We are showing a completely clear set of readings and we are on our assigned orbit. Request permission to proceed to rendezvous and transfer."

"Roger, Mars Five, you are cleared. Good luck."

Without another word, we strapped in, glanced at everything one last time, and prepared to fire the engine again. The curved edge of Earth, white smeared on blue and immense, took up the whole top half of my window (if you define top as the direction your head points), stars showing below it. I thought a personal good-bye to it. We were only going a little farther up in this next burn, but the long far road we were taking was always in my mind, and I wanted to get going.

We counted down and fired the engine, our acceleration instantly providing us with the feeling of gravity, as if the Yankee Clipper were standing on the ground on her tail. There was vibration through the floor at my feet, but with no air to carry the sound, nothing like the roar of takeoff.

I kept my eyes on the trajectory guides, keeping us right in the middle of everything, as we ascended to a higher orbit. It's a tricky process that goes against your intuition, and I'm certainly glad I've never had to try to do it without plenty of electronic helpers. But everything again stayed normal, and a few minutes later, still exactly on course, we shut off the burn and let ourselves coast upward toward apogee, where we would find our MarsHab.

3

WE CAUGHT UP WITH THE MARSHAB AN HOUR LATER. AT FIRST GLANCE it was simply a squat, thick cylinder with a long thin cylinder sticking out of one end and a big shiny dome on the other. As we drew closer you could see that central thick cylinder was a Big Can.

A lot of the success of the space effort since the Mars Project had gotten into high gear had been due to the combination of bold mission choices with extremely conservative engineering—trying always to do things at the edge of our capabilities by the safest means possible. And that in turn meant a principle of never inventing more than needed inventing. The first Big Can habitat had saved the ISS and even enhanced it; therefore, when we needed to add more parts to Star Cluster, and eventually additional space stations in LEO and at L1, we used the mature Big Can, and as a result the LEO Ports *Glenn* and *Shepherd*, and L1 Port *Armstrong* went up virtually without a hitch. Improved and more elaborate versions of the Big Can now served as the habitats on the Moon at Tranquillity, South Pole Station, and Tsiolkovsky, on Phobos (though not currently occupied), and on Mars at Crater Korolev.

Yet another incrementally improved version of it had been used for the cyclers, *Aldrin* and *Collins*, two MERCs (Mars-Earth Return Cycles, our basic long-distance ship, which shuttled back and forth between Mars and Earth) named after the pilots of the Apollo 11 mission. A LEO or L1 port was a Big Can with extra docking ports; a MERC was a Big Can with a fuel tank and engine; and a MarsHab, once it landed, was a Big Can with feet.

The Big Can assembly line in New Orleans just kept running, dribbling out a new Big Can every eight months or so, the same way that south California assembled Pigeons, Seattle built Starboosters (and later Starlifters), and Phoenix turned out Yankee Clippers—with only the necessary changes and improvements, neither rushing nor delaying.

It was hard to believe that people in the 1990s had consciously decided to go through with the vast amount of assembly in orbit needed for the ISS. The experience was valuable and had been used in any number of operations since, but nowadays we'd have realized that it was cheaper and safer to build on the ground and heave the whole thing up in one piece. This MarsHab, like other MarsHabs, had come up in one piece, heat shield, booster, and all on a single tank assembly thrown up by a Mars HLV-SL (Heavy Lift Vehicle-Starlifter) combination.

As we closed in on the MarsHab, I had that feeling of reassurance you get when you see an absolutely reliable tool in your kit. For this mission the propulsion system was a simple set of rocket engines and tanks, with a set of landing gear sticking out below the nozzle so that it could stand upright on the Martian soil. It was about the simplest spaceship possible.

As we drew close enough, I used the maneuvering jets to kill our velocity relative to the MarsHab until we were a few meters away from it, the airlock on our left side drifting slowly toward one of the Big Can's docking ports. An occasional squeeze of thrust kept us lined up, the short sharp accelerations pushing us one way and another. Finally, when the separation was less than a meter, we were drifting in at a few centimeters per second, and I fed power to the electromagnets in the coupling. We lurched slightly, and then, with a soft, shuddering thud, the airlock fit over the coupling and the ships mated, hatch to hatch.

"It's holding pressure just fine," Gander said. "All right, let's go over."

Vassily and Tsen rotated the twin dials that unlocked it, then pulled the release bar. Our air mixed with the strange metallic tang of the MarsHab's air. Tsen, Vassily, Kireiko, Dong, and Gander shifted their belongings into the MarsHab in a neat relay, passing each item through the open airlock and putting it into the locker or bin it was addressed to.

They went to arrange their personal compartments, and the rest of us carried out the same drill with our things. Shortly, all the compartments assigned to our personal possessions were empty, all the compartments for return-to-ground had what belonged in them and nothing else, and the captain's group had verified that the MarsHab's life-support systems were running well within tolerances.

Mark and I rechecked the bins once more, made sure that there were no strayed items in the Clipper, and finally went to the airlock. I stepped through the door to the MarsHab for the last time, extended my hand, and shook his. "Your ship," I said.

"Thank you, sir. And hey, good luck out there."

"Thanks. Have a safe ride down." We each reached forward, closed the hatch on our own side, and dogged it down by turning the dials. I took half a step back into the hab proper, closed the airlock's inner door, and spun the dials to dog that down. The pressure lights were showing green; neither door was leaking. I cycled the airlock to vacuum; a small pump removed the air from the little closet and put it into our crew compartment. It still held pressure.

On headset, I said to Mark, "All right, we're under correct pressure. No problems. You may release at will."

"Roger, Mars Five. Releasing."

There was a thud on the hull, and the Yankee Clipper fell away from us. Still wearing the headset, I floated to the pilot's station, checked my screen, and said, "All right, Mark, you're clear enough. Have a beer and a pizza for me down there."

"Sure, Jason. See you in a few years."

I switched to the appropriate camera and watched his engines flare to life; relative to the station he seemed to shoot violently away and dive out of sight. Relative to the ground, he had fired his rocket engine against his own direction of motion, so that instead of orbiting at the same speed as he had been, he had moved into a lower and faster orbit.

Somewhere far below he would ride down on the heat shield on the bottom of that Yankee Clipper, slowing still further from the Mach 25 of orbit down to about Mach 12 in the upper stratosphere; then the wings would deploy, and at his enormous velocity in the thin air, he could glide halfway around the world if he wanted to before descending into the troposphere and down to the landing field. That was another beauty of the Yankee Clipper over previous systems: reenter anywhere, land anywhere else. Of course you also needed to know, in a matter of a couple of minutes after you picked your reentry point, the pathway between where you came back into the air and where you touched the ground, but by using the Global Positioning System, the fast ground-based computers could generally tell you that in about ten seconds. I thought, with a faint twinge of envy, that shortly Mark would be gliding thirty miles above the Earth, at just under ten thousand miles an hour, back to Canaveral with nothing to think about except where he wanted to eat dinner.

We were to continue in this orbit for a three-hour final shakedown to look for all the possible trouble there could be while we still had an easy abort to Earth. Once we fired the booster, we would be on our way to Mars no matter what happened, and we'd get there whether or not we were alive (though we wouldn't make much of a landing if we weren't).

At the pilot's station, I checked through everything slowly and carefully; whenever my attention wandered, I went back to whatever I was sure I had gotten right, and then proceeded forward from there. Propulsion was fine, and Olga concurred. Astrogation was fine, and Captain Gander concurred. All maneuvering and control jets were fine, fired properly, gave the right calibrated thrust. I sent the camera pod, a small maneuverable robot craft, outside to look for ice forming anywhere—a sure sign of an internal leak—and to scan the heat shield for cracks. I found nothing. The camera pod returned to its place and I confirmed that it was locked down. The landing rocket checked out fine.

Each of those steps was made up of many smaller steps. I was glad I'd spent so much time drilling on them in the last few months, because it was bewilderingly complex. It had only been on the twentieth practice that I had been able to get done within three hours, and I had been past a hundred practices before I had begun to have any slack. This time, I didn't beat my record (zero gravity sort of threw me off—I had only had one training mission where I got to practice that), but I still had a good twenty minutes left over.

So did Olga, so she and I strapped into the pilot's and commander's chairs and each ate a quick sandwich, admiring the Earth by naked eye for the last time through the window. We floated in the quiet of space—or the almost quiet, for the mission specialist team and the captain were talking softly in the common room down the corridor—and watched the brilliant Moon rise over the huge blue Earth in front of us.

"They're missing quite a show," I said, indicating the people down the corridor, none of whom was bothering to look out a window, even though they too had finished their checkouts.

"It's kind of sad, don't you think, that this could be routine to anyone?" Olga asked, never moving her eyes from the window.

I hadn't thought of it that way, but I agreed. "I guess it's the price of success; we expect things to behave themselves. The scenery is probably more meaningful if you're really afraid it's the last you'll ever see."

"Perhaps. Or it may just be that no matter how wonderful something is, if we see it often enough we don't see it at all." She sighed. "Have you ever been over to our Tsiolkovsky Observatory, on the far side of the Moon?"

"I've never actually been farther than Tranquillity," I said. "I thought your country only had a regular crew of seven or eight there. I didn't think you had any foreigners as a regular thing."

"Yes, but we quite often got supply drops from your Pigeons, and usually the pilot would have time to come in for a meal. So any American pilot might have been there now and then. I was station engineer there for a few months. It's an astonishing place, because you can't see the Earth from there—the Moon at your feet blocks it forever. So Tsiolkovsky is the closest inhabited place where the only trace of home is what you brought with you. I used to sit and gaze out the window for hours, and when I had to go outside I would stop and look around, at the mountains and up at the sky, as often as I had a moment. But in their off time, the astronomers mostly played chess or watched recorded movies from home."

I nodded. "I know what you mean. Still, I bet after eight months of nothing bigger than a star except the Sun, we'll be happy enough to see Mars up close in the sky."

"Of course," she said. "Variety is the only way we ever notice what's beautiful."

We watched the Earth roll by for a while longer, and I said, "I hear you're slated to stay over on Mars for a while."

She nodded, her face very serious. "I'm needed, of course—there aren't very many general engineers, there are fewer in space, and still fewer who are as good as I am—you don't mind my being honest, do you?"

"Go right ahead."

"And also I like to see a place thoroughly; I really enjoyed spending enough time on the Moon to know what the Moon is like. And . . . well." She sighed. I looked at her closely. Naturally for space everyone's hair has to be short—longer hair is a great way to accidentally bring all sorts of bugs, parasites, and pathogens aboard—but hers was just at the edge of regulation, falling most of the way over her forehead, going a little way down into her collar, hanging over her ears. It was jet black and looked thick and clean. Her eyes were almost as dark; her skin was pale and freckled, her chin small and delicate.

I had completely forgotten the subject of the conversation, and was putting all of my concentration into raising my estimate of how attractive she was, when she finally said, "And, you know, as Earth is getting wealthy, it's becoming a better place, but it's getting dull; the new affluence is smoothing out all the differences between places. I don't regret that we don't have starvation or epidemics on the scale we once did, or that more people are safe and comfortable, but I do regret that the Earth used to have a lot of differences. Nowadays, to go somewhere different, you have to go—" she gestured toward the Moon, now well into the viewport as our orbit took us around "—you have to go beyond that."

I was trying hard to think of something intelligent to say when Captain Gander, who had come quietly up behind us, said, "Well, I quite agree. Are we ready to validate the decision?"

"Sure," I said, as Olga said, "Yes."

He smiled. "All right, let's do one last thing by the book." He lifted the headset from his chair; Olga grabbed the spare, and I took mine and put it on. "Nari, are you there?" Gander asked.

"Right here."

"All right, then." There was a click as he opened the channel to the ground and said, "Houston, this is Mars Five."

The voice crackled back "Go ahead, Mars Five."

"Houston, this is Walter Gander. We're ready for TMI."

TMI was TransMartian Injection: burning the booster to put us on course for Mars. After a couple of serious incidents the Russians had had through carelessness—including the horrible one of leaving a cosmonaut outside and boosting away during an EVA—the spacefaring nations had adopted a set of procedures to be used whenever you did a major burn in space, to make the officers more accountable for certifying that the ship was ready to go. TMI was definitely a major burn.

"Mars Five, we need concurrence of the first and second officer, plus the science team head."

"First officer concurs," Olga said.

"Second officer concurs," I added.

"Science team head concurs," Nari said.

There was a moment's pause, and then Houston said, "All verified. Mars Five, you are go for TMI. You are on your own authority for any of the precalculated burns."

"Roger, Houston. We will proceed with the next available scheduled burn. Out." Gander hung up his headset, consulted his screen, and said, "All right, people, that's just eighteen minutes forty-three seconds away. Everyone go to your compartments and eliminate, or whatever else you need to do to get comfortable, and then everyone, except the officers, get onto your bunks. We've got places to go. Olga, get out of my chair."

"Yes, sir," she said, smiling but moving quickly. "Back in a moment."

I popped out of my chair as well and swam to my compartment; I had seen it only briefly as I had been stuffing my possessions into my personal storage spaces. I closed the door and looked around; as many times as I had been in space, I had never seen a personal compartment before.

These things had been suggested by NASA's shrinks as a way of alleviating some of the stress of space voyages; they probably didn't take up much more space than a regular bunk and a large locker might have, but they gave you the feeling of a room of your own, even if you did have to enter it through a small hatch and half its floor area was your bunk. Half the remaining floor area was taken up with your personal effects locker, which was where you kept toiletries, the uniform you weren't wearing at the time, and whatever possessions you had brought from Earth. By coming up exactly as high as the bunk, the personal effects locker was also your night table, or if you wanted you could put a pad on it and make your bed a little wider for your shoulders. The whole compartment was just one and two-thirds meters tall and wide, and two meters long; not much more than a coffin, but it had its own light switch, its own door, and it was all yours.

It was also a place to use the plastic bags to eliminate in zero g; I was amused to realize that this was the first time I had been on a ship with someone else, in space, used the bathroom, and *not* had an audience. It did seem more pleasant, on the whole, although some design genius had made the bags transparent, so a moment later we all emerged simultaneously into the corridor with whatever we had done more or less on display. Carefully ignoring that, we all tossed our bags into the recycler.

The scientists went back to their compartments, the doors closed, and that would be the last we saw of them till the captain announced an all-clear. The compartments, at the moment, were oriented so that nominal "down" was toward the booster; thus the bunks could serve as acceleration couches.

I got into my seat at the pilot's station and said, "Ready, sir." The clock showed we had six minutes to go.

Gander nodded. "Well, then, here we go. Olga's back on station, and she says everything looks perfect. You've got time to recheck the board once more."

I did, again, and for the hundredth time that day everything looked perfect. I rested my hands on the controls and made myself relax; this was largely a job for the computer, just like the others, but if there were any need for me to override it would come up very suddenly.

The booster behind us would need to fire for about eleven minutes, accelerating us at just over one g, to get us onto the correct trajectory. One g is what the gravity is on Earth, of course; the purpose of putting the scientists onto their bunks was not to protect them from forces that their bodies were used to anyway, but to make sure that they could not suddenly fall when the acceleration came on, and to keep them from getting hit by anything that might shift and come loose. The captain and I in the control cabin, and Olga back near the ship's machine and farm sections, were presumed to be able to look out for ourselves.

We counted down and watched the computer screens; this needed precision in tenths of a second, faster than we could reliably handle controls, and our only function was to make sure that if something got far out of bounds we shut down before anything worse happened. I had primary responsibility for watching the trajectory, to make sure we stayed on it; Olga was watching the booster for any signs of components failing due to heat, stress, or vibration; and Gander was watching us.

Gander counted down dispassionately. We hit zero, and there was a deep, low-pitched thunder in the ship. I sank into my chair; there was an odd feeling of suddenly being back on Earth, because the gravity was the same.

Once again, things were perfectly normal; the trajectory stayed completely within bounds, and Olga later said nothing got anywhere near the critical range. The time crept by and the biggest problem I had to face was staying absolutely alert and keyed up even though nothing required me to do anything. At last, right on schedule, the engine shut down.

I took a quick look at the camera. The Earth already looked different; we had increased our distance from the surface severalfold, and now we were moving away from it at about twelve kilometers per second. We would cross the Moon's orbit in less than nine—far faster than the ballistic trajectories to the Moon that still took about three days, just as they had in 1969—but we would still take around seven months to get to Mars.

"Olga, Jason," Captain Gander said, "here's what I've got in mind: I'd like to get the whole job of orienting and spinning up done, and then let everyone take a long rest. That's probably another three hours of work, and everyone has already put in a nine-hour day. How do you feel about it?"

"I'm not badly tired yet," I said. "And the idea of getting everything into good shape so that I can really enjoy the rest afterwards seems pretty appealing."

"I feel the same," Olga added.

"All right, then, it's unanimous among the ruling class." Gander grinned. "And the reason I brought it up was that the scientists had already suggested it."

The first part of the next three hours, turning over the personal compartments, was all the hard work. Objects have no weight in zero gravity, but they still have mass, which means they still have inertia. You can easily push a ton off the floor but once it's moving it will really hurt to stop it. Furthermore, in zero gravity your footing isn't quite as secure as you might like; friction depends on the force with which the two surfaces are held together, and without gravity to create those forces automatically, you always have to think of bracing yourself.

There were several people there with experience doing physical labor in zero gravity, but I wasn't one of them. I had worked with the others twice in training, and that was all. Olga and Nari seemed impossibly graceful and efficient, finishing their allotted tasks in short order and promptly taking over and doing everyone else's. What we were doing was rotating the personal compartments 180 degrees, to the direction they would need to face from now on, with "down" being toward the heat shield. Since each of them was really not much more than a very fat, tall man's casket, and there was little that was intrinsically heavy about them, it was mostly just the sheer awkwardness that slowed us down and turned the job into real work. We had to remove the end compartments from the two racks (putting them into the common area and the lab space temporarily); flip the ones still in the racks over into the adjoining racks; rearrange so that the ends of the racks were free; then finally flip the end compartments as we put them back in. Miraculously, when we checked at the end of the process, all our little coffins were facing in the right direction, but all of us were sweating, and I know that I and a few others had some bruises.

Deploying for sustained flight was a much simpler business, because the machines did all the work. First we separated the booster stage from ourselves on a set of three-kilometer-long cables. (The fruit of the few things we had learned so far of Tiberian science: by studying some of their fabrics and fibers, we had learned how to make lighter, stronger, and more compact ropes and cables, including noncryonic superconducting cables, than anyone had known were possible.) Our power plant, which would provide our electricity through most of the voyage, was inside a fairing at the top of the booster, and that added to the mass.

Using the small jets, we gradually worked up speed until we and the booster were swinging at opposite ends of the cable, whirling around each other like two skaters holding hands, with the MarsHab moving at around 25 meters per second, so that we went around about once every eight and a half minutes. With MarsHab, landing rocket, and heat shield, we had about twice the mass of the mostly-empty booster plus power plant, so the center of mass of the whole system was on the cable about a kilometer from us. Whirling around our joint center of mass, at our rotational speed, we were producing about a third of a g of centripetal force, about the surface gravity we would experience on Mars.

We had spun up so that the cable rotated in a plane that faced the sun; now we signaled the booster, and it jettisoned the fairing around the power plant. As we watched through our cameras, arms extended automatically to stretch a thin reflective film into a large parabolic reflector.

The parabolic reflector had sat folded up inside the top of the booster. It was made of sheeting thinner than paper and long, very rigid supports made of the same Tiberian vacugel that was used for Clipper hydrogen tanks. Once deployed, the parabolic mirror that it formed, facing the Sun, was fifty meters across, a gossamer structure of the kind that can only exist in space. On another set of arms, the second parabola, inside the first and facing it, extended into place; this one was little more than a meter across.

Parabolic reflectors are useful because they will bring a beam of parallel light into a single point at their focus, and conversely if a light is placed at their focus, they will shape the light into a parallel beam. A television satellite dish is a parabolic reflector, because if an object is distant enough, the light rays coming from it will be so close to parallel that it makes no difference. The television signal comes in as radio waves from a satellite hundreds of kilometers away; these are nearly parallel, so the dish focuses them to that relatively small spot in the center where the receiver is mounted.

The same principle allowed us to have a highly efficient solar dynamic power plant. The two parabolic reflectors had been placed so their foci were identical. Parallel sunlight hit the first reflector and bounced into the focus; from the focus it hit the second reflector, and as it was reflected, was reshaped into another parallel beam. But where the large reflector had an area of 1963 square meters, the beam was now just a meter wide— and 2500 times as intense. Sunlight in space at the distance of the Earth's orbit carries about 1300 watts per square meter; this meant that a bit over two and a half million watts was in that narrow beam.

The beam in turn was focused by a Fresnel lens into a boiler; in the boiler was liquid neon. The neon boiled, expanded into white-hot gas, passed through a series of turbines, and then was expanded through a system of radiator pipes that ran down the body of the booster on the side that now would stay turned away from the Sun. By the time the neon reached the end of the pipes, it had cooled considerably; it was then compressed, releasing more heat through a second radiator, until it reliquified at cryonic temperatures.

The efficiency of a heat engine—like a turbine or internal combustion engine—depends among other things on how big a temperature difference it operates across and how much energy is lost in various turbulent processes in the working fluid—"sticky" or viscous fluids tend to absorb a lot of energy into themselves, "thin" fluids do not. We were moving heat from a two megawatt beam to the near absolute zero of space, and using one of the thinnest fluids known. Not surprisingly, we were capturing almost half of the incoming energy, something over a megawatt, which meant that the power now flowing over the cables was enough to reseparate the water the fuel cells had produced into hydrogen and oxygen, so that we were back at full charge, and to operate all the ship's equipment with plenty to spare.

That meant a lot of other things, too. With some gravity (at least enough to get water to a drain) and plenty of power, the ship's shower and clothes washer were available, and the "farm," the other technology we had copied from the Tiberians, could begin to turn out fresh vegetables.

The captain and I volunteered for the first watch; everyone else went swiftly off to sleep. Curiously, after all the hubbub of the day, in just a few minutes the ship was quiet except for the distant hum of the machinery. The stars wheeled by the windows, twice as fast as the second hand on a clock, but it gave no sense of motion since I could "feel" absolutely that the direction of my feet was down. Now we weren't confined to food that behaved itself in zero gravity, so I made coffee. For a long time we sat in the cockpit, occasionally looking at the camera images as the Earth and the Moon steadily shrank behind us. In a bare few days they would look like two bright stars, ever so slowly crawling toward each other.

But it wasn't being on an interplanetary flight that seemed strange, somehow. It was that still-large blue Earth—it seemed like an intruder into the self-contained world of the MarsHab. Already I was sensing that this new life was going to feel profoundly normal for a long time.

We were each having our second cup of coffee when Captain Gander leaned back a little and said, "Well, now that you're here, and no one else is, I suppose it's as good a time as any to discuss some things."

4

I WAITED A LONG BREATH, AND THEN SAID, "I'M LISTENING, SIR."

Gander glanced sideways at me. "Oh, don't sweat it, Jason, I'm not going to chew you out or tell you to watch your ass. Just a couple of things you need to have in the back of your brain." He stretched and yawned. "My God, twenty-five years of space missions catches up with you. Well, first off—" his voice lowered to a murmur "—I presume Lori briefed you, at least somewhat, on our political situation here. You notice that not only are you and I the only Americans on board, but we're also the nonscientists in the team."

I nodded. "I had thought of that, but people seemed to be making a big deal out of who should be the officers."

"That's what we wanted," he said. "You'll also note only one of the scientists is Russian—and he's so much the expert in the field that nobody could have left him home."

I nodded again and said, "This adds up to something, but I'm afraid I don't understand what."

Gander smiled. "Well, if you don't, then perhaps some quiet misdirection we've been doing is having a positive effect. Our diplomats tried to look very worried about the possibility of a foreign crew, and the Russians played along with us, so that it looked like we only grudgingly let Olga have the engineer's job. But the truth is just what you'd think; what really matters, what has really mattered all along, is who's going to get access to the Encyclopedia. And we do have to worry that the team that's going to dig it up and read it doesn't include an American. They may or may not give us full access to all their work, no matter what the treaty says. That applies especially to the Chinese, of course. Things aren't as bad as they were in the Cold Peace, not by a long shot, but you still can't really say we can trust them. And NASDA and ESA may well have agendas of their own, too."

"So what do we do?" I asked.

Gander smiled broadly now. "We have a little extra surprise waiting for them. Do you remember how long they're planning to take to dig down to the Encyclopedia?"

"A couple of months or so, isn't it? First they want to find out about any surprises in dealing with Martian ice, so they're going to start out by excavating at least partway to the settlement. So that means they're going to cut out the ice in numbered blocks so they can study the position of the microdebris. The kind of thing that Ilsa calls 'toothbrush and tweezers archeology.'"

"Exactly. And before that time is up, a second team of scientists will arrive—top people as good as the team we're taking, which is really saying something—four Americans and four Russians."

I started. "How are they getting to Mars? I thought *this* was the manned launch for this opposition."

"We're hoping that's what everyone else thought. They're coming out on *Aldrin*."

I gaped at him for a moment; then I almost laughed out loud. "Of course. We could have started doing that any time."

Gander nodded. "It's a new concept they've gone to, after years of talking about it. Now that living space is finally exceeding personnel at Mars, they want to use cyclers to take people out as well as to bring them back. So *Collins* will keep on doing what it always has, flying with a crew from Mars to Earth, dropping its crew off, and getting a gravity assist at Earth that sends it back to Mars for another cycle. But from now on we'll call it the REcycler—Return to Earth cycler. *Aldrin* was held over for several months at Mars, waiting for a trajectory that would allow it to return to Earth to be captured, rather than gravity assisted. From now on it's the GOcycler—the Going Out cycler—and what it will do is depart Earth with a crew, deposit the crew at Mars, be refueled here, and then return empty to Earth to pick up another crew.

"The tricky part for NASA and the Russians was hiding it from our Chinese, Japanese, and Euro friends. To make it less obvious we had to have *Aldrin* go back at the last possible minute, just as if it were a badly delayed crew return. Then we'll announce that *Aldrin* needs an emergency repair—which is consistent with that delayed return—and divert her into an aerobrake to place her in a highly elliptical orbit around the Earth. A supposed 'technical crew' of five Americans and five Russians, in two Pigeons, will go out to rendezvous with her and to supervise putting new fuel tanks on her. It'll all look perfectly normal—till instead of coming back, the Russian/American crew light *Aldrin's* engine and ride her on out to Mars. They'll get there about five weeks after we do— which is to say, the dig team here won't be more than a few layers of ice down. So we're not getting shut out of anything, and neither are the Russians."

"Slick," I said.

"Well, we can't count on the Chinese, the Japanese, or ESA taking it as good sports. If any of them were planning to share fully with us, they might very well take it as an insult; and if they weren't, they aren't going to be happy when they can't snooker us. Not to mention that if they were up to anything dishonest, their people on this ship would have to be in on it, you know. So we might have a bad situation, one way or another, on our hands, and at the least we'll probably have some wounded feelings. I just wanted to make sure you knew it was coming and weren't taken by surprise. And, of course, at least until I tell you otherwise, you *can* rely on Olga and Vassily. She'll be briefing him within the next day or so. Any questions?"

"I don't think so." I couldn't help smiling. "I know it will cause some trouble here, but it's nice to see that we can still manage not to get taken for a ride."

"That's the spirit." He looked down at his screen and said, "As usual, right when we start out, we're going to have to do some course corrections. It's not easy to get a spinning object onto a precise orbit." His fingers flew over the keys, setting up a series of bursts from the ship and the booster to get us closer to where we belonged; I watched over his shoulder, fascinated at how fast he could do that. "That's a starter," he said.

I was about to ask if I should set it up to execute when he transferred it to a genetic algorithm, defined a few parameters, and set it to optimize.

He looked up at me and grinned. "Too many people take too much pride in their work. A human being might accidentally come up with something as good as a genetic optimizer, but not likely. I can stand the thought that a machine can do this better than me."

"Same way I feel about flying the ship, captain." I stood back and waited for the output. A genetic optimizer is a fast, efficient way to do something that couldn't have been done at all a century ago. Suppose you have a problem where it's easier to tell which solution is better than it is to solve for the best solution. Then one way to solve it, if you have enough time, is to generate a hundred random solutions and keep the best ten in that group; make nine copies of each of those ten, randomly varying them, so that you bring the total back up to a hundred; and repeat the process. Stop when you have a good enough answer or when the answers stop improving. It's evolution in action: each successful solution gives birth to another generation, some of whom are "mutants." Successful mutants replace their parent-stock; sooner or later you get something successful enough.

The only catch is that that's a lot of random solutions to study, and you need a big, fast computer to do it. But nowadays, when every mission carried more computing power than the whole Earth had had in the year 2000, that was hardly a barrier anymore.

Fifteen seconds clicked by, and then the solution came out. It was remarkably close to what Captain Gander had put in in the first place, as I pointed out. "Yep. And sometimes it's not. Well, put it in and let's do it."

Once again, my job was to watch the computer and make sure that what it was doing was a good thing to do. The one thing you really can't build into machines is common sense and gut instinct, and so even as advanced as they've become, we still have to watch to make sure that what they're doing makes sense for our purposes. But once again, everything went fine, with some minor tinkering on my part, and shortly we were both closer to trajectory and at a better angle to the Sun for our power plant.

Captain Gander had been watching me closely. I didn't think much of it. If I'd been commanding a mission this important, with so many irreplaceable human beings on board and a pilot I hadn't used before, I'd have been watching pretty closely, too.

When I finished the sequence, he said, "I'm sure you're aware I knew your father."

"Well, yes, sir," I said. "The astronaut corps was pretty small in those days; I guess everyone knew everyone."

"True." He looked over at the record of the correction; I had throttled back twice when one of the small rocket motors on one booster began to run hot, but that was all. We were right in the groove. "I just wanted to mention that I don't think he ever had the patience or discipline to do the kind of job you do, as well as you do. Probably you've heard things like that from other people, before."

"Sometimes," I said. "I think it's not quite as much of an issue for me as it is for some others."

We didn't talk much more on that shift; I hoped I hadn't said the wrong thing. The truth was that I was well coordinated, with a good but not great head for math and science, and liked a challenge; very possibly I'd have been an astronaut even if Dad had been a plumber. People were always wondering what I was trying to prove, or trying to reassure me that I didn't have to prove anything. It was kindly meant, but I just didn't feel that I needed it.

The first few weeks slid by; most shifts were uneventful. Traditionally everyone brought along a few projects to study, because there simply wasn't much for a crew of ten to do between boosting out of Earth orbit and aerobraking into Martian orbit. I spent a good bit of time studying the little that was known of the Tiberian language, with help from Vassily Chebutykin, and learning from Nari and Dong the basic way a dig worked. In turn I coached Kireiko and Tsen on the flight simulators.

I spent other time reading, listening to music, or asleep. Now and again I'd find myself sitting with Olga and watching the stars wheel around from the cockpit window. We never quite broached the subject of the crews coming after us in GOcycler *Aldrin* and what effect that might have on our relations with the rest of the crew, but we'd hint at it in passing. Or we'd have a meal together and talk about what it was like to grow up rich and famous, as I had, or to struggle up from a working-class family to becoming an engineer, as she had. We had some things in common, like skiing and enjoying mysteries, and some things that the other person couldn't fathom: she had no idea what I saw in American country music, and I couldn't begin to understand what she liked about twelve-tone stuff. It seemed to be developing like any friendship does, in fits and starts, getting to know each other, becoming gradually surer that the other person really likes you.

Several of the scientists were qualified pilots, so once a week Captain Gander would have Nari or Vassily take the commander's chair, with Paul or Ilsa as pilot, while he had a meal with Olga and me in the commons, with the door closed, and we talked about things in general.

After one such meal, four days before the Mars Five Alpha crew were to intercept the MERC, back at Earth, he leaned back and said, "Well, it's getting close to the day. The best thing that could happen would be to have everyone on board here shout 'Hurray! More help!' but I'll be pretty surprised if that's what happens. I'd settle for just having it all blow over after some angry words."

Olga nodded. "Vassily thinks the Chinese are already suspicious. He says that Dong has not been as forthcoming as usual and seems sort of troubled. With private e-mail you never know what people know anymore."

The captain shrugged. "Well, I guess we'll find out soon enough. It was like this on Phobos One too, you know. We had a crew of five, one from each space agency, and sure enough there was a reason why everyone had to plant his feet on Phobos first."

Olga smiled, a tight little smile without humor. "The Russian on that mission is something of a friend of mine."

If it was a hint, it didn't seem to bother Gander. "Dmitri was one sharp guy, which was how he got the other slot in the two-man lander. I think if I hadn't had an eye on him, I'd have heard the door slide open behind me and turned around to hear our arrival announced in Russian."

"And you think he was dishonest?" Olga asked.

"Hell, no, he was perfectly straightforward about it. I respected him highly as an opponent, and if he'd pulled it off it would have done great things for his career, I'm sure. It would also have trashed mine, which is why I wasn't going to let him. No," and Gander's voice dropped low again, "that kind of thing was really more like a game than anything else. This, unfortunately, is very real. I do hope from the bottom of my heart that the planners are wrong and everyone will be friends—just like we were on Phobos eventually. But I have to think about worst cases."

Olga took a sip of her cocoa and shrugged. "Well, Dmitri Tomaso-vich always spoke highly of you, and I think he thought of it as a game as well, so I guess I can see how you managed to be friends. To me, the whole sordid business of national pride in these missions seems silly—we're in a tiny metal box that is the only place where we can survive for millions of kilometers. You'd think we'd be smart enough not to fight inside it."

"You would think so," Gander agreed. "The trouble is whether it's true or not. That we're smart enough, I mean."

"If we aren't, nature has a way of correcting the problem," Olga pointed out.

"Right again. Well, anyway, I can't think of anything else we can do to prepare, and to tell you the truth I can't think of anything that any-one else can do about it on this ship. They can be mad at us, I guess, but we still have twenty weeks left in the voyage. That ought to be time enough for them to cool down." He paused for a moment, and then said quietly, "And you know, Olga, I do understand that you're right in prin-ciple. If there's anywhere where you can get a feel for that, it's Phobos. The horizon's so close, and there you are where you can throw a rock into orbit, or with an extra heave throw it all the way to Mars, and where a hard jump leaves you hanging above the world for several min-utes and three good bounds will take you all the way around the narrow part . . . and all the time, hanging up above you, taking up almost half the sky, is that huge red planet . . . you start to notice that you're a little bit insignificant in the scheme of things. You start to wonder if you should take yourself so seriously. And, well, it still took a while, but five nations learned to share it."

"Five *people* learned to share it," Olga said. "That was the easy part.

And right now the Earth looks like a tiny shining dot, from our view-point, but the inhabitants are not much better at sharing than they were in the days of Alexander the Great."

"In fact, he got that title by not being very good at sharing the world with everyone else," I pointed out. "I don't think we can anticipate other people's reactions. We have no idea what pressures they might be under from their home countries, or how they feel about the pressure, or even whether there's any pressure at all."

They both looked at me, slightly startled. Usually at these little gatherings I only talked about technical matters, but Olga and Captain Gander loved to get into the philosophy of things. "I think," Olga said, "that it has been pointed out that we are theorizing in the advance of data."

Gander chuckled and nodded. "Yeah. And we are. All right, we'll just play it as it lays, when the time comes."

When the news came, four days later, everyone was sitting in the common area, with the door open to the cockpit so that I could hear as well. Since the ship ran on Universal Time, we had gotten into the habit, as a crew, of catching the relay of the BBC six o'clock report together, just before the evening meal. As might have been expected, it was the lead story; the moment it began, everyone fell dead silent.

I listened with half an ear; the teams of scientists coming along were indeed distinguished, and the BBC seemed to be spending a lot of time explaining how a cycler worked. They had an annoying habit of calling it a "MERC cycler," silly because the C in MERC already stood for "cycler," and I was kind of surprised at how much time they spent telling people about how orbital mechanics worked, but then I guess doctors are always surprised that the news has to tell people what the liver does, and lawyers probably wonder why the media always has to explain habeas corpus.

Whatever the reason, it stayed quiet in the common room while the BBC announcer explained that to get from Earth to Mars, you have to get into an orbit that will intersect the orbit of Mars at the time that Mars will be there. When you leave the Earth, you are already moving at its orbital speed; to catch Mars, you need to modify that orbit so that you climb out away from the Sun, reaching your peak distance from the Sun—aphelion—just at the moment that Mars passes through that point.

Mars takes almost exactly twice as long as the Earth to go around the Sun. Imagine two men running at steady speeds around two parallel circular tracks, so that the man on the inside track is running faster than the man on the outside; then the inside man "laps," or passes, the outside man at regular intervals. When the Earth passes Mars, it's called an "opposition."

When is the easiest time for the inside man to pass a football to the outside man? Just before he passes him; that way the inside man's speed is added to that of the ball, and the ball has the shortest possible distance to travel before it overtakes the outside man.

When is the easiest time for the outside man to pass the football to the inside man? Just before the inside man passes him: he can throw the ball inward toward the center of the track, using some of his speed, and let the faster inside man catch up with it.

Thus Earth-Mars missions, whether they are going to Mars from Earth or to Earth from Mars, leave some time before opposition and arrive sometime after it. Oppositions come up every 780 days, on the average (it varies because the orbits are not perfectly circular). Since the opposition of March 2010, we had been sending probes to Mars (and to its moon, Phobos) on every opposition. From the opposition of 2014 on, we had been sending equipment and supplies for bases at Crater Korolev and on Phobos. And, of course, for the opposition of July 2018, Walter Gander and his crew had departed on the MERC *Aldrin* in May 2018 and arrived at Phobos in December 2018.

NASA had hit on the idea of naming any Big Can habitat that ended up permanently in space after one of the early astronauts. When the time came to name the two that would become the Mars cyclers, *Armstrong* was already taken as the name of the space port at L1, so that made it easy to name the two Big Cans that were to become the Mars cyclers "*Aldrin*" and "*Collins*," after the two other Apollo 11 astronauts. There was something else that was appropriate about the name Aldrin being the first one to make the voyage; Aldrin himself had worked out the basic principle of the cyclers, back in the mid-1980s and added further refinements a decade later.

The point was simple in concept and difficult in execution. If you timed matters right, a spacecraft returning from Mars via a long trajectory could intercept the Earth from behind, a short time before an opposition. Since it would already be moving faster than the Earth's escape velocity, it would not go into orbit around the Earth; the Earth's gravitation would simply bend its orbit into a large ellipse around the Sun. But while this was happening, the spaceship would acquire some of the Earth's momentum, a process known as "gravity assist" that had been used since the *Voyager* missions to the outer planets in the 1970s and 1980s. The ship would be whipped up into a new orbit around the Sun—if the timing was right, one that would take it right back to Mars, without the expenditure of any fuel except minor quantities for maneuvering. Using its heat shield, the ship could then "aerocapture": slow down by passing through the Martian atmosphere, and then go into orbit around Mars.

The system was known as a REcycler (Return to Earth cycler). Theoretically you could have a "full cycler" in which the ship passed endlessly back and forth between the Earth and Mars on a twenty-six-month cycle. In a REcycler the ship always refueled in Martian orbit, boosted out of Martian orbit carrying returning crew back to Earth, dropped them off to Earth using the Pigeons it carried, and was gravity assisted back to an aerocapture, so that once again it was in orbit around Mars with its tanks empty. This had provided huge savings for the Mars program, because each crew left in a MarsHab, like the one we were in now, which it then flew down to the surface of Mars, where it became one of the buildings for the small human settlement at Crater Korolev. Returning crews always left the MarsHabs in place for future use, and came back on *Aldrin* or *Collins*. That way every crew that went out built up the size of the base at Korolev, because a new MarsHab went out with each. Crews coming back used *Aldrin* or *Collins*, and thus we not only never brought back anything that way more useful on Mars, but we always sent the cycler back with a gravity assist.

In theory crews could have ridden out to Mars on the MERCs at any time; all you had to do was catch up with them as they whipped around the Earth. But there was a lot concealed in "all you had to do." They came in and out very fast; a Pigeon with a strap-on booster could just barely catch a MERC as it whipped by, and if it missed, the Pigeon would be well above escape velocity, bound out into a solar orbit with air and power for perhaps a week at best.

If trouble happened early enough, they *might* be able to abort into a very high orbit that would take them back to L1. Otherwise, when they reached *Aldrin*, they would have to depend on its being fully functional. Telemetry of course would have assured them it was, and another crew would have gotten off just days before, but where an empty MERC coming back to Mars with problems was no big deal because crews from Phobos or Korolev could overhaul it once it reached Mars, if anything was wrong when they got on, they would have to live, or die, with it until they reached Mars more than five months later. All in all, it was a high-risk maneuver, and we and the Russians were each betting a five-person team of our very best people on getting it right the first time.

I might have expected the dead silence that greeted the announcement that Russian and American crews in augmented Pigeons had successfully overtaken and docked with *Aldrin*. Space is truly international in this: the moment you hear of anyone doing anything dangerous, no matter where they are from, the first thing you want to know is if they're all right.

What I hadn't expected next was Nari's whoop of joy, or Paul shouting "Bravo!"

I missed the first part of things, because I had a job to do and needed to keep my eyes mostly on the screens, but by the time Olga relieved me, it had turned into a full-fledged party. What all four of those of us who were in on it—me, Captain Gander, Olga, and Vassily—had forgotten was just how international science really is, and has been for a long time. Our scientists here in the MarsHab knew every one of the named group coming on Mars Five Alpha; to them they were friends and colleagues, names and faces to see again. And more than that, though they hadn't voiced the concern much, our team of specialists knew, perhaps better than anyone, that even seven of Earth's most brilliant people was a very small number for a puzzle of the scope and depth they were expecting. The effective team had just more than doubled in size, and this meant a far greater chance of success.

In the middle of the excited uproar and chatter, Gander dropped an arm around my shoulders and said, "Well, I guess everyone was wrong. And isn't that a surprise? Just out of curiosity, Jason . . . do you think there's any way we could try a radio call to Mars Five Alpha?"

"Well, you know the obvious. We'd have to get a position and course for it so we can point one of our antennae at it. Might take a day or two before we could find that out. Then there's the question whether anyone there would be on radio watch for signals from our direction, and after that I guess—"

Paul said, very loudly, "Got them!"

We all turned to look—all except Dong and Ilsa, who had been assisting him. The three of them were clustered around one of the terminals. I bounded lightly over in the one-tenth g and was startled to see a piece of e-mail on the screen—from Robert Prang, the Mars sedimentologist on *Aldrin*. "How did you—"

Paul shrugged. "I thought of it before they did, or before any of the rest of you. But it's obvious. We send a radio message, compressed data format, every fifteen minutes, back to the relay stations in Earth orbit. A lot of it is telemetry from different machines on the ship, some of it's the video recordings we made for our families and friends, and a great deal of it is Internet traffic. We all correspond with our colleagues via e-mail; the big reason why the Mars Consortium has to keep our addresses unlisted is only so we won't be deluged. Well, it occurred to me that if any of us knew a private address for any of those colleagues over on *Aldrin*, their communication arrangement was probably similar to ours. And as you can see, it happened that it was."

By the next day, all the scientists were happily corresponding. Never having been much of a writer, I didn't pay much attention.

It was two days later at dinner that Dong and Tsen announced, without any fuss, that they had indeed had orders from the PRC government to make sure that if there was a chance to secure exclusive access to part of the Encyclopedia, China got the benefits. "It was always supposed to be the top priority to get the information, even if that meant we had to share it all," Tsen explained. "But it seemed to us that now . . ." She looked sideways at Dong.

He grimaced. "We didn't like those orders much. Nobody does in the sciences, you know. Almost all of us would like to publish everything, all the time. So . . . well, now we know we can't keep any part secret, now we don't have to try."

Olga frowned. "Aren't you risking—"

Dong smiled. "Well, that is one way to look at it. By telling you this we have committed a political crime. What do you think the odds are that the Chinese secret police will come and get us where we're going? And we both know there will be decades of work for us at Crater Korolev."

"So Mars has its first refugees?" Gander asked.

"New worlds always do, eventually," Tsen said. "That's one of the reasons why they are so important."

5

SEVERAL WEEKS FOLLOWED THAT WERE PLEASANT WITH NO REALLY MEMO-
rable events at all—which was fine with me. It's only in the movies that
an astronaut wants things to get exciting en route. The shipboard routine ran smoothly, and for the most part we settled gratefully into it.

With the tension revolving around the secret *Aldrin* mission
resolved, the MarsHab became a very pleasant place; there were minor
tiffs now and then, but just the fact that people could go to a personal
compartment and close the door seemed to ease that tension. We got
e-mail from the team at Korolev Base, the outbound *Aldrin* crew and the
inbound *Collins* crew, teasing us about that "luxury," and not long after
that NASA announced that there would be an unmanned cargo ship-
ment of personal compartments sent to Mars "at the earliest opportunity."

Paul and Nari seemed to find that amusing; I asked them why.
"Because we were on the early voyages where the MarsHabs were just
one big commons, for every practical purpose. Floors for functional purposes and to increase the working area, but nothing else. You'd be
amazed how many ways there are to want privacy; there was a standing
joke about 'astronaut's dysentery' because the only place you could be by
yourself was the bathroom—sometimes I'd spend an hour in there just
reading a book or something." Nari shook his head sadly. "You know, for
space missions, we people from the advanced countries aren't really well-
suited. We aren't used to the idea of sleeping ten to a room, let alone
doing almost everything out in public all the time. It's just interesting
that it took them so long to come up with these personal compartments."

Paul added, "But it's not surprising at all that once *we* got them
everyone is demanding them. Those little people-boxes are luxury condos compared to what the current Martian stayover crew has."

Olga had just been relieved, and she came in and sat down, close to
me. I still hadn't tried to turn it into anything romantic—maybe because
I wasn't sure she'd want to, maybe because of the thought in the back of
my head that she was planning to stay on Mars, but I would be leaving a
little before the next opposition, after refueling and reprovisioning

Collins. Or, I suppose, maybe because if I got involved with her it was going to be serious, and there hadn't been anything serious in my love life in at least a decade. I was out of practice.

We sat for a long moment, the four of us just enjoying a moment's rest, till Paul said, "Nari, I've got another explanation. If it resurfaced at *any* time after the Tiberians died or abandoned their settlement, then all that happened was that the lander sank into the lake, fell sideways on the icy bottom, and then everything refroze over it."

"And the graves?"

"The corpses sank further into the slush—"

"Than a magnesium-titanium hull with several large pieces of heavy equipment? And they all sank while remaining perfectly laid out—"

"They were frozen solid."

"Not if—"

Olga glanced at me; I shrugged. She said, "Is this a private fight, or can anyone get into it?"

"It's not really a fight," Nari said. "I'm just trying to straighten out this crazed Frenchman by teaching him a little about Occam's Razor. Here we have a Tiberian lander sitting right on the discontinuity that Dr. Fleurant so brilliantly found, right? Just below that discontinuity— only a couple of meters—we have a large number of dead frozen Tiberians, and if our ultrasound and X-ray reflection tell us anything, they tell us that they are all on their backs with their arms folded over their chests—the same position we find in the lunar cemetery. So what I say is the discontinuity formed at the time the lander fell over, after the Tiberians died. The ice is structured as you'd expect if a cold lake froze on that site, so I think they were caught quite suddenly in a flood, at their campsite, where twenty-two Tiberians had already died and been buried. Quite a few of them drowned in their beds in the huts. So, I say, there is only one such discontinuity found in water ice all over Mars, wherever there is permanent ice. And the Tiberians are sitting on it. I say they did something to cause that."

Paul spread his hands out emphatically; his wrists flipped his hands upward. It was sort of an aggressive shrug. "Which is at least two huge leaps of logic, for a man who wants me to think about Occam's Razor. Suppose that when they made their camp they were on the ice of Crater Korolev, and then they got stranded and died. A thousand years, or two thousand, go by, and then there's a volcanic eruption that releases an enormous load of water onto the surface, perhaps near the equator. It might be a geyser, or maybe one of the extinct volcanoes had a huge Krakatoa-type explosion from groundwater steam. The water ends up everywhere for a while—it's a good greenhouse gas, Mars warms up a bit, and all those water-carved features we see today get laid down. Then the water gradually freezes and sublimes in the low pressure, gets carried as water vapor to the arctic, and is deposited during northern winters. That could take, oh, four thousand years. During that time, the lake in Crater Korolev gets constant sunshine for a large part of the summer—after all, it's at seventy-three degrees north—so the frost there melts and freezes over and over, forming the solid ice that so perplexes Nari. For all we know, had we known what to look for in 1200 A.D. and had the telescopes and spectroscopes to do it, the whole question would have been settled by watching the last of the water vaporize and freeze into place."

Nari sighed. "How anyone with Paul's talents got the habit of discarding so much evidence, I'll never know. Paul, nowhere on Mars is there the kind of inversion you'd expect, caused by water freezing from the top down instead of the bottom up. That means the water went in suddenly, and was already very cold, probably just at the freezing point, when it was deposited, so that unlike normal liquid water it froze from the bottom up. Now what does that look like? Mars has a very thin atmosphere made up of a gas, carbon dioxide, whose behavior is very temperature sensitive. Things can happen very suddenly planetwide; air pressure changes drastically every spring and fall, even as it is, and for example water might go into the air, and later come back out, almost instantly. So here we have a wrecked ship and many dead Tiberians— mostly dead indoors, as if something happened suddenly, probably at night, or maybe while they were all ill. We have a sudden flood, on a planet which is undoubtedly very good at producing sudden floods. We have them at the bottom of the sudden flood. And in all the eons that Mars has been there, this only happened to happen during the few brief years the Tiberians were there. And you think that the Tiberians being there and the great flood happening are completely unrelated?"

Fleurant shrugged. "Suppose there is a 'discontinuity-making event' that happens only now and then. Suppose the most recent one is the most extreme of them, so that it has erased all the older discontinuities. Perhaps it is something that causes an almost overnight thaw and freeze. Well, then the whole Tiberian camp was there—frozen and dead, two thousand or four thousand years after they all died from who knows what, whatever aliens die from. Then the whole camp sank—"

"Where all the corpses landed on their backs and all the buildings landed upright," Nari interrupted. "At least your previous silly idea had the virtue of being superficially plausible. Whereas in your present idea, *three* mysterious things happened—all the Tiberians died, their whole camp got frozen into the ice, and the discontinuity formed—all at the same time. How very unlikely can you get? On the other hand, if you assume they were all caused by the same thing, presto, the problem is simple. All we have to do is find that thing."

"But—"

By now they really weren't talking to us anymore; they didn't even look up when Olga and I got up. We went to one of the windows to sit and watch the stars wheel by, many times more than you could ever see on Earth. We'd been spending a lot of time just sitting together lately.

When we were about two weeks from Mars, it began to appear as an orange dot, distinctly round rather than a point; from then on it grew steadily. By that time the Sun had shrunk to a smaller, bright white disk, about a third of its apparent size from Earth.

By that time Olga and I had formed a habit of having at least one meal per day together, and now we generally used it as Mars-watching time. We were in the early part of northern spring—the vernal equinox had been April 9, 2034—so at least there would be sunlight, and the days would be growing longer, when we arrived at Korolev. The Martian year is about twice that of Earth, minus forty days or so, so each season there is around half an Earth year. We would have almost a full year of spring and summer before having to experience the worst of Martian arctic conditions.

We watched as dust storms swirled around the planet, and we saw the northern polar hood (the layer of clouds above the north pole) dissolving in the spring sunshine, as the southern polar hood began to form. "The reports from Korolev base say the air pressure is already falling a little," Olga said. "And the temperature is getting up above the carbon dioxide freezing point most days now."

"Knew I should've packed more summer clothing," I said.

"Silly." She looked down at the keypad, where she had been making some notes. "The thing is, Jason, I'm going to be living there for a long time. I will see some seasons, you know. And therefore, I'm trying to get myself to think of the rhythm of the Martian year. I want to be in the habit of looking forward to the next season, just the way people do on

Earth. And since air pressure and temperature are the two real signs of spring in the Martian arctic, well, then, I'm going to learn to think about them the way we do about the first robin at home."

I nodded. I was trying not to let it bother me that I would be around Olga for a bit over a year after our arrival and then would be getting back on *Collins* to return to Earth. I wasn't really emotionally involved yet—I didn't think—but then again . . .

Mars is a small planet, and though they take a long time, interplanetary journeys move fast. It was only during the last ten hours or so of our approach that Mars became larger in our windows than the Sun. Or so they told us. By that time Olga and I were far too busy to spend much time looking out the window.

None of the maneuvers involved in getting a MarsHab to the Martian surface is complicated in itself, and after all our job is mostly to make sure that there's someone there to take over in the very unlikely event of a computer failure or some kind of severe software glitch. Every now and then there's an opportunity to get a bit better than machine-optimized performance, though not often. Mostly my job was to watch the machines do the work.

Nonetheless it's nerve-wracking. We were flying toward Mars at far above its escape velocity. If we had brought fuel from home to turn around and fire a retrorocket, we would have had to bring a fully fueled rocket as big as the empty booster that now hung at the other end of our tether—and of course we'd have needed a much bigger booster to throw us and the full booster here. Thus what we were going to do was aero-capture—get down from our high interplanetary velocity, to one slow enough to be captured into Martian orbit, by interacting with the Martian atmosphere.

"Interacting" is a pretty mild term for what it involves. Essentially you're going to come in as an artificial meteor, aiming to go through the atmosphere at an angle that isn't too shallow (so you won't bounce off like a stone skipping on a pond, losing no velocity and thus continuing on into a long orbit around the Sun, as you slowly run out of food and air), or too steep (so that you don't enter the lower atmosphere, where the air is thicker, at very high speed, and burn up or hit the ground). Between those extremes there are angles where a great deal of the energy of the ship can be converted to heat in the atmosphere. You emerge after going through the outer atmosphere with a great deal of your speed lost, enough so that you go into orbit instead of continuing on endlessly.

Fortunately the Martian atmosphere is fairly friendly to the process. To begin with, it's thin. Earth's surface pressure is about a thousand millibars; Mars's is about six. Secondly, thanks to the low gravity (about a third of Earth's) and high molecular weight of the atmosphere (44 versus Earth's 14.4) Mars has a scale height of 10.8 kilometers, considerably more than Earth's 7.9. Once you grind that through the logarithmic function, it works out like this: on Earth, there's half as much air for every 5500 meters you go up. So at 5.5 kilometers up, about the height of Mount Popocatapetl, there's half as much air; at 11.1 kilometers up, about as high as the old airliners used to fly, there's one-fourth as much; and so forth. For Mars that number is not 5500 meters, but 7486—the Martian atmosphere, though very thin, thins out much more slowly than the Earth's. To do an aerocapture you have to aim for air of a specific thickness and a large scale height guarantees thickness that doesn't vary as much with altitude—and thin air farther away from the planet—so that you have a wider window you can hit, farther away from the rocks.

I wasn't thinking about any of this consciously as we got ready. The first step was to jettison the booster, which had been swinging around with us for the months of the journey, on the end of its long cables, giving us artificial gravity.

"All right," the captain said, "it looks good, Jason. Authorize the computer for jettison."

"Yes, sir." I entered the command; the computer began a countdown.

There was a slight clang, and suddenly we were in zero gravity for the first time since our Earth departure.

We had a few hours, now, for fiddling course corrections and adjustments and to send the robot outside to examine the heat shield that was now pointed toward Mars. Everything was fine and on target; it might almost have been yet one more drill.

As we drew closer and the hours crawled by, the rate at which Mars appeared to expand in our window became greater and greater. Finally, with Mars now swollen to twice the size of the full Moon seen from Earth, we strapped in and gave the final commands for the computer to take us through aerocapture.

The first pass is always the roughest because it's when you're spilling the most energy. We tore halfway around Mars in less than twelve minutes, pinned flat to our couches by several g of deceleration. I watched the instruments, but at such speeds and weighing several times my Earth-normal weight, if I had seen anything wrong I very much doubt I could have done anything. As the hab rose back into high orbit, and the glowing heat shield outside gave up its heat to space and cooled back down, we all sipped water, stretched, relaxed, and got ready for the next pass.

It took one more pass through the atmosphere to spill the energy and bring us into a low enough orbit; then we had to burn a little bit of our precious inboard fuel to get our orbit circularized, so that we passed over the Martian poles at an altitude of about 220 kilometers. "You need a break yet, Jason?"

"I'd rather take one on the ground, sir, and so far I haven't touched a control. Don't tell the taxpayers, but there's really no reason for me to be here."

"Me either, you know. Except to remind our science team to eat and sleep. Well, then, how long is it until we next have a window for a descent to Korolev? Is there time for a bathroom break and to let them know our plans?"

"The computer put us into position to do it early," I said. "We're in a one-hour-forty-nine-minute orbit, and we've got a marginal window coming up in nineteen minutes, a good opportunity coming up in two hours and ten minutes, and a not-so-good one in four hours. After that we'd have to wait a while or try to steer a lot during reentry."

"Well, we don't want to try *that*. Okay, go for the good approach. I'll call up Korolev and tell 'em to set out some extra plates."

The descent was the one part I probably could have flown manually. I guess in the old days, the stick-and-rudder early astronauts would rather have done that. But in the intervening seventy years, computers and software had improved a lot, whereas I was basically the same design as Yuri Gagarin. And I sure wasn't going to bet the lives of eight of Earth's best brains on my piloting skills unless I had to. So just as with everything else in the mission thus far, I turned it over to the machine, and sat and watched, and hoped I wouldn't have to move or act at all.

It wasn't nearly as steep a descent as you make to Earth in a Pigeon, for several reasons: the smaller Martian gravity meant orbital velocity was much slower, the greater scale height meant we could start slowing down higher up, and the thinner atmosphere simply didn't produce as much heat so we could spend longer in reentry without greatly increasing our risk. Consequently I would fire our retrorocket just as we were crossing the equator; we would pass almost directly over the north pole and finally descend to Korolev.

As I watched the computer count down, the immense Valles Marineris stretched off to my left: a great deep scar in the Martian surface, kilometers deep and longer than the United States is wide. As it passed behind us, the retrorocket fired, right on time, and we began our plunge just above the broken territory called the Iani Chaos, in the eastern part of Margaritifer Terra.

On the computer's cue, I executed the 180 that turned us with our heat shield facing in our direction of motion; minutes later we felt the giant's fist of reentry deceleration push us down into our couches. For a moment I could still see something of the pockmarked face of Arabia Terra through the white-hot plasma pouring past our window from the heat shield; then we were in true blackout, surrounded by flames, the incandescent air cutting off vision, radio, or any contact with the outside world. We sank deeper into our couches and tried not to think too much about how many things could go wrong.

We lost speed and altitude steadily, and not long before we crossed the pole, the air streaming past us stopped being superheated; suddenly it was clear again, and I looked down at the polar ice cap for just a moment, before I put my focus back on monitoring the computer. There was a short, hard thud as the heat shield jettisoned, and then a hard push in the back as the landing rocket fired. We were now a mere thirty kilometers above the surface, though still moving quite fast, and the computer was going to use the small rocket to bring us down to a reasonable speed and then to steer us, hopping over the landscape on that small tongue of flame, to our prearranged landing site.

I watched as the graphics showed us staying nicely in the center of all the curves; I never touched the controls. Crater Korolev is almost perfectly circular, and it's fifty kilometers across. It has a great deal of swollen, torn-up ground around it, probably indicating that the soil was saturated with water at the time the meteor hit. The swelling rises to sharp-edged lip, and within there's an immense frozen lake. We hovered above that surface, angled slightly to race along about a kilometer above the smooth ice, and in a matter of a few minutes we were approaching the base, a few kilometers from the dig site.

In front of us lay a small cluster of five MarsHabs, each similar to ours: a large cylinder in a steel truss, with legs mounted to the truss. Each of them sat on four long, thin legs—illogically long and thin by the standards of Earth design, where three times greater gravity had to be coped with, but more than strong enough here. And around each of them there was a starburst pattern on the ice, for when the site had been definitely established, the stayover crew had partly refueled the landing rockets and flown their MarsHabs over here. For the time being, humanity's first settlement on Mars was almost fully mobile.

We descended slowly; through the camera below I could see the fluff of dry ice on the surface of the lake flung radially outward along the plane of ice in expanding concentric circles, without enough air to cause it to billow. Then at the edge of the circle, the dry ice burst and boiled into a white "smoke ring" surrounding our landing site. We came down lower and steam began to rise from the polished black ice that had lain there for millennia; lower still, and finally, with a bump, we touched down.

Everyone got up and began talking at once, but Captain Gander held up his hand and said, "All right, everyone into pressure suits; we need to meet with the stayovers, and they've invited us to dinner. And before we do that—"

"Er, Captain," Nari said behind him, grinning broadly.

"Yes?"

"There's something important we need to do right now." He pulled out a tiny one-drink bottle of champagne, unscrewed the cap, and poured it over the bewildered Walter Gander's head. "You've been to the Moon, of course, sir, and also to Phobos . . . so welcome to the Three Worlds Club."

There was a brief delay while the captain toweled off his hair; still he didn't seem completely displeased. After that, we put on the suits that we had practiced with every week but never worn outside, verified that they were working as they were supposed to, and went, two at a time, through the airlock. Olga and I went together, climbing down from the lock on a long, thin ladder, jumping the last couple of meters in the low gravity.

My boots hit with a thud, and then flew out from under me. Polished ice, and not enough gravity to generate much friction against it. At least the helmet had some padding to cushion my head. I struggled to my feet—it was like wearing omnidirectional roller skates—and saw Olga doing the same; we leaned against each other, got up, and saw several others struggling in the same way.

The suit radio crackled. "As soon as you're away from your ship the ice won't be so slick." We turned to see a man in a pressure suit dragging what looked for all the world like an old-fashioned sleigh toward us.

"Here, all of you sit on this, and we'll pull it over to the dining hall with the winch. Welcome to mass transit, Mars-style."

Ten people was a tight fit, especially with all of us wearing bulky pressure suits, but it certainly beat falling all over the place. I looked out across the dark ice. To the west, the Sun had disappeared below the scarred red rim of Crater Korolev. The sky was nearly black, except for a deep pink/purple glow around the horizon, and many stars were already out. Naturally, just traveling within the solar system, we hadn't come far enough to change the positions of any of the fixed stars, at least not so that the naked eye could detect. The Big and Little Dippers blazed high above us, brighter than you ever see them on Earth.

The rope tightened and the sleigh glided softly across the ice, the rumble barely perceptible to the external suit microphones in the thin air. Dark fell fast and hard, so that by the time we reached the hab that would serve as the dining hall, you could barely make out the crater rim.

I got off the sleigh with the others, and looked at the wild proliferation of stars overhead, the looming crater walls, and the great sheet of ice that shone faintly in the starlight. I felt how light I was, a third of my Earth weight, and finally, truly, I believed I was on Mars.

6

I DON'T THINK I'VE EVER SEEN FIVE PEOPLE SO EAGER FOR FRESH FACES. There had been ten in the stayover crew that had arrived twenty-six months before, but five of those had departed for Earth more than eight months ago on the REcycler *Collins*. It was almost embarrassing; three of them just wanted to hear us talk, endlessly, about anything at all, and two of them couldn't shut up.

The food was standard MarsHab fare—it came out of a "farm," the little vegetable and textured-protein growing machines that were, so far, one of two major items we had gotten out of studying the Tiberians. In some ways it was like a many-times-evolved version of the "salad machines," "yogurt boxes," and "sushi makers" that the different national space agencies had been fooling around with ever since the 1980s; in other ways it was radically different. I wasn't biologist enough to understand much more than that you put sterilized human waste, carbon dioxide, and water in one side and took broccoli, carrots, tofu, and various other stuff out the other, and as a supplementary benefit it made about half the MarsHab's oxygen and scrubbed about half the carbon dioxide buildup (the rest had to be done by chemical recycling). The big problem was that the "farms" produced only about fifteen different kinds of food; within a few weeks you would know everything that could possibly be on the menu. Not that the human race hadn't lived for most of its existence on very monotonous diets for large parts of the year, but those of us from the advanced countries had grown up with very different ideas about what food should be.

Their MarsHab's food was seasoned a little differently from ours. Dr. Chalashajerian, the subsoil expert in their hab, had used his personal space for spices, and so they could do occasional curries; he had also come up with a lab procedure for extracting oil from soybeans out of the farm, and thus they had soy sauce and something that didn't taste too bad as a spread for bread. Unfortunately, we didn't have any real chefs in our crew, so there was no one for him to exchange ideas with. "Oh, well," he said. "I shall just have to wait for Mars Five Alpha, and hope."

He was dark-skinned and muscular and spoke English with a light, pleasant Indian accent; he laughed a lot, and was one of the ones who wouldn't shut up. I had to admit that after almost nine months in the ship, during which we had long since found out what everyone's favorite topic of conversation was, it was refreshing to hear something new, even if it was only a monologue about recipes for salad dressing.

There seemed to be a slight tension between Captain Gander and Yvana Borges, who had been the "mayor" of Korolev until our arrival. Arguably we didn't really need any system of government at all, and certainly five people had needed it less than fifteen would, but still there had to be someone who was in charge of picking up the phone, replying to consortium requests, and representing the tiny colony on the radio. That job was to pass to Gander, now—he was figuring it would take up about two hours per day, at most—and Yvana was to return to her particular area of expertise, the scatter-imaging X-ray equipment that had

located the Tiberian base and given us some idea of what was under the
ice. She didn't seem completely happy about it, and she kept thinking of
two more things, or ten more things, to tell Gander about.

We barely heard a word from any of the others. Pete Johnson was
an American, a very dark-skinned black man with a beard well beyond
regulation length, unusually tall for anyone who goes into space, who
smiled a lot and watched all of us acutely. He was the biophysicist and
physician for the original stayover group. So far, because there was no
access to study the Tiberians, but plenty of research he could do on the
crew, he had the record for scientific papers published as a result of
being on Mars. After a while he fell into a very quiet conversation with
Tsen, and the two of them appeared to be having a great time. As a
pilot, my first thought was that they were thinking of new excuses for
grounding me.

Akira Yamada was a meteorologist; he sat quietly, watching everyone, but particularly Nari. I formed no impression of him that first night.
Jim Flynn, a sandy-haired Texan, very slim and small, didn't say much
more; I was startled halfway through the evening to learn that he was a
pilot and engineer, since he hadn't said a word. "I would have thought
the first stayovers would have been all science specialists," I said.

"Somebody's gotta take care of them," he said. "Pete kills germs, Doc
C. grows food, and I make sure the machinery runs and drive various
things so that we don't have scientists falling into ravines because they
were looking at the mountains instead of where they were going. And
I've made a couple trips up to Phobos, mostly just hauling up loads of
volatiles to replenish stocks for them. Now, up there—*that* is weird.
Fourteen permanent residents. Almost a small city, really; there's even a
couple that's gotten married while there."

"What's weird about that?" Olga asked.

"Oh, nothing, I guess, about getting married, if you want to do that
sort of thing, but I mean all those people. They're turning it into another South Pole City; in another ten oppositions I bet they've got movie
theaters and a store up there, and probably a jail and a bar. It just isn't
the same rock that your captain landed on. Now, down here, you can
still tell we're at the edge of the frontier—though I suppose that will
change, too."

"You like it at the edge?" Olga asked.

"Oh, yes, ma'am, I do. I figure probably I'll end up buried on Triton or Charon or someplace, at least if I get my wish. You know how nice and quiet it is, and how after a few weeks you really know everyone in your crew and then you can just go about your business? Well, that's the kind of life I'd like."

Later, after we returned to our own MarsHab, Olga said, "Jim is much more extreme than I am. I only want to see new places and spend time there. I don't think he ever wants to come back."

I shrugged. "Ever hear of Daniel Boone, Roald Amundsen, David Livingston, Jim Bridger? There hasn't been much room for people like that in the last hundred years, nowhere to go where you could really be all by yourself, or at least not around anyone else like yourself. Now there's going to be again. I don't suppose there's enough of them to make much of a difference, but I'm glad that they'll have a place to go."

"It's different," Olga said. "Mostly they went on their own. People now have to pay a lot for a few to go. Still, I think everyone benefits from the few—and I'm glad there are people like Jim, who *will* volunteer."

Of course the stayovers had known when our team would be arriving, right down to the day, so they had made sure that everything was ready to get started. And we had no unpacking to do—the MarsHab was our home, just as it had been in space. So the next morning, after a breakfast just like every breakfast we'd had on the way, we suited up and met the others outside, got into the three open-topped treaded tractors that sat waiting for us, and started on our way to the site.

I rode next to Jim, so I could learn to drive one of these things. They ran entirely on indigenous propellants: methanol made from water and carbon dioxide, and hydrogen peroxide made by electrosynthesis from water. The exhaust was pure water and carbon dioxide, so what we took from Mars went back to it without any real change except its location.

The tractors were simple enough to drive—really just lightweight versions of the Sno-Cat that was the backbone of Antarctic travel on Earth. The real trick, as Jim showed me, was in getting them to behave on the slick ice, especially since much of the surface was still covered with frozen carbon dioxide from the night before. It was right on the edge of sublimating, and thus formed constant small bubbles under the treads, decreasing traction. "Just take it slow and remember nobody's ever in a hurry on this planet," he advised me. I got the hang of it pretty quickly—it was no worse than one of the manual-steering cars that had still been around when I was a teenager.

The site itself turned out to be several very large "tents": fabric-covered vault shapes under which things could be stored, with various labs and a few tiny sleeping modules inside them. "Nobody's stayed the night here yet," Pete observed. "Though I suppose now, with the dig starting, people will sometimes have reason to."

"Didn't know we could just decide to," Jim said. "I wouldn't mind moving out here, except there's nothing to eat."

"Tired of life in the busy urban center, eh?" Pete said, grinning. "I think we're going to reserve it as a resort, actually. Somewhere to go on your vacations, when you get tired of the same old place."

As we drew closer, I saw the many stakes driven into the ice, and asked if that was the site. "Yep, that's it," Jim said. "Tiberian lander, graves, huts, and what we think is the Encyclopedia is all under that, four to six meters down."

The three little tractors stopped in front of the shelters, and all of us got out. By now, the Sun was well up, and though there were still dark shadows in the crater rim south of us, the ice in front of us was brilliant white with a hint of pink, reflecting the red of the sky. Everything had a strange, sharp-edged look to it, because the smaller apparent size of the Sun, and the much thinner air, meant the light was less diffused and scattered; shadows were darker and their edges sharper. The parts of the ice plain still covered with frozen carbon dioxide were sparkling white; where boots, tractor treads, or the wind had swept away the dry ice, the water ice showed through as blue-black smears. "Hey, we're just in time," Chalashajerian said. "Look north, everyone."

We did. At first I didn't know what he was talking about, and then I saw—there was a faint puff of vapor forming a long line at the horizon. As I watched it rushed toward us at tremendous speed, a great onrushing wave that was somehow transparent, erasing the white dry ice and leaving black water ice behind it.

"One of the more interesting sights of Martian spring, or at least spring on Korolev," he explained as the line of frost bore down on us. "Watch your feet now—I don't mean keep your balance, I mean look at your feet."

I did. Seconds later, I saw the white carbon dioxide at my feet flare into a thin white cloud, boiling up at my face. When it passed, I saw black water ice in front of me—except where my shadow had been, where for a moment I saw its shape formed in white. I stepped back and away from it, and my white shadow exploded into a little cloud of vapor and was gone.

"Sublimation of CO_2 is very temperature-sensitive," Pete explained. "And the walls of Korolev are fairly high, so the shadow stretches across the black ice until well into the morning. Then after it retreats, the surface starts to warm up; the places the shadow left first, sublimate first."

That was the highlight of the morning as far as I was concerned. In a way we were paying for the things my father's generation had done at Tiber Base at the south pole of the Moon. They had gone through there so fast, with so many untrained hands, trying to find the Encyclopedia, that they had practically destroyed the site. For years archeologists had been trying to sort out what was done there by Tiberians and what was recent human activity.

Nor had humanity's mistakes on the Moon been confined to violating the archeological first principle that you never disturbed a site before extracting all the available information in your path. They had also violated another principle known to archeologists since before 1900. Ever since Schliemann had lifted the burial mask from a Mycenaen face— only to see it crumble before his eyes, before it could be photographed or sketched—it had been understood that there must be an expert on the site, as each step of the excavation, or of the unrolling of an ancient scroll, was completed, so that if anything should suddenly begin to deteriorate, there would be people on hand who knew what they were looking at and might remember something critical that would be lost forever on an untrained eye.

For that matter, the safest place to examine an object or document was often in situ; the less it was transported, the less the risk to which it was exposed. This had all become bitterly clear after the destruction of the Encyclopedia on the Moon. Dad had been an astronomer, Xiao Be a pilot, and neither had made any interesting observations or picked up a single clue for later researchers. They had merely been sent there to grab a treasure, Indiana-Jones-style. Back in 2010 it might have cost the nations of the world two extra years to train a team of archeologists, computer scientists, and cryptologists for lunar operations, then design the equipment to attempt to read the Encyclopedia in situ. They hadn't been willing to pay that price then, so now they had spent a hundred times as much money and ten times as much time to get here, and until (much later) we got down to the Encyclopedia itself (assuming that that was what was under the ice half a kilometer from the Tiberian settlement) the human race would still not know whether they had lost that precious data forever.

The problem was compounded by the scant knowledge that had been available about the Martian arctic. The actual conditions in which they would be digging had had to be painfully ascertained, measured, studied, and thoroughly understood over a period of many months, by Doc C., Yvana, and the rest of the team of experts that had already wintered over, before there was even any point in having the Tiberian archeology experts on hand for this next phase.

But now, so far as could be told, we knew everything about digging in a frozen Martian lake that we might need to know, and now, no matter what happened, trained eyes would be there to see it. So after months of waiting until we were really, truly ready, that morning we went to work with perfect confidence. We laid out a grid, using a laser transit of squares half a meter on a side, all around the site. Then, using a depth-gauged laser that constantly monitored how deep it was going, we cut out each square to a depth of half a meter. Finally, we inserted the "periscope"—a rod with mirror mounted inside its tip to horizontally deflect the cutting laser's light—into the grooves we had made, and cut the block free from the bottom. With friction grips we then lifted it out and put it into an insulated, sterilized box for the rest of the team to study.

The blocks were large and awkward, but though the mass was the same as it would be anywhere—125 kilograms—the weight, which depended on local gravity, was only 91 pounds (as opposed to the 275 it would have been on Earth). Thus the work was only hard physical labor, combined with a need for fiddling exactitude in removing blocks and labeling boxes. By the time we broke for lunch, with the sun about an hour past noon, Olga and I had cut out and boxed nineteen blocks, which was the best anyone had done; Pete and Jim were second with seventeen. Gander clapped me on the back and declared that we had saved the crew's honor; he and Fleurant had only managed to cut out eight, tying with Ilsa and Tsen.

As we ate in the largest of the overnight shelters, the analysis crew joined us. It was a tight fit, but we all wanted to hear what they had found so far.

They could do the basic processing on a block much faster than a crew could cut one out, and what they did required special skills; thus there were a lot fewer of them than there were of us. Though she was normally shy and didn't say much, Kireiko was apparently elected to tell everyone the results. She sighed, then said, "Well, you know, you always hope for something startling the first day. What we've done so far is send each block through a CT scan and an NMR scan. On the average each block has about two hundred specks of some organic material—which could be microscopic bits of dead Tiberians, or Martian life, or just various chondritic materials. The fact that so many of them are close together in size would tend to argue that they're actually spores, and if that's what they are, then they're either Tiberian or Martian, which we can probably get from looking at the DNA. If it shows up as Tiberian, great; if it isn't earthly or Tiberian, well, we've just discovered life on Mars. More likely we've discovered chondritic dirt.

"The other thing, which I'm sure will get Nari excited, is that there are a lot of microbubbles in there, and some preliminary probing suggests that just maybe the pressure in there is a bit higher than ambient."

Dr. Narihara Nigawa, probably the most distinguished scientist we had, sat straight up as if he'd received an electric shock, thumping his head against the low ceiling in the corner where he was eating, and spilling his water all over himself. It took him a moment or two to get reorganized and recover his dignity before he said, "All right, that's not fair, Kireiko. If I'd choked on my sandwich you all would have had a hell of a time explaining it back home. *How much* higher was the pressure in the microbubbles? And what was their composition?"

I had rarely seen Kireiko's puckish smile before; I realized that I had made the mistake a lot of people make of assuming that quiet and shy people don't have senses of humor. "I should have guessed you would ask about the composition. I was going to save that part to really startle you. As kind of a followup to the surprise about the pressure—"

"Will you tell me, please?" Nari said.

"I think you'd better," Gander said, grinning, "or I won't be responsible."

Kireiko's smile grew broader. "Well, then, if you really want to know . . . pressures looked to be about thirty-five millibars, and the chemical composition showed about one and a half percent free oxygen."

We all jumped at that a little bit. Ambient pressure on Mars today is something over five millibars. Oxygen is 1300 ppm, or 1/100 of what Kireiko had just said. But Akira sat up straighter than anyone else and said, "Well, at the risk of its looking like a Japanese conspiracy, I'd have to say that Dr. Nigawa's ideas are undoubtedly looking better and better. At least from a meteorological perspective."

Fleurant nodded. "Even I would have to concede that."

"For those of us who are not up on our studies," Olga said, "do you suppose you could tell us what this is about?"

"Sure," Nari said. "I think that when they came here they tried to terraform Mars, probably because the protein incompatibility was so great a problem on Earth that it seemed simpler to just come here and plant Tiberian life if they could. And then the process stopped, either because they died—or possibly because it killed them somehow. Without their intervention, Mars reverted to what it had been. The worldwide discontinuity in frozen deposits and permafrost is caused by everything thawing to that depth and then refreezing."

"I should add I don't disagree with all of that," Fleurant added. "It's just that I think it's simpler to account for it all by saying that sometime after the Tiberians moved to Mars from Phobos, and then died, there was a major thaw and refreezing. You would expect air pressure to be much higher during refreezing, so the pressure of the bubbles doesn't pose any problem to my explanation. But the free oxygen is something else. The only constituent of the atmosphere that should be undergoing gross changes in quantity, during a thaw, is water vapor. Free oxygen looks like they managed to get something growing in the open air and converted a little bit of the carbon dioxide. Nari is beginning to persuade even me."

It took Kireiko and Tsen a very long time to extract enough of the little pellets within the blocks of ice to begin a real study; meanwhile, we kept cutting blocks. Our five crews of two could cut out about three hundred blocks a day, now that we had enough practice and had perfected our techniques. The trouble was, the Tiberian site was about fifty meters square, and the tops of the Tiberian artifacts were just about four meters below the surface, so a whole month went by and we were still more than a meter, on the average, above the roofs of the huts, the side of the lander, and, half a kilometer away, the Encyclopedia that we were nominally there to get.

One evening, as we shared dinner in the mostly empty hab that everyone called the "dining hall" because it contained five farms and a sort-of kitchen Doc C. had rigged up, Nari said, "I wonder if you all would feel I was throwing my weight around, as head of the science team, if I put in a request to Mission Control to borrow Jason, Olga, and Yvana tomorrow? There's an idea that I'd really like to investigate. It will only take one day, one tractor, and some of the exploratory gear."

Gander shrugged. As head of the station he had the ultimate say in such things, but normally he deferred to Nari in any decisions that involved scientific work. "I'd say go ahead. In fact if you'll ask permission to take me, too, it's a deal. I could use a day of not cutting out ice blocks. I was going to suggest that seeing as we won't be getting down to the layer of the major objects till after the Five Alpha crew gets here, and we haven't found a lot of interesting things after the initial surface discoveries in all those blocks of ice, perhaps it's time for a little variety in our lives. Maybe we could start taking a day of rest here, say, every seventh day, since that's traditional for several of us? And Nari, if you can use extra hands productively, I'd like to let the whole team do whatever you have in mind."

Nari chuckled and stroked his chin thoughtfully. "Well, now, *that's* an interesting question. Yes, I could use a lot of hands; it's a surveying job. Okay, I'll include everyone in the request. I think I know where to look for another Tiberian site, less than twenty kilometers from the Encyclopedia site. And if we find what I think we'll find there, well, then, I would say my case is pretty well confirmed, though I will want to test one more prediction after that. So it might be great fun to have you all there while I triumphantly point at the X-ray scatters I want Yvana to do, and then say 'See, it was obvious to me all along.' On the other hand, should I prove to be wrong, I'm not sure I want you all there to watch Paul Fleurant jumping around and shouting 'I told you so.'"

Ilsa leaned back and said, "Well, Nari, now that you have assured yourself that all of us are curious, why don't you tell us about your idea?"

"Am I that transparent?"

We all nodded.

"Well, then . . . it goes back to a lot of my early work on the Moon. The question for me is always, what does it look like these people were *trying* to do? So put together the basic facts—protein incompatibility. Nobody hangs around trying to give themselves hundreds of bizarre syndromes, and that's what they had: damaged cells in every part of the body, failing joints, brain lesions, some organs badly atrophied or hypertrophied. They didn't *want* that to happen; I think we can assume the aliens are at least that much like us. So they didn't spend all those years on Earth entirely by choice, and finally they left—something changed so that they could or because something we haven't identified made the situation totally impossible. Now look at the technology mix—it doesn't look like a plan to me, it looks like what would happen if you suddenly forced the average small town back home to get along with just whatever was within city limits on a given day. Some pieces of very high-tech stuff, some fairly crude, and a lot of cobbled-up fitting of low to high. So my guess right along has been that their Earth colony failed, and for whatever reason they couldn't try to go home—certainly the landers wouldn't have had the range, which is why it seems very likely to me that the wreckage all over Phobos is what was left of the main ship. So you can't survive on Earth and you've got to survive in the solar systems. You have a lot of high-tech devices, but only a limited ability to fix them and no ability to make more. And if Earth is deadly to you in the long run, well, everywhere else is in the short run. Well, then, what do you do? You try to create a long-term habitable place for yourself and your descendants—no matter how hard that is to do. And since they were roughly like us, well, what's the most terraformable world? Okay, now we know why they came to Mars. And why Korolev? Well, that's where my guess comes in, in a big way.

"I think it's three factors. First of all, they really needed somewhere with surface water ice, so that they wouldn't have to extract water from permafrost. That argues that maybe their machines were breaking down after several decades of trying to survive in space. They wanted somewhere where their descendants could make it, even if they had to go really low tech. Well, Mars has almost no water in the equatorial regions, and not much more than none at the south pole. If you go all the way up to the ice cap, here in the arctic, then in the first place since a large part of that is going to melt, you're SOL if you don't place your base just right, and in the second place you have to deal with extreme arctic conditions—almost an Earth year of daylight followed by almost an Earth year of night, among other things. So what you want to do is go to the place farthest south in the arctic that has a significant amount of water, preferably water that isn't going anywhere too fast while it's warming up. And here we are—the best combination of southerly location and confined water available on Mars."

"Well, so far you've shown that they're at least as smart as you are, Nari," Fleurant said, teasing.

"And the proof is incontrovertible," Tsen added, "because Nari and the Tiberians both ended up at Korolev."

Nari ignored them and went on. "So, what else do we know about them? They had almost no ready-made shelters—my guess is that the two pressurized shelters on the Moon were all they had, probably one for each lander. But apparently if they had water, or even a little bit of chondrite, they could manage an adequate bioenvironment, provided they could seal it. So they used the lava tubes on the Moon, and they bored into Phobos, and then sealed those spaces with fused rock and crudely machined doors that I would bet were made in a machine shop on their starship.

"Now, take Mars. Low pressure and moderate radiation less than Phobos and the Moon. And ask the other question: why does anyone who's planning to live on a planet, that they're going to warm up to a comfortable temperature, move onto a frozen lake? My guess is, because they weren't going to stay on the ice forever. There was something more suitable somewhere nearby. So I started looking into local geology, and guess what?"

"You think you know where they were planning to move as a permanent base," Kireiko said. "And you want to go see if they got any construction done there."

"Exactly. Korolev is an almost classic case of an impact in permafrost. The meteor liquefied the soil and sent it outward in a big ripple, the ripple lost momentum and 'froze' into place, and then as water in the soil redistributed itself and refroze, the terrain around the crater softened and became lumpy. Wherever there wasn't enough water left, things collapsed or caved in, and the crater itself filled with water and later ice. Well, structures like that often have voids in the crater wall—"

"Caves," Fleurant said. "You think there are going to be caves on the crater wall, where the Tiberians were planning to dig in."

"Not only that," Nari said, "but Akira and I did a few computations that I think are very interesting. Nine thousand years ago or so—if you accept the few pieces of terrestrial wood and wool found on the Moon as evidence of the date—Mars's obliquity was considerably lower than today's. And the climate models are pretty uniformly in agreement that if Mars has low obliquity, it tends to have a thin clear atmosphere and the poles act as a cold trap for water; if Mars has a high obliquity, it tends to have a thick, dusty atmosphere and probably even some liquid water. So from a standpoint of terraforming—"

Tsen raised her hand. "I don't suppose a mere doctor and biologist can understand obliquity?"

"Tilt toward the Sun," Nari said. "Low obliquity means the poles point straight up and down, perpendicular to the orbit. High obliquity means it's really tilted steeply. Since the Martian atmosphere freezes at the poles, and weather is caused mainly by temperature differences, with low obliquity, one season is very much like another, everything that goes to the pole stays there so the air pressure drops, and temperature differences stabilize so there's not much to stir up the dust and almost no air to hang it in if it did stir up. In high obliquity the poles tilt far over, so that when one of them is pointed toward the Sun it gets a lot of heat, and at that 'summer pole' the carbon dioxide evaporates and stops acting as a cold trap for water. Meanwhile the winter pole gets colder, but that means a bigger temperature difference and so there's more wind in a thicker atmosphere, more dust to help absorb sunlight and darken the ice, and so forth. And since the winter and summer poles keep trading roles on a half-year cycle, pretty quickly you've got a lot of air moving back and forth, not much of a cold trap, big dust storms, and so forth. And what I was about to say is, if you were going to terraform—or I suppose Tiberform—Mars, you really want to arrive during high obliquity. The poor Tiberians were here at a relatively bad time to do it, when if anything happened to them, the natural equilibrium of the system was strongly biased toward freezing up.

"Also, Mars has what's known as poleward migration of water. Water tends to become part of permanent frozen deposits, and since the higher the latitude it's at the smaller chance that it will ever thaw, over long periods of time the arctic and antarctic are always gaining water. If you have thawed water anywhere on the planet, it migrates faster. So here's what I think happened: the Tiberians got partway with their terraforming, and then something happened so that they couldn't continue. As soon as they weren't pushing the climate toward warmth and thick air, things started back toward the normal—and all the water they liberated came up north and helped fill up the crater over a period of just a few years, covering what was left of their settlement and preserving everything under a blanket of ice. I'll bet the Tiberians below the discontinuity are the ones who died and were buried in the ice before the colony failed—and will be in almost perfect condition—and the ones in the huts died where they were and lay there until, that night or ten years or a century later, all that water fell back out of the north polar hood and covered them.

"But that meant one more thing to me: look for caves at the level of the discontinuity. And I've got a bunch of funny-looking echoes off the crater wall at just the right height—twenty kilometers from the landing site. So that's where I want to look."

Fleurant nodded. "And I quite agree we should look there. You spin a good story, Nari, and I'd have to concede it's even, perhaps, a true one. And a one-day excursion will do us good."

"I hope so," Nari said with a slight smile.

Three hours later, as sleep shift began, Gander announced, "Well, I did do as you requested and ask permission from Earth for a change of mission. And they read your report and okayed it, as I told you. Unfortunately," Gander said, "and I feel like a jerk for pointing this out, we can only go about ten kilometers an hour in the treaded tractors. So ten kilometers to the dig site and twenty beyond that is three hours. We have about thirteen hours of daylight at the moment, so if we leave right at dawn, that's seven hours on site. It's also risking the entire base and all of its tractors on this one excursion. So the question is, now that you've got permission from Earth, why I shouldn't just veto your plan?"

Nari frowned. "You're right, of course. And I did originally propose just four of us. I'd like to take Paul as well, and that's one tractor load. Probably that's all we should do, this time. If there's a site there, we can start working it more seriously later. And as an additional thought, I think we'll plan to return to the main site rather than all the way here— it gives us a whole extra hour at the dig." He rose and stretched. "Well, this also means a dawn departure, so I highly recommend that you lucky people get some sleep—it's what I'm going to do."

7

THE DRIVE THE NEXT DAY WAS VERY LONG, AND NOBODY WAS TALKING TO either me or Olga; Paul, Yvana, and Nari all sat in the back, arguing and calculating about where to place the X-ray and ultrasound equipment.

That left Olga and me with the front seats and a chance to enjoy the view—coupled with the pleasant realization that we wouldn't be wrestling ice blocks all over the place today.

We had managed to start just before dawn, so we got to watch the northern dawn in its most impressive form, since we were headed almost due west. The Sun came up behind us, and in the thin Martian air, there was very little that was gradual about it. The sky faded from black to blue to pink to red in mere minutes, as the stars rapidly winked out; the jagged black shape ahead of us, the crater rim, just as abruptly acquired form and definition in the morning sunlight.

We ate breakfast as we drove, swallowing the usual forgettable starch and protein. The Sun was still low and shadows still very long as we passed the dig site; we were well into the third layer there, I noted, as we swung wide to avoid disturbing the excavation.

An hour later we saw the rushing white line of sublimating carbon dioxide zoom southward toward us and pass in front of us. "That's really spectacular, isn't it?" I said to Olga. "The plumes must be five meters high."

"It's certainly the kind of thing that tourists will eventually come to see," she said.

The land reared up into the sky, its sharp-edged lip seeming to curl toward us like an oncoming wave of surf; as we drew closer to it, it loomed higher and higher.

At last we reached the point, half a kilometer from where the crater wall reared up out of the frozen lake, that Nari said was as close as we should get with the tractor for a preliminary survey. We paused and had some of the wretched freeze-dried excuse for coffee; then we got out and carefully carried our equipment in closer. I was still getting used to the gravity being three times one third of what I had grown up in. My tendency was always to try to carry too much weight and then fall over, because I could lift so much more, but it had the same momentum and my feet had only a third of their normal friction, so that it was a lot easier to get it moving than to stop it.

At last they were all set up, and now Olga and I found out what we were really there for. Though there would be only a little more heavy lifting today, there was an amazing amount of sheer running around to do. The X-ray scattering technique worked by sending a tight beam of X-rays down into the ice at an angle and seeing where they bounced back to. The receiving antenna was a 200-meter-diameter blanket that was covered with tiny sensors. We would position the source, position the blanket, fire a pulse, move the blanket, fire another pulse, and so forth, till we found an angle at which we were getting maximum power returned; then we'd move the source and start over. Meanwhile the scientists were entering results into the computer and gesticulating furiously.

Lunch was late and we were starving. There's a lot of exercise in that much running around on a slick surface, not least because it takes a lot of muscular effort to keep your balance. But the scientists were so clearly impatient to get on with it that we glanced at each other, shrugged, wolfed our food, and volunteered to get back to work. No doubt they'd tell us what was so exciting once they knew.

The Sun was creeping down toward the crater edge, and our shadows were beginning to reach pretty far to the east from us, when Nari got a call from Gander, reminding him to pack up and get moving. I had expected him to argue and had been preparing things that a very junior person like me could say to a very senior person like him, but for some reason he cooperated meekly enough. I'll even give them credit enough to say that Yvana helped fold the blanket and all of them carried a lot of the equipment back to the tractor.

"Boots are kind of senseless on this stuff," I said as I fell down for the third time. "Might as well just get a decent pair of hockey skates, or maybe cross-country skis."

Nari half turned around, then abruptly lost his footing—that's one of the best ways to make yourself fall in that environment. He landed on top of the crate of instruments, and I set my load down and helped him to his feet. "Are you hurt?"

"Sprained a dignity someplace, otherwise no. Jason, that's the kind of great idea that is seldom obvious enough. I think that it might be a genuine winner, and I'm going to send the suggestion in with your name on it."

"Suggestion?"

"Skis or skates. As long as we're working on a frozen lake, what could make more sense? Akira already tried to persuade them to send some grippers for our boot soles, and for some functions he's right—but for getting around quickly, what you really need here is runners on your feet: skis or skates. It's a *great* idea."

I shrugged. "If you say so. I was just complaining, actually." We got the last load into the treaded tractor, and I turned it around and headed back for the dig. Five minutes later we got a call from Walter Gander, pointing out that if we hadn't left yet, we were going to have a hard time getting to the main site by dark.

On the way back, they were chattering just as eagerly in the backseat, and I found myself alone for all practical purposes with Olga. "Well," I said, "that was quite a day. And at least it really was different."

"Oh, today would have been different anyway," Olga said, "or didn't you remember?"

"Remember what?"

She seemed a little impatient. "Why are we going to be looking up at the sky tonight?"

"Ahh, because—oh, right. *Aldrin* is aerocapturing. In fact, that's due in—less than an hour. Suppose it'll be visible with the Sun still up?"

"Well, if I'm figuring right, visible or not it will be right in front of us. And considerably above, of course. And the sun will be pretty far down in the sky, so it might well be visible."

"What might be visible?" Yvana asked from the backseat.

"The *Aldrin*," I said. "Its first aerobrake is in about an hour and we're guessing we'll be able to see part of it dead ahead."

"Of course it will be visible in daylight," Yvana said. "You were. Why didn't you just ask me?"

She plunged back into her ongoing loud argument with the two men without waiting for a reply. I found myself thinking, not for the first time, that I knew why so many of her crew had seemed so relieved when Captain Gander had taken over the station.

We had covered another thirty minutes worth of territory, and the shadow reaching out in front of us was considerably longer, when I heard a voice I didn't recognize—but which sounded strangely familiar—in my earphones. "Second Site Expedition, do you read me?"

"Loud and clear," I said. "Who's that calling?"

"It's Scotty Johnston, Jason. Currently piloting *Aldrin* toward our first aerobrake. I'm about ten minutes from retrorockets."

"How did you know where I was?"

"Happened to be talking with Captain Gander and mentioned that I was looking forward to seeing you; he patched me through. How the hell have you been? On the news you're always excited to be here and totally committed to the mission."

"Yeah, well, they haven't had a new tape to play of me for a while. It's not a bad planet, Scotty. I'm afraid we don't have margaritas, though."

Scotty was an old friend from Colorado Springs. We'd been doubles partners on the tennis team and spent a lot of time at the kind of bars which tended to be populated by sorority girls, where they served over-sweet drinks in funny colors. His family were what they used to call nafafs—"newly affluent Africans," meaning that they were African-American, and when the great economic boom of 2012–2025 had hit, his family had caught the rising tide and gotten rich. In the twentieth century there had been a lot of "rich man's booms"—times when business did well but employment didn't change much—but so far in the twenty-first, we were having the other kind. The vast array of new technologies and big projects to be accomplished guaranteed not only that there was always work, but that you could always get training for a better job; business was screaming for intelligent, capable people and would do whatever it took to get them. When I had been at Colorado Springs, "nafaf" had been current slang; about five years ago it had disappeared because nobody thought there was anything unusual anymore. A lot of words were disappearing from current use in those years—words like ghetto, barrio, skid row, tobacco road—because the things they referred to were disappearing.

"You know," I said, "I don't recall your being on the Five Alpha manifest."

"I was a last-minute replacement. Calvin Ho got the mumps."

"Well, if I'd known you were there, I'd have tried corresponding with you."

Scotty laughed. "You mean you'd have picked up your e-mail. Your mother, by the way, points out that not only have you not written, you haven't picked up your last ten letters from her; she always sends them to you with automatic receipt, probably because she knows what kind of correspondent you are. I could have written to Captain Gander, I guess, and told him to get you on the stick, but I thought it might be more fun to surprise you. Anyway, I'm at six minutes to my retrorocket firing, so I'll ring off for now. If they don't have margaritas, though, this is going to be one disappointing trip to the beach."

"See you soon, Scotty."

We drove on, glancing to our right when we could to watch the Sun play on the distant south wall of the crater. "That's going to be fun for you," Olga said. "I'm sure he'll be going back on *Collins*, so you can return home with your friend. And besides, you'll have someone to hang around with." It wasn't a very subtle hint, but Olga wasn't the most subtle person in the world. Most good engineers are so used to having to straighten people out before they do anything stupid that they lose whatever tact they might once have had.

"Oh, he's an okay guy," I said, "but he won't know the ropes here. When I really need to get something done I'd rather be around you. And he talks too much, anyway. He's just a guy I knew from school."

"Oh. Well, still it will be nice for you to see a familiar face."

We sat in silence, glancing occasionally at the far northern horizon, till suddenly, in the now deep red sky, a bright blazing light streaked upward. "He's in blackout for sure," I said. "Wow, when a ship's that big and going that fast, it sure makes a plume."

"Told you so," Yvana said smugly.

The great blazing fireball streaked from horizon to horizon in just a minute or so. A while afterwards, as we drew close to the main excavation site where we would bunk for the night, Scotty's voice crackled in my ear again. "Hey, Second Site Mobile. Pay up on the bet—I managed an aerocapture. One more pass will take us down to a circular orbit. We'll talk soon."

"Good to have you around, Scotty."

He was doing a job that was in some ways tougher than what I had done. *Aldrin*, as a cycler, was not intended ever to land, nor did it jettison its booster. Rather, it reeled in the booster, and instead of aerocapturing all the way down to the surface, it would use a series of aerobrakes and propulsion maneuvers until it would eventually be parked in a polar orbit around Mars, and we would ferry loads of fuel from our automated factory, down here, up to orbit to refuel the booster.

That evening, as we shared the cold supper in Number Four, the large shelter at the dig site, Olga said, "I think Jason and I would both greatly appreciate knowing what you found today."

"Well, it takes a while to put an image together," Yvana said, "and we would have to take many more pictures to refine the detail and give the computer enhancement enough to work with, but it would appear— well. For my money, Dr. Nigawa is vindicated."

Instinctively we glanced at Paul Fleurant to see what he thought; he was nodding. "It's a big cave," he said, "and from the backscatter we were able to get, it looks very much like they had a sizable facility under construction there. Looks also like two dozen Tiberian bodies in a small graveyard, and maybe a spare farm unit from some ship or other, though from the bulk of it it's probably one of those earlier-technology things that so fascinates Nari. As I said, the picture is hazy, but not so hazy that we could call it a hallucination. So what's your next step, Nari? You said you had one more thing to look at if this panned out."

Nari grinned and sipped the last of the coffee, making a face the moment he tasted it. "You know, the best reason for terraforming this ball of red dirt is that when we were done, we could grow coffee and tea here. And some rice. Just now I'd kill for rice."

"Nari—"

"All right, I'll tell you. I think we need to look at the south pole. Think about what every proposed terraforming project has ended up saying: it's where all the carbon dioxide is, and if you just darken the ice there, especially right before southern spring, you can get pressure up to thirty millibars or so, so that water will melt and run, and all that. Nine thousand years ago conditions weren't all that different from the present, except that the system was much more slanted against them than it would be against us. So I'd say there ought to be evidence of however they did it there."

"You have a candidate?"

"Well, the south pole terrain is pretty scarred up, but if you look at Craters Hutton, Rayleigh, Burroughs, and Liais—a group of four right around longitudes 240 to 260—you'll see they all are pretty good dust catchers, and they all have these interesting small craters inside them. Back in the 1990s, when guys like Zubrin were putting together the idea for how you'd do Mars missions better if you used more local materials, a guy named Mole had an idea that you could blow fine dust up into big clouds using nuclear bombs. If you do that close enough to the pole, just before southern spring, then at least in theory the dust ought to rain down and darken the ice, which in turn would mean faster evaporation and getting more of the residual cap back into the atmosphere. And at that point, well, the feedback cycle of warming that releases carbon dioxide, which causes more warming, starts, and you've got a warm, wet Mars. It's a good thing nobody tried it back in the nineties when Mole proposed it, or just possibly all the Tiberian stuff would now be in the bottom muck of Lake Korolev. But it's a cheap, easy-to-improvise way of terraforming, and I think our Tiberian friends really needed exactly that. So what I want to do is look at those craters up close—the little ones that might be right where the dust was, nine thousand years ago—and see whether there's any residual radioactivity."

"Well, I'm up for the trip anytime," Paul said, smiling. "I'd be very happy to see this work out the way you think it does, Nari. And even happier if what we find in the Encyclopedia should confirm it."

Olga rose and stretched. "Well, I thank all of you, and I'm glad to know what you found and very happy for you, Nari, but I'm about to drop. I'm afraid running around on the ice all day makes me sleepy."

"I made sure we were all set up with places to sleep right when we got here, while dinner was cooking, and that they were ready," Paul said. "There are five temporary bunks ready to go here. Nari and I are going through the tunnel here to Shelter One, Yvana gets Shelter Two to herself since it only has one bunk, and you and Jason are in Shelter Three."

I trailed after her to Shelter Three, feeling a little confused; normally, with three guys, two women, and three shelters, wouldn't you—?

When we got into the shelter and closed the door, I saw that not only were there just two bunks, but they seemed to have been shoved together. I glanced sideways at Olga; she was blushing but smiling. "Paul is a perfect example of why we Russians have always been on good terms with the French," she said. "We can move them apart if you'd, ah, rather not, but since this is likely to be our big chance for privacy—"

"We're not moving them," I said, and took her in my arms. "I'm just glad one of us was smart enough to see an opportunity. I think I owe Paul a lot of favors."

The next morning I was in much too good a mood to notice, really, but I had a distinct impression that Yvana was mad at us about something, and that Paul and Nari were as pleased as could be. The rest of the crew arrived at the usual time, and we all worked only a half day because the Five Alpha landers were due that day. Somewhere toward the end of the shift, Gander dropped back next to me and said, "Uh, Jason."

"Yes, sir?"

"Please switch to a private radio channel. Let's use channel seventeen."

I switched.

A moment later his voice crackled in my ear. "Word has reached me of a conspiracy involving Second Site Mobile. I don't like having my officers sneaking around behind my back. Therefore . . . from now on, if you and Olga should happen to decide to spend time in each other's personal compartments, you are ordered to just do so, without any effort to conceal it from anyone. And if anybody complains, he or she can walk home."

"Yes, sir." I was a little giddy with relief; he'd really thrown a scare into me for a moment.

"Back to public channel," he said.

I clicked back, just in time to hear Gander say, "Hey, Paul, you lose the bet. He didn't faint before I got to the punchline."

There was a lot of laughter from everybody on the radio. Maybe I didn't owe Paul quite as many favors as I had thought I did.

Later that afternoon, after driving back, we watched the two landers descend. They set down near the five landers that we already had fueled up and waiting to go, and we went out to greet them. There was a certain amount of fun in watching Scotty get his "ice legs."

The dinner that evening was fun and exciting, and Gander declared the next day would be our first official day of rest, because everyone stayed up way too late talking. We had set up the old MarsHab that the third expedition had left behind as Five Alpha's quarters. They made a point of telling us how nice it was, which of course was a way of telling us that they knew perfectly well what housing on Mars was likely to be like, and they weren't angry with us. We all spent the day off sitting around watching recorded movies and chatting. Scotty found time to tell me he thought Olga was "cute, but too good for you, you lucky bastard." I agreed with him.

The next few weeks went by in a blur. Normally the fuel plant ran at about a tenth of its capacity, converting carbon dioxide and water to liquid oxygen and liquid methane. But now we had to get *Aldrin* fueled for its unmanned return trip. It was slated to be the GOcycler for Mars Six, almost two years from now. That meant getting the plant running at full capacity, not just to make the needed fuel in the six months before it was due to depart, but also to provide enough fuel for the tankers that would carry *Aldrin*'s fuel up into orbit. The tankers were fairly smart, as robots go, and could handle their own rendezvous with the GOcycler and return to Korolev, but someone still had to make sure they were behaving themselves, and that someone was always me, Scotty, or Olga—and whenever we weren't operating tankers, we were still going out to the dig site. They were getting farther down now, with the added crew, closer and closer to where the precious artifacts lay. There was still nothing unusual anyone could discern in any of the ice, but we didn't abandon the protocol; if there was any information we needed in the frozen record, or anything anyone could get in future generations, we'd make sure that it was preserved.

Two months later Kireiko said she had a small announcement, adding, "It would be easier to show you. I had to do this away from the landing site."

She had set up a clear plastic tent with a black floor, and in the middle of it there was a plastic container of the same type we used in the kitchen, filled halfway with water.

"I sterilized it thoroughly before I put it in there," she said.

A thick green scum floated on its surface. "What the hell—?" Captain Gander asked.

"After I sterilized it, I put a couple of liters of Martian topsoil into the water and let it sit for a month," Kireiko said. "Nothing happened except that I got mud, and the salts in the soil plus the warmth from the tent kept the soil from freezing. Then I took the big step: I put several of those spores from the ice samples into the water. That was five days ago."

"And you're sure it's not Martian?"

"Depends on how long you have to live on Mars to get naturalized," Kireiko said. "It was certainly born here, but its DNA is Tiberian. And get this, folks: it eats carbon dioxide and releases both oxygen and nitrogen; it also excretes an enzyme that would break down iron oxides. If it isn't a tailored algae for terraforming, I don't know how we'd recognize one."

That seemed like good enough news for another celebration. Apparently the Internet was exploding with debates between people who bought Nari's theory and people who didn't, but up here on Mars we had planetary unity: we were all on Nari's side. Halfway through the celebration, Captain Gander took me aside. "I've got a little bit of news for you, Jason. I don't know how you'll feel about it. First thing, the Mars Consortium has asked me to stay on as base manager for one more opposition mission, then return to command all Mars arrivals and departures at Earth. The new transit strategy using Mars GOcyclers will start soon and more than double the launch traffic. So it's turned into sort of a great opportunity. As you know, Johnston was really the only pilot-astronaut that came out on *Aldrin*; their captain and engineer were two-hat types that are staying here as scientists. So . . . it looks like the *Collins* REcycler will return with just you, Scotty, and any of our group here who need to go back for medical or personal reasons, which might be Akira or Doc C., but probably no more than a couple of people. And that means you get to be mission commander for an interplanetary mission, if you want the job. It's a pretty big promotion, even if it's just kind of a case of being short of officers, and it would do great things to your record. I don't think NASA would mind having a new Captain Terence in its astronaut corps, and I know Lori Kirsten well enough to be sure she'd like it. Of course . . ." and now he looked me straight in the eye, "it is completely your decision. Understand? And for all I know Scotty will want to stay over, or he may decide he doesn't mind going back by himself—it's a chance to catch up on his reading, I guess. So you *can* decline, but it's up to you."

"How long do I have to decide?"

"Maybe ten days. Talk it over with friends or whoever. Sleep on it. You don't have to give me an answer right away."

The party went on a while longer, but my mind wasn't really there anymore. I had a chance to be a mission commander at a very young age, by current standards. Since the space program had been running at a high level and with a lot of missions, they had insisted on more and more qualifications before taking you up to that level, so that nowadays ten years or more was normal before you got to do it (except for the little orbital hops with cargo, where technically the pilot was the commander because he was the only one on board). For that matter, with Gander taking a permanent position here, there would be at least one command slot in the Seventh Interplanetary Squadron opening up, and though I didn't have much seniority, I'd have more experience than a lot of the candidates . . . and it would be kind of fun to see what a fuss Mom and Aunt Lori would make about it all.

Against that, there was the fact that the current research schedule didn't have them trying to bring up the Encyclopedia until right around the time *Collins* would depart, and they'd probably only turn it on, or try to, long after I was on my way back. And there was the way I was really needed here. Back home on Earth, between missions, I often just slept or went to one movie after another; here they needed everyone all the time. Back home you couldn't do anything you weren't certified for; up here, if they needed something done and you were the one available, then even if they had to talk you through it on the radio, you just did it. I'd been to the north pole in a lander, by myself, to get Akira's weather station working again, because Akira was tied up in a gas deposition experiment and everyone else was so busy. By the time I completed that mission I could have built a weather station, blindfolded, from loose parts. And while I wasn't Akira, I was on my way to being a pretty fair areometeorologist; somebody had to calibrate the station to local conditions and compare it with readouts from other stations, and Akira was still busy.

And there was Olga.

Funny thing, I'd never been a very passionate guy or anything, and Olga was pretty kicked back, too, but I'd also never been friends that way with anybody, such close friends for so long, before becoming lovers, and, well, I would miss her terribly.

On the other hand, I had a career at home that was more or less what I'd been shooting for ever since the night on Aunt Lori's back porch when I'd sat up and looked at the Moon rise and told myself that I would be an astronaut, I would go out there, and I would keep going.

I didn't sleep much that night, which may be why I wasn't quite as excited as I would normally have been when I discovered that I wasn't going to be cutting ice at all that week. First I would be flying up to go over *Aldrin* and take the notes that would lead to my plan for outfitting her for unmanned return to Earth, now just a few months away since she was the GOcycler. And upon my return I was going to be flying a lander down to the south pole, taking Akira, Nari, Paul, Gander, Chalashajerian, and Olga.

Mars Mission Control had finally decided that we needed to do the last confirming step on Nari's hypothesis before we dug all the way down to the Tiberian site, and therefore, we were to proceed to Crater Rayleigh, the one that looked most like it had been reshaped, to gather evidence of a "past Tiberian intervention"—by which Nari meant, of course, evidence that nine thousand years ago the Tiberians had set off an atom bomb there in order to get terraforming underway. A mission to the ship I might one day command, on a future return to Mars, if I said yes, and to the south pole for an important investigation—all in one week. It was another night without much sleep.

8

I'D DONE A FEW TAKEOFFS FROM MARS BEFORE. I WAS ALWAYS A LITTLE surprised at how gentle they were compared to the thundering heave of taking a Yankee Clipper up from Earth. It was a couple of hours before dawn, and I was sitting in the Pigeon by myself, running the countdown. Here, where hands were short, when Olga, Gander, Scotty, or I flew anywhere, we just made sure there was fuel in the tanks, ran the diagnostics the night before, got in and ran them again just before liftoff, had the computer generate the course—and took off. A little more complicated than pulling the car out of the driveway, but a lot less ceremony than the maglev driver puts into it when he pulls out of New York and heads for Westchester County.

The countdown hit zero and we shot upward at a steady one and a quarter g's. Everything looked fine, so I relaxed and enjoyed the view. The terminator line was swinging toward Korolev—I kind of liked the fact that home was easy to pick out from orbit, a neat white circle below the polar ice cap, roughly opposite the huge Chasma Boreale.

Though you don't have to climb as fast to get off Mars, thanks to the scale height you have to climb farther, so it was some time before I angled over and worked into the orbit that would let me intercept *Aldrin*. It gave me a little time to think, but not enough time to reach any conclusions. After a while I just looked out the window. On this outbound trajectory I was headed away from the pole, down toward Elysium Mons, an immense volcano a bit over one and a half times as tall as Everest back home—though of course it was still dwarfed by distant Olympus, the tallest mountain by far in the solar system, which I could see poking above the horizon. I climbed steadily higher, and after a while *Aldrin* appeared, first on radar (the new heads-up displays were sort of nice for that—they projected a little glowing circle on your window, enclosing where you should look to get it on visual) and then after a bit visually.

Though it bore a superficial resemblance to the Zubrin hab that we'd come to Mars in, and of course its center section was a modified HT, a Big Can like all the others that had carried us into space, a closer look revealed a lot of differences. The booster was shorter and squatter, befitting the fact that it had to hide behind the broader and flatter heat shield. There were many brackets still visible on the frame that surrounded the central living module, but I could also see that the tankers had been busy, for there were nine fuel and oxygen tanks now attached to the framework. There would be twenty before it was done with the process.

We closed in on the docking port, and I let the computer do the job. It was perfect as always; with a slight clang, the Pigeon docked to *Aldrin*. Pressure was okay on both sides, so I opened the hatches and went in to look at *Aldrin*, sister ship to the *Collins* REcycler, which I would be commanding.

It didn't have the nice personal compartments that the MarsHab did, but then there would only be four or so of us, at the very most, rattling around in here. I made my way forward to the cockpit. The cockpit of our MarsHab was long since gone, I reminded myself, torn out to make room for our small infirmary. This cockpit was in beautiful order— Scotty always had been kind of a perfectionist. . . .

I floated there in weightlessness for a long moment before I did it; I pulled myself down onto the commander's chair, belted myself in, and found myself sitting in the place where Walter Gander had sat during Phobos One. I was in one of humanity's great spaceships—part of the roll of honor that had begun more than seventy years ago, with *Vostok 1*, *Friendship 7*, *Columbia*, *Eagle*, *Aquarius*, *Challenger* . . . and Tiber Prize, my father's ship, for that matter. This was *Aldrin's* fifth trip to Mars orbit. It might have four or five more before it was given honorable retirement, whatever that might be; since it couldn't be brought down to Earth, scuttlebutt was it might end up as a space station in Martian polar orbit, doing more or less what it was doing now, but serving the needs of a growing Mars colony.

I looked around and imagined myself on the ship as commander. Funny, when I was a kid it might have been a kick, but now I was mainly thinking about the fact that the only job with less real work than being the pilot of an interplanetary mission is being the commander of one. I would be sitting in the same place in *Collins* telling Scotty to do things that he knew perfectly well it was time to do, then telling Houston he'd done them. And then, I figured, I'd go below and . . . well, I'd finally have time to catch up on my reading, and on my studying of Tiberian . . . but then there wasn't going to be much point in learning Tiberian, was there? And even less point in what I wanted to get caught up on reading. I'd finally learned enough of the specialties of enough of our scientists to want to study some things systematically and get myself up to speed on the whole project, but again . . . what would I need that for?

Well, I'd probably look pretty good in the captain's dress uniform, and it might get me some dates. If I didn't spend weekends writing to Olga.

I looked around the ship and walked her from booster end to shield end, and no matter how I sliced it, she was a great ship with a proud history, but I wouldn't be doing anything very interesting on her, and I knew in the pit of my soul that I'd be spending all my time wondering what was happening back at Korolev.

I noted down that so far as I could tell the ship was in perfect order—they'd certainly been more than careful with her—and spent a couple of hours confirming that *Aldrin* was cleared for an unmanned return as a GOcycler. I knew Scotty would want to check out *Collins* just as thoroughly before its REcycler return. I hoped he'd have a couple of extra people on board, so he could be the commander, because if he was all by himself he'd just be a pilot. And I did want him to get to be the commander—it would be such a leg up to his career.

For a long time after, whenever I let some reporter interview me on the Internet, he would ask if I had any premonitions about the Crater Rayleigh mission, and I would tell him no. Then he'd ask why everyone was strapped in and I'd say that it was because I'm a by-the-book pilot, and Captain Gander is *really* a by-the-book type, and nobody would have gotten away with not being strapped in. And we would go back and forth, and he'd think I was playing games, trying to make his life difficult.

The truth was, I had spent years and years practicing doing things exactly the way the manual said to do them. And NASA had been smart enough to design a universal ship-control software interface, so that no matter what you flew, if it had a particular control or a menu option, that was always in the same place. NASA and I were working off the same principle, the one known to martial artists, drill sergeants, paramedics, shortstops, and ballerinas: if you practice doing the right thing the right way long enough, and often enough, when the time comes when you have no time to think, you will do the right thing right.

So when at the end of an otherwise normal descent something slammed our lander violently upward and sideways, everyone was tied in, and all the equipment was tied down, and I didn't have to worry about loose bodies or lab equipment cannonballing through the space where I was trying to work. Actually I didn't worry at all because I didn't have time. I reached forward instantly and, without a thought, overrode the control software and told it to abort us to orbit.

Four g's of acceleration slammed into us as the capsule whirled about and climbed into the sky; something kicked us in the ass as we went, as if the ghosts guarding Tiberian secrets in the crater were trying to shove us along on our way. But we climbed, and I reprogrammed and got us heading back to Korolev before we actually got up to orbital velocity.

"What the hell was all that?" Gander asked, with a quiet authority that made everyone who had started to babble shut up.

"If I had to place a bet, sir," I said, "I think we came down over some fairly thick carbon dioxide ice. It's nothing up at Korolev, and there's not even much at the north pole, but the south pole is where all the carbon dioxide tends to end up, isn't it, Akira?"

"That's right," he said. "It's the pole that has winter at aphelion, so winter is longer and colder there, and it's a couple of kilometers above average level, where the north pole sits in the middle of a huge depression. And it's late fall down here. About a quarter of Mars's atmosphere is frozen onto the south pole. In that crater, it might have been half a meter deep, or more with drifting."

"And I was moving sideways, on hover, to find a spot where we could set down," I said. "Low enough so that flame was hitting the ground. Probably I heated up that big chunk of dry ice, and blooey. Sorry about that, Captain, some preplanning would have saved us all a rough ride."

He shook his head. "You couldn't have guessed everything that might go wrong. Now we know that when we go back, in a day or two, we want to have a dry, bare spot picked out, and go right for it. We'll see if any cameras on *Aldrin* can get us a precise view. Meanwhile, though, a damn fine job. If you'd let it do its regular abort, at that altitude, it would have tried to abort to ground, and very likely set off another explosion, with us lower down. We might have thrashed around from explosion to explosion until we either made a bad landing, low on fuel, or until we actually got flipped hard enough to hit."

"I didn't think about all that, sir. I just knew there was something wrong with the ground and nothing wrong with the ship—or with space."

He nodded. "That's the way it's supposed to work. In all that spare time you have, Jason, I think you should add a little subroutine to our standard Mars navigation programs, so that a carbon dioxide pressure explosion behind the lander will trigger an abort to orbit. We can't count on having every pilot as on top of things as you are."

The next trip was blissfully uneventful, from a standpoint of physical danger, and infinitely more interesting from any reasonable standpoint. We had picked out a wide piece of bare rock on the edge of what Nari was hoping would be the blast site, and I had worked out a straight-down approach, so that we wouldn't kick anything up as we approached. Still, the cursor was on the abort sequence and my hand was on the button as we descended.

This time, though, nothing happened that wasn't supposed to. We descended onto the rock in a perfectly normal landing, I shut down the engines, and the captain gave the go-ahead to Nari, who immediately started the whole crew into a dozen tasks, all urgent. Working for him was always kind of an adventure—you never knew what you'd be doing, but there would always be too much to do, and invariably it would be complicated and need to be done right away.

This time, though, there was a certain amount of common sense in it. The Martian antarctic was in winter, of course, and Rayleigh was far-ther south than Korolev was north; though the midnight Sun wouldn't start back home for a few days yet, the long night had already settled in here, and without a moon of any size, down inside a crater that lay inside a bigger crater, it was good and dark. The first hour went into setting up the small lights that would at least let us find our way around the imme-diate site.

We scrambled around on the dark slopes for about ten hours in all, tearing out soil samples, measuring radiation, running little chemical tests on the soil. As always, until he had the full set of data in hand and analyzed, Nari didn't want to tell us how it was going, but from the way Doc C. and Paul were reacting, it seemed to be going pretty well. On the flight back, they were chattering happily to Nari and Akira, getting friendly but noncommittal responses.

When we got back, we were just in time for the group dinner. Nari announced that he would know for sure, or as sure as it was going to get, in about three hours, so Olga and I decided to take a long walk. Not that you exactly had perfect privacy with having to talk to each other on radio where anyone could listen in, and carry a transponder so that they always knew where we were, but it beat crouching together in one of our personal compartments and whispering. Besides, everyone here, even all the new ones, were nice people, and our friends, and we sort of figured we could trust them not to intrude.

For a long time we just walked, in the sliding way that had become natural because it minimized falling. Holding hands in a spacesuit doesn't do much for anyone, I think, but it was a comfortable gesture.

"That was quite an expedition today," Olga said, finally. "I'm glad that mostly they plan on having us stay inside the MarsHabs and do analysis and study during the winter. I don't know if I've ever been any-where outdoors that was quite so dark before, at least not while trying to work there. I guess you'll be glad to miss the winter."

I shrugged, then realized she couldn't see that, and said, "Well, uh, um." Clearly talking about anything important wasn't going to be any easier here than it would have been on Earth. "Um, I kind of think I'm not going to take NASA up on their offer. Scotty can take *Collins* back, but I think I'm going to volunteer for permanent stationing here. That is, if it's all right with you. . . . I mean, if you were planning to break up with me or anything, I guess it would get pretty awkward with about twenty people and five buildings . . . but that doesn't mean I think you want to break up with me, I just mean that . . . oh, hell, Olga, I'm plan-ning to stay, if you'd like me to. I've gotten to like being at Korolev, and it's gotten to be home, and I might have stayed anyway, but the truth is I'm staying here to be with you."

Hugging in a pressure suit doesn't really do much for anybody, either, but I guess it's the thought that counts.

When we came back from the walk, Nari had finished his results, and everyone was babbling madly. The interior crater in Rayleigh showed unmistakable signs of having been made by a nuclear bomb, and decay of fission products dated the explosion to about 7000 B.C.E., "in perfect accord with theory," as Fleurant put it. Sometime during that party, I had a private conversation with Gander and explained that I was staying, and why. He seemed very pleased.

With that settled, the rest of the long Martian polar summer—six Earth months long—passed very pleasantly. The physical work was hard, but there were enough hands to share it. I had time enough to do some serious studying and make myself more and more a real research assistant and less a pair of hands.

About two weeks before the Encyclopedia was due to come up, Olga and I stood in front of Walter Gander, in the big MarsHab, which didn't seem so big with everyone jammed in there. Gander had had quite a discussion with Earth about the procedures for this, and that had meant involving politicians, bureaucrats, and rule makers of every conceivable stripe, each making sure that they got at least one tiny bit of input into the whole process. Walter had been threatening to begin with, "In light of conflicting orders from over twenty governmental bodies and advisory councils, we are gathered together today . . ." but he didn't.

Instead, he just talked a little about how long it had taken us to get here, and how much there was yet to do, and the future he could imagine when Crater Korolev might house one of the great cities of Mars—"No, I don't mean just of Mars. One of the great cities of the solar system." He continued on to talk about the Encylopedia, and about the Tiberian colony that had failed, and how finally, as he put it, "Nothing really stops life and intelligence. If we should fail—as we will not—like the Tiberians, there will be someone after us, no matter how long it takes, and sooner or later our galaxy—and perhaps those beyond it—will be filled with living intelligences.

"Which brings me to why what we are about to do today is so terribly important. Human beings are social creatures, and to us, no place is real until our social life can happen there. And today, we make one of the most important parts of it happen, before the assembled population of Mars. The vows Olga and Jason are going to make are important, not just for their lives, but because people getting married here is one more way of saying that humanity is on Mars to stay."

Everybody, including Olga and me, cheered, and after that it was more or less like any military wedding. Scotty served as the best man and promised that he'd make sure that rings got shipped up soon; meanwhile, as he said, it wasn't like there would be anyone in town that didn't know we were married. A couple of the Five Alpha crew had managed to ferment some of that awful orange drink mix that NASA always sends along, and produced something they called GANTH—it stood for "gross, although not technically harmful." Neither Olga nor I consumed any more of it than ceremonial purposes demanded, but several people seemed to like it a lot, and the party got livelier.

Doc C. had managed to extract sugar from the onions that the farms produced in abundance, and with that, emulsified soy oil, flour made from dried potatos, and heaven knows what else, he had fabricated something that looked quite a bit like a cake, even adding an artistic

"Best wishes Jason and Olga" in a blue dye that the bio lab supply guide at least claimed was nontoxic. (Everyone's tongue was blue for a week, but no one got sick, so I guess it was right.) The cake itself tasted like sweetened Vegemite; Olga and I each had to manage to get a whole piece down, and then to be very sincere in our thanks to Chalashajerian, who was standing there beaming with pride. At least with that cake there, GANTH wasn't the foulest-tasting stuff ever produced on Mars.

Later in the evening, I was sitting next to Dong and said, "Well, three weeks from now we get the Encyclopedia, and you'll finally get the chance to work with something besides ice-cutting tools. It must have been a little frustrating all these months."

Dong smiled, a tight, secret smile. "I suppose I can tell you. People figured the anthropologist on the mission was going to be mainly of use in understanding the Tiberians, and of course that's where the great bulk of my effort *is* going to go. But this has been an unprecedented chance for another reason; I've gotten to watch a new society coming into existence, the culture of the Crater Korolev Colony."

"Anything to note?" Olga asked from beside me.

"So far, I haven't seen much of a crime problem and there doesn't seem to be a bad part of town," he said. "It might be a surprisingly good place to raise kids, but be sure you let Earth know a couple of years in advance, and please wait until we've got adequate habitats. Other than that—" he peered up at me, and I realized he'd had quite a bit of GANTH "—here's a strange one for you to think about, Jason. There are going to be many more weddings here, eventually, and what you and Olga did will be taken as a model. Therefore, something we did here today, just out of expediency, is going to be fundamental to Martian weddings from now on. Twenty years from now it will be too much of a tradition to change."

I don't know if I believed him at the time or not. But twenty years later, so far Olga and I have been to every wedding in Martian history— and that awful cake of Doc C.'s has been at every one of them. You can't get married here without having your tongue turn blue; it's a tradition, no Martian wedding is complete without it. At least GANTH has been replaced with a decent carrot beer.

A month after our wedding, we watched as two reinforced cranes (one as a safety backup) raised the Encyclopedia from its icy grave. Later that day, with all the water apparently out of it, Nari and Vassily gave it the pulse of laser light to turn it on. A moment later Paul shouted in triumph as the first information began to pour into the receiver side he had plugged in, built carefully to Tiberian specifications from the message Earth had heard thirty years before.

Running at a steady ten megabaud, the Encyclopedia downloaded for many days, as we relayed its contents to Phobos, to Earth, and to Tiber Base. Simultaneously it was recorded onto two separate and distinct computers, and backed up to optical storage as well. Having finally gotten hold of it, we were not about to take any chances on losing it again; we had come such a long way.

Clio Trigorin: Carrying the Light— The Next Giant Leap

2082

FOR A MONTH NOW, AS ROBOTS CRAWLED OVER ITS FACE AND AS THEY wandered through it in telepresence, Tiber had filled their screens on one side, with the other side showing the immense bulk of Juno or the blackness between the stars. They had looked down on the old, eroded mountains of Palath, picked out Battle Gorges, photographed the last Palace of the Emperors from orbit; and shortly after they had looked down into the Windward Islands, and across the long, thin volcanic "string continent" of Shulath stretching nearly pole to pole.

There were no Tiberians, but they had not expected to find them. The ruins showed what had happened, clearly enough, just as the Encyclopedia had said. To preserve their world the Tiberians had put ZPE lasers onto fast little starships, and sent the starships out to work among the rocks that swarmed in the vast smear in the sky they called the Intruder. Ten years of blasting away, hitting twenty rocks per second and knocking them to bits with the fierce heat, accelerating them out of the swarm so that fewer would fall at any one time, had beaten them down to a few billion chunks no bigger than a house back home, and many times that number of smaller pieces.

The effort had been not to save their world as a place to live, which was impossible, but to preserve it as a museum from being wrecked. So many pieces of stone and iron falling into the Tiberian atmosphere every

240 years, for periods of several months, had recondensed into fine dark dust in the upper atmosphere, producing horribly low temperatures, destroying plant life, and killing the world of Tiber in something a thousand times worse than a nuclear winter. Yet because they had made the effort . . . once again, they lived, in their ruins, in the world that was more or less the same shape as it was when they had gone.

The bell sounded and Clio and Sanetomo walked forward with the others. They would go down in four landers, to four different places, for a long stayover exploring primary sites. If there were any hazard that robots had been unable to detect and they didn't know about, with luck it would not be planet wide. Captain Olshavsky would descend in the first lander, making him the first on Tiber by a matter of a few seconds.

Nor would they need to hurry, really, because word of something they had been waiting for had come in. The new starship *Excelsior*, as fast as *Egalitarian Republic* of millennia before, had passed its preliminary tests (four years ago, according to the radio-lagged news). Rather than work here for five years and then take twelve more getting home, the crew of *Tenacity* was to work seven years. At the end of that time, *Excelsior* would arrive to take them back in less than five years, if they wanted to return. *Tenacity* itself would remain here, downgraded to a mere intra-system shuttle, because rapidly advancing technology had already made it so obsolete that it was easier to wait for a faster ship than to return in the old one.

But for all the time they now had, their arrival seemed, somehow, to pass too fast. Too soon, the lander fell away from *Tenacity* and dropped into the Tiberian atmosphere; too soon, they were racing over the broad plains of Palath, ever westward toward the ocean; and before they could even appreciate that, their ship had stood on its tail and slowly descended outside the great city of Kaleps.

They wore their respirators; it would be a year before the test animals confirmed that there were no pathogens dangerous to Earth life in the air of Tiber. Indeed, Tiberian life was little more, now, than microorganisms; it was a planet of germs.

The dust in the city street was almost half a meter deep in some of its drifts and dunes. It was a mixture of dirt blown off the exposed topsoil, and of recondensed bits of the Invader drifting down out of the atmosphere, falling more than thirty times since this had been a living city. Many buildings were fallen in, probably from the many hairline fractures that must form during the repeated deep cooling they received when Tiber was blanketed in black dust every quarter of a millennium.

This first day on Tiber was more symbol than science; *and rightly so,* Clio thought, though Sanetomo had grumbled. *It's the symbols that we live by.*

They walked for a long time; Kaleps was several kilometers across, for it had been a great and important city at the time Tiber received its death sentence from space. The fine black dust blew around them and Clio was glad to be on a respirator. Above them, the vast bulk of Juno (*no,* she thought to herself, *now that I am here I want to call it Sosahy*), striped with pale bands, swirled by great dark hurricanes that probably had begun during the last bombardment a century ago, glowed overhead, lighting the sky with two thousand times the brightness of the full moon on Earth. They walked on in the swirls of dark dust, marveling at the strange, shrunken shadows that having such a wide light source in the sky caused, and at the way the dust floated so long in Tiber's thicker air, and at how every building spoke of intelligence and yet not of anything human.

Alpha Centauri B, a brilliant dot of light, was just emerging from the underside of Juno when at last they came to the park by the sea. Before them, over the sea, they could see a bright cloud that hung forever in the same part of the sky, midway between Juno's edge and the horizon—the dust and ice trapped out of the bombardment at Tiber's L4 point with Juno. The light seemed strange; it was diffuse from the huge object overhead, like fluorescent light, leaving few or no shadows.

The many bombardments of dust had left Tiber chilled to near–Ice Age conditions, even a century after the most recent one. The seacoast now was prone to ice, even though it was summer, and there was a chill down here by the water, but they kept going until they were standing beneath the two statues, one of a Shulathian and one of a Palathian: the sacred monument humans had first learned of bare decades ago, from *The Account of Zahmekoses.* There stood the great organizer and conqueror, Gurix, squat and powerful; facing him was Wahkopem, tall and thin; each with arms outstretched. Nine thousand years and so much freezing had not harmed the metal of the statue, nor had they smoothed or altered those strange alien expressions that Zahmekoses assured us were all but neutral.

Hardly knowing why she did it, Clio stepped forward, her boots crunching on the gravel that surrounded the pedestal, and then stepped up, reaching over her head to take a grip on the left statue's leg. She pulled herself up to stand between them, as Zahmekoses and Mejox had once done—

And she saw the small box, a lovely shade of off-white like the finest new ivory. On the lid of the box was a layer of the black dust found everywhere on Tiber now, the dust of the pulverized Intruder and the ruined topsoil of this world. She knew it was a most improper thing to do, that she would undoubtedly be as reviled later for having done this as the group that had torn through Tiber Base on the Moon sixty-five years before, but with a shrug, she lifted the box and brushed the black dust from its top.

Years of practice had made her as adroit at reading Tiberian script as her own handwriting.

"Greetings, lost brothers and sisters. We, the people of New Hope, came here in the 6891st year since the First Bombardment, and we found that the knowledge we have of our ancestors is true. We cannot spend much time on our dead past; we have returned to New Hope and we are pushing on with starships of our own, to twenty more worlds soon. It would give us such joy, lost ones of our species, if you came and joined us." Directions followed for how to read the memory contained in the little white box—millennia of history from these people.

"Clio, what is it?" Sanetomo asked, mounting the statue beside her. She showed him, and then everyone. With slowly dawning wonder, he said, "Then . . . some of them lived a long time, at least. They may still be out there. And New Hope is . . . er—"

"Shame on an astronomer," Clio said, "It's Zeta Tucanae. About four times as far from here as we are from home."

He took the little box from her and reverently sealed it into a sample carrier; there would be plenty of time to read it later. As he closed it up, he said, "So . . . we've come all this way just to find out that we've only started?"

Clio looked up at Juno, stretching far across the sky to the east of them, halfway down to the horizon and most of the way up to the zenith. The dark was now creeping across its face on its upper, west side; at any moment the brightening sky underneath it, to the east of them, would reveal Alpha Centauri A, as big as and the same shade of amber as Earth's Sun, climbing steadily into the sky from the land out behind the ancient city of Kaleps, the place she had come to for the first time after decades of studying it.

She waited for her first chance to see the alien sun come up behind those strange towers and to feel its warmth on her face. Finally she said, "Yes, we have come all this way just to find out that we have farther to go. And who would want it any other way?"

Dawn was everything she had hoped for and expected: dust in the air colored it deep red, and the spires and towers of Kaleps were etched against it, shimmering in the heat that rose as soon as the light touched the black dust. And yet, already, she was wondering how soon they could shake this dust from their feet and set off again. Somewhere out there was a species they needed to catch up with and join; and after that, still, they would be just beginning.

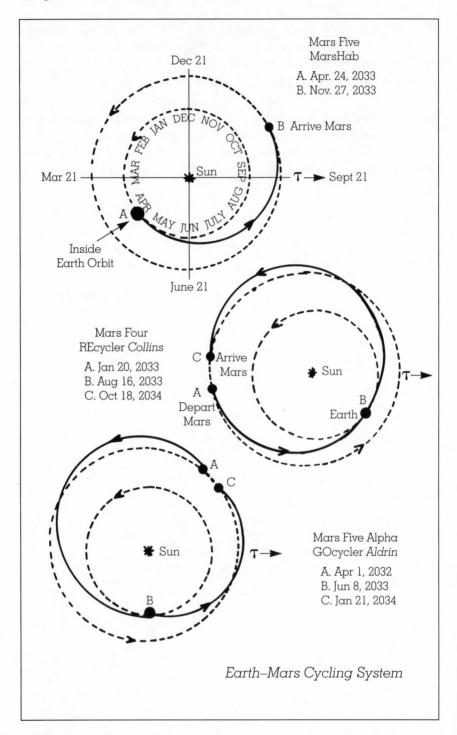

Earth–Mars Cycling System